# THE SHADOW WAND

**The Black Witch Chronicles**

LAURIE FOREST

# THE
# SHADOW
# WAND

Recycling programs
for this product may
not exist in your area.

ISBN-13: 978-1-335-21000-5

The Shadow Wand

First published in 2020. This edition published in 2021.

Copyright © 2020 by Laurie Forest

This edition published by arrangement with Harlequin Books S.A.

For questions and comments about the quality of this book, please contact us at CustomerService@Harlequin.com.

Inkyard Press
22 Adelaide St. West, 40th Floor
Toronto, Ontario M5H 4E3, Canada
www.InkyardPress.com

Printed in U.S.A.

*To Liz—who has been on this story's journey since the beginning.*

*To Mom & Diane—your feisty legacy lives on in these pages.*

North

*Icelandic Mountains*

MAELORIA

ALFSIGROTH

*Pyrran
Islands*

GARDNER

VALGARD

Malthorin Bay

*Voltic Sea*

ROTHIR

*Fae Islands*

W. Pas

GARDNERIA

# WESTERN REALM

POST ANNEXATION OF KELTANIA, VERPACIA & LUPINE TERRITORIES

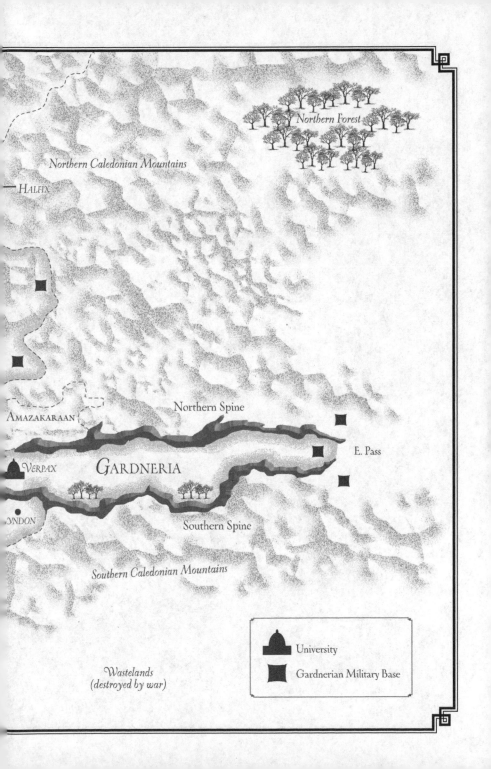

Icelandic Mountains

Northern Forest

Northern Caledonian Mountains

ALFSIGROTH

GARDNERIA

AMAZAKARAAN

•VONOR

Agolith Desert

Eastern Pass

Southern Caledonian Mountains

WESTERN OCEAN

Wastelands

WESTERN REALM

North

CONTINENT OF THE REALMS

SOUTHERN OCEAN

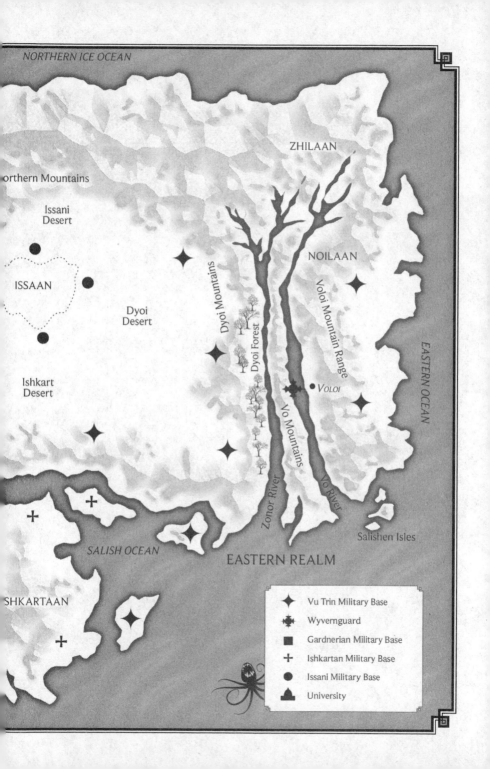

# The Gardnerian Prophecy

*(Divined from Ironwood cleromancy
by the Priest Seers of the First Children)*

**A Great Winged One will soon arise and
cast his fearsome shadow upon the land.**

**And just as Night slays Day
and Day slays Night,**

**so also shall another Black Witch
rise to meet him,**

**her powers vast beyond imagining.**

**And as their powers clash upon the field of
battle, the heavens shall open, the mountains
tremble, and the waters run crimson.**

**And their fates shall determine
the future of all Erthia.**

# The
# Noi Prophecy

*(Scried from Black Ginkgo tasseography
by the Blessed Servants of Vo)*

**A Wyvern child shall be brought forth
by the Great Goddess Vo,**

**and he shall be filled with the
dragon goddess's own fire and
power and righteousness.**

**But wreathed in Shadow,
another Black Witch shall also rise.**

**To weave horror and corruption
throughout Erthia.**

**The two shall meet on the field of battle
as all color is bled from the world.**

**And consumed by the Shadow.**

# The Amaz Prophecy

*(Foretold from Sacred Red Elm astragalomancy
by the Seers of the Goddess)*

**Daughters of the Goddess take heed!**

**A great Shadow Force rises from
the Cursed World of Men.**

**And amidst its darkness, a Wyvern male
and a Black Witch shall arise and clash,
raining destruction upon the world.**

**Take up arms, Blessed Daughters!**

**The hour to save Erthia is at hand!**

# PROLOGUE

*Fifteen years ago…*

Edwin Gardner sits on the silk-cushioned chair in a haze of grief.

He watches his distraught sister, Vyvian, pace her ornate parlor, and wishes that he could wash his hands of his family's cursed legacy of magic.

And that the news Vyvian just imparted wasn't so completely horrific.

Incredibly, in the midst of this world-altering day, Vyvian is dressed as impeccably as ever. Her long, gleaming black hair is artfully plaited, not a strand out of place. Her formfitting, midnight-colored silk tunic and long-skirt are perfectly pressed and patterned with lush pine boughs. And there's luxury everywhere in this cursedly opulent room—dark, polished Ironwood trees set into the walls, their obsidian branches tangling overhead. An oak-leaf-patterned rug beneath his feet.

Panoramic windows edged in luminous stained-glass vines that overlook Vyvian's expansive garden of bloodred roses.

*The finest of everything*, Edwin considers with bitter anguish. All this wealth secured by his mother's cruel reign of fire. Edwin sends up a prayer that future generations will not inherit her terrible, corrupting magic.

Vyvian continues to pace, not bothering to look at the three children huddled miserably in the corner, as Edwin's grief threatens to tear him apart.

His brother, Vale, and Vale's fastmate, Tessla, are dead.

Edwin's throat is tight, his breathing irregular and stifled over the loss of two of the people he loves most in all the world. He wants to rip at his hair and cry out in misery to the heavens. To shake his fist at his powerful sister, at the entire monster that is Gardneria. But he can't fall apart. He has three children who need his protection. Vale and Tessla's children.

Rafe, Trystan, and Elloren.

"You can't fight the Gardnerians," he warned Tessla just a few months ago, overcome with worry as he faced her in her Valgard home. "You don't know what cruelty my mother is capable of. Her power has turned shadowed, Tess. It's consuming her."

"I have to fight," Tessla countered, her voice rough with defiance. "They're rounding up all the Fae, Edwin! The children too. We have to help them!"

"You *can't*."

"We *have* to. Don't you see? The Gardnerians are doing the same thing that the Kelts and the Urisk did to us! Children are being seized. *Whole families.* Do you know what that's like? Watching your family, your people, herded together to be killed? The children screaming?" Tessla's cheeks were flushed, her green eyes blazing.

She was so beautiful in that moment, it was hard for Edwin to look at her.

He'd tried to reason with her. "Think of *your* children." They were being left with him for longer and longer stretches as Vale and Tessla fought this unbeatable evil. "What will Rafe and Trystan and Elloren do if something happens to you?"

Tessla shook her head. "I can't sit by and do nothing about this *horror.*"

"You can't win, Tess!"

She and Vale were tempting fate, Edwin knew. Tempting the awful power of his mother and the Gardnerian military by secretly working for the Resistance. Both Vale and Tessla were involved in smuggling Fae children and families through the Spine's Eastern Pass, the two of them in league with Beck Keeler, Fain Quillen, and Jules Kristian. And others.

The ever-present knot of dread tightened inside Edwin.

He feared it was only a matter of time before Vale and Tessla were caught and executed, then made to look like war heroes, their Resistance activities neatly covered up.

To save the reputation of the Black Witch.

Now he's sitting here, grief burning in his chest because that's exactly what happened—Vale and Tessla were apprehended three days ago, as they attempted to save a group of Asrai Fae children from being shipped to the Pyrran Islands. Both of them had been dragged to the nearest military base and executed at his mother's command, the truth of their Resistance activities hidden from all but a select few.

And this morning, trailing that catastrophe like a cataclysmic cyclone, is news that's sending shock waves through both the Western and Eastern Realms.

His mother, the Black Witch, is dead.

Slain by an Icaral who died even as he killed her with a

bolt of Wyvern flame—a fitting end to a reign of fire that had threatened to enslave the entire Western and Eastern Realms. That had destroyed leagues of forest and turned the lush plains of the East and the southern Uriskan lands to scorched desert.

Foreboding curls under Edwin's ribs, constricting his chest.

The Gardnerians will be set on vengeance. And they're not weak anymore. Because of his mother, Gardneria is now ten times its original size, and its people will be the major power in the region for a long time to come, rivaled only by their uneasy allies, the Alfsigr Elves.

And they'll be looking for their next Great Mage.

Alarm rises inside Edwin as he looks at the children.

His nephew Rafe Gardner sits on the leaf-patterned carpet, steadily watching his uncle and aunt. At five, little Rafe has the stoicism of a much older child, quickly appointing himself the protector of his younger siblings. He cries silently, his arms draped protectively around tiny Trystan.

Trystan has curled himself into a tight ball of misery as he keens and whimpers, "Poppa. Momma. Poppa. Momma," over and over.

Edwin's heart wrenches. Trystan's a fragile child, prone to tears and fear. The skinny two-year-old's eyes are dazed and frightened.

And then there's three-year-old Elloren.

She's balled up next to her brothers, hugging the quilt Tessla sewed for her, a blanket lovingly crafted for Elloren when she was still in Tessla's womb, featuring a branchy tree with bright green leaves stitched onto the fabric, with little embroidered birds and animals darting all around. Elloren is whimpering softly into its folds.

Overcome, Edwin goes to Elloren, kneels, and embraces her. She reaches out small arms to cling to both him and her quilt, her body racked with sobs.

Edwin glances at Vyvian, and his sister's expression sends an icy chill straight through him.

She's glaring at the children like they're hideous blowback, her hatred for Vale and Tessla on full display and spilling over onto these innocents. Edwin's hold on Elloren tightens as he takes in Vyvian's cruel, unforgiving expression and he realizes what he must do.

The children need him, and he loves them.

"The children will stay with me," he tells Vyvian, his voice hoarse but staunch, and he surprises himself with how unwavering he is in the face of his intimidating sister.

Vyvian's frown deepens, her fists clenching and unclenching, her glare sharpening on Edwin. She seems uncharacteristically rattled, and Edwin knows it's for all the wrong reasons.

"Very well," she says, and her mouth thins as she flashes one last resentful look toward the children, as if wanting to rid herself of this terrible business and dispose of them. She moves to leave, but pauses at the door and slowly turns, her gaze fixing on the children in a way that raises the hairs on Edwin's neck as her hateful glare morphs to one of appraisal.

She meets Edwin's gaze once more, her expression and tone hardening to a needled point. "You'll need to wandtest them," she insists. "And soon. If they have power, you're to immediately let me know. Mother would have *insisted* on it." Her voice breaks, and tears glisten in her eyes. She blinks the tears back firmly. "Our family legacy might not have died with Mother." She gestures toward the children with a flick of her elegant hand. "Their parents were traitors, but perhaps, if raised correctly, the children can grow up to be champions of our people."

Edwin blinks at his sister and, in this moment, he hates her.

*Their parents.*

*No, Vyvian*, he wants to rail against her. *Our brother and his fastmate!*

But Edwin knows that Vyvian has her blinders firmly in place. There is absolutely no nuance in her perspective. To Vyvian, the world is divided into clean halves—there are Evil Ones, and there are Gardnerians. And you have to pick one side or the other.

*No.*

Edwin knows what he will do. Not what Vyvian wants. But not what Vale and Tessla would have wanted either.

*Forgive me, Vale. Forgive me, Tessla.*

He hugs Elloren close as a fierce wave of protective love washes over him.

If any of the children has inherited his mother's power, he will hide it from the Gardnerians. He will protect the children from *all* of this.

*They* can't have them.

Not the Gardnerians. Not the Resistance.

This legacy of evil magic will end *here*.

Several months later, Edwin decides to wandtest Rafe, Trystan, and Elloren.

He tests them on three separate occasions, traveling far outside of Valgard each time and taking each child deep into the woods where no one will be able to witness any magic uncovered.

Magic that Edwin prays is not there.

So far, his uneasy prayers have been mostly answered.

Edwin had been worried that Rafe might have inherited his mother's powerful abilities. He's a kind boy, but with a surprisingly strong presence. Physically graceful and sure of himself, Rafe is filled with a steely confidence not often seen in a child of such a tender age. But he's as good as magically powerless, with only a thin sliver of earth magic.

It's clear that Trystan is going to be a powerful Mage, the precocious two-year-old already able to sound out spells and access water magic. But he's no Great Mage. He has none of the crazy, overwhelming power of his grandmother, his water magery testing at Level Five but not beyond. Also, he's a sensitive, quiet child, disinclined to violence.

And then there's Elloren.

As Edwin walks into the woods with gentle Elloren, her small hand clasped trustingly in his, he sends up a prayer.

*Ancient One, please let this child be free of power.*

She's so untroubled, skipping alongside him. So at ease in the woods. Like all powerless Gardnerians.

But it's disturbed Edwin for some time now, how drawn Elloren is to wood—gathering small pieces of it, her collections stuffed into drawers, filling her pockets, hidden under her bed.

Edwin glances down at Elloren and forces a smile that's returned a thousandfold.

She's got Vale's stark features, he muses. So angular and sharp for such a kind, sunny child. But then his thoughts shift.

*She's got her grandmother's exact features.*

Edwin pushes the frightening thought from his mind. Vale himself looked just like their powerful mother, and he was powerful, but he was no Great Mage. And Elloren might be drawn to wood, but Edwin himself can barely keep his hands off it, spending hours each day carving and creating violins. And he's only a Level One Mage.

*No, Elloren will be powerless,* he reassures himself. *Just like I am.*

Edwin stops in a small clearing, rays of sun streaking down, birds twittering. Little Elloren giggles and spins around like a whirring maple seed, her smile to the sun. She stops, teetering from the spinning, and grins at her uncle.

"Here, Elloren," Edwin says as he slides his hand into his cloak's pocket, anxiety mounting inside him. "I have something for you." He draws out the wand and hands it to his niece.

"What's that for?" she asks, taking the wand into her small hands with a look of curiosity.

"It's a game," Edwin says as he sets a candle on a nearby stump before returning to her, his finger flicking toward the wand. "And that's a magic stick, but I'll have to show you how to use it." He gets down on one knee and guides her wand hand into the proper position around the wand's hilt, his hands trembling around her small one with apprehension. "Hold the stick like this, Elloren."

Elloren looks up at him with obvious concern, clearly noting his trembling, but Edwin forces another smile and she smiles back, looking heartened, as her fingers slide into position.

"That's it, Elloren," Edwin says as he releases his hands from hers and rises. "Now I'm going to ask you to say some funny words. Can you do that?"

Elloren's smile brightens and she bobs her head up and down.

Edwin's gut tenses. She's such a compliant child. So eager to please.

*So easy to wield.*

Edwin sounds out the words to the candle-lighting spell several times, words in the Ancient Tongue—foreign words, with subtle inflections, not easily made.

"Do you think you can remember that?" he asks his niece.

Elloren nods as she points the wand out straight and true

with determined focus, and Edwin repeats the words a few more times so that she can remember.

"Go ahead, then," he gently prods as the apprehension tightens his throat, his heart hammering with both breathless hope and jagged fear.

Elloren sounds out the spell, clear and correct, her arm taking on a slight tremor, her body stiffening.

And then her head jerks backward.

A violent stream of fire bursts from the wand's tip and explodes past the stump, blasting clear through a large tree and several more behind it. Edwin stumbles backward and Elloren screams as the woods explode into a crackling, roaring monster of flame.

Edwin wrests the wand from Elloren's hand, thrusts it aside, grabs her up, and runs, racing through the woods as the forest falls apart behind them.

Edwin spends the next year trying to get Elloren to forget.

He insists, when Elloren wakes screaming from fiery nightmares, that what she remembers was a storm. A fierce, freakish storm—an inferno of fire caused by unusually violent lightning.

He insists on it again and again and again.

In time, she believes. And her true memory fades and is buried.

But the forest remembers.

The trees send out word in their creeping way, slow as sap traveling through tangled roots, one tree after another after another. And gradually, relentlessly, the message is carried toward the Northern Forest. Toward its Dryad Guardians.

Toward III.

*The Black Witch is back.*

# PRELUDE

# CHAPTER
# ONE

# EVIL ONES

## THIERREN STONE

*Present day*
*Fourth Month*
*Northern Gardnerian Forest*

Thierren's horse keeps smart pace with his unit of elite Mages, all the soldiers on horseback and following the lead of their young, confident commander, Sylus Bane, as they ride deep into Gardneria's Northern Forest.

Countless leaves rustle in the light breeze, and Thierren glances at the surrounding forest with no small amount of awe.

He's never seen trees like this before. Old growth. Ancient, untouched forest.

*Primordial.*

Trunks so large that it would take three of him to wrap his arms clear round. Rich, dark Ironwood with rustling canopies of deep emerald leaves, further darkened by the overcast day, the occasional rumbling of thunder to the west. The trees' loamy scent on the air.

And something else.

A prickling unease bristles the hairs on the back of Thierren's neck.

As the shadows of the day deepen, it's as if the trees are increasingly leaning in toward them all. And not in a welcoming way.

*The trees don't want us here.*

The thought rises unbidden, and Thierren immediately scoffs at his own imaginings. He glances sidelong at the forest, then blows out a breath and shakes his head, his body moving in sync with his horse. There's no reason to be spooked by trees, of all things. There's no reason to be spooked by anything. Thierren glances down at his brand-new soldier's uniform, spotless and edged with five gleaming silver stripes, signifying his almost unparalleled proficiency in both water and wind magery.

"Ready to hunt some Fae?" stocky, rumpled Branneth asks from beside him as he flashes an excited grin. "Make their pointy-eared heads *explode*?"

Thierren eyes Branneth, an annoyingly uncouth presence forever trying to win Thierren's favor. They're both Level Five Gardnerian Mages, but the similarities end there. Branneth is unforgivably profane and often flat-out immoral, like the rest of his family. Whereas Thierren's family is part of the Styvian sect—the most purely devout, observant Gardnerians.

The *true* Gardnerians.

Thierren glances at Branneth with barely concealed censure as they keep pace with their unit. There's no silver orb pendant around Branneth's neck, and his uniform is marked with the Erthia sphere, not the Ancient One's white bird, which the most devout Gardnerians now insist upon. Thierren feels the weight of the silver necklace gracing his own neck, the proper way to wear the Ancient One's Erthia orb, a symbol of shackling the earth below to the Holy Magedom. And Thierren's own uniform is blessedly marked with the white bird.

A stronger breeze picks up, a clear command seeming to sound on the wind.

*Leave.*

Thierren tenses as his gaze darts around warily. A creeping chill pricks at his neck and traces down his spine, like the quick brush of skeletal fingertips. *Sensing.*

It's coming from the trees.

Before he can reason away his imaginings, righteous anger flares. Thierren glares at the forest. The cursed wilds. It says right in *The Book of the Ancients* that the wilds are the lair of the Evil Ones and that trees are to be rendered to dead wood for use by Gardnerians.

Wood for wands and churches and dwellings to raise up the Holy Magedom.

And so the wilds must be razed. Subjugated and controlled, as the *Book* commands.

*We're going to tear you down,* he vows, full of pious resolve. *We'll burn you to ash, along with every evil thing hiding inside you.*

It's not an idle threat. Gardnerian forces are burning large swaths of the Northern Forest to make way for new farms and to flush out hidden Fae. Evil Fae that the Gardnerians thought had been annihilated during the Realm War, but some bands of them had survived by remaining carefully hidden in the remote forests of the North.

Until the Mages started burning the wilds in earnest.

They're monsters, these Fae—criminal, immoral beasts full of violence and depravity. Thierren has been briefed about the serious threat the Fae pose, the creatures harnessing the evil power of the wilds to attack innocent Mages in an attempt to drive them off their own land.

A heady courage ripples through Thierren.

Dangerous as these Fae are, it's exhilarating to be ready to give his own life, if needs be, to protect his people from this terrible threat. And to be part of a great, blessed story. The one true story.

The Will of the Ancient One.

"There're females, I heard," Branneth muses out of the blue. He waggles his thick brows at Thierren, his green eyes narrowing into a leer. "Best we strip them and give them a thorough inspection before disposing of them, s'what I'm thinking." He grins again, exposing wide, stained teeth, as if he and Thierren are the best of friends.

Thierren's jaw ticks as he looks away and sets his sights on the column of soldiers riding before him, two by two.

*Undressing Fae*, Thierren considers with sharp offense.

The idea is depraved and just so...*wrong*. As profane as undressing demons.

Thierren glances back at Branneth, this time with unconcealed loathing. The huge idiot must register Thierren's displeasure on some level, as his grin fades and he swallows, hacks up phlegm, spits, and then focuses on the road before them.

*What's wrong with him?* Thierren wonders. The only acceptable place for desire like that is between Mages. Among fastmates.

Elisen's face comes to mind, and Thierren's unease softens. *Lovely, wonderful Elisen.*

He glances at the fastlines on his hands and thinks of Elisen's full lips and bright green eyes. Her lustrous ebony hair. Her soft skin that glimmers deep green in the moonlight.

She's allowed him one brief, intoxicating kiss. Just two weeks back, the both of them finding a blessed, chaperone-free moment behind his estate's thick hedgerow. Thierren can still feel those soft lips, the contours of her slim waist under his palms, her body pressed against his.

He'll feel more of her soon, he muses. Both of them are newly eighteen, and their fasting is to be sealed and consummated in one week's time.

Once he gets this Fae hunt behind him.

*You're meant for great things*, Mage Sylus Bane told him only this morning.

Thierren looks at Branneth with resignation, remembering his mother's wisdom.

*Our purity and righteousness keep the Magedom in the Ancient One's graces. The non-Styvian Mages ride on our cloak-tails—but once the Reaping Times come, if they do not start to follow the Ancient One's strictures like we do, the Ancient One will shake them free and name them Evil Ones.*

Life is simple. Observe the law of the *Book*, and you are blessed. Don't, and you are cast out.

*Get out.*

A rush of hatred flashes out from the trees and straight through Thierren in an unsettling wave. A few of the horses shy, as if they, too, can sense the malice on the air. Thierren glances at the trees as he reins in his horse and sees Branneth doing the same. There's a storm moving in, the shadows around them darkening.

Branneth shoots Thierren a rattled look. "Be best when we've cut this whole forest down, I'm thinking." He swallows as he glances at the trees. There's a disturbing sense of the canopy of leaves thickening. Branches tangling. The air growing even more charged.

With hostility.

It's pouring off the trees like an ill wind, but Thierren refuses to shrink back in the face of it. He knows the *Book* backward and forward, and he knows how this story ends.

*With your complete annihilation*, he thinks at the trees. Courage and comfort wash over him, along with a fierce desire to usher in the Reaping Times and fight for the Holy Magedom.

The wind picks up, the trees seeming to loom over them even closer than before. The horses prance and whinny, needing to be reined in once more.

*Get out.*

"Can you feel it?" Branneth asks, his voice now a coarse whisper, his face edged with fear. "It's like we're surrounded. Like..." He grimaces, as if trying to convince himself that he's spinning a nonsense tale. "It's like we're headed into a *trap*." He chuckles low in his throat, but that edge of fear rims his eyes as he peers into the forest's shadows and mutters grimly to himself. "Only good Fae's a dead Fae." He turns to Thierren, as if seeking his approval. "Eh, Thierren?"

At the head of their contingent, Commander Bane raises his hand, signaling for their attention. The smell of burning wood drifts on the air.

Their collective pace slows to a halt as they come to the road's end and are met by two Mage soldiers on foot. Thierren blinks at the road's abrupt terminus, marveling at how far north they've traveled.

*Incredible*, he thinks, his skin prickling at the realization. *The end of the Northern Wayroad. Its farthest reach. Nothing but wilds beyond for leagues.*

One of the Mages walks forward, his expression serious as he salutes Commander Bane, fist to chest, then jerks his head slightly toward the wall of forest before them.

"They're just up ahead," he says. "We've flushed out a whole pack of Fae. Dryads, the lot of 'em."

*Tree Fae.*

Thierren peers at the forest before them, his heartbeat quickening, every sense sharpening in anticipation of his first engagement with Fae. He pulls in a deep, bolstering breath, feeling lit up with a renewed sense of holy purpose, eager to finally engage with the horrific Evil Ones in defense of the Magedom.

"We dismount here, Mages." Commander Bane's voice rings out from the front of their party, effortlessly dominant.

They all dismount, tether the restless horses to trees to be cared for by the Calvary Mage, and make their way into the forest on foot, following the commander's assured lead, the smell of smoke growing more pungent.

Thierren pulls out his wand and readies it as he recites wind and air spells in his mind, weaving the magery together inside his lines.

They're dangerous, these Tree Fae, some of them able to access multiple lines of elemental power and feed it through branches. And sometimes they use wildlife in their attacks. They just got word of Dryads farther south of here ambushing Mages with small cyclones and flocks of raptors in retaliation for land being cleared.

Land that belongs to the Magedom.

*No matter.* Thierren glares at the threatening trees as his unit moves deeper into the forest. *I'll be conjuring a great cyclone very soon to destroy both you and your Fae minions.*

The piercing sound of a child's scream jolts through Thierren, slowing his steps. He looks to the other soldiers in confusion, but they seem to be ignoring the sound.

Unsettled, Thierren follows his unit forward, stepping over roots, his boot heels sinking slightly into the soft, mossy soil.

The sound of a child crying.

A baby's wail splitting the air.

Women pleading in low, tortured tones in a strange language.

Thierren feels a harder stab of confusion. He steps through the trees and looks over a small meadow that ends at an even thicker band of forest. Fires are smoldering along the sides of the meadow where trees have been set ablaze by the soldiers.

And there they are.

The Dryads.

A line of pointy-eared, forest green Tree Fae are standing, side by side, before the far wall of untouched Northern Forest.

As if they're forming a barrier with their own bodies.

But...the most pathetic, easily broken barrier Thierren has ever seen.

Bewilderment whips through him. He's seen pictures of Dryads, horrific beings dripping with rotted vegetation. Crazed eyes, pointed teeth. Demonic and dangerous.

These Fae don't look anything like those pictures.

Yes, they're intensely green, their skin glimmering deep green more strongly than Gardnerian skin, their hair black, their green eyes wide, and their ears sharply pointed. And they're dressed in garments that appear to be formed from leaves melted together.

But the similarities to the monstrous pictures end there.

An old Dryad woman, her hair white as snow, has her hands pressed together as if in prayer. She's fallen to her knees, pleading in a long stream of unintelligible words. A young boy clings to her, sobbing, his face pressed into her garments. And a girl of no more than ten stands beside them both, wielding a large stone in her fist, her face a mask of hatred, her breathing labored. Sharp, hostile syllables burst from her mouth. She hurls the stone across the meadow toward the long line of Mages, but her throw is weak and the stone falls short.

Women, old people, children, teens.

And all of them appear to be covered in a black soot, the dark grains sprinkled over their skin, their clothing, as if it's been rained down on them. They're breathing heavily, their bodies slouched, as if they're tethered to the ground by some invisible force.

"What's wrong with them?" Thierren asks no one in particular.

"Tried to attack us with wind."

Thierren turns to the bearded soldier beside him.

The man throws him a jaded glance. "That young one there." He points to a boy who's perhaps all of twelve years old, shirtless and covered with the dark specks as he yells out a stream of what sounds like vicious curses at the Mages. "He threw two Mages about twenty span with a waterspout he sent out from a branch. Broke Kerlin's leg against a tree. So we covered them in iron dust. That calmed them down. Stripped them of their cursed powers."

Thierren turns back to the line of Fae, his mind storming.

There's a baby. With round cheeks. Covered in iron and screaming. Being cradled by a lovely young woman. The baby throws the Mages a look of pure horror as he tries to claw at his face with tiny hands. The young woman is desperately trying to calm the child, tears coursing down her cheeks as she attempts to both gently pry his fingers away from his skin and brush off the iron.

"And did you subdue the kelpies that were found?" Commander Bane asks the lieutenant beside him. Commander Bane's tone is bored as he looks through some papers, ignoring the pleading, threatening, crying band of Fae.

"We've poisoned them, Mage. Set down iron bolts in all the waterways."

Commander Bane nods, seeming pleased, then rolls up his parchment and thrusts it into his shoulder bag. He looks over the line of Fae, as if both resigned and satisfied.

"Pure-blooded Tree Fae," Commander Bane marvels as the children sob and the old woman keeps up her ceaseless pleading. He glances back at the lieutenant. "Good work flushing them out."

Thierren's gaze is riveted to the children, bile rising in his throat. The ones old enough to talk are speaking what must be Dryadin, but if he closes his eyes, their crying sounds unsettlingly the same as Gardnerian children's.

And their appearance is so close to *Gardnerian*.

Thierren's stomach clenches and a sense of vertigo makes him unsteady on his feet. He looks up and sees a brief flash of white in the tree limbs above the Dryads.

White birds. Translucent as mist. Watching.

Hatred pours from the trees in a staggering wave, adding to Thierren's vertigo. He feels a sharp tug on his affinity lines, as if the trees are making a play for his magery. Trying to rip the power from his very center. He struggles to set up an internal shield, whipping up air until there's a dense wall of it around his lines. He fortifies it layer upon layer, but he still feels the relentless attack of the trees, the sensation of branches slapping against the shield. Trying to pierce through it.

His mind spins as the baby cries and cries and cries.

Thierren thinks back to his unit's training. How he half listened to what seemed, at the time, like the obvious. Advice for foolish, sentimental Mages.

*They may give you the illusion of being human. It's the way the Great Shadow tricks our minds. You must see through it. And follow the Blessed Will of the* Book.

But he never expected there to be a baby. Or this lovely young woman. And Thierren senses, deep in his soul, that this is no illusion.

The young woman rocks the baby, and her movements are like a swaying branch, all smoothness and grace. Thierren's affinity power gives a hard lurch toward her.

The young woman looks up, straight into Thierren's eyes.

A rush of overwhelming shock flows through Thierren as their gazes lock, her eyes green as summer leaves, tears pooling inside them. Her deep-green lips fall open, and her misery rocks through Thierren, straight into his heart.

Heavily accented Common Tongue sounds to the side. "Mages. *Stop.*"

Thierren's head whips toward the old woman with the white hair. The woman's arms are now out in supplication, her green eyes full of a fierce urgency. She gestures toward the dark forest behind her as if she's trying to convey a vital warning.

"Leave our forest alone," the woman says, an ominous weight to the words. "If the trees die, we die. You die. We all die."

Her urgency strikes Thierren deep in his heart, and he has the disturbing sense that he's hearing something true. A fierce, disorienting urge to stop all of this wells up.

"The Shadow is coming," the old woman warns, her voice low and blazing with inescapable certainty.

"On your knees," Commander Bane orders the Fae, almost blithely, and Thierren's eyes snap to his commander's in amazement that he can remain so unaffected. There's a wicked gleam in Commander Bane's eyes. As if he's excited by all this.

A flash of revulsion rocks Thierren. He looks back to the young Fae woman, and their gazes latch again. As if they're both unwitting players in a nightmare. Suddenly, Thierren wants nothing more in the world than to grab the woman and the baby and whisk them away from here.

The young woman calls out to Thierren in her Fae dialect, her voice as melodious as it is grief-stricken. Thierren opens his mouth as if to answer her, just as Commander Bane's voice booms out.

"'By order of the Gardnerian government,'" he reads from

a scroll, "'you are hereby ordered to stand down and surrender your hold on our sovereign territory.'" Commander Bane sighs, as if this is all too easy, rolls the scroll back up, and slides it into his tunic's pocket. He steps forward, unsheathes his wand, and loosely points it at the Fae. "I *said*, get on your knees."

The line of Fae steps defiantly backward with what appears to be great effort, their arms outstretched now, as if fortifying the barrier between the Mages and the thick forest. The hatred in many of the Fae's expressions hardens. The young boy's eyes have become rage-filled slits as he hoarsely yells out a stream of furious Dryadin, and the young woman's mouth is a miserable, trembling frown as she hugs the baby to her chest.

Horror slashes through Thierren. The desperate urge to rescue the young woman and the baby swells. There's another flash of white birds in the branches above the Fae. A line of the ethereal creatures to mirror the line of birds on some of the Gardnerians' uniforms. On *his* uniform.

Thierren blinks and wonders if he's gone completely mad.

"Get on your knees," Commander Bane snarls. *"Now."*

*Wait*, Thierren wants to cry at Commander Bane, everything in the world suddenly breaking down. *Can't you see? There's been a mistake and we need to stop. This isn't what we thought. These aren't monstrous warriors.*

*These are families.*

The old woman ignores Commander Bane's threatening stance, his wand. She rises from her knees and steps forward falteringly, pushing her palms out toward Commander Bane in a halting gesture.

Viper fast, Commander Bane whips back his wand, then hurls his arm forward. A spear of ice jets from his wand's tip and plunges straight into the old woman's chest.

Her sharp cry turns to a gurgle as she falls backward to the ground with a heavy thud, blood streaming.

Chaos breaks out. Fae scream and struggle against the iron to rush to her. The terrified children shriek.

Commander Bane views the scene impassively. "By order of the Gardnerian government," he repeats, "you are hereby ordered to stand down and surrender your hold on our sovereign territory."

"We will never stand down!" the boy screams, his Common Tongue thickly accented, his skinny body rising to his full height. The power of the forest rises with him, like a dark, inescapable tide. Thierren can feel it, right through his bones.

Right through his lines.

The boy's hands bunch into fists. "We are weak now, but our Guardians are not. They will know what you do to us. The trees will tell them. And they will come for you with the full might of the forest!"

Commander Bane's eyes widen as he smiles with delighted mirth. He glances at the Mages that surround him, as if to share his incredulous glee. He sneers back at the boy. "Oh, the *trees* will come after us, will they? On their little tree legs?"

Thierren looks up, the canopy of trees on all sides leaning in. Rustling. The hard push against his affinity lines strengthens.

"We stand with the trees!" the boy yells with unbridled ferocity.

Commander Bane spits out a sound of derision and rolls his eyes at the bearded Mage next to him. "Sweet Ancient One, we need to silence them." Commander Bane stands military straight. "Mages!" he orders, looking to the left then to the right, down the line of soldiers. "Ready your wands!"

The young woman is down on her knees by the dead Fae

woman, sobbing, the baby in her arms screaming. She looks up and locks her grief-stricken gaze onto Thierren's.

Horror bubbles up, and Thierren can contain it no longer. He bursts forward into the clearing and whips around to face the line of Mages. *"Stop!"* he yells, throwing out his palm.

Commander Bane lowers his wand a fraction and eyes Thierren. "Have you lost your mind?"

*Yes*, Thierren thinks with head-spinning distress. "They've got children!" he cries at the line of Mages before him. "We have to stop!"

"They're *Fae!*" Commander Bane snarls. "Fall back, Mage Stone. *Now!*"

Thierren looks over his shoulder at the young woman. The Fae have grown silent except for the sobbing and screaming young children. All eyes are on Thierren. He meets the young woman's gaze. And suddenly, he's swept up in a sense of kinship with her that's so strong, all sense of self-preservation shatters.

Thierren turns back to Commander Bane. "We have to stop," he says, his voice hardening. "This is a mistake."

"Great Ancient One, Thierren, move aside!" Commander Bane bellows.

Thierren holds his ground. *"No."* He gestures toward the Fae, adamant. "They're not warriors. There are *children*."

Commander Bane scratches the back of his neck then shakes his head, as if he's seen this misguided foolishness before but never expected it to come from Thierren.

"Thierren, you know what we're here to do," he says with reasonable calmness. Like a parent chastising a wayward child. "And you know why." He points at the Fae without looking at them. "These heathen spawn, right here, attacked Mage farmers and soldiers doing nothing more than trying to clear *our* land for *our* farms. That 'child' there—" he points to the angry young boy without looking at him "—he tried to kill one of us." His piercing gaze bores into Thierren with righteous fire. "Do you want to give up every last part of your life...for *heathen Fae*?"

Overcome by his own righteous fury, Thierren raises his arm and points his wand at Commander Bane's chest. "We need to stop this. *Now*."

Fast as an asp, Commander Bane flicks his wand and black tendrils fly out, slapping around Thierren's wand and wresting it from his fist. Before Thierren can react, Commander Bane flicks his wand toward him again, and tendrils lash forward to wrap around Thierren's entire body, pinning his arms tight against his sides and driving the air from his lungs. Commander Bane snaps his wand backward, and the tendrils around Thierren's legs cinch tight and yank him off his feet. He lands on the damp ground with a painful thud as he strains against the bonds.

"Ready!" Sylus Bane commands the line of Mages.

The Mages lift their wands.

"*No!*" Thierren cries out, losing all control. All reason. The forest darkens.

"Aim!"

"*Stop! No!*" Thierren rages as wave upon wave of fury pours off the trees. "There are *children*!"

"*Fire!*"

Fae scream as Mage power blasts from the wands and crashes into them. Rage tears through the forest. The bloodcurdling screams of the young boy, the young woman, and the Fae baby all mingle with Thierren's own.

# CHAPTER TWO

## FOREST GUARDIANS

### VYVIAN DAMON

*Fourth Month*
*Mage Council Hall*
*Valgard, Gardneria*

Thunder cracks overhead and Mage Vyvian Damon glances up through the vaulted, stained-glass ceiling. The fierce storm brewing outside flashes lightning and slams wind against the imposing Mage Council building, steely clouds closing ranks above.

Vyvian is seated with all twelve Mage Council members around an oval Ironwood table, the inlaid image of a huge tree surrounded by a whorl of white birds set into the table-top. Her hand rests on a smooth, dark root at the table's far end as a heady anticipation builds inside her.

The chamber's arching Ironwood doors open, and Vyvian's heart quickens, a rush of heat bursting to life inside her as High Mage Marcus Vogel strides into the room trailed by two Council envoys as the Council members rise.

The young High Priest is the absolute *picture* of pious elegance, his riveting features all perfectly tapered angles, his gaze like green fire. The sensation of Vogel's contained power courses throughout the room and resonates in Vyvian's lines as all the colors of the chamber flicker to shades of black and gray.

Vyvian blinks to clear her vision, and the disorienting color change vanishes as quickly as it flashed into being.

Vogel takes a seat at the table's head, where the inlaid tree image branches into a mighty crown. His two square-jawed envoys move to stand preternaturally motionless behind him as Vyvian and the other Council members take their seats once more. Above Vogel's stilled figure hangs a huge, inverted Ironwood tree attached by chains to the supporting beams of the chamber's glass ceiling to form a massive, boreal chandelier, the tree's obsidian wood sanded and waxed to a gleam. Mage-light lanterns are set throughout the nooks and bends in the tree's branches and suffuse the storm-darkened chamber with their lambent glow.

The anticipatory tension in the air thickens as Council Mage Snowden dips his pen in a crystalline inkwell then suspends its blackened point over the parchment before him. He looks to Vogel, preparing to take down the Council's motions and rulings in compact, tidy lines.

Vyvian glances at her own neat stack of papers, the Council's *M* seal marking the top of each page. Lantern light flickers over her painstakingly put-together lists of the invaders recently uncovered on Gardnerian soil—glamoured Fae, Fae-blooded, Urisk escapees from the Fae Islands and a host of other Evil Ones bent on corrupting the sacred Magedom. All of these invaders blessedly apprehended by the Mage Guard and shipped off to the Pyrran Islands.

Much of this purification of Mage lands has been overseen by Vyvian herself.

She pulls in a discreet, steadying breath, confident that her reports are perfectly in order and that High Mage Vogel will be quite pleased with her tireless efforts.

But still, she can't shake the ever-present unease that now lives underneath her skin and heightens her desire to prove herself worthy to the shining star that is Vogel. To hold on to her newly tenuous Council seat, Vyvian knows she must prove herself perfectly loyal and devout, distinct from the reviled, traitorous members of her own family—her corrupted brother and nephews as well as her unexpectedly rebellious niece, who's run off to Ancient One knows where.

Not even Elloren's fastmate, Lukas Grey, seems to know where the wretched girl is.

The thread of unease inside Vyvian tightens and heats to anger. *I'll find you, Elloren. And when I do...*

"Let us begin, Mages," Vogel says, his pale green gaze as piercing as a hawk's, his long fingers resting on the dark gray wand he's set on the table before him.

Vyvian thrills to the sound of Vogel's silken voice, her anger brushed aside as she's caught up in her visceral awareness of his power unfurling throughout the room.

Vogel is silent for a long moment as his fervid gaze simmers with portent. "A male Icaral has been found in the Noi lands."

The words strike the room like a hammer. Exclamations of stunned outrage erupt as Vyvian is swept up in the communal, shocked dismay. Vogel remains still as death as the chamber eventually quiets and settles into an excruciating moment of suspense, all eyes fixed on Vogel.

"Where?" The breathy question escapes from Vyvian before she can bite it back, caution overridden by how stunned she is that Sage Gaffney's demon-baby is not the only male Icaral that still lives.

Vogel sets his probing gaze on Vyvian, and she feels that gaze clear down her spine, the air practically humming with Vogel's magic, her weak earthlines straining toward it.

"Our spies have located the Icaral inside the Vu Trin military's Oonlon base." Vogel's words are sinuous as they work their way through Vyvian. "The demon Icaral is a Kelt…and he is the son of the Icaral who killed our beloved Carnissa Gardner." Exclamations of outrage burst forth in the room as Vogel's gaze on Vyvian sharpens. "The name he's been going by is Yvan Guriel."

A harder shock explodes through Vyvian as the room breaks into angry murmuring.

*Yvan Guriel. The Kelt who was in bed with Elloren.*

*He's an Icaral.*

"The Icaral of Prophecy," Vyvian rasps, almost unable to breathe. Unable to move. Feeling as if the ground is giving way beneath her. The Icaral of Prophecy is not Sage Gaffney's baby after all, but the cursed son of Valentin Guryev— the very same Icaral demon who killed Mother.

Not Yvan Guriel at all.

But Yvan Guryev.

Rattled beyond measure, Vyvian struggles to hold Vogel's piercing stare. His gaze narrows intently on her as fear winds tightly around her gut and a desperate resolve coalesces—*no one can ever know that Elloren was found with Valentin Guryev's demonic son.*

"He must be slain immediately," Mage Greer insists to Vogel, his tone brusque.

Vogel's penetrating gaze slides toward the pair of Level Five Mage Guards who bracket the chamber's Ironwood doors. "Send in Mavrik Glass," he directs.

The guards open the doors, and a tall, rather dashing young Level Five Mage strides into the chamber, his dark cloak flowing behind him. He's elegantly handsome, his movements fluid, his hand curled around the handle of the mahogany wand that's sheathed at his side. Three more wands fashioned from a variety of woods are sheathed at his other hip, and two more against his upper arm.

"Wandmaster Glass," Vogel says, a shrewd smile forming on his lips, "show the Council what we've requisitioned from the Vu Trin."

Mage Glass smirks knowingly at Vogel, reaches into his tunic's pocket, and places a series of six onyx lumenstone discs on the circular table. Identical sapphire Noi runes mark each stone and send up a gauzy sapphire light.

Vyvian pulls in a surprised breath. "Are they Noi portal stones?" she asks, looking to Vogel.

"They are," he affirms.

An uncomfortable fidgeting kicks up in the room, expressions of stark confusion that Vyvian mirrors passed around. The use of heathen sorcery is flatly forbidden by *The Book of the Ancients*.

Mage Greer draws back from the stones, his black-bearded face tightening with abhorrence. "Noi sorcery is polluted magic."

"We can't risk mixing this magic with ours," elderly Mage Snowden chimes in, the white-haired man seeming overcome by indignation.

"No mixing," Vogel agrees. His grip tightens on the gray wand before him, his gaze sliding across them all. *"Consuming."*

Vogel presses his wand's tip to the stones, one by one, and Vyvian draws back, blinking in wonder as the blue glow of each circular rune is sucked into Vogel's wand leaving a dark imprint, the rune shapes then filling with undulating shadow, fingers of gray smoke twisting up from their transformed designs.

"They have power, the heathens," Vogel muses as a delicate whirl of shadow coils up from his wand. "Portal abilities and superior runic sorcery that has given them advantages for far too long. This power belongs in Mage hands. *We* are the only ones who can wield magic to do the Ancient One's will. So *we* are the only ones who should control it. *All* of it."

Vogel looks to the inverted-tree chandelier and focuses, and a flurry of dark wings appears behind a branch. A previously hidden bird flies down and alights on Vogel's shoulder.

Along with the rest of the Council, Vyvian draws back in both awe and revulsion.

The bird looks like a crow, but there's a grotesquerie of *eyes* all over its upper head, most a changeable gray color, as if they contain an incoming storm.

But the eye in the center of the bird's head...

It's the same pale, searing green as Vogel's eyes.

"What sorcery is this?" Mage Gaffney whispers, the words shot through with obvious alarm. Smoking shadow runes cover the bird's sides, its chest, the top of its dark head.

Both Vogel and the bird turn their heads toward Mage Gaffney with frightening synchronicity. A shuddering chill runs down Vyvian's spine.

"A runic eye," Vogel says, as Vyvian is filled with the certainty that Vogel is seeing not only through his own two eyes, but through the bird's central green eye, as well.

"Why does this...*thing* have so many eyes?" Mage Greer spits out, his own gaze riveted to the bird.

Vogel and the bird turn to him in a uniform motion, and Vyvian is chilled anew.

"An effect of the magic I've requisitioned," Vogel states.

An uneasy rumble of murmurs rise from the Council.

"Are there more of these altered birds?" Mage Greer asks.

"Just the one," Vogel says coolly as he lifts his chin. The bird takes flight and lands on Mavrik Glass's shoulder, the young Mage seeming unfazed by the monstrous bird, his knowing smile bright. "For now," Vogel adds, looking to the Council pointedly, as if mentally transmitting the possibilities.

"A runic spy," Mage Snowden breathes in awe, looking to Vogel as if with heightened appreciation.

"A military advantage," Mage Priest Alfex interjects reverently. "That the Ancient One has blessed us with."

Vyvian takes in the nightmare bird and Vogel's gray wand. For a moment she's overcome by the sense that they're playing with dangerous magic that should have been left alone. Magic that's corrupted and primordial and *wrong*.

Magic that can't be controlled.

But then another, stronger thought arises.

What if this magic was to fall into the hands of the heathen races?

*No*, Vyvian insists to herself, refuting her reflexive fear of this shadow magery. Vogel is right. Of course he is. The Gardnerians need to control all magic in the Realms. Because the Gardnerians are the only ones led by the Ancient One above.

"Shall I show them more, Your Excellency?" Mavrik Glass asks.

Vogel gestures his approval with a subtle tilt of his head.

Mavrik's knowing smile widens into a calculating grin. He pulls out another entirely different stone and holds it up for the Council's perusal. This dark lumenstone disc is marked with a different shadow rune, the inner, undulating designs of the complicated mark whirring against each other like clockworks fashioned from dense fog.

Mavrik clamps his fingers tightly around the stone as he unsheathes the mahogany wand at his hip. Then he closes his eyes, dips his head, and brings the tip of his wand to his own shoulder, his expression tensing with what looks like great concentration.

Vyvian lets out a small gasp as the young man's form blurs, then turns to dark mist. His body grows amorphous, then once more distinct as it re-forms into a muscular, female Vu Trin soldier with coiled black hair, angular features, and the black military uniform of a Noi soldier, the nightmare bird perched on her shoulder.

More gasps float throughout the room.

"A glamour," Mage Flood murmurs, sounding awed by Vogel's newfound advantages, glamouring having always been solely a Fae power, just as portal magic had always been the domain of the Noi's Vu Trin forces.

There's a sly look in Mavrik Glass's falsely Noi-dark eyes. "The portal stones are almost fully charged," Mavrik tells Vogel, his deep masculine voice at odds with his glamoured female form. He smirks at the entire Council. "I'll be paying a visit to the Eastern Realm this very evening."

"The Icaral has yet to come into his full power," Vogel explains as Mavrik taps his wand to his shoulder and morphs back into his Gardnerian form. "Mage Glass will journey through the portal with the runic eye," Vogel states. "He will track the Icaral creature down. And slay him."

Relief floods Vyvian's shock, overriding her fear of Vogel's new runic powers as the promise of a world-set-right burns bright in her mind.

Yes, her own niece was unconscionably mixed up with an Icaral demon. *The* Icaral demon.

*But Yvan Guryev will be dead in a matter of days*, she consoles herself, forcing even breaths. The Great Prophecy will be smashed to bits under Gardnerian might, and her mother's death will be avenged.

Gardnerian power has just become unstoppable, Vyvian

realizes, goose bumps prickling over her skin. With portal magic, aerial spies, and the ability to glamour now in Mage hands, there will be no stopping the Reaping Times.

The Council members are nodding to each other and conversing in low, reassured tones, as if rapidly adjusting to Vogel's incredible display of power, their eyes brightening with renewed purpose.

There's a single, brisk knock at the doors and everyone's attention is drawn toward the sound.

Vogel nods at the bird, and the creature closes all its eyes except the original two, its shadow runes blinking out of sight. Another wave of awe rushes through Vyvian at the bird's easy camouflage as the doors are pulled open once more.

A young, skinny military courier steps into the chamber. He seems nervous, his posture rigid as he swallows, his gaze riveted on Vogel as the two guards shut the doors behind him.

Silence descends.

"Highest Mage, we've word from the North," he says, his voice unsteady.

"What word would that be?" Vogel asks, slow and controlled.

"Commander Sylus Bane's unit...they flushed out another band of Fae from the wilds, Your Excellency." The courier's brow tightens. "Eighteen of them this time. Dryads."

Vyvian inwardly recoils from the word as troubled mutterings fill the room.

*"Dryads?"* Mage Snowden exclaims.

"The Tree Fae?" Mage Priest Alfex marvels, eyes wide. "That's not possible."

"They were supposed to be *dead*," Mage Greer spits out. "All of them *dead*. How is it we keep flushing out more of them?"

Eventually, everyone quiets and looks to Vogel, tension thick on the air.

"It has begun." Vogel's tone is low with import as it resonates through the room. His words gain an impassioned edge as he closes his eyes and recites from *The Book of the Ancients* in a priestly cadence. "'Lo, the wilds shall be corrupted and cast shadows across the land. And the Ancient One's flock shall converge on this corruption in power and in *glory*.'"

Excitement crackles inside Vyvian and she straightens, determined to be included on the righteous side of this dangerous heavenly saga—the First Children set against the full might of the Evil Ones.

There's an intricately embroidered white bird on the breast of Vogel's tunic, and on the wall behind him hangs the newly designed Gardnerian flag—the Ancient One's white bird on black.

*The Ancient One's flock*, Vyvian echoes, beatific tears sheening her eyes.

Vogel opens his eyes and peers at the courier. "Have these Dryads been dealt with?"

"Y-yes, Your Excellency," the youth sputters. "Cut down. Every last one."

Sounds of relief well up.

"But...there are threats, Your Excellency," the courier adds, casting an unwelcome note of doubt into the room.

Vyvian's pulse ratchets higher as they all stare at the courier, who seems to shrink under the combined weight of the Council's attention.

"Threats?" Vogel asks, unblinking.

"The Dryads that were flushed out," the young man says, his voice strained, "the ones that can speak the Common Tongue...well, they said they've got warriors who will fight for them."

The hall once again bursts into troubled, angered conversation. Mage Snowden and Mage Flood make the Ancient One's five-pointed star sign of protection on their chests.

"They're dangerous, these Fae," Mage Flood declares grimly.

"They're no threat to the Magedom," Mage Greer snaps back at him.

"Some of them can wield branches like wands," Mage Snowden counters, his white brow knotted. "They can draw a sizable amount of power from the forest."

"Then we'll send iron-tipped arrows through them," Mage Greer sneers. "That should tamp down their power a bit."

"What else did they say, Mage?" Vogel asks the courier, seeming impervious to the startled and livid reactions around him. The Council Mages quiet and the room falls silent once more.

The courier glances around, as if unnerved by their renewed attention. Like a cornered animal, he looks to Vogel and swallows. "They said that the Dryads threatened that they're coming for us. With the power of the trees."

Now all eyes look to Vogel, as if drawn to him for guidance in such troubled times.

Vogel extends his arms as if he's embracing the room, his expression growing pained as he closes his eyes, his gray wand clasped tight. "Pray with me, Mages."

Vyvian dips her head alongside everyone in the hushed chamber as Vogel begins the prayer and they all fall into the familiar cadence of the words.

*"Oh, most holy Ancient One, purify our minds, purify our hearts, purify Erthia. Protect us from the stain of the Evil Ones."*

Then Vyvian mirrors the entire room in making the sign of the five-pointed blessing star over her chest, one point for each affinity power.

Vogel slowly lowers his arms, but his head remains bowed, the Council silent as stone.

Waiting.

Eventually, Vogel lifts his head and opens his eyes, his stare inescapable. Drawing them all in. Filling Vyvian with a heady euphoria.

*His power.* She can still feel it emanating from Vogel and his equally powerful wand. Riding the very air.

Vogel fixes his piercing gaze on the courier as lightning flashes above in a staccato burst and a crack of thunder peals through the glass ceiling. "Instruct your commander to send a unit of Level Five Mages into the Northern Forest," Vogel orders, an ominous finality to his tone. "The Ancient One's time of reckoning is upon us. These Dryads say they'll come for our Mages? That they'll attack the Holy Magedom? That they fight with the trees? Very well. We'll raze the entire forest." His stare narrows with lethal precision. "Then we'll find these remaining Dryads. And annihilate them."

Vogel turns toward the Council and lifts the tip of his wand as another boom of thunder shakes the building. "Blessed Mages, the Ancient One has called upon us to claim Erthia, league by league. Soon the borders of the Holy Magedom will be rune magicked against every Evil Invader. And Mage soil will be cleansed of their unholy stain." Lines of shadowy magic curl up from Vogel's dark wand in an undulating helix of smoke, and Vyvian marvels at the sheer beauty of it.

"The Reaping Times are here," Vogel intones, eyes flashing along with the lightning above. "The hour has come to destroy every last Evil Invader of our blessed Mage land."

# CHAPTER THREE

# HERETIC

## THIERREN STONE

*Fifth Month*
*Valgard, Gardneria*

"Are you aware, Mage," Commander Sylus Bane asks Thierren Stone, "that a dishonorable discharge from the Mage Guard will leave you unfit for service? Lock you out of all guilds forever? Not even poor Lower River farmers hire a race traitor."

Sylus Bane sits at his desk surrounded by high-ranking soldiers, all of them glowering at Thierren.

Thierren glowers back at Sylus Bane, bleary-eyed and numbed to the censure. He doesn't care what any of them think of him. He doesn't care about anything.

When Thierren returned home, his parents were distraught and thrown into complete confusion at the staggering change in their eldest son, their golden child—terrified by his chronic nightmares, his frightening screams deep in the night, and then by his insomnia as they found Thierren up at odd hours, in odd places, staring at a wall as if watching a horrific nightmare, his face haunted, dark circles anchoring his eyes.

At first, his parents tried to understand. They even paid for a priest to perform an exorcism, sure their son had been stained by his close contact with the Evil Ones.

But soon, their concern turned to anger as Thierren spun out of control. Wandering the streets all night long. Getting hold of illegal spirits and attempting to drink them openly in their home. His parents confiscated that first bottle of spirits and destroyed it, but Thierren found more, the spirits able to dampen the ghastly scene clinging to him like a sickness.

He couldn't get the face of the young Dryad woman out of his mind.

The baby.

His parents consulted a multitude of priests and healers, his mother's face tight with humiliation, her eyes teary as she wrung her hands and recounted her son's moral weakness. How one encounter with the Evil Ones had broken him and turned him into this sinister *thing* with increasingly disturbing behavior—cutting up his Gardnerian military uniform. Setting fire to the Gardnerian flag.

Thierren drank as many spirits as he could. Bought nilantyr from a Keltish farmer and started to chew on the bitter berries, sinking into their dark oblivion. Soon it was the only thing that could even slightly alleviate the constant nightmare that was now his world.

Elisen, his fastmate, came to see him once and left hysterical, refusing to come near him ever again, her family desperate for a way to break the fasting. Thierren didn't care. All he could think about was the young Fae woman and the children. And the sound of their screams.

He started hanging white birds everywhere. Cutting them out of paper, attaching them to strings, and nailing the strings to the rafters. At first this seemed encouraging to his mother and the visiting priests. A sign that perhaps he was being led back to the Ancient One's path.

But then, perhaps worse than anything that had come before, they caught Thierren in his room surrounded by pages ripped out of *The Book of the Ancients* as he tore the page in his hands into small, curling ribbons.

That was when his parents started to talk seriously about sending Thierren to the Valgard Sanitorium.

Thierren considers all this impassively as he stands before Commander Sylus Bane and the other soldiers, looking them over as if he's watching scenery go by from inside a carriage. He doesn't care about any of this anymore. But he's not going to play along. He's not going to let them believe their own lies.

"There were *children*," Thierren says unforgivingly, his gaze fixed on Sylus Bane.

Sylus spits out a sound of derision, his mouth curling into a nasty half smile. "No, Thierren, there were *heathen spawn*. You forget who you are."

Thierren is unmoved. "There were *babies*."

Sylus's half grin disappears, his eyes narrowing to slits. "There were *Fae spawn*."

Anger wakes in Thierren, bracing as an ice storm. When it comes, these days, it's savage. Cyclonic.

Clearly Sylus Bane can sense this. He, too, knows Thierren has become some other thing. A non-Gardnerian thing. And he wants to cut him down right there. But, unfortunately, protocol is protocol.

"You're lucky you have such influential parents," Sylus says, his tone thick with disgust. "They relentlessly pled your case, and they found the only commander in the Guard willing to take you on, stripped of all rank." Sylus's mouth turns up in a sly smile, his eyes conspiratorial. "But, trust me, you'd be better placed with a swarm of kraken spawn. Because your magery is child's play compared to your new commander's. And he has a reputation for…disciplining the disloyal."

*Who?* Thierren wonders blankly. "Who is he?"

Sylus Bane's grin widens. "Mage Lukas Grey."

# CHAPTER
# FOUR

# ESCAPE
## SPARROW TRILLIUM

*Fifth Month*
*Southeastern Fae Island*

Sparrow stands on the eastern shore of the Southeastern Fae Island and looks over the turbulent Voltic Sea toward the Western Realm continent.

Storm clouds are gathering overhead. Veins of lightning flash fitfully, illuminating the waves. The boiling clouds move across the vast, wind-tossed sky, making Sparrow feel very small in the face of the threatening seascape before her.

It's unusually cold this eve. A stiff breeze buffets her thin, gray labor garments, and Sparrow wraps her arms around herself as she shivers. The salty wind tangles her violet hair against her pale, lavender face as she peers across the choppy waters at the dark, hulking landmass just beyond.

The westernmost tip of continental Gardneria.

Sparrow's brow tenses, her apprehension mounting as she

takes in the glowing deep-green line that's working its way along the edge of the distant coast like a luminescent snake.

Gardneria's new runic border. Created with the Mages' mysteriously ramped-up runic magic and fashioned from thousands upon thousands of Gardnerian runes that are being thrown up at astonishing speed.

Especially considering that the Gardnerians have only one elderly Light Mage.

Sparrow squints at the imposing rune barrier, sizing it up like a cruel, worthy foe as she pushes her hair behind her ears' arcing points.

The magical border the Gardnerians are building now limns continental Gardneria's western shore as far north as her eyes can see and extends all the way down to where she's now peering across the short stretch of kraken-infested ocean that lies between the easternmost edge of the Fae Islands and Gardneria.

The full might of Gardneria, set on keeping Urisk, like her and Effrey, on the labor islands and out of continental Gardneria.

And once the entire of Gardneria is surrounded by a runic border, no one will be able to flee through the continent to get to the Eastern Realm.

The runic border creeps farther south each week, and soon continental Gardneria's entire western coast will be impenetrable. And it's only a matter of time before the Fae Islands are surrounded by an impenetrable rune border, as well.

The time for escape is running out.

An odd shadow slips through the ocean in Sparrow's peripheral vision, and she turns her gaze north to follow it, a different chill snaking down her spine.

A kraken monster. Sliding its oily, black body through the waves, headed due north.

They used to be a rare sight here, the creatures usually encountered in deep ocean, far from shore, but for some reason the kraken are being drawn ever closer to continental Gardneria.

As if they're being summoned.

Sparrow assesses the situation as she ignores the fear that's prickling along her skin. She's used to weighing terrible, heartbreaking options. All the Urisk are.

*No. Tonight can't be the night.*

It's too dangerous for a journey across turbulent waters in a flimsy boat with kraken close. She's going to call this off. She and Effrey will have to wait.

"Plotting your escape?"

Sparrow gives a small jolt and spins around, her sandaled heels digging into the cold, wet sand, her heartbeat drumming against her chest.

Tilor is watching her with his beady eyes from the shadows of the knotty Sea Pines, just a few paces away. Revulsion floods Sparrow.

*The cruel, arrogant bastard.*

He's so pathetic, standing there leering at her in his well-pressed Gardnerian military tunic with its single stripe on the edging, a weak, magic-free Mage barely older than Sparrow's nineteen years. Yet you'd think he had the power of one of their Great Mages, the way he struts about, ordering the Urisk around.

Sparrow takes a deep, steadying breath. Normally, she wouldn't allow herself to even think these mutinous thoughts. Even a trace of defiance in the inflection of one's tone is enough to bring down the wrath of these vicious Crows.

Square-jawed Tilor strides forward, smirking, and Sparrow keeps her face carefully neutral, even though she's suddenly keenly aware of the stolen knife that's sheathed and hidden in the side of her boot, just under the hem of her long skirt.

She dips her head with deferential grace. "I like to walk by the ocean's side, Mage Bannock."

Tilor puffs up, as if visibly mollified by her submissive stance.

*If I could get away with it, I'd pull this blade and slice you clean through*, Sparrow internally rages. But there's no getting away with it, trapped as she is on this cursed island.

It's a dangerous game, to feign pleasantries with Tilor, but what choice does she have? He's the assigned Mage warden of her labor group and knows full well that she has no good options. He is increasingly taking advantage of it.

*The vile bastard.*

His gaze skims over her. "Well, I'm glad to hear you're just out for a stroll," he purrs as he comes too close. Always, lately, he's coming too close. He reaches up and slides a tendril of Sparrow's long hair behind one ear, then fondles her ear's point as Sparrow grits her teeth and fights the urge to flinch back from his repellent touch.

"You're really quite lovely," he murmurs, but then his brow knots as if he's both surprised and abashed by his own senti-ment. His hand falls away. Sparrow keeps her gaze carefully averted from his as nausea wells inside her along with the fierce urge to claw at his hated face.

The foghorn sounds, and they both glance toward the light-house just northeast of them, perched at the end of a long, rocky causeway. The impossibly high structure appears small and thin from this distance, like a pale finger pointing accus-ingly at the sky.

"I was stationed up there last night." Tilor turns back and smiles coldly at Sparrow. "Bunch of rockbats thought they'd make a try for the continent." He shakes his head, as if discussing naughty children.

Two emotions hit Sparrow at once, lightning hard. Outrage over his use of the slur that mocks both the Urisk's ears and their latent geomancy powers. And glass-sharp worry. Because she knows the Urisk he's speaking of, their whereabouts carefully concealed by Sparrow and other Urisk to buy them a day or two for their escape.

"They got about halfway to the mainland," Tilor continues, "and the kraken devoured them." He says this last part with a heavy sigh.

Shock slams into Sparrow, and it's all she can do to remain upright.

*No. No, it can't be.* Enna'lys. And Marrillya. And small Silla'nil, bundled up and loaded onto the crowded boat, clutching a cloth doll Sparrow had lovingly sewn for her. Sweet Silla'nil, with her secret collection of shells. Her rose-splotched cheeks and pale pink curls. The child singing, always singing, like a tiny bird. Even the cruel Gardnerians were unable to destroy her gentle, bubbly soul.

Tilor sniffs, frowning. "I had a good view from my scope. Watched the beast take them down. It was truly awful. Tore a child's head clear off." He makes a jaded sound. "Their own fault, really. Honestly, what were they thinking? Did they not notice the kraken out there that are visible right from the shore?" He shrugs, pursing his lips, and lets out a long breath. "Provided an evening's diversion, at least. Gruesome as it was." He glances over his shoulder at the factories, greenhouses, and farms located past the bluff and rolls his eyes. "*Anything* to break up the tedium of this godforsaken place."

Rage digs its claws into Sparrow, cold and condemning, along with a terrible, heart-shattering grief. She tries to fight it. Tries to punch it back down, but she can't this time. The outrage is too great, and it rises like a burgeoning tide.

"It's *wrong*." Her voice is as unforgiving as the ocean's black depths. "The way you treat us. It's *wrong*."

Tilor's head snaps toward her, and he looks as if she's slapped him.

*Stupid, stupid!* A remnant of sense shrilly blares a warning in the back of Sparrow's mind. But at this moment, she doesn't care. Her fingers twitch with the urge to pull her knife and take him down, even though he's too muscular for her to overpower.

Tilor's stunned expression melts away, a confrontational grin forming on his face.

"You've no souls," he declares. "It says so, right in the *Book*. You're like empty shells." His gaze flicks over her as he sighs ruefully. "A lovely shell, in your case, but an empty one. Someday, after you die, it will be like you never existed at all." His mouth twists into a bitter sneer. "So, it doesn't matter how we treat you, now, does it?"

Sparrow's fierce anger is ratcheted up by the ball of hot grief that's forming deep in her core.

*Silla'nil.* The child was supposed to be on her way to Valgard. And from there to Verpacia, and then through the Pass to the East. And, someday, to safety in Noi lands. A scream rises in Sparrow's throat, threatening to loosen.

Tilor reaches up to play with her hair again, and Sparrow digs her nails into her palms to keep from attacking him.

"I know you hate it here," he murmurs, stroking her cheek, as if sympathetic to her plight. "But you need to accept your lot. It's ordained by the Ancient One that you serve us. It says it right in the *Book*. There's no escaping us or our power. Especially now that we've got our Black Witch."

His words are like another debilitating punch to the gut.

First Vogel takes power, and now...now they have their Black Witch too?

Sparrow knows exactly who that Black Witch is likely to be.

"Fallon Bane," Tilor breathes out reverentially, a slightly besotted look in his eyes. "The Ishkart tried to kill her, but they failed. She's recuperating. And her power is growing."

Dread courses through Sparrow. It's too awful to comprehend. Fallon Bane is the reason she and Effrey are in this nightmarish place. All because of that one day, so many months ago, when Mage Elloren Gardner chose the same fabric for her dress that Fallon had chosen for her own.

Mage Florel, the kindest Mage Sparrow and Effrey had ever known, refused to be cowed by Fallon's bullying, even after Fallon returned to the shop and forbade Heloise Florel from making the dress. Incensed, Mage Florel quietly defied her, sorely underestimating Fallon Bane's capacity for vengeance.

Soon after, Fallon spread the word that no one was to do business with Mage Florel. Ever again.

And so, Heloise Florel was driven out of business and into the poorhouse. Sparrow stiffens at the memory of how both she and Effrey were purchased by the Banes in retribution for working on the forbidden dress, then shipped to this labor camp on the Fae Islands, where all the Urisk left on the Gardnerian mainland will soon be, as well.

"Finish your walk." Tilor's coldly indulgent voice snaps Sparrow from her inner storm. "Then come to my room."

Surprise flashes through Sparrow. "Your room?"

Tilor's expression sharpens. "Yes, my *room*," he spits out, as if he has a genuine grievance here. "You've put me off long enough. I brought you extra *food* this past winter. Extra *blankets* and warmer *clothing*." He straightens, his gaze sweeping over her, as if appraising something he's about to fully own. "I've been *patient*, Sparrow. More patient than any other Mage here would ever be. So, finish your walk. And get yourself to my room. I'm done waiting." There's a flash of cruelty in his expression that nearly freezes her heartbeat, as if he can sense her inner mutiny and is ready to punish her for it.

Tilor walks off in a huff, pauses just before his path disappears into the pine grove, then turns to her once more, his wretched face smug.

"Sparrow," he calls, "if you make me wait too long, I'll inform our commander of your nighttime ramblings." He shakes his head. "Don't make me do that, Sparrow."

"I won't, Mage," she promises, picturing slicing his head in two with a sharp ax.

His gaze rakes over her form once more before he turns again and walks off.

Sparrow waits for the sound of his steps to disappear as a prickling rain starts to fall. When she's finally sure that the loathsome fool is gone, she turns on her heels and runs down through another pine grove, fleet as a deer as she makes for the shore's edge.

Little Effrey looks up when Sparrow emerges from the shrubbery, the child wide-eyed and bundled into their small, hidden boat. His sizable pointed ears stick out from the cloak and blanket he's wrapped in, his violet hue darkened to a deep purple in the dim light, his purple eyes wide and watchful as a harder rain begins to pelt them both. A few supplies for their journey have already been loaded on board.

The evening's fourth horn sounds, signaling the imminent change of the guard and a temporary relaxing of the watch. Sparrow cuts a glare toward the water.

No sign of any kraken boiling through the waves. The kraken she spotted before is probably quite a ways north by now. The beasts swim in swarms, usually keeping to one direction, so that kraken was likely part of a larger group that's cleared off.

"We leave now!" Sparrow hisses in an urgent whisper. She rushes toward Effrey in a crouch. She will not stay and be forced into Tilor's bed, and it's only a matter of time before the Gardnerians find out what Effrey really is. Then they'll both be dead.

Sparrow throws one last look over her shoulder at the island's interior, watching for movement and listening for any sounds past the restless swoosh of the waves and the patter of the rain. Finding none, she hikes up her skirt and secures it under her tunic's belt. Then she pushes the boat free of the land, walking it out until cool ocean water is lapping against her upper thighs. Effrey leans away from Sparrow for balance as she heaves herself inside the boat, grabs the oars, and makes for the continent.

Sparrow doesn't pause to rest until they're halfway to the Gardnerian mainland.

There's a momentary, blessed lull in the fierce winds and the driving rain as the boat is gently jostled by the waves beneath them. Sparrow is panting heavily, raindrops coating her lips, her shoulders and arms on fire from rowing against the ocean's stiff currents—currents that want to pull them south and way off course toward the dangerous whirlpool vortexes of the Southern Voltic Sea.

She shivers, drenched in chilling rain. She glances worriedly at Effrey, the child's blanket soaked from the rain and ocean spray, his teeth chattering. He's already sporting a vicious cold.

"Will I get to be myself in the Noi lands?" Effrey asks, a question he never tires of hearing the answer to.

"Yes," Sparrow affirms, forcing optimism in her tone. "You can be your true self there."

But not here. Here, Effrey has to dress like an Urisk girl, because being an Urisk male—a male who might harbor geomancy power—brings certain death in the Western Realm.

Sparrow glances behind them at the Fae Islands as their boat bobs in the unpredictable water and flashes of lightning periodically illuminate the world. The islands are like the back of a monster, hunching in the sea. She returns her gaze to the continent, at the huge mass of malignant land that lies between them and the longed-for East.

Sparrow imagines a larger boat with a well-appointed cabin, floating somewhere on the waters of the Eastern Realm. With a comfy bed to tuck Effrey into. Soft blankets. Abundant food. Books. And all the tools of her trade—a sewing machine, threads and fabrics, and everything else a seamstress could ever need, neatly stowed away.

It's all she's ever wanted in the whole world. Paid work as a seamstress, and a home of their own, even on a small boat. Where they can be safe and warm and dry on the waters of the Eastern Realm.

She might as well wish for a palace on a mountaintop, in this unforgiving world.

Still, in this blessed, brief instant, suspended between the yawning jaws of the prison that is Gardneria, Sparrow savors a small moment of safety. No Tilor. No menacing Mage soldiers. No threats of abuse.

*Freedom.*

A small, reptilian head pops out from under Effrey's blankets, slender and bone white. The small creature sets its slitted, ruby-flaming eyes on Sparrow, and her illusion of safety shatters.

"*No,*" Sparrow gasps as she recoils. "Oh, *no.* Tell me that is *not* a stolen dragon."

The dragon's eyes narrow, its gleaming ivory horns sharp

on its head. There are bloody gashes across its face and a metallic collar around its neck marked with glowing deep-green Gardnerian runes. Runes that cost a large number of guilders to procure.

Which means this dragon is the property of one of the wealthier Mages.

Effrey's trembling mouth turns into a dejected frown. "I *had* to save him. They were using him as pit bait! He had no one. No one but me."

The dragon sinks down below the blanket, those two defiant, fiery-red eyes peering out at Sparrow.

"He's probably a full-grown dragon without that collar!" Sparrow cries, recognizing the runic collar that suppresses pit-dragon growth. "Effrey...that thing is dangerous. And the Mages pay a pretty guilder for even their bait dragons." A heightened fear slides into her. "If they catch us and find we've taken him..."

"They *won't* find him," Effrey insists, hugging the beast tight. "I'll hide him. And soon his wing will heal, and he'll be able to fly."

"He's a moonskin," Sparrow notes, feeling increasingly light-headed. "They're considered bad luck, you know. That's why the Crows are using him for bait."

Effrey hugs the ivory-hued dragon protectively to his chest as thunder cracks and the rain picks up. "Anything that's bad luck for them has to be good luck for us." Both the dragon and Effrey stare at Sparrow like they're making all the sense in the world.

Sparrow's mouth tightens into a thin, frustrated line. *Foolish child and foolish dragon.*

Their boat gives a sudden, violent pitch to the side.

Sparrow cries out from the unexpected force, scrabbling to grab on to the boat's side with one hand, grabbing tight hold of Effrey with the other as a giant fist of a head blasts up from the ocean in an explosion of white spray, huge jaws, inky eyes, and lashing tentacles.

Terror, like a hot iron, spears through Sparrow's chest.

*Kraken!*

She lunges forward and pushes Effrey and the dragon down to the boat's floor, then grasps desperate hold of the boat's edging to keep them all from being cast overboard along with their supplies, the painfully cold waves sloshing over their bodies as the boat casts wildly about.

Another hard, punching tilt. Effrey shrieks as the boat almost upends, and Sparrow whips her head over her shoulder, fear slicing through her.

Drenching water clouds the image of the kraken's gaping mouth as it opens before them, a nightmare cave of teeth large as swords, the beast like some unholy union between a giant squid, a snake, and a fanged spider. Fetid, briny breath blows a blast of chill air toward them as its head curves down, down, down. Taloned claws at the end of multiple tentacles latch on to the sides of their boat, crunching into the wood.

The kraken lets loose a multitone, ratcheting snarl that reverberates through Sparrow's entire body.

She reaches below her sodden skirts with a shaking hand and pulls her knife in a useless attempt to protect them as she hugs Effrey tight and the child whimpers, clinging to her as the great kraken beast snarls and gurgles, jostling the boat with its barbed tentacles.

Tears sheen over Sparrow's vision.

*This is how it ends.*

*I'm sorry, Effrey. I'm so sorry.*

The small dragon forces itself out of Effrey's grip and scuttles toward the mammoth beast.

The kraken spots the dragon and rears back, its oily neck

undulating, then striking forward only to come to a shuddering stop just before the small beast.

Sparrow freezes.

The dragon's silvery form is silhouetted against one of the kraken's enormous eyes as it stares the sea beast down and lets loose a torrent of tiny shrieks and hisses and clicks.

Effrey is sobbing hysterically, hiding his face in Sparrow's chest as Sparrow peers into the huge, membranous kraken eye.

The kraken's serpentine neck jerks back, as if with surprise. Then its head flows back down toward the dragon's. Effrey whimpers as the enormous beast touches its head to the small dragon's.

The boat bobs as waves slosh around them and Sparrow dazedly glances at the black talon closest to her, large as a mountain ram's horn, its point impaling the wood.

*They're talking to each other,* she realizes with amazement.

The monster's talons click back in release, and the boat slams onto the waves with a sudden, bone-jarring force as the kraken rears back, blows out a brackish huff, and sinks down, disappearing below the water's surface.

Lightning flashes and thunder sounds above as the rain pelts down.

Sparrow anxiously searches the waves for the kraken's dark form as she shivers and clings to sopping-wet Effrey.

The kraken's black, ridged island of a head reappears behind them, slowly this time, its giant eyes rising just above the waves as Sparrow's whole body goes rigid with fright. She pulls Effrey back and readies her knife as the kraken's tentacles flow back up to latch on to their boat.

And then they're moving forward, fast and then faster toward the continent, the kraken almost completely submerged. The tip of the creature's colossal black tail whips back and forth as their boat picks up speed.

It dawns on Sparrow in a dizzying rush. *It's pushing us.*

"What's happening?" Effrey implores, wide-eyed and shivering, hiccuping tears.

The small dragon shoots Sparrow a look of triumph from the boat's stern, and Sparrow stares back at him, dumbstruck. She finds her voice just as a relief so immense it's like vertigo washes over her. "The dragon. I think he talked to the kraken." She lets out an incredulous breath. "He's...he's saving us."

A peal of joyous laughter mixed with tears erupts from Effrey. "I *told* you Raz'zor was good luck!"

Sparrow gives the beast a smile of overwhelming gratitude. "Thank you," she says, impassioned. "Thank you, Raz'zor."

The dragon dips his head and gives her a fierce, toothy grin, then scuttles back to Effrey, his slender, streamlined body glowing as if lit by internal fire. Raz'zor nestles against Effrey.

"He's warm, Sparrow," Effrey says with a bright grin, hugging the reptilian beast close.

Raz'zor peeks up at Sparrow, the hope in the beast's sharp face mirroring Effrey's, and Sparrow allows herself one joyful smile. Because this moment is a staggeringly, unexpectedly, blessedly good one.

Sparrow has done the math—a young Urisk seamstress and a male Urisk child disguised as a female escaping the Fae Islands to make a break for Gardneria. And from Gardneria headed for Gardnerian-controlled Verpacia, then to the treacherous eastern desert and from there to the Noi lands.

Their chances are close to nil.

It breaks her heart, the hope in Effrey's eyes. The hope in the bad-luck dragon's eyes. There are likely to be Gardnerians patrolling the shore, border guards or volunteer bands of angry Mages eager to torment refugees.

But at least they have this blessed moment, and isn't that

all there is, anyway? A terrifying kraken shepherding them toward the shore. A bad-luck pit dragon saving Effrey from the cold. The storm moving off to the east as gray, scudding clouds thin to reveal a gibbous moon. A wilderness of stars shining down from the widening gaps, the ocean awash in silvery moonlight.

Sparrow breathes in the cold, salty air and savors their brief moment of freedom.

*Yes, let Effrey have his hope.* That will be Sparrow's gift to him.

But as they grow closer to the shore and the kraken slips away and disappears into the Voltic Sea's great depths, a burrowing vulnerability takes hold. Sparrow takes up the oars, her eyes scanning the black shore, looking for potential attackers as freedom fades and the prison of Gardneria begins to reclaim its hold.

She knows she's only buying herself and Effrey some time. Titanic forces are gathering, and their days are numbered.

Because of Fallon Bane. The next Black Witch.

Next to Marcus Vogel, she's perhaps the cruelest one of them all.

*Why does it have to be Fallon Bane?* Sparrow agonizes. But does it matter, really? She's heard the soldiers gloating about the flimsy Resistance. And the Icaral of Prophecy, the Urisk people's only hope, is a helpless babe in his mother's arms, the Mage Guard tight on his heels. It's only a matter of time before the Icaral babe is killed, the Prophecy is fulfilled, and all hope dies as the Black Witch rises.

A cold fear enfolds Sparrow in its dark wings.

A Black Witch, in her full power, with Marcus Vogel's forces by her side, will bring the Crows' Reaping Times to even the farthest reaches of Erthia. Eventually, they'll kill or enslave everyone who isn't Gardnerian.

Sparrow looks to Effrey, despair tightening her chest as she takes in the foolish hope on the child's face. She will try to save Effrey and his dragon. And she will try to save herself.

She will try.

Sparrow jumps out of the boat just before they hit the black rocks of the shore. She guides their small vessel into a small, sheltered cove as icy water sloshes around her like ink, the moonlight's illumination now a threat as the clouds continue to break apart and dissipate. She motions urgently for Effrey to be quiet as she helps the child out of the boat and Effrey conceals the pearl-skinned dragon beneath his cloak.

The sound of boot heels scuffing up sand freezes Sparrow in her crouch behind boulders.

"Stop right there!" a hard, masculine voice yells, just past the large rock to their right.

Trembling, Sparrow dares a look between boulders as she and Effrey cower in the night's shadows.

There's a young Urisk woman on her knees on the sand, blue hands raised in surrender, head down, body shaking.

In one fearful sweep of her gaze, Sparrow takes in the three male Mages that surround the woman—two young Level Three soldiers and one older, black-bearded Level Four with a lantern in hand. All pointing their wands at the young woman's head, movable bars of lantern light strafing her cowed figure.

"Papers?" the Level Four Mage demands.

The woman doesn't move.

The bearded Mage huffs out a sound of contempt and murmurs a spell. Sparrow flinches as black vines shoot out of his wand to collide with the woman's body. She gives a brief, strangled cry as the vine netting wraps around her mouth and then her entire form, wrenching her down onto the wet beach.

Outrage bolts through Sparrow as well as the desire to launch herself at the Mages as they drag the woman away, but she knows there's no winning. Not against three Mages with wand power. And Sparrow has never actually wielded a knife.

Lit up by a feral desire to survive and remain free, Sparrow grabs Effrey by the arm and they bolt in the opposite direction, the men's throaty laughs and the woman's muffled cries kindling Sparrow's panic as they run through the beach grass, ignoring their bone-deep cold.

Eventually, they spot what looks like an abandoned structure atop a small bluff.

Sparrow and Effrey scramble up the bluff and make for what turns out to be a ramshackle stable, Sparrow's heart picking up speed as men yell to each other down on the beach.

They round the weathered Ironwood structure, duck into the darkened, deserted stable, then run through it into the last stall and slide the stall's door closed.

Sparrow meets Effrey's fearful eyes in the darkness, a shaft of moonlight spearing in from a nearby window that's visible through the door's wooden slats.

The door to the barn creaks open then slams, and Sparrow's throat constricts. She hugs Effrey tight, the two of them crouching against the walls in the stall's farthest shadowy corner, the dragon still hidden beneath Effrey's wet cloak.

A tremor kicks up inside Sparrow as footsteps stalk toward them, lamplight arcing chaotically over the walls.

A young Gardnerian man with severe, elegant features and soldier's garb comes into view through the iron bars, moving in with a vengeance, the rage trailing off him a palpable thing. Breathing heavily, his jaw set tight, he roughly sets his lantern on the window's sill. There's a luminescent deep-green rune stamped on his neck and black unsealed fastlines marking his hands. He snags a crimson glass bottle from behind a hay bale, hoists it, unstoppers it, and takes an angry swig. Sparrow can smell the medicinal stink clear through the stall.

*Spirits.*

Her fear notches higher. Sparrow knows what happens when these Mages drink spirits and find themselves alone with Urisk women.

She holds her breath as Effrey's small frame trembles against her.

*Don't find us. Don't find us.*

The desperate plea slams out with every beat of Sparrow's heart. Her sweat-dampened hand slowly moves under her skirt's hem to find the hilt of her knife as she readies herself to sink her blade straight through the white bird marking the Crow's chest, even though he has a wand sheathed at his side and Level Five Mage stripes marking his uniform's sleeves.

The young man sets down the bottle and angrily yanks off his tunic.

Alarm bolts through Sparrow as his body is scandalously exposed, hard muscles flexing, his Gardnerian skin glimmering deep green in the lantern light.

Breathing heavily, the angry young man pauses to peer down at the military tunic fisted in his hand, seeming like he would murder the uniform with his blazing green eyes if he could. Then he takes hold of the bottle and pours the spirits all over the tunic, all over himself, and all over the surrounding straw. He draws his wand and murmurs a spell, and a small fire bursts to life on its tip.

Sparrow's alarm explodes into full-blown panic as she realizes what he's about to do.

She jumps up, throws the stall's gate open, and leaps forward through it, palms out. *"Stop!"*

The young man's head whips toward her as he flinches back in obvious shock, his green eyes wild with emotion as

Effrey begins to whimper behind Sparrow and Raz'zor lets out a low, threatening growl.

The Mage swallows, his eyes dazed, the fire on his wand's tip dying down then blinking out of existence.

"What are you doing?" Sparrow asks in a choked rasp, feeling as if the ground is giving way beneath her. She's used to holding her tongue, but what does it matter how she speaks to this Crow? He has them cornered, wand in hand, and likely realizes they're escapees from the islands.

The young Mage lowers the wand and stares at Sparrow like she's an apparition. His gaze slides past her as the dragon's growl kicks up. Sparrow turns. All the blood drains from her head as a sense of vertigo swamps her.

The dragon is crouched on the straw floor, pale as a beacon and coiled for attack, his slitted eyes aglow with red fire.

And Effrey, sweet Effrey.

The child is holding a rock from the beach in his quivering hand, poised to wield it, the stone shining a bright violet—revealing both Effrey's forbidden geomancy power and his forbidden gender.

*All is lost*, Sparrow realizes with a sensation of spiraling descent. *It's over.* Raz'zor and Effrey are courageous, to be sure, but a Level Five Mage stands before them.

Sparrow slowly turns back to the cursed Mage with absolutely nothing in the world left to lose.

"Why were you going to explode yourself?" Sparrow demands, ragged voiced, as tears blur her vision.

The Mage swallows, his deep-green eyes filling with what seems like a wild despair. He fists his military tunic and holds it up. "We killed them," he chokes out, a grave weight to his tone, his mouth trembling into an anguished frown. "Our Guard went into the forest and killed the Dryads. Women. Children. Babies. I *tried*..." His whole face tenses, as if against a nightmare too devastating to bear. "I tried to hold them off... I couldn't stop them..." His deep voice breaks, choking off his words.

Their eyes lock and hold, Sparrow's fear of him momentarily subdued as she takes in the abyss of horror there. Whatever happened to these Dryads is like a violent ripple on a faraway lake, telescoping out to encompass them all, leaving nothing free of its fearsome wake.

"What's on your neck?" Sparrow asks harshly as she traces a finger along her own neck, then reflexively stops. It's never a good idea with these Mages to bring attention to one's body, and this one is already half-undressed. She tightens her grip on her blade's hilt.

Ready to go down fighting.

The young man's eyes flick toward the blade impassively, as if he doesn't much care if Sparrow runs it through him. Then he meets her gaze once more, his lips twisting into a bitter scowl. "The Mage Guard marked me with a trackable rune. So I can't escape them. My parents paid a lot of money to keep me out of military prison and force me back into soldiering." His mouth curls into a mirthless smile. "But I won't be part of any of it anymore," he seethes, his voice low and impassioned, his eyes now sheening with furious tears.

A flash of understanding passes through the very air between them, and it throws Sparrow into a vortex of confusion.

She steps toward him, clear out of options as she holds his tortured stare. "If you're not a part of it," she forces out in an emphatic demand, "then *help us*." Her stomach clenches the moment she says it, knowing full well what dangers she's opening herself up to by asking for help from this Mage she just stopped from destroying himself. But what choice does she have?

A fraught silence catches between them and holds, the

young Mage's expression twisting into one of vast confusion. He has the elegant features of their upper class, Sparrow notes.

He looks her over, and unease prickles through her, even though she can't detect any lust in his eyes. Then he lifts his green gaze back to hers, his severe face tensing with what seems like genuine, baffled concern. "You're wet."

Sparrow straightens, gripping her blade's hilt tighter in response to him noticing her body. She keeps a threatening undercurrent to her tone even as her lip trembles. *Keep your distance, Mage.* "We escaped the islands," she tells him. "By boat. To try for the East."

His eyes widen a fraction. "You came all that way...*tonight?*"

Sparrow nods stiffly, unable to suppress the shivering that's kicked up from both the cold wet of her clothes and her fear of him. Her fear of all of these cursed Mages.

"There are kraken out there," he says, and Sparrow suddenly wants to scream at him. *Yes, I know full well there are kraken out there, you blazingly stupid Crow.* Effrey gives a rattly cough behind her and begins to whimper.

"Why did you do it?" the Mage suddenly implores, stepping toward her, as if the question is a lifeline. "Why did you risk dying?"

Sparrow tenses, incredulous, and spits out the truest words she's ever spoken. "Because you Mages are *monsters.*"

# CHAPTER FIVE

# SHADOW RISING
## WYNTER EIRLLYN

*Sixth Month*
*Amazakaraan*

The birds fly down to Wynter Eirllyn in great, feathery spirals.

All types of birds.

Wynter kneels on the cool, dewy grass of the elevated pasture, the darkness of night still clinging to the Caledonian wilds at her back, the Amazakaraan city of Cyme, home to her Amaz protectors, splayed out before her.

Grief lodges deep in her heart for her beloved Ariel, a grief that is a constant companion now, a yearning that can never be assuaged or comforted.

*I love you, Sweet One,* Wynter sends out toward the eastern, predawn sky, as if Ariel were subsumed in it after departing this life and the words will somehow, someday find her there.

A haze shrouds the edge of the indigo sky, the damask rose color suffusing the peaks of the pale, gleaming Spine that walls the southern edge of the city. Wynter watches the beautiful color inch higher into the sky as soft brushstrokes of rustling feathers envelop her in their caress.

Wynter has been meeting with her winged friends here in this isolated spot before every dawn these past few weeks, reading their thoughts and speaking to them through her own empathic images. Sending some of them East on a hopeful quest to search for Naga, her dragon kindred.

Wynter has sent other wingeds throughout the West to see what they will see. Now the birds are flocking to her in droves.

Wynter stills, head down, as the birds crowd around her, twitchy and excitable as they press forward to make contact with her slender frame.

So many types of birds from so many lands.

Golden Maelorin cranes and blue-eared starlings. Rose finches and silver Alfsigr doves. A pair of huge desert hawks with stripes of bright saffron and vivid scarlet for camouflage against the red sands of the east.

A tiny, violet-crowned hummingbird buzzes beside Wynter's ear, its wingbeats a blur that sends a cool breeze against Wynter's neck before the bird alights on her shoulder and presses its whole self against her alabaster skin.

Wynter bends her head down farther to listen to all of her kindreds, her eyes closed as her hands find one bird. Then another. Then another.

A spark of amorphous dread lights in Wynter, hot and urgent, as thousands of images flood her senses from the staccato minds of the birds.

Something *wrong* is being sent into nature.

Something the birds are gleaning from the trees.

Pools of inky water with no reflection. Shadowy fire that burrows down, not up. A wall of otherworldly fog creeping in, washing away all color.

A void. Dark and impenetrable, beginning its spread through the natural elements.

A shadow.

Wynter takes a deep, quavering breath and opens her empathic mind to her wingeds, willingly falling off a cliff's edge into an abyss as she surrenders herself to the birds' collective vision.

She's immediately swept into another world, crouched low on an ashen ground, her gaze furtively darting all around a nightmare landscape.

Dead trees surround her, their twisted, charred branches reaching toward a bloodred sky. And there's a wall of shadow slowly and silently closing in on the dead forest.

In her vision, Wynter rises on shaking legs and walks just past the trees into a small clearing to meet with dense, gray mist, as she pulls her wings protectively tight around herself, waiting to see what the birds are so terrified of.

A hazy figure emerges from the roiling wall of shadow— the outline of a young Gardnerian woman.

There's a steel-gray wand clenched in her hand, shadow smoke trailing from both the woman and the wand.

The woman draws closer, and a stunned recognition lights in Wynter as the birds' primal screams of warning blare through her along with a remembrance of power sensed so long ago. An astounding level of power, read in just one fleeting touch of Elloren Gardner's arm. Just as Wynter was able to read Yvan Guriel's hidden Icaral wings so many months ago in one touch of his hand.

"*No*," Wynter rasps to the birds, shaking her head against their nightmare image, her threadbare wings drawing in more tightly. "It can't be Elloren."

Wynter can sense the multitude of avian bodies and thoughts pressing themselves insistently toward her, keeping her locked in the scene as certainty rips through Wynter and tears fill her eyes.

"The Shadow is coming for you," Wynter whispers to the terrible Elloren-image before her, grief-stricken for her friend as she reads the birds, the forest. "It's going to come for you with all its might."

Because it knows. This Shadow thing knows. And so does its enemy, the forest.

The Prophecy is here and there's no escaping it.

The Icaral has risen...and the Black Witch is back.

# PART ONE

# MAGE COUNCIL
# RULING
## #366

All Icarals in the Western and Eastern Realms of Erthia
are to be hunted down and executed.
Assisting in the concealment or escape of Icarals is
hereby declared as one of the worst possible crimes
against the Holy Magedom of Gardneria.
It shall be punished without mercy.

# VU TRIN MILITARY
# INTERNAL MANDATE

Sent to Runemaster Chi Nam
Issued by Commander Vang Troi

If Mage Elloren Gardner,

heir to the power of the Black Witch,

demonstrates magical capabilities equal to
or exceeding those of her grandmother,

she is to be executed immediately.

# THE BLACK WITCH

## ELLOREN GARDNER

*Sixth Month*
*Central Agolith Desert*

I stare out over the desert, the Wand of Myth clasped in my
hand, as I pull in a long, bolstering breath, my nerves alight
with tension.

A sudden, fierce longing to have Yvan here with me for
my first true wandtesting fills me.

*Where are you, Yvan?* I wonder, my heart constricting as
I take in the sea of barren red sands before me. *Have the Vu
Trin brought you to a desert somewhere as well, to find out the full
extent of your power?*

I've been separated from Yvan for weeks now, as I've traveled east with the Vu Trin military through an elaborately
constructed runic portal and then for many days on swift
horses to get here, a secret, deserted location in the Central
Agolith Desert. A place where they can test my power and
teach me how to wield it.

A place remote enough to hide the fact that the true Black Witch has been found.

The ruddy sands of the Agolith Desert are colored a deep russet by the bloodred sun that's close to setting, the air on my face and hands already cooling as twilight starts its descent, the desert world swiftly letting go of the day's brutal heat. Clusters of small purple cacti, scrubby plants, and a few arcing stone formations dot the harsh landscape, but mostly there's just the sea of sand.

Everything is quiet and empty, except for a lone bird circling high overhead.

I grip the Wand harder as I run my thumb over its cool, spiraling handle, a sense of grim anticipation building within me.

Turning slightly, I glance over my shoulder at Commander Kam Vin, her sister, Ni Vin, beside her, both of them dressed as I am, in the black garb of the Vu Trin military. Six other stony-faced Vu Trin sorceresses stand beside them, watching me and waiting. Four of these sorceresses are young, but two of them, white-haired Chi Nam and bald Hung Xho, are Lo Voi—powerful crones adept at both rune and portal sorcery.

Runemaster Chi Nam, who leans on her rune-marked staff, watching me intently, is the most powerful sorceress of them all.

They all continue to wait, tension thick on the air.

I glance back at the empty desert before us, as the desire to have Yvan here with me in this moment leaves a longing in my heart so strong I can barely breathe.

He was with me the last time I did this. The time we both realized we were each two points of the Prophecy. But somehow with him I believed everything would be okay. That we'd make it through this. That we could make the world a better place. But as I stand on the precipice of finding out the true extent of my power, I'm not so sure.

I'm frightened.

Frightened that I might, in fact, prove to be the destructive being predicted by the Prophecy.

I desperately want to believe, as Yvan does, that prophecies are dangerous, often self-fulfilling superstitions. That the power growing inside me isn't twisted like my grandmother's. But even the sparse desert trees here—it's clear that they sense something irredeemable in me.

*Black Witch*, the trees called out ceaselessly on the wind, low and accusatory, every time we passed through forested land. Ever since I blasted a forest into flame and Yvan and I discovered what I really am, the trees have been sending their aura of hate through me with a mounting intensity, so much so that it was a relief to finally portal out of the hostile forest and into this more barren landscape.

*What if it's true?* I agonize as I ready the Wand of Myth. *What if I'm at risk of becoming just like my grandmother if I harness this power?*

*What if I'm a danger to Yvan and everything good on Erthia?*

I look back down at the Wand, suddenly filled with an overwhelming reluctance to use this wand, even though it's been dormant since we rescued Naga. Even though my brother Trystan could no longer wring the simplest candle-lighting spell from it.

"I can't use this," I tell Kam Vin, my voice shaking. I turn and hold the Wand out to her. "I've a sense it's too powerful. I told you what I can do with a little branch."

Kam Vin's expression hardens. "Elloren Gardner, that is why we are in the Agolith." She motions toward the vast expanse of desert. "There is nothing here," she points out with a sweep of her hand. "Nothing for *leagues*."

Fear gnaws at my insides as I peer back over the red desert sands and my sense that something awful is about to be unleashed grows. I remember how I conjured a great, killing fire with just a slender twig.

I remember how the forest screamed.

"Give me another wand," I insist, turning my back on the desert expanse and holding out the Wand again to Kam Vin. "A weak one. Then I'll do it."

Kam Vin makes a sound of disdain, her fist on her hip. The sun's ruby light glints off the silver star weapons strapped diagonally across her chest and does nothing to soften the severe look on her face. "You are being foolish, Elloren Gardner."

"I don't care," I counter. "I won't try the spell. Not without a weak wand."

She narrows her eyes and glares at me for a protracted moment before gesturing toward young Chim Diec with a jerk of her chin.

Chim Diec is coldly formal and graceful as a heron. Like most of our party, she seems to view me with deep suspicion and has made a point of keeping her distance. She approaches me warily, then reaches inside her black tunic's pocket and pulls out a simple wooden wand from a cluster of four, this one made of pale wood with a swirling mahogany grain.

*Mountain Ash.*

"This wand is perhaps one step up from a tree branch," Chim Diec tells me, her words crisply accented.

Heart pounding, I sheathe the Wand of Myth in the wand-belt around my waist and take this new wand in hand.

I can feel this wand's lesser power the moment I touch it, my magic drawing down, retreating through my feet and back into the earth. I can sense that the wood has fewer layers, roughly put together, shoddily done.

When I touch my Wand, I can feel layers and layers of wood going on to infinity, and, sometimes, if I have it in hand when I'm surrounded by forest, I can barely hold on to the power that strains up from Erthia to meet with it. It's been like this whenever I have a wand in my grasp ever since I sent a spell through that small branch. Ever since I discovered what I truly am.

Something within me has been unleashed. And its potential for destruction terrifies me.

And even though this wand in my hand does feel weak, it's still a wand.

"Step back," I nervously order the sorceresses, recalling the runic shields they're capable of creating. "And send up a strong, combined shield."

Kam Vin seems to be rapidly losing patience, the already tight line of her mouth drawing tighter still. "It's unnecessary," she bites out. "And will take well over an hour's time."

"Humor me," I insist.

Runemaster Chi Nam calls out something to Kam Vin in the Noi language, and Kam Vin gives a terse, reluctant nod before shooting me a glare. Then Kam Vin, Ni Vin, and the other Vu Trin back away toward where the horses are tethered to stakes.

Rune sorceresses Chi Nam and Hung Xho set down rune stones on the ground in a circle around the sorceresses, then lower themselves to each stone in turn, tapping runic codes onto the stones with their glowing blue rune styli.

Luminous sapphire lines fly from stone to stone and arc over the sorceresses, strand by delicate strand, as Chi Nam and Hung Xho painstakingly weave the shield's framework.

Eventually, both elderly sorceresses rise and Chi Nam touches her rune staff to their webbed enclosure.

The shield buzzes to life, a translucent dome of blue coursing from Chi Nam's staff and over the woven strands until it fully encompasses all of the Vu Trin sorceresses and most of their horses, the pulsating shield casting azure light in a wide radius around itself.

Both Chi Nam and Hung Xho turn to me expectantly, glowing blue rune styli in hand.

"We are shielded," Kam Vin informs me from underneath the radiant dome, an impatient edge to her sharp tone.

I survey the entire scene anxiously. Ni Vin's ebony mare is unshielded, but safely tethered far behind the shield at what looks like a safe distance away.

I turn. The sunset's colors are now dimmed to a blush of red that limns the horizon, our stretch of desert awash in blue rune light. I lower my gaze to the wand, my fastmarked hand firmly clenched around its handle. My throat tightens, and not because of the dry, sandy air.

A rapid *scritch, scritch, scritch* sounds before me and my eyes flick up. Not far from me, a small desert animal races through brush and down into a sheltering hole.

*Yes, that's right*, I think. *Run for cover. Tunnel down as far down as you can.*

I hesitate, wanting the small animal to have time to hide deep in the earth, safe from me.

And then I take a deep, quavering breath and raise the wand.

I begin to speak the words to the candle-lighting spell, the words beginning to roll off my tongue as if drawn out of me by the wand, and it begins.

Tension builds in my lower body, warm and simmering, as the words draw up Erthia's power. This sensation doesn't surprise me. I've felt it before.

But then the rumble of energy coursing through my lines coalesces in a wholly new way. The power contracts and intensifies, then makes a sudden rush for my wand hand with startling force, fire magic blazing through my affinity lines.

# THE SHADOW WAND

I gasp as my wand hand burns hot and begins to glow scarlet without pain, my fingers seeming fused to the wand as my entire body contracts toward it, driving the air from my lungs and rooting me to the spot. Tremors begin at my feet and slowly work their way up my legs as panic seizes hold. Soon, my whole body is quaking with violent energy, and I'm helpless to stop it. I gasp and strain against it, completely at the mercy of Erthia's massive, unpredictable power.

I cry out as another overwhelming surge of power shoots up from Erthia, through my body and wand arm, and courses straight through the wand.

Fire explodes from the wand's tip in a roar, rapidly furcating into thick streams of flame that fan out over the desert, the streams coalescing into a blazing flood that sets every last bit of vegetation alight as I buck and tremble, completely at the mercy of the power.

The sea of fire surges forward and engulfs the landscape, multiple exploding fireballs at its edges destroying everything in their path.

The fire flashes toward the horizon, up the distant hills, arcing skyward, its heat building. Pillars of black smoke rise as the great ocean of fire crests and then starts to curl backward, everything transformed into a cataclysmic world of flame.

Aghast, I struggle to pull my hand away from the wand, away from the power that has taken on a life of its own, as the great arc of fire starts its tidal wave roll back toward us.

A scream rises in my throat.

My savage connection to the wand abruptly gives way and I wrench my hand from it, falling backward onto the ground as the wand falls from my grip and the roaring inferno crashes down on me, a sky of fire meeting earth.

*Frantic yelling in the language of the sorceresses. Horses screaming as the searing heat plummets onto us, accompanied by the earsplitting, all-encompassing roar of the fire.*

I close my eyes tight as the fire flickers red through my lids and the heat rises, and I wait for the terrible pain. My Vu Trin garments are made to shield the wearer from fire, but they can't possibly protect me from *this*.

*I'm going to burn to death.*

I scream as the fire burns through me, and I wait to feel my own flesh melting down to exposed nerve endings, then to bone, and finally to dust. I keep screaming, the sound drowned out as the fire roars its unbearable heat through me, its force shaking me like a discarded rag doll.

And then I surrender, falling into the fire the way the drowning must eventually submit to the water, as I wait for death to turn the red to black.

The black comes, and the roar begins to die away.

Lying on the ground, I feel for my body and am shocked to find it solid and whole. The dry, crackling sound of fire is all around, the acrid taste of smoke in my mouth as a cool breeze touches my cheek.

The *skin* of my cheek.

Dazed, I reach up and touch flesh that is still miraculously there.

I feel strangely disconnected from the panicked whinnying of horses in the distance, the cries of the sorceresses frantically calling to each other in their language, the din like a faraway dream.

I open my eyes and sit up, afraid of what I'll find, not completely trusting my body to be whole.

Before me is a charred, smoldering landscape, even the stone formations rendered to ash. Small brush fires dot the desert as far as the eye can see. A bloodred sky filled with clouds of black smoke looms above it all.

Stunned, I hold up my hands and turn them over and over.

They're covered in black soot, but still there, marked by the fasting lines. I glance down at my body. My fireproof Vu Trin garb is sooty, but intact. But the travel bag and wand-belt that hung from my waist have been burned away, only a few singed leather strands remaining, the Wand of Myth nowhere in sight.

I lift my hands closer to my eyes, stunned by the sight of them. *Unharmed.*

Recklessly curious, I thrust my finger into a small brush fire that burns beside me. The heat courses through my finger as I turn it over as if coating it in rich honey, but…*nothing.* I thrust in my entire hand, then my arm. Nothing again.

I'm impervious to fire.

The reason pricks at the back of my mind.

*Yvan. His kiss.*

Realization dawns that by giving me his Wyvernfire, Yvan's made me immune to it, just like he is. But the sorceresses. And their horses…

I whip my head around, focusing in on their impassioned voices as they cry out to each other in the Noi language. My body slackens with relief as I take in their dark forms through the haze of smoke, the blue glow of the shield around them rapidly diminishing.

They've survived.

But only because of the shield.

I spot the horse that was left outside of the shield, Ni Vin's mare, and my gut churns. The mare is lying dead, half melted into the sand.

Shocked by the devastation I've wrought, my head whips back to the sorceresses as their shield dissipates. One of the Lo Voi crones, bald Hung Xho, points at me and snarls something at Commander Kam Vin in their language, both her tone and the gesture thick with accusation. She launches into what sounds like a fierce argument with Chi Nam, Kam Vin, Ni Vin, and Chim Diec, the sorceresses appearing to have split into opposing factions.

As I stand on shaky legs, Hung Xho fixes me with a look of such pure hatred that I freeze, heart racing.

Even though I can make out only a few scattered words of their language, it's clear from the way they're glaring and pointing at me that they're at complete odds over the use of my monstrous level of power. And it's then that I understand, from the fear written on all of their faces...

I'm more powerful than my grandmother ever was.

And they were wholly unprepared for it.

Shaken, I watch as they yell and rage at each other and realize I've become an agent of division and discord, setting allies against each other.

One of the younger sorceresses, Quoi Zhon, a spiky-haired, sturdy woman with a powerful stride, breaks away, like a murderous crow straying from the flock, and makes straight for me.

Confusion, then fear, explodes inside me.

"Elloren!" Kam Vin cries out as she and Ni Vin surge toward me as well, their rune swords quickly unsheathed as Quoi Zhon reaches for one of the silver stars strapped across her chest and I start a rapid retreat backward, my pulse hammering in my chest.

On instinct I flinch sideways as Quoi Zhon's hand jerks forward, and I lose my footing.

I fall to the ground, and a streak of silver strafes the side of my scalp as it whizzes past, a stinging pain exploding in its wake just as Kam Vin's sword slices in a wide arc along the back of Quoi Zhon's legs.

Quoi Zhon falls to her knees, her neck jerking back as she

cries out in pain. And then her eyes snap back to me, full of rage-fueled determination as I frantically resume my scuttling retreat backward.

Quoi Zhon reaches for another star as Kam Vin slams an elbow into the woman's arm, the silver star flashing with reflected firelight as it drops into a patch of smoldering embers. Then Kam Vin strikes the back of Quoi Zhon's head, and the sorceress collapses facedown on the sand.

Chi Nam slams the bottom of her rune staff onto the ground, and there's a loud *crack* as a brilliant flash of blue lights the world. The light quickly clears to reveal Chi Nam surrounded by what appear to be countless spears made of sapphire light, hovering around the white-haired sorceress and pointed at Hung Xho and the sorceresses who seem to have aligned themselves with Hung Xho and against me.

Kam Vin, Ni Vin, and Chim Diec all have silver stars aimed at Hung Xho and her allies. Hung Xho and the sorceresses bracketing her have drawn rune swords that glow menacingly bright with sapphire light. Clearly at a deadlock, the sorceresses launch into another volatile debate.

My heart pounds against my ribs and blood trickles down my neck as I watch the two armed groups face off, knowing full well that my life is at stake. My instinct for self-preservation kicks in, and I glance at the charred ground, searching for a wand but finding neither my Wand nor the wand Chim Diec gave to me.

I immediately realize how futile this search is.

If, by some miracle, I could find a wand that wasn't incinerated, what exactly could I do with it? Level it at all of them and kill my allies along with my enemies? As well as all of the remaining horses? I would be left alone in the desert, where I would probably starve to death.

I'm the most powerful Mage to ever walk Erthia…and I cannot use a wand to protect myself.

A few more minutes of furious discussion ensue as I pick up a sharp rock and ready it as a possible weapon, my heart thundering against my chest. But then, to my great relief, Hung Xho and her allies lower their weapons then throw them to the ground.

Chi Nam taps her rune staff on the sand, and the glowing spears disappear in a flash of light. Hung Xho snipes at both Chi Nam and Kam Vin then indicates me with a slice of her hand. Suddenly, the two young sorceresses beside Hung Xho run in my direction.

Fright jolts through me and I scuttle backward, readying my sharp rock for throwing, only to lower it again when the two sorceresses simply lift the semiconscious Quoi Zhon and carry her toward one of the surviving horses. I stare as that half of our group—the half that wants me dead—loads themselves onto three of the horses, snarls hate-filled words at me, then gallops away.

Four sorceresses remain, huddled together and talking in hushed tones.

Ni Vin's face is tense with indecision as Kam Vin makes a case to young Chim Diec. Perhaps a case for my life. Chi Nam calmly leans on her runic staff and listens.

Every now and then, Ni Vin's gaze wanders toward her mare's charred, mangled corpse, and pain twists her face.

Remorse spears me. *Ni Vin's mare. Her beloved mare.*

Unexpectedly, the mare I thought dead comes to life with a gurgling shriek, head slashing side to side, foam spraying from her mouth. Her eyes fly open, her dark gaze wild with terror as she begins to writhe in agony.

My mouth falls open as my chest seizes.

Something has to be done. She can't be left to suffer so grotesquely. As if locked in a nightmare, I glance around and, through the thinning smoke, my gaze catches on a slim, pale shape.

The Wand of Myth.

It lies on a raised, flat stone not far from my feet, unharmed, as if it's offering itself up to me. I rush to it and grab it with shaking hands, my power giving a hard lurch toward its spiraling wood. I stumble to the mare, stopping a few feet away, mesmerized by the grotesque thing I've done and sick with desperation to stop the horse's pain.

A white bird circling overhead flicks into my peripheral vision. It flashes bright as starlight and opens a dark corner of my mind.

All of a sudden, it isn't a horse I'm looking at, but a soldier, his uniform charred beyond recognition, the lower half of his body melted into the ground. His gaze is on me and filled with heart-wrenching terror. But it isn't just him. I look around, horrified to see soldiers of every race and realm, dying, burning, screaming. A battlefield full of soldiers—Gardnerians, Alfsigr, Noi, Ishkart, Amaz. But not just soldiers, no—women, men, children, even babies, all of them burned, all unspeakably injured by my terrible magic.

In that moment, I fully grasp what my power is at its malignant center.

The vision fades and is replaced by the dying horse once again.

Ni Vin stands beside her beloved animal, her rune sword unsheathed in her unscarred hand. As she considers the horse with her usual stoicism, my eyes take in her melted hand and ear, the scars that cover almost half her body.

She has tasted the same destructive magic that lives inside of me.

I flinch as Ni Vin expeditiously brings her sword down

through her mare's neck. She watches as the animal becomes motionless, her own face devoid of emotion, as if she is resigned to the death of an animal that has been her companion for years.

I look to her beseechingly. "I'm sorry, Ni Vin," I choke out. "I'm so sorry."

She turns and meets my eyes.

And there it is—a flash of grief-fueled rage, brief as a cobra's strike, gone before she turns away, wipes off her blade, and sheathes the sword once more.

Distraught, I look back at the mangled pile of flesh where a magnificent animal once stood—and all of it my doing. The vision of an entire field of death once again fills my mind and sends it spinning.

I cast the Wand away, fall to my knees, and sob.

A moment later, as my tears fall onto the charred ground, I feel Chi Nam's steady presence in front of me before she even speaks. She hovers near me, her wizened hands coming to rest on my shoulders.

"Gather yourself, child."

I look up at her, choked with tears and smoke. Her weathered body, wrinkled face, and age-thinned skin cause me to momentarily question her ability to help me learn how to handle the monstrous power lurking inside my lines. At this moment, faced with this *thing* inside me, she's like chaff in the face of a hellish storm. All of us are.

I can feel the claws of my power taking hold, sizzling through my affinity lines. Power I don't want. Horrific power.

"I'm no good to any of you," I rage. "I *cannot* control this power." I motion toward Ni Vin's dead horse. "Look what happened!" I glance at Ni Vin with fierce remorse.

Ni Vin's face tightens and she turns away.

I try to shrug off Chi Nam's hands, feeling close to hysteria. "Nothing good can come of this! The power was like a thrall once it took hold. I *can't* control it!"

A hum of energy shoots through Chi Nam's hands and courses through my shoulders in a thin line. I gasp at the line's powerful vibration as it flashes into me. My eyes jerk up to meet Chi Nam's as the energy charges through my body, riding my affinity lines as it smooths away my panic.

"That's better," Chi Nam says. The weight of the blue line of her magic pushes down harder, forcibly calming me. Suddenly, she doesn't seem so much like chaff.

Chi Nam's grip on my shoulders firms. "You push this fear aside and gather yourself."

I shake my head, and she presses her blue magic harder against the resurgence of my fear.

"*Yes*, your power is extreme," she insists with steeled certainty, "but you *will* learn to control it. You must tether yourself to that one thought, hmm?" She gently lifts her hands to my bleeding head. There's another burst of blue light, and almost immediately I can feel the throbbing pain along my scalp recede, the lacerated skin knitting itself back together.

Chi Nam releases her hold on me, picks up the Wand of Myth from the ground, and hands it to me. I hesitate, then take it from her as she regards me keenly, my affinity lines instantly straining toward it as the candle-lighting spell dances on my lips, yearning for release. "You must remember," Chi Nam says as she reaches back up to place a hand on my shoulder. "The Wand of Myth, the Zhilin, chose *you*, Elloren Gardner."

Thoughts of how much is at stake blare through my mind, making me light-headed. Both my magic and Vogel's mounting power are something born of nightmares.

I remember how Vogel murdered the Lupines, mercilessly cutting down innocent families, children. How he murdered

Diana's whole family. Agony sweeps through me over how the Gardnerians and their allies, the Alfsigr Elves, are bent on taking over the Realms and forcing their hellish worldviews on everyone.

"What do I do now?" I ask Chi Nam hoarsely as I struggle to beat back the storming anguish.

Chi Nam sits back on her haunches and clucks as she considers me, her white hair covered in ash. "Well, we must crawl before we can run, eh? Seems we must simply keep you alive for now." Chi Nam stands creakily and exchanges a look with Kam Vin as the sorceress hands her staff back to her.

"Our allies grow thin, Elloren Gardner," Kam Vin says to me, her expression troubled and hard. She glances at Chim Diec. The graceful sorceress is watching me with grim indecision. Ni Vin stands beside her, stony-faced, her focus once again inward.

"Where did the other sorceresses go?" I ask Kam Vin, reaching up to touch the dried blood over my healed scalp wound.

"To the Noi Conclave in Voloi," Kam Vin answers as she glances in the direction that the other sorceresses rode off. "They want the Conclave to send Kin Hoang assassins after you. They want you executed immediately."

The blood rushes from my face. It's what I surmised, but to hear it pronounced so starkly makes it terrifyingly real. I peer up at Kam Vin. "What should I do?"

Kam Vin hesitates then launches into a conversation in the Noi language with Chi Nam. The only words I can make out are those of a name—Lukas Grey. Surprise stings through me as a smile lights the elderly sorceress's face, and she exchanges a conspiratorial look with Kam Vin.

"Ah, yes, Lukas Grey." Chi Nam bumps my shoulder with the back of her hand and chuckles to herself. "Like a cat, that one. I used to spar with him, back when he was a lower rank. He made a game of it and tested me in turn. Seemed to enjoy it." She grows reflective. "There is an elegance to his power. And it is formidable." She eyes Kam Vin with cool calculation. "Yes, he'll do nicely. The Kin Hoang will be well matched by Lukas Grey." She turns to face me, newly serious.

I hold up a hand, disbelieving. "*Wait.* You can't be seriously considering sending me back to *Lukas?*"

"We're past considering," Kam Vin stonily affirms. "When you reach him, place yourself under his protection. *Immediately.*"

I stare at Kam Vin, Chi Nam, and silent Chim Diec, rendered speechless. This isn't how it's supposed to be. They brought me here to train with them, so that I could learn to control this power and save all the people I love. So I could learn to fight *against* the Gardnerians and their allies.

Now they want to send me back into Gardneria to the man who claimed he was a friend to me and then made use of my beloved uncle's death to fast to me against my will? And I'm supposed to go and beg him for protection?

"*No,*" I protest emphatically, sickened by the very idea of it. "I *hate* him."

"It's the best way," Kam Vin insists. "If we're going to keep you alive."

"Lukas seems to be flirting with a break from the Gardnerian military," Chi Nam tells me, a slight lift to her lip. "He and I have been in touch from time to time."

My head is spinning. *Lukas Grey? In touch with Chi Nam?* But then I remember his obvious hatred and disdain for Marcus Vogel. My own hatred for Vogel rises, hot in my gut, as I remember imploring Lukas, raging at him, to break with the Gardnerian military and his refusal.

I look to Chi Nam with fierce skepticism. "How can I learn

how to control my power if you send me back to Gardneria? If the Gardnerians find out what I am, I can't even protect myself there. I'd kill everyone around me if I tried. I might even level Valgard." *Killing countless civilians, Gardnerian and non-Gardnerian alike.*

"Which is why you'll keep your power hidden," Kam Vin states.

"If they find out what I am," I counter, facing down their level gazes, "Vogel will find a way to break me. And wield me."

We're all silent for a heartbeat.

"It's a gamble, Elloren Gardner," Chi Nam allows, a hard glint in her eyes. "But I'm convinced that your power is a tipping point. If you're killed, I fear that we're no match for what's coming."

Another terrible silence.

Perhaps responding to the anguish in my eyes, Chi Nam holds out her hand and gives me a fierce, bolstering look as she helps me to my feet. She fishes an onyx rune stone, etched with a midnight blue runic design, from her tunic's pocket. The rune glows sapphire. She places it in the palm of my hand, and it feels cool to the touch.

"Keep this hidden and with you at all times," Chi Nam says, closing her hand around mine. "It will summon me if you need me. You understand?" I nod once, and she reaches up to squeeze my arm. "*That's* it, child. Be strong. There's no other way." She gives me a penetrating look. "If we're going to defeat Vogel, we *are* going to need your power. We *will* come back for you."

"There is no more time for talking," Kam Vin cuts in, glancing worriedly toward where Hung Xho and her allies have gone. She sets her harsh gaze back on me. "You have to leave, Elloren Gardner. *Now.*" She turns to her sister, Ni

Vin. "Take her to the Phi Na Portal. Ride fast. To hesitate will seal her fate."

Panic rears. I cast a beseeching look at Kam Vin, Chi Nam, and Chim Diec. "But...where will *you* go?"

Kam Vin glances back at me with an expression of somber resignation. "We will travel to Niem and beg Vang Troi to spare your life."

Vang Troi—I remember the image of their powerful military commander, dismounting from a sapphire dragon on the North Tower's field, a silver, horned headpiece circling her brow.

"Do you think she'll listen?" I ask.

Kam Vin surveys the wreckage surrounding us, flames dotting the landscape far into the distance as the dark of night descends. She turns back to me, eyes grave, and doesn't answer as I clutch the rune stone.

"Find Lukas Grey," Chi Nam says to me. "Use your position as his fastmate to secure your protection. And, if you can, use it to find the weapon the Gardnerians used to kill the Lupines. Then give me this weapon when we come for you. If you're able to find this weapon for us, perhaps we can convince Vang Troi to spare your life. And ours."

# CHAPTER TWO

# MAGICAL ADDICTION

## ELLOREN GARDNER

*Sixth Month*
*Verpacian Province of Gardneria*

I watch Ni Vin through the flickering campfire light as I lie on my bedroll in the small forest clearing. The dark of night envelops us.

Ni Vin is sitting on a fallen tree in her black military garb, sharpening the cutting edge of her curved rune sword on a small whetstone, the blade glinting in the dancing firelight, the runes glowing Noi blue.

I've grown uneasily used to traveling with Ni Vin as we make our way west, first through the Phi Na desert portal to the Caledonian wilderness, then through a secret passage under the Northern Spine.

Headed for the newly annexed Keltish Province of Gardneria.

By now I know that, for Ni Vin, honing her weapons is her nervous tic. She sits, night after night, sharpening her rune sword and runic blades and her silver stars, even though all of these weapons are already razor-sharp.

I understand this compulsion of hers, because I'm equally drawn to wood, although I'm now actively struggling to fight my attraction to it lest I lose all control and give in to the heightened urge to send magic through it. I avoid all contact with the wrathful trees and their fallen branches as we travel through the deep wilderness of what's now the Verpacian Province of Gardneria. The forest's atmosphere of revulsion and fear zings along my affinity lines in sharp pinches.

As if the trees are quietly sizing up the enormity of my magic.

My eyes flick around as I take in the fallen branches and twigs strewn across the forest floor, some so straight and weathered that they could already pass for wands. My wand hand involuntarily clenches as the power in my lines strains toward each piece of wood I set my sights on.

I increasingly itch to touch dead wood, to feed what is increasingly feeling like some overpowering addiction that I have no control over, my yearning for wood seeming more and more like Ariel's yearning for the drug nilantyr.

To fight the urge, I clench my wand hand so tight that my nails dig into my palm, even though the longing grows stronger through my resistance. After using that wand, I finally know this compulsion of mine for what it truly is.

My access to unspeakable power that I yearn to release.

I've grown especially afraid to touch the Wand of Myth, which is rolled up in a coarse cloth and stuffed into the side of my left boot. I can sense its presence, sense the starlight tree reaching for me in the back of my mind, but I fight against the pull, scared of it.

Scared of all wands.

Scared of myself.

I lie there on my thin bedroll, thinking on these things, as I listen to the high-pitched scrape of Ni Vin's knife on stone, the blade catching the firelight and flashing in unspoken warning.

We've both been gravely silent for most of the journey, my power like a menacing third companion that we can't shake. Every so often her narrowed eyes flicker in my direction, and I wonder if she's imagining dragging the sharp edge of her knife across my throat.

She's known the true nature of this power of mine for some time. It's an enemy as familiar to her as her own melted hand and ear. And now I know it for what it is, as well. It bears no resemblance to the romanticized magic from the tales of my grandmother's battle adventures. It's the fire that killed most of Ni Vin's family, that terrorized and destroyed entire villages filled with her people. I remember how she once said that she was "cursed to live."

As she continues to scrape the blade, I realize my life balances on the razor's edge of her weapons. I should be frightened by the grim indecision in her eyes, but my resonating shock from having learned the destruction I'm capable of overrides all other concerns.

The next morning, traveling next to Ni Vin on horseback with barely a word spoken between us, I eat only to stay strong, barely tasting the square cakes of oily grain mixed with long shreds of dried fruit that have become our staple. I drink to stay alive, although the water is sour on my tongue, and all the time I wonder what evil thing I'm feeding.

Just before reaching the Southern Spine, we come to a sheltered riverbank, morning sunlight setting the water shimmering, the buzz of insects pricking at the air.

I let the heavy Vu Trin garb slide off my body with grim reluctance. The Noi weave offers protection from fire and the sharp points of arrows and knives, but almost as important, this garb provided the illusion that I could be accepted by a new people. That I could be something other than what I am.

I leave the clothing folded on the riverbank's rocky ground, grit my teeth, and quickly submerge my faintly green-glimmering body in the river, the water so cold that it sets me shivering, rigid goose bumps rising on my flesh as Ni Vin watches, impassive, from where she sits on a flat boulder. The intricate black lines of the shield-safe rune my friend Sage marked on my forearm and the demon power–sensing rune she impressed on my abdomen stand out in sharp relief on my cold skin.

Memories of my reunion with Sage a few months ago in the Amaz lands trigger a sharp longing for friends and family.

*Where are you, Sage?* I wonder. *Is your Icaral baby safe and did you make it to Noi lands? Are you there with my brothers and Diana and her brother Jarod and everyone else I love?*

*Are you there with Yvan?*

I stiffen, forcing down the fierce yearning to be with loved ones until it's buried deep inside.

My resolve steeled, I quickly finish washing. When done, I emerge from the river and wrap myself in a rough blanket then stand glaring at the fine Gardnerian clothes and cloak that Ni has set out on the flat, broad stone before me. Clothing Chi Nam was savvy enough to have at the ready in case I needed to flee.

The morning breeze picks up the edge of my blanket and sends a chill snaking around my ankles.

Feeling as if I'm voluntarily swallowing poison, I go about meticulously putting on the garb of my people—the silken undergarments and stockings, the slender, dark leather boots, the flowing black long-skirt. I thread my arms through the formfitting tunic, my breath catching as Ni firmly cinches the lacing that runs down my back and I tie it off.

She hands me the dark cloak, and I fasten it around my shoulders.

Then I slide the wrapped-up Wand of Myth back into the side of my left boot and push Chi Nam's rune stone deep into my tunic pocket, the feel of the stone through the silk the only thing able to quell my rising sense of dread.

Later that morning, Ni and I reach the Southern Spine, the ragged peaks looming overhead.

I watch as Ni Vin waves a stone marked with blue Noi runes over the flat, sun-dappled wall of rock before us, this section of Spine-stone rising higher than the Valgard Cathedral. An ache of longing cuts through me as I remember how Yvan effortlessly scaled this Spine as I clung to him with my eyes closed, terrified of how high we were.

Today, I will not be going over it.

An arc of sapphire runes similar to those on Ni Vin's stone appear on the Spine-stone, first as a faint outline, then as clear markings. Ni Vin presses her stone lightly on the series of circular runes, and part of the Spine-stone turns misty and disappears to reveal the tunnel that's to be my path into the newly annexed Keltish Province of Gardneria.

I turn to Ni Vin, my travel sack slung over my shoulder, and wait for her to hand me the dhantu stone that will illuminate my way.

Instead, her hand goes to the hilt of her sword and her expression goes raptor-hard.

The blood drains from my face in a light-headed rush as I'm pinned by Ni Vin's merciless glare. She could strike me down in an instant, and we both know it.

"I know you have considered killing me," I say, my voice low and careful.

"I consider it now," she replies without malice.

"Everyone I love," I tell her, my voice quavering with emotion, "*every single one of them* will be destroyed if the Gardnerians win."

Her hand remains firmly on the hilt of her sword. "Elloren Gardner, I know that in your right mind you are with us. But the Gardnerians...they have ways of breaking their enemies and bending their will."

What can I say in response? I know her words to be true. Images of broken Icarals and ruined Wyverns litter my mind. What methods would the Gardnerians resort to if it meant control of a Black Witch? We both know that if they discover what I am, they'll stop at nothing to own my power.

Power I don't know how to control, making me vulnerable to them.

Power that would force the Prophecy into its most nightmarish resolution.

"It is a risk to keep you alive," Ni Vin states, calm as a windless night.

"If I am dead," I force out, struggling to keep my voice from trembling, "that still leaves the problems of Marcus Vogel and Fallon Bane and the Gardnerian military. You have your Icaral, but Yvan's untrained and not powerful enough to take down the Gardnerians. Not yet."

Ni Vin holds my stare.

"And we both know Vogel's stronger than you all thought," I press, bargaining for my life.

Her hand tightens around the hilt of her sword. "Bringing you back into Gardneria..." Her lips tighten as she gives a stiff shake of her head. "It's potentially throwing you right into Vogel's hands. I question Chi Nam and my sister's plan."

We're quiet for an unbearably tense moment.

"I know," I finally say, my voice ragged. "I question this

plan too. But if my power is needed to take Vogel down, then I need to stay alive." I reach into my boot, grab the Wand of Myth from it, pull the cloth away, and hold it up, the Wand seeming to possess its own phosphorescent light. "And the Zhilin...even though I'm the Black Witch...it chose *me*."

Ni's eyes widen as they fix on the Wand, and she swallows, her slender throat bobbing.

I meet her dark stare as the power in my lines strains with disturbing intensity toward my wand hand. "It *is* a risk to keep me alive," I admit. "I know this. But my death could extinguish all hope of defeating Vogel."

I wait on a knife blade's edge while she deliberates, her brow now knotted, her hand still clenched around the hilt of her sword.

After a long, breathless moment, Ni Vin removes her hand from the hilt.

Air flows back into my lungs as she reaches into her pocket and hands me her rune-marked dhantu stone. I take it from her, already versed in the Noi words that will bring forth its sapphire light.

"Go, Elloren Gardner," she says, motioning toward the tunnel with her chin. "Take great care. And don't let the Gardnerians know what you are."

I nod in reply as her face darkens.

"If they find out and turn you," she says, her voice heavy with import, "I will have no choice but to come for you."

*To kill me*, she means.

I nod again. Then I wrap the Wand in its sheltering cloth and slide it into my travel sack, slipping it through a small tear in the seam of the layered fabric, effectively hidden and less likely to be spotted. Hoisting the sack, I set my eyes on Ni's scarred face, and we exchange one last grim look of solidarity.

Then I turn and descend into the darkness.

# THE SHADOW WAND

### ★ ★ ★

I travel through the damp tunnels for what feels like a long time, my surroundings made eerie by the blue light of the dhantu stone, and I do my best to tamp down my fear of the claustrophobic silence and scuttling insects.

When I reach the tunnel's end, a rush of relief courses through me at the sight of afternoon daylight streaming in, and I eagerly climb out of the tunnel to meet the next stretch of wilderness. I leave the dhantu stone inside the tunnel, as Ni Vin instructed, the runic symbols rimming the exit quickly vanishing as the doorway is swallowed up by Spine-stone.

Traveling for hours on foot and following the map Ni Vin gave me, I eventually reach the same horse market in what used to be Northeastern Keltania that I visited so many months ago with Yvan and Andras. I pause inside a sheltering tree line as I warily take in the late-afternoon scene, the market's convivial atmosphere disturbingly altered. There are only Gardnerian military horses in the penned fields now, black banners emblazoned with white birds hanging from their sides. They're being cared for by a few scraggly old Kelts. The younger Keltish men this market usually teems with are conspicuously absent.

Two Gardnerian soldiers lean against a fence in their smart uniforms, chortling over some joke as a white-haired, bitter-looking Kelt hands them something in a bag. As he walks off, the two men's gazes dart around before they slide the tip of a green bottle out of the bag and hastily pour its contents into the water flasks that hang from their necks.

*Spirits. Forbidden by the Mage Council.*

Heart pounding as I draw on my courage, I choose that moment to stride out to meet them.

Feeling as if I'm embarking on an irrevocable course, I emerge from the edge of the woods in my formal Gardnerian attire, the spitting image of my powerful grandmother. The men's mouths drop open in shock.

I glance pointedly at the flasks in their hands before pinning my gaze back on the two of them. "Take me to Commander Lukas Grey," I order. "I'm Elloren Gardner. His fasted partner."

Moments later, I'm in a carriage finer than my aunt Vyvian's, four Level Five Mage soldiers flanking my vehicle. I feel oddly disconnected from my surroundings, the ride so smooth, it's as if there's not a stone in the road.

Soon, the woods open up and Keltania's Central Crossroad comes into view. My eyes widen.

The broad crossroad is jammed, absolutely jammed, with Kelts all moving in one direction—toward the northeast.

Refugees, all of them, I realize, stunned by the vast number of people traveling to get out of a Keltania that's just become a province of Gardneria.

My carriage quickly traverses the distance separating us from the main road.

"Make way! Make way!" My guards call out brusque orders, and the road traffic parts before us as we travel southwest against the flow, the Kelts pulling away from us with haste, fear etched on their faces.

And hatred, carefully hidden, but it's there at the edges of everyone's eyes.

The carriage slows, and I lock eyes with a little Keltish girl who's clutching her bedraggled mother's hand. She's hugging a worn cloth doll with flaxen braids to match her own. A lump forms in my throat. She's around the age of Fernyllia's granddaughter, and there's a traumatized look on her round-cheeked face as her blue eyes stare fearfully back at me.

"How's it feel?" one of my Mage Guards suddenly booms out at the fleeing refugees, causing the little girl to flinch and blink fearfully up at him. "This is what you did to us!" he snarls. "Forced us out of our homes! Took our land! How's it feel?"

The Kelts avert their eyes as we speed up and the little girl is whisked from sight.

I'm overcome by an acute sense of the jaws of Gardneria snapping shut over the little girl. Over all these people. And the titanic forces at work all around me, disrupting the entire world.

*But there are titanic forces inside me as well,* I suddenly remember, swept up in the overpowering yearning to wrest control of my power and wield it to stop this cruelty.

My body shudders as magic fires through my affinity lines in a heated rush, along with a flash of awareness of the wooden frame of the carriage.

My wand hand clenches involuntarily. Wanting it.

Wanting the dead wood.

Wanting the power.

*You can't control it!* I desperately caution myself as I fight off the compulsion to grasp hold of the wood at the edge of my seat, voice a spell, and send my magic straight through it. *You'll be pulled under your power's thrall and kill everyone in sight! Don't touch the wood!*

I yank the window's dark velvet curtains closed and grasp my wand hand, pulling in a deep, quavering breath as Mage-fire ripples through my lines.

*You need to be patient,* I remind myself with each measured breath as fear edging toward panic makes a merciless play for me.

Fear of myself.

*You need to stay alive, or you won't be able to fight them,* I insist, battling my raging emotions and equally raging power.

I rub my wand hand, first wringing it as the fiery power

courses through me, then caressing it as my breathing slows and the fire power draws down, rapidly dissipating. I pull in a deep, wavering breath and force myself to take stock of my situation.

I need to survive.

Because I'm a weapon, whether I want to be or not.

A weapon the Resistance needs.

Soon I'll be back in the luxurious, rotted heart of Gardneria and deep in hiding. Sheltered by my connection to Lukas Grey.

Until the Resistance comes to claim me and wield me.

# CHAPTER THREE

## WYVERNGUARD MAGE

### TRYSTAN GARDNER
### AND VOTHENDRILE XANTHILE

*Sixth Month*
*Eastern Realm,*
*the Wyvernguard's North Twin Island*

Vothendrile Xanthile watches the rune ship soar toward the Wyvernguard through the night sky. The ship's huge, whirring flank runes and base runes cast the vessel in a penumbra of sapphire light that's reflected off the choppy current of the Vo River.

Every one of Vothe's predatory, Wyvern-shifter senses is on heightened alert, every sight and smell sharpened.

Blue light from runic torches encased in glass orbs gutters over Vothe and the other sapphire-uniformed Vu Trin military apprentices as they stand at attention and wait on the broad landing balcony, all eyes fixed on the incoming ship, an explosive tension—that's at full odds with their blank military bearing—crackling on the air.

A brisk wind whips against Vothendrile's strong, honed body and he pulls in a reflexive breath, his own wind magic stirring to meet the Wyvern-crafted air current that's coursing down the river. He spares a glance over his shoulder toward the towering pinnacle of the Wyvernguard's North Twin Island, the colossal, vertical island one of two towering landmasses that form the Vu Trin Wyvernguard, the huge, ore-dark Vo River splayed out all around them.

Vothe looks back at the incoming ship, his lethal determination doubling as the ship touches down, its sapphire, dragon-marked sails collapsing inward as its stairs are lowered.

Wyvernguard Commander Ung Li disembarks first, coming in like a storm.

Their tall, elegant-featured leader's face is a mask of barely concealed outrage, her steps angrily brisk as she strides down onto the landing platform, not meeting anyone's eyes, as if still caught up in a fiery argument.

Vothendrile's shifter focus homes in tight on the young man stepping off the ship behind her and into a gauntlet of simmering hostility that echoes Vothe's own.

*Trystan Gardner.*

The grandson of the Vuulnor—the Black Witch.

Vothendrile notices two things about Trystan Gardner as he draws near.

First, the Gardnerian is startlingly handsome. A thread of lightning sparks through Vothe in response to Trystan Gardner's striking looks, and Vothe quickly suppresses it, unnerved by his reflexive attraction to a Mage.

He's tall and slender, this Gardnerian, with dark green eyes and angular features. And his *skin*. It glimmers like it's dusted with deep-green gems, its verdant gleam undimmed by the flickering blue torchlight. Even his worn indigo Noi garb is unable to dispel how handsome he is.

The second thing Vothe notices about Trystan Gardner is that he seems outrageously unintimidated by the situation.

The Gardnerian's stride is strong and determined, his face expressionless, but his *eyes*—they're as fierce as white fire as he takes in the looks of pure loathing on every single Vu Trin apprentice and Vu Trin soldier lining the platform's central path.

Vothendrile wonders, with some grim, anticipatory relish, what it would be like to stare down this Mage's fervid gaze. He can't smell even a trace of fear on him.

Briefly closing his eyes, Vothe pulls in a deeper breath to read the magic simmering on the air. He gives a start as Trystan Gardner's magical aura connects with his own.

Vothe's black eyes fly open and spark with lightning.

He's got fire, this Mage. And water. Practically a whole tumultuous ocean of it—a veritable storm locked inside this Level Five grandson of the Black Witch, threatening to come unleashed.

Vothe falls into step behind Trystan Gardner, his resolve solidifying as he catches the incensed looks of his fellow military apprentices lined up on either side of the path. He sends them back a reassuringly savage look of his own.

He's as dangerous as he is beautiful, this Trystan Gardner.

And Vothendrile is determined to drive him out of the Wyvernguard.

Trystan Gardner meets Ung Li's gaze unflinchingly as she stares him down in her circular command chamber, her hands splayed on the obsidian desk before her, Trystan's subversive will to be here as entrenched as her will to see him gone.

*Go ahead*, Trystan silently conveys to her, his gaze unyielding. *Do your best to get rid of me. I'm staying, and I'm fighting with you.*

Slim onyx carvings of dragons bracket the huge windows at Ung Li's back. The arching glass offers a panoramic view of the broad Vo River, the glittering city of Voloi visible to the northeast and the dark Vo Mountain Range hulking against the river's western bank. Everything in the room is fashioned in the Wyvernguard's signature colors—sapphire, onyx, and bone.

"A guard will accompany you wherever you go," Ung Li informs Trystan as her dark gaze bores into him. Four black-clad Vu Trin soldiers bracket Ung Li and carefully study Trystan with hard-edged glares that mirror Ung Li's own.

A few additional Vu Trin apprentices have fanned out behind Trystan. He can sense their incendiary glares burning into him.

"Am I under arrest?" Trystan calmly asks Ung Li, unable to keep a trace of sarcasm from his tone. Bordering dangerously on insubordination.

Trystan immediately regrets the slip as Ung Li's eyes sharpen on him, as if she's sizing him up more closely only to find her worst suspicions confirmed.

Trystan holds her intimidating stare. It's clear that the Wyvernguard hierarchy and the Vu Trin apprentices don't want him here. Clear that he's here only because Vang Troi, the Vu Trin's brilliant and unpredictable High Commander, has ordered that he be allowed admittance into the Wyvernguard and given a chance to prove himself.

"You're a Level Five Mage," Ung Li answers, her tone low and simmering with animosity, her dark gaze unblinking. "You're also the grandson of the Vuulnor. And the threat of war between our people is in the air. If you wish to be a Vu Trin, Trystan Gardner, you will have a guard everywhere you go." Her gaze turns combative as she thrusts out her palm. "Hand over your wand."

Trystan's whole body goes taut, his water power caught up in a roiling current as Ung Li keeps her hand doggedly extended.

Invisible lightning spits through his lines as Trystan reaches down, unsheathes his wand, and surrenders it to the commander, feeling the lack of it acutely the moment the wand leaves his hand.

Suddenly, he's feeling the absence of Tierney Calix even more intensely than the loss of his wand, and wishing she were assigned to be here with him on the North Twin Island. He's grown close to Elloren's cynical Asrai-Fae friend these past few weeks as they traveled east together. But Tierney's been assigned to the Wyvernguard's South Twin Island, the two of them cast into confusion by their abrupt separation this evening.

Tierney protested vehemently, clearly sensing, as Trystan did, an ulterior motive at play, but Ung Li was unmoved, tersely informing them both that Tierney was to join the Fae Vu Trin apprentices stationed on the Wyvernguard's South Twin Island, where all the Fae divisions are located, while Trystan took his place on the Wyvernguard's North Twin Island.

Ensuring Trystan's complete isolation.

*A test*, Trystan supposes with bone-deep cynicism, *to see exactly how much the grandson of the Black Witch can take.*

Trystan's chest tightens with apprehension, but he tamps down the useless pining for friends, for family. Even though he's a renegade, he knew there would be no open-armed embrace here for the grandson of the Vuulnor.

His brother, Rafe, has fared much better, becoming Lupine during the first full moon on their journey east and casting off his Gardnerian heritage, his fierce amber eyes indisputable proof of his new allegiance. And Tierney was instantly embraced by the Vu Trin, as well—all the Fae Vu Trin military apprentices have been welcomed, their fierce loyalty to the Vu Trin unquestioned.

The Vu Trin hierarchy had initially assumed that Trystan would be eager to relinquish the echo of Black Witch power in his lines and would become Lupine during that first full moon under their protection.

They assumed wrong.

Trystan's storming, elemental power has become an intimately valued part of himself, vital as the blood that runs through his veins.

Now the Vu Trin seem unprepared to be faced with a Black Witch descendant with overwhelming fire and water magic who has no intention of being anything other than what he is—a powerful Level Five Mage.

Trystan stands there, unmoved, as Ung Li's formidable gaze sears into him.

"Vothendrile Xanthile has been assigned to guard you," Ung Li finally says, a sly look that raises Trystan's hackles slinking across her expression.

One of the Vu Trin apprentices behind Trystan strides into view.

Trystan's breath hitches, all his storming thoughts flying right out of his head as he's faced with the most dazzlingly beautiful young man he's ever seen.

The tall, dark-eyed apprentice's stance is regally assured, his sapphire Vu Trin apprentice uniform perfectly tailored to accentuate his muscular frame, the image of Vo, the starlight dragon goddess of the Noi people, emblazoned on his broad chest. He has the sculpted features and dark eyes of the Noi, his black hair short and slightly spiked, but the spikes are resplendently tipped in glittering silver, and a series of silver hoops rim his pointed ears.

And there are thin threads of lightning crackling all over his midnight-black skin.

Actual lightning.

Trystan meets Vothendrile's dark gaze and their powers collide, a flash of energy coursing through Trystan's firelines, his invisible lightning striking out in response to the palpable storm power that lives inside the young man before him.

That's in his *gaze*.

And... Vothendrile's pupils are vertically slitted. Dragonshifter slitted.

He must be a Zhilon'ile Wyvern, Trystan dazedly realizes, having read about them. A Storm Wyvern of the Eastern Realm, his people's domain to the far northeast of here. The Wyvern shifters who, along with some scattered Fae, control the weather in these lands. Who used to control the weather in *all* lands.

Before the Black Witch drove them out of the Western Realm.

Vothendrile's lips lift in a slight, hostile sneer as lightning flashes between them and Trystan snaps fully back to the situation he's in.

One of the reviled.

Trystan urgently presses down his completely unnerving attraction to Vothendrile Xanthile and holds the Wyvern's overpowering stare, the shifter's lightning now spitting through Trystan's lines in what feels like a purposefully stinging rush.

The ache that rises simply galvanizes Trystan's resolve.

*Go ahead and try to drive me out.* Trystan glowers at Vothe. *So I'm reviled here. So be it. I was reviled there too. But I'm staying. And I'm going to fight the Gardnerians alongside all of you, whether you like it or not.*

"Vothendrile will show you to your barracks," Ung Li informs Trystan, cutting into their staring contest.

Trystan staunchly salutes Ung Li, slamming his fist against his heart, as is their way here, as he meets the commander's withering stare. "Hoiyon, Nor Ung Li." There's renewed challenge in Trystan's emphatic falling in with their protocol and in his pointed use of their language.

Ung Li is unmoved. She knifes another glare at Trystan, then sets her fierce gaze on Vothendrile and flicks her finger toward the door, as if wanting, more than anything, to be completely rid of Trystan Gardner.

Vothendrile Xanthile keeps smart pace with Trystan Gardner, their boot heels echoing over the stone floor of the hallway that bores straight through the Wyvernguard's North Twin Island mountain, circular dragon emblems marked on its surface. Black dragon carvings mark the ceiling above them, carved into the obsidian stone in bas-relief, their huge reptilian forms washed in guttering blue light that emanates from rune torches affixed to the walls.

Vothe takes in the surreptitious, encouraging stares being sent to him by every Vu Trin apprentice and soldier they pass, their expressions conveying unspoken solidarity—*Drive him out*.

"So, I have a guard," Trystan Gardner says, his words edged with the slimmest trace of derision.

Vothendrile swivels his head toward the Gardnerian and is met by a quick glare, the air charged between them.

A crackle of lightning sparks through Vothe. "Of course you have a guard," Vothe shoots back, suppressing a snarl. "I'll guard you throughout the day and you'll have another guard stationed at your barracks through the night." Truly, Vothe is amazed by the contempt radiating off of this Mage. And his sheer audacity in questioning the need for a guard.

Really, how dare he? After shouldering his way in here. The grandson of the Black Witch, of all people. Here, at the esteemed Wyvernguard. Despite the protests. Despite the petition Vothe quickly organized and sent to both the Vu Trin Tribunal and the Noi Conclave. All of it ignored by High Commander Vang Troi, their highest-ranking military sorceress.

Even though close to no one wants the grandson of the Black Witch here.

"You'll shadow me, then, everywhere I go?" the Mage asks coldly as they walk.

Vothe smiles charmingly at him, even as lightning spits in his vision. "I will, Gardnerian. And if you stray one inch from the orders set down by the Wyvernguard and Ung Li, I will drag you to the Vu Trin Tribunal by the scruff of your refined Gardnerian neck."

Trystan Gardner smirks at this as they both slow to a stop, a spike of hard anger flaring in the Gardnerian's eyes as he faces Vothe, and Vothe is instantly taken aback by the sudden sense of this Mage's water power swelling, fierce and implacable.

Trystan looks Vothe up and down, and there's a flash of the Mage's own lightning in that look. "You could try," he counters, lip lifting.

*Oh, that's rich.* Vothe grins at him with cool amusement as he lets his gleaming black horns spiral up from his head. "Did they tell you who I am?" he purrs.

"I'm guessing a Zhilon'ile Wyvern-shifter of the Eastern dragonkin," Trystan states with matter-of-fact severity. "Quite powerful, I'd wager."

"That's right, Trystan Gardner, and don't you forget it," Vothe croons, leaning in, filled with the sudden urge to release his wings in a potent display. "I'm clear that you're a Level Five Mage. Of extraordinary power. *Growing* power. But don't think for a *second* that I can't best you."

Again, the Gardnerian dons that look of icy contempt with a blistering defiance riding just underneath it. Trystan's lip lifts in another slight, frigid smirk. "I'd never presume to have anything but the utmost confidence in my new guard, Vothendrile."

Vothe narrows his lightning eyes on Trystan as the Mage resumes his pace and Vothe falls in beside him.

*My, this one keeps himself carefully under wraps,* Vothe seethes as he pulls his horns back in. The sense of being faced with something completely unexpected settles over Vothe, and he's disturbed by it.

He's going to have to keep a closer eye on Trystan Gardner than he thought. It's clear that Mage Gardner answers to no one but himself, no matter how insistent the threats leveled against him. No, he's not easily intimidated, this one.

*I'll just have to try harder.*

"You're not wanted here," Vothe informs him with open venom.

Again, that wry smirk. "I'm well aware," Trystan replies. "But I *am* here, and I'm not going anywhere, so you'd best get used to me."

Vothe can't keep the caustic sarcasm out of his own tone and doesn't want to. "So, you want to be somewhere where everyone hates you?"

Trystan's face remains calm, but fire flashes in his eyes as he slows once more to a stop to face Vothe.

When it comes, Trystan Gardner's voice is controlled, almost polite, but Vothe can sense the guttering flame riding through it. "I want to be somewhere where I can join an army and fight the Gardnerians and the Alfsigr and every last one of their allies with every last shred of power in me." Trystan takes a confrontational step toward Vothe. "I don't care if you hate me. I don't care if every last person in the Wyvernguard hates me. You have no *idea* what you're up against."

The Mage turns and begins walking again at a faster clip, as if he can't wait to be rid of Vothe so he can get settled here and get on with it, and Vothe has, in that moment, a disturbing sense of the true, unbreachable, single-minded purpose in this Gardnerian.

As they ascend a large, spiraling staircase, an unpleasant edge of conflict roils in Vothendrile because the flow of this Crow's power and the emotions he can scent on him are not at odds with his words.

*What if he's telling the truth?*

"You expect me to believe that the grandson of the Black Witch is honestly on our side?" Vothe snipes at Trystan Gardner's back as they stomp up the steps.

Trystan briefly turns, his expression hard. "I really don't care what you think, Vothendrile."

They step off the staircase and start down another shadowy, arcing hallway, and Vothendrile takes the lead, both of them seemingly lost now in private, heated fuming.

Vothendrile counts down the barracks-door numbers, growing increasingly suspicious. His lightning gives a chaotic flare as they turn the corner and he realizes what Ung Li has done.

Trystan freezes at his side.

Sylla the Death Fae stands before them, her petite, dark figure surrounded by thick, gauzy spiderwebs that course over the walls, ceiling, and floor of the hallway's end like an impenetrable tunnel. She's dressed in a black version of the Wyvernguard's sapphire uniform, a gleaming black dragon embroidered on her uniform's black cloth instead of the usual white dragon on sapphire, every article of clothing these Death Fae put on instantly turning as black as night. She has tightly curled, short hair, her thickly lashed eyes large, her dark lips full, her face and pointed ears covered in onyx-metal piercings the same obsidian hue as her skin.

As Sylla stares at them with her unfathomable eyes, a disturbing clarity fills Vothe.

They're using the Deathkin to drive the Gardnerian out, lodging him near the three primordial Death Fae who scare most of the Wyvernguard with their close affinity to the terrifying aspects of nature—death, decay, sickness, and fear.

But it's wrong to use them as monstrous outcasts, Vothendrile considers, bristling. It's true that these non-elemental Fae keep to themselves, their reserve and odd ways opening them up to ridicule and superstition, but Vothendrile respects Sylla and Viger and Vesper, not out of fear, but out of the deep-rooted sense that there's something solid and necessary at the center of their power. Something just as linked to the natural order of things as Vothendrile's own weather power.

And he believes that their allegiance rests firmly with the Wyvernguard's own aims.

Spiders scuttle across the floor toward Vothe and Trystan then stream up their pants in curious spirals. All kinds of spiders. Wolf spiders and funnel-web spiders, brown recluse spiders, and a black widow or two.

Trystan calmly raises his head and looks to Sylla Vuul. "My name is Trystan Gardner," he says in a stunning display of equanimity, as if oblivious to the spiders swarming all over his body, the black widow now circling the skin of his neck. "It seems we're to be neighbors."

Sylla remains silent but cocks her head, her piercings delicately clinking against each other, her large black eyes unblinking.

The spiders abruptly circle back down both Vothendrile and Trystan and then scuttle back up the walls and into their tunnel of webs.

Trystan dips his head respectfully toward Sylla, turns, and unlocks his door, flashing Vothe a slightly indignant look as he pushes the door wide open.

Vothe freezes alongside Trystan as they peer into the room.

Bloodred graffiti is splattered on the wall. An angry, violent word that Vothe imagines Trystan Gardner can't read because it's in the Noi language. But Vothe can tell, from Trystan's briefly devastated look, that he understands nonetheless.

## ROACH

"What does it mean?" Trystan asks, his armor suddenly breached clear through, his voice thick with shock and his eyes haunted, as if by some trauma revisited.

"It means..." Vothe hesitates, not knowing why. He, himself, was idly tossing around the same word just earlier today, so bitter over being assigned to guard someone too dangerous to have here. And questioning Vang Troi's sanity.

"What?" Trystan presses, and the slash of pain in his expression inexplicably shakes Vothendrile. "What does it mean?"

Vothe fights back against his own unease. *Get hold of yourself*, he inwardly snarls. *You're a Zhilon'ile Wyvern. Don't go soft around this Gardnerian. He's dangerous.*

"It means *roach*," Vothe says, forcing an unaffected tone.

Trystan strides into the room and throws open the paint-splashed door to his black-enameled closet. More slurs are painted on the inside of the doors.

## ROACH FILTH GO HOME

Trystan Gardner's assigned uniforms lie crumpled on the closet floor. Slashed to shreds and covered in red paint.

Trystan is frozen, his devastation clear, and again, it gives Vothe serious pause.

*Remember who he is!* Vothe sharply chastises himself. *Are you honestly feeling sympathy for him? The grandson of the Black Witch? Have you gone mad?*

Trystan is quiet for a long, fraught moment, his back to Vothe. And then he shuts the closet door and turns, his eyes now blazing, and Vothe can feel the power of that gaze straight down his spine, his own lightning crackling to life in response to it.

"I'll just wear this, then," Trystan bites out, gesturing sharply toward the worn indigo Noi tunic and pants he has on.

Indignation rises in Vothe at the idea of this Mage even being allowed to wear Noi attire. "You can't dress like that here. You have to be in uniform."

Ire flashes in Trystan's eyes. "What would you suggest, then?"

Vothe bares his teeth. "That you leave."

Trystan's whole body spits invisible lightning. He strides forward, his arm brushing against Vothe's as he moves to grab hold of the door's handle, a flash of his storm magic lashing into Vothe. Overpowering magic. Possibly stronger than anything Vothe could throw at him.

Vothe's concern spikes as he steps back into the hall and Trystan slams the door in his face.

*He shouldn't be here,* Vothe rages at the door, conflict roiling inside him. *It's right to try to drive him out. He's got Her power. Or some approximation of it.*

*The Vu Trin don't know what they're dealing with.*

Trystan notes the swarm of spiders crawling in under his door as he sits down at his desk, wondering if this is some new torment devised to get him to leave a place he has no intention of leaving.

Until it's time to travel back west to fight Vogel. With the Vu Trin army.

As spiders circle him, he gets up, opens his door, and steps into the hallway to find the silent young woman, his Death Fae neighbor, still standing there amidst the thick cobwebs.

The spiders flood back to her and scuttle up her short, slender form.

Trystan and the Death Fae stare at each other for a protracted moment.

"You're afraid of Vothendrile," she finally says, her voice a midnight thrum, her dark presence seeming like the calm eye in the storm of the insects' agitated activity. Her gaze is like deep forest shadow and makes Trystan feel as if he's facing the very center of the night.

Despite her intimidating, otherworldly presence, scorn rises in Trystan in response to her pointed question. "I'm not afraid of Vothendrile," he tells her shortly. "I have a fair bit of lightning too."

She gives a small laugh that doesn't reach her gleaming black eyes. "No, not of his power. Of his beauty."

A reflexive fear strikes through Trystan, every muscle tensing over the attraction that would be a crime in Gardneria.

The Death Fae tilts her head, eyeing Trystan quizzically as a scorpion climbs from inside her tunic's collar to curl around her neck. A small lime-green scorpion.

Trystan realizes, with a small start, that it's a Deathstalker scorpion, one of the most venomous scorpions in all of Erthia.

"I am Sylla Vuul," she says with serene dignity as six more black eyes sprout around the two she has fixed on him, a tremor of surprise passing through Trystan.

Part of Trystan is amused by her polite introduction. It's

ironic, really, that the friendliest person here is so terrifyingly odd.

"I'm pleased to meet you, Sylla Vuul," Trystan replies evenly.

She cocks her head again. "You don't fear me," she says, a question in the statement.

"No," Trystan affirms.

She nods almost imperceptibly as another bright green scorpion scuttles down from inside her pant leg. "You should know, Trystan Gardner," the Fae says, her voice a lull, "that you are as beautiful as Vothendrile. I can read you."

Trystan's throat constricts. "What do you mean?"

"Deathkin can read fear. I know who you truly are."

They stand there for a long moment, eyes locked as a few spiders lower themselves down near Trystan on silken strands, peering at him through countless eyes.

"They are wrong," the Deathkin says to Trystan. "They are as wrong about you as they are about us. Be patient with them, Trystan Gardner." Her multi-eyed gaze turns almost mournful. "They fear the wrong things."

Trystan pulls in a long breath, feeling an odd solidarity with this Deathkin with her poisonous scorpions crawling over her slender frame. Scorpions that *are* a true threat. That could fell him in a heartbeat.

"You're right," he tells her grimly. "They do fear the wrong things. There's only one thing they should all be afraid of right now."

The Death Fae nods, their solidarity palpably strengthening, and when her words come, they ripple over him like inky mist, thrumming straight through his lines.

"The Great Shadow."

# CHAPTER
# FOUR

# WYVERNGUARD FAE
## TIERNEY CALIX

*Sixth Month*
*Eastern Realm,*
*the Wyvernguard's South Twin Island*

Bleary-eyed and dressed in battered Noi garb, Tierney steps down the rune ship's lowered stairs, following closely behind Kiya Wen and Soyil Vho, her young Vu Trin protectors these past few weeks. The soldiers' dark backs before her, Tierney strides onto the Wyvernguard's night-darkened landing platform at the base of the military academy's South Twin Island mountain.

Down by the mighty Vo River's edge.

As sapphire-garbed Noi military apprentices stride forward to meet them, Tierney is enveloped by a fulsome Fae awareness of the vast river that now surrounds her, its waters rushing tirelessly north to south just beyond the rune-marked landing platform and its adjacent terraces that seem to ring the island. The black-haired apprentices salute both Kiya Wen and Soyil

Vho, fist to heart, as other apprentices secure the ship to the platform's metal posts, their curious gazes darting toward the new Asrai Water Fae apprentice as they work. Two of them nod at Tierney in amiable greeting.

Tierney nods back at them self-consciously, stunned to be walking among them unglamoured, her long blue hair swinging behind her like an Asrai beacon, her skin a rippling dark blue hue, and her pointed ears dangerously exposed.

She fights the urge to hide herself. To ready herself for escape. To fight for her very existence.

But there's nothing but welcome in the young soldiers' eyes.

Feeling as if a crushing weight is slowly lifting from her shoulders, Tierney follows Kiya Wen and Soyil Vho across the broad platform, craning her neck skyward as she takes in the mammoth island-mountain before her.

Tiers upon tiers of obsidian Wyvernguard buildings circle the island-mountain, the narrow landmass rising straight through the clouds like some goddess's blunt spear. Dragons pulsing with what seems like internal lightning dart in and out of the Wyvernguard's upper reaches as rune ships encased in shimmering blue haze soar through the night sky and stream over the water like a constellation of restless sapphire stars.

A stiff breeze skimming up from the river catches Tierney in a sudden embrace, ruffling her hair and twining around her body like a beckoning call. The caress sends a ribbon of effervescent euphoria through Tierney, and every one of her senses flares to life, her exhaustion wicked away as she comes to an abrupt halt. Tierney turns to face the great river, frozen in place as she sets her gaze on its vast expanse of shimmering black water just beyond the landing platform and broad adjacent terraces, overcome by the dark grandeur of the largest river in all the Realms.

And the unassailable sense that it has set its whole focus on her.

Tierney sucks in a wavering breath, swept up in an intense emotion she doesn't fully comprehend. Everything except the river fades to the background—the Vu Trin soldiers, the glowing rune ship, the island-mountain, Voloi's glimmering coastline—all of it falls aside until there's only the water.

Only the Vo River.

Churning black waves eddy toward Tierney, first in small, tentative breakers, then larger swells, as if the Vo River's great expanse is waking up to her presence, its motion independent of the wind and distant ocean's pull.

A wave breaks over the terrace's edge, cool spray misting over Tierney, the contact triggering a bolt of sheer elation.

*Asrai.*

The word rides in on the water, sweeping through her, as tears sting Tierney's eyes.

Feeling as if she's fallen into a longed-for dream, Tierney starts for the river, rapidly closing the distance to the terrace's edge. All the Vu Trin soldiers step back and wordlessly, almost reverently, watch as wave after wave breaks over the terrace's edge.

Tierney climbs up onto the terrace's slick stone railing and throws her arms out into an impassioned greeting as the Vo ecstatically crashes against her.

As if joyfully claiming her.

A euphoric cry breaks from Tierney as she surrenders to its call and dives into the water.

The Vo closes around her in an all-encompassing, cool embrace as Tierney glides down into its depths, swept up in the river's adoration as her Asrai vision wakes, the dark waters lighting up to gleam a deep blue, fish and kelpies streaming in to swim alongside her.

Tierney opens her mouth and pulls in a huge breath of water, fusing with the river, filling her Water Fae lungs with it. Feeling as if she's finally come home.

Water slicked and still pulsing with elation, Tierney follows Kiya Wen and Soyil Vho through the countless decorated onyx and sapphire hallways of the Wyvernguard's first-tier barracks as she dries herself by drawing the sweet water from the Vo into her skin.

Their boot heels click over marble floors marked with Vu Trin martial scenes and dragon deities, the sapphire runic light emanating from glass-orb lamps transforming Tierney's new world into a surreal dreamscape.

Kiya Wen halts before a black wooden door marked, as all the doors on this wing are, with a circular metal plate bearing the design of a crashing wave. The young Vu Trin soldier turns and smiles broadly at Tierney.

"This will be your lodging here," she informs her in Noi, and Tierney can't help but touch the Noi translation rune newly emblazoned behind her ear by the Vu Trin—the shock of being able to understand so many languages still a vivid, wondrous thing.

Kiya Wen pulls a rune disc from her dark uniform's pocket and places it on the corresponding blue Noi rune marked on the center of the onyx door. "This is how you unlock it," she says to Tierney. She gives the door a brisk knock.

"Come in," a melodious voice sings out in the Noi language.

Kiya Wen takes hold of the door's black metal knob and pushes it open.

And there, whirling around in the center of the small room, is another Asrai Water Fae, as Tierney was told there would be.

"This is Apprentice Asra'leen Filor'ian," Kiya Wen formally announces. "Your Wyvernguard cohort."

Tierney's eyes widen with a visceral astonishment to be face-to-face with the water-hued, point-eared young woman. The only other unglamoured Asrai Tierney has ever seen since she, herself, was glamoured at three years old.

The dark blue of Asra'leen Filor'ian's skin is as changeable and rippling as Tierney's. Her hair is white as foam and worn in a cloud of soft, tight curls around her head, her graceful hands lowering as she twirls to a stop, a swirl of water suspended around her that quickly dissipates into a mist that encircles her slender frame.

Asra'leen's large blue eyes widen with palpable warmth as her full indigo mouth spreads into an effervescent smile.

Then the air around Asra'leen bursts into a veritable riot of crystalline rainbows.

"Tierney!" she enthuses as she springs forward and draws Tierney into an embrace, as if Tierney is a long-lost, much-beloved friend, and Tierney finds herself encircled by glittering rainbows.

Asra'leen draws back, loosely gripping Tierney's arms. "Welcome home," she says with real warmth, her smile devoid of any guile.

Tierney gapes at her, caught up in a sudden vortex of emotion.

Just like Tierney, Asra'leen is dressed in the sapphire-blue, white-dragon-marked uniform of the Vu Trin military apprentice.

And she's openly Asrai Water Fae.

A tension Tierney didn't know she was holding suddenly gives way as the full ramifications of being free of the Western Realm and free to be who she truly is strike through her.

Turbulent, dark clouds spring to life around Tierney as she furiously blinks back tears and struggles to find her voice.

Asra'leen's smile fades as she glances up at the clouds, and both understanding and compassion light in the Water Fae's rainbow-flickering eyes. "You're safe here," Asra'leen says as she holds on to Tierney. "We're all safe here." Asra'leen's gentle look hardens with significance as she glances toward the rune blade sheathed at her side. "And now we're armed."

Awe sweeps through Tierney the next morning as she follows rainbow-flecked Asra'leen into the Wyvernguard's massive central hall, the vast space cut right into the center of the South Twin Island. A towering alabaster statue of the dragongoddess Vo twines up from its middle, the dragon surrounded by carvings of Vu Trin military women raising their rune weapons outward in alliance with the goddess.

Tierney pauses to take in the countless sapphire-uniformed Vu Trin military apprentices streaming by her, some striding toward runic lifts set inside cylindrical columns that rise from tier to tier, the plate-shaped lifts able to carry Vu Trin smoothly up and down the South Twin's many stories.

Almost all of the Vu Trin apprentices passing by are young, black-haired Noi women, as the Noi men don't possess the runic sorcery needed to amplify rune weapon power or create runes. But scattered among the Vu Trin apprentices are pointed-eared, jewel-hued Urisk women and even some Urisk men. As well as blonde Issani women, dark-brown-toned Ishkartan Vu Trin apprentices with golden rune-marked headwrappings, and both male and female Elfhollen with gray hair and skin, bows slung over their shoulders.

All with a Noi translation rune emblazoned behind one ear to allow for fluency in a multitude of the Eastern and the Western Realms' major languages.

And there are dragon-shifters here—the Zhilon'ile Wyverns, tall and stunningly attractive, their onyx coloring shot through with pulses of bright white lightning, some only partially shifted, their obsidian horns and dark wings on full display.

*Now I'm part of this too,* Tierney marvels, momentarily overwhelmed by a whirlpool of grateful emotion as she glances down at her own brand-new Vu Trin apprentice uniform.

It's incredible, such diversity in one military, in one society, and the reality of it flows into Tierney in disbelieving wave after disbelieving wave.

And fills her with a fierce desire to defend it, no matter the cost.

Asra'leen sends Tierney an ebullient smile then pulls a runic watch-orb from her uniform's pocket and checks the time. She holds up the luminous blue orb for Tierney's perusal. "We need to report for roll call in an hour's time." She slides the orb back into her tunic's pocket. "You'll be partnered for a few weeks with Fyordin Lir, our division's command. He works closely with all the new Asrai."

Tierney's nervous anticipation heightens at the prospect of meeting so many of her people—their Asrai'lon division is comprised entirely of Water Fae.

"Fyordin is incredibly powerful," Asra'leen happily tells her as a sapphire Vhion'ile dragon enters the hall and walks by with a group of Noi Vu Trin apprentices.

Tierney's attention is snagged in astonishment.

*Dragons...right here in the open.*

*Unbroken dragons.*

An ache fills her heart over the remembrance of the dragon she and her friends helped to free.

*Where are you, Naga? Did you ever make it to the East?*

"...and he's claimed the Vo River as his kindred."

Tierney's head snaps back toward Asra'leen, who goes silent, her smile fading, as she seems to register Tierney's defensive flare of emotion.

Tierney's mind falls back into the feel of swimming through the Vo's dark waters, *merging* with the Vo's dark waters, the immediate bond that formed between her and the Vo last night more intimate than she imagines any lover's caress could ever be.

"Are you all right?" Asra'leen asks, her rainbow-flecked eyes glinting with concern.

Tierney can't speak for a moment, feeling deeply thrown by the idea of another Fae bonded to *her* Vo.

Tierney knows that Asra'leen has formed her own kinship with a waterfall on a small island just to the south of the Wyvernguard. Last eve they talked deep into the night, and Asra'leen spoke of the first time she made contact with her waterfall, a deeply significant Asrai bond forming between her and the falls with just that one touch, the sense of immediate connection a euphoric rush like no other. And now, Asra'leen strives to visit the lovely waterfall as often as she can, submersing herself in it and often morphing into water to become one with it, happily surrounded by its myriad fish and amphibians and aquatic insects and plant life, this small manifestation of Erthia's water now an integral and deeply cherished part of Asra'leen's heart.

Tierney knows, from her kelpies, that all Asrai eventually find their waters, a body of water that they claim as their own and are claimed by in turn.

Last night, Tierney found hers, and she isn't ready to share it.

"Did you just say that Fyordin Lir has laid claim to the Vo?" Tierney presses, an unmistakable edge to her tone.

*My river.*

Dancing mischief lights Asra'leen's eyes. "Well, he'll have

to share it now, won't he? It seems that you and Fyordin have formed the same kinship."

Every Fae instinct inside Tierney recoils at the idea.

*No. The river is mine.*

"You'll work it out," Asra'leen says soothingly, a rainbow aura glittering to life around her before her mouth turns up into another bright smile. "C'mon. Let's go meet everyone."

Tierney blinks against the bright sunlight as she pauses at the threshold of the Wyvernguard's arching exit. The broad obsidian terrace that rings the base of the South Twin Island is splayed before her and teeming with military apprentices— the shocking sight of what must be a Fire Fae division to her far right, the red-haired apprentices' conjured flames flashing in the air, and an Elfhollen Fae division to the distant left, the Mountain Fae arranged in rows as they shoot arrows at targets lined up along the terrace's edge.

But it's the division directly in front of her that wrests the air from Tierney's lungs.

"Myl'lynian'ir," Asra'leen says to Tierney brightly, beckoning her with the Asrai words for *come out, my friend* as she steps backward onto the huge sunlit terrace, one graceful blue hand playfully outstretched toward Tierney. Asra'leen's crystalline rainbow aura flashes brilliantly in the sunlight, her cloud of foam-colored hair brightened to a blinding white as it's tossed about in the breeze coming off the Vo River.

Tierney can't move. Can't speak as she takes in the fantastical scene before her, the Vo River shifting its current to greet her, flowing in to splash against the terrace's railing.

There are over twenty Asrai Water Fae assembled on a wide expanse of terrace near the river's edge, all of them with the same changeable deep-blue hue that ripples like water, curled hair, broad features, and pointed ears as Tierney's, and all of them wearing the sapphire uniforms of the Wyvernguard military apprentices, just like hers.

Stunned, Tierney takes them in, in one sweeping glance: a young Asrai woman with blue-black skin creates huge swooshes of water in the cool morning air, masses of cattails decorating her long navy-blue curls; a young man wearing a crown of ivory shells stands near the river's edge as he conjures a slim waterspout that reaches from the river toward the white clouds above; a muscular, broad young woman circles in place, her hands gyrating as she fashions river eel shapes of enormous size from sparkling water, the black shells decorating her coiled locks glittering in the sun along with the suspended water-creatures.

Everywhere, Asrai Fae are openly wielding their water power, openly displaying their allegiance to the waters of Erthia.

A sleek, androgynous-appearing Asrai is throwing bolt after bolt of water over the Vo River, their spiky blue hair festooned with pale water lilies. And a young man with a brooding expression is forming a small rainstorm off to the side, the magic flowing from his upturned palms. He meets Tierney's gaze, his indigo eyes widening as lightning spits from his storm, as if in startled response to her.

The forbidden Asrai tongue that her kelpies taught her is spoken freely, her ears thrilling to its fluid cadence. There are lines of runic weaponry propped against a weapons rack, Noi water-power runes glowing a bright sapphire on the hilts of swords and bows and spears and a host of other weapons.

For a moment, it's like the entire world tilts on its axis, and Tierney has to stifle a sound of pure emotion as the storming magic inside her rises and churns with a pained joy.

*We're all free. Free to be Asrai Fae.*

*And not just Asrai Fae...*

*Asrai Fae soldiers.*

Tierney's eyes glaze with tears and she fights back a choked-up feeling, as she thrills to the blessing that is the Eastern Realm.

"Fil'lori mir Asrai'il," Asra'leen says, compassion in her sparkling eyes, her hand still outstretched. *My Asrai sister.*

Her heart so full of emotion it feels about to burst, Tierney steps into the light.

Her presence draws more curious stares, most of the young Asrai men and some of the young women doing a double take as they catch sight of her, their water magery dissipating or splashing down onto the black marble terrace.

There's curiosity there, but also something else that Tierney is still adjusting to.

Bedazzlement.

It's a disconcerting shift for Tierney, these admiring stares that she now draws, and she doesn't know how to handle it. She had grown used to stares of repugnance and aversion in Gardneria, when she was glamoured to look like the ugliest of Mages with her pinched, severe face. But now, everything has changed.

She talked to Trystan about this during their journey here, the two of them sitting beside each other on a rock as they looked out over the Central Ishkartan Desert's crimson sands, the landscape increasingly suffused with the sunset's bloodred light.

"Have you noticed how spectacularly beautiful you are?" Trystan asked as he tossed her a wry look, his green eyes glinting.

"I'm not sure what to make of it," Tierney answered, her brow knotting over this bewildering change. "It's like no one saw me for who I really was in Gardneria," she confided in him, baring her heart fully, which was a thing so easy to do with kind, nonjudgmental Trystan. "But now, it's like I'm still being seen only for what I look like."

Trystan nodded, then glanced at her knowingly, his lip lifting as he looked over her Asrai form. "I'd imagine this is a trace better, though."

Tierney couldn't help but smile, conceding, as she shot him a sardonic look. She lifted her arm, considering the gorgeous, rippling dark blue hue of her skin, entranced by her own changeable color. Then she let her hand fall back onto her knee as she met Trystan's level gaze and a familiar, melancholy ache returned.

"I'm afraid I'll never be truly seen," she admitted, her voice barely audible even to herself.

Trystan was quiet for a long, considering moment. Then he turned to her, his eyes brimming with suppressed emotion.

"I understand," he finally said.

"Asrai'a'lore Yl'orien'ir!" the Asrai with the cattail-decorated hair calls out to Tierney from across the sunlit terrace, enthusiastically cutting through Tierney's fleeting recollection as the young woman approaches along with the androgynous, willowy Fae. *Welcome to the fold, Water Fae.*

A swirl of joyful water power rises within Tierney in response to her immediate acceptance.

"This is Torryn," Asra'leen says in Asrai as she smiles and sweeps her hand gracefully toward the cattail woman. "And Ra'in." She beams as the lily-crowned Fae throws a slender arm around Asra'leen and smiles at Tierney through lovely turquoise-lashed eyes.

"We're happy to have you among us," Ra'in says in Asrai, and Tierney is transfixed by their beauty and the lilting voice that's as melodic as an early summer stream. And by Ra'in's blaring individuality that clearly refuses to be confined, just as all their Fae natures are no longer confined here. It's an incredible thing, this freedom to be oneself without danger.

There's a huge splashing disturbance in the Vo River, just past a break in the curving railing where the terrace's stone angles down to meet the water for runic water vessels to launch.

A dragon made from water suddenly bursts from the Vo's churning knot of water, and Tierney's head jerks back in surprise. The water dragon spirals up to meet with the sky, translucent water-wings stretching out, large as sails.

A Fae male made entirely of water strides out of the spray trailing the water dragon's ascent and steps onto the terrace, a blast of his water power eddying through Tierney with the force of a hurricane. The young man's glistening form morphs from water to flesh, his spiky, wet hair glittering every shade of blue in the sun, his ears rising to points. He throws one hand over his shoulder, effortlessly wicking the water from his pants and body, his movements strong and graceful as a flowing river.

Tierney watches him, transfixed, as her water magic lurches toward the formidable young Asrai, storm clouds kicking up inside her from the sheer force of his presence, and she struggles to keep them from manifesting in the air above.

He's devastatingly handsome, with strong deep-blue features and a tall, powerful frame. And, scandalously, he's not wearing a tunic, his muscles rippling and coated in a slick stream of sweet Vo water, his dark blue nipples exposed.

Tierney's heart pounds as she quickly averts her eyes and swallows abashedly as he approaches.

"Is that Fyordin?" Tierney asks Asra'leen in a strained voice.

"It is," Asra'leen says then raises her hand toward the half-naked Fae. "Fyordin!" She gives him a friendly wave, as if his partial nudity is normal here.

Fyordin nears, and Tierney is overcome by another strong wave of his water power as it courses through her in an exhilarating rush. She pulls in a hard breath and lifts her eyes to meet Fyordin's dark blue gaze.

His power gives a palpable flare of interest as his lips quirk up, and Tierney takes in the metallic blue hoops lining his pointed ears, embarrassment sizzling through her over the fact that his brazenly exposed nipples are also pierced.

"This is Tierney Calix," Asra'leen announces, a hush falling over the entire group of Asrai as Tierney's heartbeat quickens and she averts her gaze from Fyordin's once more.

"Asrai'il," Fyordin says, breaking the silence, his authoritative voice flowing deep into her. She can feel his torrent of power in the center of that voice. And she has to draw up every storming thing inside her to keep from being submerged in it.

Fyordin holds out his hand and Tierney swallows, nerves leaping, as she reaches to grasp hold of it, suppressing a gasp as the edges of their storming power brush up against each other.

Fyordin's blue lips lift farther, his eyes sparking. "No," he states with some censure in the Asrai language. "Not like a Vor'ish'in. Like an Asrai." He slides his hand up past Tierney's grip, his fingers grasping hold of her forearm.

Water streams from Fyordin's forearm to twirl around Tierney's arm in glistening ribbons, drenching her tunic's cloth as it sends a pulsing thrill straight through her arm. "Join your water to mine, Asrai," Fyordin invites as Tierney's heartbeat quickens. "This is how Asrai'il greet one another."

Unexpectedly moved by this offer to throw off Gardnerian ways for those of the Asrai, Tierney pulls in a deep breath and summons a stream of water to flow from her skin, around their joined arms, and through Fyordin's water, the two streams colliding then coalescing and strengthening with a power that sends an intoxicating rush straight through Tierney. For a moment, she doesn't want to let go of Fyordin's arm as she looks up at him, tears glazing her eyes.

*Asrai'il. My people.*

A shimmer of warmth ripples through Tierney as Fyordin's mouth lifts into a broader smile, his grip on her arm tightening. "Welcome home, Asrai'il."

Tears escape her attempt to blink back her fierce swell of emotion as Fyordin holds on and a broader rush of water swirls around Tierney, coming not just from Fyordin, but from all the Fae converging around her.

"You're not trapped in Gardneria anymore," a young Asrai woman fiercely declares, her dark blue hair woven into spiraling braids and decorated with row upon row of small pale shells.

Tierney's heart opens as something that she's never felt in her entire life washes over her like a beloved tide.

Belonging.

"I am My'raid," the pale-shell-decorated woman says warmly as Fyordin releases Tierney, his power drawing back along with that of all the other Asrai.

"I'm Tierney Calix," Tierney says to the young woman, caught up in the communal rush of feeling. Tierney extends her arm, and the young woman grasps hold of it then sends a whoosh of warm mist around Tierney's arm that Tierney subsumes with her own rushing stream of power, not able to hold back her magic's sheer strength.

The woman looks at the water coursing around their arms with evident surprise. "You are powerful, Asrai'il," she says. "And you likely do not know the full extent of your power. Most of us did not when we first came to the East." She flashes a beaming smile. "But now you are here and freed. And you will build a new Sidhe land with us and all the Faekin."

Tierney looks to half-naked, glorious Fyordin and lets herself meet his mesmerizing gaze and even more mesmerizing smile. Fyordin's gaze locks onto hers with an intense interest that sends a ripple of warmth coursing through her. Never has a young man looked at her in quite this way. It makes Tierney feel like a heated spring, and she fleetingly wonders, as her body flushes, what it would be like to be kissed by another Asrai.

"You need to reclaim your Asrai name," Fyordin encourages, his smile dimming as his expression grows serious, "and cast off this false Gardnerian name."

Tierney hesitates. "I was never able to safely use my Asrai name, so I'm not used to it…"

"But now you can use it," My'raid points out meaningfully, a sheen of emotion flashing in her lake-blue eyes. "The Crows hold no power here."

Tierney's newfound sense of belonging is jostled as she internally winces at the slur.

*Crows.*

She heard it murmured countless times on the way here, directed at Trystan as the Vu Trin talked among themselves. And she heard it tossed out in reference to her Gardnerian family and her fifteen-year-old Asrai brother, whose Gardnerian glamour is refusing to give way. The casual use of *Crow* increasingly filled her with concern as her Gardnerian mother and father and her Asrai brother escaped East with her, her adoptive family now thrust into their new role—Gardnerian refugees settling into the nearby capital city of the Noi lands, Voloi.

Tierney's unease over hearing the slur seeps further in as she remembers what she and Asra'leen overheard during breakfast in the huge Wyvernguard dining room—that slurs were marked all over Trystan Gardner's room last night. That three primordial Death Fae were the only Vu Trin apprentices willing to welcome Trystan.

"Are you ready to fight with us, Asrai'il?" Fyordin asks with a hint of challenge, breaking into her unease as a subtle glimmer of his water power swooshes around her, a rakish glint in his dazzling deep-blue gaze.

Tierney straightens, trying to not let her thoughts scramble in response to the sight of his handsome face and his strapping, half-naked form.

"I am," Tierney replies, sending out her own whoosh of invisible water power toward Fyordin.

Fyordin gives her an intent look that Tierney feels straight down her spine.

"Your training in your Asrai for'din, your Fae power, will be fast and intense," he says, growing more serious. "We're likely to be deployed west. And soon. The Vu Trin are mobilizing for war with the Roaches."

Tierney gives a sharp, inward draw back.

*Roaches.*

Unease twists in Tierney as a storm cloud forms over her head that she's unable to tamp down. "I'm ready to fight Vogel and his forces," she says, holding Fyordin's gaze. "But you should know that there are Gardnerians who are with us in that fight."

Tierney can feel it, the energy around her instantly changing, becoming unsettled and not quite the lovely embrace it was just a moment ago.

Fyordin's lips twist into a dominant sneer, his invisible water power swelling, no longer powerfully enticing, but churning with chaotic energy. "The Roaches have no place with us."

"They're called Gardnerians," Tierney snipes back.

She can sense the combined water power all around her receding, and part of her wants to scramble to reclaim it, to reclaim the moment of belonging. Instead, she stands her cursed, obstinate, subversive ground.

*This is your special talent, isn't it?* Tierney bitterly considers. *Making yourself into an outsider everywhere you go.*

The side of Tierney's neck prickles as she senses attention homing in on her. Not the attention of the Asrai all around her, suffused with water magic. No. This is something foreign.

Something that briefly flickers her internal water power dark as night, turning its rippling blue to the murkier shades of a deeply submerged pool.

Her gaze is drawn like a compass needle to a dark, distant figure—a young man, tall and quiet, dressed all in black that matches his shock of night-black hair. His attention is wholly focused on her as he leans against the stone railing of the curving terrace just past the Lasair Fire Fae division, flames circling and rising above them.

Tierney is sure of it, even from this distance...

He's one of the three Death Fae here at the Wyvernguard.

The Death Fae, she's already ascertained from this morning's conversations, are feared outcasts, here only because the maverick commander of the Vu Trin forces, Vang Troi, wants to make use of their unique magical abilities, just as she wants to use Trystan's.

Thrown by the dark Fae's presence, Tierney turns back to Fyordin to find him giving her a blistering look.

"Half of everyone here," he snarls, his invisible water power rearing as he loses all trace of welcome, "half of all of us were glamoured and raised by Kelts. Sheltered by Kelts in the West. Kelts who saved our people from being killed by the *Gardnerians*. The other half of us were smuggled East and raised by the Noi. Who saved us from being killed by the *Gardnerians*."

Tierney's hackles rise. "My adoptive family is *Gardnerian*," she acidly refutes. "Who saved me from being killed by the

*Gardnerians.* Some of my closest friends are *Gardnerian.* All of them ready to fight Vogel."

Fyordin's narrow look tightens. "I heard you came here with Trystan Gardner."

"I did," Tierney replies with an air of confrontation that Fyordin instantly meets.

"The Roaches don't belong here," he seethes, low and threatening. "And the grandson of the Black Witch, most of all, does not belong here. If he won't leave on his own, he'll need to be driven out."

Tierney holds Fyordin's formidable gaze without flinching. "Trystan Gardner is my friend."

A deeper hush falls, the former air of welcome and acceptance whisked clear away.

"Then maybe you don't belong here either," Fyordin states coldly.

His words are like a knife straight through her. Jaggedly painful. But Tierney will be damned if she shows this arrogant Fae how much he's hurt her.

She stifles the pain and shoots Fyordin a potent glare, the storm cloud above her head gaining strength. "What ever happened to Asrai'il?" she snarls. "Or does that only apply when I don't speak my own mind?" She takes a step toward him, incensed beyond reason. "I hear you've claimed the Vo, Fyordin."

"I have," he shoots back, a storm flashing in his eyes.

Tierney gives a mirthless smile. "I challenge that claim."

A collective gasp of astonishment goes up as Fyordin takes his time looking her up and down, his lips twisting with disdain, but Tierney can feel the storm in him battering against his skin. "You don't realize what you're dealing with," he warns with a threatening smile. "You'd need an army to best me."

Tierney steps back, lowers her head, and throws out her arms, palms up, as she sounds out an Asrai call in her mind.

A call straight out to the Vo River.

*Her* Vo.

Water explodes over the terrace's edge. Shrieks sound out as more than twenty kelpies leap from the river and military apprentices all over the terrace draw back in surprise. The kelpies' bodies roil with dark water, sharp teeth forming from ice as they flow in to converge around Tierney. Her beloved kelpie, Es'tryl'lyan, comes to Tierney's side as Tierney notes the alarmed expressions of the Asrai surrounding her.

Tierney knows that her kelpies exist outside of an alliance with any Fae. And that they are aligned with the power of water to cause death, straddling the line between Asrai magic and primordial forces.

Death forces.

Tierney reaches out to touch the cool, flowing surface of Es'tryl'lyan's back as she gives Fyordin a lethal smile. "I have an army, Fyordin Lir. And we plan on fighting Marcus Vogel's forces with anyone who will ally with us."

Furious, Tierney turns on her heels and stalks away from them all, the storm cloud above her head strengthening and spitting lightning as she throws out her arm and sends her kelpies back to the water and then doggedly makes her way across the broad terrace toward the Death Fae.

"Tierney," Asra'leen calls after her, the sound of the young Fae's booted feet splashing over the water-slicked terrace.

Her water magic churning with resentment, Tierney grits her teeth and slows to a begrudging stop, her gaze still set on the Death Fae, who is steadily watching her from the terrace's farthest end.

"Tierney, please," Asra'leen pleads, her voice shot through with contrition.

Tierney lets out a long sigh and turns. She can see, from the remorseful look on Asra'leen's face, that she's genuinely concerned, her prismatic shimmer dimmed. But it's not enough to quell the angry hurt roiling inside Tierney.

"I think you're supposed to shun me now," Tierney snipes, knowing even as she says it that she's being wildly unfair to Asra'leen, who has been nothing but kind to her.

Asra'leen's face tenses with hurt, but she appears to shake it off quickly, the deep blue of her eyes darkening with a stubborn light. "I'll do no such thing."

Tierney raises a blue brow at Asra'leen's impassioned declaration, some solid will behind it.

*I've misjudged her*, Tierney considers. *She's made of sterner stuff than her dancing rainbows and affinity for a small waterfall would seem to indicate.*

"I can see that this is...complicated for you," Asra'leen falteringly offers. She glances back toward the Asrai massed on the terrace behind them.

Tierney's gaze briefly meets Fyordin's, a flash of ire passing between them as the powerful Fae sweeps up his hand and blasts a waterspout from the Vo to fly straight up and scatter amidst the clouds above.

A warning.

*Fine*, Tierney thinks, glaring at Fyordin. *It's on. I'm taking the Vo.*

"Where are you going?" Asra'leen asks Tierney, her foam-white brow crinkling. "You'll be disciplined if you leave..."

"I will not train with Fyordin Lir," Tierney snaps with an emphatic slice of her hand. "I'm going to petition to be assigned to a different division." She inclines her head toward the dark young man in the distance. "And I'm going to go over there and talk to that Death Fae."

Alarm explodes over Asra'leen's features. She swallows as she side-eyes the Death Fae. "Tierney," she warns, low and emphatic, "don't go near him. They're not like us. Their magic isn't elemental. It's primordial and dangerous. They shouldn't even be here in the Wyvernguard. All of the religions here mark them as demonic—"

"*No,*" Tierney spits out with a derisive glare. "I just came from Gardneria. You're going to have to find something better than religious arguments to get me to shun anyone. I'll figure out for myself who's a demon and who's not."

Asra'leen takes hold of her arm with a nervous glance in the Death Fae's direction. "They can read your fear and feed on it. They can pull you under a thrall, and they test you with animals that can kill you. So they can grab hold of a thread of your fear and control you." Her tone turns adamant. "Tierney, he might be stalking you. They do that. Stay away from him."

Skepticism rises in Tierney. "And yet they're the only ones willing to give Trystan Gardner a chance." Recklessly decided, Tierney turns away from Asra'leen and makes for the Death Fae.

"Tierney...wait!" Asra'leen cries out from behind her, but Tierney ignores her, ignores the collective looks of surprise from the Fire Fae division as she passes them by and homes right in on the dark figure and his unblinking stare.

# CHAPTER FIVE

# DEATH FAE
## TIERNEY CALIX

*Sixth Month*
*Eastern Realm,*
*the Wyvernguard*

Approaching the Death Fae is like approaching a void, his dark form still as Tierney strides across the Wyvernguard's stone terrace, rapidly closing the distance between them. For a moment, there's the sense of slowing down even as Tierney picks up her brisk pace, the distance between herself and the motionless Fae seeming to telescope backward as the entire world dims.

Her heartbeat quickening, Tierney continues to press on toward the Death Fae's hypnotic form as he reclines against the terrace's railing, pale hands gripping stone. He's long and slender, but she has the growing sense of vast power contained in his streamlined frame, his face all angles and shadows, his Wyvernguard uniform tinted black, as if someone has poured ink over the sapphire fabric and the embroidered dragon flowing down its center.

Tierney notes his nails are also black and sharpened to points.

Claws.

Claws that look like they could effortlessly eviscerate someone.

As she approaches, the inky color of his eyes spreads out to encompass the surrounding white, giving the impression of a bottomless abyss. Tierney pauses, the warm *whoosh* of her pulse sounding in her ears as her body stiffens with a mounting intimidation that she stubbornly ignores. She forces her feet back into motion, the world growing darker and darker as she approaches, the Death Fae now lit only by a faint silvery mist that's enfolding them both.

She stills before him.

It's as if the world has paused, only the two of them now in it, all sound muted to nothing, the terrace, the Wyvernguard mountain, and the river surrounding them plunged into darkened hues.

The Death Fae straightens slightly, his focus on Tierney seeming to sharpen with unsettling curiosity as hard obsidian horns emerge from his spiked black hair in spiraling arcs.

*Holy gods his eyes are black*, Tierney marvels, her breath tightening in her throat.

Black as the center of Erthia.

Black as the deepest reaches of the night sky.

Tierney swallows as onyx serpents slither out from under the hem of the Fae's tunic to coil around his waist, his arms, his pale neck.

He waits as his serpents raise their heads in unison, their eyes intent on Tierney, purple tongues flickering. She has the sudden, vaguely amusing thought that if the Death Fae opened his mouth, he'd push out a forked purple tongue that would flicker too.

"Why are you watching me?" Tierney asks, no accusation in her tone, only curiosity.

He cocks his head, seeming to peer at a focal point inside her. "You have kindred Deathkin," he answers, and a shiver passes through Tierney, his voice a subterranean lull that resonates in her bones. "Your kelpie kindreds are kindred to us, as well," he says, mist-shrouded. "And the Gardnerian spoke of you."

Tierney considers this as she recalls the looks of fear that came over the other Asrai when Tierney summoned her kelpies. It's clear most Water Fae don't like her vicious water horses, linked as they are to the killing power of water and known to drown anyone deemed a threat to waters they've claimed as their own.

Death rides with them.

But still, the kelpies' ferocious loyalty to the waters of Erthia resonates deep in Tierney's core, and she can't help but love them for it.

She holds the Death Fae's bottomless stare, feeling a spark of kinship based on their mutual appreciation for creatures that are both terrifying and wildly misunderstood.

She squares her shoulders against the Fae's encroaching, palpable darkness. "I heard you were kind to Trystan Gardner, and I wanted to thank you for it. He's my friend."

The Death Fae's brow tightens, his silvery mist writhing around Tierney.

A sudden flow of onyx spiders and scorpions appear over the Fae's shoulders and around his sides, coalescing to swarm down his body onto the misty stone terrace and toward Tierney. She winces from the contact as the creatures scuttle up over her pants and around her form, along with two of the black snakes.

Poisonous river spiders, cave scorpions, and water snakes.

One bite a mark of death.

Rebellion rises in Tierney in response to what feels like an attempt to intimidate. She meets the Death Fae's stare unflinchingly as the gleaming black insects and serpents encircle her, her water power rising with confrontational energy.

The Death Fae tilts his horned head, his black lips lifting, as he continues to study Tierney with those unnerving, unblinking void eyes of his.

Without warning, his dark eyes widen.

Tierney gasps, swept up in a sudden swell of vertigo, feeling as if the ground has upended to cast her straight into his bottomless eyes.

She shuts her own eyes tightly to stop from careening into his thrall, almost losing her footing as ire rises in her like a fierce tide. Struggling to regain her balance, she draws in a deep breath then opens her eyes to narrowed, livid slits and is instantly accosted, once more, by his relentless draw.

"Get your thrall off me," she seethes as the sense of hurtling straight toward him overtakes her once again. Tensing every muscle, Tierney draws a storm, dark clouds bursting from her skin, blasting away the Fae's silvery mist as her clouds whip around them both, spitting slim threads of white lightning.

The Death Fae blinks, as if surprised, and then his pull recedes.

Tierney takes a faltering step back to regain her balance, then forces herself straight as she glares at the Fae, her anger spilling over its banks. "I have an affinity for kelpies and for dark waters," she snarls. "I'm drawn to the bottom of lakes. Hidden streams. Stormy weather. It's not the clear, pretty water that I like—it's deep water with many things living in its depths. Dangerous things." Tierney flicks her eyes pointedly toward the insects still scuttling over her abdomen and the one serpent that's twined around her arm as her fury mounts.

She meets the Death Fae's black stare intently, blazing challenge in her glare. "Go ahead, Death Fae. Try to scare me. You picked the wrong Asrai to try to intimidate. I've lived in darkness for a *very* long time."

His inky gaze slides over her face as the whites of his eyes reappear and his mouth hints at a smile. "You are attracted to the dangerous things of nature?"

*Holy gods*, Tierney thinks again, the world darkening to pitch around that silken, subterranean voice, only the silver-mist-lit image of him remaining.

And those deep-cavern eyes.

Tierney stares back at him unflinchingly. "I am."

The Death Fae rises to his full, impressive height and takes a step toward Tierney, his slight smile edging higher as he draws close.

Suddenly, Tierney is once again falling into that dark gaze, mesmerized, feeling as if she's been swept up in a midnight current.

"Are you sure?" he says, his breath brushing her ear, his voice thrumming through Tierney with an odd, enticing resonance that warms the currents of her power.

The entire world dims almost to the point of full dark.

Apprehension rises in Tierney, bubbling up even as she fights against what's turned into a surprisingly alluring pull, his draw taking on the intoxicating feel of submersion in the vast river's depths.

"Why are you trying to pull me under your thrall?" she calmly asks him, holding his gaze even as her power churns warmer.

"Curiosity," he answers, his smile nocturnal as he studies her with those bottomless eyes. His brow tightens a subtle fraction, as if he's distracted by something inside her. "Your fears intrigue me."

"Is it true, then?" Tierney asks somewhat archly, striving to ignore how seductive she finds him in this moment. "Are you a demon, about to swallow me whole?"

A wicked smile lifts the Death Fae's lips, and it sends a chill down Tierney's spine. But then the smile is gone as his focus on her sharpens, an unsettled energy in it.

*Tierney Calix.*

Tierney stiffens with surprise to hear his deep voice sounding in the back of her mind.

She recoils, swiftly moving back as she exhales and blasts invisible storm power outward, striking against his invading thrall. "Get *out* of my mind," she snarls as fright ices through her.

Their powers collide, one wall of Fae magic meeting another, neither side giving way, a dark wall pressed up against a storming tide.

"No one can keep Death out," he sneers, teeth bared, as he presses against her storm. "Don't approach Death if you're timid."

"What's your name?" Tierney demands, not the least bit cowed this time as she forcefully holds his thrall at bay.

He blinks, his black lips twitching, as their powers maintain a relentless standoff. "Viger," he concedes, low in his throat. "Viger Maul."

"Well, Viger," Tierney shoots back, emphatic. "You should know that I'm not the least bit timid. But my mind is my own, and if you try to control it, I'll fight back twice as hard."

His thrall abruptly recedes. Tierney's power rushes into the unprotected space around him, his form now encircled by her unsettled clouds, threads of lightning periodically illuminating his severe features.

He stays silent as the spiders, scorpions, and snakes crawl

and slither back toward him and disappear under the hems of his garments until it's as if they were never there.

"I do not control minds," he finally says, with what sounds like a rueful note as the whites of his eyes return.

"But I'm told you feed on fear," Tierney snipes back.

A slight, bitter scowl. "No. I *read* fear," he counters with what seems like a trace of exasperation. "Better than anything. Better than your words. Better than the look on your face." Tierney is struck by the sudden, world-weary expression that tinges the Fae's coal-black eyes. He can't be much older than Tierney's nineteen years, yet, in that moment, he seems ancient.

A morbid curiosity rises in Tierney, unbidden. "What are you reading in my fears?" she ventures, feeling as if she's toying with something much more dangerous than her kelpies.

The Death Fae's lip curls back up, no mirth reaching his void eyes as he draws close once more and the whites blacken over, his misty darkness insinuating itself into her clouds.

*You fear Vogel,* sounds inside Tierney's mind. *As you should. And you fear for everyone you love.* Tierney's muscles tighten in response to the invasive feel of that deep voice resonating once more in her head.

*You fear never being seen for who you are,* the velvet voice murmurs. *And you fear not belonging.* His expression darkens further, his face closer to hers now, something approaching sympathy touching the sharp lines of his face. *You will never resolve both of these fears, Asrai. You cannot have both of these things. You stand alone.*

Tierney draws back, suddenly pierced by a sorrow she can't explain, an unsettling energy shuddering through her water power. "That's enough," she snaps, thrown by the vulnerability this stranger-Fae is stoking in her.

His black-lipped mouth falls open a fraction as if he's unearthed something that surprises him. His brow creases, a surprising tinge of compassion in his eyes. *You fear never truly being loved.*

A defensive heat sparks in Tierney and she moves farther back from him. "Get out of me."

*I can't.* The tone of the words in her mind is almost mournful as the Death Fae remains stubbornly fixated on her. *Reading fear is like breathing air to Deathkin.*

"Then get away from me, Viger."

The energy between them changes as Viger flicks out his claws and the darkness he's sent out to languidly circle around them morphs into a tempest of black smoke, roiling and storming. "You came to me," he snarls, revealing disturbingly sharp teeth as his eyes flash then turn solid black once more. "You invited me in and asked for your fears." *So face what's inside you, Asrai*, seethes in the back of Tierney's mind.

Suddenly Tierney is accosted by every last one of her fears as every terrifying moment of her life and every fear for the future gather together and rise like a cyclone inside her.

Being wrenched away from her parents at three.

Playing with her water magic as a child and nearly being found out by the Gardnerians.

The day that Vogel took power.

Finding two of her beloved kelpies dead in an iron-spiked lake.

Reading her kelpies' images of Fae refugees being impaled by iron weapons wielded by Gardnerian soldiers.

A Lasair Fae child with an iron spear thrust right through her head.

And then a vision of Vogel's dragon army flying over the Vo Mountains, straight toward where they're standing, everyone here powerless to stop the evil onslaught.

Her family and friends all ripped to shreds by soulless dragons.

Uncontrollable terror strafes through Tierney and pulls her under. Suffocating, debilitating, horrifying fear.

She lets out a strangled cry as she wrenches her gaze from the Death Fae and breaks his thrall. She turns back to face him and gives him a blazing look of anguished accusation. What appears to be deep remorse to the point of emotional pain flares in his eyes. But it's all too much.

Tierney turns on her heels and flees.

That evening, Tierney seeks out the Wyvernguard's river-level terrace once more, desperate to be close to the bobbing waters of the powerful Vo River, her emotions still running in a turbulent stream from her encounter with the Death Fae.

The cool breeze coming off the Vo ruffles her multihued-blue hair as she leans on the terrace's stone railing, her mind a storm soothed only by the Vo wakening to her presence, waves leaping then gently scrolling toward her to lap at her feet. As if the river can sense her troubled state.

Tierney exhales, her shoulders loosening in response to the water's caress.

Rune ships are streaming through the air and over the waters of the inky Vo, bright sapphire runes whirring at their sides. Beyond the stretch of river directly before her, the spiraling tiers of the Wyvernguard's North Twin Island rise up, long, rune-lit walkways connecting the North and South Twin Islands like the rungs of an enormous ladder.

Tierney turns east and takes in Noilaan's twinkling capital city of Voloi, the city rising tier after tier and built into the vertical wall of the Voloi Mountain Range, the breathtakingly high mountains that hug the eastern coast.

She pivots her head and peers west over the river at the

hulking black wall of the Vo Mountains, which hug the Vo River's western bank and wall off Noilaan from everything west of it. A fierce band of storms created by the Zhilon'ile Wyverns hangs above this ridgeline as a barrier to invaders, roiling clouds frenetically spitting blue lightning.

Tierney knows the history of this Wyvern-made band of storms.

It was created during the Realm War to keep the Black Witch out.

She frowns as she grips the cool stone railing and glances from the Vo Mountain Range to the huge city of Voloi and back west again, concerned about the vulnerability of the city.

At the base of the Vo Mountains, the Noi have fabricated a runic border that spans the Vo River's entire western bank, curving over the river's northern and southern reaches to en-circle the entire country of Noilaan. The rune border is a ribbon of blue from here, but up close, Tierney imagines it would top Valgard's cathedral in height. Its runes send up a barely visible runic dome over the entirety of Noilaan, mak-ing trespass impossible and enabling rune ship flight as well as the rune magery that powers the entire city.

Tierney looks into the night sky, needing to squint and focus hard to catch the dome-shield's slight blue shimmer and the occasional glimpse of one of the countless translucent runes that mark its gigantic surface.

Her frown deepens.

*Will it be enough to keep Vogel out?*

The skin prickles on the back of Tierney's neck, a distur-bance rippling through her water magic as the uneasy sense of someone's attention on her rises.

She turns and scans the dimly lit terrace, its obsidian stone washed a faint blue by a few rune lanterns set into the moun-tain's stone walls. Vu Trin military apprentices are strolling over the riverside terrace's broad curving surface, some alone and some in groups or pairs, taking advantage of the spectacular views and the pure joy of being so close to this most majestic of all rivers, no doubt.

None of them take much notice of the Water Fae standing by the terrace edge, enfolded in the night's shadows.

Still, Tierney can't shake the feeling of being the object of someone's unwavering focus. Her water magic whirs inside her as the sensation becomes directional, like a slight, magnetic pull.

She looks up the Wyvernguard's stone wall toward the sensation's origin, her gaze quickly zeroing in on a dark figure sitting on the leg of the huge, ivory-stone dragon sculpture that's wrapped around the base of the island and cut into the obsidian stone.

A flash of reckless interest sizzles through her as her water magic winds apprehensively tighter.

*Viger Maul.*

He looks deceptively normal, except for the fact that he's defying gravity slightly, like an elegant spider adhering to the mammoth bas-relief sculpture. His spiraling half-moon horns are absent from his short, spiked hair.

She tenses, her heartbeat quickening as she waits for Viger's mind assault of her own fears and his otherworldly, bitter voice to sound in the back of her head, but…

…nothing.

She holds Viger's intent stare, confusion and curiosity piquing inside her as she wonders whether what some of the other military apprentices told her over dinner is true.

Do Death Fae really stalk you once you draw their interest? Will they take you down by nature's most horrible means? And when you attract their attention, are you attracting Death itself?

She doesn't want to believe any of this, but here he is, staring at her.

She waits for Viger's dark thrall to descend, but it's as if he's politely, carefully holding his strange powers back. And then, never taking his eyes off her, his form turns to black smoke and twines up to be camouflaged from her sight by the obsidian stone above the dragon carving's massive form.

An inarticulate melancholy fills Tierney, overshadowing her surprise at his ability to morph into smoke.

She coughs out a sardonic laugh. *Do you truly want him to come back?* She's taken aback by her own bizarre draw toward this Fae who purposefully terrified her.

*But what did he do, really? He simply showed you your own fears.*

She stares after him for a long moment, wondering if he'll rematerialize, both intimidated by the feelings he unearthed in her as well as filled with a surprising desire to approach him again.

And not run this time.

A slight disturbance in her water magic coming from the other direction has Tierney stiffening even as she lets out a small sigh over the fulsome sensation of another Water Fae's power rippling against her own in a decadent attraction.

"Are you going to take the Death Fae as your lover?" a deep, chiding voice inquires in the Asrai tongue.

Ire churns through Tierney over the intrusion into her private space.

And because she recognizes that voice.

She wheels around to find Fyordin Lir standing there in all his Asrai Fae glory, tall and shockingly handsome, his Asrai skin mirroring the nighttime hues of the Vo River. Tierney glances down at her own hand, resting on the gleaming onyx stone.

Surprise ignites when she finds that her skin has become

a reflection of the Vo as well, a changeable dark current eddying over it.

A bit overcome, she glances back up at Fyordin. He's idly balancing a roiling globe of water above his palm as he leans on the terrace railing, his expression arrogant. His dark lips twist as he gives her a poignant look and bobs his head at something behind her, as if inviting her to see.

Tierney follows his line of vision and surprise flashes again, a deeper disturbance shivering through her water magic.

Viger has rematerialized at the far edge of the terrace, his long, lean figure now perched on its stone railing, his focus unmistakably on her.

And then he again morphs into black smoke, twining up into the night sky.

"I think he's besotted," Fyordin teases as he pulls the globe of water back into his palm.

Tierney glowers at Fyordin as she struggles to ignore how blastedly good-looking he is, but it's impossible. At least he's not half-naked anymore, blessedly garbed in his sapphire Wyvernguard tunic. Tierney forces aside the memory of how gorgeous his muscular body looks underneath it.

"I'm glad you put some clothes on, Fyordin," she tosses out in an attempt to seem unfazed by him even as her heart hammers and her water magic strains toward his, a prickling flush heating her cheeks.

Fyordin cocks a dark brow in question, and even that is dauntingly entrancing.

Tierney sighs, irritated by his powerful draw. "Men don't go around shirtless in the Western Realm," she explains in a barbed tone. "And I have very Gardnerian sensibilities. Since I was raised by *Gardnerians*. I'm quite polluted, you'll find."

Fyordin's eyes flash, his lips tightening as his vast water

magic grows as unsettled as hers, and Tierney notices, once again, that they're both a visual mirror of the Vo.

"What do you want, Fyordin?" Tierney finally snaps, struggling not to stare at his matching night-river skin in beguiled fascination. "I thought I was shunned."

Fyordin turns and leans over the stone railing and surveys the Vo, which seems to be watching them both.

Which seems to have claimed them both.

"I don't seek to shun you." He sets his piercing dark blue eyes back on Tierney with a fervid gaze that she can feel eddying straight through her power.

Hurt flares inside her, intensified by his magical pull. "I thought I don't belong," she challenges, her cursed voice breaking as she pointedly speaks in the Western Realm's Common Tongue.

Fyordin's jaw ticks, a flash of what looks like reluctant chagrin momentarily tightening his dominant gaze. He glances back over the Vo, clearly unsettled by her, as well. Tierney can feel it in the jostled currents of his power. "You belong," he states in clipped, almost impatient Asrai, as if apology is something foreign to him and this is as close as he'll edge up to it.

Tierney glares at him, and he begrudgingly meets her stare as she's swept up in the fierce, sudden urge to grab hold of his arm like before—not in Asrai-greeting this time, but to really show him the storm inside her.

Roiling with hurt, Tierney is tempted to not give this arrogant Asrai one second more of her time. To jump off the railing and spend the night at the bottom of the Vo, surrounded by the river's all-encompassing embrace.

"There's great power in you," Fyordin notes in that deep-current voice of his that seems accentuated by the night. Tierney reluctantly glances at him as he peers up at the star-blasted sky. "Enough power to control the weather, I'd wager." He gives her a significant look.

Tierney inhales, her ability to affect the weather so chaotic and linked to her storming emotions that the word *control* seems a laughable stretch.

"I can change the weather," she finally admits. "But... the power is...volatile." She stops for a moment, her throat growing tight. "My weather power put me and my family in so much danger. So many times." Memories of losing control scrape at the edges of her mind—storm clouds forming at wildly inopportune times, isolated rainstorms, small blizzards. And always, the Gardnerians lurking somewhere near, ready to swoop down.

She struggles to force the horrible memories back down.

*Go ahead. Push it all down. Stifle your fear instead of facing it.*

An unbidden image of Viger's horned head enters her mind. His dark lips and black, unfathomable gaze.

Fyordin is watching her closely now, turned fully to face her as he leans against the railing, the hard arrogance from just a moment ago now gone. Tierney is struck anew by his unglamoured Asrai-ness. His pointed ears and rippling Fae hue. Out in the open. Unafraid. Rune blades strapped to his arms. It's a heady rush just looking at his unhidden Asrai form.

"Were you raised in the West?" Tierney asks him, wondering how long it will take her to shake off the lingering spikes of terror that flash through her whenever she releases her magic. The panicked reflex to force down her power and run for cover.

Even her kelpies stay submerged most of the time, wary of coming to shore.

In hiding.

Still.

"I didn't grow up over there," Fyordin admits with a tight

look toward the storm-limned Vo Mountain Range, lightning flashing above it. "My family managed to get out before the Realm War. They were the only ones in their band of Asrai to survive." He meets Tierney's gaze once more. "I grew up here with my parents and brother."

Shock lights. "You have family here?" Tierney's throat tightens at the memory of her mother screaming her Asrai name and being dragged away by several Asrai as Tierney was placed in the arms of her Gardnerian parents.

Gardnerian parents who risked their own lives to keep her safe from the Gardnerians' Fae purge.

Her water power thrust into chaos, Tierney looks to the stone floor and furiously blinks back the wretched tears now brimming in her eyes. She can feel the storm cloud forming over her head, the crackle of lightning spitting in it as she struggles to pull it in, not wanting to bare herself to this arrogant Fae whose parents never died.

Who doesn't understand the full horror of the West.

Who never can.

"Stay in our division, Asrai'il," Fyordin says, and Tierney snaps her gaze to his, astonished by his newly compassionate tone. His deep-river eyes are searching and dark as the Vo's depths in this dim light, the metallic blue hoops in his ears catching glints of the terrace's runic light.

"So now I'm 'Asrai'il' again?" Tierney bites out, her voice fracturing as she roughly wipes away her tears.

"You always will be," Fyordin says, and this time there's unmistakable apology in his eyes.

She tightens every muscle and manages to pull the storm cloud in, wrestling control of her fitful power.

Barely.

Then she looks back at Fyordin.

"The Wyvernguard has my fealty," she says to him in Asrai

with a ferocious sincerity. "And the Asrai do, as well. No matter what. Even if you despise me for speaking my own mind."

"I don't despise you." He takes a step toward her, a hard current of his water power breaking free to course around her. "Stay in our division, Tierney Asrai'ir. I want to help you gain full mastery over your Fae power. And train you to channel it through runic weaponry."

A blaze of defiance courses through Tierney as she fixes him with a mutinous glare. "Trystan Gardner also has the full weight of my support."

Fyordin's water magic gives a hard, angry surge with an intensity to rival her own. "Gardnerians have no place here in the Eastern Realm," he declares, impassioned and dauntingly entrenched.

Tierney's face twists into a deeper scowl as the Vo's cool breeze rustles her hair and caresses her neck.

An inexplicable longing to be back with her odd circle of friends from Verpax University washes over Tierney, rapidly gaining force as she stares in the eyes of this implacable Fae. But her friends are scattered, Trystan isolated on the North Twin Island with only Death Fae for companions, the Lupines brought to a Vu Trin military base somewhere in the northeast, Wynter sheltered by the Amaz.

And both Elloren and Yvan, trapped in Gardneria as Vogel's darkness takes root there and grows.

Dread and frustration roll through Tierney as she shoots Fyordin a hard, exasperated glare.

*Stubborn, intractable fool.*

But then, she's struck by a new remembrance, of how she and her friends were able to fight Vogel effectively only when they worked together.

Despite serious differences.

*Maybe*, Tierney begrudgingly considers as she looks toward the Vo, *working together means trying to work with an arrogant, rigid Asrai who is dead wrong about what it's going to take to go head-to-head with Vogel.*

She turns back to Fyordin to find him considering her with equal frustration, both of their water powers contained but storming.

"Fyordin," she says in the Water Fae tongue, leveling with this stranger-Fae, Asrai to Asrai, "in the west, I was part of a Resistance group that included Trystan Gardner and his brother and sister too. It included hidden Fae. And Amaz. And Lupines. And Icarals. We destroyed a Gardnerian military base. Rescued an unbroken dragon. And got the remaining Lupines out of the Western Realm. But we needed *all of us* to do these things."

Fyordin shakes his head and gives her a stubborn look of refute.

"Hear me out," Tierney presses. "I do not have the luxury of uncomplicated hatred. And you need to let go of it, as well. The Gardnerians separate the world into the Blessed Ones and the Evil Ones. We can't win this fight if we think that way."

"We will never see eye to eye about the Gardnerians," Fyordin insists, and Tierney can feel his internal storm raging. His words cut to the quick, ramping up her worry for her Gardnerian family here. Her worry for Trystan.

A brushstroke of attention shivers through her roiling magic, directional and light as the brush of a dragonfly's wing. She looks past Fyordin and up.

Viger Maul is sitting on an outcropping of the island's onyx stone, his gaze set on her, and Tierney is too stirred up to be intimidated by the Death Fae's sustained attention.

*Go ahead*, Tierney thinks at him as she holds Viger's stare. *Read my fear. Read all of it.*

She turns back to implacable Fyordin, fully aware of Viger's sustained focus on her as she and Fyordin consider each other, Fae to Fae, neither side ceding any ground.

*What would it be like*, Tierney wonders as her frustration mounts, *to spend time with Viger Maul? To face every last fear, no longer hiding from any of it?*

*Every dark thing exposed.*

*Like a relief*, Tierney can't help but consider. *A cursed relief.*

And, possibly, an essential preparation for Vogel's advance on the Eastern Realm.

"You don't fully understand what's coming," Tierney says to Fyordin, dread rising. "If you did, you wouldn't be wasting your time fighting our allies, imperfect though they may be." She moves closer to him, adamant, holding his equally fierce stare. "We need to fight this thing together. Every last one of us. Or Vogel's nightmare is going to devour us all."

Their mutual storms of emotion rise, their power lashing against each other's with unbridled force.

Tierney wrenches her gaze from Fyordin's, suddenly needing to be away from him. Needing to be away from Viger Maul. Needing to be away from everything but the river.

Fyordin remains silent as she grabs hold of the terrace's railing, hoists her body up until she's balanced on top of it, then raises her arms and dives straight into the Vo.

As her body hits the cool water, she doesn't angle up to skim along the underside of its surface like she did last night as the waves of the river frolicked over her, welcoming her home.

No.

She swims straight down like an arrow, into the deepest black. Until she touches down on the river's great bed, the weight of the Vo a soothing pressure as her Asrai body strengthens against it.

She lies back and splays her arms on the riverbed's soft ground.

*Erthia.*

Tierney breathes in the clean river water, pulling it deep into her lungs as she's filled with the glorious sense of all the life thriving there—life independent of the Wyvernguard, the Noi lands. The river flows into her with every breath, connected to her now like some mammoth network of veins feeding into her own. And for the brief sliver of a moment, as her body morphs into water and unravels into beautiful chaos, Tierney considers staying there for good.

But then she feels it.

A disturbance at the outer reaches of the water that feeds into the Vo. One small point of contact reverberating out, almost imperceptible.

A faraway tendril of shadow, seeping into the water.

Slow and curling.

Life draws away from that point of contagion, plants flexing back, insects scuttling for land, fish darting for cleaner waters.

Every sense sharpening, Tierney draws herself back into corporeal form in a single snap of power.

She stills and listens to the water.

An image of a dead tree shivers to life in the back of her mind as she remembers, all too vividly, what Elloren told her of Vogel's shadowy tree and his heightened, unnatural power.

The dead forest.

She remembers, in another unsettling flash, where she encountered this Shadow power before—the night Alfsigr Marfoir assassin creatures came for Wynter.

Tierney recalls the Marfoir's rune markings, wrought from Shadow magic with the same unnatural, polluting feel as the Shadow that's begun to invade the Vo.

For a long moment, Tierney remains completely still at the bottom of the vast waters, the Vo flowing rippling images over her, piece by piece.

And then, the Vo grows quiet, focusing in on one thing and one thing alone—that touch of Shadow, making first contact with its single, slender tributary.

The threat to the river coalesces inside Tierney's mind, and everything inside her rears up to meet it, courage welling to overtake all fear.

*I'll fight for you*, Tierney vows to the river all around her, fists clenching. *I'll defend you against this Shadow power. I'll protect you from Vogel and the Gardnerians and the Alfsigr.*

Her power whirlpools inside her as love for the river gains ground.

*I won't let them poison your waters.*

Shot through with fierce resolve, Tierney pushes off from the bed of the Vo and makes for the surface.

# CHAPTER SIX

# REBELLION
## THIERREN STONE

*Sixth Month*
*Valgard, Gardneria*

Thierren stands before Lukas Grey in the command room of the Valgard military outpost as an almost irrepressible rebellion lashes through him.

Because he's no longer on the side of the Gardnerians.

*Get hold of yourself,* Thierren cautions as he holds himself military stiff. *You need to hide the fact that you've turned against the Magedom. Lukas Grey is dangerous. He'll sniff out your true feelings if you're not careful.*

Amber light gutters over the room, blazing from Verpacian Elm torches set into iron holsters that are bolted into the command room's dark Ironwood walls. Sanded Ironwood trees emerge from the walls to branch out over the ceiling, giving the room the typical Gardnerian illusion of a deep forest.

Lukas Grey is a formidable presence, Thierren considers. Lukas's aura of power mixed with his keen intellect is nothing short of intimidating. But Thierren isn't cowed. Not after witnessing the Gardnerian massacre of the Dryads. Not after meeting Sparrow.

Brave, determined Sparrow.

The young woman who is the sole reason that Thierren hasn't self-destructed, drawn his wand, and hurled an ice bolt straight through Lukas Grey and every other Gardnerian soldier on this evil base.

She brought him back from the brink of the abyss and challenged him to reformulate how he viewed a world turned on its head, everything he believed about his own people and himself wrong. Cruelly, disastrously, and heart-destroyingly *wrong*.

Now he's alive for one sole purpose—to atone for ever being part of this, and to fight against it.

And to help Sparrow and Effrey get to the Eastern Realm.

Thierren spent the past few days obtaining fraudulent work papers for Sparrow and Effrey, emptying much of his savings to do so. Both he and Sparrow have stayed up late every night for weeks now, huddled in secrecy and talking almost until dawn in the deserted stables as they've fallen into an uneasy and dauntingly complicated alliance.

It's a bond they're loath to acknowledge, and Thierren was increasingly clear on why.

"The Mages preyed on us constantly," Sparrow told him a few days back, the weighted look in her eyes speaking volumes.

They held each other's gazes for a protracted moment.

And then Thierren reached down and silently handed Sparrow his wand, giving her a look blazing with contrition, disarming himself while she remained armed with her blade. The action was a flimsy gesture, he knew, but it was all he could think of to acknowledge that he was listening to what she said as well as to what she left unsaid.

Giving her the power of being the only one armed didn't even begin to scratch the surface of what she's up against, the power imbalance the world has thrust them into a poison that can't be surmounted. Because the power of the entire oppressive system lies on the side of the Mages.

On Thierren's side.

At first, Sparrow simply looked at the wand in Thierren's outstretched palm then back up at him in a blaze of incredulity. But then her amethyst eyes lit with a more open, searching look as she accepted the wand and sheathed it alongside the blade at her hip.

And so they began every covert encounter from there on with Thierren silently offering up his wand and Sparrow silently taking it. A symbol, more than anything, that Thierren was ready to listen. Really listen. It did nothing to shift the oppressive dynamic between their cultures, but it was a start, fueling the fragile spark of friendship that had unexpectedly lit. A friendship that they're both careful to edge back from, Thierren, out of respect for Sparrow's traumatic situation, Sparrow for blaringly obvious reasons.

But still, Thierren's heart twisted with surprising force when he brought both Sparrow and Effrey, camouflaged as state-sanctioned Urisk workers, to the Indentured Labor Guild Office, their small dragon, Raz'zor, hidden with Thierren while his wing healed. As Thierren held Sparrow's gaze, he was surprised to find that she seemed loath to part from him as well, her normally guarded expression briefly igniting with fierce emotion as they bid each other a terse goodbye. As he watched them go, Thierren fought the ferocious desire to draw his wand, cut down every Mage in the room, and flee East with Sparrow and Effrey.

But he couldn't protect them, not with a Mage Guard runic brand on his neck—a brand that made it possible for the Mage Guard to kill him in an instant, even from a distance.

Instead, he kept his power in check as Sparrow and Effrey were whisked away, both of them quickly lost in a sea of Urisk being processed for labor assignments by pinch-faced Mages. Thierren stared after them for a long moment, his heart constricting in his chest, his wind and water magery whipping up into a tempest inside him as a ferocious resolve gained ground.

Yes, he'd endure whatever punishments Lukas Grey doled out and play the faithful soldier until he could get the vile mark stripped off his flesh.

Then he'd help Sparrow and Effrey get East safely. And then, he would come back West.

To fight the Mages.

Lukas Grey brusquely dismisses his Level Five Mage Guards, leaving the two of them alone in the imposing chamber. Then Lukas levels his deep-green gaze on Thierren, raptor-hard.

"I'm assigning you to a position as my personal envoy," Lukas states, his green eyes trained on Thierren, as if gauging his reaction.

Thierren gives a hard, inward start, his mind cast into confusion.

Where is the punishment for trying to stop the killing of the Dryads? For turning his wand on Sylus Bane?

He's been told again and again not to expect any mercy from Mage Lukas Grey.

A heavy silence hangs in the room.

"What are your aims, Mage Stone?" Lukas finally asks, lethally calm.

*To fight you*, Thierren inwardly snarls. *To fight every soldier in the Guard if I have to, to get Sparrow and Effrey and their small dragon out of this nightmare land.*

"I'd like to earn my way to freedom," Thierren says cautiously as he holds Lukas's penetrating gaze.

Lukas rises, strides around to the front of his desk, and unsheathes his wand.

Thierren braces himself and pulls in a strained breath, ready for whatever torture this Mage will inflict. He swallows as Lukas takes firm hold of his upper arm, presses the tip of his wand right onto the rune mark on Thierren's neck, and murmurs a series of spells.

A prickling sensation rises along the lines of the circular tracking rune, the sting quickly dissipating to nothing as Lukas removes the wand from Thierren's skin and takes a casual seat against the front edge of his broad Ironwood desk.

Thierren reaches up to rub his neck, the constant, almost imperceptible burn of the rune completely gone. A whoosh of bewilderment almost pulls him off balance. "What did you do?" he asks.

"Freed you," Lukas says, challenge in his eyes.

*It's a trick. It has to be a trick.* Thierren glares at him, cast further into cornered astonishment. "Why would you do that?" he demands, not able to keep the defensive anger from breaking through his tone.

Lukas's eyes tighten with a sly expression that reads, *Ah, good, there it is. The real Thierren.*

"Do you know why I've assigned you to be my personal envoy, Mage Stone?" Lukas asks, almost congenially.

The insubordinate words burst out of Thierren before he can rein them in. "I don't really care, Mage Grey." It's clear that Lukas has somehow found him out.

Lukas gives a short laugh, seeming impressed, as he throws Thierren a look of approval. "I assigned you to be my personal envoy because I hear that you're an unrepentant traitor to the Gardnerian cause."

Astonishment rocks through Thierren.

*This* has *to be a trick.*

He knows all about Commander Lukas Grey. He's as conniving as he is dangerous.

So, what cruel game is he playing here?

"Your magic complements mine," Lukas goes on conversationally. "Water and air, is it? My two weakest affinities." He lifts an appraising black brow and tilts his head, as if in invitation. "Together, we'd be quite the formidable weapon."

"To do what?" Thierren asks sharply.

Lukas's stare darkens, his smile now gone, his words low and unforgiving when they come. "To take down the Mage Council and kill Marcus Vogel."

# CHAPTER SEVEN

# RUNIC EYE

## YVAN GURYEV

*Sixth Month*
*Oonlon Military Base*
*Noilaan, Eastern Realm*

Yvan Guryev stares over the great Oonlon plain, the vast, dry carpet of russet shrubland giving way to the distant peaks of the Icelandic Mountains that top the entire continent.

His fire gives a heated flare of longing as his thoughts turn to Elloren, the remembrance of how she conjured an inferno with just a small branch filling his mind.

Their separation is too much to bear at times, often keeping him up tossing late into the night, his skin feverish as his fire lashes out, searching and searching for Elloren's fire to no avail, desperate to find his Wyvernfire-bonded love.

But wherever she is, she's too far away for his fire power to contact and sometimes it makes him feel like both his Wyvernfire and his heart have come untethered.

*Where are you, Elloren? Did the Vu Trin bring you somewhere isolated, as well? When will I see you again?*

Forcing away the urge to take wing and find her somehow, somewhere, Yvan looks behind him at the knot of Vu Trin soldiers massed inside the northern edge of the Spikelands, the natural rock formations that look as if thousands of great stony knives have been upthrust through Erthia and toward the sky, the stone gleaming obsidian even in the pewter light of this gloom-ridden day.

Vu Trin High Commander Vang Troi meets his gaze with her piercing black eyes and nods once.

Yvan turns and sets his sights once more on the icy mountains as wind scuffs across the tundra before him and whips his fire-red hair against his temples, ruffling the hem of his black Vu Trin uniform and the feathers of his outstretched wings.

He closes his hands into fists, draws in a deep breath of the cold air, and focuses in on the tight ball of Wyvernfire that dwells in his very center—a ball of flame that he's been strengthening for days.

He can feel himself transforming into a powerful weapon for the Resistance forces, his own desire to be a warrior for them rising along with his dragon powers.

It has been almost too much to bear, filling his center with so much fire while resisting the urge to access it. Resisting the almost irresistible desire to *feel* the fire's release as it burns through him. Instead, he has let the fire power build and build.

Now it's time to see just how powerful a weapon he's become.

Yvan drops his control, loosens the golden-hot inferno in his center, and opens himself up to it in one shuddering intake of breath.

His whole body tenses with something approaching ecstasy as fire floods him, eliminating the tundra's icy cold. His head cranes back, his mouth opening from the sheer pleasure of the burn as his vision tints gold and the whole world lights up.

And then the dragon in him breaks loose.

Fists clenching tighter, Yvan lowers his gaze toward the mountains as he exerts control over the fire and coils it into roping spirals, layer upon molten layer, through his hands, his arms, his shoulders, his whole body.

Tighter and tighter and tighter.

He snaps his wings out to their full breadth as flame crackles inside his vision, lightning hot, and Wyvern horns push up from his hair with a tight, satisfying sting. His teeth sharpen, and he bites them together with a mounting ferocity as the conflagration inside him rises, everything in him yearning for release.

A feral snarl builds in his throat as he throws his arms up and back, then violently forward, splaying his palms open.

His snarl breaks loose as fire explodes from his palms like water from a breached dam, avalanching over the tundra, filling the plains.

The horns on Yvan's head solidify, his nails lengthening to claws as he grits his sharpened teeth and loses himself to the feel of his own hot, violent power, rushing forward from his palms and over the plain with unstoppable force.

And then he's releasing the last bright tail of flame, sending it over plains that are now a lake of dancing fire, every particle of brush and grass alight. Alive with flame.

For a split second he's stunned by the extent of his own power.

*Is it like this for you, Elloren?* he wonders, aching from that familiar longing to be with his Wyvern mate. His love. His whole heart. *When you fill the world in front of you with fire?*

Spent, Yvan lowers his hands and blinks in awe at the inferno he's wrought, the flame-tint of his vision tamping down, the tension dropping from his wings and body as his horns recede and he begins to turn toward the Spikelands at his back, toward the contingent of Vu Trin behind him.

The air changes, the acrid tang of a threat suddenly on it.

Yvan freezes, midturn, nostrils flaring.

His eyes snag on something dark perched atop one of the towering obsidian formations, and every muscle instinctively tenses once more.

A bird. Watching him.

A jolt of horror strafes through him as a green eye opens in the center of the bird's forehead, then multiple eyes open as well around the three central eyes, these filled with swirling shadow. Yvan realizes, in an instant, what this is.

Vogel's dark magic.

Magic the Vu Trin have warned him to be on guard against. Vogel has come.

Yvan whips around just as a Vu Trin soldier breaks ranks and rushes for him, a glowing deep-green shield bursting to life around her as the other soldiers shout and draw weapons, the scene thrust into instant chaos.

Yvan falls into a crouch, his accessible Wyvernfire reduced to a small ember, almost all of it spread out behind him over the blazing plain.

The shielded Vu Trin running toward him pulls a wand, and Yvan realizes, in a burst of clarity, that he's looking at a glamoured Mage as the attacker throws back her wand arm and thrusts it forward, a blur of dark bolts appearing in the air and zooming straight for him.

Yvan attempts to elude the incoming spears, but they're homed in, curving as he attempts to dodge.

Shocks of pain explode through him again and again as vine spears impale his chest, his arm, his wings, his leg.

His heart.

Yvan falls to the ground, his whole body arcing against the terrible pain as Vu Trin yell and weapons fly and crash against the glamoured Mage's magical shield in a cacophony of sapphire runic explosions, the glamoured Mage battling back the Vu Trin with a fusillade of vine spears.

Yvan turns his head as the life seeps out of him, cheek to earth, his vision beginning to black out along the edges. He meets the multi-eyed gaze of the bird, only a handspan away from him now on the ground.

Watching.

Watching.

Waiting for him to die.

Defiance rises in Yvan, and he holds the bird's cruel, horrific stare even as blood flows out of him into the earth below and his internal fire ignites once more, his whole world consumed in pain and flame.

Two last impassioned thoughts fill Yvan's mind as he surrenders to his internal spike of fire and the bird takes wing.

*Be strong without me, Elloren.*

*And fight them.*

# PART TWO

# CHAPTER
# ONE

# COMMANDER LUKAS GREY
## ELLOREN GARDNER

*Sixth Month*
*The Keltish Province of Gardneria*

Yvan.

He's all I can think about as I glance down at my fastmarked hands and my carriage speeds forward, drawing me ever nearer to my reunion with Mage Lukas Grey, commander of Vogel's Fourth Division forces.

*Are you safe, Yvan?* I wonder ceaselessly, apart from him now for over a month and wishing I could find a portal straight to him.

*I'll find my way back to you*, I vow, as both determination and dread mount inside me and my carriage transports me relentlessly deeper into the newly annexed Keltish Province of Gardneria toward Lukas's military encampment.

I turn my hands over, palms up, and survey the black lines that circle every one of my fingers.

Lines that forever separate me from Yvan.

My dread ignites and sparks red-hot with frustration and anger, Wyvernfire blooming to life around my affinity lines in a sizzling rush. It's difficult to quell the fury that rises like a wildfire whenever I look at the dark, looping fastmarks now permanently and irrevocably present on my skin. They always prompt a remembrance of the last time I saw Lukas.

When he fasted to me against my will.

I wince, my outrage notching higher as I remember how Lukas, the priests, and the soldiers held me against the fasting altar and forced my hands onto it. How furious Lukas was the whole time, storming into the room and back out again afterward, barely looking at me the whole time.

Now I'm bound to him, this man who refuses to fully break with Vogel.

I clench my fists and mentally stomp back my anger, clear on what's at stake for me if I don't secure Lukas's protection. I pull in a deep, bracing breath and glance back out the carriage window, the day as storm-dark as the scenes spread out before me.

Every Keltish village we ride through has been shockingly altered by Gardneria's annexation of Keltania. The remaining Kelts appear even poorer, sicklier, and more beaten down than they did during my previous journey here with Yvan. Mage soldiers are everywhere in their black silken uniforms, standing in contrast to the bedraggled Kelts, the Mages all seeming in good spirits, laughing together outside of battered shops and taverns.

There are Gardnerians overseeing Keltish farm laborers, and more than a few well-appointed Gardnerian families living here now. The Mages seem to reside in the nicer homes that we pass. But perhaps the most chilling sights of all are the black Gardnerian flags that aggressively mark practically every dwelling and town square like the symptom of a contagious disease. And all of the flags bear the new design, the Ancient One's white bird on black.

Vogel's flag.

A worse dread sweeps over me as I take in the black pennants and long to touch the Wand of Myth, hidden inside the lining of my travel sack, which is stowed in the carriage's trunk.

Far away from my wand hand and my power.

When we reach the Gardnerian military encampment, I disembark from the carriage and am met by two new high-level Mage soldiers who beckon me forward. The day has grown even more overcast, and there's an uncomfortable chill in the air, the sea of dark, sturdy tents mirroring the somber mood of the sky.

I look around, my stomach tightening as my booted feet make contact with the damp ground, apprehension spiking at the thought of facing Lukas again. Pulling my dark cloak tight around myself, I incline my hood-covered head to keep the beginnings of rain off my face, cold drizzle speckling my hands as we set off at a brisk pace.

Every soldier who spots me stops to stare, appearing mystified by my sudden presence. Trying my best to ignore them, I press forward against the worsening rain as I scan the scene.

There's a sizable central tent up ahead, heavily guarded, and it seems to be the focus of the most regimented activity. A large Gardnerian flag flaps above it, and I notice with a start that it's the old flag, the Erthia orb marking its center like emphatic punctuation.

I know, without asking, that this is where I'll find Lukas.

Steeling myself, I follow the straight-backed soldiers toward the tent, paying little heed to the stupefied looks all around as I straighten to my full height, readying myself to face Lukas Grey.

I close my fists against my fastlines as I consider the viciously bad terms Lukas and I parted on.

*No matter,* I pledge as my resolve solidifies. *I'll win him over.*

I may not be able to lie to Lukas Grey, because of our strong Dryad natures, but I can hold back the truth and find a way to secure his protection, so that I can survive and eventually fight with the Resistance for everyone and everything that I love.

We approach the large tent's entrance, a sheltering black canvas awning now above us.

One of my escorts announces who I am to the grim-faced, bearded guard posted by the entry. The man gives me a rather resentful once-over before he curtly nods then disappears inside. His rancor unsettles me, and I try to come to terms with the number of people who might be aware of how I fought Lukas on our fasting day. How I disappeared soon after. How I have no lines of consummation on my wrists.

And how my brothers betrayed Gardneria and escaped East with the Lupines.

The bearded soldier reappears, draws the tent flap back, and ushers me in with an ill-tempered swipe of his hand.

I pull back my cloak's hood and step inside.

I'm not prepared for what a cold-water shock it is to see Lukas again, my nerves kicking up to jagged heights.

Overwhelmingly handsome as ever, Lukas is seated at a weighty table at the head of the tent's interior, surrounded by a retinue of soldiers. A few of these soldiers have the markings of the magically powerful, like Lukas, but I notice that Lukas is one of the small smattering of Mages on this base still wearing the old uniform, the silver Erthia orb marking his chest instead of the white bird.

Lukas takes his time signing papers placed before him and

talking to military underlings one by one as they approach, bow, then leave to carry out his directives. As usual, he exudes power, the deferential body language of every other soldier in the room attesting to it.

It's warm and dry in the sprawling tent, a central stove packed with smokeless Verpacian Elm blazing away, but still, I struggle to fight back the onset of a trembling chill.

If Lukas notices my presence, he gives no indication, and I've no sense of his vast affinity powers. His fire and earth magic are closed off, and I long to have the same control over my own terrible power.

Emotions storming inside me, I remain at the tent's outer margin and wait for some signal that I can approach. The other men in the tent mirror Lukas's disregard of me, averting their eyes to my presence as if they're doing their best to ignore me completely.

I flex my hands, hyperaware of the fasting marks on them, as my eyes are drawn to the same swirling black lines covering Lukas's hands. The memory slams into me anew—my hands being forced down by Lukas's, the priest's droning words as he recited the fasting spell.

And my uncle.

My beloved uncle Edwin.

Roughed up and imprisoned and essentially murdered by soldiers just like the ones who surround me now. Soldiers who would kill Rafe and Trystan if they could.

Who would kill Yvan.

Inside me swells a hatred of the Gardnerian military that's impossible to suppress. My gaze darts around, lighting on every wand, every wooden chair, running along the length of the tent's Mountain Spruce support beams.

*I may not have a wand on me,* I inwardly seethe, *but all I need is a piece of wood. Any shabby piece will do, and I could conjure a fire so great that it would destroy you all.*

As I take stock of every last piece of wood in the vicinity, the tent gradually empties until I'm alone at its periphery.

Only a single soldier now stands by Lukas. The young man's eyes meet mine, and the flash of recognition that fires in his piercing gaze sets me even further on edge. He's tall and severe looking, his angular features aristocratic, and he has Lukas's same predatory aura. Also like Lukas, his military garb is edged with the five silver lines of a Level Five Mage.

Lukas signs a few more papers and hands them off to this young man.

"You're relieved, Thierren," Lukas says, without bothering to look up as he continues to read through the stack of orders before him.

Thierren gives Lukas a perfunctory bow before he throws another quick, intent look at me. Then he strides toward the exit, studiously not looking at me as he passes by, his cloak flowing behind him as he departs.

Leaving Lukas and me alone in the tent.

I try to will myself to smile and fake pleasantries, but the weight of my anger hollows me out, and that familiar, inescapable Dryad pull to be honest with Lukas takes over. Laid bare by it, I can only stand there, fists clenched, immobilized by a sudden hatred of Lukas that's so raw it hurts.

Lukas sets down his quill, leans back in his chair, and levels his frigid green eyes at me. "What do you want, Elloren?"

*I hate you. I hate you.*

I clench and unclench my hands, wanting to strip the fastmarks clear off them. "I'm back to stay." I force the words out, completely unable to disguise my angry defiance.

Lukas narrows his eyes and makes a sound of derision, then turns his attention once more to the papers before him, signing several, taking his time, as his lips turn up in a mocking grin. "Did the Kelt boy tire of you?"

A flash of rage sends me reeling. I throw up my fasted hands, palms out, the lines still perfectly intact. *Proof* of my chastity.

Lukas glances up at them and seems unimpressed, but then his eyes meet mine in earnest and his face darkens, a violent flash of anger passing over his features as his Magefire gives a sudden, palpable flare toward me. "I asked you what you wanted," he says, his tone steel hard.

"I need a place to stay," I practically spit at him, chastising myself as I do so.

*This won't do. You have to fight this fierce urge to be so honest with him. You're supposed to be charming him so that you can secure his protection.*

I struggle for composure. "I'm… I'm ready to take my place with you." The words come out thick as boiled-down tree sap. It's no use. I can't fight the compulsion to be honest with him in tone now as well as words.

"Commander Grey, I'm sorry to interrupt."

I turn to find black-cloaked Thierren just inside the entrance, his cloak's hood rain-streaked over his head. His sharp gaze briefly darts to me. "Lieutenant Browlin has arrived."

"Show him in," Lukas orders without looking at me, his Magefire once again contained. "Mage Gardner and I are finished."

A light-headed swoop overtakes me. "But… Lukas, I…"

"Show her out," he orders, still not looking at me.

"Lukas," I choke out, my thoughts spinning into chaos as Thierren approaches and takes my arm with gentle insistence. Overcome by humiliation, I flinch away from his touch, angry tears stinging my eyes as Lukas calmly turns his attention back to signing orders and Thierren silently guides me out.

★ ★ ★

I stumble out of the tent, past the newly arrived lieutenant, who eyes me with an immediate, outraged surprise. I wrench my arm away from Thierren's loose grip and stride away.

"Mage Gardner," Thierren calls after me, sounding conflicted, but I ignore him as I swipe at the tears pooling in my eyes that I so desperately want to hide.

It's dusk now and drizzling steadily as I trudge over the wet earth, gripped by a burgeoning panic over what to do. As I pass by, the surrounding soldiers view me with evident confusion, seeming unsure whether they need to fake deference or if they're free to hold me in open contempt.

My mind in utter turmoil, I pull my cloak's hood over my damp head with tremulous hands.

*Where can I find safety if Lukas won't help me? Who will protect me from armed Vu Trin assassins that could be making their way toward me at this very moment?*

Because if I try to protect myself with absolutely no control over my magic, I'll reveal what I am to all of Gardneria. And I'll kill absolutely everyone around me, soldiers and civilians alike.

I weave around the tents blindly, not knowing where to go, where to turn.

*I don't have any money. I don't know where my belongings are.*

*I have never been so alone in my life.*

*And the Wand of Myth—*

My steps halt as a brighter spark of concern lights.

*The Wand...*it's in the carriage that was supposed to wait for me. Hidden in the lining of my travel bag.

And I have no idea where that carriage is.

Heightened alarm sizzles through every muscle as I spin around, looking for the carriage. It's nowhere in sight.

*What if the Wand is found?*

Desperately needing to calm myself, I slide into a margin-ally private space between tents and away from the groups of off-duty soldiers coming and going, then slump against a wooden support beam and attempt to steady my breathing. The rain has picked up, rivulets of water streaming down the sides of the black canvas before me in uneven lines, my cloak growing sodden.

*I need to find help. And I need to locate that carriage.*

Shivering and damp, I'm seized by a flash of remembrance of Chi Nam's rune stone. My heart picks up speed as I pull the stone from my pocket and frantically rub my fingers over the sapphire rune etched onto its gleaming onyx surface. Voice low, I recite the Noi spell that's supposed to unlock the rune and summon Chi Nam's help.

Nothing happens.

My chest tightens with urgency as I try again, rubbing the stone and sounding the spell. But strain as I may, I can't seem to get the spell's complicated pronunciation right, and the rune remains unlit.

I thrust the stone back into my tunic as my spiraling sense of alarm grows.

My only other option is one I can't stomach—seeking help from Aunt Vyvian. Just the idea of it sets a blazing, vengeful fire flashing through my lines, my wand hand twitching un-comfortably at the thought.

"Mage Gardner."

I'm startled by a deep and insistent male voice.

I turn to find Thierren, the severe-featured soldier who ushered me out of Lukas's tent. He's peering into the slim space where I'm ensconced, fierce concern evident in his rigid demeanor.

"Commander Grey has directed me to get you settled," he

informs me, but there's a storming energy churning behind the words, and I've a fleeting sense of vast wind and water power.

I hold Thierren's stare in confusion, struggling to gain hold of myself. For a moment, his words make no sense to my stressed, sleep-deprived mind.

*But... Lukas sent me away. Has he changed his mind?*

Thierren holds out a conciliatory palm. "I've been ordered to arrange a carriage for you. You'll be traveling to Commander Grey's parents' estate in Valgard. It's a little over a day's journey. I believe these are your things." He hoists my travel bag into view, and my heart leaps.

*The Wand.*

I'm momentarily frozen by this quick turn of events, and I fight the urge to leap forward and grab up the bag to get the hidden Wand away from him.

I meet his gaze and force neutrality into my tone. "So... you'll show me to the carriage, then?"

"Of course," he says, his green gaze bolted on me.

Heart racing, I force myself to straighten. "Will Lukas be joining me there?"

"Yes, Mage," Thierren replies after a short but significant pause, a caginess to his tone that makes me feel like we're both playing a part. "He has some things to attend to here. Then he'll meet you in Valgard soon after you arrive."

Foreboding snakes through me. Being separated from Lukas leaves me vulnerable to possible incoming threats. But still, if I can survive this journey, this could be a path toward Lukas's protection.

"Will I have a guard?" I press Thierren, hoping he doesn't question my expressed need for one.

Again, a pause and that same cagey look. "Yes, Mage," he concurs, a glint in his green eyes that reads like a deeper understanding of the questions behind my questions. "You'll be accompanied by myself and three other high-level Mages."

I hold his oddly knowing stare as we regard each other searchingly.

"All right, then," I concede. "Let's go."

The edge of Thierren's lip twitches up as I summon my courage and walk toward him.

I take my proffered bag, my breath suspended as I surreptitiously feel for the Wand's spiraling handle just under the fabric. Relief floods through me as I locate it there, straight and true, and I have to force my expression to remain blank.

Then I sling the bag over my shoulder, exchange one last cryptic look with Thierren, and follow him to the carriage.

# CHAPTER
# TWO

## EVELYN GREY
### ELLOREN GARDNER

*Sixth Month*
*Valgard, Gardneria*

"Mage Evelyn Grey wishes to meet with you straightaway."

A broad, dour-faced, and pale-violet-hued Urisk woman stands before me, framed by the carriage door she's just opened. She's holding a wax cloth up high to form a rain-sheltering canopy for me to step under, raindrops drumming against the top of the stiff fabric. Just beyond her I catch Thierren's eye as he rides away with the three other soldiers who guarded my carriage on the journey, his cloak's hood pulled over his head.

Concerned to see my guard moving away from me, I rise from the carriage seat, my legs cramped from so many hours of travel, then freeze before the carriage door as I take in the sheer size of the estate that lies before me. Aunt Vyvian's mansion is a small cottage in comparison to it.

The Grey estate is sprawling, and I immediately worry that it won't be possible for such an enormous structure to be adequately guarded against assassins. Although…it is placed on elevated land near the edge of a towering bluff that overlooks the Malthorin Bay.

*A huge cliff, that's good*, I consider. *Makes it difficult to approach the estate from the west.*

The estate is also encompassed by a spiky iron fence that appears to be warded against trespass by glowing Gardnerian runes affixed to its larger posts.

The mansion's two stories are supported by massive sanded Ironwood trees, and its tunneling entranceways are framed by more trees' densely woven branches, as if the entire structure has been wrought from a forest. And there's a private, cultivated forest encased in a gigantic arboretum, the huge glass structure attached to the estate, the trees inside blurred by the rain.

The estate's windows are striking, and I can't help but notice their exquisite craftsmanship as we pass them, even in my state of jumped-up surveillance—they're diamond paned and bordered by elegant stained-glass vines. And there's a roof garden with multiple potted trees and flowering vines that spill over the roof's edging in a cascade.

I frown, unsettled.

*It would be so easy for an attacker to hide amidst all that foliage.*

I am marginally relieved to find that High Commander Lachlan Grey's familial home is surrounded by more than a few Mage Guards, soldiers not only bracketing the doors but patrolling the grounds as well, Thierren now among them.

*Will this, combined with a warded gate, be enough to keep me alive?*

"Mage," the Urisk woman standing before me says, pulling me out of my momentary pause.

"I'm sorry," I hastily apologize. "Thank you."

I sling my travel bag over my shoulder and cautiously step down the carriage's slick fold-down steps, taut with anxiety but also ready to be done with close to two straight days of travel to Gardneria's capital city.

The Urisk woman shelters me under the wax cloth as I finish disembarking, her mouth set in a tight line. Rain streams off the sides of the cloth in long rivulets, soaking the woman's cloak.

Like the mist being kicked up by the rain, hostility radiates from her, and I wonder at it, even as sympathy for her sparks over what must be an impossible situation—being Urisk and indentured to High Commander Lachlan Grey.

Still, I'm both thrown and rattled by her demeanor as I keep up with her brisk stride toward the nearest sheltering archway, its roof formed by interwoven branches of Ironwood. I glance over my shoulder as the carriage pulls away.

A panoramic view of Valgard and the Malthorin Bay beyond is spread out behind me, just past the iron-barred fencing, the gauzy golden lights of Gardneria's capital city evident even in the hazy mist. My gaze catches on a faint, glowing green line that hangs over the outer edge of the bay, the Fae Islands beyond it shrouded into invisibility by the mist.

*What is that?*

I have little time to wonder at the odd sight as the rain begins to sheet down in earnest, like countless pebbles thrown at the wax cloth, the weather in this part of Gardneria famously stormy this time of year. A driving wind picks up that whips my hair around, and we quicken our pace through the torrential rain toward the archway.

The immaculate gardens that surround the Greys' mansion are being worked, even in this heavy rain, by cloaked, bent Urisk women, while knots of cloaked soldiers guard its wrought-iron entrance gate just beyond.

Remorse cuts through my worry for my own safety. What

will happen to all those women when Gardneria's mandatory eviction of all non-Mages from these lands begins at year's end?

My gaze slides to the northeastern edge of the property and the dense line of forest just beyond. I notice there's a much heavier military presence near this stretch of isolated wilds.

We step under the branchy archway, a stone walkway beneath my feet, its geometric blessing-star design cobbled in black and forest green. I notice that rain has darkened the hem of my skirt as the angry Urisk woman directs me toward a huge Ironwood door with an impatient flick of her hand.

She slows, opens the door, and ushers me into a tidy cloakroom. Then she quickly folds the wax cloth and sets it aside as I pull back my cloak's hood, but she gives me no time at all to pause and hang up my damp covering.

"Mage Evelyn is *waiting*," she practically hisses with another curt wave to prod me forward.

I follow as she rushes me through a series of lantern-lit hallways hung with impressive oil paintings depicting lush Ironwood forests. Eventually, the woman comes to a halt before a set of ornate doors, their wood carved into a rich autumn hunting scene—Gardnerians with arrows nocked in bows and aimed at a herd of elk.

"Stay there," she orders with a jab toward my feet, like I'm a dog in need of training. Then she opens one of the doors and slips inside, closes it behind her, and leaves me in the hall all alone.

I crane my ear and can make out muted conversation just beyond the thick wood. Soon, one of the doors partially opens and the Urisk woman steps back into the hallway.

"Mage Evelyn Grey will see you now." She announces this with a slight sneer, as if I'm about to get what's coming to me, then stands back and opens the door wide with a flourish, an obnoxious glint in her eyes.

I enter reluctantly and try to hide my wince when the door clicks shut behind me.

Lukas's mother, Mage Evelyn Grey, stands at the far end of the room, her back to me.

She's looking through a diamond-paned window that takes up almost an entire wall and is hung with sumptuous maroon curtains tied back with forest green tassels. She's tall, finely dressed, and holds herself in the same regal manner as Aunt Vyvian.

Heart thudding, I rally my courage, set down my travel bag by a chair, and take a few tentative steps toward the center of the room as I quickly scan my surroundings.

A large black marble fireplace blazes to one side, overpowering the day's damp chill. Richly cushioned chairs are grouped before it, an expansive bookshelf set into the adjacent wall. The soft glow of glass-encased torches on iron stands warms the dim gray light streaming in from the windows, and expensive-looking porcelain vases are placed artfully throughout the room. Everything is in the traditional Gardnerian colors—deep red for the blood of our people spilled by the Evil Ones, green for the subdued wilds, smatterings of Ironflower blue, and the ever-present black to symbolize our many years of oppression.

Thunder rumbles in the distance.

Mage Grey half turns, one hand resting gracefully on the windowsill as she gives me a slow once-over. She's intimidatingly beautiful, fine as a painting, her black velvet tunic conservatively high in the collar, and both her tunic and long-skirt devoid of embellishment. Her green eyes bore into me, hard and cold as wintry glass. I can see now where Lukas gets his stunning looks, his fiercely commanding presence. The shock of white-silver running through Mage Grey's ebony hair only intensifies her severe beauty.

I struggle to keep my confidence from wilting before her.

She continues to look me over slowly, like some unwanted insect she's fighting the urge to crush, as I wait for her to say something. After a moment, she turns away, brings one hand to her waist, and peers back out the window toward her fine gardens and view of the ocean beyond.

"Do you have any idea, Mage Gardner," she says, her voice all tight control, "how many young women would have given *anything* to fast to my son?"

My throat goes dry. I'm not sure how to respond. The black enameled clock on the fireplace mantel seems to be waiting for my answer as well, impatiently ticking to break the silence.

Evelyn Grey turns away from the window to peer at me once more. "Yet he chose someone who had to be physically restrained, actually *held down*, before she could be fasted to him."

Anger sparks like flint to steel. *Yes, well, he forced me. And I'd have struck your wretched son down and escaped if I had control of my magic.*

Her frown tightens. "He regrets fasting to you." She says it calmly enough, but I catch the desperation clawing at the edges of her tone as she glares at me like I'm some evil thing who's imprisoned her son. "You should see the look that comes over his face when your name is mentioned. He *bitterly* regrets it."

Nausea rises and burns at the back of my throat as I remember why I'm here. *If I don't secure Lukas's protection, the Vu Trin will kill me.*

"I wasn't myself at the fasting," I force out, struggling to keep my anger at bay. "My uncle had just died. It's taken me a while to get over that, and... I think Lukas will understand."

Her eyes go wide and she nods with theatrical pleasantry.

"Will he, now?" Her lip lifts, her eyes narrowing into verdant shards of ice. "A warm reception he gave you, was it?"

I shrink under her mocking glare.

"Where have you been, Mage Gardner?" Her voice has gone hard as stone.

The question catches like a hook in my throat. She's watching me, still as a cat.

"I... I just came from the Keltish Province..." I start, remembering to use Keltania's new name. "I was with Lukas..."

"No," she cuts in, acid edging her tone. "You *know* what I mean."

My mind whirls into chaos.

"He fasts to you and *seals* the fasting," she continues, "but you run off and let the Sealing spell go fallow with no consummation." Her eyes flick down at my unmarked wrists. "I can't seem to get a straight answer out of my son regarding where you went and why you rejected him in such a brazen manner," she continues, "so I'm asking *you*. This past month. Where *were* you?"

I will myself to form a coherent thought, scrabbling to unearth the excuse I've readied. "I was trying to find a way to contact my brothers," I lie.

"Ah, yes, the traitors."

I nod stiffly.

"And did you find a way?" There's cloying sarcasm in her tone.

I shake my head, grief stabbing at me. *No, you witch, I didn't,* I anguish. *I don't know where they are. I don't even know if they're still alive.* "I thought...if I could find them..." I haltingly offer. "I thought I could get them to stop."

"Stop what?" she asks, cocking her head.

"Their rebellion."

"Which you are no stranger to yourself, isn't that right?" she states as fear shoots down my spine. She stares me down before shaking her head, as if deeply disappointed in me. "What a wretched liar you are, Elloren Gardner."

I stand frozen, struggling to keep my breathing even as she moves away from the window and begins to circle me.

"I know you were found in bed with a Kelt," she says. "Do you have any idea of the lengths Vyvian and I had to go to, to try to hide that fact?" She makes a full sweep around my still form then stops directly before me. Her gaze is searing, her tight control breaking around the edges as fury seeps through. "And now, you are fasted to *my* Lukas. A girl from a family of race traitors who takes every opportunity to *spit* on her grandmother's great name, who lacks even *one shred* of moral decency." Her mouth twists into a livid grimace. "Is my son's reputation to be *so polluted*?"

"I'm not like my brothers," I stammer, the lie painful to force out.

She gets right up to my face. "You are not good enough for my son," she hisses through clenched teeth. "You are not fit to clean the mud from his *boots!*" She grabs my hands roughly with hers.

I give a small cry and try to pull away as her nails dig into my skin.

She holds on to me, glaring with furious desperation at the fasting marks. "If there was some way to break this spell," she says, seeming distraught, "I would *do* it. I've *tried* to find a way." Her voice grows rough. "In bed with a *Kelt*," she grieves, then grows silent, fixated on my hands, the wheels of her mind visibly turning. "Do you know what we do now to race traitors, Elloren Gardner?" She's speaking more to herself than to me, staring hard at my hands. "We *execute* them."

"I never slept with the Kelt," I insist, my desperation to elude this vile woman rising. "It was all a misunderstanding.

My hands. They're *proof* of it." No bloody gash marks, like on Sage's hands. Absolute proof of my chastity.

Evelyn Grey freezes, her eyes seeming to flicker in thought. A dark smile forms on her lips, and she considers my hands as if she's seeing them clearly for the very first time.

A tremor of desperate alarm streaks through me, and I tug my hands away, her nails scratching me as I do. I step back and cradle my hands protectively over my thudding heart.

Mage Grey straightens and smiles at me like a shark. "You're going to the Mage Council ball tonight." She says this with renewed purpose, as if she's terribly pleased with how clever she is, a malicious gleam in her eyes.

I swallow hard. I don't like the way she seems firmly set on some devious course of action. And I can't travel unprotected to a ball with assassins possibly on my tail. "I should ask Lukas first," I shakily insist. "I'll send a rune hawk—"

"*No,*" she grinds out, clearly incensed. "You will do as *I* say."

I'm suddenly as aware of all the wood in this room as I am of the unknown threat emanating from this woman—the Ironwood tree trunks and their tangling branches that support the room, forming wavering rafters above my head. The Ironwood planks beneath my feet.

*Dead wood. All around me.*

An image of the living Ironwood trees this wood came from flashes in my mind as power pricks at my heels and I curl and uncurl my toes against it, fire roused in my lines. I force a deep, quavering breath and fight back the feral desire to set Lukas's mother and this entire estate alight.

Something just behind me catches Evelyn's eye and I turn, blessedly distracted from the pull toward magical violence.

"Mage." A different, younger Urisk woman with lavender skin, violet hair, and amethyst eyes stands in the doorway, her features stunning, and I'm struck by the feeling that I've met her before. She looks about my age. "Oralyyr sent us." She dips her head in a graceful bow.

The bow is artlessly echoed by the skinny little Urisk girl I now see standing beside her, the child perhaps no more than eight years of age. The little girl has wide, bat-like ears and the deep-violet skin of the Urisk's most royal class. There's something troubling about the stiffness with which these two hold themselves, frozen in their deferential bow, as if they're afraid Mage Grey will have them beheaded if they make a wrong move.

Mage Grey eyes them with distaste then fixes her gaze back on me. "Sparrow and Effrey are to be your lady's maids whilst you are here, and Sparrow will accompany you every-where and report back to me as to your comings and goings. In addition, I will be sending two soldiers to accompany you to the dance. They, too, will report back to me. Do I make myself clear, Mage Gardner?"

I'm a caged bird, dangling from her elegant finger.

A mounting alarm swells. "I don't need lady's maids," I counter, barely able to disguise my apprehension.

Mage Grey pins me with her stare. "You are living under *my* roof now, Mage Gardner. You will abide by *my* rules. Not your own."

Through my tunic pocket, I finger the stone Chi Nam gave me, pressing it into my thigh. "Yes, Mage," I concede, even as anger quickly gains ground inside me. *I despise you, you witch. You and your cursed family. And especially your cursed son.*

"Effrey," Evelyn says to the younger girl, keeping her pierc-ing eyes tight on me, "take Mage Gardner's cloak. Then you and Sparrow can show her to her room."

"Yes, Mage Grey," the child hastily replies.

Effrey hurries to me as I unclip and slide off my cloak. I

hand it to her, and the child takes it then rushes back toward Sparrow, dragging a triangle of my cloak's hem artlessly across the floor. Just before she reaches Sparrow, the child knocks into a small, circular table, jostling an exquisite Ironflower-decorated vase that's set near the table's edge.

Sparrow's eyes go wide as the vase teeters precariously. Quick as a flash, she darts toward the table, catches the vase with nimble fingers, and sets it right.

Effrey is frozen, her mouth falling open as she views the vase with sheer horror. The child turns slowly to face Mage Grey, cowering and hugging my cloak as if for protection. She bows down, almost to the floor. "Please, Mage, *please*. I'm *so sorry*, Mage."

The little girl's clumsiness tugs at my memory, and recognition sparks—the Valgard dress shop. That's where I've seen these two before. Last year, when I first came to the city with Aunt Vyvian. The child was there, the clumsy little girl forever tripping over bolts of cloth. And graceful Sparrow. They were both there.

Evelyn Grey moves to a nearby refreshment table and pours herself a drink from a scarlet crystalline decanter. "Effrey," she says. "Shall I have Oralyyr beat the clumsiness out of you?"

Effrey's eyes grow wide as saucers as outrage blazes to life inside me in response to this cruelty toward a child, my wand hand flexing into a fist.

"Sparrow," Evelyn says in an even tone as she turns away from Effrey, as if she's completely lost interest in the child, "show Mage Gardner to her room. She's to attend the Victory Ball this evening at the Mage Council Hall." She sips her drink and peers back out at her storm-lit gardens, her lip twitching up into a derisive smile. "Clean her up. Try to turn her into something that at least *appears* respectable."

# CHAPTER
## THREE

# VASES

## ELLOREN GARDNER

*Sixth Month*
*Valgard, Gardneria*

I follow Sparrow and Effrey toward the far end of the estate, still reeling from my encounter with Lukas's cruel mother. We wind through countless, exquisitely appointed hallways and rooms, both my magic and my emotions as turbulent as the storm that's gaining ground outside.

Thunder cracks, the sound reverberating through the Iron-wood walls.

*Lukas needs to get here soon.* Evelyn Grey means to harm me in some way—I feel sure of it. I might be safe here from the forces of the East, surrounded as we are by a Mage military presence, but I'm not safe from the Mages.

But if I find Lukas, will he even consent to protect me?

We come to an Ironflower-embossed wooden door at the far end of a sitting room that's also a small library. Sparrow opens the door, and I go still at its threshold, my gaze transfixed by the bedroom's sizable, four-poster, canopied bed. It's topped with a luxurious emerald tree–patterned quilt, but that's not what captures my eyes and my magic. It's the canopy's posts I'm drawn to—dense columns of deep black wood, rising in smooth spirals.

Like four colossal wands.

Captivated, I step toward the bed and run my hand along the enticing wood, power simmering at my heels as a massive tree with a thickly corded trunk fills my mind and I draw in a deep, languid breath.

Ishkartan Ebony.

*Oh, this is a nice wood. Dense and strong.* My fireline gives a warm flare, heat sizzling through my lines. *It would be so easy to send magic through it…*

A flash of alarm seizes me, and I wrench my hand from the wood, my pulse quickening over how easily the wood pulls me under. I surreptitiously grasp my wand hand with the other and dig my nails into my palm, attempting to quell the almost irresistible lure of the luxurious wood.

And the almost irresistible desire to release my power.

I drag my gaze away from the bed in an effort to distract myself from the great temptation, and find Sparrow and Effrey drawing back deep-green curtains to reveal rain-battered windows, making me feel exposed to whatever could be lurking out there.

Hunting me.

"You can leave those closed," I hastily say to them, only to be met by a brief look of startled fear from Effrey followed by a slight, cautious nod from Sparrow as she draws the curtains once more. "Thank you," I amend, swallowing. "Thank you for your help."

"It's no trouble at all, Mage," Sparrow neutrally responds as she and Effrey secure the curtain ties in tidy coils.

"I've met you before, you know." I press Sparrow in the least threatening tone I can muster as I clench and unclench my wand hand. "You were at Mage Heloise's dress shop. In Valgard. Several months ago."

"It's true, Mage," Sparrow says, her expression dauntingly blank.

Reluctant to make them feel any more uncomfortable than I already have, I let the line of conversation drop and shrug my travel bag off my shoulder, then set it down on the silk-cushioned chair beside me, the cushion's fabric embroidered with an oak-leaf design. There's an intricately woven rug under my feet that mirrors the rich colors of the bed, forest greens and midnight black entwined into stylized trees. A guilty frustration swells over how much I'm drawn in by the overabundance of forest decor and dead wood in this room. I don't want to be so typically Gardnerian. I don't want any part of the wretched Magedom.

Instead, I want to crack one of those posts off the bed and fight the Gardnerians with it.

A crack of thunder cuts into my rebellious thoughts, and I glance around the room. Two doors near the bed are open, one leading to a small changing room, the other to servants' quarters. The cool air seeping in around the bedroom's windowpanes is being held back by the lush warmth emanating from an iron woodstove that faces the bed, its iron wrought into the shape of a tree, pipe chimneys branching up and over the ceiling. The room is tastefully decorated with paintings of deer in a deep forest and more of Mage Evelyn's seemingly beloved vases—vases that seem more important to her than the people working in her household.

I frown at the vase closest to me, made of parchment-thin onyx-glazed porcelain with a hand-painted scene depicting the slaying of an Icaral by several Mage soldiers.

I want to knock it clear off the table and watch it shatter into tiny, unfixable bits.

Sparrow brings my travel bag to the bed, sets it on the tree quilt, and moves to open it.

Anxiety swiftly overtakes me.

"I'll unpack my things," I say as I take a quick step toward Sparrow. I can't risk her finding the Wand—and possibly handing it over to Lukas's loathsome mother.

Which would immediately raise questions regarding why, exactly, I'm armed without the Council approval that is required of all Mages. Especially women.

Sparrow gives me an odd look as she acquiesces and instead begins turning down the bedsheets and quilt.

My heart thudding against my chest, I open the travel sack and lift my sparse belongings from it, piece by piece, placing them neatly on the bed. Then I fasten the sack and slide it far under the bed.

"I'd like that kept there," I say, pointing underneath the bed while hating my dominant position over the two of them. They both nod in solemn deference, which only notches my remorse higher.

*They shouldn't be here.* Not with the Gardnerians about to ship every last Urisk to the Fae Islands in a matter of months to remove non-Gardnerians from "Mage soil." I look to skinny Effrey, who's busy placing my clothes in the drawers of a nearby dresser, my outrage on her behalf rising.

*She's just a child. She shouldn't be working as a virtual slave in this house for this cruel woman in this hostile land. What she needs is to get to the Eastern Realm, and fast.*

"Let me do that, Effrey," I offer, and she flinches, hunches down, and looks at me once more with obvious fright. I immediately regret scaring her.

There's a perfunctory knock at the door, and we all pause

and turn toward the sound as Sparrow smoothly hastens across the room and opens it.

Oralyyr, the dour Urisk woman who met me at the carriage, stands in the hall.

She shoots me a withering glare then thrusts a parchment-wrapped bundle into Sparrow's arms. "I'll be back for the clothing she's wearing after she changes into this," Oralyyr snipes to Sparrow before scowling at me once more and stalking off.

Sparrow closes the door, turns, and folds back the parchment to reveal a glittering gown. She walks back to the bed, pulls the garment fully free of its covering, and lays it out on the bed's quilted surface. Her expression puzzled, she draws back and blinks at the dress as if thrown by it, but seems to quickly collect herself.

"For tonight's ball, Mage," she informs me with a slight bow and a formal air, but I can sense her lingering confusion in the tightness around her eyes.

Apprehension constricts my throat as I scrutinize the garment, even as part of me can't help but be awed by its spectacular beauty.

It's blazingly scandalous.

The sumptuous black silk of the dress's formfitting tunic and long-skirt shimmers a lustrous red at the folds as the room's lantern and woodstove light flicker over it. Rubies are splashed over the entire garment in a blessing-star design, the scarlet constellation thickening at the hems, and I note that the tunic is both close-fitting and low-cut, black lace edging the collar.

Deeply perplexed, I run a finger over the bumpy, glittering clusters of gems along the tunic's edging as the Urisk girls return to the bustle of organizing my things and preparing the room.

My apprehension sharpens.

Both the overabundance of red and the fit are bound to attract censure in an increasingly strict Gardneria. And it's clear from the design of this estate and from Evelyn Grey's own garb that Lukas's mother is even stricter than my aunt in all things. So, why would she want me to wear this outrageous, borderline-scarlet dress? And how did Mage Grey guess my size? Has she been in touch with my vile aunt?

"Sparrow," I ask as I study the dress uneasily, "do you know if Lukas is expected at tonight's ball?"

"Yes, Mage," she affirms, her gaze fixed on the dress, as well.

A brittle crash sounds out, startling us both, and we turn to find Effrey surrounded by pieces of the horrible Icaral vase. The child bursts into tears, appearing as if she just stepped into the middle of her most dreaded nightmare. Sparrow freezes, staring at the shattered bits, her mouth agape.

The longer Effrey cries, the smaller and skinnier she starts to look.

I hold up a hand. "I broke it," I say firmly, my voice louder than usual as I struggle to be heard over Effrey's distraught sobs.

Effrey swallows back her tears and stares at me, her whole body convulsing with hiccups. Sparrow has grown several shades paler and is also staring at me, wide-eyed.

"I broke it," I insist again. "I didn't like it, so it's no great loss. We'll clean it up and tell Mage Grey that I'm not fond of all these vases and would prefer that they be removed from the room." My heart is racing. *This certainly won't help me deal with Lukas's awful mother.*

It takes Sparrow a moment to find her voice. "Y-yes, Mage," she finally stammers.

Effrey is still quietly hiccuping and blinking at me in evident confusion as I lower myself and begin picking up the knifelike shards.

"No, Mage," Sparrow insists. "You shouldn't be doing that. Come, Effrey," she says, placing her hand gently on the child's back. "Let's clean up the pieces."

A moment later, the child is crying again, having cut herself on a shard of vase.

I go to Effrey and kneel down before her, pull a handkerchief from my tunic's pocket, and apply pressure to her trembling, cut palm. A bloodstain quickly fans out over the white linen, overtaking the fine Ironflower embroidery.

"Get some Singeroot tonic and a bandage," I direct Sparrow, flabbergasted at little Effrey's ability to get herself into one scrape after another. "I've some apothecary training. I can take care of her." Keeping pressure on the wound, I indicate the chair beside us with a tilt of my head. "Effrey," I say gently, holding the child's cowering gaze, "we're going to get this all fixed up, and then you'll sit down and rest while I help Sparrow get things done."

"Singeroot tonic is expensive, Mage," Sparrow tells me, her tone surprisingly blunt. "Mage Grey will *never* approve of its use on servants."

"Ancient One," I mutter, disgusted by these horrible rules and by Lukas's repulsive mother. I meet Sparrow's level gaze. "Then tell Oralyyr that I cut myself when I broke the vase," I offer.

A grim understanding seems to pass between us, and Sparrow nods then leaves to gather the healing supplies.

Not too long after, Effrey is patched up and whimpering softly, curled into a tight ball on the chair, the tree quilt wrapped around her small form.

I peer closely at the child. There's something odd and unfocused about the way she's staring at me. "The child needs glasses," I mumble to myself, the light dawning.

"Oh, Mage," Sparrow breathes, her tone gaining a somber, pleading edge. Effrey begins to cry again in earnest as she looks to Sparrow, clearly frightened by my observation.

I turn to Sparrow as well, surprised by the stark fear that's now etched across her expression.

"Effrey's eyes are weak, it's true," Sparrow says, her tone imploring, her composure faltering, "but please don't tell Mage Grey. I can do the work of two. *Please*, Mage."

My heart wrenches, a dart of sympathy piercing me. The situation these two are in is just so *wrong* on every level. Of course, I know what my answer will be and that I'll help them in any way I can.

And I know something else, as well.

Sparrow and Effrey aren't Mage Grey's allies. They're terrified of the woman. And I need all the allies I can get.

Even if the only ones I can find are two powerless servant girls.

# CHAPTER FOUR

## VICTORY BALL
### ELLOREN GARDNER

*Sixth Month*
*Valgard, Gardneria*

I let my thumbnail slip under the rough piece of lantern-lit wood just under the carriage seat-cushion beneath me. A dark-leafed tree opens up in my mind.

*Black Maple. From the Northern Wilds.*

I carefully pry the small shard loose from the trim, my gaze darting out the carriage's twilight-dimmed windows, acutely aware of the pair of Level Four Mage Guards flanking the carriage on horseback as we journey toward tonight's Mage Council ball.

Acutely aware of what could be hunting me this eve.

*Will these soldiers be enough to keep me alive until I can find Lukas?*

I nervously roll the splinter of wood between my fingers. It's no bigger than a pine needle, but still, a small shudder of power courses through me.

*A tiny little wand.*

Sparrow is sitting across from me, her expression blank as new-fallen snow and set on the middle of the distance between us.

I roll the wooden sliver in slow circles across my fingers and take stock of my situation.

If Lukas remains hostile toward me, I'll have no protection, apart from my wits, from forces that will close in on me.

Likely soon.

Chi Nam could well be imprisoned for allowing me to flee, as could Kam Vin, Ni Vin, and Chim Diec. If that happens, the Resistance won't be coming to fetch me anytime in the near future. And I have no way of getting hold of my brothers or Yvan or anyone else who could help me.

I have no one to lean on but myself.

As hard as that is to come to terms with, there it is.

I inhale and pinch the wooden shard between my thumb and forefinger, considering...

I've learned that my magic grows with a wand's layered focus. The difference in the fire conjured with a small branch versus a wand made of pressed, laminated wood is extreme.

*What about a sliver of wood?*

I carefully keep my other hand away from my seat's maple edging as I evaluate the shard's straightness with my wand hand, the sliver of wood so tiny that I feel tenuously in control of my temptation to send magic through it.

*What if I tried this tiny wand?*

I would have to be extraordinarily careful to hide who I am from the Gardnerians. But I can't help wondering—could I tamp down my power enough to control it if I used small enough shards of wood?

Could I find a way to train myself?

Set on this new course of action, I clasp the small shard

tight as my gaze lifts to rest on Sparrow, a new question rising. "Why aren't you working at the dress shop anymore?"

Sparrow's amethyst eyes snap into tight focus on me and, for a moment, I've a sense of her beating back some strong emotion.

"Evelyn Grey is awful," I press, wondering how she and little Effrey ever wound up working for the vile woman.

"Mage Grey was kind enough to indenture us," Sparrow states carefully, the words chilling in their neutrality. But then a glint of stony courage breaks through in Sparrow's large amethyst eyes as she considers me for a brazenly long moment, momentarily letting me see through her servile demeanor.

What I see there is formidable.

"You helped Effrey," she finally says, surprisingly forthright. "It was kind of you. Very few Mages would do what you did."

I purse my lips and shake my head, both confused by her train of thought and uncomfortable over being given credit for the barest minimum of humane behavior.

Sparrow's brow furrows, her violet-lashed eyes still fixed on me as her hands grip the edge of her seat. "Mage Gardner... Fallon Bane's looking for you," she blurts out stiffly. "She's still in love with Lukas Grey."

I blink at her, my fingers tightening around the wooden shard in my hand, a jolt of power shuddering through my lines. I hold up my other hand for her to peruse, my palm out to reveal the web of black fastlines marked across it. "Well, that's just too bad for her, isn't it?" I bitterly counter. "It's done. I'm fasted to him."

Sparrow's grave stare is unwavering. "A priest can lift Lukas's fasting if you die."

A tense silence descends.

Sparrow's expression remains dead serious as I take in her

obvious warning with all the gravity it deserves, a rush of concern prickling my whole body with gooseflesh.

It's true. Whereas the fastmarks of a female Mage are permanent no matter what, a Mage Priest is able to lift a male's fasting spell if his fastmate dies. It's worked right into the spell's language.

My breath grows strained in my chest as I realize the very plausible reason that Evelyn has me dressed like a scarlet beacon, so easy to find amidst a sea of black.

So easy for Fallon Bane to find.

So that she can break this fasting the only way possible.

*No*, I argue with myself. *That's too extreme. Even for Fallon.*

I'm filled with a sudden, urgent longing to have the Wand of Myth in my hand. But it's back in my bedroom, hidden in my travel sack under the bed.

Even if I had the Wand—or any wand, for that matter—how could I possibly protect myself with it? I don't know how to control the devastating power I'd release.

I lean toward Sparrow, my pulse quickening. "If Fallon uses magic to attack a fellow Mage, they'll strip her of military ranking and throw her in prison."

Sparrow hesitates, then leans in as well, throwing a quick glance at the guards that flank our carriage before setting her gaze back on me. Her lips twist. "She's the Black Witch. They'll never throw her in prison." Her expression darkens, her brow creasing. "She was at the estate earlier," she says, her tone ominous. "She and Mage Evelyn Grey, they spoke."

A cold sweat breaks out along the back of my neck. "Did you hear what they said?"

Sparrow shakes her head, the warning in her eyes undiminished.

My mind whirls. "My aunt... Vyvian Damon," I press. "Do you know if she'll be at tonight's ball?" My stomach lurches at the thought of seeing Aunt Vyvian again, a slash of vengeful fire knifing through my affinity lines. But as much as I despise her and she likely despises me, I know that Aunt Vyvian has a vested interest in my living long enough for Lukas Grey to sire powerful Mage children with me.

"Mage Damon is in the Verpacian Province with a few Mage Council members," Sparrow grimly tells me. "They're meeting with the Alfsigr Royal Council, to finalize the division of the Lupine territories between the Gardnerians and the Alfsigr. She doesn't return until tomorrow."

My sense of urgency heightens. "Do you have any idea when Lukas is arriving at the ball?" I ask.

"I don't know. But he has to come. Vogel has required that several of his commanders, including Lukas, be there tonight. Vogel has some important announcement to make, and the Mages are celebrating Gardneria's annexation of huge swaths of the Western Realm. Lukas is the commander who oversaw Keltania's annexation. He *has* to be there. He might have already come."

I don't have time to wonder at Sparrow knowing all of this in so much detail as fierce apprehension whips up inside me. *Fallon can't hurt me*, I desperately reason with myself. *She absolutely cannot hurt me.* Hated or not, I'm Carnissa Gardner's granddaughter, and my fastmarks are chastely intact.

But will Fallon really lose anything if she comes after me? Especially if she does it in some covert way, like she did back when we were both scholars at university?

I remember the chilling smile on Mage Evelyn Grey's lips when she informed me I was to go to the ball. Is that what Lukas's mother was plotting? To send me into Fallon Bane's path?

Am I being sent to my own execution?

"I can't make a run for it," I say in a constricted voice, my eyes flicking toward the soldiers outside. "Not with how Lukas's mother has me guarded. I'm going to have to go into the Council Hall."

"It's a large hall, Mage, and I know it well," Sparrow says evenly, her gaze tight on mine as I sense us falling in with each other.

"I need your help," I admit.

"I know," she says with a grim nod. "I'll help you."

I'm stunned by the aid she's offering. She's taking an incredible risk, throwing her lot in with mine. And I realize, as my mind whirls, that Sparrow's own situation must be almost as monstrously bad as mine to make the possibility of me as an ally worth risking everything for.

"You'll need to stay out of Fallon's sight," Sparrow warns. "Try to avoid her any way you can."

I cock a disbelieving brow at her, nerves churning. "That's going to be a bit tricky, don't you think? Seeing as how I'm wearing the most scarlet Gardnerian dress ever made."

Sparrow's gaze flicks over my flamboyant, ruby-glittering garb before it meets mine once more, an impressive level of resolve burning in her eyes. "Then you'll just have to find Lukas before she finds you."

And perhaps I'll have a chance of saving my own life.

I clutch the wooden shard in my hand so hard that it slices into my skin, my magic roaring to life and racing toward the wood as the terrifying realization crashes over me.

I'm about to be thrust into a game of cat and mouse. Against a Level Five Mage in full control of her power.

The carriage climbs the long, winding hill that leads to the immense Mage Council Hall as I struggle to prepare myself, my whole body bowstring-tight with tension.

The Council Hall is carved into the mountainous face of the Styvius Bluff, the Hall's bluff-stone walls and arches chiseled to appear as if we're approaching a dense stone forest. Massive rock trunks support the six stories of the Hall and their curving outdoor balconies. A forest of stone-tree statues brackets the stone road leading toward the Hall, the trees' carved branches twining overhead to form a porous tunnel.

I push the carriage window open a crack and breathe in the salty air, the rain having passed, the turbulent Voltic Sea just beyond the bluff. Seagulls cry out and circle the Hall, which is newly cast in the sunset's rose light as the clouds break up, everything lit by flickering torchlight.

There are Gardnerian flags everywhere, the new white bird design on black hung over balconies and flowing from windows. One of monstrous size is affixed between the two mammoth stone trees that support the second-story balcony, and the windows all around this level are lit the brightest with a festive yellow glow.

Elegant Gardnerians dressed in various shades and sheens of black are packed onto this wide, sweeping second-story balcony and inside its ornate interior. Large doors are thrown open and orchestral music streams out, conversation and laughter gelling into one loud buzz. And there's a military presence—quite a sizable one. Powerful Mage soldiers with Level Four and Five stripes practically ring the base of the Council Hall.

An army of Mages.

Countless torches on iron stands illuminate the walkways, and the hot, musky scent of the torches' Verpacian Elm oil wafts through the air. The torches cut through the remaining dampness from the rain, the deepening twilight newly warm and balmy, the breaks in the clouds beginning to glitter with sparkling stars.

A perfect night for celebration.

I ready myself for flight as we near the Council Hall and I

take in the Gardnerians—their splendid garb, the jubilant swell of their conversation, how many of them there are.

And the white armbands around every Mage's upper arm, blaring their support of High Mage Marcus Vogel.

It's hard to fight off a dizzying sense of doom. I've never seen so many carriages in one place before, clogging up the road in front of the Hall. As I gape at the size of the crowd, my own carriage comes to an abrupt halt near a broad curving staircase leading to the raised first floor.

I flinch as one of my guards jerks open the carriage door, a disconcerting sneer on his bearded face as his gaze rakes my blazingly scarlet dress and lingers on my arm, probably noticing my lack of a white armband.

I close my fist around the shard of wood and step out, my pulse galloping as the guard brusquely motions me forward. Tensed for attack, I set out toward the flow of the crowd, flanked by my guards and with Sparrow close on my heels, a heady sense of my formidable magic streaming through me.

One of my guards smirks and shoots his bearded cohort a smug look that sets the hairs on the back of my neck on end.

Behind us the carriage pulls away, and its absence leaves a stark void inside me, depriving me of my only avenue of escape. But the wood in my palm gives me some uneasy comfort; it's only a sliver, but it might as well be a broadsword. Or a hundred broadswords.

Or maybe thousands more.

I follow the crowd toward the huge staircase, keeping my head down and hugging tight to the rail as I ascend, but it's pointless to try to be inconspicuous when I look like a blaze of red torchlight.

I inadvertently bump into an older woman in an opulent black velvet gown that winks emerald. The woman turns to me with a ready smile that quickly morphs into an expression of complete mortification as she takes in both my famous face and my shockingly red-accented tunic and long-skirt. She whips her elegant head away, clinging to the arm of the Mage beside her as she whispers and he steals a glance at me. This scenario begins to repeat itself as I make my way up the stairs, through the throngs of Mages. Their judgments, not whispered quietly enough, waft backward on the warm night air.

"Carnissa's own granddaughter! Fought her own fasting!"

"Tried to run off with a Kelt!"

"Family took an evil turn."

"Vyvian's disgrace."

"Brothers ran off with the Lupines!"

"Race traitors!"

"And how she's *dressed*."

"Like a heathen whore!"

Each new comment is like the sting of a whip, hooking my steps. I quickly realize that Fallon isn't the only one set against me. This entire crowd is hostile.

I have to find Lukas. And fast.

Unsteady, I glance over my shoulder, searching for my guards as the crowd streams up the stairs. I spot them stationed at the foot of the staircase, hands on sword hilts and wand handles, their gazes set on me.

*Blocking my exit.*

I peer past my guards, past the multitude of carriages, toward a small plaza encircled by the stone forest.

Shock overtakes me.

There's a statue there, almost identical to the one in front of the Valgard Cathedral, its ivory marble glowing silver in the bright moonlight. The figures are spectral, like two ghosts back from the dead. A larger-than-life depiction of my grandmother, the Black Witch, towers over Yvan's Icaral father. My grandmother's wand is pointed at Yvan's father's heart, her foot grinding hard into his chest.

A wave of nausea washes over me as I clench my hand around the wooden shard, my power shuddering through my lines as the full gravity of my situation takes hold.

I can't use this power. Not yet. Not even to protect myself.

I'm surrounded by Mage soldiers. If I make even one mistake and the Gardnerians find out that I'm the Black Witch of Prophecy, it will all be over. They will bring me straight to Vogel, who will stop at *nothing* to control my power and use me to destroy Yvan and everyone that I love.

No, right now all I can do is survive.

With great reluctance, I extend my fist over the balcony's edge and open my hand, watching as the wooden shard twirls away to disappear into some ornamental bushes far below.

My power immediately draws down.

*There. Temptation gone.*

I start back up the stairs, but Sparrow's hand clenches tight around my arm, halting my ascent.

I turn to her and am instantly alarmed when I take in her stark, dread-filled gaze. She gives a swift glance up and I follow her line of vision up one flight to the second-story balcony.

To the three dark-clad figures standing at its edge.

My throat cinches tight.

*Fallon Bane.* Her Level Five brothers, Sylus and Damion, in uniform flanking her.

And she's looking straight at me.

Fallon flashes me a wicked smile that sends ice down my spine. She points at me, her devious smile echoed by her equally devious brothers. Then all three Banes turn and head for the balcony's doors, the brothers' silver-striped cloaks sweeping out behind them.

"Follow me," Sparrow breathlessly orders, her grip on my arm firming. "I know where the high-ranking military usually enter."

We set off at a fast clip, darting around the crowd on the stairs, over the first-floor balcony's terrace, and into the festive hall.

We're engulfed in the crowd of dark-clad Mages, the scent of expensive perfume and rich food heavy on the air. My fear-addled mind takes in details as I follow Sparrow through a maze of hallways and packed rooms, my affinity lines lurching hard toward one type of luxurious wood after another—

Black Cherry tree trunks that form the central support of several rooms, their branches hung with black crystal leaves and small crimson lanterns.

Mountain Oak that frames countless oil paintings of former Mage Council members and Guild heads.

A Bloodwood grand piano that sits prominently in a parlor, the rare scarlet wood gleaming with varnish and ruby swirls.

I clench and unclench my wand hand, desperate to send my power through every last piece of wood we come upon, and struggle mightily to resist the powerful urge.

A young, blue-hued Urisk woman slides in front of us, blocking our way. My gaze darts around her, searching for Fallon, as the woman offers up a delicacy wrapped in baby lettuce and impaled with a coarse toothpick. I glance down at the hors d'oeuvres, and for a moment, I'm transfixed. Not hungry for the food.

Hungry for the wood.

*Another tiny wand.*

Sparrow tugs my arm insistently, breaking the wood's thrall as she pulls me back into motion and we swerve around the Urisk woman.

The music dampens as we rush, just on the edge of running, through room after room, the crowds thinning as we go. We hurry down a narrow, dimly lit hall and then into the expansive Council library. Small knots of Gardnerian soldiers and military apprentices are congregating there, some bearing the markings of the highly ranked, their conversations low and dignified. Dotting the crowd are a few soldiers wearing the silver-striped cloaks of the powerful Level Five Mages.

*Like Lukas.*

Breathing hard, every sense on heightened alert, I search them over, desperate to locate Lukas.

"Excuse me," I say to a white-haired Mage with lieutenant markings on the shoulder of his military tunic.

He turns to me, contempt washing over his face and the faces of the other Mage soldiers in his small grouping as they take in my face and obvious recognition lights.

I swallow back my anxiety. "Might you know if my fast-mate, Lukas Grey, has arrived?"

The Mage's gaze flicks unkindly over my scarlet dress and he huffs out a short sound of disgust. "I haven't seen him."

I politely excuse myself and step away from the Mages.

Sparrow leans in close as we leave the room. "There's a balcony where we can spot new arrivals," she tells me, her tone one of forced calm, her hand firm around my arm as she guides me forward. "We can watch for Lukas there."

I follow her through a side door at the far end of the room and down a long, deserted hallway.

Sparrow and I duck into a smaller library, and I catch hold of my bearings as Sparrow moves to open a glass door leading to a small balcony that overlooks the front of the Council Hall. The library is as deserted as the hallway was, the orchestral music now far away, and a frisson of anxiety crawls down my spine at our sudden isolation.

Sparrow jostles the glass door's handle, but it won't budge.

She turns to me, her voice growing taut with apprehension. "It's locked. We'll have to get there another way."

Footsteps sound in the hallway, and my pulse quickens.

A saffron-hued Urisk maid strides into view and pauses just outside the door. She narrows her citrine eyes at me, then glances toward something or someone down the hall as she points insistently at us.

Fallon Bane sweeps into the room, and my legs almost give out from under me.

Fallon is magnificently terrifying, dressed in a gleaming black velvet tunic and long-skirt embroidered with a stylized onyx dragon that flows down her entire side. Black opal jewelry graces her neck and ears, and her hair is artfully pulled back with a gleaming, jewel-encrusted dragon's talon, her wand sheathed at her side.

"Don't I know you?" Fallon asks Sparrow with a cruel smile. "You're supposed to be in the Fae Islands, isn't that right?"

Sparrow has gone stock-still, her breathing tight and uneven.

"You're dismissed," Fallon blithely orders.

Outrage rears, overtaking my fear. Forcing my posture taller, I look Fallon straight in the eye. "She's not yours to dismiss."

Fallon's eyes go incredulously wide as she lets out a throaty laugh and swivels her gaze back to me. "You have no allies here." She glares back at Sparrow threateningly, losing the smile. *"Leave."*

Sparrow shoots me a look of intense reluctance but I give her a quick nod, knowing it's safer for her to be far away from here. The other Urisk maid steps into the room and unceremoniously ushers Sparrow out.

Leaving Fallon and me alone.

Fallon unsheathes her wand and taps it rhythmically onto her palm, her lips curling into a slow grin.

Frantic, my gaze darts toward a door at the back of the room.

Fallon glances that way, her eyes narrowing to mocking slits. "You think you can escape *me*? And go *where*?" She spits out a derisive laugh. "You're *all alone*. No friends. No *Lukas*. *Everyone* has abandoned you." A gleam of savage glee lights her eyes as she takes in my scandalously red-accented dress. "You look like a whore, which is exactly what you are." She glances down at my fastmarked hands and her expression of triumph curdles.

I can practically feel the envy radiating from her in thick waves, and I'm suddenly acutely aware of the Ironwood lamppost beside me, magic firing through my lines, my wand hand clenching against the draw of the wood.

And the desire to send my fire straight through Fallon Bane.

*Keep hold of yourself!* I frantically caution. *You wouldn't just take her down. You'd kill everyone. Sparrow too.*

"No one will care if I hurt you," Fallon crows with vicious smugness, baring her teeth in an aggressive smile. "Lukas and I are with each other now. Did you know that? With his mother's *full* blessing." Her smile turns openly hostile. "We're meant for each other. He sees that now. He's no longer *blinded* by how much you look like your grandmother. No one is."

She's posturing, one hand on her hip, her chin high, her foot thrust forward along with her wand. My gaze flits toward her delicately laced shoe, its slim heel so very poorly suited for running.

An idea lights.

Slowly…carefully… I slip my feet from my own pinching, elegant shoes, my heart hammering so hard that it's dizzying.

The moment the stockinged soles of my feet make contact with the Black Walnut flooring, my power gives a hard flare.

Perhaps sensing my inward flare of defiance, Fallon loses her smile, her gaze once again perusing the fastmarks on my hands. "Do you feel the fastlines tighten when Lukas and I embrace?" she taunts, stalking closer and keeping her wand pointed at me. "When he touches me?"

She's becoming alarmingly aggressive, like a wolf defending its territory, ready to rip me to shreds over it.

Over *him*.

Fallon springs forward, grabs hold of my arm, and jabs her wand against my throat. I flinch back and freeze, swallowing hard as the cold embrace of her magic pricks ice all over my skin, my stockinged feet tensing against the wooden floor, fire blazing through my lines.

Fallon's lip curls down into a snarl. "I will not allow you to ruin his life."

There's a tussle in the hallway, two women arguing in the Uriskal language. Fallon's wand is still at my throat as I turn my head a fraction and Sparrow sprints into view.

"Mage!" Sparrow calls out, her eyes wide.

Fallon turns toward Sparrow, her wand dropping down a fraction.

Seizing on Fallon's split-second loss of focus, I smack her hands away from me, and her wand skitters across the floor.

Then I throw my fist forward and punch her in the face as hard as I can.

Fallon cries out and falls sideways.

Panic rearing, I turn and break into a run through the room, out its back door, and into another long hallway, my heart racing, pain knifing through my wand hand's knuckles from the punch. I almost lose my footing on the lacquered flooring beneath me but find sudden purchase on a carpet. I hoist my skirts and sprint down the hallway.

Fallon's scream sends a bolt of fear exploding inside me. *"You BITCH!"*

I throw myself around a bend just as several icicles slam into the wall behind me, decimating a portrait of our former High Mage.

Stunned by her use of attack magic and fueled by a desperate will to survive, I fly down another hallway, then another, then dive into a populated room, shoving people aside as I run, a gray-haired matron sending up a cry of alarm. I bump into a Urisk woman, her tray of hors d'oeuvres flying clear out of her hands.

There's a trail of exclamations and crashing in my wake, room after room.

*"You SLUT!"* Fallon cries out from behind me, fueling my speed. *"I'm going to KILL you!"*

Ice streams over the crowded floor, the frosty edge of it speeding under my stockinged feet, the room erupting into chaos. I almost slide backward, but my reflexes are prey-sharp. Pulse racing, I duck down, splay my arms out to maintain my balance, and slide over the ice and straight through a side exit.

I smack into the wall before me and roll quickly away from the exit as more ice spikes hurl through it to impale several potted ferns, the pots shattering in a fusillade of porcelain.

More crashing and cursing behind me as I renew my flight, breathlessly realizing that I've gained a small time advantage.

*She can't cross the ice quickly in her fancy shoes.*

With renewed vigor I take a sharp turn left and loop back in the direction I've come from, then duck into a hall going the other direction, with no pattern, desperate to throw her off my trail.

Fallon's yelling becomes fainter. The music and exclamations of distress muted. The hallway I'm now running down is deserted, the sound of my labored breathing dangerously loud to my ears. A cramp stabs into my side as I run and run, the music now nonexistent. I race down countless hallways and rooms, the lighting increasingly dim, wooden walls giving way to stone.

I spot a door ahead and duck into a deserted room, then stumble to a stop and grasp at the back of a broad chair in the faintly lit room. Doubled over, I catch my breath and listen.

*Nothing.*

I stare at the black tree pattern on the stone floor as my breathing slows, the cramp in my side loosening to almost tolerable.

I slowly raise my head only to come face-to-face with the oil painting that dominates the entire wall before me.

It depicts an Icaral. An Icaral like Yvan. Being impaled by multiple spears as Gardnerian soldiers lord over him. And above them all, the Ancient One, in the familiar form of the white bird. Looking down upon the gruesome scene with benevolent approval.

My gut wrenches and I fall back as nausea sweeps through me.

*I have to get away from here. Away from all of them.*

I stumble out of the room's back exit and lurch down another deserted hall, everything now carved in stone. I race under the elaborate vaulted ceiling, the image of trees embossed on its surface, the smell of salt water growing sharp on the air. Stripes of moonlight mark the stone floor, streaming in from repeating arched windows high up on the stone walls. The sound of the rhythmic lapping of waves is now present, the temperature cooling.

I round a corner, exit through a heavy wooden door, and step onto a deserted balcony.

Wind whips at my hair and I'm immediately accosted by vertigo, waves crashing on rocks far below, the turbulent Voltic Sea spread out before me, that odd line of glowing green stretching over the water in the far distance.

I realize I'm at the rear of the Mage Council Hall, which is built right inside the bluff, the windows on every level of this side blessedly dark. I draw back in awe at the overpowering height of the Styvius Bluff.

Gigantic trees are cut into the flat bluff stone. They rise from a turbulent ocean that crashes against night-blackened rocks at the bluff's faraway bottom, the waves' crests a foamy silver in the moonlight. A series of stone stairs and balconies to my left lead ever upward, winding through carved branches and limbs, toward the top of the staggeringly high wall of stone. The network of stairs and balconies terminates close to the bluff's apex, this last balcony sheltered by a stone canopy of carved leaves. I squint up at the terminal balcony. It curves clear around the bluff, and I wonder where it leads.

Perhaps to a way out.

Trying to ignore the dizzying height, I avoid looking down at the crashing surf and set off at a run up the stone stairs, across a balcony, then up more stairs and another balcony, ever upward toward the top.

When I reach the highest balcony, I sprint around the bluff's corner and skid to a dead end.

The balcony is bathed in moonlight. A bench is cut right into the bluff's stone, carved vines framing it. The view from this balcony is incredible, the height unfathomable. Breathing hard, I cautiously move toward the balcony's stone balustrade.

I can't see the Council Hall anymore; the bend in the bluff is too sharp. And I can't see the city of Valgard, which lies just beyond another sharp, irregular bend in the bluff. I wince as a huge wave crashes onto the black rocks below. More stars make an appearance as the moonlight-limned clouds continue to move out.

I listen carefully for the sound of pursuit.

Nothing.

All voices and music are erased by the ocean and the cliff's sheer heft.

A brittle panic floods in and I lean in against the balcony edge, gasping in big gulps of air as I look around for something, *anything* that could be used as a weapon. But there's nothing but carved stone and some flowers planted in the recesses.

*Please, Dear Ancient One, don't let Fallon follow me up here,* I pray as I grasp the railing for support, wishing I'd had the sense to at least bring a knife or any sharp thing.

A harsher panic overtakes me.

*How am I going to get out of here? And what happened to Sparrow? If Fallon has lost my trail, will she level her vengeance on her instead?* Remorse courses through me at the thought as I realize what a huge mistake it was to come back to Gardneria.

Kam Vin and Chi Nam were so very wrong.

But where else could I go?

Reflexively, I feel for Chi Nam's rune stone hidden in the base of my dress's pocket, relying on the subtle calming energy of the smooth stone as my only support as I'm rocked by a sudden, fierce desire to not be so alone in this.

*Where are you, Yvan? What are you doing now?*

A knot of profound longing for him gathers in my throat as I stare at the pinpoints of stars, at the inky blackness of the Voltic Sea. A sweet aroma rises on the breeze.

Roses.

I turn to regard the moonlit blossoms planted all along the balcony's inner periphery. Their heady perfume makes me think of my uncle's flower garden, and another vicious ache takes hold. I press my eyelids firmly together, holding back tears.

I know that if Yvan were here, he'd wrap me in his warm arms, spread his wings, and fly me far away from this awful place. With him, I wouldn't be trapped.

Something shifts in the air around me and an uneasy tingle starts at the base of my neck. It's quickly followed by the uncomfortable certainty that I'm being watched.

I turn slowly and search the irregular shadows cast by the overhanging stone-branches, sure that I heard the whisper of something rough moving against stone. Just around the bend.

Silence.

I can't see anyone, but still the feeling grows.

I peer across the balcony, searching the shadows of the many alcoves cut into the sculpted trees.

*It's my imagination. There's no one there.*

But still, I swear I heard something.

Someone.

The sense that I'm being watched morphs into a palpable feeling of danger so strong that I break out in a cold sweat.

How could I be so foolish as to come up here unprotected? Far away from everyone. So far away that no one would be able to hear me scream.

Who would question it if I were tossed into the ocean and later found washed up on the shore? Who would doubt that it was suicide? An unstable girl, infected by the same evil seed, the same madness as her brothers. And killing me would make it possible for a priest to strip the fasting right from Lukas's hands, freeing him to fast to Fallon Bane. Just as Sparrow warned me.

The shadows shift...and a figure emerges from around the bend.

I stumble backward as terror swamps me.

*Ancient One, have mercy.*

It's not Fallon Bane. It's worse than her. *Much* worse.

Damion Bane stands there watching me, wand in hand, his eyes bright with interest.

My gaze darts around as my muscles tense and I ready myself to flee past him.

Damion is staring at me as if he can read my mind, a slow grin forming on his coldly handsome face, and I've a stark remembrance of how he used to prey on the Urisk kitchen workers.

"You…you startled me," I stammer, struggling to keep my tone light.

"Where's Lukas?" he asks pleasantly, as if playing with me, as if he already knows the answer. I notice his hands and wrists are marked with sealed fastlines.

"He'll be here shortly," I lie, my heart pounding. "We… we're supposed to meet here." I sweep my hand out toward the ocean. "It's so beautiful. He wanted to show me the view."

"Funny," Damion says as he slowly approaches me, rolling his wand idly in his palm. "I thought he wasn't supposed to arrive until later." He draws ever closer and I instinctively step back only to be halted by the stone railing of the balcony behind me. Hyperaware of his wand.

Everything in me wanting to grab hold of it.

*You can't use his wand*, I desperately caution myself.

Damion comes to a stop in front of me, an evil glint in his eyes. I recoil as he reaches up to lightly stroke my hair.

"Lukas wouldn't want you doing that," I snap, outrage seeping through.

Damion makes no move to back away. "Oh, I *know*," he says, as he continues to play with a long strand. "Your devotion to Lukas Grey is *so* touching." He leans in closer. "Everyone knows your aunt found you in bed with a Kelt." He reaches down to grab hold of my hand, eyeing the fasting marks with interest as I wrench my hand away from his. "Vyvian arrived in the nick of time, I'd say." He laughs and leers at my too-tight, low-cut scarlet clothing. "I heard you were half-naked." His eyes narrow. "No, Lukas is quite done with you."

Panic rising, I move to sidestep away from him, but he reacts quickly, sidestepping as well, and grasps hold of my arm, his wand now pointed at my neck.

I freeze, the tip of his wand sharp on my skin.

"You were almost mine, did you know that?" he whispers, leaning in, his breath sickeningly warm on my face.

"What do you mean?" I gasp, the top of the stone railing jutting hard against my lower back.

"Your aunt gave consent for you to fast to *me*," he says silkily. "I was there, ready to bind myself to you, when *he* showed up. It was quite the surprise. No one expected Lukas to be so doggedly persistent in his...*affections* for you." His grin fades and his brow furrows in consternation. "I really don't understand what my sister sees in him. She's quite upset, you know."

I give a hoarse cry as he jabs the wand under my chin, forcing my head up. He shoves his body against me, pushing me against the banister, a viciously suggestive gleam in his eyes. "She thinks you should be punished."

"You're fasted," I croak, defiance rising as I grit my teeth. "I'll tell your fastmate and everyone in that hall if you don't get off me."

Damion lets out another contemptuous laugh and pushes the wand even harder into my throat. "You think your little friend Aislinn will defend you? That skinny little thing? All the fight's beaten out of that pathetic fastmate of mine."

Aislinn's face lights in my mind as rage explodes inside me. *"You bastard!"*

I slam my whole weight against him and lunge for his wand,

but he anticipates me, tightening his grip on the wand as my hand closes around his and my forefinger makes direct contact with the wood.

My affinity lines crackle into the shape of jagged tree limbs as power flashes up from the ground, through the stone, fire magic racing toward me, rushing through my affinity lines and suffusing them with pulsating, killing power.

Damion's eyes go wide with surprise.

The words to the candle-lighting spell dance on my lips, my body trembling with a vengeance begging to be unleashed. But I battle against the fierce urge to let loose with the spell that would incinerate not just Damion, but possibly the whole city of Valgard.

Taking advantage of my hesitation, Damion narrows his eyes with wicked purpose. In the blink of an eye he sends out a spell.

I cry out as vine bindings fly from his wand and cinch tight around my body, the breath forced from my lungs, my limbs instantly trussed tight. Damion hurls me to the ground, and my head hits the stone with a heavy thud.

He's on top of me in an instant, his eyes bright with excitement as he jabs his wand into my side, his other hand coming around my throat. I struggle for breath as his fingers tighten, his whole body pushed crushingly down on me.

"Oh, I'm going to enjoy breaking you," he croons as spots flash before my eyes.

I'm beginning to black out as boot heels thud on the balcony floor.

Damion is suddenly lifted off me, and breath rushes back into my lungs in jagged heaves, my vision returning as the vines restraining me dissipate into black smoke.

Lukas is there, his face wild with anger, dragging a stumbling Damion across the stone floor as I pull in great gulps of air. Damion's wand is now in Lukas's hand, and is promptly hurled off the balcony. Lukas pushes Damion roughly against one of the stone trees.

"She's *mine!*" Lukas snarls before punching Damion in the face so hard that I can hear something crack. Then Damion is lying on the floor, Lukas straddling him and savagely punching him in the face over and over as Damion cries out, blood streaming from his nose and mouth.

I push myself away from the two of them and scurry backward to avoid the flying limbs.

Lukas stops, rises to his feet, and steps back, his fists clenched as he looms over Damion.

Coughing and spitting blood, Damion rolls over, whimpering, then struggles onto his knees. He holds up his palms in surrender.

I hold my breath, thinking it's over.

To my surprise, Lukas starts in on Damion once more, kicking him to the ground and then kicking him in the side again and again as Damion cries for mercy.

I'm afraid that Lukas won't stop. There's something so wildly violent in his expression that I'm worried he's actually going to kill Damion Bane.

Damion tries, pathetically, to crawl away from Lukas, but Lukas attacks even more savagely, Damion's weakness seeming to provoke rather than calm him.

I turn away as I hear the sickening sound of a bone breaking.

Footsteps sound on the stairs and then on the balcony, running toward us and around the bend as a deep male voice booms out, "Lukas, *stop!*"

Lukas pauses, his gaze fixed on Damion, his hand a bloodied fist. He stands like that for a long moment before slowly lifting his gaze to meet that of his father, High Commander Lachlan Grey.

Lukas's father is flanked by four Gardnerian soldiers, my guards among them, all of the soldiers wearing shocked expressions as they survey the situation. Sparrow comes into view behind them, and I realize, in a staggeringly grateful rush, that she must be the one who summoned Lukas and the other soldiers.

Still breathing hard, Lukas seems undaunted by their presence, and the soldiers shrink back from his glare. Only Lukas's father is uncowed.

"You *cannot* kill the son of a Mage Council member." Lachlan bites off each word, rage brimming in his eyes.

Lukas glances down at Damion, then back to his father, the side of his mouth curling up.

"He is a fellow commander." Lachlan scowls.

Lukas is unmoved, his fists clenched tight.

"I *will* strip you of your command," his father threatens, but I notice he makes no move toward Lukas, and neither do the other soldiers.

Lukas lets out a short laugh of contempt.

"And I will *arrest* you," Lachlan stubbornly continues.

Lukas shoots his father an incredulous look and glances back at Damion, who is now unconscious on the floor.

We watch, breathlessly, as Lukas deliberates for a long moment then steps back.

The soldiers all let out a sigh of relief and step back in turn. It seems that no one wanted to be the one to try to arrest Lukas Grey.

"Take him to my physician," Lachlan directs the soldiers, motioning toward Damion but keeping his gaze blazing on his son.

The soldiers jump to retrieve and then carry a limp, bloody Damion across the balcony and down the stairs.

*Damion sensed my power.* The panicked thought whirls in my mind. *Sweet Ancient One, the Banes can't know what I am.*

Lachlan Grey gestures for Sparrow to leave, and Sparrow's eyes briefly meet mine. She gives me a deeply cautionary look before quietly following the soldiers.

I slowly pull myself up, my legs trembling, power singing through my affinity lines.

Lachlan glances at me, his expression full of disgust, then turns back to his son. "Lukas. We need to talk," he says tersely, eyeing me again with disdain. *"Privately."* Lachlan walks a few steps away, turns briefly to indicate with his glare that he expects Lukas to follow, then leaves. His heavy, angry steps sound on the stone stairs.

Lukas glances at me, his expression and magic unreadable, but an echo of violence still burns in his eyes. He turns and strides off after his father.

I struggle to catch my breath, still rasping through my lungs. I hoist myself up and away from the balcony and follow them, hearing their voices below, the cool breeze coming in from the ocean chilling my face and neck.

I make my way down two levels and crouch behind a stone trunk as their voices become audible from the balcony's far end.

"…throw away your entire career for *what?*" Lachlan's harsh voice demands. "A girl who doesn't want you?"

"She's *mine.*"

"She was all but Damion's before you stormed into the fasting, threatening everyone in the room. For a girl who had to be forcibly restrained to fast to you. Vyvian Damon *played* you! To get you to fast to a girl that no one but Damion would have wanted. Did I raise you to be such a fool?"

*He saved me. Lukas saved me. Holy Ancient One, he saved me from being fasted to Damion Bane.* Nausea churns in my stomach as a dizzying clarity descends.

"She's a troublemaker and a whore," his father continues. "One step up from a Selkie—"

"Careful." Lukas's voice is low and threatening.

They're both quiet for a moment, and I've a sense of both the tension simmering on the air and that Lachlan Grey is intimidated by his son.

"You are a fool," Lachlan finally says. "This girl is a traitor to her own kind. Is this your way of thumbing your nose at our traditions? I know you didn't want to be fasted, but to make such a mockery of a *sacred rite*, choosing a girl who has disgraced herself in such a wanton, disgusting manner, from a family full of *race traitors*..."

"Are you finished?" Lukas's voice has become cold, disinterested.

"No, I'm *not* done," Lachlan snaps angrily. "You *will not* kill Damion Bane. *Promise* me!"

"If he touches her again, I *will* kill him," Lukas answers calmly, irrefutably.

Again, they're quiet.

"You should have let Damion have her," Lachlan bites out, as if through clenched teeth. "He'd have beaten some sense into her. I suggest you do just that."

There's the sound of footsteps, and Lachlan storms by without noticing me, making his way to the descending staircase. And then Lukas strides into view.

He catches sight of me and stops dead in his tracks.

I freeze, wholly unprepared to face him, my heart pounding against my chest.

Fire power blasts through his lines and out toward me, his face taking on a look that's so impassioned it stuns me. "Elloren, are you all right?"

So much power is swirling through my lines in response to his that I'm light-headed. "I am," I force out with a stiff nod.

He extends his hand to me, his gaze fervent. "Come inside with me," he offers as I'm encircled by his out-of-control flame.

My fire leaps toward his, and for a moment I want nothing more than to clasp his wand hand to mine and surrender to our all-encompassing, magical pull.

But I hesitate.

Our fire power is running feverishly hot, and I can feel Lukas's emotion in it, blazing just as hot and raw.

I curl my wand hand into a tight fist and press it to my side, fighting against our draw. Because if our wand hands touch and he gets a full sense of my power, I know that he'll likely realize, beyond a shadow of a doubt, that I'm the next Black Witch.

# CHAPTER
# FIVE

# ALLY

## ELLOREN GARDNER

*Sixth Month*
*Valgard, Gardneria*

I sit on the stone balcony for a protracted moment, my eyes locked with Lukas's. He keeps his hand extended to me as his fire whips around me in an uncharacteristically discordant rush.

My power strains toward his to the point where I feel that, if I give in to the pull, my body might slide to his of its own accord.

I do not take his hand.

A disturbance shudders through Lukas's fire as his face takes on a look of intense confusion. His fire dampens in a flash, and his searching look is replaced by a more severe demeanor as he withdraws his hand and I rise on my own. I smooth my tousled skirts with shaking hands, then reach up to touch my aching neck, an echo of horror rising.

Lukas's fire gives a pulsing flare. "I should have killed him," he says, and I meet his gaze once more, green fire spitting in his eyes.

I hold his fervid stare as my trembling lessens and the lashing flow of my power slowly dissipates.

Nothing is as it seemed, and my head is spinning from so many new realizations.

Lukas saved me from being fasted to a monster. He never conspired with my aunt to destroy my uncle and force me into fasting. It was all Aunt Vyvian's doing—playing Damion Bane and Lukas off each other as a means to her wretched ends.

And Lukas stepped into her trap to save me from a truly nightmarish fate.

A sharper realization sweeps over me.

I remember all the Level Five Mages I was surrounded by on that day, my depraved aunt's strategy so clear to me now. Aunt Vyvian not only arranged for me to be fasted to Damion Bane.She was careful to organize a guard large enough that Lukas wouldn't be able to fight his way through it. Once there was no possibility of my escape, she likely called in Lukas at the very last minute and gave him an ultimatum—

Fast to Elloren...or see her fasted to Damion Bane.

I let out a long, shuddering breath, both astonished and newly decided. "I need to speak with you, Lukas." I receive no response but a creasing of his brow, and in that moment I rue the divide between us.

*I wish I could tell you everything*, I agonize. *I need a friend, and I need help. You don't have any idea how high the stakes are. If I can survive, I'm a weapon that could bring down Vogel.*

I remember how Lukas told me he considers Vogel to be unhinged. How he disapproves of the religious intolerance sweeping through Gardneria that Vogel is emboldening.

"Is there somewhere we can go?" I press, ready to plead if necessary.

Lukas's jaw tenses and he looks just past me, as if trying to rein in some strong emotion.

But then his eyes meet mine and he silently holds out his arm to me.

For a split second I hesitate, unnerved by his piercing look and the memory of his out-of-control violence toward Damion.

*Damion Bane.*

Whom I'd be bound to without Lukas's intervention.

*For life.*

I reach out and thread my hand through Lukas's arm, careful to not let my hand brush against his.

I match Lukas's long stride through the Mage Council Hall, the distant sound of orchestral music and the buzz of crowds growing louder as we step into a populated, tree-lined atrium with a constellation-imprinted ceiling. A sense of the surreal envelops me as I walk, arm in arm, with Lukas Grey, the memory of our fasting now viewed with such a drastically altered lens. I internally wince, remembering how I screamed *I'll hate you* forever! at him.

And how everyone in this room likely knows it.

Mages drinking scarlet punch cast me looks of censure and narrow-eyed dislike as we cross the room, and I'm acutely aware of both the tension burning in Lukas's banked-back fire as well as the scuff of my raw, shoeless feet on the smooth tile beneath me. A young soldier with aristocratic features approaches with the air of someone who has been looking for Lukas. I recognize Thierren, the Level Five Mage who guided me out of Lukas's command tent in the Keltish Province and was part of my escort to the Greys' estate.

"Where are the Banes?" Lukas asks him in an aggressive tone that implies *So I can kill them.*

Thierren's gaze darts to me, his face remaining as impassive as Sparrow's before he looks back at Lukas. "Commander Damion Bane has been brought to a physician," he states succinctly, "and Commander Sylus Bane left with him. Mage Fallon Bane has been brought to the Valgard military base for questioning." He glances at me again. "For attacking a fellow Mage with wand magic."

Worry for Sparrow rises in me. "Have you seen a young Urisk woman with lavender features?" I ask him, concerned that the Banes could have enacted some vengeance upon her before they left. "She's my lady's maid, and she needs an escort home."

Thierren loses his impassive look for a moment, his brow tensing hard as he views me searchingly. "She's fine and is in a carriage traveling back to the Greys' estate," he assures me.

"Report to the Valgard Base," Lukas directs Thierren, and the young Mage instantly regains his military-blank expression. "I'll check in with you later."

Thierren nods, then shoots me one last questioning look, turns, and departs, leaving Lukas and me both alone and surrounded by a candlelit swirl of strangers, most of them glaring at me with unconcealed animosity.

I look up into Lukas's raptor-sharp gaze, a flash of affinity heat igniting between us and sending a shiver through my lines, our magical draw impossible to fully suppress.

"I know of a deserted library," Lukas says, clearly ignoring our sparking magic.

"Good," I reply, attempting to ignore his unnerving draw, as well. "Take me there."

I keep pace with Lukas down a lengthy hallway, his posture stiff, his jaw set tight, as he holds his unsettled magic more firmly at bay. He remains dauntingly silent as he leads me through winding corridors, up staircases, and down more hallways, the sound of music and conversation rapidly fading.

Eventually, we come to an isolated, lantern-lit hallway far away from the crowds, and he guides me into a small, darkened library.

Lukas releases my arm and unsheathes his wand, my affinity lines immediately straining toward it. He turns, walks to a wall lantern, and mutters the candle-lighting spell. The candle inside bursts into a reddened flame.

I watch as he stalks around the room lighting crimson glass lanterns with an air of severe purpose, the rich details of the library gradually coming alive, Lukas's black cloak swirling behind him.

He cuts a fine figure, I have to admit, tall and broad shouldered, an athletic grace to his movements. My magic continues its relentless pull toward his matching lines, and it makes me uneasy. His magic's draw is nothing at all like Yvan's alluring and bolstering fire. Lukas's magic is like a force I have to push against to stay whole.

Ill at ease, I turn away, my gaze drawn to the marble mantel of the unlit fireplace beside me. It's glossy black with thin green veins tracing through it, the emerald of the lines so bright that they almost glow, and the surface is so finely polished that it's nearly as reflective as a mirror. For a moment, I'm overcome by the sheer beauty of the craftsmanship.

"This marble is beautiful," I comment absently as I trace the green lines, strangely attracted to it.

My face grows warm with surprise as I instantly realize what this is.

It's not marble. It's *wood*.

Alfsigr Spruce, from the upper reaches of the northern Borial Forest. Dense as granite. I've heard about this wood, read about it, but I've never seen or touched it before. As I slide my finger along its gleaming surface, a static-riddled warmth flows up my arm as my earthlines shudder to pulsing, branching life, the image of a deep-green spruce tree with a silvery sheen to its needles unfolding in my mind.

"This is Elfin wood," I murmur, transfixed by the effect the piece is having on my lines. I turn when there's no answer from Lukas, my finger still caressing the enthralling wood.

Lukas is watching me from a few steps away, his arms crossed, his expression jaded. "What do you want, Elloren?" His fire gives a brief flare toward me and I can sense the conflicted energy in it.

I hold his confrontational stare, dauntingly aware of our difficult history with each other. I've no doubt hurt his reputation. Probably made him the object of more than a small bit of ridicule. It's likely that everyone in this building knows that I resisted being fasted. Priests gossip, as do lower-ranking guards. And I imagine the Banes told everyone in Valgard about my behavior.

Lukas knew full well that this would be the outcome of permanently Sealing himself to me. But still, he did it to protect me. Even though he likely knows that I'm in love with someone else.

I swallow as my hand falls away from the wood and the larger issues I'm faced with come rushing in. Issues that are bigger than Lukas and Yvan and I.

*Can I trust you, Lukas?* I agonize as I study his tall form. *I need to be able to trust you.*

"I…need your help," I haltingly admit.

"With *what*?" His tone is sharp and wary.

I struggle to come up with a plausible lie, but the words get tangled in the back of my throat, because we cannot lie to each other. Lukas stares me down, his lip lifting with a trace of amusement that doesn't reach his eyes, and both frustration and anger flare in me in response to his unreceptive demeanor.

*Calm down, Elloren*, I chastise myself. *You need him. And Chi Nam said he might well be on the Resistance's side.*

"I'm ready to take my place with you," I force out, the words stilted and stiff. It's not quite a lie, though. Just the truth artfully picked through. Covering up the larger, explosive, world-altering truth.

Lukas gives a bitter laugh. "Really, Elloren. As my fasted partner? Shall we truly seal our fasting and consummate it this evening?" He looks at me cynically, like he knows the answer.

My angry desperation notches higher. "You once said you were my *friend*." My voice breaks against the word as I step toward him. "Lukas, I need help. And I need to know what side you're truly on." I hold my breath, knowing that last question is dangerous.

Lukas looks away and shakes his head as if at war with himself.

Heated frustration mounts in me over his refusal to bend. "Fallon said you two are together." I'm unable to keep the abhorrence from bleeding into my tone.

He coughs out a contemptuous laugh as he throws me a sarcastic look. "No, Elloren, we are not. Are you with the Kelt?" His smile is gone, and something like jealousy flashes through his eyes. He looks away again, his jaw ticking.

*Yes, Lukas*, I want to cry at him as pain strafes through me. *I'm with Yvan. But I also can never be fully with him.*

*Because I'm fasted to* you.

We're both silent for a long moment. And when he brings his gaze back to mine, his brow is furrowed with both bitterness and something I've never seen in him before—profound hurt.

My anger caves in on itself.

His wretched mother is right—he could have fasted to practically any young woman in Gardneria. He didn't want to be fasted any more than I did. But still, he did it.

For me.

I slump and exhale, looking to Lukas with a new, chastened understanding. "If you hadn't stepped in, Damion would have forced me to fast to him," I say, my voice rough with outrage as my heart aches for what Aislinn has likely endured. "Then he would have taken me back to his estate and raped me. And that would be my life. Every day."

Lukas's mouth tenses as he stares at me.

A stark realization takes hold. "That's twice you've saved my life."

Lukas cuts me a glare. "He wouldn't have killed you, Elloren."

"I'd be as good as dead."

"No," he says, shaking his head, serious. "You'd have found a way to fight him."

"Maybe. But still, you were right. When you forced me to fast to you, you were being a friend to me."

Lukas lets out a long breath and loses the last trace of his antagonistic demeanor. "What is it that you want?"

*I'm the next Black Witch and I need protection* comes close to escaping my lips. "I told you," I say instead, "I'm ready to take my place with you."

"No. Why are you here? Why are you back in Gardneria?"

It all crashes through me—my impossible task, my uncontrollable and therefore useless power, everyone I love in danger.

My life in serious danger.

"Because," I say, my voice cracking, "I have nowhere else to go."

Lukas studies me, his expression now searching. "I'll help you," he finally says, his voice low and adamant.

Tears burn in my eyes and I pull in a shaky breath, overcome with gratitude and wanting to find some way to express it. "Let's go back in there," I offer, gesturing in the direction of the Council's Main Hall, "and I'll dance with you. I'll tell everyone in the room how happy I am to be fasted to you. I realize... I realize how much fasting to me, especially after how I fought you...the things I said... I realize how much I must have hurt your reputation."

Lukas looks up at the ceiling and shakes his head before once again meeting my eyes, his expression going hard. "I don't care what anyone thinks—" he motions between us "—about *this*. Whatever it is."

A familiar, heated tension lights between us, and I can sense, by the intent way he's now looking at me, that he feels it too. My uncomfortable awareness of his magic rises as I remember how many times the two of us have kissed, and quite passionately, the pull of our matching affinity lines an enticing, palpable thing.

I step back a fraction, abashed by my reflexive attraction to Lukas and his power when I've given my heart completely to Yvan.

"I'm to meet with Marcus Vogel before he makes his address," Lukas says, breaking what felt like a momentary spell cast between us.

"Why?"

"He wants to meet with all the commanders of our Guard. Although I don't think Damion Bane will be attending." There's no humor in his voice when he says this, only a volatile hatred swimming in his eyes.

Fear of what Damion might now suspect about me spikes.

*I'm going to have to tell you what I am, Lukas. But...where do you stand? I have to know where you truly stand.*

"When are you to meet with Vogel?" I ask.

He frowns and glances at a clock. "Now."

It's odd how dismissive he is. His whole demeanor is strangely brazen, and I have the sense that something significant within him has changed.

"Then you should go," I prod, worried that my only ally here with any real power might be flirting with a dangerously open rebellion.

Lukas makes no move to leave. "Let him wait," he says in a harsh, subversive tone that leaves me wondering. No one leaves a High Mage waiting. *No one.* Not even an incredibly gifted Mage. Not even a military commander.

"Don't make him wait," I caution, my own tone now one of undisguised warning.

Lukas considers me closely, a tendril of his fire loosening and flaring toward me. I can tell he understands that I sense how he feels about Vogel and that I agree, and it feels good, this meeting of our minds. Lukas nods, as if in acknowledgment of it.

"I'll find you after Vogel's address," he promises.

"I'll look for you."

He holds out his hand. "Give me one of the hairs from your head, Elloren."

Confusion flares and I draw slightly back from him. "Why?"

His mouth tightens. "I have a Noi tracking rune," he says. "I can amplify my wand magic with it to cast a search spell." He gives me a poignant look. "It might be a good idea for me not to lose track of you."

I consider this, my brow lifting at his use of Noi sorcery. It's flatly forbidden for Gardnerians to mix their magic with the sorcery of other lands. And Lukas can't charge runes, since he's not a Light Mage, so a Vu Trin with runic sorcery must have charged whatever runes he's using.

"Are you allied with the Vu Trin?" I ask him boldly, my pulse speeding up as I wait for his answer.

Lukas looks as if it's his turn to try to stamp down a lie that he's unable to voice. "We share similar aims," he answers, a cagey look flashing over his expression.

Emboldened by this and by Lukas's defiance of Gardneria's magical strictures, I reach up and pull a hair from my scalp, wincing slightly at the sting, then hand it to him.

Lukas places the hair in his tunic's pocket, shoots me a look of fervent, unspoken solidarity, and leaves.

# CHAPTER SIX

# SHADOW WAND

## ELLOREN GARDNER

*Sixth Month*
*Valgard, Gardneria*

*Ironflowers.*

They've been brought in for Vogel's address, the blossoms rising from countless black lacquered vases that now ring the Mage Council's entire Main Hall and the foyer it spills into.

The lights have been dimmed to enhance the sacred flowers' ethereal sapphire glow, and the darkness provides me some measure of anonymity as I weave through the overflow crowd of Gardnerians. They're gathered just outside the packed Main Hall's open, arching doors, white-armbanded Mages straining to get a look inside as they murmur with bright anticipation.

Waiting for Vogel.

The scarlet of my dress has been muted to black by the deep-blue light, the green glimmer of my skin heightened, muting my individuality and subsuming me into the great sea of Mages.

A nightmare of conformity.

Rattled by how well I blend in, I reach for the vase beside me and pinch off one of the delicate Ironflowers, holding it between my fingers as I rub my thumb and forefinger against it in an effort to soothe my storming emotions. Soft as velvet, the petals move in a lazy spiral, their soft blue glow momentarily carrying my thoughts back to a gentler time.

There was a large Ironwood tree grove near my family's cottage in Halfix, just behind our horses' small stable. Every year, as spring became gloriously entrenched, the floor of the forest beneath the Ironwood trees would erupt in a carpet of small, glowing blue flowers, the trees flowering days later. I remember how happy and entranced Rafe, Trystan, and I would be when the flowers were finally in bloom, and can almost hear little Trystan's voice—*Ren! They've bloomed! Come see!*

Grief slices into me, triggering a longing for my brothers so raw that it sends an ache through me. I stare down at the luminescent flower cupped in my palm, my grief rapidly morphing into a mounting outrage that focuses in like a lightning strike on this potent religious symbol of Gardnerian power.

*Gardneria. The monster about to consume the world.*

A troubled fire kicks up along my affinity lines as I close my fist around the flower, crush it, then cast it to the ground, the pulp's glow now a muted midnight blue. Eyes narrowed, I peer back toward the Council's packed Main Hall.

Blue torches on long iron poles stand around the raised dais at the hall's far end, the orchestra that was there now absent, the music gone. Behind the dais, a huge Gardnerian flag hangs from the dark Ironwood trees set into the walls, the entire scene bathed in flickering blue torchlight.

I weave my way to the hall's open doorway and slip inside. Splayed before me is a sea of black-clad Gardnerians, packed together beneath the hall's high domed ceiling. The ceiling is supported by Ironwood tree branches, a dense canopy of leaves painted on the dome's curved surface.

"Vogel's bringing back order to the world," a Mage before me murmurs reverentially to the Gardnerians that surround him, as I catch snippets of hushed, jubilant conversation throughout the room.

"Manifesting the Ancient One's light…"

"Ensuring safety for our children…"

"Beating back the tide of evil. Getting the invaders off of Mage soil."

"Ushering in the Blessed Reaping Times…"

Resentment claws at me as I listen to them spin their religious delusions, all of them so sheltered from the misery they're supporting.

An image of Gardnerian mobs rampaging through Verpacia assaults my mind. My fellow kitchen worker, Bleddyn, lying half-conscious in the shadows of an alley. Olilly's bloodied face and mutilated ears. Little Fern's terror as she clutched at her doll, guarding her toy's pointed ears.

Andras's small son, Konnor, hiding his face against Brendan's chest the day his Lupine parents were murdered. Diana's entire people slaughtered.

Embers spark to a slow burn inside my lines as I lurk in the shadows of the Ironwood trees at the back of the room and beat down the desire to thrust my wand hand against the trunk at my back and burn this entire hall to the ground.

I pull in one deep, quavering breath, then another, and let Chi Nam's steadying words echo in the back of my mind.

*Gather yourself, child.*

But I'm in so far over my head, there's no clear way out.

I look to the leaves painted on the domed ceiling far above me as both fury and desperation swell. Aislinn is somewhere in Valgard and wandfasted to Damion Bane. My beloved friend is caught in the jaws of an unimaginable nightmare that could have been mine.

*I'll come for you, Aislinn*, I vow, sending the pledge throughout Valgard with the force of a solemn promise. *I swear it on the Ancient One. Somehow, I will get you out of here.*

My thoughts turn to Sparrow, also trapped here in Valgard along with Effrey.

Sparrow, who saved my life this evening.

*I'll help you get out too, Sparrow. Both you and Effrey.*

There's movement onto the dais, and I straighten as everyone's attention snaps toward the front of the hall. Excitement ripples through the air.

A procession of Level Five Mage soldiers streams in to line the back of the dais, followed by a throng of military commanders, Lukas and his father among them, followed by priests and Mage Council members, all assembling themselves in a long arc in front of the soldiers.

Marcus Vogel sweeps into the room and onto the dais, two Council envoys striding in behind him, and the room explodes into a frenzy of veneration.

The cheers are deafening, the Mages around me crying out his name, a woman beside me breaking into joyful tears as she calls out, "May the Ancient One's Blessing be upon you forever!" again and again.

I'm unprepared for the furious emotion that overtakes me as I'm faced with High Mage Marcus Vogel for the first time since Diana and Jarod's people were massacred. Affinity fire roars through my lines, my wand hand tingling then burning hot, and I pull it into my sleeve, fearing my hand might take on a molten glow.

Vogel steps to the front of the dais and raises one hand as if in blessing, and the massive crowd grows preternaturally silent and still, all eyes looking to their Blessed High Mage. Vogel's features are raptor-sharp as he scans the crowd, his priestly robes black as a charred forest and marked with the white bird.

In his lowered hand, he holds a dark gray wand.

The vengeful fire in my lines rears hotter at the sight of it, my wand hand fisting as a crackling energy fills the demon-sensing rune Sage marked on my abdomen.

I freeze, alarm overtaking me as I consider what that might mean.

And then Vogel lifts his wand.

A wave of invisible black affinity fire hits me from clear across the room, its knifelike sting shooting straight through my lines. My whole body constricts, my gut cinching tight as I'm rendered suddenly immobile.

A flash of crimson lights my vision, and the room goes dark.

I inhale, cast into a sudden, claustrophobic panic, the image of the hall, the giant flag, the crowd of Mages—all of it disappears.

Roiling dark shadows now surround me.

An image forms in the shadow that's closing in—the black silhouette of burned branches against a red sky, the dead tree rapidly melding back into the smoking, undulating shadow. And then, *poof*, both the smoky darkness and the shadow tree blink out of sight, the room once again lit up sapphire before me as I'm released from Vogel's grip.

I reel, unsteady on my feet as I struggle to control my panic, hollowed out as the terrifying certainty fills me…

Vogel's grown even more powerful. And it's because of the wand.

That shadowy wand in his hand.

I can feel it in the way his magic is pulsing over the room in an odd, spiraling coil.

My gaze darts frantically across the hall, the Mages around

me seeming oblivious to the reality of the creature that stands before them.

Marcus Vogel raises both hands once more and I flinch down, ready for another shadow assault. But Vogel's power remains firmly contained.

The Council's sole Light Mage steps forward, his dark garb marked with glowing deep-green runes, his white hair and beard flowing over his tunic's back and front like a pale river. He lifts his wand and marks a suspended, verdant amplification rune to hover in the air before Vogel.

"Pray with me, Mages," Vogel intones over the crowd, his words amplified by the light magery, his elegantly inflected voice resonating through me. Vogel closes his eyes as he begins to recite the Ancient One's blessing, the entire crowd joining in with impassioned force.

*Oh, Blessed Ancient One. Purify our minds. Purify our hearts. Purify Erthia from the stain of the Evil Ones.*

In unison, everyone brings their right fists to their hearts with an all-encompassing thud. Everyone, that is, except me... and Lukas, who remains stiff as an iron rod, his hand gripping the handle of the wand sheathed at his side as he eyes High Mage Vogel boldly. It surprises me, Lukas's refusal to pretend to be part of this communal piety, and strikes me as potentially foolhardy. As it did when I first saw him in his tent, a heightened awareness hits me that Lukas is in a very small minority of Mages still wearing the old military uniform.

Vogel opens his eyes and looks over the crowd. "Blessed Mages," he says with simmering import. "Tonight is a night to celebrate what the Ancient One has wrought." He pauses, and his devotees wait breathlessly, the faint noise of the entire crowd reduced to an almost imperceptible rustle of silken fabric.

"The Ancient One has brought us victory after victory over the heathen races who seek to destroy us," Vogel proclaims. "Who seek to pollute our lands. Enslave us. And corrupt all that is sacred. And so the Ancient One has enhanced our runic magic, calling upon us to wall out the Evil Ones with border runes and holy purpose." Vogel pauses as he takes in the crowd, and the Mages around me strain forward as if to breathe in his every word. "Beloved Mages," Vogel calls out, his tone resonating with vengeful force, "we will drive the Evil Ones from our lands. We will wall them away from our children. We will cleanse this land and bring the Reaping Times to all of Erthia."

Thunderous applause breaks out and swells, aggressive cheers sounding as my mind snaps back to the image of the odd, glowing green line stretched out over the Malthorin Bay.

A terrible realization coalesces.

*He's building a runic border.*

To magically keep non-Gardnerians out. To keep the Urisk imprisoned on the Fae Islands with no chance of escape East. And, eventually, to keep anyone who wants to flee East trapped in Gardneria.

*Including me.*

"A new day has dawned, Mages," Vogel says as the applause and raucous cheers fade and the crowd settles back down into enraptured silence. "The Reaping Times are here," Vogel says, his tone so ominous that it fuels the dread in my heart. He pauses, the room his, every ear straining toward him. "The Great Prophecy has been struck down," he states with terrible finality.

Surprise bolts through me as a confused murmuring rises throughout the entire hall. Mages look to Vogel and to each other in sudden, obvious astonishment. Even most of the Mages on the dais seem thrown, including Lukas, who seems to be scanning everyone around him for some clue as to what Vogel means.

Only the attending members of the Mage Council seem unsurprised, their serene posture exuding confidence and triumph.

A crow flies down from the branches woven across the domed ceiling and alights on Vogel's shoulder, and the sting along the rune on my abdomen abruptly worsens. Foreboding sweeps through me.

"The Great Icaral Demon of Prophecy has been found," Vogel announces, his voice booming throughout the room.

Gasps hiss throughout the hall, and for a moment, I don't fully comprehend Vogel's words.

"The Winged Demon was located in Noi lands," Vogel continues. "Glamoured as a Kelt and known by the name Yvan Guriel."

The words strike like hammer blows straight to my heart. All the blood rushes from my head.

*No. No.*

"The heathen Noi were harboring the Great Demon on their Oonlan military base," Vogel continues, his tone sharpening to a blade's edge, "honing his power, intent on unleashing this weapon of fiery destruction upon the Holy Magedom."

Vogel pauses as I struggle to breathe, struggle to think.

"The Demon is the son of Valentin Guryev," Vogel says, slow and seething. "Not Yvan Guriel at all, but Yvan Guryev. Son of the Demon who killed Carnissa Gardner, our Great Black Witch."

My stomach lurches and vertigo rushes over me as vengeful rage breaks out across the room. I can feel Lukas's flash of fiery surprise from clear across the hall as every beat of my heart sounds out one word.

*Yvan. Yvan. Yvan.*

"By the grace of the Holy Ancient One," Vogel cries over the restless crowd, "the Icaral Demon has been struck down. Yvan Guryev, cursed son of Valentin Guryev, is *dead*."

# CHAPTER SEVEN

# IRONFLOWERS

## ELLOREN GARDNER

*Sixth Month*
*Valgard, Gardneria*

A violent roar of triumph breaks through the crowd like a wave, everyone yelling and crying out as fists are thrown into the air in support of Yvan's death.

Shock rips through me as my knees go weak and I take a faltering step backward, my legs almost buckling beneath me. I throw my hand back and grab hold of the Ironwood trunk behind me, my wand hand meeting wood.

The invisible magic in my lines detonates.

Power rushes through me in a savage inferno, heat flooding my lines as a murderous rage overtakes me that's fueled by ferocity and grief and my destroyed heart. The urge to draw up my fire power and level the entire city of Valgard takes hold with incredible force, and I know that if I stay a second more, I *will* burn this city to ash.

I turn on my heels and flee.

★ ★ ★

I run and run, bursting through the Council Hall's entrance, past shocked-looking soldiers and down the sweeping staircase. Clear past the Council Hall and into a grove of Ironwood trees, not caring when rough roots scrape my feet.

I run until I'm past the back edge of the grove, past all the wood, racing toward the ocean until there's cold bluff stone beneath my feet, a rocky cliff before me and the ocean below, the ledge lit sapphire by the glow of the grove's Ironflower blooms.

I pause, my breath suspended as my eyes latch on to the glowing green line that crosses the bay in the distance.

Bile rises in my throat.

My legs buckle and I drop to my knees against the ledge's raised stone, my whole body racked with ferocious sobs as the stiff ocean breeze strafes over me and black waves crash violently against the rocks below.

I cry until I can barely breathe. Until my eyes are almost swollen shut. Until pain clenches my chest and throat and eyes.

*Yvan.*

*My love. My only love.*

*Gone.*

*Murdered.*

*I'll never see you again.*

I cry, devastated, wanting to scream at the heavens. Wanting to send my fire over Vogel and every soldier in Gardneria before they can cut me down in turn.

"Yvan," I sob aloud, breaking apart. "Yvan."

I cry for a long time, crumpled forward, my eyes tightly closed, my forehead pressed to the chill bluff stone.

*Yvan...* I agonize, lost and unmoored and suddenly landed in terrain too brutal to navigate on my own.

*What would you want me to do?* I finally ask, as if the thought can reach him.

Yvan's unwavering answer sounds bright in my mind.

*Fight them.*

I grow still, a sob catching tight in my throat as merciless clarity descends.

Vogel's power is horrific, and it's growing.

The power of his wand is growing. His wand of shadows…

The Shadow Wand.

I can feel residual stinging along the demon-sensing rune on my abdomen.

Vogel will wield the evil power of that Wand against everyone and everything I love. Against everything good in the world.

Nothing and no one is safe.

Yvan's words from the day I found out I'm the Black Witch light up like a beacon in my mind.

*This is bigger than just us, Elloren. If no one steps forward, they'll win.*

I remember the exact look on Yvan's beautiful face when he said this to me. A face I'll never see again.

Grief makes another play to tear me apart, a wail threatening to pull loose from my throat as an orb of sapphire light rolls up beside me, a glowing blue line trailing behind it from the grove as a sudden awareness of Lukas's fire blazes through my lines.

*The Noi tracking rune.*

As I look behind me, Lukas bursts through the grove and onto the rocky bluff.

Our eyes meet, and fire ignites in my lines, the sight of his Mage uniform triggering a rage in me that's so raw, I might have stricken him down had I wood in my hand.

I bolt to my feet, fury thick and potent in my blood as

Lukas's fire intensifies along with mine, both of us abruptly caught up in a violent, chaotic blaze.

"Elloren," Lukas says with blistering urgency, accentuating each word, "does anyone other than your aunt and me know that you were with the Icaral of Prophecy?"

Fire explodes through my lines as I raise the palm of my wand hand. *"Stop,"* I demand of him in a teeth-clenched snarl, my other hand balling into a fist as my Dryad compulsion to be honest with him grips me fiercely "Tell me," I command Lukas, my voice breaking around my fury. "Tell me that you've broken with Vogel. Tell me that you're only standing here, in that vile uniform, because you're planning to use your position to destroy him."

Lukas's gaze is as ferocious as mine as we stare each other down.

"Yes, Elloren," he finally says, his voice ironhard.

A blast of shock hits me, the world altered yet again. Because Lukas Grey cannot lie to me and I can read the truth of his words in the forceful current of his fire.

I blink at him, rapidly adjusting to his stunning admission. I can sense him holding back a broader explanation—an explanation I need from him.

Because he is still wearing their uniform. And I need to know that he hasn't just broken with Vogel, but with Gardneria as a whole.

Because Vogel's evil is bigger than Vogel alone.

Lukas takes a step toward me. "Elloren," he says, his tone gaining urgency, "who else knows?"

*I don't care*, I want to snarl at him as tears sheen my eyes. *I loved him.*

But then another voice sounds in my mind.

Yvan's.

*Survive, Elloren.*

*Survive and fight them.*

"I... I don't know," I force out, misery threatening to break loose from my throat.

*I love you, Yvan. I love you.*

"We need to leave," Lukas says, still urgent but gentler this time. "Elloren, if they find out about this, they'll kill you. You shouldn't even be in Gardneria."

My eyes stay locked with his as horror infuses my voice. "I'm not safe anywhere." Fear rises, and I struggle not to succumb to its clawing grip.

*Lukas, I'm in so much danger I don't know what to do.*

*But if I fight back, I'll kill everyone. Even you.*

"I need your protection." I level with him. *Or I'm going to be killed.*

"I meant what I said," he says, his tone blazingly heartfelt. "If you need my protection, you have it."

The inescapable urge toward honesty swells, and I'm unable to contain it.

"I loved him," I say, my voice breaking. "I loved Yvan."

A flash of stark pain passes over Lukas's expression. "I know," he finally says, an edge to the words, but then his gaze turns unexpectedly ardent. "I *am* your friend, Elloren. I always will be. Let me help you."

I look away, overcome by Lukas's show of alliance as I wrestle with overwhelming grief. Tears burn my cheeks as I'm swept up in a yearning for Yvan so powerful that it threatens to undo me.

Lukas moves closer and gently takes my hands in his, and I let him. I keep hold of him, his own grip firming around mine as I cry and the waves crash onto the rocks below us. Lukas reaches up to caress my cheek, and I tip my head against his palm as I sob, his green eyes fixed on mine and filled with an unexpected compassion that feels like a lifeline. Then he reaches down to take my other hand again in his as he slightly loosens his fire and earthlines, letting his invisible branches twine around me protectively. His fire affinity seeks out mine in small, bolstering flares, then, meeting no resistance from me, courses through my lines in a rippling stream.

It's like flame to spirits.

A reflexive shudder flashes through my body as fire lights in my vision and my magic surges with monstrous force, colliding and meshing with Lukas's in a sudden wave—fire, earth, air, and water power avalanching into his magery.

Lukas sucks in a hard breath, his whole body tensing as his grip around my hands tightens and my power overtakes him.

And I realize in this one brief, staggering moment...

*I've become much more powerful than Lukas Grey.*

Alarm gains hold and I jerk my hands away from Lukas's then stagger backward, balling my stinging wand hand into a fist as power continues to course through my lines, straining toward Lukas, my hand glowing scarlet and burning hot.

The world around us has grown dim, the grove's sapphire glow gone.

I glance wildly around, my breathing erratic.

The Ironflower blossoms behind us have all darkened, a palpable terror now emanating from the trees.

Lukas glares at the grove then sets his fervid gaze back on me, his own breath unsteady, his fire a lashing blaze. "Holy gods, Elloren. Your power's grown."

My mind is cast into full-blown war with itself.

*Tell him what you are. You need to tell him. Damion suspects, and he won't be unconscious forever.*

But I can't get the words out. Instead, I'm caught up in agonizing indecision as Ni Vin's warning blares in my mind—

*Don't let the Gardnerians know what you are.*

"Elloren," Lukas insists, stepping closer to me, his tone now rough and brooking no argument. "Tell me what's happened to you. What's quickened your affinity power to that level? If you could access it, that's Black Witch–level power."

I look to him, violently shaken by the force of my own magic as Lukas's hand comes tight around my arm, his own gaze catching fire. "I know you're back here for some reason that you're hiding from me," he says in a razor-sharp whisper, dire concern breaking through. *Tell me what's going on.*

I doggedly hold back.

*No, Lukas. Not until I know you've broken with all of Gardneria, not just Vogel.*

Lukas abruptly releases my arm and steps away from me, visibly upset.

My head is starting to throb, and Lukas's obvious frustration sets off a spiraling void deep inside.

*Rafe, Trystan, where are you? Yvan is dead and I need you. I don't know who to trust.*

"Where are my brothers, Lukas?" I demand, my voice cracking as anguish overtakes me. "Do you know anything about where they are? Are they even alive?"

Lukas glares as if furious with himself for being drawn in by me. "Yes," he finally says, and his anger seems to dampen. "To my knowledge, they are."

Jagged relief explodes through me as fresh tears sting my eyes.

Lukas looks up at the darkened trees and studies them for a moment. He looks back to me, one brow raised in strident question.

"Lukas…" I say, my head a pulsating ache, the thoughts coming in a rush. *I'm the Black Witch. And everyone is going to want to kill me or wield me. I want to tell you the truth. I want to trust you.* I close my eyes and press my forehead against my palms.

I can feel Lukas steadily watching me. "I don't know what to do," I relent, knowing I'm in over my head.

Leagues and leagues over my head.

Lukas remains quiet.

"You're right." I finally level with him as I open my eyes and glower in the Council Hall's direction. "I do need to get out of here." I meet his gaze once more. "With you."

Lukas nods as I hold his impassioned gaze, feeling scoured by sorrow and the lingering scald of so much power racing through my lines. "I'll need shoes," I admit. *Along with the ability to control world-destroying power.*

Lukas cocks a questioning eyebrow then considers the stockinged foot I kick out from under my skirts. He gives me an incredulous look, then nods, lifts his arm, and holds it out for me to take.

A flare of fire power passes between us as I thread my arm through his, my eyes wandering toward Lukas's identically fastmarked hands. But then a harder surge of my power drags my gaze to his *wand.*

I clench my wand hand tight and fight the urge to reach for his wand as my power continues to ratchet up.

Inhaling and exhaling breath after breath, I struggle to keep the power at bay as we set off together and I keep pace with Lukas's long stride.

We walk away from the ocean, through the eerie, still-darkened grove. As we stride out of the grove and toward a thin line of pine trees stretched out before us, I'm filled with a prickling sense of being watched.

I glance back over my shoulder and fear trills through me.

The dense Ironwood grove has regained its glow as if re-suscitated, its luminescent sapphire shimmer even stronger than before.

*Black Witch.*

The words scrape through me like dry leaves, and I turn quickly away, my body breaking into gooseflesh. I can feel the trees' smug defiance, as if the grove is making a show of power.

A sudden, harsh tug on my lines has my abdomen clenching. A tug emanating from the trees.

"The trees are pulling on my lines," I tell Lukas.

"They can't hurt you," he reassures me, voice low. He throws a quick glance back at the trees. "I can feel their hostility as well, but it's just an aura. Push it back with your fire."

Outrage sparking, I dredge up affinity fire and blaze it in an invisible wave toward the trees.

The entire grove recoils. I can feel it, deep inside, as tension releases from my lines.

As if the trees have lost their grip on me, but I can feel them scrabbling to regain their hold.

Outrage spikes to fury and I throw out another blast of invisible flame.

*Be my enemy*, I seethe at the forest. *Go ahead and try. What's one more? You're playing with fire if you try to come at me.*

Even as I think this, I can sense my grandmother's mounting power infusing my affinity lines.

Settling in.

Forming dark branches, a heightened fire, a stronger current of wind, and a steadier trickle of water.

I glance back down at the handle of Lukas's wand, both caught up in and terrified by my burgeoning desire to take his wand in hand and unleash my power through it.

# CHAPTER EIGHT

# PORTAL

## ELLOREN GARDNER

*Sixth Month*
*Valgard, Gardneria*

During the ride back to the Grey estate, Lukas is quiet, and so am I, both of us seemingly caught up in a silent struggle over how much to divulge to each other as I wrestle with a grief that threatens to tear me apart. Bars of light from a hanging lamp slide back and forth over Lukas's sculpted face, the two of us sitting opposite each other in his family's elegant carriage.

Lukas looks out the window as if lost in storming thoughts of his own, his brow deeply furrowed as the carriage makes its way through the vast farm fields that lie between the main city and his family's estate.

There's a grim weightiness to Lukas's demeanor that trumps his usual cool arrogance. Every so often he looks over, his jaw set tight, and considers me as if trying to work out a particularly vexing puzzle. Then he looks away again as I scrutinize him in the same conflicted manner, gutted by unassuageable sorrow.

And overwhelmed by the knowledge of Vogel's demonic power.

Power that's growing and rapidly becoming unstoppable. Vogel's forces are organized and aligned, whereas the forces that could stand against him are being pushed farther and farther east. And the Resistance seems intent on destroying one of its most powerful weapons.

Me.

I peer out the window and let my gaze wander across an expansive cornfield, the full moon casting a pallor over the small stalks, the scene as bleak as my emotions.

When I turn back to Lukas, he's watching me with an unblinking focus that's so intense it unnerves me. I drop my gaze and absentmindedly trace the swirling fastlines of one hand with the index finger of the other, considering the absolute permanence of the intricate, looping design.

They're beautiful, these fastmarks. There's no denying it.

A beautiful cage that would have kept me forever from Yvan.

Suddenly, the carriage jerks.

My hands splay against the carriage walls as I struggle to keep from pitching forward.

Before I have a chance to react, the carriage jerks again, hard, and I brace myself as the vehicle markedly speeds up and begins wobbling precariously from side to side. The movement of the lamplight bars is chaotic now, casting wildly about the carriage interior.

My eyes meet Lukas's. He's also braced himself and looks as surprised as I am.

A man's howl of terror slashes through the night air, and

the horses shriek. Lukas pulls his wand, his gaze fierce as he peers out the windows and motions for me to stay back.

Wide-eyed, I, too, look out the windows and frantically search the dark as a sickening realization washes over me. "Lukas—"

The carriage gives another violent jerk to the side.

Lukas reaches for me, his hand coming tight around my arm, steadying me as we both struggle for balance, his body tense and coiled as the carriage lurches about haphazardly and begins to veer on and off the road.

We hit a particularly painful bump, and the carriage pitches clear over and falls hard on its side.

Pain bursts as my head slams into the window and Lukas falls onto me. The hanging lamp smashes into shards that rain over us as its light snuffs out.

I look around, dazed, as Lukas shifts, lifting his weight off me in a shower of glass. I sit up. Stars wink in my eyes then give way to stars shining through the window that's now above me, the carriage's floor to my back, its roof before me as my heart thuds against my ribs. For a split second, all is ominously quiet but for the tinkle of broken glass falling from our bodies.

"They've come for me," I say, my throat cinching with fear, only half able to make out Lukas's features in the dark.

"Who's come for you?" he asks with confusion.

"The Kin Hoang."

Lukas's eyes widen. He grabs my arm, sending glass shards everywhere. Then he jerks me backward and tightens his grip on his wand. "Hold on to me," he orders, his voice sharp. "Don't let go!"

My hand grasps the side of his tunic as he raises his wand slightly higher and murmurs a spell through clenched teeth.

A fuzzy, glowing mist flies out of the tip of the wand, over him then over me like a second skin, the magical shield's buzzing energy coating me like millions of tiny flies bouncing uncomfortably off my skin as a metallic, whirring noise slices through the outside air.

The center of the carriage's roof explodes inward with a spray of sawdust as a small, silvery blur flies toward my head and slams straight into my shielded nose.

My head jerks back as pain blossoms, my eyes temporarily crossed from the blow as the sharp object bounces off Lukas's shield, ricochets back against the carriage's base, and comes to a clattering stop at our feet.

My stomach lurches.

*A silver star.* A Kin Hoang assassin's killing star.

Lukas turns to me just as a barrage of stars explode through the carriage's roof. I cry out as they strike my chest, my head, my limbs, beating me backward toward the carriage's base as Lukas holds on tight to me. It's like being hit by rocks while covered by a blanket, each blow leaving behind a new, throbbing ache, the stars clinking against each other as they fall to the carriage's side in a sharp pile.

And then it's over. The roof of the carriage before us now resembles a slice of salty Krillen cheese, full of irregular holes slashed liberally by the killing stars.

Lukas thrusts his wand straight out of the carriage's roof, grasps me tight, grows stone-still, and forcefully murmurs the words to another spell.

I recoil as an explosion of fire rips from his wand, cutting out all visibility as the flames engulf us and flow tight around the magic shield. It's like my one attempt to use a real wand, my desert inferno, all other sound cut off by the roar of the fire. The brightness of the flames forces my eyes shut and fills the world with red heat. The carriage wall beneath me gives way and we fall down into a concavity I can't see, the buzzing of Lukas's shield against my skin now hot and stinging.

Lukas clutches me close and I keep hold of him. I can't open my eyes. It's still too painfully bright.

Behind my eyelids, red rapidly turns to orange then yellow then blue. And finally black.

I open my eyes and gasp.

We're crouched in a smoldering pile of ash and rubble, a radius of charred ground all around, only one blackened carriage wheel still identifiable and spinning pathetically in the air. The horses are dead, their charred necks exploded, and so is our unlucky driver, whose burned body lies sprawled out on the singed ground, his neck a bloody mess and slashed almost clear through. Horror slashes through me at the sight of this innocent man so gruesomely slain.

Retreating hoofbeats sound, and movement catches our attention through the haze of smoke—a woman on horseback, both her rune-marked uniform and her horse dark as ash, racing up the sloping cornfield before us, her horse's hoofbeats muffled by the loamy soil.

Racing straight toward the moon.

Lukas tightens his hold on my arm and pulls me to my feet, the buzzing shield still uncomfortably pasted around us.

"Come on," he orders as he sets off in hot pursuit of the Kin Hoang, dragging me beside him.

Our attacker is bent low on her horse, rapidly gaining distance, and I recognize the style of her dark gray tunic marked with glowing blue Noi runes. There's a gray headband tied around her head and rune swords fastened to her back.

The uniform of the Kin Hoang—she's definitely one of the Vu Trin's elite assassins.

I stumble over jagged cornstalks as I struggle to keep up with Lukas, half running, half being dragged, the fancy embroidered shoes Lukas obtained for me just the wrong sort of footwear for chasing down assassins.

Lukas halts, one hand still clenched around my arm as he raises his wand and grinds out the words to another spell before the rider can crest the long hill.

Fire shoots from his wand, focused in a stream aimed directly at the woman's back.

Just before the stream of fire reaches her, a shimmering runic portal edged with luminous sapphire runes appears out of nowhere at the hill's crest, its gilded interior flowing like molten glass and blocking the moon from view.

The sorceress rides straight into the portal and is engulfed in the golden liquid, both rider and horse disappearing from view as Lukas's fire slams into the portal with a fierce roar. The fire curls up and around the portal's frame, setting the surrounding cornstalks alight.

Lukas releases my arm and runs to the portal, cursing angrily to himself.

I glance around with disbelieving eyes. The decimated carriage at the bottom of the field is still smoking, the dead horses and driver dark mounds on the road.

Remorse stabs through me once more over the death of this innocent stranger and the animals too.

I turn back to Lukas, who's come to a frustrated halt just in front of the shimmering portal and smoldering stalks of corn.

Breathing hard and dazed from the trauma of the attack, I slump and let my hands fall to my knees, my legs close to buckling as questions assault my mind.

Have the Vu Trin sent more assassins to strike me down? What happened to Chi Nam and my other Vu Trin allies? Will the entire Vu Trin army come after me now?

Should I tell Lukas what I am?

The remnants of Lukas's shield are now a faint buzz on my skin that rapidly dissipates to nothing. As the shield fades, the acrid smell of smoke comes rushing in.

# THE SHADOW WAND

I remain hunched over for a long moment, catching my breath. My emotions a blaze of mounting alarm, I lift my skirts to check my badly scratched ankles, then take a deep breath, straighten, and make my way up the hill toward Lukas. Everything hurts, from my star-bruised body to my scraped ankles to my throbbing head and nose.

When I reach him, Lukas is quietly stalking around the fading portal. Only a hazy wisp of its shape remains and shimmers in the air. Lukas passes his hand through it, as if evaluating it with equal parts admiration and frustration.

"The Noi are talented with portals," he says flatly, his lips taking on a rigid line.

He takes a deep, resigned breath, sheathes his wand, then pulls another wand out from under his tunic.

A wand that's marked with glowing Noi runes.

Lukas lifts this wand and murmurs a new spell at the misty portal. It promptly explodes into finer mist, then disappears.

For a moment, we both stand there, looking at the place where the portal once was.

"Couldn't you have used it?" I finally ask, since he's clearly no stranger to combining magical systems.

"No," he replies with a shake of his head. "There was no opening this portal. It's beyond me, anyway. The Vu Trin have a firm lock on portal magic. Well done, really."

In a rattled daze, I look down at the singed ground, at the marks the horses' hooves gouged out of the soil, the line of tracks coming straight from our destroyed carriage to where the portal once stood, where the hoof marks abruptly disappear.

"Elloren," Lukas says, his voice all tight control.

I look up, my stomach clenching at the unmistakable edge to his tone.

His eyes are fixed hard on mine. "Why was an elite assassin trying to kill you?"

I open my mouth…but nothing comes out. I'm still not sure I trust his allegiances enough to tell him the truth, and I'm unable to voice every lie that comes to mind.

He stands there waiting, as if he's ready to wait all night if he has to.

I fidget my foot away from the back of my shoe, where I can feel a blister forming, my mind a mess, unable to form a coherent thought. "Maybe…maybe I remind her of my grandmother?" I finally manage.

Lukas considers this as his eyes continue to bore a hole into me. "Elloren," he says again, as if desperately trying to remain civilized, "how long have you known that the Kin Hoang are targeting you?"

I hesitate, realizing how terribly foolish it was to not tell him. "A few days now."

He looks up to the sky as if praying for composure before bringing his gaze back to mine. "Perhaps, in the future," he says, "'Kin Hoang assassins are after me' could be among the very first things you say to me. Just after your initial greeting."

I nod in rattled agreement, the side of my head still throbbing from its collision with the carriage wall.

"Is anyone else after you?" he inquires. "Assassins of any type? Anything at all?"

"I don't know," I admit. I go silent, and Lukas's jaw tenses as he stares me down. I can tell he knows there's so much more that I'm not telling him.

Lukas lets out a measured sigh and rubs the bridge of his nose. Then he resheathes his rune-marked wand under his tunic and peers closely at me. "Come," he finally says, gesturing for me to follow him back down to the road. "This is a main route. We'll requisition the first carriage that comes along and set you up with a proper guard."

# CHAPTER
# NINE

# PREY

## ELLOREN GARDNER

*Sixth Month*
*Valgard, Gardneria*

It's not long before a carriage comes along and I'm sitting across from an elderly Gardnerian couple, the two of them staring at me with unwavering dubious expressions during the journey back toward Valgard. Lukas is seated outside with the driver where he can keep watch, wand in hand.

As the carriage bumps along, the feeling of overwhelming shock that initially buffered my emotions gives way to a stifling terror that I won't live to see another day.

I grip the Scarlet Elm of my seat's edging in a desperate attempt to stop the full-body trembling that's kicked up, my thoughts swirling in chaos. An image of the wood's source tree unfolds in the back of my mind—red serrated leaves, deeply furrowed trunk. But the beautiful image is able to shear only a slim edge off my panic.

Before long I'm disembarking in front of a military post on the outskirts of Valgard, unsteady on my shaking legs.

The garrison is lit by torches set on long iron poles and is made up of a collection of dark structures with walls formed from Ironwood trunks, twisting branches weaving into tangled roofs. A well-guarded central tree-building lies just ahead. This building is larger than the others and has the distinction of Gardneria's flag raised atop it, flapping in the evening's warm breeze.

Lukas strides to this central building, his tall form illuminated by the torches' wavering amber glow as he launches into conversation with a hard-eyed Level Five Mage who has come out to meet us, his uniform bearing the markings of a post captain.

The captain nods grimly as Lukas describes a significantly altered version of what transpired. In this new version, the Kin Hoang sorceress brutally killed our carriage driver and the horses, then attacked Lukas. Quickly realizing she was seriously outmatched, the sorceress turned and fled through a runic portal. Just before escaping, she threatened not only to come back for Lukas, but to come after me, his fasted partner.

Lukas tells the story smoothly, and it's accepted without question with grave nods and growled murmurs. I'm both relieved and alarmed by the fact that Lukas can lie so well to others.

The captain turns toward a sentry and barks out a list of soldiers' names. The sentry strides purposefully away. He soon returns flanked by a small contingent of young Mages, severe-featured Thierren among them.

Thierren's gaze catches mine for a moment, a flash of caution in the look that roils my emotions even more.

Most of the young soldiers nod with solemn deference as Lukas gives firm orders. Thierren simply listens, his face now impassive until I see him exchange a private, blazingly intense look with Lukas.

I ponder the exact nature of Lukas and Thierren's obvious alliance as I wait nearby in the night's shadows, sleeves pulled low to hide my bruised forearms, no longer able to hear all of what Lukas is saying over the clatter of our rescuers' carriage leaving and a new one arriving along with more soldiers on horseback. Six more soldiers emerge from the command structure, two of them wearing black cloaks bearing the five silver stripes of the magical elite.

They all make their way straight to Lukas with a determined cadence.

A young, expressionless soldier presents himself before me, momentarily cutting off my view of Lukas.

"Your carriage, Mage Gardner," he directs, hard insistence in his tone as he motions for me to follow him to the newly arrived carriage.

I hesitate, my heart picking up speed as I look to Lukas to make sure stepping into that carriage won't put me in more danger.

Lukas briefly meets my gaze and nods toward the carriage, his message clear.

*Yes. Get in.*

Capitulating, I incline my head and trail the young soldier, hoping the shadows of the night will hide the bruise pulsating between my eyes. Glancing up, I notice the new carriage is not being driven by a civilian but by two additional soldiers, and it bears the crest of the Mage Guard.

As I'm ushered to the carriage door's threshold, even more soldiers arrive on horseback. Panic builds as I worry that I'm teetering precariously on the line between guarded aristocracy and military prisoner.

*Do these soldiers suspect what I am? Where are they going to take me? Is Lukas completely in control of this situation?*

I climb in and sit on a velvet-cushioned seat, tensing at the sound of the door clicking shut as I clench and unclench my trembling hands in a futile effort to calm myself.

I flinch as the door abruptly reopens.

Lukas swings inside and sits down on the opposite seat. Then he shuts the door and levels his gaze at me.

My breath grows shallow. "Aren't you going to ride out there?" I ask, gesturing toward the front of the carriage. "To guard us?"

"No," he says, an edge of challenge in his expression. "We need to talk."

The carriage lurches forward, and we're quickly engulfed by soldiers on horseback. Thierren and the two black-cloaked Level Five Mages are among them, coming in and out of view through the carriage's side windows.

"Are we still going back to your family's estate?" I ask, my voice tight with nerves.

Lukas tilts his head and takes in my guarded demeanor. "We are." He fixes me with a look that reads, *Why? Should we be going somewhere else?* Then he reaches over and jerks first one window curtain shut, then the other.

I swallow.

Lukas sits back, his stare coldly serious, one hand loosely fingering the hilt of his sheathed wand. "Your nose," he says, pointing to the bridge of his own, "it has a bruise on it."

I reach up to touch it. It's sore, but not as sore as the rest of me.

"Tell me again why the Vu Trin's most elite band of assassins want to kill you," he presses.

I stare at him, my mind falling into a panicked whirl as my

lips part, the world-altering truth readying itself. But I hesitate as I remember again Ni Vin's stark warning.

Lukas seems to be an enemy of Marcus Vogel, that much is clear, and I believe him to be my friend and ally. But he also seems entrenched in the Gardnerian military.

Entrenched in being a Gardnerian.

And I won't be drawn in as a weapon for a faction of the Gardnerian army with questionable motives.

I'll fight for the Resistance and the Resistance alone.

Stalling, I let my head fall into my hands and rub my eyes and then the bruised side of my head, wanting a magicked portal of my own leading right to my brothers. "I hit my head really hard, Lukas," I bemoan, heart racing, desperate to divert his attention until I can learn more about where he stands. I peek up to see if I've roused his sympathy.

Lukas seems unmoved, his eyes narrowed on me.

I fidget and drop my hands to clutch the edge of my seat, feeling like an ant caught under the point of a stick. My fingers instinctively find the wood along the edge of my seat, just under the black velvet cushion. I restlessly scratch at it.

*Lacebark Pine.*

Soft and flimsy. And cheap. The whole carriage is cheaply made, nothing at all like Lukas's family's fine carriage with its even finer wood. Little pieces of the friable pine find their way beneath my nails.

*Delicious and porous.* Airy as a spring breeze and full of tiny places to fill with magic.

Small sparks of invisible magic flare under my nails, up my arm, cutting through my fear and grief, the feel of it like sparkling sunlight on water, inviting the power into my hands, my fingers, and straight through my lines. My nervous trembling smooths out, the throbbing all over my body cut in half as fire and earth magic sizzle through me. I bite the side of my mouth and flex my fingers, attempting to hide the effect the wood is having on me, feeling as exposed as if I had ten wands sticking out from under my nails.

"You lied to the soldiers," I say, fighting to ignore the sparks.

Lukas considers this, his brow tightening in thought. "If the Gardnerians find out the Kin Hoang have come for you, they'll grow suspicious of the power they sense in you. They'd immediately bring you to Vogel." He looks at my hands, and I self-consciously cease flexing them, realizing how odd the repetitive scratching must seem. And what conclusions he might draw from it.

"*You're* Gardnerian, Lukas," I remind him, taking a chance of feeling out whether he's still aligned with Gardneria, even though he's not with Vogel. He's talking about Gardnerians as if they're a group he's firmly on the periphery of, which gives me hope.

But he isn't listening. He's watching me, lost in an idea. "I'm going to wandtest you."

Power again sparks over my fingers like pine branches catching invisible fire. I can feel the entire framework of the carriage all at once, right down to the wheels making contact with rough road. "It's a waste of time," I scoff, heart pounding. "I've been tested several times."

*Once by my uncle, who quickly discovered that his three-year-old charge was the Black Witch and promptly went into hiding; once at university with a blocked wand; once with Yvan when I burned down a forest. And once by Vu Trin sorceresses who are now intent on killing me.*

Lukas's eyes harden. "Give me your wand hand," he insists, holding out his own.

"Why?" I curl my hands protectively in my lap, balling them into tight fists to try to douse the sparking power.

Lukas keeps his hand extended, insistent.

I eye his hand, realizing that if I refuse, I'll inflame his suspicions. Reluctantly, I reach out, filled with the acute sense that I'm rapidly sinking under a deep, inescapable tide.

Lukas takes my wand hand in his and gently pushes up the sleeve of my dress.

My arm is covered in angry bruises from the assassin's barrage of stars.

"She *really* wanted to kill you," he observes, sounding slightly mystified as he turns my arm over for inspection.

"You think so?" I nervously snipe. "I thought she meant it only as a warning. She seemed so *half-hearted* about it."

He glances up at me and purses his lips, as if mocking an assassination attempt is in poor taste, then goes back to studying my arm, the wheels of his mind visibly turning.

"I can feel it." His hand slides around my wrist, his thumb tracing an arc just below my palm. Small sparks trail in the wake of his touch, setting me further on edge. "There's power just below your skin," he murmurs. "More than in the past. *Much* more."

I pull my wand hand back toward me as I struggle to find a way to withhold the truth. "My uncle wandtested me," I insist, leaving out the giant explosion part. "I was tested at university. And... I tried out a wand while I was gone. All with the same results. *No more testing.*"

His brow furrows searchingly. "Are you back as a spy, then?"

"What?" I cough out. "For the same people who're trying to kill me?"

"You tell me, Elloren."

"I'm here for protection," I insist.

Lukas settles back in his seat. "I'd be willing to wager you're back for more than protection." His unflinching gaze is formidable. "I think you're back for information." He reaches into his tunic, pulls out Chi Nam's blue rune stone, and holds it up for my inspection.

Panic jolts through me. My hand reflexively slides over my pocket and the blood drains from my face when I find it flat and empty.

Lukas's mouth turns up in a dark grin. "Did you lose something?"

*I don't know. I've never seen it before. It's not mine.* The lying words stick tight to the base of my throat, caught there like fish in a net.

Lukas's smile inches wider. He tilts his head and holds the stone loosely, his hand resting on his thigh. "Did Chi Nam tell you we're acquainted?" He turns the stone over in his fingers. "We've been sparring for years. It's like a game of cat and mouse with her."

"Who's the mouse?" I shakily ask.

Lukas laughs and shoots me a sly grin. "We switch off." He narrows his eyes in consideration. "If Chi Nam wanted you dead, you'd be quite dead. So you must be in her favor for some reason. She certainly wouldn't have given you this if you weren't." He rubs slowly along the stone, trying to work it out. "Yet her people want to kill you. Interesting."

"Not all of them," I blurt, the compulsion to be honest with him building. "Maybe only…the one who came after me…"

"And that one was after you *because*…" he prompts.

I bite my lip in an effort to force back the truth, the wood shards under my nails now sending small spirals of fiery energy up through my wrists. The almost irrepressible urge to tell him everything is like an avalanche straining to break free.

For a long, agonizing moment Lukas studies me as he turns the stone over and over in his palm. Then, seeming to have worked out the puzzle, he clenches the stone tight and leans forward, his green eyes searing.

"Here's what I think. I think you're working for the Resistance and you've aligned yourself with the Vu Trin. But somehow they've sensed the growing power in your lines. Power that could easily be passed on to your children and lead to another Black Witch's emergence. Perhaps they toyed with the idea of killing you." He pauses, watching for a reaction. "But Chi Nam thought better of it, didn't she? She's letting you live because she wants something." He seems to take my troubled, stubborn silence as an affirmation and sits back, looking satisfied. "In any case, at least one sorceress was deeply alarmed by the power in your bloodline. Alarmed enough to go against Chi Nam's wishes."

I thrum my fingers, my dueling thoughts waging war on each other. Not telling Lukas the truth leaves me more vulnerable to further attack. *And Damion might suspect what I am.* But telling Lukas the truth would be just as dangerous if he's still aligned with the Gardnerians in any way. Part of me desperately wants to cling tight to him and not let go. Part of me wants to wrest the rune stone from his hand, leap from the carriage, and make a run for it.

"Will you go after her?" I ask. "The sorceress who escaped through the portal?"

Lukas shakes his head dismissively. "I have no idea where that portal led. And I suspect she'll be disciplined by her own kind if she did, in fact, go against Chi Nam's orders. Chi Nam's decisions carry a fair bit of weight." He rolls the stone to the tips of his fingers then raises it level with his eye, drawing my gaze to his. "Elloren, why did Chi Nam give this rune stone to you?"

*Dance around the truth, Elloren. Let him believe his version of events.* "Chi Nam gave it to me...in case there was trouble. To help me..."

"No," he cuts in, shaking his head. "Chi Nam's not one for

charity. She's ruthless in the defense of her people." He slips the stone into his pocket and leans in, his expression taking on a harder edge. "What did she send you here to find out?"

I bite at the sides of my mouth, trying to hold the answer back, but it bursts from my lips before I can contain it. "What is it that killed the Lupines, Lukas? It's that Wand, isn't it? Vogel's Shadow Wand."

Silence.

The question hangs in the air between us, dark and terrible.

Lukas's smug look has disappeared, his eyes turned to flint. And there's something else in his gaze that sends trepidation straight through me—fear.

"That wand," Lukas levels with me, "is the most powerful wand I've ever encountered. Yes, I think it was involved in the slaughter of the Lupines."

A chill snakes down my back as I remember the immobilizing effect Vogel's Wand has on me. The sudden destruction of Diana's people, all in one night, sent shock waves through all the Realms. It's monstrous, the power of that Wand—monstrous enough for even Lukas to fear it.

"You told me you're not aligned with Vogel," I say, leaning toward him as well, my voice hardening as I pin him with my stare. My gaze flicks over the silver Erthia orb on his chest. "Yet here you are, dressed in a Gardnerian military uniform after having overseen the annexation of Keltania. Lukas, I have to know. Are you still aligned with the Gardnerians *in any way?*"

Lukas withdraws, his mouth a tight line as if he's now struggling to hold back the truth from me as much as I've been struggling to hold it back from him.

"What are you hiding from me?" I press.

We hit a bump in the road, the wall lamp swinging. For a moment, we both freeze, our eyes locked. Lukas pulls back the window's curtain a fraction and glances out. Seeming satisfied that everything is fine, he lets the curtain fall shut and leans back in close.

"No, Elloren," he says succinctly, "I am not aligned with Vogel or the Gardnerians. I've been trying to work out the complicated wards that Vogel has placed around himself for some time now. So I can kill him. And I've just begun recruiting high-level Mages to work for the Vu Trin for the eventual overthrow of the Gardnerian government."

I stare at him, astonished and wildly relieved. Because I know what he says to be true since Lukas and I are unable to lie to each other.

"Your turn," he challenges, his gaze weighted. "Tell me *exactly* what's going on with your power."

My throat goes dry and tight. "It's grown," I admit in a rasp, barely able to voice the overwhelming truth that strains to break free. "More than you know."

"Then show me," he says.

I draw back at this. "What do you mean?"

"Kiss me," he says, his voice hard.

My eyes widen as an almost affronted confusion whips up inside me as well as an instant refusal to betray Yvan's memory so egregiously.

But there's nothing suggestive in Lukas's tone.

It's a challenge. A charge. And suddenly, I understand exactly what he's asking for.

"I can read the full extent of your power in a kiss," he says. "You know I can. Better than any other way. Kiss me once, Elloren. Show me what you're holding inside you. Show me *exactly* what scared the sorceress."

I can feel the blood rushing from my face as apprehension sweeps through me, my mind dazed by the power that the wood under my nails is drawing up through my lines.

*Show him, Elloren. He's not aligned with Vogel or the Gardneri-ans. And Yvan would want you to live and be protected. Let Lukas sense your power fully. It will take only one kiss for him to see.*

"I have more power than my grandmother," I caution, fully leveling with him as my throat constricts tight, my heart hammering as if I'm bracing myself for a lethal dive off a cliff.

Lukas's eyes narrow further. He slides forward into the slim space between us, his hand coming up to gently touch the nape of my neck. "Elloren," he says, softer now, his green eyes compassionate, "*show* me."

I reach up to touch the side of Lukas's face with my trembling wand hand.

As soon as my fingers make contact with the skin of his cheek, the splinters beneath my nails give a hard spark in response to Lukas's internal fire power, my whole hand unnervingly sensitized by the wood. I can feel Lukas's every line of magic, blazing with power just underneath his skin.

Fire, earth, air, and a slim line of water.

Our magery a perfect match, line for line.

Sinuous sparks of my own invisible magic trace through my arm, catching fire as they stream through the fingertips of my wand hand to flow straight into Lukas, my magic colliding with his in a heated, explosive rush, a back draft of fire searing through me.

Overwhelmed by the sensation, I move to pull my wand hand away, but Lukas catches my wrist and keeps my palm to his skin, his eyes widening.

"There's fire in your touch," he says, his voice husky. "Like a *torch*." Looking dazed, he brings my hand to his lips and kisses my fastmarked palm, as if trying to sense something in it, before pressing it back onto the side of his face.

My power gives another hard flare, and another burst of magic flashes through me and toward Lukas in a shuddering rush, fanning out over the skin of his cheek, my palm suddenly fused to him and taking on a molten glow as our lines strive to merge and weave through each other.

It's impossible to fight my fierce draw to his power, to hide the sudden magical craving in my lines, the savage pull of our matching affinities burning through all my grief and fear.

Only the magic remaining.

"Your fire was only in your kiss before." Lukas's words are rough with an obvious desire for my power, as well. "Now it's all over you."

We stare at each other as I struggle to keep control of the cataclysmic power that so desperately wants to fuse with his. That *strains* toward his lines.

Lukas closes in, his lips coming down on mine.

I gasp against his mouth as my obliterating power rushes toward his, rapidly merging with it and escalating into a wave of fiery, branching magic that forces my eyes wide and rocks me to the core.

Lukas draws back. "Put your other hand on my skin," he says raggedly as he grabs the sides of my skirts and pulls me closer.

I slide my hand up along the side of his neck, another rampant burst of my fire rushing to meet his.

Lukas kisses me deeply, the feel of our powers merging both startling and all-consuming. On some dim level, I know we're crossing too many dangerous lines and too fast, but the fire makes it impossible to care.

It builds, deliriously hot, a spiral of flame winding around us. Our affinity lines grab hold of each other with unrestrained force. Fire meeting fire. Branches winding. Air joining in a storming rush to fan the flames hotter. Our combined power caressing every line, impossible to resist.

Lukas pulls my body hard against his. I gasp against his

kiss as everything shudders and blazes crimson. The fire is everywhere, coursing through me, coursing into him, a roar in my ears blocking out sound, and I can feel every muscle of his body tighten, feel his deep groan in my mouth. Nothing exists but our combined fire, cutting out every last thing in the world.

Overcome, I yank my hands away from his skin, the fire fading enough for us both to suddenly realize that the carriage has stopped.

We break our kiss and turn to find the carriage's door being held open by Oralyyr, the Greys' stern-faced Urisk servant. She's regarding us both with a wide-eyed, stunned expression.

I freeze as the torchlit image just beyond her sears into my mind.

Just beyond Oralyyr stands High Mage Marcus Vogel, his green serpentine eyes fixed on Lukas, his dark Shadow Wand sheathed at his side.

Terror, like a hot iron, spears through me.

Vogel is flanked by Lukas's father, a young priest, and a sizable guard of Level Five Mages. And even more soldiers beyond.

Vogel's eyes meet mine for a split second, and the image of his dead Shadow tree crashes into my mind.

"Congratulations, Commander Grey," Vogel says, his reptilian stare sliding back to Lukas. "It seems you've triggered a war."

Lukas's gaze flies to mine as I lean back from him, desperately trying to blink away the image of the dead tree. Lukas cautiously exits the carriage and I follow him, my heart thundering against my chest. I watch Lukas as he takes it all in—the number of soldiers, his father's severe expression, and Vogel's surprising presence. No one dares even a smirk at our tousled state, and I'm overcome by the sense that some evil thing's hand is about to grab hold of me.

"We were attacked by a Kin Hoang," Lukas tells Vogel, his gaze darting around watchfully as he explains his false version of events. Lukas pulls Chi Nam's rune stone out of his pocket and casually holds it out for Vogel's inspection. "I suspect she was looking for this."

Vogel takes the glowing rune stone and turns it over in his hand before fixing his penetrating gaze back on Lukas. "Such a large sacrifice of Vu Trin for so small a prize."

Lukas's brow tightens in confusion. "There was only one Kin Hoang. Not an army." His response is met only by Vogel's withering stare. Lukas turns to his father for clarification, but Lachlan Grey only glowers back at his son with furious intensity.

The young, slender priest to Lachlan's left sneers. His priestly tunic is finely made, and he has Lukas's same riveting green eyes. "What are you playing at, Lukas?" he demands.

By now, Lukas has relaxed his expression into his usual impenetrable calm. He turns to me and loosely gestures toward the young priest. "Elloren, I don't believe you've had the pleasure of meeting my brother, Silvern."

Silvern ignores Lukas's attempt at pleasantries. "You were attacked by a Kin Hoang," he rages, "which is the equivalent of a call for *all-out war* on Gardneria, and *this* is how you behave?" He thrusts a hand out at me as if I'm the source of all trouble and disgrace that could possibly be visited upon his illustrious family.

"She escaped through a portal, Silvern," Lukas replies, as if humoring a fool. "There's not much to be done about it at the moment."

Silvern seems as if he momentarily loses the ability to speak and all the words ball up in his throat, threatening to explode.

"They've taken out a portion of our Eastern Command," Lukas's father states grimly.

For a moment, Lukas's careful veneer of calm is breached. "Who has?"

"The Vu Trin," his father replies. "They wiped out our base at the Spine's Eastern Pass. And now the Vu Trin are massing near the Pass, ready for movement. They're flying in dragons."

Shock explodes through me.

*An army. They're sending an army after me.*

Vogel tilts his head, his gaze fixed on Lukas.

A terrifying dread worms its way into me. I think of small desert vipers. There's that same look in Vogel's eyes—fast, deadly, and completely devoid of mercy.

"We've just apprehended a sizable contingent of Kin Hoang, moving in the direction of your carriage," Vogel says to Lukas, his voice smooth as a blade. "They were carrying maps of your family's estate. And they had records containing every last detail regarding your command and your travels." Vogel's gaze intensifies. "So, Commander Grey, all this begs the obvious question—what could you *possibly* have, besides this one rune stone, that the Vu Trin want?"

Everything slows to a dreamlike pace, everything around us muffled, receding. Lukas swivels his head to meet my gaze for a split second, each blink a wave of deepening comprehension washing over him as his eyes lock on to mine with ferocious urgency.

*He knows. Lukas knows.*

*He knows I'm the Black Witch.*

There's no chance to react as everything snaps back into vivid focus.

Lukas's face morphs into an impassive mask as he turns back to Vogel. "I don't know, Your Excellency."

I inwardly shrink, like a mouse backed against a wall watching the cats convene, knowing it's only a matter of time before they take a very strong interest in me.

"It's one thing to play at war games with Chi Nam," Vogel says to Lukas. "Quite another to stage an arbitrary attack on her. When were you planning on reporting the stolen rune stone?"

Lukas's jaw tightens. "When it became relevant."

It's clear from Vogel's icy grin that this is *exactly* the wrong answer. He turns to Lukas's father. "Send out the Fourth Division to help secure the Pass." He fixes his gaze back on Lukas. "Commander Grey, you're to accompany me back to the Valgard Base. We have quite a bit to discuss."

Vogel's guards move in around us.

Lukas bows respectfully to Vogel. "Of course, Your Excellency. May I request a moment to secure my fastmate's protection?"

Vogel sets his serpent eyes back on me, and tendrils of Shadow snakes rush through my lines. I stiffen, frozen in place and unable to even pull in a breath, all my focus wrenched toward the Shadow Wand Vogel has sheathed at his side, his fist curled around its hilt. Vogel turns back to Lukas, and the spell breaks, air rushing back into my lungs as my body is freed up and Vogel nods his assent.

Lukas strides to Thierren, who is standing to one side with the guards who accompanied us here. He gives Thierren a series of instructions I can only half make out as Vogel watches them both with malefic intensity.

Lukas and Thierren speak for a moment longer, the other soldiers, Lachlan Grey, and priestly Silvern falling into low conversation with each other. Lachlan deferentially asks Vogel a question, drawing his serpent gaze.

Seemingly taking advantage of Vogel's break in focus, Lukas strides back to me with a quick glance toward Vogel. "I'll come for you when I can," he states, his expression and tone oddly formal. He embraces me stiffly and leans in for a farewell kiss.

As his lips make contact with my cheek, his hand clenches around my arm, tight as a vise. *"Your power,"* he hisses into my ear, too low for anyone to hear. *"How much can you access?"*

I choke out my whispered answer, terrified. *"All of it."*

Lukas pulls back. And when his eyes lock on to mine, I'm horrified to see fear there. Fear for me. He leans in again, his hand clenching harder, his whisper full of fierce urgency. *"Tell no one."*

Feeling unable to breathe, I force a nod. I can see him trying to convey an extreme sense of danger with his expression alone.

Mage Vogel's Level Five guards close in around us, waiting for Lukas to follow.

Lukas releases my arm and shoots me one more brief, intense look. It scares me, how hesitant he is to leave. Without him I'm incredibly vulnerable. But there's no choice. Not with Vogel waiting.

Masking his feelings, Lukas gives me one final perfunctory bow.

And then he's gone.

# CHAPTER
# TEN

# ORDERS

## ELLOREN GARDNER

*Sixth Month*
*Valgard, Gardneria*

*Escape.*

It's foremost in my mind as I scan the stout backs of the guards stationed outside my bedroom's diamond-paned windows.

Anxiety tightens my chest.

More soldiers on horseback are riding in just beyond the guards outside. I turn and take in my bedroom's heavy Iron-wood door, knowing two more soldiers are posted just outside this room.

*A trap closing in on both me and Lukas.*

An image of Vogel's malevolent Shadow Wand fills my mind as well as a remembrance of his terrifying magic. Magic he'll consume me with if he finds out what I am.

But then the vision of another Wand blazes into being—a

Wand able to send out the image of a starlight tree to wind around and destroy Vogel's Shadow tree.

The Wand I'm a Bearer of.

The Wand of Myth.

My actions hidden by the bed's side, I kneel down and hastily retrieve the Wand of Myth from inside the lining of my travel sack, lantern and woodstove light flickering over me as, with trembling hands, I fold back the edges of the handkerchief the Wand is wrapped in. Even though its ability to channel magic went dormant when Trystan last tried to wield it, power leaps through my lines at the sight of it, straining toward the Wand's pale wood.

Everything in me yearns to touch it, and I'm careful not to let its spiraling wood make contact with the skin of my wand hand. Instead, I stare at the Wand, almost mesmerized. Its wood is so beautiful—opalescent with an underlying glow.

As if it contains a guiding star in its bright depths.

A frisson passes through my lines as I'm caught up in the sense that the Wand is staring back at me.

Without warning, an image of white birds explodes into my vision, then a Shadow tree, then a flash of bright light, one image after another in staccato bursts. My head jerks back, a rush of energy coursing over me as I'm filled with the sudden, innate sense that it's desperately important to keep this Wand close.

And to not let Vogel get hold of it.

My pulse thundering, I wrap the handkerchief tight around the Wand, shove it into the side of my boot, and pull my skirts down over it.

My sense of danger surges, triggering the fearsome desire to press my hands onto every piece of wood in sight and release an inferno of fire.

Curling my wand hand into a fist, I sit down on one of

the cushioned chairs set by the woodstove and pry the slivers of pine from the carriage out from under my nails. Then I slump forward and press my palms hard against my eyes, my breaths coming in a tight, irregular rhythm as I struggle to keep hold of myself.

*Calm down, Elloren. You need to be strong. What would your brothers want you to do? What would all your loved ones want you to do?*

Diana Ulrich's fierce image fills my mind, my Lupine sister always so courageous in the face of any threat. I cling to the remembrance of Diana's unflappable bravery as my breathing steadies and my heartbeat tamps down to a more normal rhythm.

My savage yearning for wood slightly abated, I sit up and rest my wand hand, palm up, on my knee and take in the curling black fastlines.

My gaze flits toward the guards stationed just outside the windows.

*If Lukas doesn't return, I can slink out the window and crouch down behind the maze of shrubs and then flee.*

*And they'll promptly catch me.*

I clench my wand hand tighter, snared by desperation.

*Will Vogel send you to find me, Lukas? What am I going to do if he's sent you away instead?*

*I'll escape is what I'll do.*

*Ha! If the Vu Trin don't kill me first! And if they don't succeed, the Gardnerians will quickly figure out the Vu Trin aren't after Lukas—they're after me.*

I sit there, mired in a fierce back-and-forth war with myself, as the sound of a door opening breaks into my thoughts and my pulse speeds up.

Heavy footsteps thud into the sitting room that abuts my

bedroom, and I bolt up from the chair and quietly creep to my bedroom's door.

Lachlan Grey's ironhard voice booms out. "You're dismissed."

More heavy boots sound as the guards just outside my bedroom door walk away, their steps growing fainter until the door at the far end of the sitting room closes once more with a firm thud.

Quiet descends.

"So," Lachlan Grey finally says, his words slow and even. "You've been stripped of rank."

"Temporarily."

Relief explodes through me at the sound of Lukas's unfazed voice.

*Sweet Ancient One, he's here.*

I slowly unfasten the door's lock, praying Lukas's father won't hear the soft click of metal disengaging metal. I open the door a parchment-slim crack and peer through.

Lukas is standing by the room's crackling fireplace, its guttering light cast over the bookshelves and tree-supported walls. There's a clink of crystal on crystal as he pours himself a drink from a bloodred carafe. He picks up the flask and casually rests one elbow on the fireplace's black granite mantel, his side to me as he sips his drink and watches his father through hawk-steady eyes.

His father matches his son's coolly casual demeanor, one hand on the back of a chair, the other loosely on his hip, but I can feel the pent-up anger coming off of Lachlan Grey in waves.

"May I ask you why you had Chi Nam's rune stone?" Lachlan's words are dangerously clipped.

Lukas shoots him a cagey smirk. "A trophy." He pulls the stone from his tunic's pocket and tosses it to his father, who deftly catches it.

Lachlan considers the small onyx stone, its imprinted rune

activated to glow a soft, otherworldly sapphire, and I wonder if Lukas has been testing its sorcery. Lachlan's gaze darts back to his son. "Vogel allowed you to keep this?"

"For now."

Lachlan frowns and turns the stone over in his hand. "The Vu Trin moved on the Thirteenth Division for *one stolen rune stone*?"

"I've made three recent attempts on Chi Nam's life. Mock attempts, mind you. To make a point." Lukas's eyes gleam with mischief. "It seems to have annoyed them."

*Oh, Lukas. You cool liar.*

Lachlan scowls, his voice taut with anger as he tosses the stone back. "Wipe that smirk off your face. You've provoked a war."

"That they cannot win. That they're exhausting all their Western forces on. For an ill-guided suicide mission fueled by pride."

Lachlan glares at his son. "What did Vogel make of your games?"

Lukas considers his glass. "I think he was partly amused." His expression darkens. "Partly not."

"You have been sparring with that woman *far too long.*"

Lukas smiles, catlike. "She's clever. Delightfully unpredictable."

"This is *no game.*"

"So I've been told. I'm to redeem myself by killing her." He shakes his head in obvious dismay. "A waste."

"Lukas, you have talent and power, to be sure." Lachlan's biting off the words now. "But you would do well to have some of your brother's commitment and his gravity. That woman is *Vu Trin.* And their most powerful sorceress, at that. And now, thanks to you, we're embroiled in a war with her kind. Yet you speak of her with fondness. Where is your loyalty?"

Lukas's expression hardens. "By sparring with her, Father, I learn what they can do. The limits of their rune sorcery."

Lachlan grows quiet, seeming to consider the point.

Lukas swirls his glass absently, flashes of gold from the firelight reflecting off the crystal. "I have one month to assassinate Chi Nam, or Vogel's revoking my command. And he'll place me under the command of Damion Bane."

"Perhaps an incentive you'll understand and heed."

The side of Lukas's mouth lifts. "And I need to control my lovely fastmate."

The hairs on the back of my neck bristle with alarm.

"The Gardner girl is trouble." Lachlan scowls. "Your mother's distraught over this fasting, and you know how I feel about the girl."

"Yes, well, you've both forgotten what's in her blood."

Lachlan tips his head in consideration as the fireplace crackles. "She's from the strongest of bloodlines, to be sure," he tersely allows. "There is no finer line."

"Vogel senses the power in her," Lukas says, matter-of-fact. "He knows she can't access it, but our children would likely be quite powerful. Vogel wants me to sire an army of Mages brimming with Carnissa Gardner's blood." He raises his glass slightly in a loose toast. "He's insisting on a Sealing ceremony. Tomorrow night."

The blood rushes from my head.

*He's lying. He has to be lying.*

"Vogel will preside over the sacred occasion himself and reset the spell," Lukas continues.

Shock blasts through me anew, the room seeming to shift, the walls closing in.

*No. I can't have that Shadow Wand anywhere near me.*

Lukas takes another sip from his glass and looks at his father through narrowed eyes. "That's how much power Vogel senses in her, Father. Enough to take an evening to see us properly sealed, even with Vu Trin staging war games along the Eastern Pass."

When Lachlan finally speaks, his tone is astonished. "So, we're to pull together your Sealing ceremony in one day's time? With war breaking out?"

"The Vu Trin attack has been all but put down. And the Sealing can be a small affair."

Lachlan's tone grows rigid with anger. "Have you forgotten who you are?"

"I don't have time for the nonsense attached to Sealing ceremonies."

"High Mage Vogel is presiding!"

Stunned, I move a fraction away from the door, the full implications of a formal Sealing rushing over me, along with the fear of an army intent on destroying me.

Shaken, I peer back out at them.

They're staring at each other, neither one relenting.

Lachlan finally lets out a heavy sigh. "Well, as much as your mother hates the girl, she does want grandchildren to carry on our line of power. And we're *certainly* not going to get them from your pious brother."

Lukas sips his drink, his green eyes glinting. "See, Father, there are some advantages to my lack of piety."

A harder anger flashes across Lachlan's face. "Well, then, seal the fasting and breed on the girl. And quickly." Outrage bursts inside me as Lachlan shoots Lukas a look of derision. "From what we saw earlier, at least in *that* you won't have much of a fight."

Lukas smiles lazily at him as anger rises in me, swift and potent, wildfire racing through my lines.

Lachlan shakes his head, his expression of ire softening. "A grandchild *will* lessen the blow of this disastrous fasting and placate your mother. She despises the girl."

"Her attempt to set the Banes on Elloren made that quite clear." Lukas's tone is meticulously pleasant, but I sense the sudden surge of his fire, as well.

Lachlan glowers at him. "Your mother senses defiance, and so do I. The girl needs a firm hand to bring her to heel."

"Compared to Chi Nam, I don't imagine she'll pose much of a challenge."

Lachlan shoots him a wry look. "No, I imagine not."

*Oh, Lachlan, you bastard. You have* no *idea.*

The two men stare at each other for a protracted moment.

Lachlan narrows his eyes at Lukas. "Why did you let her run loose for more than a month? Be honest with me this time." He says it calmly enough, but there's steel underneath his tone, and I wait, my breath suspended.

Lukas meets Lachlan's gaze squarely. "I was rather busy with the annexation of Keltania." His expression darkens as he looks down at the glass in his hand. "And I was deciding whether or not to dispose of her." He fixes his gaze once more on his father, who nods, seeming somewhat satisfied by this as my fury grows.

"She's quite bruised," Lachlan says. "Is that all from the Vu Trin?"

"Some," Lukas acknowledges. His jaw tightens. "I took her in hand."

Lachlan averts his eyes. "Ah. Unfortunate. But necessary." He looks sidelong at his son. "There is potential for power there," Lachlan considers. "Vogel's right. Your children could claim quite the magical inheritance. As long as you *control* them."

"We'll raise them here," Lukas says, seeming disinterested. "You and Mother can control them as you see fit."

Loathing takes hold. *What exactly are you plotting here, Lukas?*

Lachlan nods, seeming satisfied. "That uncle of theirs let the Gardner girl and her brothers run loose and wild. You can see what came of that."

And that's when the rage unfurls.

I grasp quick hold of my wand hand, digging my nails into it as I battle back the urge to send fire straight through the door and Lachlan Grey, my fierce grief for Uncle Edwin fueling an urge to violence that's almost impossible to suppress.

Lukas gives his father a chilly smile. "Are we quite done, Father? I've matters to attend to."

Lachlan stiffens. "Where are you going?"

Lukas sets down his drink, shoots his father a knowing look, then gestures to my room with his chin. "To bring her further to heel."

Power roars through my lines, and I dig my nails deeper into my wand hand.

"Keep her pure till tomorrow eve," Lachlan insists. "Do you hear me? Take your sport with her how you like, but keep her fastinglines pure for the Sealing. You've bucked tradition *enough*."

"I'll keep her pure," Lukas promises unconvincingly as he starts for my room.

The second his face is out of his father's sight, Lukas drops his grin. It's quickly replaced by an expression of intense urgency.

I click the door shut, my heart hammering in my chest, an inferno coursing through my lines. I need time to disperse my power. And to sort out what's true and what's false in what I've just heard.

*It was a terrible mistake, coming back here.*

The thought gains traction as the magic strafing through me ratchets higher, a stiff thread of defiance tightening my gut.

On impulse, I reach out toward the door and throw the lock firmly into place.

# CHAPTER ELEVEN

# ALLIANCE

## ELLOREN GARDNER

*Sixth Month*
*Valgard, Gardneria*

Tiny black vines curl through the door's brass lock, and it clicks open.

Lukas opens the door, strides into the room, and shuts it, then sets the lock back into place as the vines disappear.

He cocks a brow at me. "You honestly thought you could lock me out?" He glances back at the door's lock before shooting me a look of incredulity.

I grab a wooden-handled hairbrush from the vanity beside me and level it at him threateningly, my power streaming toward the wood in a staggering rush.

My arm trembles as I back away a step, a cornered defiance whipping through me. "I heard everything you and your father just said, Lukas. And now you're going to listen to *me*. There's no way I'm going to let you or Vogel or anyone else control me. And I am *not* fully Sealing this fasting."

Lukas calmly takes in the hairbrush. He nods, his gaze darting once more to the door, then back to me. "Elloren," he says, a sliver of urgency running through his measured tone, "put the hairbrush down."

"I don't know what to believe," I throw out at him as chaotic power sparks through my arm, straining toward the River Maple brush, "but if one single thing that you told your father is true, I *will* fight you, Lukas. You have no idea what I'm capable of."

Lukas splays his hands out in a conciliatory gesture. "I kissed you. I have a pretty good idea." He turns one hand over and holds it out, palm up, his tone calm but firm. "Elloren, give me the brush."

Jaw clenched, my hand trembling with indecision, I lower the brush a fraction.

Lukas loses his easy expression, strides over to me, takes the brush in hand, then opens the woodstove's glass door and throws it into the fire, flames rearing as the brush ignites. Then he moves to the windows and tugs the curtains shut.

He turns and closes in on me, his voice a determined whisper. "You need to tell me *everything*."

My outrage hardens. "Was anything you just said to your father true?"

Lukas's face tenses with concern. "No. Except the part about Vogel insisting on a formal Sealing."

My thoughts cyclone as I glare up at him. "I want to be able to trust you."

He loosens a breath, his gaze steady on mine. "Elloren," he calmly but firmly says, "I can't lie to you. You know that. Just like you can't lie to me." His lips quirk into a jaded half smile. "Believe me, I've tried."

I turn this over in my harrowed mind. He's right. If anything, our Dryad pull to honesty seems to be getting stronger.

The corner of Lukas's mouth lifts further. "Go ahead. Try it," he prods. "Try lying to me. Tell me…" He pauses, his gaze turning inward as if he's searching for a suitable lie. He levels his eyes back on mine, his smile playing at the edges of his mouth. "Tell me that you don't find me attractive."

I gape at Lukas, deeply put off by humor at such a time. I square my shoulders and narrow a glare at him. "I don't find…" The words cinch in like a wall closing in around my throat. Like choking without the loss of air. I struggle to push the false words out, to fling them at him, but they stay caught. I force out a growl of frustration instead.

Lukas's feral grin widens. "I wouldn't be able to say it either."

"I find you *infuriating*!" I spit out. "*There*, that's easy to say." I pull back from him, my emotions a tumult as I shoot him a potent glare. "Chi Nam is my *friend*. I don't want you to kill her even if you're ordered to. She was kind to me when no one else was."

Lukas gives a wry laugh. He pulls Chi Nam's rune stone from his tunic's pocket and hands it to me.

I take it from him and thrust the rune stone protectively into my tunic's pocket, running my fingers over the smooth stone, yearning for its calming aura as my emotions churn.

Lukas leans in. "Chi Nam is a friend to the Vu Trin political agenda. Period." He lifts a finger to swiftly trace the side of my neck. "Thwart that, and she'll slit this pretty little throat of yours without a moment's hesitation."

I back away from his touch and toward the canopy post behind me.

It's all too much, such matter-of-fact talk of someone murdering me. I glance around blankly, the whole situation surreal and bearing down on me. My hand finds the canopy post and I grip the Ironwood, my unstable power flaring violently inside of me.

Lukas's hand comes back to my arm, his look of urgency back. "Tell me *exactly* how much power you can access."

Tears sting at my eyes as I cling to the post. "More than my grandmother ever had," I say, my voice a low rasp. "They took me to the desert. To train me."

"The Vu Trin?"

I nod tightly. "They gave me a flimsy wand. I said the candle-lighting spell." I pause, remembering. My mouth pulls down into a trembling grimace. "There was an ocean of fire. If they hadn't put up a shield, I would have killed everyone I was with. I killed Ni Vin's horse. I *melted* it."

Surprise lights Lukas's eyes. He pulls in a deep breath. "You did *that*. With the *candle-lighting spell*?"

I nod and tell him everything.

When Lukas speaks, it's slow and with emphasis, his tone disturbingly matter-of-fact. "We have at most two days before the Vu Trin kill you or Vogel figures out you're the Black Witch."

A harder panic takes hold and I swallow, desperation surging. "Can we get out of here?"

"We're surrounded by Vogel's entire guard."

"So, what do we do?"

He sharpens his gaze on me. "We stage a diversion and escape."

Clarity descends. "The Sealing ceremony."

"Yes," Lukas affirms. "Vogel might have just handed us a way past him by forcing this on us."

Dread rises at the thought of that Shadow Wand anywhere near us both.

"Lukas, Vogel's Wand has demonic power in it, and he'll use it to reset the Sealing spell."

He nods, jaw tense, a hard look in his eyes. "We're going to have to risk having the magic reset with that Wand. I can't think of a way around it."

A maelstrom of emotions war inside me. "But you think we might have a chance of escaping?"

"We might. I think a formal Sealing will provide the *ultimate* distraction. Gardnerians love Sealing ceremonies. The vicarious thrill of a virgin's deflowering. And not just any virgin, mind you—Carnissa Gardner's granddaughter."

Ire rises, overtaking my near panic. "That's in really poor taste, Lukas."

"The whole thing is in incredibly poor taste," Lukas concurs, surprising me. "And we're going to use it against them."

A hard spark of triumph lights within me at the idea of using the Gardnerians' awful wandfasting traditions as a weapon aimed squarely at them.

"When would we leave?" I venture.

Lukas hesitates. "I can think of only one window."

My mind casts about, quickly lighting on that window.

The Blessing of Dominion. It would have to be then. The morning after the Sealing ceremony and just after the Sealing breakfast. When the couple is required, by *The Book of the Ancients*, to enter the wilds alone and scatter the ashes of a destroyed tree to symbolize the Magedom's dominion over Erthia, the time spent in the woods open-ended.

"The Blessing of Dominion," I say.

He gives me a weighted look. "It would have to be then."

The full implications of this wash over me. We wouldn't just be resealing our fasting as a ruse. To get past Vogel, we'll have to really seal it this time, the consummation of our union absolutely required to fully set the magic, our fastlines flowing down our wrists afterward and blessed by the priest at the Sealing breakfast.

Blessed by Vogel.

And after that, the Blessing of Dominion.

An uncomfortable flush heats my neck as an aching grief takes hold. Nothing was supposed to be like this. I was supposed to be with Yvan.

*Who would want me to survive.* Even if it means putting aside my shattered heart to align with someone else in every way.

"The Blessing provides a good window," I say, the tenacious will to escape hardening inside me even as grief shears through my emotions.

"It's the only gap in their defenses I can find," Lukas says, his brow tensed. "I'd leave now if we could. But we're surrounded. And being carefully watched. Both of us."

A new fear sparks. "Do you think Vogel suspects what I am?"

Lukas's split-second hesitation causes that spark of fear to catch flame.

"No," he finally says. "If he did, he'd have brought you into custody by now. But I think he suspects that you're a traitor like your brothers. Vogel can sniff out rebellion and, Elloren, you reek of it."

My defiance heats up. "Unlike you, with your unquestioning obedience?"

"They don't question my loyalty," Lukas counters. "Just my morality and gravity."

"And your piety," I acerbically note.

Lukas spits out a bitter sound. "There is my complete lack of piety."

Our gazes lock and hold for a brief moment, a new understanding seeming to solidify between us.

"A Sealing will likely dampen their suspicions about both of us," I cede, giving him a jaded look.

Lukas nods, meeting my look with a cynical one of his own. "You'll need to act broken. And firmly under my control."

"I know," I snipe, fire ratcheting up at the thought. "But one thing needs to be clear, Lukas. Regardless of what they'll all think, I *won't* let you control me. And you'll never own me. Even if we seal this fasting."

Lukas's look turns blazing in its intensity. "We are *friends*," he says emphatically. "And as such, equals. I want you to control *yourself*. And I want you to come into full control of your power."

Moved by his sentiment, I think on how Lukas relinquished all control over me after our fasting. When he could have, by law, mandated my every move.

I study him, his intense gaze unwavering, as some of the force of my defiance lessens. I believe him. And I know that we've fallen into an unexpected but genuine alliance.

An alliance that could serve something far bigger and more important than us both.

As if sensing my changing feelings, Lukas's lips form a grim smile. "Play the submissive fastmate for the moment. Once you're trained in the use of your power, Vogel will be intimidated by *you*. Along with everyone else on Erthia."

I cast him an edgy look, unable to keep the resurgence of outrage from my tone. "I heard your whole conversation with your father, you know. He really loves the idea of you beating me."

Lukas lets out a short laugh, tinged with disgust. "Because that works so well. He beat me regularly throughout my entire childhood."

I inwardly wince at this as I hold his gaze, a moment of emotional candor passing between us. Outraged now on his behalf, I give him a look of solidarity. "You are the absolute *picture* of docile submission."

Lukas gives another short laugh but then his smile fades. There's genuine concern in his gaze now. Concern for me.

I inhale as I glance down at our fastmarked hands. "I will admit," I say as rebellion simmers inside me, "part of me likes the idea of using the Magedom's horrid fasting traditions against them. It's awful. Especially for women."

"It is," Lukas firmly concurs, a shrewd glint forming in his eyes. "So, we weaponize it. And aim it directly at them."

His words stoke my rebellion as I glance once more at the matching lines on our hands, feeling heartened that Lukas holds as much contempt for the "Sacred" Sacraments of Fasting and Sealing as I do.

Agreement settles between us, surprising in its strength.

"There was a time," I admit, "when I seriously considered fasting to you. You should know that. And it wasn't just for your money. Or your power."

A flash of warmth ignites in Lukas's eyes as his affinity fire momentarily escapes his control. "Elloren," he says, his tone gaining an impassioned edge, "I wanted to fast to you from the moment I first laid eyes on you."

Remorse and grief well up inside me in response to his heated admission. My eyes prick with tears that I struggle to blink back. Because I do have feelings for Lukas, but the loss of Yvan is a spear clear through my heart.

Overwhelmed by conflict and sorrow, I look at Lukas, staring into those forest green eyes of his. Lukas reaches up to caress my cheek, my hair, his touch featherlight, his expression slightly pained. Moved by his attempt to comfort me, I wipe away my brimming tears and pause at the brink of this new thing between us as I take in the level of emotion in Lukas's eyes.

I feel devastated by the loss of Yvan. But circumstances will not allow time for my heart to recover. And Lukas is here, ready to fight alongside me. Ready to risk his own life for me and bind himself to me in every way.

"I want you to know," I haltingly tell Lukas, "that in time... I feel like I could care for you as more than a friend. Possibly a great deal. But right now..." Grief for Yvan constricts my chest, choking off the words.

Lukas's eyes tighten, the pain in them edged with understanding. His arm drops to my shoulder, but his touch remains gentle and comforting, his thumb tracing a short line back and forth across the silk of my tunic.

My voice is throaty with tears when it comes. "I can't seal to you purely for escape. Not if we're going to consummate it. I know we're both being forced into this, but...if I'm going to be sealed to you, I have to actually be *sealed* to you."

Lukas stays quiet, and it feels like we can both sense the seismic emotional shift happening between us.

"I want to be sealed to you," Lukas states unequivocally. "Truly sealed."

Feeling like I'm quietly taking a dive off an impossibly high cliff, I press back my grief and meet his deep-green gaze steadily.

"All right, Lukas," I say, holding his fervent stare. "Let's truly seal this fasting."

Lukas's expression shifts, the gravity of this decision stark in it, stark in us both. "Tomorrow eve," he finally says, his voice pitched low. "Mother will arrange things."

My hackles rise, the mention of his mother reminding me of the dangers at hand and slicing through this moment of closeness between us. "Lukas, I'm certain your mother arranged for the Banes to attack me."

Lukas frowns. "Damion Bane won't be attacking anyone anytime soon," he says, a hard glint forming in his eyes. "I won't be killing Chi Nam, but he *is* on my list."

Trepidation spikes. "Damion may be suspicious about me. He sensed my power when he attacked me."

"We'll be long gone before his suspicions are of any consequence."

"But your mother...she's a real threat. She wants to drive me out of the Realm. Or worse."

"Well, she can't drive you out," he says shortly. "Not with Vogel presiding at the Sealing. And the minute there's a possibility that I've got you with child, she'll leave you alone."

I cough and emphatically slice through the air with both hands. "*No one* is getting me with child."

Lukas shoots me a look of incredulity. "Elloren, of course not. I've Sanjire root."

I'm relieved to hear he has the pregnancy-preventing root, but still, anger churns hot over Evelyn and Lachlan Grey's cruelty, particularly toward women. "Your family is *vile*," I spit out at him.

Lukas's face tenses and the anger and bottomless hurt that's momentarily laid bare in his expression is so intense that I instantly regret saying this.

His mouth rearranges itself into a tight line. "Yes, Elloren. I *know* my family is vile."

Instantly abashed, I hold Lukas's intense gaze, trying to convey that I'm sorry for the harshness of my words even though the sentiment is true. Understanding seems to pass between us, his expression losing its severe edge. I bring my hand up to massage my newly aching forehead as my mind casts about, attempting to piece together this plan for escape.

"So...we'll be sealed tomorrow night," I say.

Lukas nods. "And leave the next morning."

I cough out a laugh in response to his brazen level of understatement. "You mean we'll run for our lives."

Lukas's confident aura doesn't budge. "We'll have to travel

over the mountains to avoid the current hostilities at the Pass, but yes, we'll need to get East as fast as we can. And from there to Noi lands, where I'll train you in the use of your magic and organize an army."

I eye him with disbelief. "The Vu Trin want me dead, Lukas."

"We'll win them over."

"But…"

"We'll convince them by force if necessary. We need their dragons."

"You think we can make it through the desert all the way to Noi lands?"

"That's the wild card in all this, but I believe we can get there. If we're lucky. The Sealing might buy us enough time and enough of a lead to get to the Eastern Realm." Lukas lets out a long breath. "We have to get out soon in any case because Vogel is rune warding the entire border."

My heart twists as I think of Sparrow and Effrey and of all the Urisk and Smaragdalfar and Fae still trapped here in the Western Realm. Anyone who doesn't make it out in time will be horrifically imprisoned by Vogel's runes.

Imprisoned by that Shadow Wand.

But if he can imprison a whole country with his newfound power, what happens when he sets our Sealing spell with his Wand?

"Lukas, I want you to tell me every last thing you know about Vogel's Wand," I press.

"I will," he promises, "but for now, you and I need to focus on getting out of here and east of the Pass. Then we can prepare to wage open warfare on Vogel and his Shadow Wand. Now that we're properly armed."

Hope sparks. "You have a weapon, as well?"

Lukas's mouth lifts, as if amused by the question. "Yes, El-loren. *You*."

I startle as I struggle to adjust to this new reality I'm faced with—

Allied with Lukas Grey. About to flee to the Eastern Realm. About to run for my life as both Realms come after me.

Because I'm a weapon.

My mind whirls as I'm hit by a remembrance of something else I need to tell him. "I have a Wand, as well." I reach down and pull the cloth-wrapped Wand of Myth from my boot and then hold it up for his inspection, the pale Wand holding its faint, luminescent glow. "I know this is going to sound impossible, but I think this is truly the Wand of Myth. Although...it might be dormant. Trystan wasn't able to cast spells with it the last time he tried it." I frown with frustration. "I have no way of proving this. But... I think it might contain a primordial force, like Vogel's Shadow Wand." I've a sudden, strong recollection of how I was rendered immobile by Vogel's Wand on the North Tower's field...and how my Wand seemed to fill me with starlight branches to break Vogel's Shadow hold on me. A new idea rises. "I think the two Wands might be enemies."

Lukas lifts a brow. "Enemies?"

"I think my Wand might be a counterforce to Vogel's Wand. Like in the myths."

"A dormant counterforce?"

I slump, fully aware of how outlandish this must sound, his expression unreadable as he seems to consider my fantastical theory.

"Perhaps some of the myths are true," he offers, "and we've landed in mythic territory. I *will* test your wand, Elloren. Once we get out of here. All right?"

Loosening a relieved breath, I nod and push the Wand back

into the side of my boot, my gaze sliding toward my servants' quarters. My thoughts latch on to how I'd be dead if Sparrow hadn't summoned Lukas's help while Damion attacked me. And Effrey is just an innocent child. If we escape and leave them behind…

"My maids," I say. "We can't abandon them here when we leave. Sparrow saved my life."

Lukas nods. "I've already arranged for them to come. Elloren, Sparrow's offered to organize a network of Urisk spies for me."

This catches me completely off guard, but I find myself rapidly adjusting to the idea. Sparrow seems to be all self-protective barriers and facade. I've glimpsed only a slim piece of the steel inside her, but it's clear to me that there's something fierce and unyielding beneath her guise of the subservient, compliant maid.

"Aislinn Greer's coming with us too," I suddenly insist. "I won't leave without her."

Lukas stills. "Damion Bane's fastmate?"

"Well, he's rather incapacitated at the moment."

The side of Lukas's mouth curls up, a hard glint forming in his eyes.

*Oh, he likes this idea—sticking it to Damion while he's laid up.*

"Is that a yes?" I press.

"It will lure him to me." His smile widens, and it raises the hairs on the back of my neck. His chilling look is the face of a predator in the brush just before an attack. "He and I seem to have left matters *unfinished* between us. Yes, Elloren. We can bring Aislinn Greer."

For a moment, I sense the full extent of the vast power that thrums beneath his skin—the full, unbridled danger of him. Yes, my power dwarfs his, but his is still staggering in its potency. And firmly under his control. Unlike mine.

Intimidation rises over the thought of being intimate with him. It's bad enough to be jumping into bed with someone mainly to escape from the Western Realm, but this…this will be like bedding a tiger. A tiger with overwhelming fire power.

"Lukas… I…" For a moment, I can't collect myself, the memory of how overwhelmingly explosive it feels just to kiss him only heightening my apprehension. "I've never been with anyone before." I gesture vaguely from him to me. "Not in the way we're planning." I search for some glimmer in his eyes that he grasps what I'm alluding to.

He cocks an eyebrow.

"It's just…" I try again, to no avail. It's difficult and embarrassing to try to share such private thoughts with him, as Gardnerians just don't speak of such things. And if I can't even *talk* about this, how in the world am I going to jump clear into bed with him?

I straighten and unsuccessfully try to equal his penetrating gaze. "I want to be *clear*. You need to take things at my pace with this."

Lukas looks surprised, but his voice, when it comes, is low and reassuring. "Of course."

"You can be unpredictable and aggressive," I counter.

His expression has turned serious, his deep-green eyes gilded by the firelight. "Elloren, I won't be. Not with this."

His unexpectedly caring tone dredges up something raw and vulnerable inside me. I bite my lip as tears sting my eyes once more.

Lukas pushes a loose strand of my hair behind my shoulder and moves closer, his gaze searching, his words low and firm. "We won't fully seal our fasting until I've set you at ease."

"Bring spirits," I say, remembering the soothing effect of Valasca's tirag.

"I'll bring some wine," Lukas offers.

"*Strong* wine," I press.

"Elloren," Lukas says as he caresses the side of my neck, his touch featherlight, his expression kind, "you won't need it."

My whole body is tense, but I manage a tight nod.

Lukas looks at me quizzically, his brow furrowed. The side of his lip pulls up a fraction as his silken voice lowers to a more intimate register and he leans in close. "You don't need to worry, Elloren. I'm skilled at this."

His attempt at reassurance has exactly the opposite effect. Mortification spikes and I take a step back from him. "I don't want to know that about you. I don't want to be one more... *conquest* of yours." Images of Lukas with other women flit through my mind. I swallow, wildly uncomfortable as I look toward the curtained window, at the firelit floor, anywhere but at him as I'm faced with the uneasy realization that Lukas has never once told me that he loves me. And I've never once said it to him. "I wanted to share this with someone who it *matters* to," I say, my voice catching.

Lukas caresses my arm. "It *will*." His voice is strong and sure, a tendril of his fire reaching out for me.

I shake my head, not able to meet his eyes. "You don't understand. You can't *possibly*. I wanted this...to be *significant*."

*With someone I love and who loves me.*

*With Yvan.*

When I finally look back up at Lukas, there's a storm of emotion in his eyes that's so intense a flush spreads down my neck. There's strong hurt there. And I'm surprised and chastened by the realization that I've inadvertently landed such a stinging blow.

"Lukas, I'm sorry..."

His hand falls away and he straightens, as if collecting himself. But I can feel the turbulent emotions that are now coming off of him in waves. His struggle for control is visible in the rigid way he's holding himself, in his palpable attempt to bring his suddenly unbridled fire under rein.

When his words finally come, they're clipped. "Tomorrow, stay here until I send for you."

"I will," I concede, filled with remorse and feeling uncomfortably formal toward him.

"Try to get some sleep," he says, averting his gaze from mine. "You'll need to be sharp."

I swallow and eye him searchingly. "You too."

Lukas shoots me an enigmatic look, turns, and walks out the door.

✷

# PART THREE

✷

# CHAPTER
# ONE

# THREAT

## SPARROW TRILLIUM

*Sixth Month*
*Valgard, Gardneria*

Sparrow stares at Lukas Grey in sheer astonishment. What he's just revealed to her and Thierren is a life-altering thing.

A world-altering thing.

"Elloren Gardner is...*the Black Witch*?" Sparrow can barely get the words out, her mind spinning as if caught in a maelstrom.

"Are you sure?" Thierren asks Lukas. The light from a single lantern set on the storeroom table flickers over them all, midnight's shadows darkening the estate.

"She's told me everything about her power," Lukas answers him with a poignant look. "And I've felt its magnitude. It's leagues stronger than mine."

Sparrow takes in the gravity that washes over Thierren's face, his chiseled features stark in the lantern's flickering light.

"You take her at her word that she's on our side?" Sparrow presses them both. She meets Thierren's pine green gaze, seeking the reason that jaded, cynical Thierren would believe this without question.

"Strong earth magery means they both have strong Dryad lineages," Thierren explains, his gaze flicking toward Lukas. "Which means they can't lie to each other. It's physically impossible."

Sparrow's deep-seated rebellious streak gives a flare as she eyes these two Mages, gratified to hear them speak with such easy blasphemy about their Tree Fae blood—blood the Mage holy book staunchly denies. Blood that's blaringly obvious to Sparrow from the Gardnerian fixation on trees and forests and dominating the wilds. As well as in the green glimmer of their skin.

Sparrow turns this new knowledge about Dryad lineage over in her mind, Lukas's news still reverberating through her like a runic blast, shortening her breath. "So, there's absolutely no way for you and Elloren Gardner to speak a lie to each other?" she presses.

"No, there isn't," Lukas states emphatically. "And I can read Elloren's affinities when I touch her, which means I can read her emotions and her magic clearly. She's the most powerful Mage the Gardnerians have ever seen. She can create an ocean of fire with the candle-lighting spell alone. And she's fully set against Vogel."

Sparrow sucks in a wavering breath, all of them quiet for a moment, the air crackling with the explosive ramifications.

The Black Witch is not Fallon Bane after all.

*Holy Am'eth.*

Holy *all* of the Ge'o deities.

"So, the true Black Witch…is ready to fight for our side?" Sparrow finally manages to say, still barely able to believe it. And yet…she does believe it. She's overheard Evelyn Grey railing against Elloren Gardner's "traitorous" brothers. And against Elloren's penchant for forming forbidden friendships with Lupines and Elves.

And Icarals.

"Elloren may well be the only thing that can tip the balance of power against Vogel," Lukas says, calm and slow, as if waiting for it to thoroughly sink in.

"But Vogel doesn't know what she is," Thierren voices, clearly piecing together the same conclusions that are forming in Sparrow's mind.

"No, he doesn't," Lukas concurs, his eyes like twin blades. "But he will soon. And I need to get Elloren out of here before he realizes the Black Witch is *right here*."

A sharper understanding of the situation Elloren Gardner is faced with emerges in Sparrow's mind.

"The Vu Trin know what she is, don't they," Sparrow postulates, eyeing Lukas. "Which is why they tried to kill her. They weren't after you at all."

Lukas's lip quirks as he holds Sparrow's gaze, obviously impressed. "Elloren has an army of Vu Trin hunting her," he confirms. "And soon, several more armies will be after her, as well."

Sparrow raises her brow at this and briefly meets Thierren's eyes, an awareness of the extreme danger obvious in his tense expression.

"So, she's the most powerful weapon on Erthia," Sparrow says to Lukas as she pins him with her stare. "And you want us to help you smuggle her out of here. With multiple armies about to descend."

"Help me get her out," Lukas rejoins, "and I'll get you and Thierren and Effrey East. Along with Elloren. Who I will then train in the use of her power so that she can strike down Vogel and the entire Mage Guard." Lukas's mouth tilts up a notch more as he holds Sparrow's gaze, challenge sparking in his eyes. "I'm assuming that holds some appeal for you."

The possibilities course through Sparrow, her pulse quickening as she turns the broader situation over in her mind.

Vogel's power is growing to monstrous levels, shocking everyone in both Realms, his rapid creation of a runic border taking everyone off guard. As has his annexation of so much of the Western Realm in only a matter of weeks, his sights beginning to turn East.

Inevitably to the East.

If he's not stopped, and soon, there won't be a speck of safe ground left anywhere on Erthia.

*But a Black Witch*, Sparrow thinks, her lip twitching up. *That could put a nice dent in Vogel's plans.*

Sparrow considers Elloren Gardner's kindness to Effrey, such a contrast to vicious Fallon Bane. She can barely suppress her smile as she considers how Fallon Bane will react to the news that Elloren Gardner is, in fact, the true Black Witch.

*That alone is worth helping Elloren Gardner dodge several armies.*

Along with the fact that the East is going to need every single weapon they can get their hands on to stop Vogel.

Sparrow's chest tightens with urgency. Because she desperately wants to keep Effrey safe from what's coming.

She meets Thierren's gaze once more, holding his fierce stare as a silent conversation rages between them. Neither of them holds any illusions about the risks at play here. The difficult odds.

The power of the foul Magedom.

Thierren's sharp features solidify with resolve, and Sparrow can sense they're falling into one mind on this.

"Are you sure?" she asks Thierren, the words weighted with portent.

"Let's go east," Thierren responds, and for a brief moment, Sparrow is swept up in the power and comfort of their alliance.

Bolstered, Sparrow turns to Lukas. "All right," she says. "Let's chance it. Let's smuggle the Black Witch out of here."

Lukas nods, growing serious as his gaze flicks over them both, as if gauging their commitment. Seeming satisfied, his eyes take on a hard glint. "The window of escape will be very slim. Here's what I need you to do."

A few hours later, dawn filters into one of the estate's upper-story hallways through stained-glass skylights, washing Sparrow in its muted light. She hurries down the narrow, tree-lined hallway, a lantern in hand, as her mind brims with knowledge.

Lightning flashes, briefly brightening the hall with white light.

Sparrow stops at the hallway's end, opens the linen closet's door, and steps inside the sizable storage closet. She sets down her lantern and gathers a pile of neatly folded milk-white sheets from the shelf before her, racing to finish the morning's tasks with her usual pristine competence so that Oralyyr and Mage Evelyn Grey don't become suspicious that anything could be amiss.

Leaving Sparrow time to pilfer food and supplies for a long journey—a journey Sparrow prays she and Effrey and Thierren survive, a fragile hope now cradled in her chest.

Until this moment, Sparrow's outlook has been a morbid one, but now...

If Elloren Gardner can learn to wield her power for the Resistance, everything is suddenly in play—

The defeat of Vogel and his forces.

The defeat of Fallon Bane and her brothers.

The liberation of the Fae Islands.

*And Effrey and Thierren and I are getting out of the Western Realm tomorrow morn,* Sparrow marvels.

*Finally.*

This elusive, longed-for dream of escape is unattainable no more.

Sparrow is ready, her heart practically singing with courage as she hugs the sheets close and moves to pick up her lantern.

"You're new here, aren't you?"

Sparrow startles at the question, her movements instantly halted by the deep, silken voice. She turns, her heartbeat quickening as she's suddenly faced with Lukas's priest brother.

Silvern Grey.

She clutches the clean linens protectively against her chest, wanting to form a wall between herself and this Mage as her alarm rises.

Silvern Grey is like a leaner, meaner, and powerless version of Lukas, lesser in every way and, from what little she's gleaned about him, deeply resentful of it. His sculpted Gardnerian features are square jawed and aristocratic, his priestly tunic well pressed and of the finest silk, his icy-green gaze identical to Evelyn Grey's.

And he's leaning against the door's frame, intentionally blocking her way out. Disturbingly bright eyed and...*interested.*

Sparrow's gaze darts around him as thunder rumbles through the estate's Ironwood walls, her heartbeat quickening to a faster rhythm.

She's seen this look too many times before.

And the priests are the worst ones.

She ducks her head deferentially, pulling her figure inward, careful to sound neutral and not the least bit friendly. "Mage Evelyn wants the linens changed right away." She cautiously moves toward the door, toward his side, waiting for him to step back, but Silvern doesn't budge, the interest in his eyes taking on a glazed sheen, his breathing deepening as he swallows and looks her over.

Sparrow's alarm strengthens. "I need to go, Mage," she insists, avoiding eye contact as she moves toward his side once more, hoping he'll move.

Instead, Silvern steps inside the closet and takes hold of her arm as she attempts to dart around him. Sparrow's gut clenches at the threatening touch.

"Stay a bit," he croons, looking at her but not really *looking* at her, and Sparrow knows exactly what she is to him in this moment. "Or we'll need to speak about the Fae Islands. I might need to see your work papers. To make sure they're in order."

His threat is lightly but devastatingly leveled. Panic crests in Sparrow as she moves to slip from his grip, but his fingers grip tighter.

"Please, Mage," Sparrow pleads, feeling as if she's sinking into dark waters with no ground beneath her. "Mage Evelyn will be looking for me," she insists, trying to force truth into the lie.

"Shh," Silvern croons as he traces the base of Sparrow's neck with his finger.

Sparrow recoils, backing into the shelf behind her, and Silvern closes in, yanks the sheets from her grasp, and grabs hold of her arms.

Outrage gaining fierce ground, Sparrow slams her palms against Silvern's bird-marked chest and pushes hard, keeping him at bay.

Anger flashes across Silvern's face, his free hand flying up to grab her wrists, wrenching them away from his chest. "Stop," he hisses as he forces her roughly against the shelving, the entire shelf thumping against the wall behind her. "You be quiet," he demands, looking her over, lecherous heat in his gaze, his sour breath warm on her face.

Sparrow's mind whirls around his mention of the Fae Islands and her forged work papers as she desperately considers going for the blade she has concealed in a calf-sheath under her skirts. The blade Thierren has taught her to wield.

*You can't pull a blade on him,* Sparrow agonizes. *He'll have both you and Effrey arrested and shipped to the Pyrran Prison Isles if he finds out you're armed. And if you kill him, you won't just be destroying Effrey's and your chance of escaping east…*

*You might destroy Elloren Gardner's chances of escape, as well.*

*Which could deliver the Black Witch straight into Vogel's hands.*

If Thierren was here, Sparrow agonizes, or if Lukas was here, they'd stop Silvern.

But no one is here.

Emboldened, Silvern pushes himself against her, nuzzling her neck, and Sparrow tries to squirm away, desperation mounting.

Silvern slams himself against her, as if for emphasis. "Do you want to go back to the islands?" he snarls, wild desire sparking in his eyes as he reaches down to grab hold of her skirts, pulling them up even as Sparrow frantically struggles to push them back down. "Right back where you came from?"

*He can't find the blade. If he finds the blade…*

"Silvern." An imperious female voice sounds from the open doorway.

Silvern freezes as both his and Sparrow's heads turn toward the dim hall and surprise rips through Sparrow.

Mage Evelyn Grey is looming in the shadows.

Silvern is off Sparrow in a flash as he faces his mother, looking for all the world like a cornered feral animal.

"Your father has need of you," Evelyn coldly states, her green gaze boring into her priest son.

Sparrow can barely breathe, can barely move as she prays that Evelyn Grey did not see the blade strapped to her calf.

Silvern gives his mother a curt nod and strides out of the room, leaving Sparrow alone with Mage Evelyn Grey.

The room grows silent save for a distant peal of thunder.

Evelyn's gaze does a slow slide over Sparrow, and Sparrow struggles not to wither from the sheer force of that icy stare.

"You need to wear looser clothing and get that violet hair under a cap," Evelyn says, leveling the order lightly but firmly. "And get your chores done earlier to avoid being alone with the men of this house. You're here to serve, not to tempt."

Outrage volcanoes in Sparrow as the urge to grab up her blade takes furious hold.

"Stay away from my son." Evelyn Grey bites out each word with deadly emphasis. "If I find that you continue to be a distraction for him, it won't matter that you're indentured to Lukas. I'll take full possession of your work contract and drag you to the Fae Islands myself. *Do you understand?*"

Sparrow forces back the trembling that's kicked up all over her body, the desire to lash out in pure rage. To push this woman to the floor and fight back.

But Evelyn Grey holds all the power in the world.

The Gardnerians hold all the power in the world.

Blinking back vengeful tears and keeping her hand far away from the hilt of her knife, Sparrow nods.

"I'll kill him," Thierren growls, anger flashing in his pine green eyes as he takes hold of his wand's hilt.

Sparrow shakes her head emphatically as she struggles to force back the furious tears that are threatening to storm loose, her whole face tensed as she huddles in an isolated hallway with Thierren.

Thierren's angular features are sharpened with anger, his

Level Five magic practically storming off him. Sparrow can feel the churning energy of it on the very air.

There are times, like this, that Sparrow struggles not to hate the image of him—his distinctly Gardnerian looks, the green glimmer of his skin accentuated by the darkness of the storeroom.

His vile Mage Guard uniform.

Their alliance is so complicated that Sparrow can't bend her mind around it, her anger at the Mages so raw and leagues deep that it's impossible for Thierren to escape getting snared in it.

They're both so damaged from what they've been through. Thierren with his constant nightmares and debilitating guilt and fierce desire to fight for the Fae—Fae who will likely want to smite him if he ever does find them. And Sparrow, with her own constant nightmares of predatory Mages and the threats they pose to both herself and her beloved Effrey as well as the small rune-collared dragon she's become increasingly fond of.

"You can't kill Silvern Grey," she insists, adamant, her tone gaining steel.

"He *can't* treat you like that," Thierren rages, as his fist tightens on the hilt of his wand.

Anger spikes through Sparrow. "Of course he can," she snarls, the anger erupting. Years and years of pent-up anger. "What do you think it's been like for me? What do you think it's like for all of my people? You Mages treat us like this all the time." On some level, Sparrow knows that Thierren doesn't deserve the full brunt of her fury, but she's having trouble holding back what's been kept at bay for far too long. "It's a miracle that I haven't been raped. *Repeatedly.*"

Pain flashes in Thierren's eyes as a storm of emotion rages in Sparrow and she finds she needs to look away from his Mage face.

"Sparrow," Thierren says after a pause, his tone gentler this time.

She looks up at him, the moment suspended as their eyes lock. Sparrow holds his distraught stare as her heart twists and the anger storms.

He's proved himself to be a true ally to both her and Effrey over these past weeks, finding a way to see her almost every day. Never once touching her or giving her that *look*. He's been so kind that there have been fleeting times when Sparrow has almost forgotten that he's a Mage, a fragile bond of friendship struggling to form between them.

Sparrow moves a fraction toward Thierren, yearning for consolation but unable to shake her awareness of him as a Mage.

The dam inside her cracks, and Sparrow can't hold back the deluge.

"Thierren," she rasps as she closes her eyes and closes out his uniform and tears spring to life, an abyss of misery opening.

"You're so brave," Thierren says, as Sparrow cries tears of outrage, keeping her eyes tightly shut as emotion pummels through her. "I admire you more than you could ever know," he admits, his voice breaking.

The dam inside Sparrow breaks clear apart as a small, safe space takes root between them. Sparrow nods in acknowledgment of it.

"We'll make it East," Thierren says, his tone hardening with resolve. "I'll make sure you and Effrey make it East."

"When do we leave?" Sparrow chokes out as she opens her tear-slicked eyes to look up at him, the concern in his gaze making it easier to ignore his Mage looks, his horrid uniform.

"Tomorrow morning," Thierren says. His expression takes on a violent edge. "And if Silvern comes near you again, I *will* kill him."

"You won't." Sparrow holds his gaze. "And I can avoid him for just one more day."

A look of fierce struggle overtakes Thierren, but Sparrow knows he respects her enough to listen.

And that he knows this is not his battle to lead.

"Get me and Effrey East," Sparrow says, determination rising. "And get Lukas and the Gardner girl East." Simmering fury takes hold once more, infusing her words. "Then come back with them and the Vu Trin forces and anyone else who will fight with you. And *liberate* the Fae Islands."

# NEXT OF KIN

## ELLOREN GARDNER

*Sixth Month*
*Valgard, Gardneria*

I stare at myself in the opulent vine-cloisonné-edged mirror before me as Sparrow brushes my hair with a Black Oak brush she's retrieved from another room. She pulls my head gently and rhythmically back with each deft stroke, the two of us alone in my bedroom. Effrey is ensconced in their nearby servants' quarters, polishing silver cutlery for the Sealing dinner, and I can hear the *clink* of silver through the closed door.

Gray early-evening light filters through the windows, the next storm gathering in the distance, thunder a faraway rumble. The gardens are preternaturally still, bloodred roses standing at attention, buds pointed to the sky. No wind, no rain.

The whole world suspended.

But bearing down like the storm-charged air is the trap about to close in on Lukas and me.

I feel lost without Lukas and wish he was here, despite the

tension between us and the ever-present grief for Yvan that pulls at my heart.

I draw in a shaky breath and eye the remote young woman in the reflection with me.

There's a subtle tightness to Sparrow's lavender-hued face that wasn't there last night. She's like Trystan, I realize, protecting herself behind a facade that hides all of her emotions save small clues. Growing up with Trystan has made me adept at reading such subtleties, and it's clear to me that Sparrow's having trouble maintaining her perpetually blank visage.

"I imagine Lukas has told you that we're all leaving," I venture, deciding it's best at this point to just bluntly state the facts.

Sparrow lowers the brush and stills.

Our eyes meet in the mirror, the tension in the air growing suddenly taut.

"We're coming with you tomorrow morn," she whispers, her tone equal parts girded hope and trepidation.

My heart picks up speed in response to her forthright approach and I nod, abruptly thrown into a close alliance with this young woman.

Sparrow holds my stare, her servile look vanished, her mouth now set in a tenacious line. It's a relief to not be staring at the wall she so expertly puts up, but at the real Sparrow—a young woman brimming with rock-hard defiance in the face of the Gardnerian nightmare.

"He said you have power," she whispers.

I can feel the sweep of blood draining from my face. It's an enormous shift, to have this explosive fact voiced by her, the two of us suddenly stripped of all artifice.

I nod.

A spark of rebellion lights her amethyst eyes. She lowers her voice to a barely there murmur. "Lukas says you're more powerful than Fallon Bane."

I can read a desire for vengeance in her tone, and I'm certain, in that moment, that there's something raw festering inside Sparrow when it comes to Fallon.

"I am," I tentatively whisper back. *But I've no control over my power*, I want to caution her. *I'm not the boon you might think I am.* I almost say it, but wonder if it would be confiding too much.

We stare at each other in the reflection, the elaborate Ironwood clock on the shelf behind us ticking out the seconds, delicate Ironflowers carved onto its gleaming, lacquered surface. It's all so Gardnerian-perfect in here, in glaring contrast to the chaotic fire that's whipping through my lines.

"If you tell anyone what I am," I say to Sparrow in a hoarse whisper, "they will either kill me or turn me over to Vogel."

Her unblinking stare doesn't waver. "The Eastern forces are going to need every weapon they can get hold of to fight the Mages," she states with emphatic certainty. "I won't tell anyone." Raising the brush, she resumes its strokes down my long black tresses. She flashes me a slight, mirthless smile of solidarity, and the unyielding look in her eyes eases a trace of my apprehension.

Sparrow begins to artfully weave elaborate braids through the sides of my hair, pausing every so often to place sparkling emerald leaves affixed to slim silver hairpins into the braids. I watch, trying to tamp down my anxiety and my simmering fire magic, as my hair begins to take on a resplendent, verdant glimmer.

I glance toward the bedroom's closed Ironwood door, aware of Level Five Mage Thierren Stone stationed on its other side.

"Thierren is aligned with Lukas, isn't he," I say. The young guard's demeanor around Lukas suggests some type of deep alliance.

A wary expression crosses her face. "Yes," she says, clearly unsettled, and I wonder at this.

Thierren's deep, muffled voice sounds through the door, and Sparrow's fingers halt in their motion on my hair. We both turn toward the sound as my bedroom's door abruptly swings open.

Surprise rams through me as Aunt Vyvian strides into the room, her gaze fixating on me.

Sparrow's hands fall away from my hair, and my lungs constrict so hard that for a moment I can't breathe.

Aunt Vyvian's expression is polished, but her eyes are full of resolute, unforgiving purpose. She's as severely stunning as ever, her black velvet tunic and long-skirt embroidered with curling fiddlehead ferns, the necklace and earrings that grace her elegant ears and slender neck fashioned from tiny lacquered real-life ferns.

"Leave us," she directs Sparrow as she removes her black calfskin gloves and motions to the side doorway to the servants' quarters with a quick tilt of her head.

Sparrow's usual blank look is firmly back in place. She gives my aunt a deferential nod, eyes looking to the floor, gracefully sets down the brush, and leaves.

I'm frozen as Aunt Vyvian walks up behind me, picks up the brush, and starts to work on the unbraided back of my hair, sending me a chilling smile in the mirror.

The memory of Uncle Edwin, beaten and slumped on the floor, cyclones through my mind and whips up a wrathful anger that's so fierce, a wave of magic surges through my feet and races to my wand hand. The rush of power is so consuming that I'm scared it will jump from my wand hand to all the wood in the room without any need for a spell.

My wand hand flexes as every piece of wood in the room brightens in my mind, including the brush in Aunt Vyvian's hand.

"You've been gone for some time, Elloren," Aunt Vyvian says with icy pleasantry. She pulls the brush through my hair with such force that my head jerks back, a flash of pain stinging along my scalp. My heart speeds up, defiance rising as I meet her menacing gaze in the mirror.

*You think you have me in a trap, you witch,* I seethe, *but you don't know what you're dealing with.*

"You fasted me against my will," I return, just as icy, barely able to resist the urge to grab the brush from her hands, level it at her, and envelop her in a churning ball of fire.

She relaxes the brush, and I jerk my head forward, glaring at her. But then she takes hold of my hair in her fist and yanks my head back once more.

I gasp, my neck aching, as she leans in and bares her teeth.

"I know what you are," she hisses. "You and your uncle and your *brothers*. Worse than traitors." Her face tightens into a pitiless grimace. "You're staen'en, the lot of you, just like your parents were." I glower back at her, unyielding in the face of the Ancient Tongue slur. "And you're the worst one of all, aren't you?" Her voice breaks as she lowers it to an enraged whisper. "Not just in bed with a *Kelt*. In bed with the *Icaral* son of the *Icaral demon* that killed my mother."

Pain spikes through me at her mention of Yvan, followed by a rapid resurgence of fury.

Her grip on my hair tightens. "All of this started with Edwin," she bites out. "He turned you and your brothers into traitors, didn't he? Tried to destroy our family line. All because of that Urisk *bitch* he fell in with."

Bewilderment roils through me. *What is she talking about?*

Her gaze sharpens on me, her lip lifting. "Oh, you didn't know about the Urisk bitch?" she croons, as if she's read my shock in the mirror's reflection. "I'm not surprised. I only just found out about it myself. It seems that, years ago, Edwin claimed a little heathen shopgirl as his own to pleasure himself with, then sent her East with all his money. Didn't you ever wonder why your uncle was so poor? How he squandered his entire inheritance?"

My confusion grows. And so many conflicting emotions that it's hard to find my bearings. In the space of a second, a hundred pieces of the puzzle that was Uncle Edwin fall into place in my mind.

Uncle Edwin refusing to have Urisk servants.

Uncle Edwin tearing up when hearing reports of Urisk or anyone else being deported.

Uncle Edwin keeping me and my power hidden from the Mage Council—a Council that would use my power against the Urisk and anyone else who is not Gardnerian.

Tears sting my eyes as realization washes over me and grief rises in its wake. *Why didn't you tell us what was in your heart, Uncle Edwin?* I agonize. *You should have told us.*

Aunt Vyvian yanks my hair again, and I grit my teeth against the swell of anger.

"He had us so fooled with all his pretense," she sneers. "His bumbling ways. All the while, he was lying in wait, with plans to corrupt our family with that Urisk whore. But Edwin's betrayal ends *here*. As does yours."

She releases her grip on my hair and straightens, her expression rearranging itself into a calm, collected mask, but the fury in her eyes remains.

"You're to be kept under guard at all times," she says. "We're all in agreement—Evelyn, Lachlan, Lukas, and I. Lukas is to breed on you as many times as he can. Because Mother's line *will* go on. Our people's legacy of power does *not* rest with the Banes." She raises the hairbrush and resumes brushing the back of my hair, this time with normal strokes, but my whole body is tense, fire blazing through my lines as I wait for her to rip my hair clear out of my head.

"You and Lukas will mingle your blood to bring forth Mages of incredible power," she says with import, as if she's suddenly in some type of twisted solidarity with me. "Your child, Elloren, will be the next Black Witch."

I spit out a laugh of defiance, my fiery hatred of her scalding through me.

Aunt Vyvian's eyes widen a fraction, as if she's finally seeing me with crystal clarity. Her smile returns, the smile of a player who knows she's ten steps further along in the game than her opponent. "We have a good idea where your brothers are, Elloren," she says, smooth as silk.

My heart constricts, my defiance instantly imploding. *Rafe. Trystan. Where? Where are they?*

She resumes brushing, gentler this time, then takes up Sparrow's braid work at the sides of my hair with nimble fingers. "We have spies everywhere." Her eyes flash as fear knifes through me. "I want to see those Sealinglines flowing down your wrists tomorrow morning," she says lightly. "If you fight Lukas Grey or refuse him in any way, if you try to escape, or if you ever step *one toe out of line* ever again, I will see that your brothers are hunted down and slain in the bloodiest way possible. Do you understand?"

My pulse rushes in my ears as fear streams through me. I nod, suppressing the slight tremor that's kicked up.

Aunt Vyvian has lost her vicious look, her smile now one of triumph.

*Enjoy your moment while it lasts, you witch*, I inwardly hurl at her. *You won't have to wait for our children to manifest the Black Witch heritage.*

*I am the line.*

I *am the power.*

Aunt Vyvian works another braid into my hair and places a few more gem leaves into the woven design as power courses into me from the ground to lash through my affinity lines. My aunt sets down the comb and gives me a pleased smile, her dominance reestablished, her family's shocking rebellion squelched. And a new trajectory set where she can look forward to reclaiming her high social standing.

She inclines her head. *"Girl,"* she calls sharply, and, miraculously, Sparrow enters the room, head lowered.

I'm amazed by how perfectly Sparrow has honed her submissive servility, and also deeply disturbed by this. I realize that this talent has probably come at a brutal price. And I wonder what Sparrow's life story is.

Sparrow waits, head down, her face blank.

"Finish up here," Aunt Vyvian blithely orders Sparrow as she dismissively sweeps her hand toward me. "I'll be back with the dressmaker at the seventeenth hour." She straightens and smooths out her skirt. It's as if I'm no longer in the room. A prisoner, with no say at all.

"Yes, Mage," Sparrow says with a deferential dip of her head.

Aunt Vyvian's gaze rakes over me, victorious.

And then she turns and sails out of the room, shutting the door firmly behind her.

I let out a great shuddering breath as I stare at Sparrow's reflection in the mirror, my fire affinity lines fair exploding with stinging flame. I look down and realize my hands are trembling.

Perhaps noticing this, Sparrow turns to the tea service beside us, picks up a teacup, and sets it lightly down in front of me, then pours me a fragrant cup of vanilla tea.

The steam wafts up as she pours, the sweet, comforting scent steadying me. I pull my trembling hands into my lap, massaging the palm of my wand hand as I inwardly tighten my fire affinity lines, attempting to gain some semblance of control.

My eyes meet Sparrow's in the mirror.

"She killed my uncle," I tell her, my voice coarse and un-forgiving.

Sparrow pauses for a moment, teapot in hand, her voice calm and controlled when it comes. "And they'll kill every-one else you care about if you don't survive to fight them." Her amethyst eyes hold mine in the reflection with a poignant intensity that lays bare in the clearest of terms how high the stakes are.

Vengeful tears prick at the corners of my eyes as I nod stiffly back at her.

"You'll best them," Sparrow tells me as she pours some milk into my tea, her reflection flashing me an ironhard look. "Because you have to."

"I don't know how to control my magic," I admit, my breath tight in my throat.

"Then you'll learn," she replies, setting down the pot and mixing the milk into my tea with a silver spoon. She picks up a porcelain plate holding two currant scones from the side table along with a silver dish of clotted cream, sets it all down on the dressing table before me, and begins to lather the thick cream onto one of the scones for me.

"Please stop," I say, holding up a palm, suddenly not able to bear her waiting on me. I've done nothing to deserve her fawning attention. "Please stop serving me and sit down." I motion toward the cushioned chair beside mine, my voice strained. "Draw the blinds if you have to, but please, sit down and have some tea. And some food if you'd like."

Sparrow stops and considers me, her eyes narrowing. But then she sets down the spoon, goes to the window, pulls the blinds shut, and returns to the side table that holds the tea service. She calmly pours herself some tea then takes a seat beside me. I take a sip of the hot tea as she prepares a scone for herself and takes a neat bite of it.

For a moment, we drink tea and eat the scones in a weighty, companionable silence, considering each other.

I set down my cup and glance at my fastmarked hands, the knot of stress in my stomach tightening. Soon those lines will flow down my wrists.

Tonight.

Thoughts of Yvan crop up, sending an ache through me. Yvan's intense, compassionate eyes. His beloved voice. His kiss.

How much I loved him.

"Lukas and I have to fully seal this fasting," I tell Sparrow, my face heating as I broach the forbidden topic. "There's no other way."

Sparrow nods, a stoic gravity in her expression. "No. There isn't." She hesitates, giving me a shrewd look, but it's not unkind. "Is there someone else?" she gently asks.

Anguish rises and my voice cracks under the weight of it. "He's dead."

She's quiet and still for a long moment. "I'm sorry," she finally says.

I nod, tears clouding my vision, not able to speak for a bit.

Sparrow goes back to sipping her tea, and I realize she shares my aunt's regal elegance. She's so lovely. Stunningly lovely. With her lavender hair and hue, her graceful, aristocratic bearing. She is, without question, one of the most beautiful people I've ever seen.

My thoughts darken as I remember how Mage soldiers used to prey on the Verpax University kitchen workers. Especially the young, pretty ones.

"How do they treat you here?" I ask, the blunt question rising, unbidden.

Sparrow stills, then lowers her teacup and returns my frank look. "Lukas is good to me." She grows thoughtful. "I suspect he would be even if we weren't allied. He wants things done correctly. But he's fair. And he doesn't think the Urisk should be held down like we are."

I'm deeply heartened by this, but also not surprised. I remember Lukas's apparent friendship with Elfhollen Orin. It's becoming increasingly clear that Lukas has a rebellious streak that's leagues wide.

"And the rest of the family?" I press.

She gives a subtle wince, the line of her mouth tensing. "Evelyn Grey is unkind and so is her fastmate. But Lukas's brother…he's a particular problem. His…*attentions*…are hard to avoid." Her meaning is clear from the pained disgust that tightens her gaze and the outrage inflecting her tone.

I remember Silvern Grey's haughty, unforgiving air as righteous anger flares inside me. "Sparrow…"

She shakes her head, as if forcing my concern away. "We're leaving in time," she says, her lip suddenly quivering, and it pierces me, this glimpse of her pain. She shakes her head again, grimacing. "Silvern…tried to go after me this morning." She takes in my look of horrified distress, her own expression one of lingering revulsion. "It's good we're leaving. If I stayed here much longer, I would have to get Lukas involved to keep his brother away from me, and that would…complicate things."

I nod grimly, clear that the stakes are higher for Sparrow than I comprehended. Yes, I'm about to bind myself in every way to Lukas Grey so that we can slip past the Holy Magedom tomorrow morn and flee from this dangerous place. But this course of action means escape for Effrey and Sparrow and Aislinn too.

Escape from this whole sordid, twisted society.

*The perfect, pious Holy Magedom.*

My firelines simmer hot as I cradle my teacup, the trembling in my hands now gone. I don't know how Lukas is going to get Aislinn out, but I trust him at his word. And I trust that he'll try to get Sparrow and Effrey out, as well.

"How did you get here?" I ask Sparrow, wondering why she's not still employed by the dress shop.

Her gaze turns flinty. "Fallon Bane sensed rebellion in me. That day you came to Mage Florel's shop and defied Fallon, I smirked. She noticed. And then, I worked on your dress."

A light-headed rush sweeps over me as I remember that day when I insisted on Mage Florel using a fabric for my dress that Fallon had laid claim to.

"Ancient One," I breathe, swamped with remorse. "I'm so sorry."

"It's not your fault," Sparrow sharply insists. "It was all Fallon's doing. She drove Mage Florel out of business and indentured Effrey and me. Then she had us shipped to the Fae Islands. A few months later, Effrey and I escaped by boat."

*Great Ancient One*, I think. *By boat?* The Voltic Sea is notorious for its dangerous, unpredictable currents. Not to mention the occasional kraken. I try to imagine Sparrow and gentle little Effrey clinging to a flimsy boat, lashed by a cold current, risking their lives to escape the Fae Islands.

"Tell me what it was like," I say. "On the Fae Islands. If you're able to."

I want to know the truth. The full truth about where the expensive silks of my Sealing dress were made. Where much of the food I'm eating has been grown. I know there are vast stretches of factories and farms on the Fae Islands. And the Gardnerians paint a glowing picture of these faraway endeavors—the Urisk kept busy and blessedly productive as they serve the benevolent Holy Magedom.

"Please," I press. "Tell me the truth of it."

Sparrow stares at me, as if sizing me up. Then she sets her tea aside, folds her hands together in her lap...and tells me her full and unabashedly ugly story.

Later that evening, I'm standing in front of my reflection, this time before a long, gilded mirror in the opulent changing room just off my bedroom's side, the entrancing scent of the Ironflower perfume I've been dabbed with gracing the air. Veins of lightning periodically fork across the room's small window, the storm continuing to hold off.

Aunt Vyvian and Mage Zinya Blythe, Evelyn Grey's white-haired dressmaker, look me over with icy appraisal, their glacial stares reflected back to me in the mirror.

My aunt looks like a star-dusted night.

She's changed into a glittering affair of midnight velvet decorated with the familiar Gardnerian constellations formed from diamonds, the star patterns echoing stories from our holy book. And diamond jewelry set into the shape of the Galliana's Raven constellation, which resembles a bird spreading its wings if you connect the stars, graces my aunt's ears and neck.

I set my gaze back on myself in the full-length mirror and take in the elegant, lethal creature before me.

My hair is splashed with a sparkling riot of emerald leaves, a wreath of gem foliage gracing my brow, the bruising on my face and neck gone from the Arnican tonic that's been provided for me.

And my Sealing tunic and long-skirt...

They're perfectly fitted, and all deep forest greens, this

much color allowed only for Sealing ceremonies, the verdant Sealing color meant to highlight and enhance the deep-green shimmer of Mage skin, the so-called mark of the Ancient One's favor upon us. Embroidered, emerald-dusted leaves swirl over me, my tunic tied snugly back and laced with a black silk ribbon. My eyes are heavily lined with black kohl, my lips and eyelids and nails painted dark green.

The overall effect is riveting. Severe and powerful and beautiful.

And the Wand of Myth is tucked under my skirts, wrapped in its cloth and pushed into my emerald lace stocking, snug against the side of my right thigh, my wand hand itching to take hold of it.

"You're lovely," Aunt Vyvian says, seeming momentarily overcome in spite of herself. And I note that the dressmaker seems a bit drawn in by me as well, her frosty green eyes softening in appreciation.

A feeling of surrealness washes over me as I stare back at myself and remember the last time I was transformed by Aunt Vyvian and made to look like my powerful grandmother.

*And now I am the Black Witch.*

I wonder, if there was some alternate Erthia where I was not raised by my uncle but by Aunt Vyvian instead…

What type of monster would I be?

"She's ready," Aunt Vyvian says to Mage Blythe, her eyes homing in on me. "Leave us."

Mage Blythe politely dips her head and exits along with Sparrow, who quietly closes the changing room door behind her.

Aunt Vyvian comes up behind me and fingers the lacing down my back as my spine tingles with revulsion in response to her proprietary touch. Then she smiles at me in the mirror, unties the top lace, and yanks the strands even tighter, tighter than is seemly, my shape on brazen display, my breasts now straining against the silken tunic as she ties the laces.

"This is the moment," she croons as I struggle to pull in a full breath, "that I'm supposed to tell you what to expect on your Blessed Sealing night." She leans in and gently brushes a few stray tendrils of my hair back behind my shoulder. Then she arches her brow suggestively and lowers her voice to a purr. "It is my duty, as your oldest female kin, to impart the secrets of the Sealing chamber so you know what to expect from a man's attentions on this sacred night." Her smile fades and is replaced by a look of animosity, her gaze pinned to mine in the mirror. "But I will impart no such knowledge to you. It is my fondest wish that he *shocks* you in every way. That he *binds* you if he has to. *Beats* you if he must. And is as *rough* with you as possible."

Suddenly, she reins herself in. Her eyes still blaze with hate, but her mouth turns up in a cruel smile as she reaches out and runs one perfectly manicured finger over the fastlined hand at my side.

I flinch away, resisting the urge to strike her.

"I want to see those lines thick on your wrists tomorrow morn," she tells me. "After he's taken you repeatedly." She straightens and sighs. "But you'll get no advice from me this eve. No quiet, soothing conversation to prepare you for what's to come. You *certainly* deserve none."

She leans over my shoulder, eyes narrowed maliciously as she voices the traditional Sealing phrase, teeth bared. "Sanguin'in, Elloren."

*Bloody the sheets.*

And then she gives me one last chilling look, turns, and sweeps out of the room in an elegant cloud of menace, shutting the door behind her.

Furious, chaotic magic is lashing so hot through my lines

that I suddenly yearn to go find Lukas, but I can't. Because while I'm being kept prisoner here, he's preparing for our escape. As Sparrow and Effrey and probably Thierren will be all through the night.

While Lukas and I become true fastmates, binding ourselves to each other in every way.

Sorrow overtakes me as I stare at myself in the mirror. I remember the feel of Yvan's arms and wings around me when I last saw him, and the words he whispered in my ear.

*Wait for me.*

My heart constricts, the swell of grief momentarily unbearable.

*He's gone, Elloren. You have to let him go.*

I battle back the tears as I force my grief for Yvan roughly to the back of my mind. And when my eyes settle once more on my reflected visage, an impassioned, hardened look stares back at me.

There are threats from every side bearing down on me, Vogel and his Shadow Wand about to close in.

And Yvan would want me to survive all of it.

Because he loved me. And because he always knew that this fight is bigger than us.

I know all these things with as much rock-solid certainty as I know one other thing. Something that I know Yvan would want me to grasp tight hold of, as well.

There is no time for grieving if I'm going to survive.

# CHAPTER THREE

# FEALTY

## ELLOREN GARDNER

*Sixth Month*
*Valgard, Gardneria*

*Tick, tick, tick.*

A small clock set on the dressing room's Ironwood armoire ticks down the minutes left before Lukas and I are formally sealed…before I have to face Vogel. I take one last look in the full-length mirror at the leaf-decorated, glitteringly verdant creature I've become.

A creature who looks just like my terrifying grandmother.

A multitude of emotions spiral up inside me as I take in my reflection—fear, awe, rebellion. Along with an acute aware-ness of the Black Witch power contained in my lines. And of the walls rapidly closing in around me and that power.

Low voices sound, and I head for the changing room's door and open it. Surprise ripples through me as I pause at the room's threshold.

My guard, Thierren Stone, is just inside my bedroom door,

huddled close to Sparrow, the two of them talking in low, indecipherable tones, engrossed in serious conversation.

They're standing much too close to be only passingly acquainted.

Thierren is leaning toward Sparrow, his broad shoulder resting against the closed door's frame, his green eyes riveted on her, and she's looking at him with equal fervency. Thierren reaches out to gently touch Sparrow's arm just as Sparrow catches sight of me.

She startles, her amethyst eyes widening just as Thierren notices me as well, the two of them immediately stepping back from each other, as if attempting to conceal their bond. I remain standing there, blinking at them.

*Are they close friends? Lovers even?*

I think of Uncle Edwin and his Urisk love. Such dangerous lines to cross here in the Western Realm.

*Is this why Thierren broke with the Gardnerians?*

He's fasted, I notice, but the fasting was never consummated, his looping black fastlines stopping just short of his wrist.

"You should leave us," Sparrow tells Thierren as she glances uneasily at me.

Thierren gives her a brief, reluctant look, then nods stiffly. He throws an unreadable parting glance at me and leaves the room, shutting the door behind him as he takes up his guard post once more.

I step into the room. "Sparrow," I say, wanting to reassure her, "if you and Thierren are together..."

Sparrow shoots me a quelling look. "We're allies, nothing more."

A flash of yellow light bursts through the room from above, cutting off her words, and my head jerks back from its intensity. Startled, we both look up.

A luminescent golden circle has flamed to life on the Iron-wood ceiling.

There's a muted *pop* as the circle's interior bursts into a geometric, runic pattern, and both Sparrow and I take a quick step back.

I look to her, alarm rising. "What's this...?"

Another sizzling flash of gold as the wood beneath the huge rune disappears and a man drops down through the hole and hits the floor with barely a thump.

My heart almost jumps out of my chest as I stagger back and a split-second impression takes hold—pale skin, sand-blond hair, kohl-rimmed eyes, blackened lips, dark garb. And a curved rune sword grasped in his black-gloved hands.

A northern Ishkart assassin.

"Thierren!" Sparrow shrieks as horror bolts through me.

The assassin lets out a growl and launches himself at me as I stumble backward and everything happens at once.

Thierren bursts into the room, wand out as the door to the servants' quarters flings open and Effrey runs in, palm extended and flashing a purple gleam. The assassin grabs my arm and I struggle to fight him off as he pulls his sword back, a cry of terror escaping my lips.

Just before the assassin is about to bring the sword down on me, a white creature flies diagonally in from a corner ceiling branch to collide with the assassin's throat, the impact driving him away from me. I stagger back a step just as a line of violet fire streaks toward the assassin from Effrey's palm and a spear of ice flies from Thierren's wand to impale the assassin's chest, his whole body arcing backward as he bursts into violet flame.

The assassin's runic sword clunks onto the carpet as he falls to the floor. He lets out a wet, gurgling cry as he kicks his

feet out and desperately claws at the small white dragon affixed to his throat.

*A dragon. There's a* dragon *in my room...*

I take another step away, the assassin gasping and flailing as
the carpet begins to catch fire, the sides of his clothing consumed by the violet flame as the dragon mercilessly tears at
his neck, and I fleetingly note that there's a collar around the
dragon's neck marked with glowing deep-green runes.

Another flash of purple fire streaks toward the man, and
my head whips around toward the violet flame's origin, to
find Effrey's purple-glowing palm still extended toward the
assassin, her other hand raised and fisted around a large amethyst, her purple eyes wide with fear.

"Hold your geofire!" Thierren orders Effrey as he simul-
taneously unsheathes his sword and plunges it into the assassin's chest while sending out a stream of water from his wand
to douse all purple fire as the assassin's body convulses, shudders, and goes limp.

Effrey's frightened purple eyes meet mine as realization
slams into me.

*Effrey's a geomancer.*

*Only male Urisk are geomancers.*

*Which means Effrey is male.*

I look to Sparrow and find her poised for battle, a runic
blade grasped in her fist, her eyes riveted on the gory scene, a
line of blood splashed across her white servant's tunic.

Thierren throws down his sword and moves toward Sparrow as she lowers her blade. "Sparrow," he says, his tone impassioned, "are you hurt?"

"I'm all right. I'm all right," Sparrow breathlessly insists
as she dazedly looks to Effrey. "Effrey," she says to the child,
her face tightening with concern as she takes in Effrey's fear-
stricken stance. "He's dead. We're all right."

Thierren turns to me, his wand still gripped in his hand. "Elloren, are you hurt?"

The words refuse to form, so I shake my head disjointedly, my heart racing.

*He almost killed me. He almost killed me.*

My fireline rears with chaotic heat.

The dragon's head whips up, as if it can sense my sudden flare of affinity fire, its bone-white muzzle shockingly red with blood. The creature's ruby eyes narrow, and I'm hit with a lashing tendril of the beast's invisible fire power that's so strong I gasp, its bloodred Wyvernfire searing through my affinity lines.

The dragon jerks its head back, as if in extreme surprise. Then it lowers its head and goes very still, its entire focus on me, its body coiling as a sense of danger builds in the air.

*"No, Raz'zor!"* Effrey cries, lurching toward me.

I recoil as the beast flaps its wings and takes to the air, darting toward me at the same moment that Effrey leaps forward to catch hold of its legs.

The dragon gives an outraged shriek as it's yanked backward to hang upside down in Effrey's grip, like a large chicken being brought for slaughter.

The creature growls ferociously as it writhes and gnashes its teeth at Effrey and Effrey struggles to avoid the dragon's bite. Both Effrey and Sparrow let loose a stream of pleading Uriskal aimed at the dragon.

The dragon hisses back at them what sounds like a stream of obscenities in Wyvern.

"Order him to stand down," Thierren insists of Effrey, his wand now pointed at the dragon.

Effrey looks to the dragon with an unnatural level of focus, the beast glaring back at Effrey just as fixedly, and I realize, in that moment, that Effrey is not only a Urisk male, but one of the rare Urisk males who can mindlink to dragons.

I point a shaking finger at the dragon. "How did you get hold of a dragon?"

They all fall silent as the suspended dragon growls and snaps and glares at me from upside down.

I look to Effrey, my voice quavering. "You're talking to the dragon with your mind. Aren't you?"

The small dragon lets loose what seems like another stream of vicious expletives.

"Can you tell me what he's saying?" I ask Effrey, who looks ready to burst into tears.

The dragon is now panting, fury in its glowing ruby eyes as it spits out a small, sparking line of red fire toward me. I glance at the clock with no small amount of alarm. I'm to face Vogel in less than an hour's time.

I turn back to Effrey, urgency rising. "Please, Effrey. Tell me what the dragon is saying."

Effrey hesitates, the child's eyes flicking to Sparrow before he capitulates. "Raz'zor says that he senses your power and that he knows you're the Black Witch. He says he's heard warnings of your existence from the forest. And that dragonkin stands with the forest."

Outrage born of desperation whips through me. I take a step toward the small beast and meet the dragon's murderous, glowing stare. "Tell your dragon that the damnable forest is wrong about me. I'm a friend to Wyvernkin."

Effrey, Sparrow, and Thierren all blink at me, as if thrown by my sudden show of defiance.

Effrey turns and looks intently at the dragon, who lets loose with even more hissing and spitting.

Suddenly, the beast gives a violent twist, breaking free of Effrey's grip.

Effrey cries out in alarm and I jerk backward as the dragon flashes toward me in a pale blur.

Raz'zor collides with my chest with surprising strength, and my feet slip out from underneath me as I'm knocked to the carpeted floor, grappling with the creature as he sinks his teeth into my shoulder.

I yelp from the jolt of pain, my affinity fire rushing out to the dragon in a powerful *whoosh* as Effrey, Sparrow, and Thierren all swoop in to pull the dragon off me and the small beast abruptly unclamps his jaws from my shoulder, his body going slack as he lets himself be pulled away into Effrey's arms and I push myself up.

The dragon's eyes blaze with red flame as he stares at me, wide-eyed, as if stunned. Then the dragon begins to hiss out another string of unintelligible sounds, eyes fierce on me, as if he's both outraged and wildly confused.

Effrey looks to me with amazement, one of the child's hands clenched around the top of one of the dragon's wings as I shakily push myself up from the floor.

"Raz'zor says you are *bonded* to Wyvernkin," Effrey translates. "He says that you have Wyvernfire coursing through your Magelines."

I clutch the stinging bite on my shoulder as the meaning of the dragon's words becomes devastatingly clear.

*Yvan.*

"How can this be?" Sparrow asks. They're all looking at me in complete confusion, the dragon most of all, its slitted eyes locked on to mine.

"I *am* allied with Wyvernkin," I tell the dragon, my voice suddenly rough with grief over the remembrance of Yvan's passionate, fiery kiss.

When he gave me his Wyvernfire.

"If you kill me," I tell the dragon, my voice breaking over the memories of Yvan, "then you're a *fool*."

The creature lets out a long, wavering hiss, but then stills and stares probingly at me.

"He will not kill you," Effrey shakily translates, "but…he wants to know the truth of things. He wants for his mind to touch yours."

I gape at Effrey. "How?"

Effrey brings two fingers to his own forehead. "Skin to scales."

I meet the dragon's blazing stare as the memory of how I once feared Naga fills my mind and a reckless courage takes hold.

"All right," I say, taking a chance. "Let him go."

Sparrow hesitates, but Raz'zor wastes no time deliberating. The creature thrusts his body violently forward, breaking Sparrow's hold once more as he flies to me and lands heavily against my chest, pushing me back until I stagger down onto the carpeted floor again.

"*Raz'zor,*" Thierren snaps as he steps forward, wand raised.

I go very still, my pulse thudding as the dragon stares me down, claws on my shoulders, his eyes like two fiery red pits and heat searing off him. Ignoring Thierren, the dragon presses his warm, scaled forehead against mine, my fireline whipping up in response to the dragon's proximity, his teeth too close.

Invisible tendrils of the dragon's flame stream into me, and I gasp as the full brunt of his power rushes into my lines, blazing hot. Raz'zor may be only the size of a small lamb, but there's a torrent of power buried deep within his compact, reptilian body. Enormous power. Deep veins of it, like he's connected to a volcano. Like he's tapped into the center of Erthia itself.

And I realize that this small dragon might hold more power than Naga.

The dragon hisses.

"Raz'zor says," Effrey translates, wonder in the child's tone, "that you saved Naga the Unbroken."

The dragon's head draws back, his murderous look gone, confused awe remaining in his fiery eyes.

I pull in a long breath to steady myself. "Yes, Raz'zor," I affirm, the remembrance raw and bittersweet. "I helped to free Naga."

*With Yvan. And my family and friends*, I think, an ache cutting through me as I realize the dragon is able to skim only the surface of my thoughts and read just a scattered few.

Raz'zor presses his forehead back onto mine, another rush of his fire searing through my lines. Then he pushes away from me, wings flapping as he rises then lands on the floor before me.

For a moment, I remain seated on the floor, his gaze still pinned on me, and I've a sense of his internal red fire whipping up with indignant fury as he lets loose with an emphatic hiss.

"Raz'zor says—" Effrey looks to me with evident confusion "—that you are the bonded mate of a dragonkin...yet you are Sealing to another."

There's a storm of bewildered outrage in the dragon's small ruby eyes, the flame in his gaze amplifying as I slowly rise to my feet. The dragon spits red sparks as he bares his teeth and growls at me.

Effrey's expression has turned to one of grave concern. "He says that the Wyvernkin gave you his fire and that you should not bind to another. He's very upset about this."

I glare at the dragon, outraged myself as both a fierce grief for Yvan and a heated indignation rise within me.

"I do not accept your censure, dragon," I lash out as angry tears burn my eyes. "He's *dead*."

Raz'zor cocks his head and goes very still, his gaze now fiercely questioning, his ruby eyes locked on to mine with unblinking intensity.

"Elloren," Thierren says, a shocked sympathy in his gaze, "were you with the Icaral? Yvan Guryev?"

My emotions tense with pain over hearing the beloved name. I nod.

Raz'zor lets out a series of low, whistling hisses and everyone grows quiet for a moment.

"Raz'zor says," Effrey translates, full of solemnity, "that he pays tribute to your loss."

"Thank you," I force out, my voice rough as a tear streaks down my cheek and I brusquely wipe it away.

When I look back at the dragon, he's staring at me in a new way, a simmering gravity in his eyes.

"Raz'zor says to you," Effrey continues, "'Take heart, friend of Wyvernkin. Naga the Unbroken sends forth the wingeds as her messengers. She will gather the dragons of the West and the East. And she will be our savior.'"

A sudden rush of hope takes hold.

"Do you know where Naga is, then?" I'm suddenly imploring the small dragon, almost forgetting he came close to ripping out my throat just a moment ago.

*Naga's alive. Sweet Ancient One, she's alive.*

Tears prick at my eyes as I hold the dragon's fierce stare and he lets loose with a series of rough growls.

Then grows silent.

"Raz'zor says he will hold his fire," Effrey finally announces. "He says he will break with the forest in this and he will not slay you, even though you are the Black Witch."

My breathless hope gives way to incredulity and I glare at the dragon. "That's much appreciated, Raz'zor."

The dragon narrows his eyes, as if reconsidering, and hisses again, more forceful now.

"But he makes no pledge of fealty," Effrey amends with cautioning gravity.

*What?* I'm at a complete loss. It's like I've landed in some strange, formal dragon court, ignorant of the rules.

Whatever it is, this pledge of fealty sounds useful.

They grow to be quite large, these dragons. I picture Raz'zor grown to the size of Naga. And I remember how Naga, even diminished by her long recuperation, was able to take out most of the guard of the Valgard Prison in a fiery inferno.

"You know what, Raz'zor?" I throw out, worn to a frayed nerve. "*Fine.* You go ahead and deliberate about your fealty while the Gardnerians get stronger and stronger. But, *please*," I snipe, my own fire rising, "take all the time you need. Really. While the Gardnerians burn down your beloved forest, enslave all the Wyverns, and slowly take over the entire of Erthia."

The dragon blinks at me, his small head pulling back, as if affronted.

Fuming, I turn to Sparrow and Thierren. "How did you ever manage to get hold of an unbroken dragon?"

"He was bait," Effrey chimes in.

"Pit dragon bait," Sparrow adds.

"I freed him," Effrey adds with a touch of defiance that surprises me.

I look to Effrey in confusion. "But...he's powerful. I can sense it. Even though he's so small."

"He's not small," Effrey counters with an emphatic shake of his head. "He's full grown. He's kept small by the rune collar. But when we get to Noi lands, we will find a way to free him of it."

My eyes widen at this as I turn back to Raz'zor, taking in the collar around the dragon's neck, the metallic band marked with glowing deep-green runes.

"Why in the world would they waste such a powerful dragon as bait?" I ask them all.

Raz'zor's fire flares, as if in hot appreciation of my words, his reptilian stance lengthening.

Effrey's lip tenses with obvious reluctance to answer, and he glances at Raz'zor. "He's a moonskin. They're unlucky."

*Ah.* I'd forgotten about that age-old Western Realm superstition. Because white dragons resemble the Eastern Realm's dragon goddess. Making him lucky in the East and unlucky in the West.

I let out a long sigh and rub my newly throbbing head.

"So," I say, massaging my temple as I look to Effrey. "You're a geomancer and a boy." I turn to Sparrow and Thierren. "You two are allies." I give Raz'zor a pointed look. "And you're a full-grown dragon who was pit bait and who is also empathic." My gaze darts back to Effrey. "*And* you can talk to dragons with your mind." Everyone is quiet, considering me in their guarded, unified way, which I find somewhat infuriating right now. "Just figured I'd state *all* the obvious things." I set my gaze back on Sparrow and gesture toward Raz'zor. "I wish you'd told me about all this."

Sparrow nods, her expression grim. "Perhaps I should have."

I blow out a breath and turn back to Raz'zor, resigned to this new bizarre situation, as I make the split-second decision to go for broke. "We should join forces, Raz'zor."

The dragon glares at me, seeming a bit startled.

"What do you have to lose?" I press. "I'm perhaps the only being on Erthia who is even more unlucky than you."

I have a sudden sense of this small dragon's pain in how jaggedly his core fire is now whipping about. His head lowers slightly in an almost cower. And I realize that part of him, deep inside, is beaten down low. It prompts a remembrance of how Ariel was treated by the Gardnerians and, unexpectedly, my heart goes out to this small, threatening dragon as I come to a rapid, reckless decision.

If this small dragon wants formality, formality is what he'll get.

And if I'm the Black Witch, then it's time to *be* the Black Witch.

I straighten to my full height as I hold Raz'zor's ruby stare. "Pledge fealty to me, dragon," I challenge. "If I ever gain control of my power and get to Noi lands in one piece, I'll find Naga and fight for Wyvernkin. *Unbroken* Wyvernkin."

The dragon gives me a long measuring look as if considering a very dangerous thing. We stare at each other, everyone silent, tension vibrating on the air.

And then Raz'zor's fire solidifies into one hot, churning stream, his eyes narrowing to slits. He steps toward me, his talons scuffing against the carpeted floor as he sniffs the air, as if scenting me. He comes to a stop before me, his small head rising as he sends out a stream of hissing and clicks.

Effrey's eyes widen with obvious surprise as the child translates, "He says, 'I will pledge fealty to you, Black Witch, friend to Naga the Unbroken.'"

I blink at the dragon in astonishment, amazed this formal approach actually worked. I quickly compose myself as I consider him. I push a tendril of my invisible affinity fire toward the dragon, who responds by sending his own tendril of reddened fire out to meet mine.

"Free Dragon," I tell him. "I accept your pledge." I exhale, my shoulders slumping. "I could use all the fealty I can get, Raz'zor."

Raz'zor looks to Effrey.

"You need to hold out your arm," Effrey tells me somberly. "The bond of fealty requires a blood bond."

I eye the dragon with guarded surprise. "How much blood? You already bit me."

"Only a few drops," Effrey explains, but I don't like how the dragon is now smirking at me.

But...a dragon ally.

I think of Rhys, Cael's second, and wonder if that relationship is what fealty means to a dragon. Rashly decided, I pull up the bejeweled silk of my sleeve and hold the wrist of my wand arm out to the dragon.

Raz'zor springs forward in a flash, and before I can even think to jerk away, his teeth are locked on my wrist, his fangs puncturing my skin with a heated sting, but only a little, like a cat biting in warning. He holds on, and I can feel him pulling on my fire power. I close my eyes and take a deep, warm breath, my whole body momentarily suffused with a delicious, ruddy heat that feels like sheer power.

Raz'zor releases me, his eyes burning hot. A small amount of blood trickles from puncture wounds that glow as red as the small dragon's fire, then disappear along with the sting on my shoulder as more powerful heat rushes through me and my vision flashes red.

As if I've absorbed his flame.

*Black Witch, we are bound.*

Startled, I feel my eyes widen at the sound of a razor-edged, hissing voice in my mind.

Raz'zor gives me a smug, knowing look.

I blink in surprise and look to Effrey. "He just spoke to me," I say, breathless. "In my mind."

"You can do it too," Effrey tells me eagerly. "Concentrate on what you want to say, then send it forward with a breath. Right toward him."

I think my question. Really focus on it with everything in me. Then push it toward the dragon with a hard exhalation. *What does the pledge of fealty mean, Raz'zor?*

*You have my fire,* comes the assured reply.

I pause, shocked to be communicating this way, but quickly steady myself.

*I need your help,* I send out to him with renewed purpose. *I need allies.*

*You have my fealty.*

Reflexively, I send out a rush of invisible golden Wyvern-fire to Raz'zor, and he meets my fire once more, bolstering it in a heady rush of his red flame, our fire power joining and blazing to a vivid orange. All of a sudden all my muscles feel stronger. My blood is running hotter, my fire affinity line coursing with heightened deep-orange Wyvernfire.

*Our fires,* I marvel to him, *they strengthen each other.*

*As is the way with hordes,* Raz'zor tells me. *A Wyvern horde shares fire and feeds fire. We are a horde now.*

A horde of two.

I look to the Ishkart assassin sprawled out on the ground. The hour is growing late, and not only is there a dead body in the middle of the room, but in a few minutes' time, Aunt Vyvian will return to escort me to the Sealing ceremony.

The longing to have competent, steel-nerved Lukas here with me rises.

"Lukas needs to know about the assassin," I say to Thierren, who nods.

"I'll get word to him," he assures me.

"What will you do with the body?" I ask.

"I'll put a freeze spell around it and we'll slide it under the bed. We'll all be gone before the spell fades." He glances at the hole in the ceiling, the crawl space revealed, then glances down at the charred, bloodied carpet.

"I'll keep anyone from coming in here," Sparrow says to Thierren, who nods in unspoken agreement.

I glance again at the assassin and his discarded rune sword, the golden runes burning bright along its length. I swallow, an icy fear working its way up my spine. "Thierren, what are the chances that they've sent more than one assassin after me?"

"Quite good," he replies without hesitation as he gives me a frank look. "Since the eastern forces clearly know that you're the Black Witch."

*So, there it is.* Everyone in the room knows that I'm the Black Witch, but they're still here, none of them running from the Witch of Prophecy. They're a surprising group of allies, but allies nonetheless.

Allies that I'm grateful for.

Sparrow looks to the tree clock that's on a nearby shelf then sets her unflinching gaze on me. "We need to get you cleaned up and mend your dress. Fast. It's almost time to go."

# CHAPTER
# FOUR

# THE SEALING
## ELLOREN GARDNER

*Sixth Month*
*Valgard, Gardneria*

Aunt Vyvian's grip on my arm tightens as she guides me down the night-darkened main hall of the Grey estate, my leaf-decorated skirts swishing. She says nothing to me, her eyes focused militantly forward, as if I've ceased to be worthy of any conversation, and her silence unnerves me as my fear of Vogel mounts.

Emerald fire torches set on iron vine-decorated poles bracket us on both sides, the broad, dark corridor washed in their green illumination. The verdant flames lick the darkness, creating the illusion that the carpet's twisting root pattern is undulating like snakes beneath my feet. Ironwood trunks and branches rise on either side of us and curve over the hallway's domed ceiling. Interlocking glass panes are set between the tangling branches overhead to reveal the evening's stormy sky, all the decor creating the illusion that we're engulfed in an ancient forest.

Lightning forks overhead, followed by a low roll of thunder.

My gaze darts warily around the shadowed alcoves as I imagine the shapes of assassins lurking, my chest tight with jumped-up apprehension as tempestuous fire gutters through my lines. High-level Mage soldiers stand motionless by each torch, their green-lit faces carefully blank as their eyes track me.

So many Level Five Mages in one place.

Aunt Vyvian guides me toward a huge archway formed by two enormous bending Ironwood trees, and we pause at the threshold.

The ballroom's entrance is bracketed by six Level Five soldiers, but all this pales in comparison to what lies before me.

A forest tunnel.

Created by two long lines of high-level Mages, each soldier holding a large curving pine branch angled toward the central path before me. The soldiers at the farthest end of the aisle are angling their branches down, blocking what lies at the end of the path from view.

It's traditional, this dark tunnel, symbolic of the dark times when Mages were cast into the shadows of the "Heathen Wilds." But knowing this does nothing to diminish the wave of fright that swamps me as Aunt Vyvian releases her tight grip on my arm.

It has the look of an inescapable cave.

A cave I know Vogel is lurking at the end of.

My pulse spikes as Aunt Vyvian gives my back a light shove and I step into the tunnel, willing myself forward, the branches behind and above me closing in so that I'm cast in almost total darkness. The smell of pine sap is sharp on the warm air, only a hazy tracery of deep-green light filtering through the dense branches as I warily move closer to what lies beyond.

As I reach the center of the path, the branches ahead of me pull back in a wave to reveal Marcus Vogel standing at the far end of the tunnel.

His pale green gaze hits me like a blow and I freeze, the force of it igniting both a raw, primal fear as well as a hard spike of defiance.

Vogel is standing behind an altar wrought from a twisted Ironwood trunk, two military envoys standing behind him. He's bathed in green torchlight, the planes of his elegant face glimmering emerald.

His Shadow Wand in hand.

The Wand sheathed against my thigh thrums with a sudden, urgent energy that quickly blinks out, as if the Wand is in rapid retreat.

As if it's hiding from a monster.

I repress a surge of stifling, amorphous fright and will my legs to move toward Vogel, my defiance hardening.

The branches tunneling over me suddenly pull back, the wave of greenery retreating on both sides as Lukas steps toward the altar and into full view.

My heart arrests at the sight of him. He's stunning, and I can't tear my eyes away from his tall form.

Lukas's gaze latches on to mine, and he does a double take, as well. His gaze slides over me with an ardent flash of intensity as both my fear and my blazing defiance are swept aside. It's a shock to see Lukas in something other than black. Like me, he's dressed in deep Sealing greens that heighten the forest green of his eyes and the green glimmer of his skin, his silks perfectly tailored to complement his strong physique.

*My ally. A rebel, just like me.*

A fierce longing to escape with Lukas grips me as Vogel's

oppressive stare tracks me like prey. Keeping my gaze firmly on Lukas, I close the distance between us, noticing a hard urgency in Lukas's expression that's mirrored by the vibrating tension of his affinity fire.

I stop beside Lukas, our hands immediately finding each other's and taking firm hold. Lukas's grip on me tightens as his branching magery rushes through me and around my magic in tendriling lines, his fire riding over my earth magery in a hot, bolstering wave.

Strengthened by Lukas's controlled magic, I glance around.

A dome of pine boughs forms a low ceiling that flows down to the blessing-star-patterned floor. Countless small green glass lanterns hang from the boughs to form a verdant constellation, a veritable sea of Mages seated underneath in the torch-encircled space, all of them tinted a more vibrant green by the emerald torchlight and the lanterns above.

I swallow as I steel myself.

It's as if every influential Gardnerian and most of the high-ranking military were hastily invited to Lukas Grey's Sealing ceremony. Lukas's family and Aunt Vyvian are seated in the first, arcing row, their glares on me raptor-hard. A line of priests, soldiers, and two envoys stand behind Vogel in an arcing row.

There are only Gardnerians in the room, as the presence of "heathens" is banned during the sacred Sealing ceremony, the Gardnerian glimmer purposefully amplified by all the green light. The impact is dramatic, as if someone scattered brilliant deep-green starlight over everyone in the room, but I'm unsettled by the oppressive uniformity.

Our fingers intertwined, Lukas gently guides me to take my place across from him at the altar then lets go. Heart thundering, I struggle to maintain my courage in such close proximity to Vogel, the High Priest looming beside us, no trace of his Shadow magic on the air.

Palms up, Lukas holds out his hands to me over the altar, his gaze fixed on mine as I place my hands back in his and grasp tight as Lukas sends another bolstering wave of his affinity power through my lines.

But then another set of hands comes to the altar, the dark gray spiraling Shadow Wand loosely clasped in elegant fingers.

For a split second, my vision warps toward the Wand, everything surrounding it blurring, as if diffracted. I wait, breathlessly, for the terrible sense of Vogel's dark, invading tree, his terrifying void, but...

Nothing.

Absolutely no sense of Vogel's eclipsing power.

I glance at Vogel, and his pale eyes meet mine. His lips curl in a slight smile that sends ice straight down my spine. He's like a snake, coiled and biding its time, and I'm struck by the remembrance of the full extent of his evil. How he led the Gardnerians to murder the Lupines, using our religion to justify the horrific massacre. Diana's whole family mercilessly killed. Her parents. Her little sister, Kendra...

Vengeful wrath surges to life inside me like a storm yearning to burst through my skin. A sudden surge of power whips through me and strains to the Ironwood altar under my palm. Lukas's hand clamps down tight around my wand hand, pulling it slightly up to break contact with the wood as I meet Lukas's searing gaze and draw in a shuddering breath, the power tempered slightly.

"Blessed Mages," Vogel announces beatifically as he looks over the silent, anticipatory crowd, "we gather this night for the Sacred Sealing Ceremony." He pauses as his gaze passes once more over the room, his expression growing solemn. "We gather in the sight of the Holy Ancient One to celebrate the joining of these two Mages. In union with each other and in union with the Holy Magedom. Ever in dominion over earth, fire, water, wind, and light." Vogel turns to face a nearby knot of priests and nods. "Bring forth the element of fire."

One of the priests steps forward, gripping a candle on a long silver stand. He sets the candle in the center of the semicircular area that lies just before the altar, then rejoins the other priests.

Lukas shoots me a fierce look of solidarity, releases my hands, and then steps back and pulls his wand from its sheath in one smooth, practiced motion. He strides to the candle and calmly considers it as Vogel raises his hands, closes his eyes, and intones the traditional fire blessing.

*"May the Ancient One bless your union and grant you dominion over fire. May you bring forth Mages who own fire for the glory of the Ancient One."*

Lukas is supposed to either put the candle out with his fingertips or snuff it out with a quick spell. It's symbolic, all of this, as most Mages are magically powerless.

Instead, Lukas is looking at the candle as if he finds it amusing. As if he's mentally toying with it. He murmurs a series of spells under his breath, then gives a quick flick of his wand toward the candle.

The candle's flame leaps from the wick and into the air, then explodes outward into a suspended inferno big as a miller's wheel, and the entire crowd gasps. Lukas pulls back his wand hand, and the inferno blazes into his wand in a long stream, the wand taking on a golden glow as Lukas whips the stream of fire around his head like a lasso. He throws his arm out in a wide, sweeping arc, and the fire courses out toward all the torches encircling the room. Another collective gasp goes up as Lukas's fire lights all the torches gold instead of green, a rush of heat and flaxen light washing over us all.

Lukas steps back and casually lowers his wand. Then he turns and grins wolfishly at Vogel, who returns his smile coolly. Outwardly, Lukas emanates his usual calm, but I can sense the Magefire contained in his center coalescing into a tightly contained inferno.

I stare at Lukas in awe as the torches flicker back to green, a heightened gratitude rising in me to be so fully aligned with him. I knew he was powerful, well trained, and in control of his Level Five magic. But I had no idea he had this level of control.

A priest comes forward and expeditiously takes away the candle as two priests bring out a small table and a closed glass vial magicked to hold a small cyclone of air in its interior. They set down the table and place the vial on top of it, then step away as Vogel intones the second elemental prayer.

*"May the Ancient One bless your union and grant you dominion over wind. May you bring forth Mages who own wind for the glory of the Ancient One."*

Lukas smiles slightly then murmurs a series of spells under his breath and points his wand.

The vial takes on a white-hot glow that explodes into raying light as the glass dissolves. I draw back along with everyone else as the cyclone springs free and rises into the air, wind now whipping through the room and through my hair, the torchlight wildly guttering as the cyclone draws upward and then expands over the room into a low ceiling of roiling clouds.

Lukas whips his wand outward and throws a tight line of fire into the clouds, the flame forking into horizontal streaks of bright white lightning. Lukas jerks his wand backward, and the clouds swoop down and contract into a tight, rotating ball suspended just before him and spitting lightning. Then Lukas murmurs a spell, and the contained storm morphs to wispy smoke and dissipates, the crowd of Mages emitting sounds of gratified awe.

I turn toward the onlookers to find Evelyn Grey's gaze set on her son with a look of fervent pride. And then her eyes shift and meet mine. Her expression transforms into a venomous glare.

Vogel begins intoning the prayer for dominion over light as one of the priests carries out a brick of golden lumenstone and sets it on the floor. Lukas pulls his sword and brings it down on the lumenstone in a shower of yellow sparks, deftly rendering it to ash with one focused blow. Water is then brought out, and Lukas throws fire at it and sends it up into a rush of steam.

Lukas lowers his wand to his side and faces Vogel.

"Mage," Vogel says with a formal cadence, "you have shown us your dominion over fire and wind and air and light." Vogel swivels his head toward the priests, who come forward once more, this time hoisting a small potted tree between them. I'm enthralled by the sight of it.

The exquisitely gnarled fir tree has an ancient look about it, as if a huge old-growth tree was shrunk down to size and set in a black porcelain container, its needles resplendently limned in gleaming silver.

The priests set down the tree in the clearing, and I'm mesmerized as a wave of the small tree's love washes over me. A returning love wells up deep inside me as I'm overtaken by a surprisingly potent feeling of kinship.

"Mages," Vogel intones, "please rise."

The sea of Mages stands.

I know this is a pivotal part of the Sealing ceremony—the male Mage always ends the ceremony by killing a tree, the higher the status of the family, the rarer the tree. The next day the couple walks alone into the woods to perform the Blessing of Dominion and scatters the dead tree's ashes in the forest over the largest tree they can find as a stark warning to the "Heathen Wilds."

Unease rises as an inexplicable commiseration with this tree blossoms within me.

It's been sheltered, this miniature tree. This rare Silver Spruce. I can sense its mournful isolation. Grown in captivity and cut off from its woods...

*Dryad.*

I startle as the tree's whispered word fills the back of my mind, prompting an ecstatic wave of affection for this small tree to swell inside me, quickly followed by a tremor of fear.

*Don't kill it*, everything in me rises up to implore.

Vogel lifts his arms.

*"May the Ancient One bless your union and grant you dominion over earth. May you bring forth Mages who own Erthia for the glory of the Ancient One."*

Panic assails me, fueled by my enraptured connection to the small tree as Lukas steps toward it, grasping his wand.

*No. Don't kill it*, I silently rail, barely able to hold myself back.

A single word reaches out to me, lancing through my heart.

*Dryad.*

Wave upon wave of adoration courses over me as I whip my head to Vogel to find he's taken a sudden, strong interest in me. In my peripheral vision, Lukas lifts his wand.

Panic explodes as I round on Lukas. *No, Lukas. No...*

Flame shoots from Lukas's wand just before I can stage a protest, engulfing the small tree in an explosion of fire.

The tree screams in my head, its agony spearing into me as my affinity lines contract, devastation ripping through my heart.

*Ancient One. No.*

Grief grips hold. Inconsolable grief. I'm barely aware of Vogel's final prayer as it's intoned by the entire hall. Of Lukas's arm coming around me as I stare at the pile of ashes in the center of the clearing.

My gaze jerks to Lukas, my breathing erratic, my eyes brimming with furious tears.

Lukas's eyes narrow as he takes me in with a long, searching look and I struggle to get hold of myself. I need to get away from all of this *right now*. Away from Vogel and all of these Mages.

Away from this vicious ceremony that mercilessly kills innocent trees.

"Elloren," Lukas whispers, his gaze locked on mine with unmistakable urgency, as if prompting me to remember the danger we face.

I glance back at the tree's ashes, a heightened awareness flooding into me of what's at stake. I can't fall apart over the killing of this tree.

Tears obscure my vision as I let Lukas guide me back to the altar, his hands reaching out to grasp tight hold of mine once more, his fire and earth magic flowing into me and threading through my lines in what I know is an attempt to comfort me. But I'm beyond comfort.

Vogel raises his Shadow Wand above our hands.

"Lukas Grey and Elloren Gardner," he intones, "I seal you with the Ancient One's power. I seal you with the Ancient One's glory. I seal you before the Ancient One's Holy Magedom."

His lips lift in an infinitesimal smile as he presses the tip of his Wand to our clasped hands.

As soon as Vogel's Wand makes contact with the skin of my wand hand, a slight sting prickles through my fastlines and the torches all around us crackle and spit green flame, as if unsettled by the flare of magic in the air.

Without warning, Vogel's Shadow tree punches through my lines and all the breath is wrenched from my lungs. Lukas's hands tremble around mine as the rune on my abdomen begins to sting.

The world bends, my mind overtaken by a warping sensation as Shadow roils in from all sides and annihilates the light, only the image of a huge dark tree remaining.

The tree abruptly enlarges, and I've the sudden, strong sense of being lifted clear into the air, suspended from its limbs like a marionette, dangling and terrified as tendrils of Shadow twist around me.

I hang there in the darkness, with no control over my body, held completely in Vogel's thrall. I want to scream, but I can't breathe, the scream forcibly arrested in my throat.

And then…something slithers into me.

Another Shadow, like a snake twining out from Vogel's Wand and into my earth affinity lines as I'm filled with the petrifying sense of Vogel's disembodied pale green eyes set on me along with multiple pale gray eyes lurking in the dark tree's hollows.

Watching me.

I sense, with staggering horror, that it's not just Vogel in my lines, but an entire army of slithering, many-eyed Shadow things riding alongside Vogel's power.

All of it coming from the dark gray Wand in Vogel's hand.

The Shadow things slither along my affinity lines, testing,

plucking. Then sharpening, like the slicing edge of countless knives cutting into my lines.

I gasp from the pain, desperate to cry out, but Vogel's Shadow wraps around my throat and pulls taut.

And then, as abruptly as the invasion came, it falls away in one world-tilting swoop as the Shadow Wand pulls away from my wand hand, Vogel's invisible grip on my throat releases, and the Shadow tree vanishes, everything around me blinking back into sight.

My hand flies to my throat as I gulp for air and Lukas does the same, one of his hands braced on the altar he's now slumped into, his breath rasping and uneven.

Lukas's gaze meets mine in stunned horror as he reaches out to grab desperate, protective hold of me. But my focus is ripped away from him as all of the affinity power in the room suddenly blasts toward me and I'm whipped up in it, instantly consumed.

I'm like a boat caught in a storming whirl of magic. Whereas I used to only be able to sense some of Lukas's power because of our matching lines and had a growing sense of Yvan's fire, I'm suddenly hyperaware of every line of elemental power in every Mage around me, save Vogel. My eyes cast about in a wild, unfocused panic as the elemental magic of so many high-level Mages assaults me, wind magic roaring in my ears.

There are four Level Five Mage soldiers bracketing Vogel, and I've a clear sense of their wind, fire, earth, and water power being tethered to him, their affinity lines streaming from their bodies and into Vogel's Wand like a fast-moving current sucked into a dark abyss.

Straight toward those many-eyed things.

I look to Lukas, disoriented from the battering onslaught of affinities. Tears burn in my eyes as I cling to Lukas and struggle to convey to him with my gaze alone that Vogel has truly become a monster.

The skin of my hands prickles, and I look down as both my fastlines and Lukas's begin to branch out, curling and looping, the lines gradually thickening but stopping just short of our wrists. I release one of Lukas's hands and look dazedly at my Sealing-magicked palm, and then Lukas and I exchange a dire glance as the power in the room carves hurricane paths through my lines, my balance unsteady.

I throw my palm back down on the altar to brace myself and startle as Vogel abruptly brings his own hand down on mine and Lukas's fire explodes outward to whip protectively around me.

I flinch back from Vogel's touch, but he smiles and holds on, seeming pleased by my reaction and wanting to draw me into a confrontation. His long fingers dig into my skin, his eyes bright as his lurid, dark Shadow rushes into me once more, pushing back all the magic in the room.

"So much power," Vogel croons. He closes his eyes and inhales deeply, his magic pulling on my affinity lines, and I've the horrible sense that, although he's holding back, he could easily pull my lines clear out of me and into his possession, like the tethered Mages behind him.

"It's all there," he tells me, and it's as if we're suddenly the only Mages in the room, his merciless gaze locked on to mine, everything around us blurring. "Carnissa's power is in you. And *more*. Your fire. It rivals hers."

Lukas's power abruptly ramps up as he tightens his grip on me, as if he's assessed Vogel and is ready for him this time. Lukas's fire takes on a wrathful force as it flows out to encompass me and force back Vogel's thrall—and I worry that Vogel will sense this rebellion for what it is if he possesses my rare magic-sensing abilities, a skill he's somehow quickened.

Vogel releases my hand and wrests his power from my lines with whiplike force, and a whoosh of dizziness overtakes me as all the affinities in the room rush toward me with renewed strength to batter through my lines.

Vogel turns to Lukas and gives him a narrow look, as if reading his defiance. His lip lifts, as if he's amused by it. "You'll bring her to me tomorrow morn," he says, his voice keen with interest. "For wandtesting."

Another flash of Lukas's fire blasts through me as my fear surges through the maelstrom of power accosting me.

Lukas's voice, when it comes, betrays nothing. "I've recently wandtested her," he placidly states. "She has no access to her power."

Vogel's pale eyes shift back to me and I avert my gaze as I struggle to contain a violent swell of my magic that mingles with the onslaught of magic in the room.

"Bring her to me after the Blessing of Dominion," Vogel says, ignoring Lukas's attempt at deflection. "I will test her myself."

Lukas hesitates for a split second. "Of course, Your Excellency," he capitulates with a graceful dip of his head, but I can feel his earth magery rearranging itself into spears pointed directly at Vogel.

"I want to see her fastlines changed by morning," Vogel says. "Your Magelines combined will be a formidable thing. I will take an acute interest in the Mage children you bring forth."

Lukas is furious now; I can sense it in how wildly his fire is scything around me as he holds Vogel's piercing stare.

Vogel's mouth lifts, a gleam in his eyes. "Sanguin'in," he says to Lukas.

*Bloody the sheets.*

Outrage swells along with my magic. The traditional saying

is like some vicious charge. As if Vogel's challenging Lukas to force me down and bloody me in the most invasive way possible.

Lukas holds Vogel's terrible, bottomless stare. "Sanguin'in," he says back to Vogel like it's his own threat, only leveled at Vogel instead of me.

Vogel's mouth turns up in a chilling, vulpine smile, and he steps back, sheathes his Wand, and stretches out his arms for the final Sealing prayer. I can barely form the words around the storm of elemental magic that's engulfing me, invisible flame scorching through me, branches and shards of ice spearing, the roar of wind in my ears.

"Elloren," Lukas says, his voice cutting through the swirl of magery. There's fierce urgency in his gaze, and I latch on to it with desperation as the cacophony of magic lashes against my lines.

We're supposed to kiss, I distantly remember.

Lukas moves around the altar, pulls me into his arms, and brings his lips firmly to mine, his hand splaying out over my back as he draws me tight against his body.

I shudder as a hard stream of his fire blasts through me, his dark branches rushing out to twine through my battered earthlines and meld them together in a way that was never possible before. My dizziness dissipates as Lukas grips hold of my wand hand and kisses me, pulsing his magery through my lines, and bolstering my affinities with his. Pushing the room's invading power out and drawing my own magery back into my center.

And, incredibly, forming a shield from our combined magic just under my skin.

When he pulls away, his eyes are blazing, his expression steeled.

Steeled for me.

As the crowd applauds, I've a sense of my branches restoring themselves as Lukas's residual fire whips through my lines. My head is still swirling, and I'm still hyperaware of the magic in the room, but I'm steadier on my feet.

Lukas keeps firm hold of my wand hand as we face the crowd, my tempestuous power fused to his.

We're truly sealed, I realize. But not in the way Vogel imagines. Lukas is not set on dominating me. He's my ally, and together we're a joint force.

Against the Magedom.

My grip around Lukas's hand tightens and he responds in kind, our perfectly matched affinity magic twining tight.

Fire to fire. Earth to earth. Air to air and water to water.

One vast wall of Mage power.

# CHAPTER FIVE

# PRIVATE FOREST

## ELLOREN GREY

*Sixth Month*
*Valgard, Gardneria*

Lukas and I enter our Sealing reception under heavy guard. Two Level Five Mage soldiers stride before us, four keeping close to our heels as we enter the estate's huge glass-enclosed arboretum. Anxiety, sharp and acrid, burns through my chest, my sense of mortal threat so all-encompassing that it's beginning to feel like calm.

Lukas holds tight to my wand hand and I cling just as tightly to him, keeping our magic fused in a shield over my lines as we step into the greenhouse-contained forest. Countless trees are spread out before us, the path beneath our feet seamlessly cobbled with gleaming obsidian stone. Deep-green light emanates from emerald glass lanterns hung from the trees' branches and mottles the indoor forest with an otherworldly latticework of shadow and verdant light, the scene undeniably beautiful.

But nothing can dampen my turbulent unease.

My deeper well of magic roils with volatile force just under the shield Lukas wove around my lines, battering relentlessly against it. Lukas's strong magic sizzles over my power like a densely woven net, holding my power firmly at bay and protecting me from the storm of magic in the room as the diffuse miasma of power emanating from the surrounding high-level Mages strains to get in.

But still, Lukas's shield isn't able to protect me from one of the most dangerous things in this whole estate.

Myself.

Because my hunger for wood has grown savage.

My hand tenses around Lukas's to stave off my shockingly ramped-up desire to grab hold of every piece of wood my eyes light on.

Every branch.

Every tree trunk.

The Ironwood frame of the arboretum.

Every *wand*.

Vogel's changed my power in some intrinsic way; I'm sure of it. When he touched his Shadow Wand to my hand and invaded my lines with his terrifying magic, he quickened my fledgling ability to sense power and made me more vulnerable at the same time. If I release my hold on Lukas and his power, I can feel Lukas's shield begin to degrade like a net unraveling as the power around me pummels in.

I keep a tight grip on Lukas as I glance around the arboretum. My leaf-patterned skirts swish around me, glittering in the emerald light, the smell of greenery lush on the air. I'm surrounded by a decadent variety of trees, some of which I've never seen before but have envisioned when touching their wood, now suddenly magnificently before me in all their branching glory.

Rainbow Eucalyptus trees from the Salish Islands with color-striped trunks.

Dragon's Blood trees with dramatically upturned crowns.

Uriskal Beech trees draped in gauzy moss.

Lukas and I pass under a grove of Alfsigr Wisteria trees in full bloom, their fragrant silver flowers hanging down in pendulous, emerald-tinted clusters, the trees so beautiful they make my heart ache, even in this dire situation.

With their roots pruned and cut off from the wilds, these trees have no hatred emanating from them. Only a palpable curiosity and a gentle murmuring as I pass, like the feathery brush of a light wind.

*Dryad.*

Remorse takes hold as I think of the small tree from the Sealing ceremony and its rush of love. How it embraced me as a Dryad only to find itself in the clutches of tree-killing monsters. The nightmarish memory of Lukas exploding the miniature tree makes me wince, and I have to battle back the rise of a disorienting conflict.

I glance up at the branching wisteria canopy, suddenly struck by the realization that it would be the perfect place for an assassin to hide and creep over me through the tangle of limbs. Thierren said he'd tell Lukas about the attack, but did he?

We near the edge of the forest and my chest tightens.

Lukas meets my fraught gaze with a look that reads, *Are you ready?* I tighten my grip on him and nod.

We emerge from the trees, and applause breaks out as we're faced with a huge green-lit crowd of Mages who all rise to their feet and call out congratulations as we stride down the center aisle. They're gathered around multiple tables that fill the luxurious open space at the western edge of the arboretum.

An orchestra is assembled just behind the crowd and in front of the greenhouse's huge glass wall, a dance floor just before it.

The tables are covered in raw silk dyed a rich forest green and set with cut-glass goblets and gleaming black china. Candelabras fashioned from small polished trees stripped of their leaves stand in the center of each table, their candles magicked to send out a green-fire glow.

Evelyn Grey, Lachlan Grey, and Aunt Vyvian all view me with cold formality as we pass, Silvern with an out-and-out contempt that I struggle not to mirror as the applause continues and Lukas leads me toward the dance floor for the traditional first Sealing dance.

Concern mounts as I take in the number of Mage soldiers stationed outside the arboretum, their rigid forms visible through the glass.

A veritable army.

Just beyond them lies an expansive view over the Valgard bluff, the lights of Valgard glittering in the distance, the curving city edging the Malthorin Bay. And streaking over the water lies the green line of Gardneria's new runic border, a threateningly bright reminder of Gardneria's increasing power.

My courage falters. *How will Lukas and I get past so many soldiers? And where is Vogel and his guard and the knot of priests that were at the Sealing?*

The orchestra launches into "Deep Forest," the traditional post-Sealing song. Lukas guides me onto the dance floor, takes me in his arms, and swings us into a waltz as Mages gather around the floor's periphery. I catch Evelyn Grey's resentful glare as well as Aunt Vyvian's look of smug triumph, her eyes set on her grand prize, Lukas Grey.

Lukas deftly turns me around, one hand firm on my waist, the other wrapped tight around my wand hand as the crowd breaks into restrained applause and sends up a collective, polite murmur of appreciation.

Lukas seems as unfazed as ever, but I can feel the forceful current of every line of his power blazing with lethal tension.

Breathless with concern, I draw close to Lukas, leaning in to whisper in his ear. Lukas immediately responds by pulling me closer.

"Did Thierren speak with you?"

Lightning flashes through the glass ceiling.

"Yes," Lukas replies, his tone emphatic, the response of someone who has assessed the threat and somehow handled it. He gives me a sharp look as if to caution me to silence, and I surmise that he likely knows about the dragon and Effrey's geomancy, as well.

"Keep hold of me," he whispers, tightening his grip on my wand hand for emphasis as we dance, "so I can pull on your magic and feed power into the shield." He gives me a brief, crucial look as my worry mounts that Vogel has permanently altered my magic in some intrinsic way.

Possibly in some corrupting way.

Without Lukas's shield, my rare ability to read magic has been rendered into a debilitating skill by Vogel's Shadow power. I'm like a book cracked open, all the overlapping elemental magic in the room able to flow straight in, my lines on full display and disastrously vulnerable.

The orchestral piece's violin crescendo rises like a tide as Lukas glides us over the dance floor, the two of us having fallen seamlessly into our musical bond the way we did when we played music together, but the yearning to speak freely to him grips nearly as tight as his magical shield sizzling over my lines.

The crowd applauds once more as the piece draws to its finale and Lukas pulls me dramatically close, his searing gaze holding mine as the back of my neck begins to creep with an indefinable dread. The Wand of Myth in my stocking shudders against my thigh as a disquieting tang of magic rises in the air like fog and the rune Sage marked on my abdomen prickles with energy.

I turn as Marcus Vogel emerges from the edge of the indoor forest and starts down the reception's central aisle, drawing everyone's attention.

Fear mounts, quickly followed by the rise of a cornered defiance.

Vogel is trailed by a large military contingent, the four tethered Mages tight on his heels, his two young envoys just behind them, Vogel's long stride practically radiating power. And his fist is tight around the hilt of his sheathed Shadow Wand.

Lukas keeps decisive hold of my wand hand, his power running hot over mine, as Vogel nears and his pale eyes flick over me, quick as an asp, a palpable sting lashing against my shielded lines.

A stab of terror knifes through me as surprise flickers in Vogel's gaze.

*You're trying to get in, aren't you*, I realize as I tighten my grip around Lukas's hand. *You're trying to get into my lines. But you didn't expect a shield, did you?*

Vogel passes by and takes his place at a well-guarded table near the wall of glass. He smiles benevolently at Lukas and me, then raises a permissive hand to the orchestra. The musicians launch into another waltz as Vogel takes a seat and couples spill onto the dance floor, my heart threatening to pound a hole straight through my chest.

Stamping down the urge to bolt, I follow Lukas as he guides me away from Vogel and toward a long receiving table set by a green-lit waterfall and to a seat near its center, where I'm surrounded by Lukas's family and placed next to Aunt Vyvian.

She rises as I approach, her constellation gown glittering, the diamonds reflecting green sparks of light. Her ever-smug expression makes my stomach churn.

But even my aversion to Aunt Vyvian can't cut through my awareness of Vogel's attention. I've a subtle sense of invisible Shadow magic rolling over the floor, like writhing mist, flowing up against the fire and earth magery Lukas has woven around my lines. Almost caressing the shield before drawing back like a sinister tide.

"May the Ancient One's blessing be upon you," my aunt croons as she takes hold of my arm and kisses me on both cheeks, everything in me recoiling from her touch. She draws back and gives me a look of gloating import as she accentuates each word. *"Mage Elloren Grey."*

A sliver of shock ripples through me as I hear my new name for the first time.

The finality of it punches through my defensive haze and unearths a stab of grief for Yvan, but I quickly gain hold of myself. I could have been Elloren Bane, I bleakly consider. If Lukas didn't intervene, I *would* be Elloren Bane. And Damion would have sussed out my power and thrust me straight into Vogel's grip.

Into the grip of that Shadow Wand.

Appreciation for Lukas's staunch friendship stirs in me as my aunt greets him, her gaze sweeping over his tall frame. Lukas's stance is casually dominant as they briefly embrace, but he keeps tight hold of my hand as his fire gives a combative flare.

Aimed at my aunt.

"Finally," Aunt Vyvian says to Lukas, smooth as silk. "Congratulations to you both. May your union be a fruitful one."

"Oh, I've no doubt of it," Lukas counters, a subversive glint in his gaze.

*It'll be fruitful, all right*, I silently hurl at my aunt. *And I'll come after you with everything in me if you try to harm my brothers.*

Urisk servants emerge from the greenhouse's central forest, carrying tray after tray of food and drink. We all take our seats, and I'm glad for the sudden bustle of activity.

A willowy, blue-hued Urisk woman of about my age approaches the table, sets down a large silver tray on a nearby stand, and begins placing one exquisite forest-themed platter after another before us. She announces each one in a strained, formal tone as rich scents fill the air.

"Grouse in a spruce tip glaze, Mages," she says as she sets down the black china plate, the glistening meat dusted with tender spruce needles. "Pine pollen dumplings stuffed with deep forest morels. Linden leaf salad with braised burdock root." She lifts an emerald glass decanter and pours the traditional Sealing drink, a tree cordial made from elderflowers, sassafras leaves, and birch syrup, into our crystalline green glasses. My eyes briefly meet hers as she pours the golden cordial. She quickly looks away, her blue eyes bright with fear, her posture desperately careful.

My gut clenches as I consider her situation. With the runic border closing in and non-Gardnerians about to be "cleansed" from mainland Mage soil by year's end, will she be forcibly brought to the Fae Islands? And then what? Vogel speaks openly of the Reaping Times, when all non-Gardnerians are supposed to be annihilated or forced into servitude. How will this young woman survive?

I glance through the glass wall toward the glowing borderline of green stretching across the Malthorin Bay. Sparrow's shocking depiction of the Fae Islands fills my mind as renewed purpose overtakes me.

Vogel and his forces need to be struck down and the Fae Islands need to be liberated. This entire system of oppression needs to be rendered to ash. That's the only way to truly free this woman. To free everyone caught under Vogel's heel.

Including myself.

Newly bent on rebellion, I fake a submissive posture, head lowered, shoulders hunched, as the servant leaves and the murmur of convivial conversation and the *clink* of silverware on china fill the air. Lukas pretends to ignore me as he launches into a discussion about the current political situation with his father, who is seated beside him, but his hand remains firmly clasped around mine under the table.

I glance at all the food set before me as my stomach clenches into a knot. I can feel my shield's edges beginning to degrade from the effect of my churning emotions on my affinity fire as well as the ceaseless press of magic in the room.

Perhaps sensing how troubled my fire is running, Lukas's hand firms around mine and he sends a new line of his own fire out to me, and then a potent line of earth magery to flow around my jostled affinity lines. His shield pulls in taut, taking firm hold of my magic and smoothing it into calmer lines.

*I can feel what you're doing,* I try to convey to him with a wordless glance. *Thank you.*

Lukas nods and sends me a knowing look.

The traditional line of guests begins to stream by to offer up their obligatory congratulations, a knot of Level Five soldiers pausing before us as Aunt Vyvian gets up and steps away to converse with a small group of Mage Council members.

"A Blessed Sealing to you, Commander Grey," a black-bearded Mage heartily congratulates Lukas as he salutes him. I draw back from the strong water and air power rushing off him, a fusillade of magic almost powerful enough to cut through Lukas's shield. The Mage's eyes flick toward me with unkind mischief. "Looks a bit spooked, your maiden."

"Of course she does," the soldier beside him says, smirking

good-naturedly at me. "She'll be seeing his sword work first-hand tonight, won't she now?" They all look to Lukas, since he's the only one of us included in their jesting.

My cheeks heat, resentment curdling my emotions as I keep my eyes militantly focused on the table before me. I've no desire to take in the gloating looks on their faces as they revel in their private knowledge of this thing they're alluding to, the finer details of which have been kept from me solely because I'm female. And it strikes me—it's not *right* that they all know so much and I know so little.

"That's quite enough, Hale." Lukas says it pleasantly enough, but there's an unmistakable edge to his tone that unsettles their collective magic.

"A Blessed Sealing," the soldier beside Hale amends with a slight bow, quickly retreating into formality. "May your union bring forth Mages for the power and glory of the Ancient One." The sentiment is echoed by the other soldiers as they take their leave from us.

"Sanguin'in," Hale rakishly tosses out in parting, his eyes flicking toward me with a look that borders on a leer, and the others echo the traditional cheer.

My fire rouses in response, uncomfortably hot, and I look to Lukas, wanting to lash fire at the next person who utters the phrase Sanguin'in.

Lukas's fingers trace mine as if reading the angry flare of my lines. He gives me a decisive look and gets up, gently tugging my hand. "Come with me, Elloren."

Feeling both besieged by the threats bearing down and incensed by our traditions, I rise and let Lukas steer me down a side aisle, his shield rapidly shredding as my magic slashes against it. We duck into the indoor forest until we're ensconced in a small grove of Silver Pines, their smell a sharp, spicy tang on the air that barely registers through the angry flow of my magic and the onslaught of external power clamoring against my lines.

Lukas pulls me into an embrace, his fire running in a hot, urgent stream as I immediately realize he's feigning our sneaking off to kiss.

"I can read more than just your magic now," I frantically whisper, my lips brushing against his ear. "I can read *everyone's* magic. When Vogel pushed his power inside us during the Sealing—it triggered something. I can read every single affinity line in this room."

"I gathered as much," Lukas whispers back, drawing away slightly and giving me a serious look. "He's amplified something in us both. I've a much clearer sense of your magic. I can sense its strength and flow even when I'm not touching you."

A rattled surprise takes hold, since I know Lukas has never been able to read my magic without touching me, and he's never been able to read anyone else's magic but mine. "Can you sense the magic in the room, as well?" I ask.

He shakes his head. "No. Only yours. And only faintly when I'm not touching you. When we kiss, though…" He pauses, his fire surging toward me. "It's like your lines are as clear to me as my own."

"I've a clearer sense of your affinity lines as well," I shakily tell him, "and it's heightened when we touch."

Lukas smiles slightly at this, his brow lifting. "Should make for an interesting evening."

I frown at him, put off by his penchant for humor at fraught times. And really concerned about Vogel's effect on our power. "What if Vogel's permanently corrupted our magic?"

Lukas frowns. "I don't think he's seeded any magic in us. I don't sense any lingering thrall. He probably tried to permanently invade our lines but wound up amplifying our perception of external power instead."

"That Wand he has," I whisper, "Lukas…he can tether Mages to his power with it."

Lukas draws back a fraction and meets my eyes, his expression darkening. "Are you sure?"

I nod. "The four soldiers Vogel keeps behind him—their power flows right into his wand. When I'm not shielded by you, I can sense it clearly. I think that Wand he carries gives him the ability to bind others' magic and control it."

Lukas considers this, his jaw ticking. "I've noticed he's rarely apart from those soldiers. And his two envoys, as well." His gaze narrows in thought. "I don't have any sense of his power tethered to ours."

"I don't either, but if he can tether those Mages to his Wand, that means he might be able to tether us. And possibly, the entire Gardnerian Guard."

My anxiety gains ground as I turn these new realizations over in my mind, along with our odds of escape.

Lukas and I are surrounded by an army of Gardnerians, and yet another army of Vu Trin could be making its way toward me to strike at any moment. Assassins of every stripe could be closing in.

And Vogel might be close to realizing that I'm the Black Witch.

If he hasn't already.

"Vogel's…sending power out to me," I tell Lukas falteringly. "I can feel it. He's testing the shield. Lukas… I'm scared."

Lukas looks closely at me, his thumb tracing over the back of my wand hand with slow deliberation, as if he's reading the flow of my magic in it. My power has revved up so chaotically hot beneath his shield that I can barely think around its force.

Lukas caresses my back, his green eyes intent. "Kiss me, Elloren," he says, his voice a slow, gentle thrum. He reaches up to stroke my cheek as he gives a swift glance at the crowd beyond the pines. "You're so worked up that you're laying waste to the shield. And I can access your magic more intensely when we're close." I nod, and Lukas brings his lips to mine.

Our magic bucks hard toward each other, his breath hitching as I grip his hand and tunic more fiercely. Lukas tightens his hold on me, one hand coming up to cup the back of my head as his fire sears into me in a hot, blazing stream.

I gasp against his mouth, my breath shuddering through my lungs as I cling to him, and Lukas kisses me so intensely that every one of my affinity lines tightens and grows as molten as wildfire, then becomes more contained as Lukas coaxes my fire magic into a controlled stream and the violent rush of my fire steadies. I pull in a tremulous breath as he kisses me long and deep and twines his magery around my lines.

Lukas draws back a fraction, his gaze fervid with heat, both of us breathing hard. "Better?" he asks.

I nod as he holds me, his molten heat reverberating through my reshielded lines. "Much better," I say, giving him a slight appreciative smile as my skin prickles with heat.

"Good." His lip lifts. "I'll kiss you more later."

"All right," I manage, breathless from the strength of our magical pull.

We're quiet for a moment, the dire nature of our situation cutting through our haze of affinity desire.

"Are you ready to leave?" Lukas asks, his fervid gaze turning searching and serious.

"Ancient One, yes." My flush deepens as soon as I say it, every last boundary between us about to fall. A heightened awareness of his body takes hold, his hand loosely on my waist, our bodies pressed against each other, and I can feel the hunger our affinity attraction has kicked up in both of us.

A different type of trepidation rises.

Lukas and I have kissed on more than one occasion to the point of wrapping around each other quite passionately.

But this is a big step for us both.

"You know," I say, "Aunt Vyvian met with me earlier. To let me know she wouldn't tell me any of the 'secrets of the Sealing night.' Instead, I got the impression that I was about to endure a military attack on my body."

Lukas raises his brow, his lip tilting up. "Certainly not the evening I've envisioned."

"Well, that's a relief, Lukas." A complex vexation rises within me, my brow tightening against it. "It's not right, you know. How I've been kept ignorant about all this because I'm female."

Lukas takes my other hand and rubs the back of it gently, affection warming his gaze. "I imagine you'll catch on quickly enough."

I glower at him. "That's not the point."

Lukas looks closely at me. "I know that's not the point."

"I'm angry. About a lot of things."

"Good," he says succinctly, losing the smile. "Hold on to that. Because it's much better than fear."

I study him. My subversive, warrior fastmate.

Wicked mischief lights his eyes. "When I'm done 'ravaging' you," he says, clearly mocking the idea, "I'm going to reshield your lines with a tighter weave of magic." He gives me a significant look. "But as soon as I can, I need to teach you how to shield them *yourself*. You're too vulnerable, dependent on my magic like this."

I throw him an appreciative look, both his humor and his frank offer steadying. Gratitude for his friendship rises as it hits me, just how much he's sacrificing, jumping over to the side of the Resistance and now throwing his lot in with mine. Ready to risk his life to help me escape and survive Vogel.

And it strikes me that I don't mind, so much, being Elloren Grey while I face down my destiny.

"All right, then," I tell Lukas as I glance at our clasped, fastmarked hands then raise my eyes to meet his compelling stare once more. "I trust you. Let's get out of here. And go change these lines."

We approach Vogel's table, and I've a sense of every other magical force in the room suddenly being pulled to the side.

Vogel sets his penetrating, pale-eyed gaze on me, and I have to fight the urge to fold inward. He's like a dark star, everything in the world now orbiting around him and that Shadow Wand.

"We're to take our leave now, Your Excellency," Lukas impassively states as I hold Vogel's unflinching stare and wait for his Shadow power to crash through me, but he holds it back.

I think of the Lupines, of the refugees running for their lives, the wreckage Vogel is visiting upon the world, as my affinity fire rears and kicks up to a blaze just under Lukas's tightened shield.

*Enjoy your moment while you can,* I silently rage. *If I ever get hold of what's inside me, I'm coming for you.*

A shriek sounds above. My head jerks up along with Lukas's and most everyone around us, unsettled murmuring rising as more shrieks sound and the orchestral music dies off.

A broken dragon horde tears through the sky overhead as sounds of surprise burst forth from all directions, the incoming dragons visible through the glass ceiling, the arboretum's green light washing over their scaled black bodies. The ground thuds as first one, then another, then another dragon lands, lit by the surrounding green torchlight just outside the arboretum's glass wall. Mage soldiers are astride the dragons' backs, more soldiers riding in on horseback to ring the estate.

Lukas and I exchange a swift glance, his fire giving a quick, urgent pulse as mine surges under his shield, and I surmise that this is unexpected for him, as well.

Lukas rapidly collects himself. "Is there new concern about a Vu Trin attack?" he asks Vogel.

Vogel narrows his pale eyes at Lukas. "The Vu Trin seem to have been effectively subdued. But we need to ensure the safety of so many Council members and high-ranking military until we're sure." Vogel smiles as he casts me a knowing look. "And we need to keep Carnissa Gardner's granddaughter well protected. Wouldn't you agree?"

I catch the rush of tension in Lukas's fire as my hope for escape implodes and fear overtakes me.

This goes beyond a guard to ensure safety during a Sealing night and Sealing breakfast.

This is an army to guard a Black Witch.

"Escort Mage Lukas Grey and his lovely fastmate, Elloren Grey, to their Sealing chambers," Vogel intones, his pale gaze flicking toward the soldiers to his left. He gives me a narrow look, a flash of his power slithering over my shielded lines, an unsettling sting racing over the rune on my abdomen.

Ten Level Five Mage soldiers break off from the surrounding guard and stride toward Lukas and me, and I blanch at the feel of their combined power. It's devastating, the sheer pressure of its incoming force close to blasting right through Lukas's shield. And none of it is aimed at Lukas.

It's all aimed at me.

"Thank you, Your Excellency," Lukas says to Vogel with a polite dip of his head, "but such a large guard is unnecessary."

"I insist," Vogel counters. "For your protection. They'll escort you to your chambers and to the Sealing breakfast tomorrow morning." He looks to me. "And then, to your wand-testing. We can't be too safe now, can we?"

Lukas stares at Vogel for a beat, then stiffly bows. "Thank you, Your Excellency."

Vogel's steady smile is the smile of someone ten steps ahead of us all. "Sanguin'in," he says, looking straight at me.

My pulse kicks up to a violent rhythm as Lukas tightens his grip on my wand hand and leads me away, a stream of his fire shuddering through my lines. My own fire lashes out toward Lukas in response as I match his long, determined stride with ten Level Five Mage soldiers tight on our heels.

# CHAPTER SIX

## SEALING NIGHT

### ELLOREN GREY

*Sixth Month*
*Valgard, Gardneria*

When we get to his bedroom chambers, Lukas escorts me inside the heavy Ironwood door, motions with his finger to his lips for me to remain quiet, all the while keeping his hand tight around mine. Then he locks the door and bolts it against the ten Level Five Mage soldiers on guard outside.

It doesn't keep the unyielding press of their magic out.

Magic aimed at me.

The aura of their combined magery has my affinity lines in an unsettled uproar and tangling around each other, and I can feel the edges of my shield beginning to degrade once more from the ceaseless assault of so much power.

My body sings with tension as Lukas holds tight to my wand hand and guides me down an Ironwood tree–lined hallway, through another door and into his bedroom. He bolts and locks this door too. Then he unsheathes his wand and uses it to unlock a black-lacquered box set on a shelf built into the tree-embedded walls, the trees' dark gleaming limbs branching out over our heads. He opens the box to reveal a sizable number of black Noi rune stones, the hazy sapphire glow of the runes illuminating the air above them in a puff of blue.

Lukas pulls out four of the rune stones and places them on the shelf, then sheathes his wand, reaches under the hem of his pant leg, and pulls out a hidden wand—a wand marked with Noi runes. He taps this wand's tip to each rune stone in turn, murmuring spells, and the glow of the runes intensifies. I follow beside him, our hands still clasped to maintain my shield, as he places one of the stones at the base of the room's door and the others at the bottom of each of the room's remaining walls.

We move to the center of the room and Lukas raises his arm, points his wand at the rune at the base of the door, and murmurs another spell.

Static sizzles over our clasped hands as a thread of white lightning flashes from Lukas's wand toward the rune. The moment it hits the rune, faint, luminous blue lines, like a spider's web, fly up from all three stones and cobweb over the surface of the door and the walls and the room's ceiling, then appear to melt into the surfaces.

I blink at the vanishing lines, stunned by Lukas's display of yet more cross-magic as the prickles coursing over our hands recede. The press of the magic coursing in from outside the room abruptly vanishes, only my sense of Lukas's magic remaining, both his magic and mine able to traverse my internal shield since it's woven from our combined magic.

Lukas lets go of my hand, and apprehension leaps inside me as I prepare myself for our guards' affinity power to flood back into me, but...*nothing*.

"We can speak freely now." Lukas turns and focuses on me.

"I can't sense the magic of our guards anymore," I marvel.

"That's because I set up a runic barrier."

I stare at him, amazed. "You're pretty adept in the use of forbidden Noi magic," I note with a touch of wry challenge.

Lukas's lips lift as he gives me a smoky look. "Are you disappointed in my lack of magical purity?"

The rakish gleam in his eyes sends a shot of unsettled warmth through my lines. I give him an arch look. "You continue to be a very bad Gardnerian."

A laugh erupts from him. "True." He looks me over. "But then, so do you."

Our eyes catch and hold, a spark of tension lighting between us that has me remembering just how closely allied we're about to be.

Cheeks heating, I look around and let out a shuddering sigh, nervous about crossing so many lines with him but deeply relieved to be away from Vogel and the rest of the Mages.

"One night here," I think out loud, turning to look at him, this man I'm about to give myself to.

"Yes, Elloren," Lukas says as he moves to take another rune stone from the box and sets it against the base of the wall before him. "One night until all hell breaks loose. Enjoy the very brief respite." He touches his rune wand to the stone and murmurs another spell. The walls around us briefly shimmer with a gauzy, wavering blue film.

I tighten my brow in question. "What does that rune do?"

Lukas rises and turns to me. "Holds the barrier magic. At least until we're gone." He glances up at the ceiling's lingering blue shimmer. Seeming satisfied with his work, he sets his rune wand down beside the box of rune stones. "I've broken down their magery." He cocks a brow at me. "*Someone* had a Light Mage set up echo runes in my bedroom."

"What are those?"

"They absorb sound and allow its echo to be accessed at a later time. Tricky magic. The runes take months for a Light Mage to build and can be used only once."

Comprehension lights. "Did Vogel have them placed to listen in on us?"

"I suspect so," Lukas somberly concurs, apparent disgust tightening his features. "And, perhaps, to hear all that transpires between us this night." Revulsion surges in me as Lukas gives me a poignant look. "I, for one, would prefer that everything that happens between us remains *private*."

"Does this mean they brought the Council's Light Mage here?"

"Yes, Elloren," Lukas grimly answers. "It also means that Vogel thinks you're important enough to spend complex runic magery on. So he can anticipate your next move."

His use of *your* instead of *our* catches troubling hold.

"You think Vogel has figured out what I am?" I murmur.

"Perhaps," comes Lukas's unvarnished reply.

"Why hasn't he confronted me, then?" I challenge.

"Because he's a religious zealot, above all else." Lukas's lips tighten with derision. "It says right in *The Book of the Ancients* that no new spells are to be cast from the time of Sealing until the Blessing of Dominion. And I don't think Vogel realized what you are until he cast the Sealing spell."

Fear makes a harder play for me, and I force a wavering breath, struggling to not let it pull me under.

"Lukas," I say, my voice constricting, "how are we going to get past so many soldiers? Vogel's got an army of Level Five Mages surrounding this estate. And dragons too."

Lukas gives me a predatory look. "When they see our changed fastlines tomorrow morning, their defenses will be down." His gaze darkens. "Ours won't."

"But how can we possibly outrun them? Will the Blessing of Dominion give us enough time?"

Lukas takes a step toward me, a lethal glint in his eyes. "We'll be allowed the open-ended solitary time in the woods that *The Book of the Ancients* demands during the Blessing. Vogel is fanatical about following the *Book* to the letter. That's his weak spot, and we're going to take full advantage of it. We'll gain a lead on them and take to the high ground."

I shake my head in desperate refute. "They've got *dragons*. Our odds are not good."

Lukas draws closer and gently touches my arm, a pulse of his warmth rippling through my lines. "Elloren," he says, his voice low and emphatic, "do you trust me?"

Pressing back my haze of fear, I glance around the room at all the unexpected rune stones and take in Lukas's creative melding of magical systems, my confidence in him reinforced. I know he wouldn't have brought us both down this path if he didn't truly believe we have a real chance of escape.

Our eyes meet, and Lukas gives me a slight smile, his green gaze warm and full of resolve.

"I trust you," I tell him.

He sends a caress of earth magery around my lines. "Good," he says, and I'm overwhelmed by the level of emotion in his eyes.

I look away, eager to distract myself from thoughts of what tomorrow could bring, focusing instead on the fine craftsman-ship of everything in Lukas's bedroom. It's all fashioned in midnight black and forest greens, with a sizable library built into one wall. A fire roars in the fireplace, which faces the foot of a very large bed.

I swallow at the sight of the bed, a dart of nerves tingling through me.

It's made up with elegant coverings—a dark green quilt

with an intricate fabric depiction of a River Maple, midnight-black sheets underneath. There's a forest green canopy held aloft by ebony branches, sanded and worked in beeswax until they gleam.

Two side tables bracket the bed, stained-glass lamps set on them with Ironwood stands carved into the shape of tree trunks, their glass lampshades a gorgeous canopy of leaves. A black-velvet-cushioned mahogany chair faces one side of the bed, and an artfully woven rug lies beneath my feet, green vines on black. The intricacy of the weaving brings to mind the North Tower tapestries that Wynter fashioned, and a small ache gathers in my chest.

*Where are you now, Wynter? Are you still in Amaz lands?*
*Please don't be lost to me like Yvan.*

Before misery can take hold, I press my longing for my family and friends firmly away, everything in the outside world needing to be stamped down this eve. This room and Lukas. That's all there is. There's no better choice. I'm Elloren Grey now, and Lukas and I need to be fully sealed so that we can escape.

Setting my focus back on the luxury surrounding me, I move toward the bed and finger the black embroidery on the edging of the canopy curtain. The silk is smooth beneath my fingers, small black tassels hanging from corners. I run my hand along the wood of the canopy post, a shiver of magic passing through my lines. *Black Oak.*

Lukas is watching me, his hand resting on the back of the velvet-cushioned chair. His fire is banked, but I can sense its presence, molten and simmering.

I glance uneasily at the bed and back to him again as vulnerability takes hold.

"Lukas," I say, feeling tremulous, "I want to stay sealed once we make it to Noi lands."

Lukas holds my gaze. "I want to stay sealed to you no matter where we go."

"No, I mean…if we make it to Noi lands," I haltingly continue, "I want you to be as bound to me as I am to you."

"Elloren, our fasting is permanent. And after tonight, the Sealing spell will be too."

"No, it's only permanent for *me*," I counter, resentment breaking through. "Because I'm female. You can be with other people."

Comprehension lights in his deep-green eyes. "I won't be," he says definitively. "I want only you."

He says it so absolutely that something inside me loosens. I nod as I hold his gaze in what feels like joint understanding.

"Sit down. Relax," he offers. "You're safe here tonight. And this evening won't be anything like your aunt told you. I'm not going to force myself on you, regardless of what she said."

I frown at him. "You can be pretty aggressive when you want to be."

"I can be," he agrees as he opens a cabinet at the base of a bookshelf and retrieves two long smoked-glass bottles and a corkscrew from it. He rises and meets my gaze once more. "But I would never force myself on anyone. *Ever.*"

I nod and pull in a deep breath as I sit down on the edge of the bed facing him, running my fingers over a delicate fabric branch embroidered on the quilt beneath me. Lukas has assuaged some of my anxiety, but the outside threats have my whole body tensed and primed for flight. And as reassuring as he's being, I'm apprehensive about tonight.

Lukas sets down the bottles and the corkscrew on a small table by the chair, his brow furrowing as he takes me in. "Elloren," he says with understanding, "I know this situation is not ideal. I've told you that. It's much too fast, and I'd have preferred to court you first."

I nod, my own brow tight as a bowstring, unable to easily shed the danger and trauma of the evening. And the intrusive Gardnerian traditions that muscle in on something so personal and intimate.

"I didn't like all the jokes about this," I blurt out in a rush of honesty as I motion loosely toward the bed, unable to keep a swell of outrage from my voice. "All those jokes about your 'sword' being used on me and *sanguin'in* said over and over." I can still feel the embarrassing sting of it all, a sting that makes me want to lash out in retaliation for how Gardnerian traditions have taken ownership of this away from me.

Lukas gives me a weighted look, obviously taking this seriously as he comes to me. He reaches out and caresses my shoulder, his thumb tracing a gentle arc on it.

"It's like some joke I'm the target of but not in on," I say, my resentment breaking free. I frown at the bed then look back up at him. "I've been kept ignorant about this and left out of all the humor because I'm female and...it feels *wrong*." It dawns on me, how intimately I'm confiding in Lukas right now. Lukas seems surprised by my candor, but his focus remains unwavering. I'm angered—*really* angered—a tremor taking hold in response to how unforgivably *unfair* our traditions are toward women.

"Elloren," Lukas says as he takes both my hands in his and gently pulls me up, his voice deep and emphatic when it comes. "We're together in all things. Including this. And it's not a joke. Not to me."

My lip curls in disgust. "Tomorrow they'll be asking you about your 'sword work' while they leer at me."

"And someday you can ram your overpowering magic straight down their throats and envelop them in fire."

I give him an arch look, unexpectedly and deeply warmed by the violent sentiment. And by his understanding. By how he's not taking this lightly. "You're saying all the right things tonight, Lukas."

Lukas gives a low laugh as he reaches up to caress my cheek, giving me an affectionate look. "Good. I mean them."

My angry trembling fades under his comforting touch as I make a conscious effort to breathe evenly. I gesture with my chin toward the bottles, remembering that I asked him to bring strong spirits. "So...we've spirits?" I note. "That's good."

Lukas smiles as he releases my hands. "I think you'll like these."

I eye him quizzically as he moves to pick up one of the bottles along with the corkscrew.

He flashes me a subversive look as he winds the screw into the bottle's corked top. "They're tree-based wines." I raise a brow at this as he pulls the cork from the bottle with a suctioned pop.

"I hope they're strong."

"They're not," he admits as he sets the bottle back on the table. "We need to be sharp tomorrow. They aren't intoxicating, but they're relaxing in other ways. There's a slight wood thrall in each of them."

"That's...good," I say as he removes the cork from the screw. "Lukas... I'm incredibly nervous."

He pauses, his eyes flicking up to meet mine. "I'll do my best to set you at ease," he says reassuringly. He places the cork loosely back into its opening. "This is very good wine, Elloren. I'm guessing you've never had wine before?"

*I've had tirag with Valasca*, I think. *Way too much of it.*

"No, I've never had wine."

"Well, I think you'll like this." He retrieves two crystalline glasses from a nearby shelf.

I sit back down on the bed and pick up a crystal bottle that sits on the side table nearest me. It's tied with a golden ribbon that's embroidered with Ishkart letters. "What's this?"

"Ellusian oil." He pauses, as if unsure what to say. "For later."

I lift the glass stopper and breathe it in. *Vanilla. Rose. Jasmine.* "What's it for?" I ask, replacing the stopper.

He hesitates again, wine bottle in hand. "I've no desire to hurt you, Elloren."

For a moment, I'm confused. Then a light dawns and my face warms. "Well practiced in deflowering virgins, are you?" I ask edgily, embarrassed now.

He smiles and pours a small amount of the wine into the two glasses. "No. You'll be my first." He picks up both glasses, moves toward the bed, and holds one out to me.

Flustered, I take the glass, the liquid the color of honey in the soft lamplight.

"We're unique, you and I," Lukas says, taking a seat on the velvet-cushioned chair facing me, his glass held loosely in hand. "Our affinity lines match, line for line." He gestures to the bed with the glass. "I suspect we'll be a good match in this, as well."

Feeling wrapped up in apprehension, I take a small sip of the wine.

Its subtle sweetness permeates my mouth and my eyes widen in surprise. It's startlingly good. Dry and smooth, with an undercurrent of wood.

"What *is* this?" I marvel, running my tongue lightly over my upper lip, the spirits decadently warming my earthlines. My eyes brighten. "Oh, I know." I close my eyes, enraptured, as the image of coniferous trees with low-hung branches suffuses my mind. "Mmm. Cedar."

When I open my eyes Lukas is sipping his wine, his gaze intent on me. "Very good. It's aged in cedar barrels for several years. Only Mages with very strong earthlines can sense the trees in it."

"Oh, Lukas." I take another sip and let the wine roll over my tongue, the trees' sensuous limbs caressing my lines. "It's so good."

Lukas is smiling appreciatively, no small amount of affection in his gaze. "I like that you can recognize fine things. Good music, good wine." He considers his glass. "They're fools to make this illegal. Gardnerians are idiots."

I take another small sip, the awareness of the beautiful cedar grove like an embrace, relaxing the tension in my body and my emotions to the point that suppressed thoughts begin to rise to the surface. Yvan's beautiful face lights in my mind along with the remembrance of his embrace, his Wyvernfire kiss, his wings wrapped around me...

*Yvan.*

Grief engulfs me, uncomfortably sharp, as the pained thought arises—

*This was supposed to be with you, Yvan. We were supposed to be together.*

I sip the wine again, desperate to let the all-encompassing feel of the cedar grove push back my grief.

*He's gone, Elloren. You have to let him go.*

I pull in a long, shuddering breath as the wine's tree-effect settles in deeper, the beautiful vision of the trees calming my flare of sorrow.

I slip off my leaf-embroidered shoes and curl my stocking-clad feet into the carpet, my knees almost touching Lukas's as I set down my glass on the side table and consider him—the easy way he sits, hips thrust forward, leaning casually on one elbow, his glass loose in his hand. "Have you been with many women?" I ask him, growing hesitant.

Lukas sips his wine, his eyes now guarded. "A few."

It stings to hear this. *Which is absurd*, I chastise myself. He's been clear that he's experienced.

He must sense that this rattles me as his brow tightens. "I've never been with another Mage, for what it's worth."

I try to shrug off the ridiculous hurt that's strong enough to cut through the wine's lull. "That's surprising," I say.

He barks out a laugh. "I don't interfere with the Gardnerian cult of virginity." He swirls the wine in his glass, reflective. "Our whole society is touchy about it."

I bristle at the remaining options. "So, Urisk serving girls?" I ask him warily, thinking of how Silvern went after Sparrow.

Lukas throws me an incredulous look. "No, Elloren. I don't approve of that."

Confusion mounts. "Please tell me you've never been with a Selkie."

"Of course not. I've told you that before."

I furrow my brow at him. "If you haven't been with Selkies or serving girls, then who?" I know I'm being intrusive, but this entire situation is intrusive.

Lukas lets out a long sigh. "Is this really important for you to know, Elloren?"

*No, it's probably best I don't know*, I think. *But still, I don't think I can be with you if you've been abusive in the past.*

"Yes," I tell him. "I need to know."

He tips his glass, watching the play of light on it. "There were new Vu Trin soldiers at their Verpacian base every year. Far away from home. Quite lonely. And they have a different moral viewpoint regarding…" He gestures loosely toward the bed with his glass. "There were two instances where a soldier of similar rank to mine felt a mutual attraction. And we pursued it."

I gape at him.

He laughs. "Don't ask questions you don't want answered, Elloren."

I narrow my eyes. "You have a very complicated love life."

He sighs and gives me a slow once-over. "Yes. I do."

"Vu Trin soldiers?" I can't quite get my mind around it. "With their killing stars and rune swords and blades?"

He gives a short laugh. "I like dangerous women." He raises his glass to me in a slight toast. "Obviously."

"Well, that's good," I wryly comment, "since you might be risking your life tonight. Seeing as how my power bests yours in almost every way."

"I'm ready for you this time," Lukas returns, a mischievous gleam in his eyes. "And your power's tamped down since it's shielded." He sets down his glass and moves to open the second bottle, flashing me a sultry smile that sends a ripple of warmth through my lines. "I have another one for you to taste."

I look Lukas over as he pours a small amount of the scarlet wine into our glasses. Fully noticing him as my fireline rouses. Imagining the shape of his body under his tunic. Taking in his smooth, muscular movements. His deep—forest green eyes.

He picks up his own glass and hands me mine.

I take a sip. "Mmm." I slide my tongue decadently over my lips. "It tastes like…smoked cherries. And…oh, it's *oak*." I close my eyes and breathe in deeply as the dark branched tree unfurls itself for me, my earthlines curling around its every limb. I open my eyes and smile at Lukas.

He leans forward, pressing his knees lightly against mine. "I want to kiss your lips with the taste of this wine on them."

My eyes widen, my face growing warmer as my fireline gives a strong flare.

Lukas slides his gaze down my body then up to meet my eyes. "We should enjoy fine things while we can, Elloren. We've a difficult road ahead of us. With few luxuries." He sighs, as if resigned. "After tonight, our bed is likely to be the ground for some time."

I consider this as we both grow quiet, sipping the wine together in companionable silence, the burning firewood crackling softly, the lushness of the wine further soothing my lines. *He's being so careful with me*, I realize. Keeping his fire pressed firmly back. But I also know I don't want to stall all night.

I take a deep breath, stand up, and turn my back, then look at him over my shoulder. "I'll need help with the laces," I tell him, my heartbeat quickening as my magic reaches out to shimmer through his.

Lukas's fire gives an intense flare that sparks against then feeds into mine, the flames in our lines rapidly surging and licking around each other's.

I watch breathlessly as he sets down his glass and rises in one smooth motion, his fire encircling mine as he comes to me.

Lukas gently caresses the sides of my arms, and I draw in a shuddering breath, his touch intensifying the decadent heat, my lines straining toward his. He slides his palms up my arms and rests them lightly on my shoulders.

I can feel his warmth radiating all along my back, my breath hitching in response to it. And I love the smell of him. I close my eyes, lean back against his chest, and breathe him in, turning to nuzzle my cheek against his warm neck as his fire gives another heated flare.

*Deep forest wood. Pine.*

Lukas slides his hands between us, moving back a fraction as his pianist fingers make deft work of my laces, quickly unfastening them. Then he tugs up my elaborate Sealing tunic, and I raise my arms as he pulls it smoothly over my head and drops it on the floor, revealing the deep-green camisole underneath. I lower my arms as Lukas's arms slide back around me, his hard body pressing against me, a hot rush of his fire breaking free.

I look at him again over my shoulder, my breathing erratic as I'm swept up in sudden anticipation and the entrancing feel of his flame searing through mine.

Lukas's breath is warm against my ear, his deep voice an inviting whisper. "Take off the skirt. Please."

My own fire quickens in response, our magic newly charged.

I turn and sit on the bed, amused by how unsteady I am from nerves and desire and the hot draw of his magic.

Reaching behind me, I clumsily unfasten my skirt, push it down, and wriggle out of it.

Dressed now in only my thin, silken green camisole, pantalets, and deep-green silk stockings, I meet Lukas's molten gaze, my cloth-wrapped Wand still pressed to my thigh in one of my stockings. I slide the Wand out and place it on the side table beside me, then lie back on the bed, basking in the feel of Lukas's fire sparking against mine as I stretch, the linen quilt bumpy against the bare stripes of skin above my stockings. I close my eyes and delight in the taste of cherries still on my tongue, the feel of the trees caressing my lines.

Lukas's fire draws down for a moment, and I open my eyes just as he retrieves something from the leather bag by the chair. A small bottle. He pulls what looks like a tiny sliver of root out of the bottle and hands it to me.

"Here, Elloren."

"Sanjire root?" I ask.

Lukas nods.

I hold out my palm, and he drops the dark pregnancy-preventing root into it. I place it in my mouth.

It's bitter on my tongue, and I flush over the need for it.

Over what's about to transpire. I throw Lukas an arch look. "I thought you were supposed to 'breed on me.'"

He shakes his head and sits back down, picking up his glass. "That is, perhaps, the least sensual phrase ever uttered in the entire history of Erthia."

"Hmm," I agree as I finger the embroidery of the quilt beneath me.

Lukas's expression grows serious as his gaze slides over me, a pulse of his fire stroking my lines. "That fabric is thin."

"It's soft too," I tease as I bite my lip softly.

"Hmm." His fire gives another hot pulse in my direction, the heat growing more insistent.

"Your fire," I say as his heat stirs up my own. "It's starting to make me feel very relaxed."

"Good," he says. "Because I'm starting to want to take that camisole off of you."

I swallow, the tension picking up in the room.

Flushed from our affinity draw, I sit up and swing my legs over the side of the bed. I pick up my glass and take a small sip of the wine, then swirl the liquid and consider it as its oak limbs twine through me, soothing every line.

"Where did you get the rune on your forearm?" Lukas lightly inquires, his focus intent.

"Sagellyn Gaffney placed it on me," I explain. "When I visited Cyme. It turns out she's a Light Mage. She placed a demon-sensing rune on me, as well." I brazenly pull up my camisole to show him and can sense Lukas's focus scattering for a moment as he stares at the rune on my naked abdomen, his gaze growing a bit liquid before he raises his eyes to meet mine.

"You were in Cyme?" he asks, seeming a bit breathless.

I nod as I glance down at my glass, the wine such a lovely crystalline scarlet color, the firelight dancing in it. "I had spirits for the first time there too," I confide in him with a mischievous smile. "I drank too much tirag one night with Valasca Xanthrir."

Astonishment ripples through Lukas's lines. He sits forward, his invisible fire guttering. "Did you just say you drank tirag in Cyme with... *Valasca Xanthrir*?"

"Mmm-hmm." I grin at him and take another sip.

Lukas pulls in a deep breath, pondering. "Well, the odds of our survival just got a whole lot better. If we can get you through the Pass, that is."

"Why do you say that?"

"Because the Vu Trin are aligned with the Amaz. And once they tell them that you're the Black Witch, the Amaz will send the head of the Queen's Guard for you."

I raise a brow at this. "Well, that's a lucky stroke of fate. She's my friend."

Lukas cocks his head and lets out a long sigh. "It's a relief to know that Valasca Xanthrir is not likely to kill us. How did you ever come to drink tirag with her?"

I tell him the story of Marina, the Selkie, and how we had to travel to the Amaz city of Cyme to enlist the help of the Amaz to free all the Selkies, and how I encountered Sage Gaffney there. "I had a headache that evening," I tell him, "so Valasca gave me some tirag. I drank quite a lot, and quickly found that spirits make me feel..." I give him a slow smile. "...quite loosened up. Much like your fire."

Lukas's eyes take on a suggestive gleam. He sends out a warm, embracing line of flame. "Would you like to feel more of it?"

My magic flares toward him, a hard stream of it flashing into his lines, and Lukas shudders slightly in response. I smile at him. "I would."

Lukas seems amused by my brazen gaze. He stands, takes

the glass from my hand, sets it on the table, then pulls off his tunic in one smooth motion and throws it over the back of the chair.

It's a shock, his partial nudity, and a hard spike of desire flashes through me. I swallow as my gaze wanders over his handsome frame.

There's a knife marked with Noi runes strapped to one of his upper arms. Another small spare wand that's rune marked strapped to the other. His chest is muscular. Mostly smooth and shimmering green in the dim light, dark hair shadowing its center.

A line of black hair disappears down his pants.

My lines warming, I quickly look back up at his face and find that his smile has turned feral.

Lukas removes his wand, his knife, and the sheaths, then sets them all on the table next to my Wand. He sits, removes his boots, and reaches under each pant leg, removing rune blades strapped just underneath.

"Sure you won't need them?" I challenge, attempting a fierce look.

"As dangerous as you are, I highly doubt it," he jests. He sets the second knife next to the first one and flashes me a grin. "You seem increasingly friendly."

"You're incredibly attractive."

He smiles at me and picks up his wand. "Lie back," he gently prompts.

I comply, and he softly murmurs a spell. Thin, dark lines flow from his wand and encircle my body, brushing lightly over me in a caressing net, sending out delicious sparks, some muted by the clothing, some startlingly pleasurable where they touch down on bare skin.

My breathing deepens, the sparks radiating a delicious vibration down through the core of me, and a moan escapes my lips. "Oh, that's nice, Lukas."

His eyes take on a carnal light. "It's a lot more fun with your clothes off."

I stare at him for a long tension-fraught moment as the lines dissolve then disappear, my words soft and sly when they come. "Then take them off."

For an instant all is still. The fire crackles in the fireplace. Neither of us moves.

Lukas is next to me in one streamlined movement, the bed dipping from his weight. He focuses on me with searing intensity, his hand sliding up the center of my camisole as if he's determining where to start first.

The camisole is off in three gentle decided tugs. The rest of my clothes in a single smooth motion. He has the ardent intensity of an artist. No hesitation. No awkwardness.

He leans down and his mouth claims mine as he lowers himself onto me, his long, muscular body pressed decadently against mine, excitingly hard and warm to the touch. Our affinity fires race toward each other, earthlines rapidly interweaving, and I can sense Lukas's affinity flames straining against his careful control.

He seems to get hold of himself and pulls back the way he did when we played music together. His touch is lighter now, his firelines more contained. He waits for me, letting the intensity build as he kisses me ardently and his fire strokes down my lines, the heat surging forward, then pulling back again—a dance. Rise and fall. Teasing me by withdrawing. Then giving me a heated glimpse of his full power.

Slowly, I catch on, and we begin to find each other's rhythm, faltering less and less, exploring each other's bodies and magic. I revel in the hard muscle of his thigh beneath my palm. The jut of his hip bone under his pants. The caress of my power on him here, his hands firm on me where my magic sparks with a burgeoning longing for him.

And surprising things that cut clear through the fiery haze of our power.

His fingernails, lightly grazing my outstretched palms, sending tingling waves of heat through my body. His mouth, shockingly on my nipple, his tongue spiraling in ever-tighter circles. The delicious warmth of him. The decadent glimpses of his half-naked body moving against mine.

His weight shifts on the bed and he sits up, his eyes hot on me. His wand is now lightly in his palm. "Lie on your back," he hoarsely invites.

Ensnared by him, I eagerly comply. Lukas murmurs a spell, his voice throaty with desire, and sends the sparking lines out over me again.

"Mmm." I'm like a cat in sunlight, languidly stretching into the pleasure he's flowing through my lines. He's all tight focus as he slowly moves the wand down my body, sending the sizzling magic ever lower as a delicious tension builds.

The lines coalesce in one spot between my legs, and I'm overcome by a sudden explosion of shuddering ecstasy, my neck arching as I cry out, and a throbbing heat envelops me. Wave after wave of it. Taking its time receding. I close my eyes, crane my neck, and let out a long, shuddering breath.

Only then does he come to me.

His half-clothed body slides over mine, his own hard desire pressing where pleasure still echoes, my eyes still dreamily closed. I bask in the incredible sensation he created, pivoting my hips to hold on to the edges of it. Pressing against him as I do.

He rolls half off of me, and I hear a small click and feel him unfastening his belt.

I open my eyes then turn quickly away, the room unsteady,

my heart thudding in my chest, his fire racing through my lines. I bite gently at my lower lip, the taste of cherries and oak still lingering there. Then I swallow and venture a glance at his body. Heat burns along my neck and I look away again as a raw trepidation cuts through my haze of desire.

Lukas gently slides back over me, the skin of the entire length of his body enticingly warm against mine.

I turn and catch the glint of firelight reflected through the bottle of oil. With one hand, Lukas unstoppers the bottle, tips it, and pours some onto his fingers.

I breathe in the oil's warm floral-vanilla scent.

He props himself up on one elbow, his palm now on my stomach, sliding down, the oil's soft heat flaring in his palm's wake. His fingers leave a trail of warmth where they travel, the sensation flaring. Lukas traces spirals on the naked skin of my hips with the oil, the heat reverberating, then slides his fingers lower, holding my gaze to confirm my permission the whole time.

I nod and let out a ragged breath, my hands tightening on him.

I catch another glimpse of him, and nervous surprise mingles with a hard flash of want as heat rises on my face, my chest. It's so intimate, the sight of him. My breathing deepens in response.

A man's body. Aroused.

Lukas positions himself just over and against me as he kisses me long and sensuously. A tighter hunger takes hold as our fires blaze toward each other and I pull him closer.

And then the full pressure of him. A jolt of stretching pain that arches my neck as I gasp in surprise.

Lukas pauses, now deep inside me, one hand grasping my hip, his mouth almost touching mine. He's breathing hard as he waits for me, all tight control, the sting of his entry receding. He brings his mouth back to mine and kisses me deeply, sending twining, soothing roots through my lines.

He waits for my grip on him to loosen, for my chaotic lines to smooth out and warm. Then he moves in me, slowly at first.

I gasp at the fullness of him. It's overwhelming. But a heated pleasure reverberates to balance the hurt, and I arch toward him as his fire shudders through me and pleasure takes hold and builds anew.

Lukas's movements are smooth and in delicious concert with the motion of his mouth and tongue, the loosening then tightening of his grip on me.

The loosening of his magic.

I slowly fall into sync with him, finding his rhythm as strengthening waves of pleasure and his fire eddy through me. I press my hips forward to meet him and feel his smile on my mouth.

When the explosive rush finally comes again, it's not as ecstatic as before, the slight sting at the edges of him holding me back. But a more mellow, decadent pleasure courses through me, blending roots, sinuous branches, and shuddering fire, dampening the hurt. I let out a sigh and glide my fingers down his muscular back.

Lukas's control begins to fracture as he picks up the intensity of his rhythm, his touch becoming increasingly impassioned with a growing hunger as his fire rushes through his lines and into mine, the heat building.

On instinct, I wrap my legs tight around him, my mouth pressed to the heated skin of his neck as he moves. I summon my power and push blazing fire and branching magic straight into his lines.

Lukas loses all control.

He thrusts hard, his breathing hot and ragged, as he grips at me fiercely.

"Elloren…"

He drives a gasp from my lungs with one final thrust that floods me with warmth as he groans and grips me, his fire spiraling all around my body, scorching through my lines.

His jaw presses into my shoulder, his breath hot. Every muscle in his body rock-hard.

His eyes meet mine.

Open. Wide-open. Unguarded.

The wild yearning in his eyes stuns me, and I almost shrink back from the intensity of it.

After a long moment, Lukas's breathing evens out, and the raw, ardent intensity in his gaze dampens.

We lie embracing like this for a moment, both of us seeming stunned.

He pulls out in one smooth motion as I cling to him, still in a haze of magic and heat. "No, don't go," I protest.

Lukas gives a low laugh as he moves off me and onto his back, now staring at the ceiling, one hand on his muscular stomach, his breathing deep and ragged.

I sense a void opening between us, and I cling to him, hugging his arm. But he seems suddenly lost in thought, elusive.

I'm still affected by the force of our combined magic, overcome by a pleasurable, heated daze, but I'm clear that he's been incredibly thoughtful in how he's handled me. There's only a small, throbbing ache where he's been, mingled with the hot, lingering pleasure.

He turns and meets my eyes.

"I'm still caught up in your fire," I tell him.

One finger traces lightly along my side. "I'm caught up in everything about you," he says, his voice throaty. "You're so lovely, Elloren. Just…*beautiful*." He's looking at my body with deep appreciation, like it's a fine work of art. His gaze lifts to mine and the affection in his eyes strikes a chord deep inside my heart.

I hold up my hand and marvel at how the fasting marks have changed, intricate new spirals flowing down my glimmering-green wrist.

Lukas holds his similarly marked wrist up and then traces the lines of my wrist with a fingertip. "Have I brought you sufficiently to heel," he teases, sending a shiver through me as he traces the line.

I cough out a laugh, and even through our magical thrall, I manage a look of white-hot defiance. "No."

Lukas's laugh is low and satisfied. "Good." He lightly touches the tip of my nose, smiling wickedly before his eyes grow serious. "Hold on to that." His smile fades, and that ardent fire is suddenly back in his eyes.

Then conflict.

Lukas eases onto his back and stares at the ceiling again, his expression unreadable.

I'm too relaxed from the fire still coursing through me to feel any sting at his withdrawal. The pull of his magic, the wild pleasure of being with him—it all spirals together and sweeps me into a black, dreamless sleep.

# CHAPTER
# SEVEN

# ASHES

## ELLOREN GREY

*Sixth Month*
*Valgard, Gardneria*

When my eyes flutter open, dawn is illuminating the edges of the drawn curtains.

Lukas is up. Even in the early-morning light, I can tell that he's bathed. I smell soap mingled with that deep-forest scent of his. He's in newly pressed pants, his chest bare as he pulls his belt through the loops.

I stir, disoriented, and meet Lukas's intent gaze. His eyes flick toward my chest, and I see a spark of interest in them as he buckles his belt.

I glance down at myself and jolt fully awake, mortified to realize I'm completely naked. I jerk the sheet that's haphazardly wrapped around me up over my breasts.

*This is all wrong* is my first thought. *This isn't what this is supposed to be.* The uneasy remembrance slams down that we've never even told each other *I love you.*

My pulse quickens as my emotions churn.

Lukas is all business. He looks to be thinking hard on something as he grabs his tunic and throws it on, then leans to write something on a list he's started on the side table. His eyes flick toward me every now and then, his expression unreadable.

Emptiness drops through my center, hollowing me out. I lie there, motionless, my messy nakedness jarring in contrast to his cold, crisp efficiency.

*This was a mistake. A terrible mistake.*

And even worse, I enjoyed it.

Remorse whips through me, along with the certainty that something precious has been lost to me forever. I run my fingers back to clutch at my tangled hair.

I was supposed to experience this with Yvan. Instead I threw it away on a man who might care for me and respect me, but who's never once said he's in love with me.

For escape.

My rational mind is clear that Lukas and I didn't do this on a whim. That we've allied ourselves as true friends to escape from Gardneria and fight for everything that's good in the world. But I'm unable to escape the fierce tide of grief and emotion as it captures me in its undertow.

There will be no sweet discovering of this with Yvan, everything new and fresh to both of us. No holding me afterward and whispering endearments. It's lost forever. That first time with someone who truly loves me.

I ball up in the bed, chilled by my nudity, close my eyes, and struggle not to cry.

*I want my uncle back. I want to tell him that everything has gone wrong and is spinning out of control. That he was right to shelter me. And I don't know what to do, because I'm being faced with impossible choices. I want to talk to him and have him comfort me.*

*I want to go home.*

Lukas has gone very still. I can't hear him moving at all. But I can feel his gaze on me.

I brace myself, remembering how unsympathetic Lukas was when I was attacked by Icarals in Valgard. How he snarled at me that I had to be tough. I feel like I'll hate him with an unstoppable fury if he tells me that right now.

"Elloren." His voice is softer than usual when it comes.

I open my tear-blurred eyes to find him standing before me by the edge of the bed, holding his hand out to me.

"I can't get up," I tell him roughly. "I'm naked." Regret rips through me. I close my eyes tight, trying to block everything out.

*What have I done? Why did I decide to do this?*

*To save your own life*, a quiet part of my mind reminds me. *And to fight to save countless others.*

I hear his body shift.

"Elloren." He's close to me now.

I open my eyes to find him kneeling down almost to my eye level.

His gaze is steady on me. "After I've gotten you to safety, I *will* court you properly."

I want to laugh at the sheer impossibility of his offer.

*Safety?*

The word breaks through my misery, our impossible situation rushing in. There is no safety for me. Only unspeakable, terrible danger. People who hate me. People who want to kill me and watch me suffer.

People who see me only as a weapon to wield or destroy.

It all floods through me. The very real danger to so many lives if I don't survive and learn how to fight. But my odds of survival…they're so horrifically bad.

*I don't want to die, I don't want to die*, I anguish with every beat of my heart.

I'm scared. Not just scared. Terrified. I start to tremble.

Lukas's hand takes firm hold of my arm. "You are *not alone*."

The way he says it stops me short. I open my eyes to meet his gaze full on. He's so sure. Like it's a simple, unassailable fact.

It's not enough to heal the gaping wound in my heart, or to extinguish my debilitating fear, but the certainty in his voice bolsters some central part of me. Enough for me to roughly wipe away my tears and take the robe he's now holding out to me.

I contort myself to try to put the robe on under the sheet, giving him a look of censure when he does not avert his eyes. But when he holds out his hand again, I take it.

Lukas gives me a slow once-over as I rise, and I marvel at him, stunned that he can be so brazen. I shoot him a grimace as I pull my robe tight.

Heat flares in Lukas's eyes. He lifts his hand and gently slides it along the nape of my neck and up through my hair, his thumb caressing my jaw as he sends a stream of his affinity fire through me, both the fire and the motion of his hand soothing.

I close my eyes and intentionally pull on his flame, my breathing and my mortal panic loosening. Steadied, I look up at him.

Lukas nods with a look of calm approval, as if acknowledging that I've steeled myself. He smiles. "If the world were not about to end and I'd already courted you properly, I'd peel that robe off you, pull you onto the bed, and ravish you again." His finger idly traces the skin along my robe's neckline as I gape at him.

His simple, straightforward lust at a time like this is so outrageous that it makes me cough out an incredulous laugh in spite of myself. I can tell by the amusement dancing in his eyes that this bawdy humor is his attempt to comfort me.

It strikes me that trying to be close to Lukas is like being allied with a cobra. It's unsettling comfort, but comfort nonetheless.

And as much as I want someone to hold me, I don't need a sentimental ally right now. Lukas may be cold and harsh at times, but I need someone hard. And this dangerous, ruthless man is promising to help me get out of the Western Realm alive. At great personal risk.

An unexpected wave of gratitude washes over me.

I reach up to rest my hand gently on his shoulder, stand on my toes, lean in, and softly kiss his mouth.

Lukas's eyes darken with yearning as I draw back a fraction.

"If you kiss me like that one more time," he says teasingly, his voice velvet smooth, "I *will* take you again. Vogel be damned."

I slide my hand back through his hair and run my thumb lightly over his lower lip, a flare of desire rising in me that takes me by surprise. I let my hand fall away and step back from him.

He's watching me closely with those predator eyes of his.

I take a deep breath, determination rising. "I'm ready. Let's get out of here."

"Elloren…" he says, hesitating, serious now. "I need to shield your magic. To prepare you to face Vogel. It will be easier to do if I kiss you."

I nod, understanding that this is suddenly a very different thing.

Lukas slides his hand behind my head, pulls me in, and brings his lips decisively to mine. I gasp as he sends a rush of his power through me, then gasp again as his power tugs hard on my earthlines, wresting control of my branch magic and weaving it over my other lines, his own magic encircling then coalescing around it. To slowly, methodically create a wall, layer by layer, just under my skin.

Of solid, impenetrable magery.

Lukas and I stride through the center of the arboretum's forest, our hands tightly clasped, my Wand wrapped in cloth and hidden again in the side of my stocking, Chi Nam's rune stone in Lukas's pocket. Our small army of Level Five guards is tight on our heels. My whole body itches for escape, and I can sense the bowstring-tight tension that's vibrating through Lukas's contained fire.

Everything is washed in ruby light, the green illumination from last night replaced with innumerable red glass lanterns hanging from countless branches, suffusing the world in a lurid scarlet glow. Outside the windows, storm clouds hang so low that their bulbous, steely forms almost touch the arboretum's glass ceiling.

It's as if the very sky is closing on us.

My fireline gives an anxious flare against Lukas's tight shield as we near the edge of the indoor forest then emerge past it to face down the dense crowd of Mages spread out before us.

Thunder rumbles overhead as I take it all in.

The huge glass-enclosed space has been transformed for the Sealing breakfast, all the decor now awash with red accents symbolic of my deflowering, and I grit my teeth against this intrusive tradition.

Vases of red roses grace the center of every bloodred table-cloth, and ruby glass lanterns hang from the iron stands set beside each table. Even the traditional black silk garb Lukas and I are wearing is edged with intricate, bloodred embroidery, all the red heightened by the dark morning sky with its ominous steel-gray clouds.

As we enter, everyone stands and breaks into subdued applause.

My eyes meet Vogel's across the room, and a defensive fire rears inside me and bucks hard against Lukas's shield.

Vogel is standing before the small Ironwood altar from our Sealing ceremony near the arboretum's western-facing glass wall. An army of soldiers is massed just outside the glass, along with a horde of broken dragons, the dragons' large black forms facing outward and preternaturally still, like demonic statues.

My gaze slides to the Shadow Wand in Vogel's hand.

My Wand flares to life against my thigh in an urgent hum that I can feel straight through the cloth it's wrapped in. A sudden pull accosts me, like a cord giving a small yank from my Wand, through my lines, out through my wand hand toward Vogel's Wand.

And then my Wand's tremulous hum blinks out of existence, and the Wand renders itself into deadened, inert wood yet again. As if it's desperately thrown itself back into hiding.

Aunt Vyvian and Lukas's family are seated at a table near Vogel, along with what seems like most of the Mage Council. Behind them stand Vogel's two envoys, the four soldiers magically tethered to him, and an arcing line of Level Five soldiers, all of them regarding Lukas and me with intense focus.

Apprehension grips my throat, pulling it taut.

So many Level Five soldiers, Vogel's personal guard tripled from last night.

I've an amorphous sense of the powerful magery thrumming in the air, the feel of it like a ferocious storm about to blow through, but it doesn't overwhelm me. Their collective magic hovers around the powerful shield Lukas wove under my skin, reducing their magical press to a slight, uncomfortable pressure and a static tang on the air.

Heart thudding, I lower my gaze to the obsidian-stone tile

work on the floor beneath my feet, holding tight to Lukas as we stride down the center aisle toward Vogel.

The polite applause continues as we come to a stop before the altar and I keep my eyes cast submissively down, my breath hitched tight in my chest.

I can sense Vogel's malefic gaze locked on me.

I can sense his Shadow Wand, its power a low, tide-like pulse.

He seems to have shuttered his magic as tightly as Lukas has walled back his own, no trace of his vast power revealed. For a moment, I frustratedly yearn to possess such control.

Control that would hand me magical dominance over all the Mages in this room, save perhaps Vogel.

I dare a glance up to find Lukas's parents and self-righteous brother staring at me coldly, while Aunt Vyvian looks me over with conceited triumph, all gazes flowing to the hand I have clasped around Lukas's.

A stinging flush warms my face. I know what they're all scrutinizing so intently—the Sealing marks that now flow around both our wrists, our changed lines proof of consummation.

Angry humiliation flares, running hot through my lines. I feel exposed, used.

Like their communal plaything.

Lukas tightens his grip around my hand and lifts it straight into the air, as tradition dictates. The applause surges to life once more, some of the men cheering Lukas on, and I'm aware that I've ceased to be a person to all of them save Lukas, who I know despises all this as much as I do. But to them I'm nothing but a thing to be bred on. A conduit of my grandmother's power, seized for the Grey line. Seized by a family loyal to Marcus Vogel.

Lukas lowers our hands, and the applause and cheers die down.

Vogel smiles at me, then at Lukas, seeming charmed by us. He holds out his hand for mine, and I let him take it as I struggle to suppress a slight tremble, his long fingers oddly warm as they close around mine, and I hold tight to Lukas with my other hand.

I don't attempt to hide how upset I feel, my lips trembling along with my hand. I know they'll all read this as proper maidenly anguish—the secrets of the Sealing chamber laid bare and foisted upon innocent me. But, suddenly, I'm boiling with a bottomless fury as Vogel studies my Sealinglines with leering focus.

This man killed Diana's family. And standing nearby, watching me coldly, is the aunt who killed my beloved uncle Edwin. These are the people responsible for driving everyone I love East, to a fate unknown to me. These are the people forcing me into an escape I don't even know if I'll survive.

Fire whips up in my lines and rears against Lukas's compact shield, one violent tendril of flame breaking clear through it.

Vogel's lips pull back over his teeth, as if he's sensed my sudden rush of fire. His eyes flick toward Lukas with approval as he keeps hold of me. "So, you've made her yours?"

Anger continues to lash into a conflagration through my lines, even as I struggle to rein myself in.

"I have," Lukas calmly returns.

"Her fireline," Vogel says, fondling my hand. "It's strong. Can you feel her grandmother's power in her?"

Lukas smiles. "I can."

Vogel's penetrating gaze falls back on me as he abruptly tightens his grip, his nails digging into the skin of my wand hand.

I shiver and pull in a shocked breath as dark branches snake through me, relentlessly flowing through my escaped fire and over Lukas's shield as I'm suddenly pinned in place and unable to push Vogel out. Vogel's Shadow power contracts around Lukas's shield, sending a slash of pain through my lines.

Vogel narrows his chilling gaze on me, then gives me a disturbingly knowing look as he withdraws his probe. Seeming satisfied, he releases my hand, and I pull in a breath of air, my lungs freed from the suffocating press of his power.

Vogel suddenly presses his Shadow Wand against my hand, and I recoil in fear.

Lukas's reaction is immediate—his invisible affinity branches make a quick, lethal orientation toward Vogel, and I tighten my grip on Lukas's hand to caution him to hold back his power.

"It is written," Vogel tells me, as the wood of his Wand digs into my skin. "'To be disciplined by an honest Mage is a blessing for his fastmate.'"

Lukas's fire gives another savage flare, looping around me with protective ferocity. I glance at him only to find his gaze pinned on Vogel with startlingly open fury.

Shock cuts through my terror. I've rarely seen Lukas's calm breached like it is right now.

Ignoring Lukas, Vogel studies me intently. And then presses his Wand harder into my hand. His magic slams into me like a bolt of angry fire to collide with bone-heating force against Lukas's shield.

Lukas's shield sags violently inward, and I clutch harder to his hand, nearly buckling in half as Vogel's Shadow fire roars over the surface of Lukas's tightly woven shield. Bombarding it. As if Vogel is attempting to slaughter it into oblivion and take control of me.

And then he abruptly withdraws his attack.

I teeter on my feet and would have fallen if not for Lukas's steadying grip and his strengthening rush of fire.

"Bring her to me after the Blessing of Dominion," Vogel says, a fanatical gleam entering the pale eyes he has trained on me. "For wandtesting."

Lukas's grip on my hand and my shield remains firm. "Of course, Your Excellency," he replies, calm as a storm's eye.

I wait, breathless, as Vogel dips his head toward Lukas in solemn acknowledgment. "I've arranged an escort. To accompany you to the forest for the Blessing."

Fear, like a hot iron, sears into my chest.

*We have to enter the forest alone. Our escape hinges on it.*

"Your Excellency," Lukas calmly counters, sounding only mildly surprised, "it is written in the *Book* that the sealed Mages must face the wilds in solitude."

Vogel's mouth curls up. "It is also written that 'it is a blessing to hold a Mage to a straight and righteous path.'" Vogel flicks one hand, and two Level Five Mages step forward. They look young but tough, and I've a sense, straight through Lukas's shield, of the incredibly powerful air and water affinities that are lashing inside the two of them in a gale-force storm.

I realize, as a starker fear accosts me, that Vogel has read both my lines and Lukas's with exacting focus. The affinity powers of these two Mage soldiers are the exact opposite of Lukas's and mine, with enough water and air between them to dominate Lukas's fire and blow apart his earth magery.

I know, deep in my pounding heart, that if I could control my magic, Lukas and I could easily take down these two lethal guards. But Lukas can't best them alone.

Lukas's earthlines tighten around mine with fearsome urgency, as if he's striving to maintain hold of his magical barrier between us and them. But his efforts are futile.

We're trapped.

And we're completely outmatched…because I can't control my power.

Lukas and I step out of the arboretum and into the large, manicured rose garden that abuts the forest greenhouse, the wilds just beyond the gardens and the warded iron gate that encircles the estate.

Lukas's fire whips around me with rigorous force as we're trailed by the two Water and Air Mages, along with an additional four Level Five guards. The army of Mages and military dragons that surround the estate are all magically focused on us.

The skin of my arms prickles from the tempest of affinity power at our backs as I internally wage war against my spiking apprehension.

The wind picks up as the low storm clouds overhead thicken and Lukas and I stride down the onyx-stone path that cuts through the garden. The slim scarlet heels of the shoes Aunt Vyvian provided click against the stone, the morning air laden with the smell of bloodred roses. I throw a glance over my shoulder to find Vogel, Aunt Vyvian, Lachlan Grey, and the rest of Lukas's family staring at us through the arboretum's glass wall with intense scrutiny.

A stiff breeze cuts through the gardens and pushes the surrounding roses into a unified tilt as we approach the iron fence. Lukas presses his wand to the deep-green rune that marks the gate and murmurs a spell, then resheathes the wand as he pushes the gate open.

We step through and approach the rustling line of forest.

*Black Witch.*

The hostile words sound in my mind, riding in from the wilds before us—wilds we're supposed to escape into.

Lukas gives me a significant look just before we step into the trees, his fire blisteringly hot and tightly held at bay. Wordlessly, we stride into the wilds, fingers entwined, as Lukas pushes his invisible fire aura out toward the hostile trees in firm warning.

Shadows close around us as Lukas pulls me deeper and deeper into the woods, practically dragging me now as I struggle to keep up with him on my thin-heeled shoes, our guards close at our backs.

Lightning flashes overhead and thunder booms.

After a while, Lukas halts and draws a velvet bag from his tunic's pocket that contains the ashes of the tree we destroyed during our Sealing ceremony. He pretends to survey the forest for just the right tree to throw the ashes onto in sacred warning, as I ready myself for the ruse we came up with as a contingency plan just before we left for the Sealing breakfast.

A ruse that will turn the way Gardnerians treat females against them.

Lukas focuses on a towering Black Oak. But instead of throwing the ashes onto its textured trunk and reciting the Dominion Blessing, Lukas drops the bag to the ground, yanks me around, and grabs hold of my arm as he clamps his mouth down on mine. My feet skid against the forest floor as he presses me against the tree's rough trunk, and the tree's essence recoils violently from us.

I whimper dramatically and pretend to fight Lukas, but he holds on tight, "forcing" his mouth onto mine as he reinforces my internal shield and draws hard on my power.

I mock struggle against him, finally wrenching myself free. "Stop!" I plead with a beseeching look toward our guards who stand in an arcing row nearby. Predictably, they turn away, clearly both surprised and uncomfortable. And somewhat amused.

Lukas's hold on me tightens, his face twisting into an intimidating snarl. "You don't tell me to *stop*. You are my *fastmate*. Shall I take the lash to you like I did last night?"

I'm trembling, and it's good. Even though the trembling is from nerves set alight because I know what we're about to attempt.

"You listen to me," Lukas snarls as he leans toward my ear and surreptitiously reaches for his wand. He leans in closer, whispering spell after spell after spell after spell too low for the guards to hear, flooding his lines with both his magic and mine.

Then Lukas pushes me roughly aside, whirls around, and throws his wand arm out in a sweeping arc.

Dense vines shoot from his wand's tip in a fusillade of spears, raying out to impale every guard straight through their heads before they have a chance to raise their wands.

The guards fall to the ground in heavy *thumps*, but one manages a sharp, rasping cry that I know will carry.

Lukas and I exchange one fiercely determined look as I scuttle around the tree to retrieve the sturdy boots that Lukas had Thierren leave there for me. I cast off my flimsy shoes and pull on the boots.

Lukas grabs my hand, and we set off at a fast clip through the woods.

A male voice booms out from the direction of the estate. "That way!"

Fear slices through me as Lukas and I sprint up a rocky incline, rapidly gaining a higher vantage point as we crest a wooded hill. A clearing just beyond two sizable boulders allows us a sweeping view of the gardens below.

A large number of Level Five Mages are running toward the spot where we entered the wilds, wands raised, several more leaping astride broken dragons and rapidly tracking us.

Fear crests inside me. "Lukas—there're too many of them. We don't have enough of a lead to—"

A huge explosion booms and rocks the world into nothing but a flash of blinding blue light.

Lukas throws his body over mine protectively, pressing us both onto the ground, a dark negative of the blast spotting my vision. My heartbeat slams against my ribs as no new blast sounds and we rise and look out over the scene.

The entire estate and its surrounding grounds churn with bright sapphire flames. Dragons shriek. Soldiers scream as vivid blue flames and indigo smoke rise high into the air.

I tense and gasp, not believing what I see next. Close to twenty black-clad Vu Trin soldiers stream in around the inferno, storming the estate from its eastern side, hurling stars and picking off soldiers and broken dragons with streaks of blue rune fire and whirring rune weapons.

Through the dark blue smoke, I catch a glimpse of a Mage soldier throwing out a hard jet of water from his wand. It knocks two Vu Trin down just as the Vu Trin soldier advancing behind him throws a glinting silver star that slices straight into his neck. She darts forward and slashes his back with a sword at the same time that he's hit by a barrage of silver stars from his opposite side. The Mage arcs back and falls to the ground in an explosion of sapphire fire.

A ferocious roar sounds above, and I jerk my head up as six sapphire Noi dragons pierce the storm clouds like arrows aimed at the estate, jets of golden fire spearing down to take out the remaining soldiers and dragons.

I gape at the roaring inferno, astounded. Vu Trin soldiers at the explosion's periphery shout to each other in the Noi language as their sapphire dragons circle and land.

*They're all dead*, I dazedly realize.

Vogel.

Most of the Mage Council.

Aunt Vyvian.

Lukas's entire family.

*Gone. They're all gone. Everyone who attended the Sealing.*

I'm paralyzed, my legs unsteady beneath me. Because I know what the true target of the Vu Trin invasion is.

*Me.*

I turn to Lukas to find him staring at the scene with a stunned look, and when he turns to me, his eyes flash with a momentary devastation.

*His whole family.*

"Lukas...your family..."

"*Stop.*" His expression goes hard, the word silencing me. "We just got the diversion we needed," he rasps. He glances back at the huge fire that has engulfed his family's estate. "And I don't think the Vu Trin saw us."

There's another explosion at the edge of the churning blue flame, but this conflagration is gray flame that spits silver.

Bolts of silver-gray fire spear out of the strange conflagration toward the Vu Trin and their dragons, rapidly killing them, as a smoke-darkened figure emerges from the compact silver-gray inferno. His wand is raised as he slashes out shadowy fire, the Vu Trin's runic weapons seeming powerless against him.

A fresh terror bolts through me.

*Marcus Vogel.*

*Sweet Ancient One, no.*

Impossibly, incredibly, and horrifically...he's survived.

Marcus Vogel turns and scans the smoldering landscape, the many Mages and Vu Trin and dragons now lying dead, strewn all over the gardens.

Vogel raises his eyes toward the elevated wilds where we're hidden as he lifts his Shadow Wand.

Lukas wrenches me to the ground and throws himself on top of me, gripping my head with both hands as he brings his mouth down hard on mine and forces all his affinity power into my shield in one overpowering surge.

I clutch Lukas's arms, pulling on his power as it spirals tightly around my lines and forces every last shred of my magic down behind it.

I gasp as I'm hit by a blast of Vogel's Shadow power from clear across the grounds and through the wilds, my whole body shuddering against Lukas's as Vogel's magic streams over us like an inescapable tide and grays out my vision, even as Lukas sends magic through me and holds on tight.

And then...the tide of Shadow magic passes over us and streams into the wilds, fanning out in a continued search for me as Shadow fire roars and the whole world changes.

# CHAPTER EIGHT

# ESCAPE

## ELLOREN GREY

*Sixth Month*
*Valgard, Gardneria*

I cling to Lukas's hand as we rush uphill through the woods, sticks and brush scraping against my cheeks and arms, desperation fueling my steps. The *whoosh* of wingbeats sounds from above, and I duck as three sapphire forms shoot by overhead.

*More Vu Trin dragons!*

Lukas adjusts our course, and I do my best to push through a painful stitch in my side, my lungs feeling like they're full of glass shards as we run, the red beadwork on my skirts repeatedly catching on brush and tearing away whenever I yank up my hem to free my steps.

The roar of dragons and the *boom* of explosions coming from the direction of Valgard's ports spike my pulse, my heart attempting to punch a hole through my chest as we pick up our pace and Lukas meets my panic-stricken gaze with a steely look of his own.

We rush over a road that cuts through the forest, then sprint back into the wrathful trees as another explosion sounds. I keep hold of Lukas's hand as we run up a wooded hill, then down a steep embankment where I briefly lose my footing and Lukas catches me as I start to skid.

After righting my balance, we dart toward a hemlock grove, and I startle and slide to an abrupt stop alongside Lukas as a hooded Gardnerian figure emerges from the shadows of the towering evergreen trees—a young man with a severe, elegant face, blistering urgency in his pine green eyes.

*Thierren!*

He motions us forward, and we follow him into the hemlock shadows and around a large, rocky outcropping to find three horses saddled and ready to go.

Mahogany-haired Malthorin Thoroughbreds. Built for sustained speed. Travel packs hanging from their sides.

Thierren tosses Lukas a stuffed sack, which Lukas deftly catches then pulls clothing out of and hands a simple black woolen tunic and dark riding skirt to me.

"Where are Sparrow and Effrey?" I ask. "And Aislinn?"

"Safe," Thierren reassures me.

"Put these on," Lukas directs as I take the clothing. He gestures with a sweep of his finger along his face. "Wipe off all that face paint. And get rid of the jewelry."

"What happened?" Thierren asks Lukas, seeming rattled, as Lukas throws off his own silk red-embroidered tunic. There are weapons strapped all over Lukas's body. More weapons than he had on last night, most of them Noi rune blades marked with glowing sapphire runes on their hilts. And his extra wand with Noi runes worked into its ebony wood is sheathed against his side.

"The Vu Trin took out the entire estate," Lukas harshly recounts to Thierren, his jaw set as he pulls on a plain woolen tunic.

I turn away from them, yank off my Sealing tunic, hastily throw on the new one, and wipe off my makeup with the discarded tunic as another explosion sounds in the direction of the city.

"Vogel survived," Lukas says to Thierren, giving him a quick, portentous look as I tug on the long riding skirt under my Sealing skirt. "He knows what Elloren is. And he suspects she's alive. He sent out a search spell."

Thierren stills, as if he's been physically hit with this information. "During the day?" he asks, low and weighted as I tug off the Sealing skirt.

Lukas nods, his returning look one of such grave import that it spikes my urgency as I quickly remove my glittering ruby earrings, necklace, and hair decorations and shove them into my pocket.

"We need to get Elloren out of the Western Realm." Lukas draws the rune-marked wand from its sheath strapped just under his tunic's side. "And *fast*." He turns to me, his eyes blazing with purpose. "Pull up your sleeve, Elloren," he says, his tone brooking no argument. "I'm going to create another shield just under your skin, to make it difficult for the Vu Trin to track you, as well."

Wordlessly I draw back my sleeve and hold out my forearm to him.

Lukas presses the rune wand's tip to my skin and murmurs a spell in the back of his throat.

A stream of thready blue lightning flows from his wand's tip and forks around my wrist and up my arm, tickling my skin as the thin, forking veins crackle over me. Then Lukas goes to one knee and lowers his wand to the forest floor, angling his head down as he murmurs another spell.

Another flash of blue lines courses from his wand's tip. They fan out over the forest floor in a glowing net that courses in the direction we came from, the lines vanishing almost as quickly as they were sent out.

"What was that?" I ask Lukas.

"Noi anti-tracking sorcery." He rises and surveys the forest floor. "One of the runes on the wand is precharged with it."

His knowledge of mixed magery is like a door to the unknown thrown open. "You need to teach me how to do all of that," I say, insistent.

Lukas flashes me a look of approval. "I will," he promises as he pulls up the side of his tunic, flashing his glimmering-green skin in the dark gloom as he resheathes the wand.

Thierren stuffs our discarded clothing into one of the horses' packs then hands both Lukas and me dark cloaks that match his own. We throw them on, then mount the horses, pull on our cloaks' hoods, and take off through the woods down a rough, winding path as explosions and the roar of dragons reverberate in the distance.

Eventually we come to what looks like a long-abandoned Keltish guard tower, the top of the structure charred to oblivion, lichen growing over its crumbling stone walls. The explosions booming from the direction of the city are now faint disturbances that mingle with the muted roll of thunder from the storm that's been gathering for more than a day. A storm that, I imagine, will be quite violent when it finally breaks.

We ride around the structure's stone corner, and my heart leaps.

*Aislinn.*

An almost debilitating surge of relief sweeps through me.

She's standing beside Sparrow and Effrey alongside two more horses tethered to a rusted hitching post. The large black Frezian steeds are loaded with saddlebags, and brand-new silver wire spectacles frame Effrey's fear-stricken purple eyes. Just above them all, Raz'zor perches on an overhanging tree limb like some bone-white, reptilian bird, his ruby eyes set fervidly on me.

Aislinn is dressed as I am, in simple, homespun garb, a cloak fastened over her shoulders, her hood casting her face in shadows. Dark circles anchor her eyes as she stares at me with a jagged intensity that speaks of prolonged, horrific struggle.

"Aislinn," I rasp, my voice breaking as we all dismount and I go to her, the two of us falling into a tight, emotional embrace. "Lukas got you out," I say as we hug each other close. "Thank the Ancient One."

Aislinn pulls away, clutching my arms as she glances at Lukas and Thierren, who are recounting to Sparrow what happened as they boost Effrey onto one of the Frezians. "Sparrow got me out," Aislinn tells me, her voice tremulous. "And she brought my two servants, as well. We're to meet them and take them East too." Stark urgency lights Aislinn's green eyes. "Elloren... Sparrow told me that you're the Black Witch. That it's been you all this time."

I bite my lip and nod as my eyes catch on what looks like a healing bruise on Aislinn's cheek and a fresher ring of bruising around the base of her neck.

A flash of outrage spears through me. "You're hurt," I say as red-hot fire sparks and crackles through my lines. "Did Damion do that to you?"

Aislinn's face twists into a pained grimace, the answer clear in her expression as she looks away. The desire for vengeance courses through me, along with the urge to grab every branch that litters the forest floor.

I want to find Damion Bane. I want to stalk him, branch or wand in hand, and finish what Lukas started.

Fury burns in my throat, followed by a rush of guilt. *It was supposed to be me fasted to that monster. Not you.*

"I'm so sorry, Aislinn," I tell her, my voice trembling with outrage. "He'll pay for this. I swear to you, someday he'll pay for this."

Aislinn shakes her head, her expression brittle. There's a deep line between her eyes that wasn't there before. But when she brings her gaze back to mine, her green eyes fire with rebellion. "I'm going to join the Lupines, Elloren."

I pull in a harsh breath in response to her unflinching declaration, a welter of emotions rolling through me. "We'll get to the Eastern Realm," I say, choked up now. "And you'll be with Jarod again."

Aislinn's face tightens with anguish as her voice lowers to a hoarse whisper. "Jarod will never want me now. Damion *did* things...made me do things..." She looks away, her frown quavering with disgust, the compounded weight of her pain in her expression. "He threatened to hurt my servant if I didn't obey." She meets my eyes again, and her gaze is so haunted, a chill runs through me. "Yillya is only twelve years old. I had to protect her..." She looks away again, as if she can't bear for me to see the extent of her shame. "Lupines mate for life," she says roughly as she wipes away a tear with the back of her trembling hand. "No. Jarod won't want me anymore." She looks back at me, her expression turning vengeful. "But I want Jarod to make me Lupine. So I can come back and find Damion Bane. As a Lupine."

A tremor runs down my spine, so lethal is Aislinn's expression. I'm reminded of Diana's ferocity.

"Elloren." Lukas's urgent tone pulls my attention from Aislinn. He's gripping the reins of our two Thoroughbreds, his green eyes fixed tight on me. I notice that he's standing apart from Thierren and Sparrow, who are waiting by the Frezians and Thierren's Thoroughbred. Effrey clutches the mane of his Frezian, looking nervous. "You and I need to go, *now*," Lukas insists.

Shock flashes through me as I realize he means just me and him. Leaving Aislinn and the others to travel East on their own.

A sudden spiral of clarity descends.

We have to separate.

The full might of Gardnerian and the Vu Trin forces are bent on trying to catch or kill *me*. If we all travel together, I might bring those forces down on the heads of Aislinn, Sparrow, Effrey, and Thierren. And Lukas and I can move faster alone.

*Black Witch*, a low, snarling voice sounds in my mind.

Mind reeling, I glance up to find Raz'zor peering at me from his perch, calm as a predator on watch. The words he's sending me are fierce, but devoid of any ire.

They're a challenge. A call to battle.

I hold the dragon's red gaze, a flash of his scarlet fire sizzling through me, prompting a deep, bolstering breath.

I turn back to Aislinn, forcing courage even as the walls of Erthia close around me, inspired by Raz'zor's steady ferocity and his fire.

"I *will* see you in the Eastern lands," I say to Aislinn. "And your eyes will glow *amber*."

Aislinn nods, tears glazing her vision as she embraces me, and I realize, in a sudden clutch of anguish, that there's a very real possibility we're embracing for the last time. There are no guarantees that we'll survive the journey East.

My head jerks toward the city as another faint explosion sounds in the distance.

We mount our horses, Lukas giving first Aislinn and then me a leg up, and I take one last look at our allies. Aislinn,

Sparrow, Thierren, and Effrey, sitting in front of Sparrow and staring at me through his new spectacles with an expression of wide-eyed fright.

My heart clenches at the sight of such a young, gentle child thrust into fleeing for his life.

No child should be forced to flee for their life.

I meet Sparrow's gaze from where she sits behind Effrey, reins in her hand. Determination blazes in her amethyst eyes.

"Uush'ayil moreethin orma'thur," she calls to me in Uris-kal, and I don't need to speak her language to guess what she's saying.

*Be safe. Escape.*

*Live to fight them.*

I nod back to her, my throat constricting as I turn to Aislinn and she gives me one last fierce look before we all prod our horses into motion, Aislinn, Sparrow, Thierren, and Effrey setting off in one direction, Lukas and I in another, an aching void hollowing out my chest as I lose sight of Aislinn.

Raz'zor shadows me, flying from branch to branch as I follow Lukas's lead. Lukas glances at the dragon, then back to me, caution in his eyes.

*Black Witch.*

I feel Raz'zor's greeting in the back of my mind, along with a sudden swell of kinship and the visceral pull of fealty. The warm glow of red Wyvernfire lights up my shielded lines.

A protective concern rises for this fierce dragon, along with a certainty that he needs to get out of the Western Realm.

And far away from me.

*Go with Sparrow and Effrey and the rest*, I think to Raz'zor as Lukas hastens our pace. *You need to protect them. Get them to Noi lands. Fight for them if needed.*

Images of red revenge flash through my mind.

Bloodshed. Slashing claws. Ruddy flames streaking through the air.

And then one word.

*Fealty.*

A rush of ruby fire sizzles through me and flashes bright red against my vision. The bloodred fire rushes straight through Lukas's shield to wind around my fireline, and I pull in a deep breath as a sense of heightened strength floods me. Suddenly, I understand the powerful advantage of this oath of fealty as I sense the full weight of Raz'zor's alliance.

*If you've given me your fealty,* I think out to him, *then follow me in this. Go with them. Keep them safe.*

Raz'zor takes flight, darting higher into the forest's canopy, a flash of pale white against the storm-darkened green.

*I will find you in the Noi lands,* he sends down to me. *And I will fight with you.*

*You'll be one of the few,* I think back at the small dragon.

*So be it, Liberator of Naga the Unbroken.*

Another image of red fire, and the dragon rises past the canopy in a flash, wings flapping. A hard growl and then a white blur.

Another distant explosion startles the horses as a hard pulse of Lukas's fire whips protectively around me. He glances back at me, his eyes burning with a determined light, before he turns away and veers slightly to the right as I follow, riding tight on his heels.

# CHAPTER
# NINE

# WAR

## ELLOREN GREY

*Sixth Month*
*Caledonian Forest, Gardneria*

Lukas and I ride hard down narrow, deserted roads, the dark woods closing in around us, the forest's barely suppressed hostility palpable on the lightning-charged air. The hoods of our cloaks are pulled up over our heads, the rune lanterns attached to our saddles emitting soft halos of scarlet light.

The sounds of explosions and roaring dragons have been muffled by the distance, but every now and then sapphire Vu Trin dragons streak overhead, spearing west, arresting my heart each time. I have to remind myself that our lantern light is magicked with Amaz runes to stay invisible to all but those who are very close to its glow.

Undetectable to the dragons flying overhead.

That are hunting for me.

After a while, Lukas waves me to a stop, swings off his

horse, and secures the mare by a small stream, then motions for me to dismount, as well.

"I need to replenish the anti-tracking sorcery," he tells me, "so the Vu Trin can't locate you. And the horses need rest." I slide off my mare and bring her to the stream as well, taking a moment to thank the animal, then draw closer to Lukas as he unsheathes his runic wand from underneath his tunic's side.

Lukas gives my forearm a pointed look as lightning flashes and a peal of thunder breaks.

I slide up my tunic's sleeve and hold out my forearm to him, the sight of my sealed fastmarks triggering the harrowing memory of his family's estate being swallowed up in blue fire.

"Lukas," I say as he takes hold of my arm, places his rune-marked wand's tip to my skin, and murmurs a spell. "I'm sorry about your family."

Lukas's gaze flicks up to mine, a flash of anguished conflict passing through them. His affinity fire rears then abates, as if he's violently stamped it down. "Do you mourn your aunt?" His voice is full of virulent emotion as he keeps his wand's tip pressed to my skin.

Discord wrests hold of me.

Aunt Vyvian was family. Someone who had been in my life since I was a young child. But how could I possibly mourn the woman who threatened to harm my brothers? Who used me as a tool to maintain her political power and gloated at the thought of my pain?

Who was responsible for the death of my beloved uncle Edwin?

My angry conflict morphs into a knifepoint of grief for my uncle.

"No," I force out roughly, my fire now a disjointed mess that's running chaotically hot against the underside of Lukas's shield. "I don't mourn her."

Lukas slides his fingers dexterously along the small runes worked onto his wand's hilt as if he's playing a complicated instrument. Threads of glowing blue course from his wand to flow across my skin.

I study him with concern as runic sorcery tingles over me. "But, Lukas," I press, "this was your *whole family...*"

Lukas's firelines spike with a surprising level of ferocity. But then his invisible flame pulls in taut once more as a hard wall of his earth magery clamps down around his lines and his searing green gaze flashes to mine. "I do not mourn them," he spits out in a blaze of conflicted pain, then focuses back down on the work at hand.

My mind reels from his admission, which is even more jarring, because we can't lie to each other and I can feel the truth in his words. But then I try to imagine a family with only Aunt Vyvians in it. And I realize, with deep remorse, that Lukas's entire life has been that way. No one to truly care about him. Everyone around him worshipping and loving power and prestige above all else.

"Would you mourn me?" I ask, the question escaping me as rune sorcery courses over my skin.

Lukas is silent for a moment, his gaze pinned on the blue magic branching along my wrist.

"Yes, Elloren." His gaze lifts to mine. "I would mourn you for the rest of my life." I send an answering rush of warmth toward him as I take in the impassioned look in his eyes. The very same look he gave me last night, when he merged every last part of his desire and his magic with mine.

Raw longing.

And something even stronger than that.

Our fires mingle in a heartfelt caress, tears stinging my eyes as I hold Lukas's emotional gaze and the web of blue lines pulls into my arm, teasing through the shield just under my skin to form a stronger barrier.

Another crack of thunder booms, breaking through our momentary bond.

Lukas glances at the storm-darkening sky then cuts me an uneasy look as he gently releases my arm and resheathes his rune wand. "We need to go," he says as he briefly caresses my arm.

"How far do you think we can get before the storm breaks?" This part of Gardneria is famous for its storms, and the longer they gather, the fiercer they are when they finally let loose.

This one has been gathering for a while.

"To the base of the Caledonian Range," Lukas says, as white bursts of lightning briefly illuminate the angles of his face, giving him a stark look. "We need to put more distance between us and Vogel. We've only a small window of time."

Dread wells up inside me. "Before what?" Thunder cracks as lightning skitters across the sky.

Lukas's eyes are a flash of warning. "Before night falls and he's able to hunt you with stronger magic."

The storm continues to gather, like some enormous beast that's patiently tracking us. As the day slides closer to night, the clouds thicken and billow angrily, shaking out thunder and lightning like an enraged fist but still holding back the torrent.

Every so often, Lukas signals for me to halt beside him, an urgent look in his eyes as we dismount. He slides his arm around me and pulls me into an impassioned kiss, sending his fire and earth magery into me to bolster the shield beneath my skin in a hard, tangling rush. His all-encompassing magic never fails to make me gasp and shudder against him as the horses fidget beside us. And every time, the trees' oppressive aura draws back, as if they can sense the staggering level of magic at play.

As we advance through the forest, I find myself hungering for the next time Lukas will pause and pull me into his fiery kiss, the terrible world around us momentarily singed away whenever Lukas's magic fuses with mine.

A lightning-riddled dusk descends as the forest changes and staggeringly immense trees loom over us, their gigantic, crenulated trunks washed a sullen, flickering red by our Amaz runic lanterns.

The Caledonian Sithoy forest.

I glance around with no small amount of awe and trepidation as we enter forest that's famed all across Erthia. A forest I've only read about in books and sensed when touching its bloodred wood.

We're only a few paces into the Sithoy when the trees' surrounding aura begins to change. Their ire begins to envelop us with claustrophobic force, like a deep, weighted rumble pressing against my lines.

I crane my neck up, a slight vertigo taking hold as I view the Sithoy's distant, lightning-illuminated canopy with mounting concern.

The black-needled Sithoy trees rise taller than Valgard's cathedral, and both Lukas and I have to force back their hostile aura with double the usual magical effort or it starts to feel like a weighted invasion of our minds, difficult to think around. Even with both of us lashing invisible fire magery in periodic streams, it's as if we can barely contain these trees.

I've the strong sense of them watching us with deep-seated hatred as we weave around their massive trunks. And I've the disturbing sensation of their collective aura not only pressing against my lines, but plucking them gently. Directionally.

As if mapping my magic's flow.

"The trees here," I say to Lukas as I glance warily around. "They're dangerous."

Lukas glances back at me as we ride, giving me a significant look. "I can feel their press of power as well, Elloren. But they're like a Level One Mage. All power with no access. Don't let them intimidate you."

He sends out another blast of his invisible magic, but it barely puts a dent in the trees' encroaching rancor.

And still, that disturbingly subtle brush against my lines that so easily traverses Lukas's shield.

*You're not easily intimidated, are you*, I sullenly think at the colossal trees, feeling besieged by their rippling invasion.

Thunder has begun a low, more insistent roll, the sky webbed with constant, forking lightning as the storm-dampened air rapidly cools. I'm having a hard time shaking the chill that's seeped into my bones, no matter how forcefully I pull on my fire affinity or press my hands against my horse's warm neck.

Night descends as the storm's winds rise then strengthen with punishing force against the forest's distant canopy, huge branches swaying overhead as the wind howls through the trees and the sky begins to spit a needling rain. The red-lantern-illuminated landscape grows rocky and hillier as Lukas and I draw ever closer to the edge of the Caledonian Mountain Range, blessedly leaving the Sithoy portion of the forest behind.

The oak, maple, and evergreen trees that now surround us are smaller and sparser.

And less able to infiltrate my magic.

A small clearing opens before us. It's haphazardly strewn with dark boulders, a rocky hillock at its edge. I flinch as lightning creates an earsplitting crack of thunder and the horses startle, the cold, misting rain turning to harder drops that splatter against the trees and dampen my cloak and my face.

Lukas stops then dismounts, motioning for me to follow his lead as he takes a moment to soothe his fidgety mare. We tether our horses inside the forest edge, under an isolated grove of oak trees with a thick, sheltering canopy.

"Stay with the horses for a moment," Lukas directs and I comply, wind whipping at my hair as it begins to send up a disconcerting howl and I do my best to calm the restless animals.

Lukas moves to the center of the small clearing, holds his wand aloft, and sounds out a series of spells, low in his throat, as his strong, red-lit form is buffeted by the intensifying rain and wind.

I give a start as loose branches fly in from the woods and circle Lukas in a tight spiral, more branches soaring in to join the cyclone of wood until I can't make Lukas out. And then the *whooshing* spiral abruptly flows toward an indentation in the hillock's wall of rock, Lukas's tall form visible once more. Wood crackles against stone as Lukas rapidly weaves the branches into a domed structure against the concavity, lines of his earth magery flowing around the wood in slender vines that cinch the branches tightly together.

Lukas is coldly efficient as the storm turns into a violent deluge, and I find both his stunning display of earth magery and his ability to remain so calmly competent in the face of everything to be deeply steadying.

As I watch through the sheeting rain, he burns a door into the structure and angles its top outward to create an awning of sorts. Then he strides toward the dwelling he's created, points his wand at the entrance, and sounds another spell.

Debris flies out of the enclosure, and Lukas hurls it at the forest with a sweep of his arm. Then he sounds another spell, and a rush of thick fog billows out, lit eerily red by our lantern light.

Another ear-piercing crack of thunder sounds as lightning forks down from the clouds, slamming into the forest not far from where we're standing, and my pulse skitters in response to its proximity. I continue to soothe the spooked horses, patting necks and speaking to them in low, calm tones as rain batters down, the smell of scorched storm energy on the air.

"We should get our packs out of the rain," Lukas calls out as he strides over to me, his hood off, his black hair curled into wet tendrils.

We unhitch our rain-drenched packs and our lanterns from the horses, and then loosen the girths of their saddles. I give mine an apologetic pat for not taking the tack off and giving it a proper grooming, but we have to be able to go quickly if needed. Gathering my pack and lantern, I follow Lukas, half running, into the shelter, hoping the horses will be all right with the natural covering they have. At least with the amount of rain here, there's plenty of grass for them to eat.

Ducking down, we both slide into the enclosure just as the storm fully unleashes and turns violent, the rain an impenetrable curtain shot through with lightning flashing and thunder booming in a fierce, overlapping chorus.

Lukas lowers himself to one knee in the dwelling's center, his face and form lit by the flickering scarlet glow of the lanterns he's set down beside him. He raises his wand and murmurs a spell as he draws his other hand back, palm forward, as if drawing something into the wand.

My whole body warms as rain is drawn from my cloak, my skirts, my skin, and flies toward Lukas's wand to be instantly consumed into a tight, churning ball of water that's suspended in the air, just over his wand's tip.

Lukas pulls the water off himself as well and feeds it into

the expanding sphere, then hurls the ball of water out of the dwelling through its small entrance, my body and clothes now dry and much warmer, the smell of damp diminished.

With a look of deep concentration, Lukas points his wand at the shelter's domed ceiling and gracefully moves it back and forth, his motion as precise as an orchestra conductor's. A slim stream of black vines courses out from his wand's tip and threads all through the structure's roof, creating an increasingly watertight surface. Then he sheathes his wand, pulls off his cloak, and hangs it across the entrance.

It's not a large structure he's fashioned. Just big enough for the two of us to lie in comfortably on the dry moss, and just high enough for Lukas to stand if he stoops a bit.

"Lukas," I venture as the immensity of the situation bears down. His eyes meet mine. "Do you think Vogel will find us here?"

"I think it's unlikely. This is a big stretch of wilderness we've crossed. I don't know of any search spell with that range. And a tracking beast would need to follow your scent, which is near impossible with this rain." He regards me squarely. "But it seems as if Vogel's tapped into some primordial system of magic…"

"Demonic magic," I amend firmly.

Lukas nods in grim agreement. "Perhaps. The old magical rules might not apply. Vogel's wand seems to be amplifying his magic, so I'm not sure what he's capable of."

A chill ripples down the sides of my neck just as a resonant *whump, whump, whump* sounds overhead, cutting through the storm's sheeting chorus.

A frisson of alarm streaks through me as we both look swiftly up, the sound like a more forceful, rhythmic thunder. My eyes meet Lukas's in a flash of sudden, urgent concern as a succession of shrieks split the air.

Lukas and I move swifly toward our shelter's opening, push away the cloak's edge, and peer up into the rain.

My spark of alarm detonates as repeated flashes of lightning illuminate the sky to reveal a horde of Gardnerian military dragons tearing through the storm, just above the forest's canopy.

Countless broken dragons, soaring relentlessly East.

"What does this mean?" I say after the gigantic horde finally seems to have passed.

"The Gardnerians have cut down all the Vu Trin," Lukas gravely reasons, his lightning-lit eyes narrowed and his face slick with rain as he scans the sky. "Mage forces are likely massing near the Eastern Pass in preparation for an invasion of the Eastern Realm."

The ramifications of this hit home with devastating force.

The Realm that holds almost everyone I love. The Realm that's the only hope for thousands upon thousands of people.

I remember the stories Yvan told me of Gardnerian dragon horde attacks on Keltish villages. Children and families torn to shreds. Entire villages decimated. Horror takes hold of me as I imagine this nightmare visited down on the people of the Eastern Realm.

"I've caused this," I rasp, my fire affinity rearing against Lukas's shield with anguished force. "There's now all-out war because of me. Thousands of people are going to see their lives destroyed. And I have no way of stopping it."

Lukas shoots me an incredulous look then takes hold of my arm and guides me back into the shelter. He yanks his cloak back down over the shelter's entrance.

"Elloren," he says firmly, still holding my arm, "this war would have come to the Realms *with or without you*. Do you think Vogel would have left the Eastern Realm alone if you hadn't come along?" His brow lifts in further incredulity. "*No.*

He would have marched in and enslaved them. If he had his Black Witch, it would only have happened that much faster." His gaze on me sharpens. "Right now, he's likely bringing in Fifth Division trackers so they can locate our trail as soon as this storm passes. Mark my words. You're the only significant threat that stands in Vogel's way, and you *will* learn how to fight back. You're potentially the deadliest weapon that both Realms have ever seen."

*The only weapon of the Prophecy left*, I think with terrible clarity as an aching grief twists my heart. But I'm a weapon rendered useless by my lack of control over my magic, while Vogel's dragon army bears down on my family and friends and countless innocents.

What if Vogel catches up to me before I gain any control over my magic?

"Vogel can't find me," I roughly insist, grabbing hold of Lukas's hand. "If he does, he'll force me East. He'll turn me into a *monster...*"

Lukas eyes the hand I'm clutching him with, his brow tightening as he takes my wand hand into his, his fingers weaving through mine as his grip on me tightens. "Elloren," he says, giving me an intense look as my magic cyclones through my lines and clamors against his shield, "you've *got* to get hold of your magic. You're going to punch right through my shield. And if Vogel chooses to send out a search spell and happens to guess our direction correctly, you'll bring about everything you fear."

I struggle to do what he's asking of me. To gain control of my magic and tighten my lines against it, but my affinity flame is whipping out in chaotic streaks too powerful to subdue. My mind circles into panic as my magic slashes fiery tears in Lukas's shield and I rail against the nightmare I'm caught up in.

There's a massive forest around me filled with trees that

would strangle me with their limbs if they could and rip the affinity lines clear from my body. Beyond that, I have no truly safe place to train. Even the Eastern Realm is a danger to me. We'll have to sneak in somehow, since the Vu Trin want me dead.

And the Wand in my stocking, the Mythical Force for Good, is no match for Vogel's Shadow Wand.

It *hides* from Vogel's Wand.

My heartbeat ratchets up as I face the full horror of the situation head-on. "I'm scared, Lukas," I confess, my voice growing hoarse as my magic slams against his shield with riotous force. "I can't control it. I can't control the magic in me."

A look of deep concern flashes over Lukas's features as he holds on to me, the line of his jaw hardening.

In one decided movement, he closes the distance between us, pulls me in, and brings his mouth to mine, blasting fire straight through my lines.

I gasp against him as Lukas's magic blazes through me, staggeringly hot and strong, his fingers threading through my hair then clenching tight, keeping my mouth firmly against his. The full strength of his affinities flashes through me, feeding into my violently out-of-control power with scorching heat. Melding with it then reining it tightly in, rapidly restoring the shield.

I cling to Lukas as he kisses me deeply and his magic sears through me in a fierce, contained inferno. Wave after wave of blisteringly hot magic. Burning away my fear as the heady sense of his controlled power keeps rushing in to take hold of my own.

Then Lukas draws back, his green eyes blazing.

I'm thrumming with magic now, my breathing uneven and my skin feverishly hot, every part of me lit up by our combined power. But with Lukas's control now coursing over and through my lines, my magic is no longer chaotic and fitful.

It's reined in and deadly.

Lukas's mouth lifts into a half smile as he moves back a fraction and reaches up to gently caress my cheek with his hot palm. "That's better."

I swallow, flushed and overwhelmed by the strength of our combined power. And desperate to maintain control over it so that Vogel won't find me. "I need your power to survive this," I say, coming to a full reckoning.

"You won't always," Lukas firmly counters. "Not after you have some control over your own magic. And, Elloren, you *will* gain control over it. But you need to get hold of your emotions, and fast. Once we're out of the Realm, I'll teach you how to control your power and shield *yourself.* It's complicated magery, but we'll work through it. I'll teach you every last thing I know about magic."

I nod stiffly at this and force myself to breathe evenly as Lukas's thumb strokes my shoulder, a line of sparks chasing his warm caress. I hold his stare, his eyes set tight on me in the deep-red light.

"Elloren, you're stronger than you think," he insists, adamant. "I'm sure of it. I always have been. Even though you don't think you're equal to this. You are."

I want to believe him. I want to be strong enough to face this and fight back. And Lukas's unwavering faith in me fortifies a small piece of my battered courage. He's never coddled me, even though, sometimes, I've hated him for it. But he's always believed in me.

"Sometimes I feel like you understand me better than anyone else," I confess. "Better than I understand myself."

His lips lift with a slight trace of amusement. "That's because I do understand you better than anyone else. Elloren, our affinities are a perfect match. I know you inside and out, as I suspect you know me. And I can read your emotions in your fire."

I nod, the prickling flush heating my neck as affection for Lukas warms my lines. "It's more than that."

"I know it is," he agrees, a rakish glint in his eyes. "We're both rebels from the same background."

*Gardnerians.* Born into the same oppressive culture. Both of us forced to wrestle with the same lies and myths and religious strictures.

"That's part of it," I agree, "but it's more than that too, Lukas."

Something deep with import flashes in Lukas's gaze, the silence between us growing emotional and charged. "I know," he admits.

"You help me to be strong."

Lukas shakes his head, his brow creasing. "No. We help each other be strong."

His sentiment is so kind and so heartfelt that my warm affection strikes into a blaze, and I yearn, in that moment, for a way to bring down the wall of grief around my heart, even though I know that the wall may never fully come down.

I loved Yvan with everything in me, and I might never recover from his loss, but I can feel my battered heart opening up a small space for Lukas.

And I realize, in that moment, that a heart is a thing not so easily destroyed by the shadows.

"I want you to kiss me," I tell Lukas, yearning to fill up that space in my heart with him and his fire and keep hold of him there. Wanting to drive back the shadows.

Lukas gives me an impassioned look. "Elloren, I'll kiss you all night if you want me to."

The ache to be close to him ignites and quickly fires up to a blaze.

"Did you bring the Sanjire root?" I ask throatily, my heart-beat deepening.

The question flickers on the air between us, as if writ in flame, our magic giving an insistent pull toward each other.

Lukas breathes out a sound of disbelief as he gives me a heated, significant look. Then he reaches into his tunic's pocket, draws out the vial, and hands it to me. The vial's glass catches the crimson lantern light as I unstopper it, pull out a tendril of the root, and place it in my mouth.

Lukas's gaze turns molten as I chew the root and swallow.

We stare at each other for a long moment as heat flares in the air between us. Then Lukas draws me into an embrace, his lips grazing my ear. "Are you sure, Elloren?"

"I'm sure," I say as our magic weaves together and every inch between us sparks with heat. "I want you," I tell him, certain. "And we're stronger together."

"For the good of the Realms, then?" Lukas purrs, his deep voice thrumming straight through me along with a shimmering flash of his power.

"For the good of the Realms," I agree, surrendering to the pull as our affinities spiral around each other.

Lukas brings his mouth to mine, and it sends a heated charge through us both as thunder cracks, our magic fuses, and the whole world catches fire.

# CHAPTER TEN

# TRACKED

## ELLOREN GREY

*Sixth Month*
*Caledonian Forest, Gardneria*

I wake up to find Lukas gone from the shelter, his steps scuffing the ground outside, the rain ceased. No sounds of dragonflight above.

My affinity lines are all wrong.

It's as if, during the night, the forest pierced through each line with a minuscule hook then pulled the lines taut in every direction away from my wand hand, giving me the sensation of being a fly caught in a spider's vast web.

Caught by the trees.

Stiff from sleeping on the ground as well as the disquieting sensation of being tethered to the trees, I clumsily throw on my clothing and push my cloth-wrapped Wand into the side of my boot, then step out of the hut into the cool, damp air.

Lukas is tightening the girths and securing our packs to the horses, his masculine form washed in the otherworldly gray light of dawn, a gauzy mist hanging in the air, rendering the surrounding forest dreamlike, as if all its hard lines have been erased.

Our eyes meet.

Lukas's eyes narrow. "Elloren, what's wrong?"

I glance around at the wilds, disturbed by the sudden absence of the forest's ire. "The trees," I say, my throat tightening with distress, "I can feel them pulling on my lines. Stronger than before. It's like they're actively trying to distort my power so that it can't reach my wand hand." I survey the ground around us. Then, finding a wand-like branch, I pick it up, the affinity power inside me leaping toward it.

"Elloren, they can't harm you," Lukas insists. "They're conduits of power, nothing more—"

"Hold my wand hand," I cut in. "Tell me what you feel."

Lukas comes over to stand just behind me as he places both his hands around mine. I tighten my fist around the branch in turn and point it at the forest in front of us.

Just that action prompts a palpable cinching of my magic. The threads of power hooked to my lines pull stingingly taut into what feels like a binding weave, and I look back at Lukas.

His eyes have tightened with grim appraisal as his gaze flicks from the branch then out toward the mist-shrouded trees.

The eerily calm trees.

"Do you sense their hostility anymore?" I challenge him, my voice tight from the pain cinching my wand arm.

And from my rising alarm.

Lukas considers this as he grows quiet with apparent concentration, as if listening to the air. "No," he finally says.

A dread of certainty takes hold. "That's because I've been bound."

Lukas shakes his head. "It doesn't make sense. Trees can't wield magic."

"Can an entire forest bind it?"

Lukas grows still, a dark sense of realization enveloping us. He scans the forest surrounding us, as if sizing up a foe he's vastly underestimated before he brings his piercing green eyes back to mine. "We'll get past the forest and unbind whatever they've done to your lines. How's the shield?" he asks, still holding my hands.

"It's strong." Of course it is, with the amount of power we generated last night. My face warms just to think of it as I shoot a glare at the wilds, feeling as if we're surrounded for leagues and leagues by a wrathful army.

That's patiently waiting to strike.

A chill snakes down my spine. "I need to get out of the forest, Lukas."

Lukas nods and finishes securing our packs as I move to mount my horse and lift my foot to the stirrup.

Suddenly, my back is hit by a blast of magic and the world goes dark.

My body arches and I fall to the ground as the breath is forced from my lungs and every muscle goes rigid. The image of the Shadow tree crashes through my vision, its limbs forking like lightning over Lukas's shield, rattling it as it strikes.

And then the blast of magic is torn away, like bindings viciously ripped off, as fire races over my lines and the darkness blinks out, the sensation of Lukas's embrace and fiery kiss sweeping in, feeding power into my shield.

I gasp for breath against Lukas's mouth, surprised to find myself on my knees along with Lukas, my whole body trembling against his.

The trees have drawn back, their hold on me loosened, as if they, too, have been blown back by terror. As if they felt Vogel's power.

But my shield is intact.

Lukas draws back and presses his forehead to mine, both of us breathing hard, his arms tight around me as I keep desperate hold of him and his fire pulses through me. But his magic and his shield around my lines can't assuage the horror that's taken hold.

"Vogel knows I'm alive."

Lukas swallows and pulls back a fraction more, and I notice there's a line of sweat along his hairline, his face still tensed from obvious magical effort. "He does," he says, his tone rattled. "And he must have some idea of our direction."

"He's coming for me."

Lukas nods, his mouth a tight line. "Yes. But hopefully we'll be out of the Realm and ready for him before he finds us. We need to leave. *Now.*"

Lukas and I rise and swiftly mount our horses.

Doubt claws at me as I take hold of my mare's reins. "How can we possibly get over the Caledonian Mountain Range before Vogel finds us?" Morbid sarcasm bubbles up, fueled by desperation. "Do you have a dragon hidden somewhere who can fly us over the mountains?"

Lukas doesn't smile as he prods his horse into motion. "We'll go east through a Noi portal. We'll use it to bypass the mountains completely and transport straight into the Eastern Desert."

Surprise lights like flint sparks on steel in response to this revelation.

"How long have you known about a portal?" I ask.

"Not long," he says as he pulls into the lead. "I read its location in your rune stone."

"Is the portal close?" I ask.

"A day's ride," he answers, his tone that of someone ready to face down an army of demons to get us out of here.

"Well, let's find that portal, then," I say, as we pick up the pace and a fierce determination rises within me. "Let's get the hell away from Vogel and all these trees."

We head due north throughout the day as we skirt the imposing side of the Caledonian Range, its snowcapped peaks becoming visible through the forest's canopy. The trees seem to be ignoring us after being hit by Vogel's spell, their hold on my lines diminished to a loose sting.

*Hold on to me while you can*, I fume at the trees. *Soon I'm going to step through a portal and rip myself clear out of your grasp.*

As a steel-gray twilight is taking hold, I follow Lukas's lead as he veers out of the woods and onto a forest-bracketed road, the shadows of encroaching night rapidly lengthening as we take off at a faster clip.

After a time, the faint thud of galloping hoofbeats sounds behind us, rapidly growing louder.

Fright spears through me, but Lukas doesn't deviate. He glances back once and stays the course, but I notice he holds the reins in one hand and keeps the other close to the wand sheathed at his side.

My pulse racing, I glance back and see two cloaked figures astride dark green Uriskal Thoroughbreds, closing in on us with what seems like an unsettling aura of purpose.

I pull in a tight breath, wishing I could wield the Wand in my boot.

"Lukas," I say in a coarse whisper as we speed forward, but before I can get more words out, the riders are upon us, one drawing up on either side, their faces obscured by their cloaks' hoods. My lungs constrict, all my muscles tensing as I ready myself for flight.

"Hello, Chi Nam, Valasca," Lukas calmly calls out, relaxing his hold on his wand.

Shock takes hold as one of the riders pulls down her hood, and I realize, in a harder explosion of surprise, that's it *is* Valasca, her spiked hair glistening blue and black in the dim light, her pointed ears and blue, sharp-featured, rune-marked face lit with an expression of amusement. Her dark eyes, full of mischief, meet mine.

"Why, hello there, Elloren," she says playfully as we all slow to a brisk canter. "Fancy meeting you here."

Heart pounding, I whip my head to my other side to find Chi Nam's hood now down, as well. The Noi rune sorceress's wizened, deep-brown face and shrewd black eyes meet mine briefly, a small smile on her lips as she rides up beside Lukas, her white hair tied back in a coiled braid, her rune staff wrapped in a black cloth sleeve and secured against her horse's side.

I turn back to Valasca. "Ancient One," I gasp as I'm flooded with relief. I glance at the hilts of Valasca's rune blades, the weapons briefly visible as her cloak shifts, the runes on them glowing Noi blue and Amaz scarlet. "How did you find us?" I ask, stunned.

Chi Nam gestures toward Lukas with her thumb. "This one. He contacted me through the rune stone I gave you." She gives Lukas a calculating smile. "So, Mage Grey, what do you think our chances are of keeping her alive, hmm?"

Lukas laughs. "Better now."

His tone is shot through with more relief than I've ever heard him express, and I realize that finding Chi Nam and Valasca in time was a long shot that Lukas took.

Because it was likely our only shot.

Chi Nam's smile widens as she looks him over. "You're finally coming over to the right side, I see."

Lukas gives another short laugh. "I'd say we're on the universally unpopular side at the moment."

Valasca makes a dismissive sound. "Long odds are more interesting."

"I'm so glad to see you," I say to Valasca, still breathless with surprise.

"You do know the Amaz sent me to kill you?" Valasca wryly returns, and a streak of unease races through me.

"I can't believe the Amaz are after me too," I say, the whole situation feeling more surreal than ever.

Valasca cocks a brow at me. "You definitely know how to make an entrance onto the world's stage." Her mouth quirks into a grin as she glances around at our small party, then sets her irreverent gaze back on me and shakes her head. "Well, Black Witch, this is certainly nothing I could have ever imagined." Her gaze flits down to take in my fast-and Sealing-marked hands. Her gaze flicks to Lukas then back to me as she shoots me a knowing smile. "Difficult times make for interesting bedfellows, wouldn't you say?"

Before I can feel embarrassed by her jest, Valasca tightens her legs, signals to her horse in the Noi language, and speeds up to a gallop, quickly passing Lukas.

"Come on," Valasca calls back to all of us with a beckoning wave. "If we're going to keep Elloren alive, we need to make a portal jump to the Eastern Desert."

# CHAPTER ELEVEN

# RUNE SORCERY

## ELLOREN GREY

*Sixth Month*
*Caledonian Forest, Gardneria*

We ride northeast via a dirt road that cuts through dense pine forest, Lukas and Chi Nam in the lead, Valasca taking up the rear as night descends. Our path is lit by crimson light from our Amaz runic lanterns as well as a ball of blue light that Chi Nam has conjured to float above the tip of the rune staff that's now strapped diagonally across her back. Every so often, Valasca draws her rune stylus, murmurs a Noi spell, and throws out a net of blue lines to magically cover our tracks.

Words brush up against my mind, limned with malice.

*Black Witch.*

My neck prickles as I glance sidelong at the pine forest, the immense Sitka Spruce trees rising almost as tall as the Sithoy evergreens. I recognize the Sitkas' thick needles, scaled trunks, and pendulous cones. I saw these trees in visions throughout my childhood, as I cut and sanded wood with Uncle Edwin, the Sitka wood perfect for transmitting sound.

Perfect for fashioning into violins.

The happy memory vanishes as we ride through their spiteful legions. The trees' accusatory words are a gust of relentless wind in the back of my mind as a disturbing awareness grows of their aura straining to draw my lines into a snarl.

I remind myself that we'll be out of the forest soon and away from its ability to bind magic.

"Any word of what's happened?" Lukas asks Chi Nam.

"Our forces took out most of the Mage Council when they hit your family's estate," she tells him, then hesitates. "I heard that your family was killed."

Lukas looks away, and I can feel the slash of intense emotion that flickers through his fireline. My heart twists for him and his lack of any loving family, ever. He turns back to Chi Nam and tells her something in fluent Noi, to which she responds in Noi, just as seriously, as if offering a condolence.

"Did they take out the Mage Council building?" Lukas asks, switching back to the Common Tongue.

Chi Nam nods. "And its archives as well as the Valgard and Verpacian bases before our Western forces were cut down by the Mage Guard. Now Vogel's mobilizing his own ranks east of the Verpacian Pass to prepare for deployment across the desert." She throws Lukas a weighted look. "He's declared war on Noilaan and has sent out draft notices to all adult male Mages. And he's imposed martial law on Gardneria and taken sole control of the government."

"That was inevitable," Lukas cynically returns.

"Apparently there wasn't even any mention of trying to form a new Council," Chi Nam notes, a jaded cast to her tone, as well. "And the Gardnerians aren't questioning it. In any case, war has begun. Vogel is holding a giant rally tonight in Valgard. Rune hawks have been dispatched to every one of his military bases."

"He won't wait long before he advances on the Eastern Realm," Lukas warns.

"Well, he can't advance on us just yet," Chi Nam sharply counters, her clipped accent further barbing her words. "He's got a wide expanse of desert he needs to get through first. And even with his broken dragons, it's a challenge to get through the central desert's storm bands." She purses her lips and shakes her head. "But you're right. He'll be coming for our Realm. And we'll need to meet him with overwhelming power." Chi Nam turns and gives me a significant look over her shoulder that I strive to fully meet.

It's mind-bendingly significant that she's here. Guarding me against the express command of her own military, when she could have been fighting with the now decimated Vu Trin regiment against Vogel's army and their dragons.

Which means that Chi Nam is gambling that I'm strategically more important to the coming fight than the Vu Trin's entire Western Realm force.

My lungs tighten as I imagine how she's viewing me right now—as a cataclysmic weapon.

Or, perhaps, every weapon on Erthia shoved into human form.

"Are Kam Vin and Ni Vin all right?" I ask Chi Nam. "And Chim Diec?" I add, concerned to know what became of the women who saved my life in the desert when the other Vu Trin moved to cut me down. Valasca turns her blue-hued face toward me, her expression tensing at the mention of her love, Ni Vin.

"Nilon is fine," Valasca informs me, her teasing manner whisked clear away. "She's back in Noi lands with Kamitra. Chimlon is back in Noi lands too." Valasca uses the longer, informal version of Ni Vin's, Kam Vin's, and Chim Diec's first names, indicating that she's on close terms with all three of them.

"Were they disciplined for helping me escape?" I worriedly ask.

Valasca shakes her head. "They were simply following Chi Nam's orders." She raises a black brow in Chi Nam's direction. "There's a warrant out for Chi Nam's arrest, though. Thing is, they'd have to catch her first." Valasca shoots Chi Nam a wicked grin, which the powerful sorceress meets with a look of unfazed authority.

"I think we found the weapon that took down the Lupines," I say, and they all glance back at me, a harder tension suddenly in the air.

Chi Nam's deep-brown lips lower into a frown. "Vogel's Wand of Shadow. We know of this. It appears Marcus Vogel has resurrected a thing that should never have been brought back into this world. A thing not seen since the Elfin Wars."

"It sends me a vision of a Shadow tree," I tell her. "And a dead forest. And there's demonic power in it." I tell Valasca and Chi Nam of the Smaragdalfar demon-sensing rune Sage marked on my stomach, and how Vogel's power lights it up like a stinging beacon.

"I believe it to be the Wor," Chi Nam states with forbidding gravity.

My brow tenses in confusion. "What's that?"

"The counterforce to the Zhilin," Valasca explains, setting her black-eyed stare on me with piercing intensity.

I remember the Noi word for the Wand of Myth—the Zhilin. The sacred tooth of their dragon goddess, Vo, that can be wielded as a rune stylus only by the goddess's chosen bearer—the Vhion.

To Valasca and Chi Nam, I am the Vhion bearer of the Zhilin.

But I've never heard of the Wor.

"Do you still hold the Zhilin," Valasca asks me, an edge of concern creeping into her normally unflappable tone.

"It's in my boot."

Valasca lets out a relieved sigh as she and Chi Nam exchange a quick look.

"You should know that my Wand…it seems like it's become powerless," I confess. "I've a sense that it's hiding from Vogel's Wand."

"The Wor is powerful," Chi Nam agrees as she shoots me a sober look over her shoulder. "But have faith in the Zhilin, toiya. Perhaps its power at the moment lies in its faith in you."

I want to hold tight to these words and draw comfort from them, but there's no comfort to be found. Control over my power is what I need at the moment. Not faith.

"Vogel's hunting Elloren with his Wand," Lukas informs Chi Nam. "He's sending out search spells. And he can do it during the day as well as the night."

"And the forest is trying to bind up my magic," I add. "It thinks I'm aligned with Vogel."

"Sounds like we better hightail it to that portal," Valasca throws out to us.

Chi Nam prods her horse into a fast gallop, rapidly pulling into the lead.

Before long, we're veering off the road and riding into the Sitka forest single file, our pace slowing as we skirt the spruce trees' large trunks.

As we're enveloped in forest, the sensation of the trees plucking at my lines grows more pronounced, and I look worriedly to Lukas, who rides in front of me. As if sensing my attention, he glances back and meets my gaze, his tense expression echoing my concern, as if he can perceive the trees' aggressive shift, as well. His shoulders stiffen as he lowers his head and throws out a burst of invisible fire power at the forest, the plucking sensation along my lines easing a bit.

Before long, we reach a clearing near a stony outcropping at the western edge of the Caledonian Range.

Chi Nam rides up to a mammoth wall of rock. The sapphire ball of light hovering over the staff strapped to her back casts bobbing blue illumination over the landmass.

She dismounts, and we all follow her lead.

"Send the horses to the nearest village," Chi Nam directs Valasca before looking to Lukas and me. "We can't bring the animals with us, and they can sometimes spook at what I'm about to do."

As efficiently as we can, we remove the packs from the horses but leave their tack on. Valasca murmurs affectionately to them as she leads them back into the forest, the horses whinnying animatedly as if in conversation with her as she gently talks to them in Uriskal. I'm reminded that Valasca, like all the Amaz, has been rune marked with the ability to speak to horses with her mind.

Chi Nam pulls out a series of Noi rune stones from her pocket as she advances toward the stone wall. She stoops and arranges the stones along its base, then rises and sounds a Noi spell, the fingers of one hand dancing along the luminescent blue runes that mark her staff.

The rune stones at the base of the wall light up.

Chi Nam unsheathes a stylus and begins tapping it against the stone wall's flat surface in a sweeping arc.

My brow lifts in surprise as a line of incandescent runes whoosh into existence, trailing her stylus's motion, the shape of a doorway made entirely of rotating sapphire runes taking form.

The portal's frame is similar to the Noi portals I was led through during my journey from Verpacia to the Eastern Desert and back again.

"It will take about an hour's time for the portal to charge," Chi Nam says to Lukas over her shoulder, then resumes tapping her stylus along the portal's frame, the action bringing smaller runes to glowing life.

"Who else knows about this portal?" Lukas asks her as he strides up beside me, an edge to his tone that sets the hairs on the back of my neck prickling.

"Only me," she assures him.

"Where does it lead?" I ask.

Chi Nam smiles cryptically. "Somewhere Vogel will have a hard time locating and an even harder time getting to."

Valasca strides back into our blue-lit clearing with an air of purpose, a black leather sack slung over one muscular shoulder. She walks to me.

"Take off your cloak and tunic," she orders.

Confusion lights. "Why?"

"I'm going to glamour you."

My eyes widen, but I comply, shrugging out of both my cloak and my loose woolen tunic, dressed only in my thin forest green camisole, riding skirt, and underthings now.

Valasca reaches into the sack and withdraws a fist that's now bunched around several long, slim golden chains. The chains reflect pricks of blue light from Chi Nam's runic sorcery as Valasca sets to work unraveling them. There are tiny, bright green, circular runes attached all along the chains at repeating intervals.

"Are those Smaragdalfar runes?" I ask.

Valasca doesn't look up from her work of untangling. "Yep."

My brow lifts at this. Subland Elf runes.

I remember Professor Fyon Hawkkyn, my Smaragdalfar

metallurgy professor, driven out of the university and now covertly active in the Resistance. And the Smaragdalfar refugees I've seen, most of them on the run from the Alfsigr Elves. Many of them children and all of them headed East. Just like us.

Valasca flicks her finger at my camisole. "That needs to come off too."

Heat blooms on my cheeks. "You want me to undress... right here?"

I look at Lukas, who cocks an eyebrow, as if amused that I would care if he saw me without my camisole, considering how wantonly we were wrapped around each other last night, our clothing quite absent.

"Elloren," Valasca insists as she holds up the now untangled chains that are draped over her palm and dangling down from her hand. "This is no time for modesty. We've got to protect you, and *fast*."

My flush deepening, I reach down and unbutton my camisole, then let it fall off my shoulders, my exposed chest cooled by the night air, a prickle of gooseflesh rising.

Valasca eyes the runes on my abdomen and forearm with a nod of approval. "Sage Gaffney does nice work," she says conversationally, which strikes me as bizarre. As if I'm supposed to have a casual conversation about demon-sensing and shield-passage runes while I'm half-naked.

I nod, so mortified I'm unable to form a coherent sentence.

Valasca carefully places one of the chains over my head, a look of intense concentration on her face, the necklace draping outrageously around one of my breasts. Then she pulls her rune stylus out and taps it to one of the runes as she sounds a spell. All of the runes on the necklace whir to life and take on a more luminescent emerald glow.

My skin's natural deep-green shimmer blinks out of sight, and I gasp.

Valasca drapes another one of the necklaces over me and touches her stylus to it. The runes spring to glowing life as my skin tone morphs to a pale storm-cloud gray.

"Are you glamouring me to look like I'm Elfhollen?" I ask her, so astonished I almost forget about my bare-chested state.

Valasca nods. "I am. Because there's quite a bit of sympathy for the Elfhollen in Noi lands. And they're allowed safe passage through the desert." She places another chain over me and activates it with her stylus.

A prickle swarms over my scalp. I grab some of my hair and stare at it, stunned to find it's turned a pale gray hue.

Another chain is looped over my head, and my ears give a painful stretch. I reach up to find them elongated, with long arcing points.

Another chain, and a brief sting courses over my eyes, a flash of silver momentarily bursting through my vision.

And then another chain that's accompanied by a sharp pinch along my hands and arms. I look down to find both my fastlines and my rune marks fading to nothing.

I hold up one of my fastmark-free gray hands, astonished. "Does this mean…?"

"No," Valasca cuts me off succinctly with a brief glance toward Lukas. "You're still fasted." She turns back to me. "And you're still imprinted with Sage's runes. It's all hidden under the glamour." She gives a few last taps on the chains' runes, and the necklaces sink into my skin with a static prickle then flatten into tattoos of their design, the runes losing their bright glow.

Valasca eyes the crumpled camisole I'm now holding against my naked chest. "You won't be needing any of that clothing." She leans down and pulls a traditional Elfhollen pale gray tunic and gray pants from her sack, the edges embroidered with a geometric white-star design. She straightens and hands the clothing to me. "Put this on."

I slide on the traditional Elfhollen garments, amazed to both appear like and be garbed like one of the Mountain Fae Elves.

"Is this permanent?" I ask Valasca as I button up the long, formfitting tunic, the Wand of Myth in the side of my boot now hidden under gray pants instead of a long black riding skirt.

Valasca shakes her head. "I can remove the glamour down the road. But for now, it's best that you don't look so much like the Black Witch."

"How did you get hold of that glamour?" Lukas asks, seeming deeply impressed as I fasten my cloak over my new garments. "I wasn't even aware that could be done."

She turns to him. "It's one of a kind. It belonged to Ra'Ven Za'Nor."

Recognition rises inside me.

"Ah, yes," Lukas says, returning Valasca's loaded glance. "The Smaragdalfar prince who's giving the Alfsigr so much trouble."

Sage Gaffney's love. The father of her baby Icaral.

Valasca's mouth tilts up as she eyes Lukas shrewdly. "Mmm. He's stirring things up a bit in both Realms." She gestures toward my chest. "Ra'Ven used those rune chains to glamour himself as a Kelt for a few years while on the run from the Gardnerians and Alfsigr both. I pulled his glamour out of the necklaces and implanted a new one. And strengthened the binding."

"But if we meet any Elfhollen," I point out, concerned, "they'll know I'm a fraud. I don't speak their language." I look to Lukas, remembering his fluency in Elfhollen and other languages.

"Ah," Chi Nam says as she works on the fledgling portal, "we can fix that." She straightens and surveys her work, the brightening arc of rotating runes now spitting out small veins of blue lightning. Seeming satisfied, she resheathes her stylus, grabs her staff, and walks over to take Valasca's place in front of me, handing her staff off to Lukas, the ball of blue light still hovering over its top.

Chi Nam reaches into her cloak's inner pocket and pulls out a flat, crystalline rune stone that's marked by the most intricate Noi rune I've yet seen, a seemingly infinite number of rotating, circular designs marked inside it, the lines sapphire bright.

She reaches up to hold the stone just behind my right ear, then closes her eyes and murmurs a stream of Noi that's unintelligible to me, save for a smattering of disjointed words.

Lines of warmth radiate out from the stone and fan out through my head to encompass my ears in a heated rush.

"Koi na vu'lon nishun ta'noi. Koi na vu'lon nishun ta'noi. Koi na vu'lon nishunderstand me. Tell me when you can understand me."

I startle as the words of her Noi tongue morph into meaning.

"I understand you!" I blurt out, flabbergasted.

Chi Nam pulls the stone away from my head then steps back a fraction and speaks to me in Noi. "I've placed a koi'lon rune just behind your ear. So now you will understand all of the major tongues of both Realms." She holds the crystalline stone up, loosely gripped in her palm, its sapphire runes rotating slowly, their bright glow now dampened as if spent. "These koi'lon are powerful. It takes years of concentrated sorcery to form the translation power embedded in them. And the power in this stone is now in you."

I gape at her, not able to get over my amazement of being able to understand her.

Fluently.

"Place your fingers over the rune behind your ear," Chi Nam encourages, seeming amused by my shock. "And think of a word you know in Noi. This will trigger the translation, and you'll be able to speak Noi as well as understand it. Then say something to me in my language."

My heartbeat quickens with excitement. I reach up and press my fingers to the rune, sounding out the Noi words for *no* and *thank you* in my mind—nush and khuy lon. Then I take a deep breath and say, "I'm going to speak Noi to you now..." I suck in a hard inhalation of surprise. The Noi words are flowing right off my tongue. "I can't believe I can do this!" I marvel in Noi, breathless. I glance at Lukas. "Are you going to mark him with the koi'lon?" I ask, looking to Chi Nam.

"I speak Noi," Lukas tells me in effortless, fluent Noi, amusement dancing in his eyes. He gestures toward my ear with his finger, continuing on in Chi Nam's language. "And the koi'lon she used to mark you will have to be recharged with translations before it can be used again. That takes years." He looks to Chi Nam. "You don't have additional koi'lon, I'm assuming? With the tight hold your Wyvernguard keeps on them."

Chi Nam shakes her head. "No. We'll have to get one for you in Noilaan."

"Why would they keep a tight hold on them?" I ask in Noi, thrown.

Lukas looks to me. "Language is powerful. This sorcery gives their military and their ruling council an advantage."

I turn to Valasca. "Do you have one of these rune marks?"

"Of course," Valasca replies in Noi with an incredulous twist to her smile. "I'm the head of the Queen's Guard. A guard allied with the Noi Wyvernguard." She pushes her spiky blue-streaked hair behind her pointed ear and turns the side of her head to me.

And there they are, the faint blue lines of a circular koi'lon rune, nestled inside the black lines of the runic tattoos that mark her skin.

Valasca grins. "But I'm part Noi and part Urisk. I speak both Noi and two Uriskal dialects even without the koi'lon."

I marvel at them all, deeply impressed by their abilities with languages and language sorcery. But then, an uneasy thought comes to mind. "Is my koi'lon mark visible?"

Chi Nam shakes her head. "It's been absorbed under the glamour spell. Completely hidden from view."

Chi Nam slides the spent koi'lon stone back into her cloak and pulls out a flat, star-shaped stone that's marked with whirring sapphire runes on its points, a larger rune rotating in its center.

"Hold still," Chi Nam directs as she reaches up to grasp the back of my head. "This might hurt a bit." She practically slams the star-stone against my forehead.

I arch backward against her hand and let out a rough gasp, a streak of painful energy shooting through me, straight through Lukas's shield and through all of my lines, the pain quickly morphing into a rippling sting that pools just under my skin. I flinch as a flash of blue light rays out from me in all directions before disappearing along with the lingering sting.

"Vogel and the Vu Trin both will attempt to track you," Chi Nam says as she withdraws the star-stone and briefly grips my shoulder. "I've strengthened the Mage-shield you two have so clearly been working on." She peers appreciatively at Lukas as she takes back her rune staff from him. "Nicely done, Young One."

Lukas's mouth lifts, his hand coming to the small of my back, a trace of our fire power connecting at the point of contact in a warm rush.

I look up at Lukas. "Do I look very different?" I ask him in the Common Tongue, oddly reticent to hear his answer. Wanting Lukas to be able to recognize me as me.

Lukas gives me a crooked, knowing smile as his deep-green eyes flick over me. "Your features are mostly the same. Except for your ears. And you'd look lovely in any form, El- loren. Slate suits you."

An appreciative warmth slides through me as my earth magery reaches for his and he responds in kind, our branches twining, the motion quickly turning into a mutual caress. Lukas's head bobs in a silent laugh, his gaze on me briefly full of suggestion.

I glance down at my wand hand, turning it over and over. Gray as a storm.

I fidget a bit, feeling refreshingly free in clothes I can really move in after spending so long in the restrictive, long-skirted Gardnerian attire.

"Mage Grey and I should check the periphery," Chi Nam declares, leaning on her rune staff as she gives Lukas a mea- suring look.

"You're drafting me into your service, then?" Lukas asks Chi Nam, seeming amused.

"That I am." Chi Nam's eyes glint with good humor as she starts for the line of woods and motions for Lukas to follow. "Come, Young Mage. We'll send out a web of your magic combined with my sorcery and see if there's anything stalking Elloren this eve." Her words are lightly said, but there's an ominous undercurrent to the look that passes between them.

"Stay close to Valasca," Lukas directs as he caresses my arm, but there's true warning in his tone, and I nod.

"Be careful," I tell him, my branching affinity lines grasp- ing tighter hold of his.

Emotion flickers in Lukas's eyes. "I'll be careful," he as- sures me.

And then Lukas gently pushes my magic back as he and Chi Nam disappear into the darkness of the wilds.

# CHAPTER TWELVE

## SHADOW EYES

### ELLOREN GREY

*Sixth Month*
*Caledonian Forest, Gardneria*

Valasca and I stare at each other, both of us washed in the portal's flickering sapphire light, the only sound the insects chirring. Tiny lights flash in the cool night air as fireflies zip around and wink their beckoning glow.

"So," Valasca says from where she leans against one of the clearing's boulders, her stance casual, but her gaze weighted with steel. "You're the Black Witch."

I nod, holding her hardened look. "Are you tempted to kill me?"

Valasca spits out a laugh that doesn't reach her eyes. "No."

"Is it because I have this?" I reach down and pull the Wand from the side of my boot, peel away the top of its cloth wrapping, and hold it up. It has a subtle glow, often seeming like there's an ethereal light trapped inside it. Like someone has encased starlight in the very center of a wand.

So beautiful and mysterious. Yet so powerless in the scheme of things, I mournfully consider.

Powerless compared to Vogel's Shadow Wand.

Valasca studies the Wand reverentially for a moment. Her brow creases as she shakes her head. "I know you're not with the Gardnerians, Elloren."

My tone takes on a bitter cast. "So, you believe in the Wand but you don't believe in the Prophecy?"

Valasca inhales and regards me squarely. "I think the Prophecy comes from the trees." She glances at the night-blackened forest before setting her dark eyes back on mine. "And from what you've told us, it seems the trees are not inclined in your favor."

"That's an understatement."

"All the divination tools the Seers use, Elloren...they all come from the trees. Your priests cast sticks etched with sacred symbols. The Noi scry from Black Ginkgo leaves. The Ishkartan cast wooden lots. I could go on and on." She straightens and walks to me. "But the point is, it's all *wood*. It's all from the trees. So the trees must know about your power and fear you for it. Because of what your grandmother did and what the Gardnerians are currently doing to large swaths of the wilds." She nods as if in agreement with herself and shoots me a smug look, as if she's pleased with herself for figuring this all out. "I think the various takes on the Prophecy are based in truth, but I think they're biased."

"Are you saying," I ask her, stunned, "that you think all these Prophecies are...prejudiced against me?"

"That's *exactly* what I think."

I blink at her, my mind cast into turmoil over the ramifications of that possibility. Different versions of the same, flawed Prophecy being upheld by practically every religion in both Realms.

"So, what do we do now?" I ask, deeply thrown. "With both Realms and the wilds set against me."

Valasca flashes a rebellious grin. "We subvert the Prophecy. We get the Black Witch out of the Western Realm, and then we prove the trees and everyone else wrong."

I think about the killing sea of fire that I can conjure. Ni Vin's dead horse. The vision of the field of battle, countless people dead on it. "They might not be wrong," I caution. "My power...it's horrible, Valasca."

She steps closer, her jawline firming. "And we're going to need every bit of that horrible, awful, terrible power to crush Vogel."

I shake my head emphatically. "You don't understand. My power is worse than my grandmother's. And the trees..." I glance at the night-darkened wilds. "They know it. So they're actively fighting against it. I think that's why they're trying to bind my magic in some way."

"So, we bring you somewhere far away from them."

Back to the desert.

I rewrap the cloth around my Wand and slide it into my tunic's pocket. When I meet Valasca's gaze once more, she's studying me with a probing look.

"I noticed your fastmarks have changed," she says with some wariness. "You and Lukas...you're lovers now?"

I nod, heat prickling along my neck in response to this admission.

"I'm assuming your Sealing was a mutual decision, based on how you're acting around each other?"

I take a deep breath. "It was. I've grown to really care for him in a short amount of time. And you should know that he hasn't been aligned with the Gardnerians for a while. I learned that he saved me from being fasted to Damion Bane."

Valasca's face tightens with shock.

"You know what Damion's like, then?" I say.

"He's a complete sadist," she spits out. "All of the Banes are."

"Well, Lukas stopped me from being fasted to him."

She's scrutinizing me again, her brow creasing as if in question.

"Lukas and I needed a diversion," I explain, answering her unspoken query. "We had to seal the fasting to get away from Vogel."

"So, you're Elloren Grey now."

I nod, acutely aware of the momentous shift that's happened in my relationship with Lukas. "I am. I truly am."

"Well, felicitations, then." Valasca cocks one black brow as she eyes me with evident interest. Her mouth tilts into a half smile as she lowers her voice to a more private register. "So. How was he?"

I stare at her, perplexed. And then my cheeks warm. Valasca's offhanded way of asking about intimate matters that Gardnerians just do not speak of catches me off guard.

*Overwhelming. Incredible. And we took each other again last night.* "Practiced," I say obliquely, my blush heating to a burn.

Valasca gives a short laugh and grins, her eyes lighting with mischief. And as mortified as I am by her blunt ways, I'm also bolstered by her tendency to fall back into humor, even in dire circumstances, much like my brother Rafe. A pang of longing cuts through me, the desire to see my brothers again an ever-present yearning.

I glance at my pale gray hand, the Sealing marks hidden under the glamour. "Lukas has been a good friend to me," I tell Valasca, my voice catching as I remember the last conversation she and I had about love. About both Lukas and Yvan.

The grief that's always waiting for me in shallow waters sweeps in.

Valasca seems to note my change of mood, her eyes taking on a look of concern. "Elloren," she says, her voice pitching lower with compassion. "I heard about what happened to Yvan Guriel. And… I know what he was. And what he was to you. I'm sorry."

I nod, tears welling in my eyes and threatening to spill over. And all of a sudden, the full force of the grief I've been suppressing rushes in and I'm being choked by it.

I shake my head as my throat tightens, making it impossible to speak for a moment.

"I loved him," I finally force out in a rasp. "I loved him with all my heart." I pause again, overcome as tears glaze my eyes and my lips tremble with emotion, and I'm only half able to voice my heart. "I lost something really important." The words break off as tears fall.

After a moment, Valasca comes to me and takes gentle hold of my arms. "Elloren," she says, her voice both serious and kind, "look at me."

I meet her gaze, my face tense with agony.

She gives me a fiercely significant look. "You will lose important things." She says this emphatically, her words hard and raw. And terrible in their finality. She stands spear straight as she keeps her gaze locked on mine, as if willing me to really look at her, to really listen to what she's telling me. "You will *lose and lose and lose* one thing after another. Do you understand? That's what this war is. That's what it means to fight something like Vogel."

I nod as tears streak down my face and she holds on tight to me.

"You will likely lose every last thing that's precious to you. And so will I. And so will Lukas Grey. And so will Chi Nam. And so will everyone who really commits to this fight. But you'll do it so that others won't lose these things."

I nod again, my face rigid with misery as I recognize the

awful truth of her words. I think of how she's lost Ni Vin already, choosing the protection of her people over going East.

"Listen to me, Elloren," she says, firming her grip on me. "My people, they need to get out of this Realm. I need to get *all* of them to the Eastern Realm. And once they're there, I need you to use your power to protect them. Now, you've met my people. You've seen the children. The mothers. The old women. You saw them with your own eyes."

I think of all the Amaz I met, the women laughing and singing, the little girls and their pet deer. The babies. And my beloved friend Wynter being sheltered in their lands.

Valasca's expression turns starkly ominous. "Now tell me what you think Vogel and his allies want to do to them."

I don't need to. I hold her level stare as I swallow back my tears.

"I believe in you," she states adamantly. "That's why I'm here by your side. So, I need you to let go of *everything* that's precious to you for something much greater than all of it. Do you understand what I'm asking of you?"

I hold her fierce stare, fear of my own magic welling up. "I can't control my power."

"You're going to learn to. You need to keep the faith. The time in your life for weakness of any sort is *over*. We're going to need you."

Her passionately insistent tone rocks me to the core, and the chance she's taking on me fully sinks in—the chance Lukas and Chi Nam are taking too.

"You know," I tell her, bitterness rising even as resolve gains ground, "this would all be a whole lot easier if the side I've chosen to fight for wasn't trying to kill me."

Valasca spits out a laugh. "Take heart, Elloren. Just because the good side is trying to destroy you doesn't mean we don't need you."

I shoot her a sardonic look. "That is no comfort whatsoever."

She grins warmly. "If you're in this fight for the accolades, you're going to be sorely disappointed."

"I'd settle for just a little less outright hostility."

Valasca's head suddenly lifts as if she's heard something that's caught her attention. Her gaze flicks toward the forest as the fireflies blink and the insects softly chirr.

Her face tenses in confusion as she cocks her head to the side, as if listening to the air. "The horses... I can sense them in the distance. They're picking up something," she says distractedly. "Something *wrong*..."

Brush rustles behind us and we both turn, Valasca releasing me as the sound of Lukas's deep voice and Chi Nam's scratchy tone become audible from the woods, the two of them engaged in hushed conversation in the Noi language.

My abdomen starts to prickle with a swirling sting.

Panic floods me as my hands fly up to clutch at my stomach. "The rune..." My head whips toward Lukas and Chi Nam just as they step into our clearing, my gaze snagging on something moving behind them. It's barely visible, save for the rune light glinting off it—a black angular thing, tight on their tail, scuttling predatorily through the trees with terrifying speed. And it's *tall*...monstrously tall.

"Behind you!" I cry, pointing sharply at the thing.

Glittering, insectile eyes emerge from the shadows, way above Lukas's head, a twitching, monstrous jaw and cretinous, segmented body below.

It all happens in a horrific blur.

Lukas and Chi Nam leap sideways and swing around just as the horrific thing bursts from the forest, like some giant, grotesque mantis-scorpion hybrid that's bizarrely stretched out. It has a black chitinous body and powerful forelimbs. And its head—its horrible, terrifying head. Shovel-like, with large, gleaming black compound eyes and smaller swirling gray eyes spread out around its main eyes, as if it has a sickness. As if its eyes are multiplying. Smaller eyes dot the thing's neck, and the sides of its body are covered in a combination of deep-green runes and runes made of undulating gray shadow.

The thing's powerful, serrated forelimb slashes down toward Lukas, who ducks and slides out of the thing's reach as he yanks off his cloak and draws his sword.

Valasca whips out a rune blade and Chi Nam lifts her rune staff.

"Don't throw sorcery!" Lukas yells at Valasca and Chi Nam as the thing lets out a piercing, horrific shriek and Lukas dodges to the side once more to avoid another powerful swipe of the beast's massive forelimb. "It's got a deflection rune on it!"

Lukas slides into a berserker rage that's stunning to witness. He leaps forward and slashes at the thing with savage intensity, deftly darting away from the beast's swiping blows like he's locked in a violent dance with it as I grab up a sharp-edged rock in my fist and back up to the rune-marked wall.

Valasca throws off her own cloak and hoists her rune blade, seeming coiled for an entry point. And that's when I notice the stinger at the tips of the mantis thing's scorpion-like tail, the gleaming black barb quivering above its head.

"Watch the stinger!" I cry out to them as I hurl my rock at it and hit it right in the center of its head.

Stunned that my aim was true, I take another step back as the thing sets all of its malignant eyes on me.

A dark tree blasts into the back of my mind, Shadow rising from its limbs like steam, the feel of Vogel's malefic void rushing in, like a million spiders scuttling along my shielded lines.

The mantis thing leaps toward me and I dodge, a scream

loosening from my throat as I lose my footing and fall onto hard stone. Lukas lunges forward and swipes his sword, teeth gritted as he growls and hacks off two of the thing's back legs in one arcing cut.

The mantis comes crashing down sideways with a rasping shriek as black ichor spurts out its mutilated body. Lukas keeps slashing until he's cut off the top of the thing's lashing, venomous tail and half of the foreclaw closest to him.

The thing keeps its eyes on me as the taloned edge of its remaining forelimb crashes down and relentlessly drags its shredded body toward me, its chitinous form scraping the ground as Lukas pulls back his arm and slices the sword through the thing's neck in a powerful blow.

The thing's head flies off as its body collapses in a heap, the whole mass twitching and gurgling in a mess of black fluid and guts that smell like sickeningly sweet rotted carrion.

Lukas drops his sword, cursing under his breath and breathing heavily as he glares at the decimated creature.

Valasca and Chi Nam go to him, but I can't move. I can barely breathe. My back is pressed against the stone, and I'm trembling so hard that I can barely control my limbs. Paralyzed with terror over that *thing*. And Vogel's power…it's still writhing around in my lines.

Lukas sets his intense gaze on me. "Elloren," he says sharply. "Are you injured?"

"No," I choke out.

"Then get hold of yourself," he commands.

I look to the huge, headless monster, another wave of gut-wrenching horror slashing through me.

"Vogel's going to enslave my magic," I rasp, my voice and body trembling, lost to a panic that's quickly edging into hysteria. Vogel is *here*. I can feel his dark power still clinging to my lines, slithering through me. "He's going to take over my lines and kill all of you…"

"Stop it, Elloren," Lukas snarls as he takes a step toward me. "This is a *long fight*. And it just ramped up. You need to be tougher. *Right now*."

"He's in my *lines*," I cry, the panic overtaking me, Vogel's Shadow tree still reverberating in my mind. "Don't you understand? He's going to take over my power…"

"He's not here," Lukas growls. "You're feeling a thrall. Throw it off."

"It's not a thrall! It's *real*!"

Lukas's expression turns vicious as he whips his wand out and I'm hit with a blast of Lukas's affinity power that's so strong, it's like being slammed into by a gale-force wind. I recoil against the stone wall, gasping as Lukas's invisible affinity fire rages through my lines, burning to a scald, overtaking the Shadow tree and singeing it away, his earth magery pummeling in, wresting hold of my branches, pinning me against the stone where I'm crumpled in a trembling mass.

Shock spirals through me as he keeps hurling magic at me, only strengthening its force, even after he's burned Vogel's power from my lines.

"Fight back!" Lukas growls out. "Fight back against my thrall!"

My shock intensifies over Lukas's unexpected magical attack. I look to Valasca for help, imploring. But Valasca's gaze has gone as hard as Lukas's. She pulls her rune stylus and levels the tip in my direction, a scarlet Amaz rune springing to life above its tip that she throws toward me, the rune blasting into my chest in a shower of red sparks, forcing my magery back even further.

Desperate, I turn to Chi Nam, who clamps her fists around her rune staff and jabs it in my direction, a brilliant ray of blue scything from it and into my lines, flattening them until I can barely breathe.

I gasp for air as their cruel, combined attack relentlessly assaults my lines.

But then my fear and anguish start a rapid slide into a rage that builds and builds as my fear is burned away by the force of my mounting anger. I draw in a constricted breath, my eyes tight on them, as I pull up power from the earth, from the roots snaking through the ground.

Forcing power to flow straight into me from the cursed trees as I rise.

The power grows and grows inside me, just under Lukas and Valasca and Chi Nam's combined power, until I'm trembling from the force of it, my hands balling into fists, my nails digging into my skin as I tense my whole body. And then I blow out a hard breath that turns into a guttural cry of rage as I force all of my power out toward them in one overwhelming rush.

Lukas stumbles back, nearly falling over as his fire-and earthlines contract and all of the runes on Chi Nam's rune staff and Valasca's rune blades blink out of sight.

I stalk toward them all, power whipping through me along with my overpowering rage as I close in on them, my anger over being attacked seeming to have taken on a life of its own.

"Get back!" I cry at them, furious over their cruelty, my words the lash of a whip. "Keep your magic away from me!" My face twists into a grimace, magic slashing through my lines as I stalk to Lukas, furious.

Lukas is flushed, a sheen of sweat on his skin, his eyes fierce. He leans closer to me, his lips twisting into a feral smile. "Ah, finally. *Finally.* The Black Witch is here! I wondered when she'd finally show herself!"

Another flash of rage overtakes me in a blinding rush. I

pull my Wand, rip the cloth off it, and jab it to Lukas's throat, my magic rushing to it. "Don't ever attack me again," I snarl as power courses through me with lethal force. "I could cut you down right here, if I wanted to."

Lukas moves closer, ignoring the Wand pressed into his neck. "Yes, Elloren," he hisses back. "You *could*. Which is why you need to stop acting like you're weak and start acting like a warrior, no matter what monstrous thing comes at you!"

A sudden reckoning bears down on me, my anger imploding under the sheer weight of its immensity.

I pull the Wand away from Lukas's neck and take a faltering step back, thrown into turmoil over being faced with my first military attack.

I'm on a collision course with Vogel and the entire Gardnerian military and probably the whole of Alfsigroth and Noilaan and Ishkartaan—and they're going to send every nightmare thing they can think of out to subdue me.

I'm disastrously ill prepared to face even a small fraction of this fate.

*How can I be the Black Witch with even my allies set against me?* I rage as my emotions circle down toward the rapid loss of faith.

A face suddenly lights in my mind, halting the descent.

Fernyllia's granddaughter—little Fern.

An image of the child fills my thoughts, her small hand clutching my skirts as she sobbed and protectively hugged her cloth doll, Mee'na. That terrible night when the Gardnerian mobs were attacking Urisk and cutting off the tips of their ears.

*I'll protect you. We all will*, I promised her that night.

I wonder—is Fern in the Noi lands right now, clutching her beloved doll? Safe for the moment?

Not safe for long if these insect beasts come for her.

Not if Vogel comes for her.

Another vision accosts my mind—an army of the many-eyed insect monsters swarming into the Eastern Realm. And Fern, running from them as a massive foreclaw slams down toward her small frame...

*No.*

I inhale and flex my hand against the Wand.

*I'll protect you. We all will.*

I scan the darkness of the wilds, the hostile trees, knowing that Lukas is right.

I need to be strong. Even in the face of impossible odds. Even in the face of a monstrous attack.

Because this is bigger than all of us.

A shimmer of light catches my eye, and I look up to find a Watcher sitting high in the dark canopy of forest, the gleaming ivory bird there and then vanishing from sight.

I pull in a surprised breath, both chastened and inspired by the sight. There's an echo of anguish still swimming in me, but I find the strength to tamp it down.

"I need your help in learning how to fight like a soldier," I admit to Lukas, to all of them. "I'm not trained like all of you. I'm a violin maker and an apothecary. I've never seen combat. I need your help."

"We'll train you," Lukas says, passionate resolve in his gaze as he steps toward me.

"How much longer until we can get out of here?" Valasca asks Chi Nam, her tone urgent. "We can't train anyone if we're eaten by demonic insects." The portal's center is now lit with a silver sheen, and I notice that the runes on Chi Nam's staff and the hilts of Valasca's rune blades are brightly charged once more.

"Any minute now," Chi Nam answers as she scrutinizes the brightening portal, and I push my Wand back into my tunic's pocket, my magic's pull toward it drawing down.

Lukas cuts a hard look at Chi Nam and Valasca. "Stay sharp. There could be more scorpios. They normally swarm."

Valasca brings her black gaze to me. "If that rune on your stomach so much as pricks, you tell us. Understand?"

I nod as Lukas comes down to one knee and studies the wreckage of the mantis's body, prodding it with his wand. Revulsion ripples through me at the sight of the grotesque corpse. Tendrils of smoke are curling up from the shadowy runes on its thorax like undulating steam.

"What is that thing?" I ask, forcing myself to keep looking at it.

"A desert scorpio," Lukas says as he eyes the creature's mangled carcass. "They're not indigenous to the Western Realm."

"They're common in much of the Eastern Desert, though," Valasca adds. "But this one...it's corrupted by some kind of twisted magic. Its appearance is distorted."

I look to her. "They're normally different from this?"

"Oh, they're nothing you want to meet without a weapon." Valasca gives a grim chuckle, not taking her eyes off the thing. "But this one..." She narrows her eyes at the beast's remains. "This one is bizarrely stretched out."

I think of the Marfoir—the horrible Elfin assassins that came for Wynter—and how unnaturally tall and stretched out they were, with horns of undulating smoke and gray insectile eyes...

I take in the eyes swarming around the scorpio's two main eyes. "Do they normally have so many eyes?"

Valasca shakes her head. "No. Normal scorpios have two compound eyes and that's it."

Lukas points to one of the deep-green Gardnerian runes that mark the scorpio's body. He looks to me. "Elloren, this is a deflection rune. You need to be able to recognize these."

I study the circular deep-green rune and its internal telescoping pattern. "What does it do?" I ask, remembering his strident warning to Chi Nam and Valasca.

"Deflection runes cause wand magic or sorcery to double back and attack the person who cast it," he explains, poking at the green design. "They take years to charge. It's very complicated rune sorcery." His brow tightens as he looks to Chi Nam, a suspicious glint in his eyes. "Quite a lot of runic fabrication going on in the Western Realm when there's only one Council Light Mage."

"Are you thinking Vogel possesses light magery?" Valasca asks, one black brow raised.

"Possibly," Lukas answers as he studies the creature. "In addition to possessing a wand that can amplify it." Lukas slides his wand's tip over one of the shadowy runes emblazoned on the thing's huge thorax. Tendrils of smoke still twist up from those runes. Lukas looks to Chi Nam. "I haven't seen runes like this before."

"They must be based in demonic magery." Chi Nam studies the runes alongside Lukas. "They triggered Elloren's rune." She places the tip of her rune staff on one of the Shadow runes. Wraithlike smoke trails up her rune staff, momentarily turning all the blue Noi runes a smoking gray, their internal designs morphing to spiraling shapes that give the illusion of tunneling down into some dark infinity.

Chi Nam pulls her staff away, seeming uncharacteristically thrown. "These runes are filled with odd elementals." The runes on Chi Nam's rune staff snap back to Noi blue and begin to flash out changeable shapes, as if pulsing a complicated warning. Chi Nam sets her dark gaze directly on Lukas. "I think we're dealing with something new."

"Or something very old," Valasca amends grimly as she eyes the scorpio with heightened alarm. "Cast by the Shadow Wand. Like in the myths."

An animalistic shriek sounds in the distance, and all our heads whip toward the sound.

"The *horses*," Valasca rasps out, eyes widened.

More heart-wrenching shrieks are followed by a chorus of tinny, insectile screeching as a hard sting lights on my abdomen and my gaze whips toward Lukas. "There're more. They're coming."

Lukas hoists his sword and slides in front of me as Chi Nam moves closer to the portal and I hastily grab more stones, shoving some in my pocket. Valasca pulls a second blade and tightens her grip on both of the weapons, slowly stepping backward toward me as a multi-eyed, rune-covered scorpio slides into the clearing, teeth chattering, its head jerking this way and that.

Then another.

And another.

And another.

All of them with deflection runes marked on their huge abdomens. All of them bizarrely elongated.

The creatures pause as they loom over Lukas and Valasca, tilting their heads jerkily as they study them. Lukas and Valasca lower themselves into fighting stances before me, their sword and blades raised.

"Chi," Lukas says calmly. Too calmly. "We need that portal to be ready *now*."

"It's almost fully charged," Chi Nam says with Lukas's same unnerving calm, her rune-marked hand, held to the portal's frame, taking on a blue glow as the ripple of silver in the portal's center gains strength and begins to streak with gold.

Strangely, the scorpios all wait, limbs twitching, as they stare Lukas down, stingers raised and quivering.

Three more of the horrific things slip into the clearing and my pulse ratchets higher.

Valasca's gaze darts toward the portal as she takes a step backward, her hand closing tight around my arm, as if she's ready to hurl me through the portal the second it sets.

The things are chattering now, their horrible jaws making rapid-fire clicking sounds. I notice the one nearest Lukas, the most stretched-out one, has the biggest swarm of eyes, spread clear down its neck. Two more eyes dot the thing's forelimb like a disease.

It turns, a pale green eye in the center of its head riveting onto me.

I take one small, faltering step back as all the beasts swivel their heads and set their countless eyes on me.

Terror explodes as they all lunge for me in a unified stampede.

Valasca yanks me backward, and the largest one knocks Lukas sideways with the blunt side of its forelimb, stingers lashing forward like whips. A cursing Valasca wrenches me farther to the side then releases me and springs forward in a whirlwind of slicing blades as Lukas battles three of the beasts, his sword whirling as he lops off limbs and venomous tails, creatures shrieking and falling as they descend into an unfocused, scuttling attack.

I pull back my arm to hurl my rock at an advancing scorpio just as its huge pointed forelimb slams down through my cloak and tunic, grazing my shoulder to impale the edge of the cloth, pinning me against the stone wall behind me. I frantically struggle to beat back its forelimb with my rock and pull my arm free as the largest scorpio closes in to peer down at me and I'm overtaken with a horror.

It's the most hideous one, with eyes clear down its neck.

The insect monster slinks its head forward only a hand's length from mine as every one of its eyes pivot forward to stare hard at me.

I stare back into the single pale green eye in the center of the thing's head as recognition blasts through my mind.

*A Vogel eye.*

I cry out as Vogel's Shadow limbs punch into me in an explosion of pain, Lukas's shield fracturing, the violent assault quickly followed by the ghastly feel of Vogel's power slithering into me and around my lines, his invading Shadow rooting me to the spot and wresting away my control over my own body. I'm trapped inside Vogel's Shadow magic, trapped within his terrifying thrall as wraithlike Shadow smoke rises all around me.

But then, as I stare into Vogel's cruel, soulless eye, my fear gives way as an explosion of pure fury sparks then detonates inside me. Fury for the Lupines. Fury for little Fern. Fury for every last person who is running for their lives because of this monster.

*Fight back,* everything inside me screams as the fury whips through my lines and ramps up my magic. *Fight Vogel with every last shred of magic inside you.*

*Throw off the thrall.*

Vengeful energy rises, like an inescapable tide, as I pull in a deep breath and gather my power against Vogel's shadowy grip, my fire rising as my earth magery arranges itself into killing spears.

Eyes fixed on Vogel's eye, I exhale hard and force my power toward him in a savage rush.

The image of Vogel's dark tree shatters, his Shadow power flying off me as I break through his paralysis with a stinging burst of agony.

Suddenly and shockingly freed from the thrall, my power whips through my lines, rapidly dampening the pain. I grit my teeth, tighten my grip on my rock, and slam it straight into Vogel's eye.

The huge Vogel scorpio rears back with a furious shriek just as

Lukas advances, swinging his sword in a flashing arc that cleaves straight through the beast's neck. The scorpio scuttles sideways then crashes to the ground as Lukas hacks at it in a blur of motion.

The smaller scorpio closes in, jaws snapping, but I'm ready to fight now. With a snarling cry, I swing my arm at it, aiming my rock at its mass of eyes. The creature flinches, dodging my attack, still pinning me to the wall as its jaws click and a fierce battle cry sounds behind it.

Valasca leaps onto the creature's back, throws her arm around its neck, and slices her blade clear across the thing's large compound eyes. The scorpio rears backward, Valasca hurled off its back as it releases my arm. Dark ichor sprays from its head, the beast shrieking so loudly that I fear my ears will burst.

Abruptly freed, I lurch away from the scorpio as it levers its forelimb back at me, its limb colliding with the rock wall and just missing my shoulder, as two more scorpios close in and slash their forelimbs at Valasca.

A brilliant flash of golden light rays out from the portal.

"It's charged!" Chi Nam calls out in Noi.

Valasca turns just as the largest of the remaining scorpios closes in and slashes its serrated forelimb at her with blinding speed. A metallic streak arcs through the air as Lukas's sword slices through the limb and sends it skittering away before it can impale Valasca. Another scorpio limb swoops toward Lukas in a blur, the forelimb's knife-edge slamming into his shoulder in a spray of blood, the blow knocking him to the ground as my heart bolts through my body.

"Lukas!" I scream, lurching forward just as Valasca darts toward me, her expression ruthless as she grabs rough hold of my arms, swings me around, and shoves me headfirst into the portal's rippling lake of gold.

✳

# PART FOUR

✳

# CHAPTER
# ONE

# VONOR
## ELLOREN GREY

*Sixth Month*
*Northwestern Agolith Desert*

Everything flashes gold as I fall through the portal's shimmering depths. My hands slam down onto night-darkened stone as I collide with the ground, fine sand coating my body in a choking cloud.

I cough and whip my gaze across the scene, wildly disoriented.

I'm on a greatly elevated ledge and encased in a translucent, runic dome, a dramatically surreal desert landscape with lurid, blood-colored sands splayed out before me. Giant, arcing red rock formations and smatterings of bulbous trees mark the view as far as I can see. They're washed in dim ruby light that emanates from the blazing stars and moon, which are not glowing their familiar white but a luminescent crimson. An impossibly long band of dark clouds is massed along the entire eastern horizon, lightning scything through it.

Desperation for Lukas roars through me.

I force myself to my feet just as Chi Nam rushes through the portal interior, golden rays blasting from a runic frame that's now marked on the mountainous ridge before me. A bloody Valasca bursts through next, dragging an even bloodier Lukas, a burst of his untethered affinity fire hitting me like a hot, violent wave.

"Lukas!" I cry as I rush to him and he drops his sword and staggers to his knees.

I fall to one knee beside him and grasp his arm as I take in the deep gash that's slashed clear across his chest and shoulder. His tunic is shredded, his power lashing and untethered. He's frighteningly pale, his normal deep-green shimmer reduced to a sickly white-green.

A chittering shriek sounds from the portal as a scorpio's massive forelimb thrusts through its shimmering center, and I flinch protectively over Lukas just as Chi Nam lunges forward and slams her staff onto the portal in another explosion of golden light. The portal's rippling interior vanishes in a shower of yellow sparks, the serrated limb thumping to the ground beside her.

"We need alluriem to stop the bleeding," I implore Chi Nam, invoking my apothecary training as I tear open Lukas's shredded tunic to better view his injury. My gut tightens as I take in the depth of the wound slashed across his chest and shoulder, his chest slick with blood. So much blood...

"Support his back," Chi Nam orders, her face a mask of determination as she lowers herself before Lukas, blue rune stylus in hand, and I recall how she healed my scalp after it was slashed by a killing star.

I throw one arm around Lukas, his out-of-control fire power whipping out of him and rapidly depleting, like a great star burning out. Lukas is panting, every muscle tensed, his expression agonized.

His vastly weakened magic seizes mine like he's a drowning man as Chi Nam draws a blue rune in the air just over Lukas's chest and shoulder, then swiftly pierces the rune with her rune stylus's tip and drags the stylus down the entire length of Lukas's bloody gash, trailing a golden wavering glow that sizzles with heat.

Lukas groans, his back arching against my arm as he throws back his head, his whole body seeming strained to the breaking point as his remaining magic scrabbles to keep hold of mine, power draining out of him.

*"No!"* I snarl, ready to rip through Erthia itself to save his life.

I grab hold of both sides of Lukas's head and turn it toward me. *"Kiss me,"* I growl ferociously.

Teeth gritted and eyes glazed with pain, Lukas angles his mouth toward mine.

I capture his mouth and bear down, boring power into his lines in a shuddering bolt. A burn races along my skin and into him as Lukas's hand grasps the back of my tunic and his depleted lines connect with my power. Chi Nam's sizzling magic courses over us both as I hold tight to him, feeding and feeding the power into him.

After a long moment, my flood of magic starts to meet some resistance from his lines. I pull back, sweat lining my brow and his. His color has deepened to a darker green, and his fireline now pulses with the same heat that's scorching through my lines as Chi Nam swiftly marks a line of blue runes on either side of his gold-glowing wound.

I can feel it clearly—Lukas's magic is stronger but still too depleted to fully stand on its own.

"I *will* kiss you again if I need to," I tell him, my voice a riot of fear.

Flame sparks in Lukas's eyes as he reaches up to take hold of the back of my head and pulls me into another feverish kiss. I twine my tongue around his and force blast after blast of fire into his lines, his rapidly thickening earthlines spiraling over mine with clenching intensity.

"Stop," Chi Nam says when I draw back once more, my fire whipping around Lukas's burgeoning flame and solidifying earthlines. "Any more and you'll make him Magedrunk. Just keep hold of his hand and let his power restore itself."

I grasp Lukas's hand, my heart thudding with passionate concern as Chi Nam connects the pairs of runes that span Lukas's entire wound with lines of blue sorcery. The wound is now a streak of glowing gold, his skin charred but no longer gushing blood, and I realize she's magically cauterized it.

Chi Nam taps the top pair of runes, and the lines of blue sorcery abruptly stitch tight.

Lukas lets out a hard, short cry, and I wince at his obvious pain even as the joyous realization circles through me that he's going to live. I can't swallow past the staggering relief that's balling up in my throat.

"Stay still and let that set," Chi Nam says as she rises. "That wound should be mostly healed in a few hours." She moves to tend to Valasca, her sorcery still flowing over Lukas's wound in a blue aqueous current.

Lukas's eyes flash toward mine. "Did you force off his thrall?" he grits out through clenched teeth.

I realize he means Vogel. During the scorpio attack.

"Yes," I say, tears pooling in my eyes to hear Lukas's ragged voice, to feel his magic gaining ground.

He gives me a quick wolfish smile through his obvious haze of pain.

"One of the scorpios," I tell him, as tears of relief streak down my face, "it was marked with Vogel's eye."

Lukas's expression shutters as he maintains his tight grip on me and draws on my power in fits and starts.

Valasca lets out a partly stifled cry, and I turn to her. She's slumped down, her leg splayed on the stony ground, her pant leg shredded to expose a long slash on the side of her thigh. Her face is tight with misery as Chi Nam expeditiously sends luminous blue sorcery over the bloody cut and stitches it up tight.

Concern fills me as I take in her tear-slicked cheeks. "Valasca..."

Valasca's distressed eyes meet mine, and she shakes her head, as if refuting my fears. "My wound isn't deep. It's not that. It's..." She closes her eyes tightly, her chest heaving as she begins to sob. "The *horses*. Vogel didn't kill them. He *took* them."

A chill ruffles through me.

I think of the beautiful horses we escaped on and remember Valasca's ability to read horses' minds. Which means she sensed their terror as they were attacked by those...*things*.

If Vogel took them...what horrific creatures will he turn them into? Some elongated, multi-eyed, and soulless version of themselves?

I let out a shuddering breath as Lukas continues to draw steadily on my magic, replenishing his own.

"Where are we?" I ask Chi Nam.

She rises from where she was crouched by Valasca and walks to the portal, the dimmed runes of its frame still rotating against the mountain's stone wall. She raises her rune stylus, sounds a spell, and begins to tap sorcery codes into the runes. "We are in the Northwestern Agolith Desert," she says in the Noi language as she taps. "Welcome to my Vonor."

I mentally place us on the map of the Realms.

The Northwestern Agolith Desert. Just east of the Caledonian Mountain Range.

Disturbingly close to Gardneria.

"I don't understand what *Vonor* means," I say, the translation rune marked behind my ear seeming unable to find a word in the Common Tongue to morph the sound into.

Chi Nam throws me a cunning smile. "A Vonor is a Lo Voi sanctuary." She turns back to the portal, the runes brightening in response to the motion of her stylus. "Most portal crones have a Vonor. A place known to no one else where we can practice our craft in isolation, in a location so remote it's unlikely that anyone could ever find it. This Vonor is set amidst a large stretch of wilderness and bordered on all sides by deadly storm bands." She gestures to the horizon with a pointed glance over her shoulder.

The band of dark clouds hugging the horizon is spitting lightning along its length, and I view it with trepidation, the gloom of it seeming impenetrable. The storm band has the appearance of a line of mountains traveling parallel to us. The scarlet moon hangs above it as if in bloodred warning.

"Ancient One," I breathe out, turning back to Chi Nam as she reaches the last rune on the portal's arcing frame and taps a code into it.

"Those storm bands are called ha'voor," Chi Nam tells me as she straightens and turns around, narrowing her gaze at the horizon. "They were created by the Zhilon'ile Wyverns after the last Realm War. They're virtually impassable." She leans into her runic staff and points at the horizon's band of darkest gray. "That storm band is part of the much larger net of storms that are cast over the entire desert. Fly over them, and you're hit with the entirety of their lightning. No matter how high you come in." She casts me a sly smile. "Difficult for both Gardnerians and Vu Trin to get through."

"Vogel marked one of those scorpios that attacked us with his eye," I warn. "He was watching us through it. He also formed multiple deflection runes that all of you were surprised by. It seems to me that we don't know what he's capable of."

"I've ward-illusioned this entire area," Chi Nam says, her tone hardening, as if in direct challenge to Marcus Vogel. She flicks her gaze up. "And the runic shield above us is military grade. Much like the dome that protects both the Amaz and the Noi lands."

I raise my brow at this as I take in the translucent runic dome just above us, remembering the dome-shielded Amaz city of Cyme. This shield encases our immediate area like a huge bubble, the barely visible sphere liberally splashed with dim, curving Noi runes.

"When you say this area is 'ward-illusioned'…does that mean it's glamoured?" I ask.

Chi Nam's head bobs in affirmation. "That's an apt description. If you were to look down at us from above or from a distance, you'd see only a rocky mountain. Unless you got very close."

It's reassuring, but only to a point. I've an intrinsic sense that it's only a matter of time before Vogel finds a way around all of this sorcery and swoops down to claim his Black Witch.

"Vogel might send out search spells," Lukas bites out through his pain. "And Elloren is currently unshielded."

"We're too far away for any search spell to reach from Gardneria," Chi Nam counters. "And search spells cannot penetrate this dome, even amplified."

"We don't know what he can do," Lukas presses. "We need to get her farther east as quickly as possible." Lukas glances at the portal, and I follow his gaze, the brightened runes of its frame slowly rotating against the mountain's stone wall.

My eyes stop on the severed scorpio forelimb strewn before it, and a shiver passes through me. "I'm assuming you're charging it again?" I ask Chi Nam. "To get farther east?"

"I am," she says as she moves toward the mouth of a shallow cave that lies beside the portal and taps her stylus along the cave's flat inner wall.

A door springs to life, made up of a solid mass of multiple rotating blue runes, the cave's shadows now infused with sapphire light.

"The portal's trajectory is newly set for the Noi lands," Chi Nam tells me as small threads of blue lightning fork from the door's edge. "Toward a corresponding rune in the Dyoi Forest. But it takes time to charge it for one passage. More for four. And it's not precharged like the portal we used to get here. Even using the bulk of my stored magic, it will take weeks to charge this portal powerfully enough for us all to get through the bands of storm magic and to the Eastern Realm."

*Weeks?*

Worry mounts. "How many weeks?"

"Perhaps four." There's a flicker of grim indecision in her dark eyes that I don't want to catch but do. She, Valasca, and Lukas exchange somber glances, and my apprehension flares higher. I can read in their shared expressions how unlikely it is that we'll reach the end of so much time without Vogel finding us here. And I realize…we're gambling.

It's a bet that we might lose.

*Who needs good odds? Where would the fun be in that?*

A sliver of morbid amusement rises as I remember saying that to Trystan, the thought prompting a familiar pang of longing for my brothers as I glance up and follow the crimson constellations east.

*Where are you, Rafe and Trystan?* I wonder, as I'm seized with a desire to be reunited with my brothers that's so strong I'm ready to fight through every horrific thing Vogel can throw at me just to get back to them.

"I'll do a perimeter check," Valasca announces, and she forces herself to her feet with a tense groan, her rune blade fisted in her hand. She tests her leg, bouncing slightly on it, her gash still encased in a streak of glowing blue, a fringe of shredded fabric framing it.

"Be mindful of the wraith bats," Chi Nam cautions just as the interior of the cavern's door ripples blue and the stone disappears, revealing the Vonor's sapphire-lit passageway.

Valasca smirks at Chi Nam, a lethal gleam entering her dark eyes as she deftly flips the blade in her hand. "You should be warning *them*, Chilon."

Chi Nam cuts Valasca a look of censure over her cheeky use of the sorceress's informal name, a tang of power flaring in the air that sends a frisson of bright blue energy through my lines. But then Chi Nam's expression quickly morphs to one of narrow-eyed amusement and she lets out a long sigh, as if resigning herself to the rebellious company she's keeping.

Valasca tightens her hold on her rune blade, strides toward the runic dome, and raises her palm to it. Her rune-marked palm rays blue light as it makes contact with the dome, and she effortlessly passes through it, then makes her way to a twisting path that switchbacks down the long incline set directly before our stony platform, sheer cliff drops to either side of it.

"What are wraith bats?" I ask Chi Nam, nerves jittering.

"Bat-like predators," Lukas answers, his voice deepened by his labored breathing.

"Bred during the Elfin Wars using twisted magic. They're not difficult to take down if you can resist their psychic attack."

I meet his pain-glazed eyes with concern as he sends a tendril of his fire out to embrace mine, solid strength in his magic now that I'm heartened by.

"They feed on fear," he adds, an edge of challenge in his eyes. "Catch hold of it. Amplify it." The side of his mouth quirks up slightly. "Which means *you* need to hunt them."

To learn how to control my fear, he means.

I consider this, along with our short window for me to train before we take the portal farther east.

*I drove Vogel out of me*, I think as I glance down at the gray hand I have wrapped around Lukas's shimmering green one. *I drove Vogel straight out of me with my magic.*

And by finding my courage.

"All right, Mage Grey," I tell Lukas, suddenly ready to face whatever he and Valasca and Chi Nam want to throw at me. "I'll hunt some wraith bats."

Sparks light throughout Lukas's restored firelines and send a charge through us both, a sardonic look coloring his gaze. "You'll be slaying wraith bats in no time, Mage Grey."

Another shiver of his heat rushes through me as I unexpectedly warm to my new name.

"Both the wildlife and the weather here are quite dangerous," Chi Nam says, giving me a canny look. She steps toward Lukas and me, supported by her staff. "But they're our good friends, toiya. They're what keeps Vogel and the Alfsigr from being able to easily bring an aerial or ground force to the East." Her lips curl into a lethal smile. "And they're what will enable us to train you, during this short respite. So you can fight with us to take down both Vogel and his Shadow Wand."

# CHAPTER TWO

# DESERT LAIR

## ELLOREN GREY

*Sixth Month*
*Northwestern Agolith Desert*

"I got us some dinner!" Valasca announces as she climbs up the switchback path to our broad stone ledge, her spiky blue-and-black-haired head bobbing in the gaps between boulders.

A cool breeze rising from the desert ruffles my own pale gray hair as I watch her ascend, her slender form washed in crimson moon and starlight.

Lukas's arm is draped diagonally along my back, his hand snug against the curve of my waist. Chi Nam, Lukas, and I are all gathered around a blazing-red metal firepit, my blood-stained cloak balled up beside me.

Valasca throws her rune-marked palm against the dome-shield in a spray of blue light, then steps through it and onto the ledge, a sizable python marked with a stunning blue-and-violet-diamond pattern slung over her shoulder, some slim branches tucked under her other arm.

Valasca throws the dead snake and the branches onto a flat stone, then pulls a knife and begins to skin the serpent. "I took a look around," she blithely tells us, and I'm relieved to find her natural bravado so quickly restored. "No hydreenas or wraith bats. I did spot a small herd of scorpios, though."

"S-scorpios?" I sputter, almost dropping the warm mug of tea I'm cradling in my hands.

"They'll be normal scorpios here," Valasca counters with a dismissive wave of her knife. "We're likely to eat a few."

I raise a brow as her eyes flick to mine, mischief in them, as if gauging my reaction to this.

"Fine," I tell her unflinchingly. "I'd like my scorpio well seasoned."

Valasca cracks a smile. "That's the spirit."

"So, this cave is to be our home?" Lukas asks Chi Nam. He angles his head toward its sapphire-lit entrance.

"It will be, Young Mage." There's some friendly challenge in Chi Nam's tone as she sips her tea.

"Welcome to the Resistance, Mage Grey," Valasca crows to Lukas with a laugh as she carves up the snake. "Did you expect a Valgard level of luxury?"

Lukas gives her a tight smile. "No. But a glass of Issani wine would be good right about now." He shifts his position slightly and gives a sharp wince. Chi Nam's line of blue sorcery still burns bright along the diagonal wound that spans his bare chest and shoulder, and I can read how much pain he's feeling in the spiking flare of his magic around the scar.

Valasca pulls a flask from her tunic's pocket and hands it to Lukas, her expression more subdued now, as if she can read the pain in his gaze. "Tirag," she says.

Lukas gives her an appreciative look, accepts the flask, unstoppers it, and takes a surprisingly long swig for someone who's told me he drinks spirits in careful moderation.

He lets out a long, shuddering sigh as I survey his wounds. Lukas's gash looks much improved, the edges cleanly knit together now. My eyes snag on his muscular chest, lingering as I take in his handsome form. A prickle of heat rises in me, independent of my lines, and I'm instantly embarrassed to be noticing him in this way at this time, but when I meet his eye, he's smirking wickedly at me, as if he can read my mind. Despite the pain he's in, he intentionally sends a rippling pulse of heat through me, and I color hotly then look away.

"You shouldn't do that," I murmur to him, almost in a whisper. "You should conserve your fire for healing."

He gives me a sultry look, grins, then throws back another long drink of the tirag.

Both unsettled and drawn in by him, I hold both my palms up to the firepit's blaze, surprised anew by the storm-gray color of my hands, and of my entire self.

When I glance back at Lukas, his expression appears once more strained from physical discomfort. He takes another long swig of the tirag, and the chaotic force of his fire power around the wound dampens a bit.

Valasca lays the branch-skewered meat over the bowl-shaped firepit, shiny globules of fat dripping from the white snake flesh to crackle and pop on the flame.

An owl's sonorous call reverberates in the distance.

After a time, Valasca hands me a skewer that's pierced through several large chunks of meat. "Go ahead, Gardnerian," she says, her dark eyes glittering with amusement. "It won't bite. At least, not anymore."

It smells good, I have to admit. I take a small, hesitant bite and am immediately filled with surprise. It's like a buttery, greasy cross between poultry and white fish. "It's...*good*."

Lukas eyes me with slight humor. He leans into me as his

fire reaches for me with sudden, untethered boldness, possibly loosened up by the sizable amount of tirag he's consuming.

For a moment, my vision feels blurred by the heat he's sending through me as it caresses my lines in an enticing rush. I struggle to keep my breathing even as Chi Nam pours more hot tea for everyone.

"Are you drunk?" I ask him.

"Maybe a little," he admits. "But the pain's more tolerable now."

"You're sending huge waves of fire power into me."

His lip turns up. "That I pulled from you."

"You seem a bit restored," I archly observe.

He breathes out a laugh and gives me a smoky look before growing serious. "Does the fire bother you? I'm not sure I can hold it back."

I consider this. It's a whole new experience, being around a Lukas who isn't so tightly controlled. "No," I tell him. "I'm glad you're not in so much pain."

"You saved my life," he says, suddenly intense.

I hold up the inside of my wrist, the bumpy scar from the Icaral attack in Valgard visible through the glamour. "It was well past my turn."

He smiles again and takes another drink of the tirag as we all eat and Chi Nam and Valasca fall into a detailed conversation about the evening's watch and the shield's warding.

I let my gaze wander over the arcing rock formations of the Agolith Desert as I sip Chi Nam's bitter tea in a handleless black mug marked with an ivory dragon design. Everything is lit a soft red by the moon's scarlet glow, the constellations splashed across the sky like countless luminescent rubies, the red a fabled trick of the skies here. And lining the horizon, the roiling stormwall flashes lightning, lying in wait like a serpent made of violent weather.

Valasca throws more wood on the fire, and my attention is drawn toward the remnants of snakeskin cracking in it.

"Will you and Valasca be teaching me to hunt pythons too?" I ask Lukas, red firelight dancing over the hard, wildly attractive planes of his face and form.

He gives me a slow, lazy smile, his gaze increasingly hooded from the drink. "Elloren, you'll be able to lay waste to cities. I suspect you'll be able to take down a python or two."

*Lay waste to cities.*

I know he means it partially in jest, but the reality of what I am comes rushing back in with the words, jostling my emotions, and suddenly I'm aware of the waves of emotional and physical exhaustion breaking over me. I lean against Lukas's good shoulder, and he responds by pulling me closer, his cheek brushing my hair as he angles his head down to nuzzle against me. He inhales deeply, and then, to my great surprise, he kisses my temple, soft and lingering, as his fire shudders through my lines.

Lukas certainly isn't the least bit shy in private, but he's always been reserved and formal in public, and I'm both flustered and drawn in by his open display of affection.

"Would you like some?" His tone is light as he offers me Valasca's flask of tirag.

"I think you need that more than I do," I wryly observe, declining, even though it's tempting. Part of me wants to deaden my ever-present grief and my fear of the future and the horrific memories of this evening. I want to forget that there are evil Shadow forces ready to destroy me and everything and everyone that I love. And I want to forget Lukas almost died tonight and how that shook me to the core.

But I also want to stay clearheaded, especially with Lukas injured and increasingly affected by the drink.

"How long do you think it will take me to learn to use a wand?" I ask him.

Lukas pulls in a long, languid breath, growing thoughtful. "It might take a while." He focuses his glazed eyes on me, and my gaze is drawn to the sensual curve of his mouth, his lips shimmering green in this dark. "I've been training intensively in wand magic since I was a young child," he says. "Elemental magic is complicated and difficult to master. And shielding is some of the most difficult magic of all. But we'll simply take you out tomorrow morning and start from the beginning."

"And we'll pool what we know about mixed magical systems to protect her," Chi Nam adds, throwing pointed looks at both Lukas and Valasca, her expression made even more formidable by the flickering red firelight. "The forces of all the Realms will throw everything they have at us," she says. "We can't afford to just be lethal. We need to be one step ahead of them at all times and know their magical systems better than they do."

"I'll have the advantage there," Valasca boasts as she cradles her tea, her elbows resting on her knees as she leans toward the guttering fire. "Because my people link all the runic systems. None of this nonsense about magical mixing being against the gods. And we're stronger for it. We actually value diversity in Amazakaraan."

Lukas laughs then winces as he gives her an arch look. "To a *point*."

Valasca gives a conceding shrug. "All right, to a point. Minus men."

Lukas's sardonic smile widens. "That's a sizable subtraction."

Valasca rolls her eyes at him. "Yes, well, I'm here, aren't I? Not killing you." Her expression turns feline. "Not yet, anyway."

Lukas nods, grinning. "Point taken."

I look to Lukas in surprise. "Could she really kill you?"

Lukas glances at Valasca, their eyes meeting again for a long moment, as if they're calmly sizing each other up, his gaze flicking over the blades she has sheathed on her arms, at her waist, across her chest. Lukas turns back to me and nods amiably. "Most probably. She's the head of the Queen's Guard. That's not a position that goes to the talentless. She's likely able to deflect any spell I could throw out."

"You could try to run a sword through me," Valasca offers helpfully.

Lukas shoots her a sarcastic look. "I imagine I can't."

Valasca barks out a laugh. "I imagine you can't either."

Lukas gives her a wolfish look and takes another swig from the flask of tirag, wincing a bit as he lifts his arm.

"Is the pain still bad?" I ask him as Valasca and Chi Nam fall into a conversation about how to link runes from different magical systems.

"It *was* bad," Lukas says then pulls in another draft, his gaze on me serious, but then his mouth curves into a lazy grin. "But I'm feeling better and better." His gaze does a slow slide over my newly gray form as his earth magic brushes my lines. "That gray on you... You're so beautiful," he muses throatily. "You look like a storm sweeping in." He smiles at this, as if amused by his own sentiment, passion firing in his eyes. "You're going to pull me clear under."

I raise a brow at this effusive expression of his feelings, charmed by this more open, unrestrained Lukas. His thumb begins to trace a provocative spiral along the side of my waist. I glance at Valasca and flush at the amused, knowing look she's giving me through the red flames.

"Have you ever drunk this much before?" I ask Lukas, meeting his gaze as his pianist fingers trace over me.

"No," he says. "But I've never been in this much pain before." His gaze changes, heating as it fixes on mine. "Or wanted anything this much."

I swallow, caught in the fervency of his look, a deeper tension lighting the air between us. "What is it you want?" I ask, half knowing what his answer will be.

Lukas's smile fades. "You."

There's frustrated yearning in his words. And I'm acutely aware of Chi Nam and Valasca's silence, their attention clearly settled on us, even though they're keeping their eyes averted.

"Everyone should get a few hours' sleep, hmm?" Chi Nam says as she sets aside her tea and gets up with the support of her rune staff. "Valasca and I will take turns as sentry, but there's likely no need. We're well protected here." She unsheathes her rune stylus and holds it up.

The runes on the dome surrounding us brighten, and we're all bathed in flickering sapphire light as the runes begin to rotate slowly, a brisk current of magic passing through my body.

Chi Nam lowers her stylus, and the dome blinks almost completely out of view, only the dim imprint of a few scattered runes once again hovering in the air.

"These are the same runes that protect the Wyvernguard," Chi Nam informs us in Noi. "So, rest a bit tonight. We're safe for the moment." She motions toward me with a tilt of her rune staff. "Tomorrow, your training begins."

Lukas holds Valasca's flask of tirag out to her, and she gets up and accepts it from him, jostling it a bit before turning the flask upside down to show its emptiness, her lips quirking.

"Well, I bet you're feeling no pain, Gardnerian," she chides him in Noi, her grin met with Lukas's own enigmatic smile as she slides the flask back into her tunic's pocket. "You best sleep this off, Mage Grey. Thanks for saving our asses."

"I think it was a group effort," Lukas returns in fluent Noi with a cordial dip of his head.

Valasca huffs out a laugh and shoots him a wry look before throwing sand onto the firepit, casting the ledge into a deeper darkness lit only by the runes on Chi Nam's glowing staff and the crimson moonlight and constellations. The nighttime desert chill rushes in, swirling around me, but it's well countered by Lukas's insistent fire coursing brazenly through my lines.

I look down at my gray skin, my slate nails, dark blue in this light, still a bit astonished to find my coloring devoid of its normal green glow.

I stand up and offer Lukas my hand, but he rises on his own, balling his fist as he carefully flexes his injured arm, then lets out a long, shuddering sigh of relief as he cautiously tests his arm and shoulder's range of motion, the rune magery coating his wounds dampened to a mellow blue glow, the gash across his chest no longer a broad, gaping wound, but miraculously knit together and already mostly healed.

We follow Chi Nam and Valasca toward the cave, Lukas right behind me.

I glance back at his tall form to find his eyes homed in on me, a rush of his fire simmering through my lines. An unsettling thrill sizzles through me, mixed with bone-deep gratitude for what he's risked for all of us tonight.

Blue light and warmth envelop us the second we step into the interior of Chi Nam's Vonor. The light and the heat emanate from sizable crystal orbs hung from iron hooks attached to the walls, Noi runes rotating inside them. We're surrounded by an indigo-carpeted circular room that appears to be a combined library, armory, and kitchen, bookshelves blasted into stone walls stuffed with volumes in a multitude of languages, a large variety of runic weaponry hung on the walls along with a huge map of the entire Continent of the Realms.

There are additional Noi runes all over the cave, brightening the space with their sapphire light, some drawn on the cave's walls, some hanging suspended in the air along the periphery of the room, some lining the entire frame of the door we just passed through. And there are other runes as well—a few scarlet Amaz runes, and scattered, suspended emerald runes that I recognize as Smaragdalfar, one of them identical to the rune Sage placed on my abdomen.

"Is this place demon warded?" I ask Chi Nam, pointing to the emerald rune.

Chi Nam smiles approvingly and nods. "Ah, you're paying attention. Good. You'll be learning the various runic systems. So we can teach you how to use wands marked with combined sorcery."

We follow Chi Nam through an entranceway that has a black rune-marked curtain hung over it, through a narrow stone hallway and a small library, then past a dedicated armory.

When we come to another curtained doorway, Chi Nam holds back the rune-marked fabric to reveal what appears to be a sleeping area, the stone floor covered with another circular indigo carpet. A few bedrolls are piled neatly against a wall along with some square embroidered pillows, one bedroll already laid out on the carpeted floor.

"You can each take bedding," Chi Nam tells us. "Val," she says to Valasca, "you're welcome to sleep here in my room." She turns to Lukas and me and points toward a slim hallway that leads deeper into her network of caves. "I've a meditation chamber." Her eyes flick to me then back to Lukas again, as if trying to gauge the situation between us. "Lukas, you may use that room, and, Elloren, you are free to stay there or here with us."

My face warms over this formal acknowledgment of Lukas's and my sealed fasting.

*Mage Elloren Grey.*

It strikes me anew that Lukas and I have seriously bound ourselves to each other, which kicks up a whole host of conflicting, powerful emotions.

I glance at Lukas to find him steadily watching me, his

expression unreadable, but there's no subtlety in the way his power is running. It's not the least bit controlled, as it usually is, because of the tirag, no doubt. Instead, it's blazing hot and rippling through my every line.

The invitation in it clear.

My thoughts scrambled by Lukas's sultry magical caress, I swallow and pick up two bedrolls and pillows before Lukas can offer to help.

"Well...thank you," I say awkwardly to Chi Nam, growing flustered. "I'm sure your meditation room will be fine for us."

Valasca coughs out an amused laugh and gives me a knowing look as she rolls out her own bedding. Chi Nam simply nods, her savvy gaze passing over both Lukas and me once more before she leaves to stand sentry.

I hug the bedding to my chest as I venture down the slim hall, acutely aware of Lukas quietly following, his out-of-control heat lapping at my back as we step through another curtained doorway into Chi Nam's dimly lit meditation room.

Unlike all the other halls and rooms, there are no glowing runes marking the walls or suspended in the air of this small room. Only a single rune lamp emits a soft blue glow.

A low-set altar is placed against the rocky wall. It holds a silver incense brazier and a small statue of an ivory dragon wreathed by white birds, and I'm reminded of Raz'zor. There's what appears to be a Noi religious text placed by the dragon, its black leather imprinted with the image of Vo, the ivory dragon goddess the statue depicts, as well as a series of several small metallic bells of various colors.

"I can take that, Elloren," Lukas offers, his voice a low thrum as he holds his hand out for some bedding, the crooked smile on his lips tangling my thoughts.

My hand trembles as I give Lukas a bedroll and pillow,

acutely aware of the smoldering look he's giving me and how hot his fire's running.

Lukas sets down his bedroll by a wall and rolls it out in one smooth motion, then languidly sits down on it, looking relaxed as he watches me.

I set up my own bedding near the opposite wall, a few hand-spans away from him, and lie down on it, growing ever more flustered by how intensely Lukas's fire is reaching for mine.

Lukas smirks at me. "Keeping a polite distance?"

I swallow, unsettled by my awareness of his maleness and how gorgeous his emerald-dusted body looks in the soft blue light. I can barely hold my fire and earth power back from his insistent draw.

I watch as Lukas removes the rune blades strapped under his pant legs and places his two wands beside his pillow, then lies down and turns his head toward me, his gaze steady, his fire beckoning as I stare into his eyes.

Regaining some control over his power, Lukas sends out one tendril of his fire, slow and teasing. Caressing me, but in a deeper way than usual. Stroking. Long and slow. I glance uneasily toward the curtained door, heat prickling to life on my cheeks, along my neck.

Then he pulls back, smiling, as if he's waiting for me.

We're both quiet for a protracted moment, the stillness broken only by the deepening rise and fall of my chest as tension sizzles in the air between us.

Feeling reckless, I throw out my own line of fire.

Lukas smiles as he catches my line and pulls it in. Then he sends out an answering rush of magic, teasing it down my lines, his magic now caressing every part of me quite wantonly as I struggle to keep my breathing even.

I lie there, every part of me pulsing with heat, the pleasure radiating until it's low inside me. Both of us are breathing deeply as his earth magery flows into me and mine into him, branches curling and twining. I throw out another slim line of my fire, then send a harder blaze along it, searing it into his entire body. Lukas gives me a deeply carnal look, then flows a cascading blaze of fire out to me, his magic torching through my lines.

We lie there for some time, our fire and earth magic caressing every part of each other with increasingly brazen intimacy as Lukas shudders and looks at me with a desire so fierce that I know it will override any concerns about other people just down the hallway.

He holds his hand out to me with firm insistence. "Come here."

There's nothing gentle in the request. There's a demand in it, fueled by overwhelming want that's both wildly enticing and intimidating all at the same time.

I glance toward the rune-curtained doorway. "Lukas, no. They'll hear…"

He half smiles, desire swimming in his gaze as he keeps his hand extended toward me. "Then let's go somewhere else." Again, there's a command in it. A rough edge to this desire of his.

"You're hurt," I remind him, dazed from the desire he's sparking in me.

"My shoulder's a bit sore still," he says, a wicked gleam in his eyes. "The rest of me isn't."

For a moment I want to be reckless. To throw myself into his overwhelming passion and let him take me any way he wants. As if sensing my hesitation, Lukas reaches out more insistently, losing all vestiges of amusement. But he's too intense and affected by the tirag and too full of a domineering want at the moment. I don't take his hand.

His expression tenses with frustration, and he balls his outstretched hand into a fist and withdraws it, breathing deeply.

A torrent of his fire rushes through my lines, and when I meet Lukas's gaze, there's a hunger in it so intense that it stuns me.

Lukas's voice is low and impassioned when it comes. "I want you more than I've ever wanted anything in my entire life."

I know he's not just talking about this moment. He's not just talking about wanting to take me, right now. He's saying something of far greater significance.

Moved by his open display of both his feelings and his desire, I lift my hand, ever aware of the lines that mark me just under the glamour. "We're fasted. You have me."

His fire gives a harsh flare as he finally looks away. "No, Elloren," he says, a different pain clear in his tone. "I don't." He stares at the ceiling, his torrent of fire wrenched away, only the slight chill of the cave remaining as a pang of grief spears through me.

Because I know it's true. I've grown to care for Lukas. A great deal in a short amount of time. In so many ways. And I gave myself to him last night with no reservations, surrendering to our fierce attraction and my longing to fall into our perfect affinity match. Yearning to let go of the shard of grief that's lodged so deep and love him back fully.

Because even though Lukas won't profess his love, I can read it in his fire. Staggering in its strength, blazingly ardent and unfractured.

But I can give him only a small piece of my heart in return because the rest of it is shattered over my loss of Yvan and might always be. And I know he can sense that truth too.

I lie there for a long time, lost in conflict and guilt and horrific imaginings of Vogel's pale green eye staring down at us all, until finally, my eyes fall shut and a dreamless sleep takes hold.

# CHAPTER THREE

# DESERT TREES

## ELLOREN GREY

*Sixth Month*
*Northwestern Agolith Desert*

I bolt awake, momentarily disoriented when I find myself alone in a cave. My mind rapidly catches up as I take in Chi Nam's meditation altar, the small statue of the Dragon Goddess Vo, the Noi military garb that's folded beside me, and the black leather weapons belt set atop it.

And Lukas's neatly rolled-up bedding.

I glance down at my blood-speckled Elfhollen garb. My storm-gray skin.

Everything rushes back in—a world descending into war, the scorpio attack, Vogel's terrible thrall, our escape through a portal. Lukas's passionate words and unchecked fire.

My inability to return his feelings wholly.

I get up, feeling Lukas's absence keenly as the desire to find him rouses in my emotions and in my tumultuous, un-shielded lines.

I catch my reflection in the silver meditation bell that hangs from the wall and give a small start at my vastly altered appearance. I look like a living storm, my pale gray hair wildly mussed, silver eyes and lashes glimmering, my skin the color of thunderheads, my lips a deeper gray.

And my ears as curved as twin sickle moons.

I throw off my Elfhollen garb and put on the black Noi uniform, my boots and weapons belt, then dare to touch the Wand's surface with my wand hand, the feel of its spiraling handle refusing to prompt any flare of power in me. Thrown by the Wand of Myth's quixotic nature, I slide it into its belt sheath, then glance down at the sapphire military runes that mark my uniform's edging and pause, a sense of the momentous overtaking me.

The time to be a soldier has come.

To face my destiny full on.

*Today.*

*Today I will wield my magic.*

Emboldened by the threat of Vogel closing in on both me and the wider world, I fold up my bedding, then stride through the narrow stone hallway and through Chi Nam's bedroom, down more hallways, and into the Vonor's main living space.

The passageway to the outdoors reveals a spot of purple-edged predawn sky, the sound of Lukas's deep voice speaking Noi filtering in.

I look through the doorway and find Lukas sitting with Chi Nam and Valasca around a low circular table they must have dragged onto the ledge, a rune lamp in the table's center. The lit firepit beside them crackles with bright red flame. The air is cool, the sky half-tinted a dreamy dark purple that stands out in stunning contrast to the fading crimson stars.

I take in Lukas's unbelted Vu Trin tunic, his chest, abdomen, and palms newly marked with multiple glowing sapphire Noi runes and a few scarlet Amaz. He's poring over a thick text marked with runic diagrams, deep in conversation with Valasca, as they point at pages from several more texts splayed open on the table before them. Chi Nam quietly listens to them as she sips a steaming mug of tea, her rune staff propped against the rocky outgrowth beside her and glowing with a wider variety of runes than it was last night—emerald Smaragdalfar, scarlet Amaz, and golden Ishkart runes mixed in with the sapphire Noi.

Multiple wands hewn from a variety of wood are strewn among the texts, a glimmer of magic racing through my lines as my fingers itch to touch them.

Lukas looks up, obviously sensing my roused fire, and meets my eyes.

His black hair is spiked from washing, his distractingly muscular chest almost completely healed, only a slim red scar slashed horizontally across it. My fireline gives a reflexive flare toward his.

A flash of searing intensity passes between us, his own fire rearing then immediately wrenched back and forced to heel.

I feel the sharp sting of his guarded behavior as I step outside, flustered by my new knowledge of how strongly Lukas feels for me. And saddened to know the reason he's closing himself off.

But none of this matters compared to what we're all faced with, and I know that Lukas and I will have to set our complicated emotions aside and focus on the coming fight.

"I'm ready," I tell them as I hold Lukas's intense gaze. "Teach me how to use a wand."

"Relax your grip." Lukas's deep voice is soft in my ear as he traces a slow line down the thumb I have pressed against the wand. "You're not trying to crush it. Pretend it's a violin bow."

My firelines shiver toward his, unrestrained, as Lukas's arm slides around my waist, pulling me closer, his pianist fingers curling around my wand hand. His sinuous movements spark a tingling warmth that's rippling through me in slow strokes, and I struggle to keep my focus.

He's *so close*, his rigidly contained power only a fraction away from mine. And he's left his shield off my lines, which only makes it harder to resist being consumed by his draw.

I know he feels it too, his skin as feverishly hot as mine.

I loosen my fingers under Lukas's caressing grip as I prepare to let him send his magic through me in a demonstration of control over the candle-lighting spell.

Brow tensed, I set my eyes on the predawn desert before us as magic shivers along my heels and shudders up through my lines as it reaches for the wood.

*Red Manzanita*, Lukas informed me when he handed me this wand. Wood harvested from the bloodred trees that dot the edge of the sands stretched out before us, the trees' thick oval leaves a vivid plum that burns bright against dawn's gentle glow. Beside the sparse Manzanita grove stand three Striped Baobab trees with dark, ballooning, water-filled trunks. And to our other side, Black Date trees twist under one of the desert's multitude of arcing crimson-stone formations, a few Golden Yucca trees thrown into their mix. Knots of what appear to be dead, desiccated trees are interspersed throughout.

They're so silent and still, all of the living trees. No trace of hostility in the air.

A chill snakes up my spine.

Because I can sense them watching.

"A wand is like an instrument," Lukas says, ignoring our strong affinity draw, "and the magic is the music."

I glance at him askance over my shoulder. "Music that can level cities."

Lukas's mouth tilts up. "Even so. You're a musician. This is something you can intuitively understand."

Determined to focus past Lukas's seductive pull, I squint at the landscape. The dawn sun is tinting the arches of crimson stone with a soft blush of rose as it breaks free of the dark storm band.

Silver lightning crackles through the murky horizon of storm.

"I'm ready," I say, nerves spiking.

"Good," Lukas says, his voice a low thrall that threatens to scatter my magical focus into oblivion. "Now, sound the candle-lighting spell."

Surprise flashes through me, sharp as a blade.

I round on him as I vehemently shake my head. "You said you were going to send your own magic through my hand," I insist. "I can't release my power. It's not safe."

"I'll control it," he calmly returns.

"*No*, Lukas." I step out of his arms and turn to face him fully as I slash the air with my free hand. "If you want *me* to do this, every one of you needs to get far away from me and shield yourselves."

Lukas gives me a cynical look. "Elloren, you used an actual wand for that testing. You're holding a single layer wand carved from a branch. Besides..." He drops his voice and gives me a poignant look. "...I have a pretty good working knowledge of your power."

I shake my head, unmoved, remembering the river of fire. *My* river of fire. "No," I emphatically protest. "You *don't* know, Lukas."

Chi Nam cuts in from where she and Valasca are watching. "She's right. If you're going to have her use her own magic, you need to step back, and we'll form a combined shield. I've witnessed what she can do."

"Apparently, she makes her grandmother look like a baby Dryad playing with sticks," Valasca crows. "I'd take care if I were you." She mock toasts me with her water flask, smiling broadly.

Lukas eyes Valasca appraisingly. Then he gives me the trace of a humoring smile, turns, and strides to where Chi Nam is leaning on her rune staff and Valasca is perched atop a red boulder that lies at the base of a huge stone arch. Valasca's mouth is set in its usual rakish half smile, anticipation narrowing her sharp eyes.

Chi Nam taps her staff, and an aqueous blue haze flies out to envelop all three of them. Then Lukas draws his wand, murmurs a spell, and sends dark lightning forking through Chi Nam's shield. Valasca pulls out her rune blade and idly touches it to the shield, and the entire thing, including the sparking lightning, turns Amaz crimson.

Lukas leans against Valasca's boulder with his usual casual grace, his eyes trained on me.

"Are you sure you're well shielded?" I shrilly ask Chi Nam, remembering how much longer it took the Vu Trin to shield themselves properly against the devastating onslaught of my magic.

Chi Nam leans into her staff and nods. "There's much more power at work here between the three of us."

I swallow hard and turn again toward the vast stretch of crimson desert before me, heat gaining ground as the sun rises farther from the horizon's storm band.

Battling back my intense trepidation, I grit my teeth, raise the branch, and begin to speak the candle-lighting spell.

Power starts its whooshing rumble up from the ground beneath my feet, then branches through my legs in a tingling rush, like a fast-moving current.

Then all of the power streams toward my wand hand like an arrow shot from a crossbow then whips backward.

My power gives a hard flare, my eyes widening as my affinity lines cinch painfully inward with a brutal force that drives the breath from my lungs. My lines contract more intensely, and I double over, forced to my knees and onto the sandy ground as if yanked there by a savagely coordinated attack. And I can feel where the multiple points of cruel tension are originating from.

The desert trees.

I gasp for air, immobilized by my own lines as Lukas distantly calls my name and the power continues to ricochet backward from my wand hand, flying right into the affinity lines balled up in my center. Unbearable heat flares deep inside me, then gives a sudden, violent burst outward, and the world explodes into flames.

I cry out to Lukas as fire cuts off my vision and scalds through me. The whole world enveloped in fire.

I can hear Lukas yelling an incoherent spell through the inferno's fierce roar as a punishing wind lashes against me, knocking me onto my side and rapidly snuffing out the conflagration, a choking black smoke rising into the heated air.

Lukas rushes in through the smoke, drops down to his knees, and grabs hold of me. Chi Nam and Valasca are tight on his heels, their shield dropped, as Lukas flicks his wand and snarls out urgent spells, clearing the rest of the smoke away with a spiraling rush of wind.

"*Elloren,*" he says with ferocious urgency, more rattled than I've ever seen him, his eyes blazing as I cough and gasp for breath.

Wildly alarmed, I look around frantically.

The landscape is unharmed. Lukas and Chi Nam and Valasca are unharmed. And they're all gaping at me in obvious shock.

"What happened?" I ask breathlessly, my voice rough from the rising smoke. "There was fire everywhere…"

"You burst into flames," Valasca explains. "*A lot* of flames."

"You exploded," Chi Nam says.

My gaze flits toward the trees as I'm swept into a terrible certainty.

"The trees did this," I tell them, outrage kindling as a deeper realization takes root. "They mapped my lines. They've been mapping them for weeks and finally got a clear view of them. They forced the flow of my power inward, away from my wand hand. Then they waited for the right moment and attacked."

I meet Lukas's eyes, a terrible comprehension passing between us.

Lukas's jaw tenses as he turns and narrows his gaze at the trees, then looks back to me, seeming rattled. "Are you saying that they've completely infiltrated your lines?"

My outrage explodes. "I'm saying that they tried to *murder* me! The only reason I'm alive is because…" The reason strikes home.

*Because Yvan kissed me and I'm immune to fire.*

I take a deep, shuddering breath and flex my wand hand, then meet Lukas's gaze once more. "I survived because I have Wyvernfire in my lines and I *can't* be burned."

A lash of invisible affinity fire flashes out from Lukas, jealous heat in it, there and gone again in a heartbeat.

"Let me read them," Lukas says. "Let me read your lines."

I nod, realizing what he's asking. Lukas's grip on me firms and he pulls me close and brings his lips to mine. His fire rushes into me, his branches spiraling over my painfully knotted lines. But it's all wrong, the map of my lines completely skewed and tangled.

He pulls back and sets his severe gaze on Chi Nam. "She's right. The trees must have mapped her affinity lines while she was traveling through the forest. Then they waited until now, when she was unshielded, and attacked." He sends the trees a vicious look, as if sizing them up in a new way. "Clever," he says under his breath.

"What are you reading in her?" Chi Nam asks Lukas.

Lukas sets his piercing gaze back on the sorceress. "They've tied her lines in a way that orients them toward her center."

"Which means *what*?" Valasca demands.

"If Elloren tries to work a spell using an affinity other than fire, her magic will double back and kill her."

The terrible fact crystallizes in a light-headed rush. "Lukas," I bite out, "how am I going to learn to control my power?"

"You can't," comes his stone-hard reply. "Not for the moment."

Anger lights like blinding fire, the power inside me rearing.

Incensed and covered in soot, I bolt up and stalk over the red sands to the tree I felt the strongest pull radiating from—the large Baobab that stands before the Manzanita grove.

Teeth gritted in fury, I throw my wand hand's palm out against the tree's black ballooning trunk and hurl a wave of invisible affinity power out from my balled-up lines and straight into the massive tree.

The tree's aura shudders all through its huge form down through its roots.

A fury roars into existence inside the tree to match my own, the Baobab tree's rage soon mirrored by all the desert trees that surround us as I'm gripped by an acute awareness of how deep their taproots go down, and how all the trees' roots tangle around each other.

Down…
Down…
And down…

Leagues and leagues of connected roots leading over the entire expanse of the desert and toward the denser forests of all the Realms.

*Black Witch.*
*Black Witch.*
*Black Witch.*

The words ring out clear in the back of my head. Echoing over and over and over from all of the trees with relentless accusation.

My anger heats to blistering rage.

"Do you want Vogel to win?" I cry at the tree, at all the trees, as I press my wand hand against the Baobab's trunk and desperately struggle against their collective hold on my lines. "Is that what you want for the world?"

Suddenly, the image of rough trunk before me blinks out of sight to be replaced by an all-encompassing vision of trees screaming all around me.

Black fire raging through a forest.

Red smoking skies.

Leagues and leagues of forests being burned down.

And striding through the forest's ashes is a cloaked and hooded Gardnerian priest, a wand made from compressed, roiling Shadow in his hand. His pale green eyes searching and searching, a steaming Shadow trailing in his wake.

Another figure moves in behind him, rapidly becoming visible through the haze of swirling darkness. A young woman dressed in Gardnerian blacks, a spiraling wand in her fist. Horns made of Shadow spiraling from her head.

Her eyes a solid mass of roiling gray.

It's me.

Horror rises like bile in my throat as the corrupted image of myself vanishes.

I stumble backward as the terrible sense strafes through me that this is no mere vision. It's the forests of the Western Realm being burned down by Vogel. And Vogel searching for me to bring forth an even more rapid destruction.

When he turns me into one of his Shadow things.

"I'm not aligned with him!" I cry at the trees with desperate vehemence. "Let my magic go! I'm not what you think I am!"

"Elloren." Lukas's hand clasps hold of my shoulder.

"Let me *go*!" I cry out again at the trees as I yank my shoulder from Lukas's grip and face down the forest.

*Are you happy?* I lash out at the trees with my mind. *I'm set completely* against *the Magedom, and you've bound my power!*

*Well played, idiot trees!*

Lukas's hand comes to my arm again, but I'm engulfed in such a haze of anger that it's hard to focus on him.

"Elloren." His tone is calm but firm as he guides me around to face him.

I roughly swipe away angry tears. "It's no use." I throw my hand out toward the massive Baobab tree, outrage whipping through me. "I can't break free. I can't access *any* of my magic."

"Not for the moment, no," Lukas agrees. "Or you'll kill yourself. I'm sorry, Elloren. But wands are off-limits for now."

# CHAPTER FOUR

## MILITARY APPRENTICE

### ELLOREN GREY

*Sixth Month*
*Northwestern Agolith Desert*

"So, that's that, then," Valasca says as she crosses her arms in front of herself and glances at Chi Nam. "Can we break Elloren free of the trees' hold?"

Incensed, I stare over the red sands toward the trees and mentally hurl curses at them.

Chi Nam takes firm hold of my wand hand, the fingers of her other hand sliding over the runes of her staff. I flinch as blue energy flashes in my vision and through my lines in a tingling rush.

Every Noi rune on Chi Nam's staff bursts into sparking sapphire light.

Chi Nam releases my hand, the Noi runes on her staff instantly dimming, her expression tightening with what seems like an ominous realization as she looks to Lukas and Valasca. "We don't possess enough power to break the hold of the entire forest," she says. "We'll need to wait until we go East. We'll need to enlist the aid of multiple sorcerers and Mages to break Elloren's magic free and shield her lines from the forest's manipulation."

"They'll need to be talented in counter-runic resonance," Lukas notes.

"What's that?" I ask.

He looks at me. "The ability to build runes to counter every part of a complex magical system. Sorcerers competent in this can break down elemental spells into their components and fabricate runes to dismantle each part of a spell. Tree magic is complex."

"We could simply kill all these trees," Valasca offers, glowering at them.

"That's not a bad idea," I snap, though I'm swept into an oddly strong, almost instinctual conflict over the thought.

"The damage is done," Lukas counters, his jaw tight with frustration. "It would be a waste of effort and magic. And it might diminish the magical power I can access."

"It also won't untangle Elloren's lines," Chi Nam calmly adds.

Lukas sighs. "The trees are the source of our power, since we're part Dryad. Gardnerians work very hard to deny this fact, but there's no way around it."

"Vogel's cutting down large swaths of the Western Realm forests," Valasca notes, her tone hardening. "You are aware of that, aren't you?"

"Yes, well, he seems to be sourcing his magic from a new place," Lukas states.

Valasca blows out a frustrated breath. "Time for an alternate plan, then." A stubborn light sparks in her eyes. She looks me over speculatively, cocking her head. "We'll train her in the use of runic weaponry."

"I think that's the best we can do right now," Lukas agrees.

Chi Nam leans heavily on her staff as she gives Lukas a keen look. "She might be able to amplify the runes that line up with her affinities. Much like you can."

"Won't that make me explode?" I snipe, glaring at the trees.

"No," Chi Nam says. "You wouldn't be directly accessing your magic. Just firing up runes with the auras of your affinities." Her eyes flick toward Lukas, a knowing light in them. "Much like you two send magic through each other."

Valasca's brow creases in thought. "Have you ever used a weapon, Elloren?"

I shake my head in frustration, feeling terribly daunted. It may well prove impossible to break free of the entire unified forest of the entire of Erthia.

So, I'm powerless. Yet again.

Possibly for good.

Because the trees are ignorant fools who have just sealed their own fate along with ours.

Lukas and Chi Nam and Valasca have all grown quiet and are looking at me with concern as my troubled affinity fire knifes out from my knotted magic in slashing rays.

"Elloren…" Lukas touches my arm but I shrug him off.

I don't deserve his comfort. I've put him in terrible danger. I've put them *all* in terrible danger.

For nothing.

Chi Nam clucks her tongue, then steps toward me. She wraps her arm around my shoulder, doggedly holding on when I stiffen, my emotions overcome with fierce remorse.

"Toiya," Chi Nam says, the word firm but kind, "you need to decide right now to simply never give up. *Ever.*"

"Well, that's not so easy," I say, my voice fracturing.

She chuckles under her breath as she squeezes my shoulder. "Did any of us promise you 'easy'?"

I cough out a bitter sound as Lukas's and Valasca's mouths twitch up. "No," I begrudgingly concede. "You most certainly did not."

Chi Nam smiles slightly. "We have a saying in Noilaan—when fate locks a door, sometimes it's the most unlikely key on the ring that reopens the lock, hmm? Don't forget that."

A ripple of fire shivers through me, and I glance at Lukas, who's watching me with a subtle, knowing look. The heat from his invisible, fiery embrace cuts into my frustrated anger and despair, prompting me to rally slightly.

The odds just went from terrible to impossible, but still, they're all here. Believing in me.

Not giving up.

"All right, then," I capitulate, moved by their collective support, "let's try a few keys."

"We'll just have to jump in and start somewhere," Valasca says, rapidly shifting gears with her usual tart efficiency. She unsheathes one of her rune blades, the weapon's onyx handle marked with three rotating runes that glow Noi sapphire. "Here," she offers, holding the knife out to me handle-first.

I take it from her, the runes buzzing with a static sting against my fingers.

"Let's see what level of novice we're dealing with." Valasca flicks a finger toward a cluster of dead Baobab trees, their leafless branches browned and splintery against the brightening rose sky. She points to the largest and closest one. "Throw the blade at that trunk."

I glare at the living trees who are holding me prisoner and briefly consider throwing the blade at one of them instead, but my instinctual reluctance to harm them flares.

*We could be allies*, I mentally lash out at them, frustrated beyond belief.

Valasca slides behind me, takes hold of my arm, and demonstrates how to position the knife in my hand. I follow her directions, holding the hilt loosely against my palm, my index finger pressed against the dull edge of the blade.

Valasca points to a rune on the blade's hilt that encases a telescoping design with a small dot of what looks like a flickering blue flame in its center. 'Place your thumb on this central rune." Valasca gives me a significant look. "It's a fire elemental."

"You're sure I won't explode?" I ask her mirthlessly.

Valasca gives a short laugh. "The blade won't pull on your power. You'll simply amplify the runes that match your affinities. If you were Water Fae, you'd naturally amplify a rune containing water power."

"I'll mark a target," Chi Nam says as she angles her rune staff at the dead Baobab tree's trunk. Blue light bolts from the staff to the tree, a glowing blue circle blasting onto the wide trunk, a smaller circle glowing in its center.

"Watch me carefully," Valasca directs. "I'll show you the proper form."

As soon as Chi Nam steps away, Valasca unsheathes a similar blade, throws her thumb over the fire rune, pulls back her arm, then whips her blade into the air, lightning fast.

The blade spears forward to impale the target near its center with a clean, snappish *thwack*, a small burst of blue fire flashing out from it like a transient star.

Valasca shoots me a slight grin, then sweeps her arm toward the target in graceful invitation.

I step forward, grasping my blade's hilt tighter as I eye my target like it's a formidable adversary.

"Go ahead, Gardnerian," Valasca prods.

Bleakly skeptical that I'll be able to land this blade anywhere near the tree, much less hit the target, I pull my arm backward and artlessly ready the throw.

# THE SHADOW WAND

The Wand of Myth starts an insistent buzz where it's sheathed against the side of my waist. Translucent green lines burst from the knife and arc through the air toward the tree, like a glimmering track that spans from weapon to target.

Thrown by the odd vision and the Wand's sudden awakening, I blink my eyes and lower the blade.

The shimmering green lines blink out of sight.

"Did you see that?" I ask Lukas, Chi Nam, and Valasca, flummoxed.

"See what?" Valasca asks, tensing her brow quizzically.

"The lines," I say, acutely aware of the Wand's buzz tamping down. I point at the tree. "I saw green lines. And my Wand was buzzing against my waist."

Chi Nam straightens as her grip tightens around her staff, her gaze sharpening on me. "Try again," she prompts. "Throw the blade this time."

I pull my hand back, and the Wand's insistent buzz kicks up once more. Shimmering green lines fly toward the tree in a visible trajectory, everything surrounding it blurring. I thrust my arm forward as the lines contract, and I'm filled with an intrinsic sense of when to let the blade go, just as everything but the slender path to the target blurs to a haze.

I release my grip…and the blade sails through the air, following the bright lines and cartwheeling twice before impaling the trunk with a pronounced *thwack* right through the bull's-eye.

Everything snaps back into clarity as the dead tree bursts into an explosion of sapphire flame.

Astonished, I whip around to face Lukas, Valasca, and Chi Nam.

Valasca lets out a long, low whistle and turns to Lukas, who seems just as astonished, his mouth open as he blinks at the tree.

"Well, that's a game changer," Valasca crows with a laugh as she nods to me appreciatively. "And a hell of a nice throw."

"It was my Wand," I marvel, a bit overcome as the tree crackles with spitting, swirling blue flame. "It guided my aim."

"Give me the Wand, Elloren," Lukas says, holding his hand out for it.

I unsheathe the Wand of Myth and pause.

Its usual starlight glow has been replaced by a green luminescence, its spiraling handle warm to the touch instead of cool.

"It's turned green," I marvel, the Wand's energy pulsing faintly against my palm.

Like it's emerging from dormancy.

"It feels like it's waking up," I tell Lukas, a bit breathless with surprise as I hand it to him.

Gripping the Wand, Lukas strides away from us over the red sands until he's a fair distance away. He stills, raises his wand arm, then brings it down, pointing the wand at the stormwall lining the horizon.

Nothing.

He tries this a few more times to no effect, the Wand's vivid green glow settling into a deeper green luminescence.

Lukas turns and walks back to us. "It seems to slip back into a state of dormancy when I hold it," he says to Chi Nam as he hands the Wand back to me and I resheathe it.

"Because you are not the true bearer of the Zhilin," Chi Nam says before regarding me with a probing, quizzical look. "Give her another target to aim for," she directs Lukas and Valasca, not taking her eyes off me.

Lukas unsheathes the Noi rune blades strapped to his arms. "Here," he says before handing them both to me, hilt-first.

He motions to another dead Baobab tree with a hollowed-out center, his other hand touching the back of my waist lightly. "Aim toward either side of that hole," he says. "Halfway down. Both blades at the same time. No rune power."

I take a moment, fumbling, as I position the fingers of both my hands on the blades just like Valasca showed me as Lukas steps back.

I straighten, take a long look at the tree, then rear both my arms back as the luminous green lines spring to life once more, this time forming two clear tracks that arc from the blades to either side of the tree's hollow middle, everything else blurring beyond the twin trajectories. Teeth gritted, I thrust my arms forward and release the blades just as the verdant paths contract, the blades zooming along the lines to impale my targets with a firm *crack* at exactly the same time.

Stunned, I turn back to them all, my heart racing as Valasca spits out an expletive in the Noi language that's so outrageously off-color that it warms my cheeks.

Lukas laughs and shoots Valasca an incredulous look. "Do they let you say that in Amazakaraan?"

Valasca snorts and eyes him sideways. "We're not there, are we?"

"Well, this presents some interesting possibilities," Chi Nam says as her lip quirks up.

"That it does," Valasca agrees slyly. "Perfect aim and advanced rune amplification." She turns to me and grins. "It appears we have a new plan, Elloren Grey, since you can't be the Black Witch as of yet."

I blink at her in question, stunned by my new abilities.

Valasca's grin widens. "We're going to turn you into the equivalent of an Amaz warrior."

For the rest of the morning, Valasca and Lukas have me deploy a variety of weapons on the cluster of dead Baobab trees as Chi Nam quietly watches, all with the same results.

Perfect aim.

The bright sunlight beats warmth down on us like a kiln, as I step back and eye the rune spear I've just thrown. It has impaled the center of a circle Valasca chalked onto the dark trunk quite a distance away from me.

And the results are the same even if I hand the Wand off to Lukas.

Perfect aim. Fully conferred to me by the Wand of Myth. Even if I'm not in contact with it or holding it.

Like a gift of power.

My mind struggles to adjust to my sudden transformation.

I've felt physically powerless my whole life. And I was so quickly thrust back into that state by my total lack of control over my magic, and then by the trees wresting hold of it. But now, the Wand has granted me some *real power*. Small, compared to the power of a Black Witch, but power nonetheless.

A heady sense of possibility rises within me, impossible to contain.

Valasca throws Lukas and Chi Nam a dangerous grin. "Let's throw rune sorcery back into the mix."

She pulls out the large blade sheathed against her thigh. There are countless very small, rotating Amaz runes along one side of the hilt, an intricate etching of the Amaz goddess on the other, the goddess's image gorgeously worked in gleaming mother-of-pearl and decorated with small garnets. Valasca hands the blade to me.

I close my fingers around the hilt and press my fingertip onto one of the runes. The motion briefly stops the runes' rotation.

"This is the Ash'rion," Valasca tells me pointedly. "It is a sacred blade. One of the most powerful rune blades my people have ever fabricated. Its elemental power is unparalleled."

Lukas eyes her with amusement. "Now, how did you ever get hold of that?"

Valasca flashes him a slightly irritated look. "I borrowed it."

Lukas laughs. "You heretic. That's used in your religious ceremonies, isn't it?"

Valasca shrugs noncommittally.

He arches a black brow at her. "Interfering with deep-seated religious boundaries and handing a sacred religious object over to the Black Witch. That's sure to win the Amaz to our side."

Chi Nam cuts Lukas an arch look. "The future belongs to those who can move past their preconceived, rigid lines."

Lukas flashes her a feral grin. "I think the future belongs to those who can learn to decimate Vogel and his Shadow creatures."

Chi Nam nods at this, chuckling as she says something to Lukas in an obscure dialect not translated by my runes that prompts a knowing smile from Lukas and his own nod of obvious, wry agreement.

"But I've known for some time that you're a complete heathen," Chi Nam says to him, switching to the Common Tongue. "It's a reason I've always liked you, quite in spite of myself."

"You like me because I can almost best you," Lukas shoots back with another grin.

"Careful, child," Chi Nam says, smiling coolly. "This battle will not go to the recklessly overconfident."

"How do I use the blade?" I ask them, gripping its hilt as the runes whiz against my skin and send out a static *whoosh*.

"Shall we demonstrate?" Lukas asks Valasca with a relishing look of challenge as he draws his own rune blade.

"Oh, I thought you'd never ask," Valasca says with a grin, reclaiming the Ash'rion from me. She eyes Lukas wickedly as they face off a few paces away from each other. "You're on my territory now, Gardnerian." Her predatory smile broadens. "This is going to be fun. I've imagined this moment so many times. It's a real shame we're on the same side now."

Lukas gives her a look of mock caution as he fingers his blade's hilt then gracefully pulls his arm back, coiled for attack. "Do not permanently maim me."

Valasca shakes her head as if ruing the situation. "I *so* wish we were still mortal enemies." She drops into a fighting stance. "All right, Crow. Give it up. Show me what you've got."

Lukas smiles, and I've the sudden sense of his firelines heating to a scald. Whip-fast, he hurls his blade at Valasca, a rush of golden fire bursting to life around the knife and blasting ahead of it toward Valasca.

In a flash Valasca sweeps up her own blade, the image of fractured mirrors crackling into my mind as Lukas's stream of fire hits her blade's glinting side. Valasca sweeps her blade down, throwing the fire off to the side as she dodges Lukas's incoming blade, the streak of fire colliding with a small knot of brush that bursts into a bright blue conflagration.

"I win," Valasca gloats, her eyes full of confrontational glee.

"I'm just warming up," Lukas spars back with the trace of a smile, as I'm hit with the vision of silvery fire rushing through his lines. Without warning, Lukas pulls his wand and flicks it toward Valasca, veins of white lightning spearing out ahead of it.

In a blur, Valasca pulls a second blade, her fingers dancing against runes as she holds both blades up in an X before her. Lukas's lightning slams into the center of the X and doubles back at him.

Lukas flips his wand toward himself and conjures a rippling golden shield over his body, the lightning crackling over him in a shower of sparks before dissipating.

"Show me how to do that," he says to Valasca as he drops his shield, obviously impressed.

Valasca eyes him incredulously. "Mage-power deflection is an Amaz military secret."

Lukas is undaunted. "Teach me."

Valasca snorts out a laugh and narrows a cheeky glare at him. "There are some things I will never share with you, Gardnerian."

Lukas grins and shoots Valasca a suggestive look. "There are *many* things you will never share with me, Valasca."

A spike of jealousy flares in me. "Hey now!"

Both of them turn to me with looks of amused incredulity in response to my territorial outburst. I bite my lip, abashed by my reaction to their mutual teasing as heat blooms on my cheeks.

Lukas gives me a warm look and sends out an invisible tendril of fire to caress my lines. I shiver from the pleasurable rush of his fire and sheepishly meet his gaze, unable to suppress a slight smile as affection for him rises.

My fastmate.

My fastlines are hidden by my glamour, but suddenly, they don't feel so much like a cage anymore, even though I'm bound to Lukas by them. My flush heats further as Lukas's fire sizzles through me and I briefly consider the many ways I don't mind being paired with Lukas.

"Stop flirting, you two," Chi Nam chides then gestures to Valasca. "Give Elloren the Ash'rion."

Grinning, Valasca strides toward me and hands me the Ash'rion blade, the static energy in the runes prickling against my hand.

I look to Chi Nam. "Can you fight like them?" I ask her, curious about her abilities. Lukas and Valasca turn to Chi Nam as well, like two panthers looking to the lead panther.

Chi Nam's lip twitches up, as if she's amused by my question. She glances at Lukas and Valasca. "Attack me," she says, almost fondly.

"Stand back, Elloren," Lukas says as he pulls both a wand and a blade, eyeing Chi Nam with a level look of respect.

I step back as Valasca takes two blades in hand as both she and Lukas crouch down and Chi Nam's fingers slide over the runes on her staff.

Lukas and Valasca exchange a quick look.

I've a split-second sense of Lukas's fire blasting into his wand and blade as well as Valasca's press of runic lightning energy into her knives, before they hurl their weapons and magic at Chi Nam with such ferocity, I recoil, their fire power bolting and forking through the air.

Their combined magic slams into Chi Nam, and an ear-splitting *crack* sounds, painful in my ears, as a shield springs to life around the sorceress and she's briefly encased in a web of chaotic blue lightning.

Chi Nam angles her staff, and the web of lightning flies out toward Lukas and Valasca, knocking them both onto their backs and pinning them to the ground like two fish caught in a net, their weapons thrown from their hands and now beyond their reach.

Chi Nam turns to me and calmly leans on her staff as if she's expended no energy at all, some small threads of blue lightning still crackling over her form as she gives me a shrewd look. Her fingers move slightly over the runes on her staff, and the nets of energy around Lukas and Valasca blink out of sight.

Both Lukas and Valasca stand, brush the red sand off themselves, and retrieve their weapons. Then they pause to incline their heads toward Chi Nam in an obvious showing of respect.

Chi Nam focuses in on Valasca and motions toward me with a flick of her finger. "Test her elemental power."

Valasca returns to my side as I hold up the blade between us, the multitude of scarlet Amaz runes gleaming on the side of its hilt.

"So, Elloren," she says, "this is perhaps our most complicated elemental blade. These runes all correspond to elemental forces in one form or another—fire, lightning, water, ice, and so on—and they've been precharged with spells. You can throw out elemental force with the blade by placing your fingers on specific runes." She gives Lukas a scrutinizing look, head to toe. "You need to size up your opponent and try to figure out what type of magery he's likely to attack you with so that you can choose the most effective counter-element. For example, water neutralizes fire."

"That should be easy," I say. "I could sense your magic before you used it." I gesture toward Lukas. "I felt his fire powering up before he threw his blade, and I sensed his lightning forming before he released it from his wand." I lift the Ash'rion blade. "And I had a vision of some type of mirror sorcery before you used this to deflect his fire power."

Lukas steps toward me, serious now. "You sensed all that?"

I nod. "Like I can sense affinity power in Mages and Fae."

He sets his calculating gaze on Valasca and Chi Nam, his eyes blazing with possibility.

"She's magically empathic," Chi Nam says to Lukas. "It's rare for it to be this strong. I've encountered only a lower level of magical empathy in a few powerful Mages and Fae, and only the ability to sense other affinities or Fae thralls. A sense of runic charging means that Elloren must possess latent light magery."

Valasca lets out a swooping whistle. "Hell of a battle skill."

Chi Nam's mouth curves into a cunning smile as she turns to me. "You do realize what this means, Elloren?"

Giddiness rises up. "That I might turn out to be pretty good with rune weapons?"

Chi Nam gives a laugh, teeth bared. "It means that once you learn the runic systems and correct finger positioning—" she gestures toward Lukas and Valasca "—you'll be able to take down these two." Both Lukas and Valasca give me looks of lethal delight.

"We'll need to retrieve all the Noi and Amaz rune manuals," Chi Nam directs Lukas and Valasca, her eyes fixed on me like I'm a door that's suddenly been thrown wide-open. "Drill her in all the elemental combinations." She looks to me. "I'm hoping you're as dexterous as this one." She points to Lukas with her thumb and flashes him a broader smile. "He's got some of the nicest runic fingerwork I've ever seen."

"Pianist," Lukas comments, holding up a hand. "It has applications in the runic martial arts." He looks to me, his mouth tilting. "Elloren has pretty deft fingerwork too, being an accomplished violinist. She's very good with her hands." The suggestive glint in his eyes has me flushing anew, but I'm also warmed through by his approval.

"This isn't going to be all cerebral runic exercises," Valasca says to me, warning in her tone. "We're going to train you hard. We'll start with runic systems today, but be ready. First thing tomorrow morn, I'm going to start treating you like I'd treat any Amaz military apprentice. Becoming a warrior is not just about the magic and weapons mastery. You need to become mentally and physically tough."

I meet Valasca's hardened gaze, sobered by the memory of how I folded when faced with the first scorpio that attacked us.

"I want that," I agree, lit up by the idea of becoming tougher in every way and gaining control of some true power. "Train me like the Amaz."

Valasca's eyes flash with a feral light. "You won't like it, Gardnerian."

Defiance sparks as I bristle at her certainty.

And at the feeling that she's probably right.

An incoming flock of purple-flecked ravens snags my attention and I look past her, the birds swooping down to light on branches of the dead Baobab trees. Their wings settle as they turn toward us and grow still.

I'm suddenly filled with the unsettling sense that all the birds are watching me.

Along with the trees.

# PART FIVE

# HIGH MAGE RULING

Declaring that a State of War exists
between the Holy Magedom of
Gardneria and Noilaan.
All necessary force will be used
to subdue the Noi aggressors and
their Vu Trin forces to protect
the Holy Magedom.

# Gardnerian Guard Internal Mandate

## Issued by High Mage Marcus Vogel

Initiating a military search for Elloren Gardner, heir to Carnissa Gardner's power.

# NOI CONCLAVE MANDATE
## 6'203'68

Ruling War against Gardneria and all those
who align with them in their aggressions
against the people of the Eastern Realm.
The full might of the Vu Trin forces shall be
employed to cut down all threats to Noilaan.

# VU TRIN MILITARY
# INTERNAL MANDATE

Set down by Vang Troi,
Commander of the Vu Trin Forces

Mandating a hunt for Elloren Gardner,
the next Black Witch.

# CHAPTER ONE

# ZALYN'OR

## WYNTER EIRLLYN

*Sixth Month*
*Amazakaraan,*
*Capital City of Cyme*

Wynter wraps her threadbare wings around herself, tight as a blanket, as she makes her way through the Queenhall's archways of deep-purple curtains, hemmed in by two Amaz soldiers before her and two behind.

Her fluttering trepidation mounts as she prepares to answer this unexpected summons to Queen Alkaia's Council Chambers, her mind casting about like a small boat in a storm, unable to anchor itself on what could have possibly prompted this most urgent call to stand before the Amaz queen, a call issued on the same evening that war between Noilaan and Gardneria has been declared.

Wynter can feel the new defiant tension that this declaration of war has shot through the air of Cyme, the entire Amaz Guard mobilizing for potential hostilities with both Gardneria and the Alfsigr Elves. All of the Amaz soldiers and soldier apprentices she's gotten to know have already been summoned to the military bases on the periphery of the Amaz territories.

Amazakaraan.

The last holdout. The only land in the Western Realm not annexed by Gardneria or Alfsigroth.

The Lupine lands have fallen.

Verpacia has fallen.

Keltania has fallen.

And now, two monstrously powerful armies are looming on Amazakaraan's doorstep, and the Amaz's only remaining military ally is gone—Noilaan's entire Western Vu Trin force decimated in one day by the Gardnerians.

Wynter winces as she recalls the fearful questions asked by Amaz children in a multitude of languages.

*Mamma, will the Gardnerians and the Alfsigr come and hurt us?*

*Muth'li, will they send the broken dragons? What happens if they send the broken dragons?*

*Auntie, if Mamma Tith'lin goes to fight the Gardnerians, will they kill her? Make her stay home. I don't want them to kill her.*

And always the same answers, said in a variety of ways and languages in the same forced, reassuring tones—

*The rune shield over our lands will hold, sweet one. You need to trust our brave queen and our brave soldiers.*

*You're safe, toiya. The shield will keep the dragons out.*

*Nothing will happen to you, my love. Our brave soldiers will protect us. I'll protect you too.*

But the children catch the undercurrent of doubt, their fear not assuaged.

Because the situation is an encroaching nightmare.

The Amazakaraan military is formidable. But they're vastly outnumbered by combined Gardnerian and Alfsigroth armies. Which means the runic dome-shield cast over the Amaz territories is the only thing standing between the Amaz and complete annihilation.

Wynter's birds sweep in around her as she wrestles with her troubled thoughts and advances through the curtained hall. All types of birds, in an avian wave that seems to always move with Wynter now wherever she goes, surrounding her with their dazzling spectacle of color.

Orioles with persimmon feathers bright as fire.

Black swallows with backs dusted a sparkling blue.

Tiny jewel-toned hummingbirds in a shimmering palette of emerald, sapphire, and ruby.

Golden finches, bright as the sun.

And the raptors—three owls now, even in the daylight. And hawks and falcons, the predator and prey birds in a wary truce with each other as they bring their messages to Wynter, some frantic and chattering, some in a flash of dire imaging. But all with the same dread-filled tenor—

*Warning. Warning. Warning.*

*Burning forests! Corrupted elements! The priest with a Wand of twisting Shadow!*

It's always there now, the fear that the complete unraveling of the natural world has begun.

And in the center of it all…the dreaded fire bringer. Killer of Forests.

*The Black Witch.*

Wynter has tried to send reassuring thoughts of her friend Elloren Gardner back to the birds, only to be met with an explosion of fluttering panic each time.

*Black Witch! Black Witch! Black Witch!*

*Destroyer of trees!*

*Destroyer of all!*

The soldiers before Wynter slow their brisk gait, and Wynter slows along with them to stop before the curtained entrance to the queen's Council Chambers as Wynter's multitude of avian kindreds alight on every carved wooden rafter above, the Goddess's serpent form worked into the Verpacian Elm beams.

Muted conversation sounds through the violet snake-patterned curtain before Wynter.

One of the soldiers in front of her turns and gives her a poignant look, as if to say, *Are you ready?*

Steeling herself, Wynter gives a slight answering nod, even though her heart feels as if it will patter straight through her throat.

The soldier reaches out with one strong blue hand and pulls back the curtain.

Surprise bursts through Wynter. An Alfsigr Elf stands in the center of the crimson-tapestried room before Queen Alkaia and her Council. The young Elf girl is wearing russet Keltish garb, her alabaster hair chopped into short spikes, the unadorned tips of her white ears swiftly pointing through her tousled hair.

The Elf girl turns her head to peer over her shoulder, meeting Wynter's gaze with intense silver eyes.

Recognition bolts through Wynter.

*Sylmire Talonir.* One of the few Alfsigr brave enough to be openly kind to Wynter when she was in Alfsigroth. The daughter of nobility and cousin to the rebellious rune sorcerer Rivyr'el Talonir.

She must be around thirteen years of age now. She's taller than the last time Wynter saw her, more woman than child. But she's clearly the same fierce, defiant Sylmire, or she wouldn't be standing in the center of this crimson tapestry-covered room in front of Queen Alkaia and her Council of crones.

The Council is seated in a semicircle in front of Sylmire. The formidable Queen's Guard is present too, standing military stiff at the Council's backs, weapons at the ready, all of the Amaz's faces marked with runic tattoos. The queen's most formidable warrior, Alcippe Feyir, stands just behind Queen Alkaia, the huge warrior's pale pink face emblazoned with densely applied runic tattoos, her rose hair tied up in multiple knots, the tattoos on the right side of her face and neck obscured by a large healing burn scar.

Wynter hesitates at the chamber's threshold as her birds sweep into the room and alight on the radiating star of rafters that support the tapestried ceiling and walls. The image of the great Goddess rises up behind Queen Alkaia, larger-than-life against the deep-scarlet fabric, a swirl of birds made of starlight circling the Goddess and flowing up toward the ceiling to blend in behind Wynter's own unsettled flock.

"Wynter Eirllyn," Sylmire says by way of greeting, her silver eyes like confrontational stars. She keeps them unblinkingly trained on Wynter as Wynter pads forward over the carpeted floor toward the girl, her wings hugged tight around her thin, hunched frame.

Sylmire's sardonic tone and proud stance is just as Wynter remembers, but she's stressed, this girl. Deeply. Wynter can read it in the haunted look that edges her white-lashed gaze, the tight set of her pale mouth.

And in the ripple of agitation she sets off in the birds.

Wynter turns to look questioningly at Queen Alkaia, then lowers herself to her knees and bows to the ground before the queen, her forehead meeting the woven carpet.

"You may rise, Wynter Eirllyn," Queen Alkaia kindly but firmly directs.

Wynter rises but remains on her knees.

Sylmire hasn't budged from her defiantly upright position, one fist on her hip.

*How did she ever get here?* Wynter wonders, still astonished by her presence. Sylmire is right around the age of her Elian'thir, her coming-of-age ceremony. A time when she'd be surrounded by family and priestesses—the hardest time of all to slip out of Alfsigroth and journey to Amaz lands.

"You *must* kneel before the queen before you make your petition," Alcippe slowly states in that low, resonant voice of hers, her rose-quartz eyes pinned on Sylmire, each word enunciated, a command best obeyed.

Sylmire's sharp gaze flicks to the massive, ax-armed warrior. "I'll do no such thing," she fearlessly snaps. Her lip curls with defiance. "I grovel before *no one*."

Alcippe makes a slight, threatening move forward, but Queen Alkaia raises a quelling hand.

"Let her stand," Queen Alkaia calmly orders, her shrewd emerald eyes set on the girl, black runic tattoos swirling over the queen's green-hued face. "Sometimes the truth requires strong words. And even stronger actions. She has journeyed a long way. A journey that I imagine involved quite a bit of risk." She flicks up her palm. "Speak, child."

"I petition you for protection," Sylmire declares, a challenge in the plea.

"From who?" Queen Alkaia serenely inquires.

"The Alfsigr Elves." Sylmire's courage seems to falter, her lip wobbling slightly even as her body tenses as if she's primed for a fight. "They're coming for me. And they'll kill me if they find me."

Murmuring breaks out among the Council crones as they eye the girl warily. Wynter catches the grim gaze of the only other Alfsigr Elf in the room save herself and young Sylmire.

Ysilldir Illyrindor.

The tall, willowy member of the Queen's Guard who stands beside Alcippe.

Ysilldir's long snow-hued hair is styled in multiple looping braids, the dark lines of her runic Amaz tattoos stark against the alabaster skin of her face, her neck, her hands. A bow and quiver are secured on her back.

"Why will the Alfsigr kill you, child?" Queen Alkaia asks.

Sylmire reaches into her tunic's pocket and withdraws a gleaming silver necklace, fisting its chain as she raises it for the queen to view, its shiny runic pendant reflecting flashes of lamplight as it sways.

"I escaped Alfsigroth before I turned thirteen," Sylmire says. "Right before my Elian'thir. To keep them from forcing me to wear *this*."

"This is a Zalyn'or, yes?" Queen Alkaia inquires, nodding to herself. "I know of this necklace. All Alfsigr are given this to wear when you come of age. It is part of your religious rituals, is it not?" The queen turns to Ysilldir for confirmation.

"Yes, my queen," Ysilldir replies, her elegant voice heavily accented like Wynter's own, an Alfsigr inflection that's undimmed even though she's spent five of her twenty-one years here. Ysilldir looks to Sylmire, her white brow creasing in question. "We all receive the necklace during our twelfth year. It is set into our skin permanently with runic power."

Ysilldir pulls down the center of her tunic's collar with both hands, exposing her upper chest. The tattoo of a necklace and its pendant are emblazoned on her chalky skin, the flat impression of a silver chain and an oval disc marked with multiple Alfsigr runes.

Wynter's skin prickles as she considers her own Zalyn'or imprint, just under her tunic's fabric.

"The Zalyn'or is fused to us," Ysilldir continues, "by the Alfsigr Royal Council's rune sorcerer. It imprints us with knowledge of our religion and our traditions." Wynter catches the trace of disdain that's entered Ysilldir's tone, and she's clear on its origin.

Wynter has walked with Ysilldir more than once during her

patrols of Cyme, her soldier friend quietly laying out her reasons for escaping Alfsigroth. Confiding how glimpses of the oppression of the subland Smaragdalfar Elves seared through her desire to remain docile and please her family, her people. Over time, Ysilldir started to notice that the rare Elves who questioned any of the edicts thrown down by the Alfsigr monarchy or priestesses either disappeared or were cast into the sublands to be imprisoned there along with the Smaragdalfar Elves.

Then, one day, Ysilldir overheard her parents discussing their plans to forcibly bond her to a mate chosen for her by the Alfsigr Circle of Priestesses. A mate with a stern face and rigid ways, twenty years her senior.

She left for Amaz lands that very same day, barely able to withstand the overwhelming desire to turn back, the pull like a fierce undertow that almost subverted her will to escape.

"The Zalyn'or is not just a way to impart Alfsigr ways," Sylmire cuts in, almost a snarl. "It's infected with primordial power. *Shadow* power. And it controls minds."

A susurrus of uneasy murmuring rises.

Queen Alkaia patiently waits for it to subside, her probing gaze fixed on the girl. "How can this be true?" Queen Alkaia asks. "Two of your Alfsigr sistren stand before and beside you, the Zalyn'or imprinted on both of them. Both of their own minds."

"Not completely." Sylmire eyes both Wynter and Ysilldir. "They are not what they appear to be. They are not even what *they* think they are."

Queen Alkaia's expression grows severe. "What do you mean, child?"

Sylmire's fist tightens around the necklace as she raises it a fraction higher. "This necklace doesn't just impart knowledge of Alfsigr religion and culture. It forces *complete belief* in the supremacy of those things. And it suppresses all rebellious thoughts, and all physical desire too." Sylmire's mouth turns down into a disgusted grimace as she briefly eyes the necklace like it's a dangerous serpent. "It turns the wearer into an obedient eunuch for the Alfsigr state."

It's as if a fire rune has been detonated in the chamber, all the Council members erupting into conversation at once in urgent tones.

Queen Alkaia flips up a hand and waits, her green gaze fixed on Sylmire as everyone grows silent.

"Both Wynter Eirllyn and Ysilldir Illyrindor have escaped Alfsigroth and stand at odds with many of the Alfsigr ways," Queen Alkaia sharply points out. "How could they dissent if this necklace has the control that you say it does?"

"Only the most rebellious have minds that partially survive." Sylmire turns to Ysilldir and then Wynter with looks of impassioned concern. "You are ghosts of your true selves. Imprisoned in Shadow runes."

A stunned, disbelieving shock spears through Wynter.

*No.* That can't be true.

The only thing Wynter is sure she's imprisoned in is her fate as one of the demonic—a Deargdul Icaral beast.

Silver fire ignites in young Sylmire's eyes. "These two must be some of the most strong-willed people of all the lands. That's the only way some of their free will has survived the Zalyn'or."

An outbreak of more troubled murmuring.

Sylmire meets Wynter's gaze once more. "Your brother, Cael, and his second, Rhys…they're rebels too. Or they would *never* have been able to fight back against the Zalyn'or's pull. It's the only reason they were able to break with Alfsigroth and support you like they did, even though the Alfsigr want all Icarals slain." Sylmire pauses, her bold words turning hesitant, her pale brow tightening with obvious concern. "Wynter… Cael and Rhys were renounced by the Alfsigr Royal Council shortly after they returned to Alfsigroth. Right before I escaped. They were taken into military custody." She swallows, lapsing into Alfsigr. "It's likely they'll be sentenced to the sublands for helping an Icaral to escape capture."

Wynter gasps, the news a staggering blow straight to the heart. Her beloved older brother, Cael—her protector and unwavering supporter. And kind, gentle Rhys, with his searing intellect and bookish ways, her loyal friend since childhood.

Both of them members of the Alfsigr royal class.

Fear rises at the thought of them being cast into the sublands, where they would be at great risk of being slain by the Smaragdalfar in retribution for the terrible cruelty the Alfsigr have rained down upon the subland Smaragdalfar Elves.

For a moment, Wynter can't move. She can barely breathe as tears pool in her eyes.

"What this girl says about the Zalyn'or," Ysilldir interjects, "it cannot be true, my queen." She glances protectively at Wynter before sweeping her silvered gaze toward Sylmire. "I am a warrior for the Amaz," she says, raising her sharp white chin. "I left everything behind to escape and come here. Even though I bear the Zalyn'or imprint."

"Because your free mind is *iron strong*," Sylmire doggedly insists, not ceding an inch. "Strong enough for a piece of it to resist control."

Ysilldir ignores this as she looks to Queen Alkaia. "My queen—I do not see the truth of this—"

"Do you struggle to let go of the Shining Ones?" Sylmire harshly challenges Ysilldir.

Ysilldir freezes, seeming stunned into silence as verses from the Alfsigr holy book swarm through Wynter's mind and sweep her into a rancid certainty of her own sinful nature—a beast with vile wings. Cast out forever by the Shining Ones.

A Cursed Icaral.

The familiar, irrepressible urge bubbles up…

*Atone. Atone. Atone.*

"Does the fear that you are cast out of the One True Faith give you nightmares?" Sylmire presses Ysilldir, and Wynter feels the truth of Sylmire's words straight through to her bones, her own sleep plagued by nightmares where she's cast out by the Shining Ones' light and into the Evil Abyss under the surface of the world.

*Atone. Atone. Atone.*

Ysilldir's silver eyes are riveted on Sylmire, her expression stark, as if this young Alfsigr girl is peering straight into Ysilldir's very soul.

"And the Zalyn'or doesn't just control them by controlling religious belief," Sylmire tells Queen Alkaia. "It controls by removing romantic urges, as well." She looks once more to Ysilldir. "Do you wonder at your complete lack of desire for anyone?"

"There are many who feel no desire," Ysilldir counters, clearly rattled. "It is normal for some—"

"Not for an entire country." Sylmire cuts her off. She turns to Wynter. "Did you ever see your brother, Cael, yearn for anyone? Or Rhys?"

"There are many, many Alfsigr," Queen Alkaia counters with some impatience. "Clearly there is desire among them."

"Only when the Alfsigr Royal Council and the priestesses allow it," Sylmire argues. "The Council's rune mage lifts a portion of the Zalyn'or's power only when they grant a couple the right to conceive a child. And they lift the Zalyn'or's rune power for only one day."

Wynter considers this through her haze of misery and worry for Cael and Rhys. And her reflexive desire to draw sharply away from everything Sylmire is saying.

*Mind control.*

Wynter tightens her frail shoulders and forces herself to face these ideas head-on, even as every emotion inside her revolts against the subversive thoughts.

Yes, it's true that Cael and Rhys and Ysilldir and she, herself, never seem to have felt that spark of desire or romantic love that almost all of the non-Alfsigr around them seem to fall into. Wynter has always supposed that the Alfsigr were simply different that way. Refined and removed from such messy, turbulent feelings.

But what if it's because huge swaths of their thoughts and desires have been suppressed?

Wynter's hand reflexively rises toward the Zalyn'or imprint on her chest, just below her purple Amaz tunic's fabric. Purple that she struggles to wear—all clothes that aren't Alfsigr clothing seeming *wrong*.

"They forced one of those necklaces on my sister a year ago," Sylmire tells Queen Alkaia, her mouth drawing down in a trembling grimace. "And she *changed*. She's like a ghost of herself now. Like she's all chained up inside. I've spent over a year trying to save her, sneaking into the Alfsigr Royal Council and Guild halls. Looking through their secret archives. And I've found out *things*."

"What things?" Queen Alkaia prompts.

"The Alfsigr Priestess class got hold of Deargdul'thil runes during the Elfin Wars, when the nations of Erthia rose up against the power of the Deargdul'thil demons and their Shadow Stylus. The priestesses knew that this was wicked sorcery, but felt that they, as the bearers of the One True Faith, had the power to wield it for 'the good.'" Sylmire's lips twist with derision. "They used it to create the Zalyn'or and force obedience to our faith and our culture and our Council hierarchy. And so we have grown strong and imprisoned the

Smaragdalfar Elves without any effective dissent, their labors making us rich.

"But now the Alfsigr Royal Council and the priestess class are worried. There's talk that Marcus Vogel has obtained the primordial Shadow tool that was used during the Elfin Wars and that he's wielding it as a Shadow Wand. Which could make it possible for him to create his own Zalyn'or spells." Sylmire glances at each Council member in turn. "Which could make it possible for him to control the minds of everyone imprinted with the Zalyn'or necklace. Eventually imprisoning everyone in every Realm inside his vision of Gardnerian supremacy and placing two armies under his control."

A tense silence descends.

Wynter's eyes meet Ysilldir's, the Elfin warrior mirroring her look of concern, and Wynter realizes in another terrible flash that what Sylmire is telling them has a deep ring of truth to it. And that both she and Ysilldir might actually be imprisoned by the Zalyn'or and rendered mere specks of themselves.

Mind controlled.

"We have tried to lift this Zalyn'or from Ysilldir's skin to study its runes," Queen Alkaia says carefully, as if the full ramifications are settling into her mind. "All our rune sorceresses working together could not lift this runic mark."

Sylmire returns the queen's piercing stare without flinching. "Only an Alfsigr rune sorcerer can remove this mark. It is set into the spell. And there are only two of them in all the lands."

Queen Alkaia's mouth twitches into a grim smile. "Do you propose, then, that we request the aid of the Alfsigr Royal Council's rune sorcerer in this task?"

"No," Sylmire sharply returns. "Seek the aid of my cousin, Rivyr'el Talonir. The only other Alfisgr rune sorcerer. He may be the only one who can save those marked with the Zalyn'or."

Sounds of outrage rise all around.

Queen Alkaia's expression has become a locked door. "He is male."

Sylmire's star-eyes ignite. "He has removed his own Zalyn'or and set himself against the Alfsigr! He has fled East to align himself with the Noi Wyvernguard! He can break these runes! He *must* break these runes!"

Queen Alkaia's expression tightens, her green eyes narrowing. "He is a male. And as such, an abomination. We cannot fight an abomination with an abomination. We would lose the Goddess's favor. We must find another way." She grows silent again as she studies a frustrated-looking Sylmire. "Sylmire Talonir," the queen finally says, "it is of extreme importance to find out if what you say is true, beyond the shadow of all doubt."

Sylmire boldly holds the queen's stare, her jaw set stubbornly tight. "The proof stands before you and beside you." She looks to Ysilldir. "Ysilldir Illyrindor—do you struggle against the idea that everything that is non-Alfsigr is corrupted and impure and evil?"

Ysilldir winces as every set of eyes moves to her, the Alfsigr warrior clearly battling against this airing of her own oppressive thoughts. "I… I always assumed it would take time," she stammers, "to break through the lies I had been taught by the Alfsigr…"

Sylmire levels her gaze on Wynter, a pained compassion softening her hard look. "Wynter Eirllyn, do you see yourself as the worst of demons, even though I have never seen you do a single unkind thing?"

A storm of emotional pain wells up inside Wynter, threatening to choke her into oblivion.

"Are you filled with guilt over your very existence?" Sylmire relentlessly presses on. "Repulsed by your wings simply because the *Ealaiontorian* tells you to be?"

"Stop, please, I beg of you," Wynter pleads, her whole body contracting into a devastated ball, tears slashing across her vision as birds fly toward her in a tweeting, chattering, screeching rush that she can barely hear over her storm of emotion as the verse from the Alfisgr holy book sounds in her head—

*Lo, the Shining Ones will come to smite the evil wingeds and cleanse the earth of their depravity and sin.*

"Don't you ever wonder," Sylmire rages on, clearly incensed on Wynter's behalf, "why you can't fly? Why you have no fire?" Her gaze turns incendiary. "It's because they fed you *lies* about yourself and stole your fire from you!"

"*I don't want to fly!*" Wynter cries out fiercely as she's choked with an overwhelming anguish and shame over her grotesque wings. Yearning to be what she can never be—a pure, wingless Alfsigr, her back unmarred. Wishing someone could take a knife and slice the wings from her back...

*Shining Ones forgive me for my great sin.*
*Shining Ones forgive me for my great sin.*
*Shining Ones forgive me for my being born a monstrous Icaral.*

"I'm cursed!" Wynter cries out, weeping in great, choking spasms. "One of the wretched ones! It would have been better if I had never been born!"

"*Enough!*" Queen Alkaia orders, immediately silencing the room as a red-tailed hawk, a small pygmy owl, and several starlings swoop onto Wynter's shoulders, her lap, the edge of her wings and flood Wynter with their fierce affection.

Wynter looks to Sylmire as she hangs on to the tether of the birds' collective adoration. The young Elf meets her gaze, all ferocity gone, the girl's expression turned mournful, her own eyes now glazed with tears.

"Look around you," Sylmire says to Wynter, her voice breaking with emotion. "You could have an army of falcons ready to do your bidding. All the wingeds in all of the lands ready to follow you into battle against Marcus Vogel."

Before Wynter can respond, there's a sudden jostling of curtains to the side of the Queen's Council dais, then an explosion of fabric as an Icaral child flies into the room, her black wings flapping in a flurry of motion, bright excitement in four-year-old Pyrgomanche's face as she makes straight for Alcippe and birds rustle excitedly, a contagious rush of avian joy shooting through the room.

"Muth'li Alcippe!" Pyrgo cries happily as Alcippe catches the child in her strong arms, a swirl of hummingbirds whirling around the child like a jeweled constellation.

Wynter takes in the slash of vicious burn scars, nearly healed, that obscure the runic tattoos on half of Alcippe's pale rose face and neck. Healing burn scars mark the side of her arm as well, little Pyrgomanche prone to nightmares from the trauma she endured that causes her to burst into flame in response to both the nightmares and her fits of uncontrollable rage over losing her Gardnerian mother and being thrown in the Mages' prison before being freed by Yvan and Elloren. Wynter and the Amaz Fire Fae all helped Alcippe care for the child on more than one occasion, as they have an immunity to fire whereas Alcippe does not. And the Amaz rune sorceresses have labored to mark Alcippe with runes to give her some immunity to fire and speed the healing of burns.

But no matter how many times Alcippe is burned by the Pyrgo, the huge warrior never once shrinks back from raising this child she's developed a fierce parental love for.

A slight, teenage Elfhollen-Amaz girl rushes in behind

Pyrgomanche, pausing to bow low before the queen. "I'm so sorry, Queen Mother. The child escaped me."

Queen Alkaia holds up a bemused hand as birds fly about the room and assemble on the rafters above the child and around Wynter. "Sometimes the Goddess does not stand on convention," Queen Alkaia tells the girl with a benevolent smile. "Sometimes she speaks to us through a child."

The rustling of birds dies down, an emerald hummingbird lighting on Pyrgomanche's shoulder as Pyrgo grins at the queen and hugs Alcippe tight.

"Come to me, child," Queen Alkaia says warmly to Pyrgo, holding out wizened hands.

Pyrgo's wings give an excited flutter, her smile widening with delight as she lets herself be passed from Alcippe to the queen and she falls into Queen Alkaia's warm embrace.

After a moment the queen pulls back and looks closely at the child, beaming. "Tell me, Pyrgomanche," she says. "Does the Goddess want you to diminish your fire?"

"No!" Pyrgo yells, answering the question she's been asked many times by joyful rote, variations of these questions asked regularly to all Amaz children. Pyrgo glances searchingly at Alcippe, as if slightly abashed by how loudly she answered.

Queen Alkaia's smile twitches up. "And tell me, child. Does the Goddess want you to lower your voice?"

Pyrgo grins. "No!" she shouts.

"Or hide your power?"

"No!"

"Or believe in lies about yourself?"

"NO!" The last *no* comes out in a roar.

Queen Alkaia's head bobs with satisfaction. "And tell me, Pyrgomanche, does the Goddess want you to hide your wings?"

"*NO!*" Pyrgo bellows, louder than a storm, looking as if

she'll burst into joyful flame right there as Wynter is cast into deeper pain and conflict.

For a moment, both Queen Alkaia and Pyrgomanche are quiet as they smile at each other vigorously.

"Who are you, child?" Queen Alkaia prompts, her face taking a turn for the serious.

"The Goddess's beloved warrior!" Pyrgo cries out.

Queen Alkaia nods solemnly. "And who loves you, Pyrgomanche Feyir?"

"The Free People of Amazakaraan!"

Queen Alkaia's face takes on a look of fierce triumph as she prods the child forward. "Show us, Pyrgomanche Feyir, beloved of Amazakaraan. Show us your wings!"

Pyrgo hops up from the queen's lap and steps forward, looking once to the queen for approval, and Queen Alkaia gives her a bolstering nod. Pyrgo's innocent face bursts into a look of joyful pride as she unfurls her wings, gleaming like opals, to their full size, her eyes lighting with golden flame as a small hawk swoops down to land on her shoulder.

The entire Queen's Council rises as one and bursts into whoops and cheers, every soldier in the room moving, as one, to salute Pyrgomanche, fists to chests. Tears flow down Alcippe's cheeks as she places a broad, bolstering hand on the child's head and Pyrgo glances up at Alcippe with a look of pure devotion.

Something stirs in Wynter's devastated mind—something small and chained that's looking to throw off the shackles.

"Who are the Icarals, Pyrgomanche Feyir?" Queen Alkaia says above the ongoing chanting of Goddess blessings.

*"Dragonkin!"* Pyrgo heartily answers as she ruffles her wings. "Beloved ones of the Goddess!"

Queen Alkaia sets her eyes on Wynter and holds her faltering stare, even as Wynter is caught up in unrelenting agony. *"This* is your future, Wynter Eirllyn," Queen Alkaia vehemently insists, glancing pointedly at the child. "*This* is your truth. Not the poison the Alfsigr fed you. Not the lies this Zalyn'or sends into your very soul." Queen Alkaia's gaze moves to the knot of heavily tattooed women assembled to the Council's side.

"Circle of Sorcerers," Queen Alkaia booms out. The room grows silent as the women all rise, each bearing multiple rune styli attached to belt sheaths.

"Yes, Queen Mother," the most elderly of the women answers, her skin a deep blue, her hair salt white. Glowing scarlet Amaz runes decorate her pointed ears.

"Set your Circle to work on breaking the power of the Zalyn'or," Queen Alkaia charges. She turns her vivid green eyes on Sylmire. "Sylmire Talonir, I grant you amnesty in Amaz lands. You will work with the Circle and tell them all that you know." Queen Alkaia's gaze hardens. "The time has come to free Wynter Eirllyn and Ysilldir Illyrindor and raise a force to free all of the women of sunland Elfinkin."

Wynter's small spark of hope blinks out of existence even as sounds of vigorous support for the queen's declaration go up all around.

Wynter can barely hear anything above the roiling agony overtaking her.

If the Zalyn'or is imprisoning her, she wants to be freed. And she wants all the women of Alfsigroth to be freed, as well.

But she desperately wants Cael and Rhys to be freed too.

And they are *male*.

The tears coating Wynter's face are cool on her cheeks as she sits by Ysilldir on a large, broad rock overlooking the city of Cyme as twilight descends. Dense wilds are at their backs and a broad field slopes down before them, the city splayed out just beyond to fill the enormous bowl-shaped valley.

It seems as if every owl in the forest has come to Wynter this eve, a small screech owl with pale gold eyes and caramel feathers perching on her shoulder, countless other owls settled in the surrounding trees.

Their steady aura of warning bears down against Wynter and Ysilldir's combined silence. Along with their projected image of an unnatural, twisting Shadow.

Wrapped up in both the birds' foreboding and a near-debilitating worry for Cael and Rhys, Wynter turns and takes in the tense lines of Ysilldir's face as the Elfin warrior peers over the city, her friend's reed-straight back unmarred and unpolluted by wings.

All too aware of her own cursed wings, Wynter pulls them in, painfully tight, as if seeking to punish them. To force pain into them as her own penance for being born an Icaral.

*Shame. Shame. Shame.*

"What do you think we would be like without the Zalyn'or?" Ysilldir asks Wynter in Alfsigr, breaking into the joint quiet and Wynter's tortured thoughts.

"I...don't know," Wynter hesitantly answers, her words strained as the owls send their constant stream of warning through her, their low undercurrent of foreboding a much more intimidating thing than the excitable chittering of so many of their avian brethren.

Ysilldir turns, her silver gaze lit with urgency. "We need to get these necklaces off."

Wynter hesitates, stopped short by an internal pull that fills her with the desire to remain silent. "You speak the truth, Ysilldir," she forces out. She draws in a hard breath and says the next words in a rush before her throat can close in on them. "I believe what Sylmire says about the Zalyn'or to be true."

Ysilldir's whole face tightens, as if she, too, is wrestling mightily to voice forbidden thoughts. "We changed when they put these necklaces on us. My elder brother, he changed, as well. Everyone I knew was deeply altered."

Wynter's head is suddenly spinning with memories, as if a rock has been kicked over to reveal one small shard-like part of her mind. "I remember my brother, Cael...from before the Zalyn'or."

Fierce Cael. Brought early to receive the Zalyn'or necklace, just on the cusp of eleven years old instead of the customary twelve. Because he was out of control. Fighting with everyone who dared call his beloved younger sister a filthy Icaral.

Fresh tears fill Wynter's eyes at the memory.

And at the memory of quiet, bookish Rhys, Cael's closest friend, also brought early to the priestesses to have the Zalyn'or placed. After he wrote a long tract supporting Wynter, signed the bottom of it, and quietly nailed it to the front door of their school, to the horror of his parents, the priestesses, the whole school, and the entire Alfsigr Royal Council.

Both young Alfsigr boys were promptly and roughly hauled to the Alfsigr Ealaiontor'lian Shrine that day.

Wynter winces at the terrible memory of her beloved brother viciously cursing at their parents and at the Alfsigr soldiers as they dragged him away, and the wild, pleading look in Cael's eyes as his gaze met hers.

*There's nothing wrong with you!* he'd cried to her. *They're lying to you! There is nothing wrong with your wings and I love you! Don't forget that! Don't ever forget that!*

Wynter remains silent for a long moment, unable to say more as she's lanced through with pain, her owls rustling and drawing nearer, as if pulling a cloak of support around her.

"What were Cael and Rhys like after they came back?" Ysilldir asks in a low, careful tone.

A tear drops from Wynter's eye and slides down her cheek. "It was as if a peace had descended on Cael. His unhappiness...his anger...they were muted. He stopped fighting with everyone. He stopped fighting with Mother and Father. But still, both he and Rhysindor would secretly tell me that the Alfsigr were wrong about me. Wrong about my being one of the Evil Cursed Ones."

Ysilldir looks to Wynter, a poignant look in her silver eyes. "Their rebellion still broke through."

Wynter considers this as the immensity of Sylmire's revelations begin to gain full traction in that free sliver of her mind, even as the larger part recoils from the ideas. But still, the thoughts are dredged to light by that spark of rebellion that burns inside Wynter and refuses to be snuffed out.

"What were you like before the Zalyn'or?" Ysilldir asks, her voice so strained it sounds like it's weighted down.

Wynter forces her thoughts deeper, that childhood time hazy, like a barely remembered dream.

Like a partly erased dream.

The small owl on Wynter's shoulder nuzzles her neck and sends out an aura of affectionate concern, as if prompting her to delve deep.

"I hid in my room," Wynter quietly admits. "It was...too hard to go out and see the hatred in everyone's faces when they looked at my wings. To see Mother and Father's misery over what I am. But...sometimes, I was content. Cael and Rhys would bring me art supplies and sit with me. And with them, there were moments that I was almost...happy."

Wynter's voice breaks off again as other childhood memories intrude.

Sorrowful memories.

*Of her secret attempts to fly into the air and into the white blossoms of the wild plum trees, spring filling her heart with joy as her bird friends flitted about, happily calling for her. And then rising, rising straight up* toward the center of the celestial canopy, the cloud-white flowers surrounding her in an embrace as warm sunlight kissed her wings.

And then the painful grip around the ankle, wrenching her to the ground. The blows rained down on her as she cried out and screamed and writhed on the grassy ground, her beloved wingeds chittering their alarm, diving for the priestesses only to be struck.

To be killed.

The memory of the silver robin felled beside her, one wing torn asunder.

The terrified look in the bird's eyes shattered Wynter's heart as blows connected with her own wings, the pain excruciating as she screamed and begged and promised she would never, ever fly again.

And then, she was dragged off to be educated by the priestesses. Forced to read passages in the Alfsigr holy book, the Ealaiontorian, again and again and again.

Passages that spoke of the evil of the wingeds, and that her whole spirit railed against.

And then, the rapid shift to another memory.

She wandered into a room where a brazier was lit, her whole self entranced by the fire leaping in it and toward her, as if in happy greeting, the fire power inside Wynter growing warm and golden.

Her small finger thrusting into the flame, unharmed by the lovely warming fire that sparked straight through her body and bristled through her wings.

Her whole self coming alive.

Her wings coming alive.

And then the shock of cold hands. Wrenching her away from the flame. Hauling her to the head priestess. Then being thrown into a cell where her small form was doused with icy water again and again as she cried out for her brother and cowered on the floor in penitent robes. Struck with sticks. Made to recite verses about abominations who play with hellish fire.

Verses every shred of her being recoiled from.

★ ★ ★

But then, the cruelest memory of all.

When her own time to wear the Zalyn'or came.

*The minute the necklace touched her skin, a terrible knowing descended. And she finally understood, beyond the shadow of a doubt, that every last passage about the "wingeds" in the* Ealaiontorian *was true. And that the priestesses had been right all along.*

*She was an abomination. Dirty and evil and unclean to the bone. Even a lifetime of penance could never wash away her terrible stain.*

*Newly subdued and distraught with contrition, she threw herself into her art, glorifying the whole unwinged Alfsigr—that group she could never be part of. That shining, blessed thing.*

*Unlike her.*

*But there was something else flowing from deep inside her. Something the Zalyn'or could not extinguish—her love for her kind brother, Cael, and for Rhys, who refused to give up on her even after the necklace claimed them all.*

"Did you have fire?" Ysilldir asks, breaking through Wynter's tormented thoughts. "Before the Zalyn'or?"

Wynter winces with contrition and nods, almost imperceptibly. Wanting to disappear from the cruel weight of her shame laid bare.

"I want to get this Zalyn'or off," Wynter says, feeling as if the words might detonate the end of Erthia. Her gut cinches, her wings tightening to the point they risk a tear.

Ysilldir's silver eyes widen, fierce struggle in them. "I, as well."

"I can barely think it," Wynter admits tightly.

"Nor I," Ysilldir says in grim agreement. "Wynter..." Ysilldir starts then stops, and this hesitancy catches Wynter's attention, cutting through the owls' collective drone of warning. "Do you think the other things that Sylmire said could be true? If the Alfsigr were all free of the Zalyn'ors..." Ysilldir stops again, then looks at Wynter dead-on. "Do you think we would feel desire?"

This surprises Wynter—not only the nature of the question, but the idea that the Alfsigr would cease to be such a uniformly chaste group if they were freed from the Zalyn'ors.

"Perhaps," Wynter concedes, although just the idea of that type of desire seems too intense for Wynter to fully consider. Just touching people brings on such a rush of intimate memory and emotion; to experience yet more intimacy, and possibly a stronger pull and bond...

"Tamalyyn spoke to me after the Queen's Council adjourned," Ysilldir tells her, an unsettled gravity to the words. "She is convinced that if these Zalyn'ors are removed...that she and I are destined to formally pair as Goddess-bonded am'ior. And it is true that I have never felt a spark of friendship that is as strong as what I feel for Tamal."

Wynter considers this, her heart going out to both Ysilldir and Tamalyyn, the young Smaragdalfar woman as passionate and boisterous as Ysilldir is reserved and contained.

It's clear that Tamalyyn is madly in love with Ysilldir.

"Perhaps you will feel the pull of a closer bond to Tamalyyn if we gain our freedom," Wynter considers, pushing past the thicket of bindings in her mind. "And perhaps you will be as some here, naturally free of desire and content in that path."

"And you, Wynter Eirllyn?" Ysilldir asks, slipping into the Alfsigr's casual use of full names. "Is there someone who you might love in a more passionate way?"

Wynter's heart seizes at the question, instantly overcome by an upswell of grief.

*Ariel.*

"She's gone," Wynter finally says, barely able to get the words out. "She was killed by the Gardnerians."

Ysilldir gives her a sympathetic look as Wynter reels from sorrow over her loved ones falling away, one by one.

*Cael, Rhys. Where are you, my beloved ones? Have the Alfsigr locked you in a cold prison? Will they hurl you into the sublands below?*

They both grow quiet as fireflies begin to light the skies, the gem-like tones of sunset brushed across the eastern sky, a soft crimson rune haze settling over the city.

"The Gardnerians are going to come after these lands," Ysilldir says, her voice thick with a foreboding that mirrors that of Wynter's owls.

Wynter looks to the sky, able to make out the glimmering edges of the multitude of huge garnet runes that are imprinted on the city's nearly invisible dome-shield. "They won't be able to get through the runic shield," Wynter says.

"Then they'll choke us off," Ysilldir counters, frowning at the Spine. "No trade. No way to get out. All of us imprisoned in the Caledonian Mountains." She fixes her eyes on Wynter's. "Until Vogel finds a way in."

*A way past Amaz runes.*

A shudder passes through Wynter in response to the horrifying idea.

"Vogel is growing in power," Wynter reluctantly concedes, the thought like a crushing, submerging wave. "The things my wingeds show me, they are...unfathomable." Wynter holds Ysilldier's silver gaze. "His power is lapping at the edge of the natural world."

Ysilldir throws Wynter a significant look. "And soon he'll be lapping at the edge of our minds."

Apprehension mounts inside Wynter. "But...a piece of our minds is our own."

"What if he finds a way in and we lose that piece?" Ysilldir shakes her head, the rows of metallic hoops pierced through her pointed ears catching the city's scarlet rune light. "Wynter Eirllyn, I have been loyal to the Amaz ever since I came here five years ago. And I have *never* broken with their ways." Her white brow furrows tighter. "But this time, I fear our queen is wrong. We need to find the rune sorcerer Rivyr'el Talonir. We need his help to break the Zalyn'or hold. Even if he is male."

There's a rustle in the trees and Wynter looks up, flocks of sparrows and starlings and countless other wingeds zooming down to land in thick rows on the tree limbs all around them, the birds' incoming message gaining strength.

> *Warning. Warning. Warning.*
> *The Shadow Thing is coming.*
> *It's coming. It's coming.*
> *It's here.*

Images flood Wynter's mind, of a Shadow touching down on the wilds, all around the corners of things. Poised to slither its corruption deep into the natural world and subsume the elements that flow through it.

*Hurry up, Elloren*, Wynter agonizes as her sense of urgency mounts. *Hurry up and come into your power before Vogel finds you.*

She looks to the jagged peaks of the Spine.

*The Shadow is coming for you, Elloren*, Wynter thinks as she sends out a message with her flock of birds.

*Warn her*, she charges them, pushing against their reflexive protest and fear of the Black Witch.

*You're wrong about her*, Wynter doggedly insists. *You're wrong. So, find her and warn her.*

*Tell her that the Shadow is here.*

# CHAPTER TWO

# SHUNNED

## RHYSINDOR THORIM

*Sixth Month*
*Alfsigroth*

Rhys Thorim's whole body is alive with pain. He glances down at the streaks of livid scarlet blood slashed across his frost-white Alfsigr clothing, his vision blurred and crackling with stars from so many blows. Bright rays of sunlight flash against his eyes.

Alfsigr soldiers in gleaming silver armor impassively stand by holding bone-white runic whips, ready to strike again at the command of the Alfsigroth monarch, Iolrath Talonir.

Rhys pulls in a shuddering breath, the outdoor air startlingly sweet after being trapped in a prison cell for so many weeks, only their royal lineage dragging out the verdict's final resolution.

Shunning.

Sentenced to the sublands below.

Two Alfsigr doves circle overhead, their arcing flight sweeping Rhys into a more intense sensation of vertigo.

A greater pain pierces his heart as he worries that these birds could be kindred messengers, able to send heartbreaking images of himself and Cael bloodied on the ground to his beloved one, Wynter Eirllyn.

Rhys's love for Wynter Eirllyn is so strong, not even the Zalyn'or imprint around his neck has been able to subdue it.

The taste of blood thick in his mouth, Rhys turns toward Cael Eirllyn, Wynter's brother and the Elf he's a bonded Second to.

Cael is also down on his hands and knees on the white marble ground, streaked in bright lines of blood and breathing heavily, his face defiant. A rope of bloody saliva hangs from the corner of Cael's mouth, his strong, muscular form no match for the slashing power of runic whips.

Monarch Talonir's rune sorceress steps forward.

The tall, dour Elf raises a silver rune stylus as she glares down at Cael and Rhys.

Rhys flinches as a translucent dome made of faint, whirling silver runes springs to life above him and Cael to encompass a large circle of marble beneath them. The ground under the dome begins to take on the fantastical appearance of a rippling silver lake, even as it remains solid to the touch.

*But not for long*, Rhys considers with great foreboding.

No. They're about to be hurled down into the subland abyss. For their support of Wynter Eirllyn.

An Icaral.

Anguish sparks in Rhys's core, matched in intensity by the pain streaking through his back.

But his resolve is unmoved.

They could whip him completely to shreds and he'd never turn Wynter over to the Alfsigr. He only regrets not getting to see her one last time to tell her how much he loves her. How much he's always loved her.

"Caelidon Eirllyn and Rhysindor Thorim," the ivory-robed monarch booms, his silver eyes glacially cold as the line of white-robed Alfsigr Royal Council Elves look on along with their cold-eyed soldiers, all of them grouped around the Royal Council's guarded entry into the Subland Realm, the pale marble walls around them carved into a swirling design.

"You have set yourselves against both Alfsigroth and our Blessed Shining Ones by sheltering a Deargdul demon," Monarch Talonir mercilessly continues. "You are hereby shunned by Alfsigroth, not fit to stand on the blessed, sunland soil of the High Elfkin—the unblemished Elfdom. You are infected with the evil of the Deargdul, corrupted beyond redemption and a danger to Alfsigroth."

The monarch straightens, his prismatic eyes flashing sunlight as his tone takes on a hard-edged, official cadence. "For the crime of refuting a clear summons to bring the winged Deargdul demon Wynter Eirllyn to Alfsigroth, I sentence you, Caelidon Eirllyn, and you, Rhysindor Thorim, to banishment in the sublands. You are hereby cast out of all Elfindom, in this life and the next."

A white-robed priestess steps forward, an ivory crown set on her long snowy hair, its silver wrought into the shapes of the Shining Ones' sacred flock of starlight birds flying in a swirl. Sacred silver runes are marked on her flowing garments, and she's bracketed by several Alfsigr soldiers in silver-plated armor.

The dour rune sorceress falls in behind her.

All of them pass through the runic dome as if it's made of air, the runes flashing silver as they make contact with it, but Rhys knows that he and Cael would run into a solid wall if they tried to get out.

The soldiers descend on Rhys and Cael, strong hands gripping their arms as they yank them both over and force their backs to the ground.

Fresh sparks explode in Rhys's vision as horrific pain streaks down the lash wounds on his back. Cael groans low in his throat and Rhys turns to him, his friend's head tipped back in obvious distress, the misery in his pale silver eyes so intense that Rhys's heart gives an agonized twist.

The priestess unsheathes the sacred runic blade at her side and strides to Cael as he's held pinned to the ground. She drops down to one knee, takes firm hold of the center of Cael's tunic, and slashes her blade straight down its length, exposing his pale, bruised chest and his Zalyn'or marking. Then the priestess expeditiously moves to Rhys and does the same, triggering a fresh explosion of pain through Rhys's body as he bites back the urge to cry out.

And then, the rune sorceress presses her rune stylus into Rhys's Zalyn'or tattoo, the tattoo giving a painful sizzle before morphing into a three-dimension runic necklace, a shadowy rune pendant dangling from a slim silver chain. Then she moves to Cael and repeats the process before gracefully rising.

"You are hereby no longer a child of Alfsigroth," the priestess declares to Rhys and Cael both, disgust swimming in her gleaming eyes. "You are vile creatures of the Deargdul and, as our *Ealaiontorian* commands, are to be cast down into their pit of corruption."

Dazed from his crippling haze of pain, Rhys looks up at the gem-like blue of the sky, the pale birds wheeling, the blinding white of the sun, its rays fracturing in his vision.

The most horrible realization bolts through him, devastation spearing in with it—

After he and Cael are thrown into the sublands, Wynter will be all alone when she needs them the most.

He and Cael know that the priestesses have been given new

powers to enforce every rule of the *Ealaiontorian*, with no deviation from the holy book's rigid words allowed.

And so they've sent the Marfoir after Wynter again.

But not just two this time. Thirteen of the horrific Alfsigr assassins.

Rhys struggles against the soldiers' restraining grip as the priestess kneels before him once more, grabs up the chain of his Zalyn'or, and slides her rune blade's edge just under it, then pulls the chain taut.

Panic rears inside Rhys at the thought of losing the Zalyn'or, along with the sudden, desperate desire to beg and plead to keep the necklace. To recant every blasphemy and do penance for his corruption, for his traitorous thoughts.

To scour his own mind.

But he grits his teeth and battles the feeling back, his love for Wynter stronger than the pull to keep hold of the Zalyn'or.

The priestess slices through the necklace's chain, silver sparks flying off it as Rhys has the sense of his whole body momentarily losing its form. Then the priestess wrenches the necklace from Rhys's neck as she drones the shunning words from the *Ealaiontorian* holy book, branding him as forever non-Alfsigr.

One of the polluted.

Rhys can barely hear her.

Emotion surges up, up, up inside him with volcanic force, his entire mind sharpening as grief, rage, and rebellion gather into a whirling storm within him and the image of a white bird made of blinding light blazes for a split second behind his eyes.

He whips his head toward Cael as the priestess rips the necklace from Cael and the arms that grip Rhys fall away, the soldiers and priestess and rune sorceress all retreating through the silvery shield dome.

Rhys draws in a hard breath, lit up by the incandescent outrage rising within him. Defiance rising, he quickly regains his sense of balance and starts to push himself up from the ground as Cael also gets to his feet and straightens to his full, intimidating height.

There's a look of sudden, raging shock in Cael's silver eyes as he levels them at the Council and the priestess. His gaze narrows and flashes like a volcanic storm, his pale fists clenched, a cataclysmic level of rebellion firing in his eyes.

Rhys straightens as well, ignoring the slashing pain.

As they both face down the entire Alfsigroth hierarchy.

"What have you done?" Cael seethes, the force of his tone like a blizzard, sweeping in with monstrous force. "What have you done to your own people?"

"Silence the Evil Ones," the priestess demands of Monarch Talonir.

"You're not trying to silence us because we're Evil," Cael snarls. "You're throwing us into the sublands because even your Zalyn'or was not enough to subdue our minds. You're afraid of us. Because you can't control what I say—" he jabs a finger toward Rhys "—or what he writes."

Rhys is mesmerized by Cael's open rebellion, at the beautiful, vengeful creature before him. Gone is subdued Elfin Cael. He's like some magnificent other being.

The Cael that Rhys remembers from before the Zalyn'ors.

Angry Cael.

"You can *never* control us," Cael rages. "Because our power of free thought is too strong."

"Cast them into the sublands," Iolrath Talonir orders the rune sorceress. "Where the Evil things reside."

The rune sorceress steps forward and points her stylus at the ground beneath Rhys and Cael.

"Long live the Resistance!" Cael cries with enough rage to shake the heavens as the ground gives way.

Rhys's arms fly up, his stomach lurching, as he falls along with Cael into subland darkness, hurtling down as the circle of sunlit world above them flies up and away, the birds small, circling dots on its receding palette of blue.

Rhys cries out as he hits the ground, his wounds a blaze of pain as the sunlit hole far above them shudders to a close, like a mist quickly solidifying.

Silence.

And then…a sudden flash of bright green light, as the surprisingly sharp emotion of fear cuts through Rhys's pain.

Along with Cael, Rhys turns toward the source of the light.

It's coming from runic arrows, nocked into bows, as several Smaragdalfar Elves close in, murderous expressions on their emerald-patterned faces.

Their weapons aimed at Cael's and Rhys's heads.

# STORM RISING
## VOTHENDRILE XANTHILE

*Sixth Month*
*Eastern Realm,*
*the Wyvernguard*

"Your sister, Elloren Gardner, is the Black Witch."

Trystan Gardner stills as Commander Ung Li grimly conveys this world-altering news, Trystan's water power instantly suspended inside him.

Vothendrile Xanthile's own power freezes as well, and he understands fully, in that moment, why they're standing in Ung Li's private meeting room, a circular tower at the pinnacle of the Wyvernguard's North Twin Island. Why they're surrounded by soldiers.

Why they confiscated Trystan's wand before they entered.

A bright slash of lightning threads across the inky sky outside, momentarily brightening the sapphire hues of the rune lantern–lit room. Thunder rumbles over the Vo Mountains.

"That can't be," Trystan finally says, his voice strained, his face pale. "Elloren has no power. She's a Level *One* Mage…"

"She's not," Commander Li throws down, her gaze pinned on Trystan and piercing with import. "She's been wandtested by the Vu Trin."

"I don't understand."

"Your sister is more powerful than your grandmother ever was."

The finality of Ung Li's words sends a rush of shock through Vothendrile that's echoed by the jolt of lightning he can sense bolting through Trystan's internal magic.

Vothe can also feel, with his Wyvern-shifter senses, that Ung Li is truly certain about this. There's fear there. Real fear.

And she's one of the most fearless Vu Trin in the entire Noi guard.

Vothendrile's mind reels.

Not only is the Black Witch back—she's a more powerful Black Witch.

As if that were even possible.

A storm of alarm is now slashing through Trystan, invisible lightning exploding along his affinity lines, and Vothe looks to him, the conflicting emotions he's begun to feel for this Mage whipping into a near frenzy.

Vothe's initial animosity toward Trystan Gardner has proved to be frustratingly hard to hold on to as he's witnessed, again and again, how Trystan has met abuse with resolve, refusing to be driven away from the Wyvernguard. Honestly dedicated to the fight against Vogel and his forces. Offering up his magic to the Vu Trin to test and figure out defenses against, even though he ends each day of magical sparring with savage bruising up and down his wand arm.

But a Black Witch sister. A sister who could destroy the Eastern Realm.

That changes everything.

"Where is she?" Trystan asks in a choked rasp, obviously understanding the potential ramifications of this.

There's a beat of hesitation. Ung Li's smooth, wide brow creases, and Vothendrile takes a deep breath as he realizes that she's about to relay potentially devastating news to Trystan.

Because Ung Li rarely hesitates with anything.

"She's likely dead," Ung Li says.

Trystan pulls in a hard breath and doubles over slightly as his invisible water magic comes untethered, his hands flying up to clutch at his abdomen as if he's sustained an actual physical blow.

Vothe almost takes a step toward him in troubled concern but sternly forces himself to keep back. A tempest kicks up inside Vothe as his heart twists for Trystan, even as he's cursing himself for giving in to this ferocious sympathy.

*Get hold of yourself, Zhilon'ile,* Vothe internally rages. *Be clear on who your enemies have to be.*

"Your sister was caught in the cross fire when our Western forces attacked the Mage Council." Commander Li conveys all this in a flat military tone, but Vothendrile can read her unease as she's faced with Trystan's obvious devastation.

Trystan lifts his green eyes to meet hers. "But you don't know for a fact that she's dead?" he asks, almost a plea, his voice fractured as palpable anguish storms through him. The note of aching hope in the question is difficult for Vothe to witness.

Ung Li's dark eyes narrow. "There's a slim chance that she's still alive."

Vothe is stopped short as he reads the false note in Ung Li's words with his Wyvern senses.

Smelling the lie.

*No*, Vothe thinks, rattled. *There's more than a slim chance that she's alive, isn't there?*

Vothendrile's own powers whip up inside him, water and wind suddenly churning, the immensity of what this could mean for the Eastern Realm rapidly cycloning together.

*A more powerful Black Witch...*

*Alive.*

"You will see postings going up throughout the Wyvern-guard and the city with your sister's likeness on them," Ung Li states, her guarded energy increasing as she buries her ferocity deep.

"Postings?" Trystan asks, and Vothe can sense the jolt of his confusion.

"If your sister has survived," Ung Li says, her tone and expression downplaying the possibility, "and if she makes her way to the Eastern Realm, then we need to make it clear that she's to be brought to the Vu Trin immediately." There's a pause, a split second too long. "For her protection." There's the trace of a comforting smile on her lips, but her dark eyes are hard as stone.

Vothe can sense all the water magic in Trystan freezing.

Vothe glances at him sideways with no small amount of alarm, realizing that Trystan is reading everything in this suspended moment as clearly as he is.

The postings aren't for Elloren Gardner's protection. Because if Trystan's sister is more powerful than their grandmother...

...that means that Elloren Gardner is the most powerful weapon the Realms have ever seen.

And the Vu Trin will almost certainly want to find her and kill her.

*Immediately.*

Her gaze raptor-sharp, Ung Li studies Trystan. "If your sister makes it to Noi lands," she says, her tone carefully neutral, "it is likely that she will seek out you or your brother, Rafe. If this happens, you need to bring her to us without delay. Do you understand, Mage Gardner?"

A whoosh of Trystan's invisible water power breaks over the room, and it sets Vothe's heart beating harder. And then all of Trystan's magic is suddenly yanked back inside him, his vast water and fire magic instantly buried to the point that Vothe's Zhilon'ile powers can't detect even a trace of it.

Trystan gives Ung Li a stiff, formal salute, striking his fist firmly to his chest. "Yes, Commander," he affirms, grim-faced. "If my sister has survived and she seeks me out, I'll bring her right to you."

*Liar*, Vothe senses, his roiling conflict heating up, lightning crackling through his internal Zhilon'ile power as he vows to double down on how closely he guards this Mage, regardless of how sincere Trystan's Vu Trin alliance has been up to this point.

Because it's clear that he's even more powerfully aligned with his family.

With his sister.

And that alliance has just put him at odds with the entire Eastern Realm.

Elloren Gardner is now the Eastern Realm's most sought-after enemy, potentially more dangerous than Marcus Vogel, and the entirety of the Vu Trin and Zhilon'ile forces will be set on finding her.

Vothendrile will be set on finding her.

And if Elloren Gardner is not dead, she will be soon.

# CHAPTER FOUR

## SHADOW INVASION
### TIERNEY CALIX

*Sixth Month*
*Eastern Realm,*
*the Wyvernguard*

Tierney looks over the choppy Vo as rain lashes the deserted Wyvernguard terrace, a storm-black night closing in. Both the rain and the chill wind are picking up as the tempest moves in from the north, the Vo's waves as unsettled as Tierney's rioting emotions.

Tierney closes her eyes, links her Asrai power to the water around her, and forces the rain slightly away to create a misty shield just past her form. Encased in dry air, she reaches into her uniform's pocket, pulls out the posting she's torn down from the wall, and unfolds it. The terrace's rain-dampened sapphire lantern light spills faintly over the paper.

Elloren Gardner's exact likeness stares back at Tierney, rendered in black ink. With instructions to bring her to the Vu Trin if she is found in the Eastern Realm.

By force of military edict.

Every muscle in her body tenses as Tierney's mind roils. She balls up the posting and hurls it to the ground as she lets the rain beat back down on her.

A collective gasp went up when Commander Ung Li informed the Vu Trin apprentices that the Black Witch had been found. A weighty horror immediately descended over the Wyvernguard's huge central hall.

Tierney had to force even breaths as she came to terms with the stunning news. And the unbearable tension that rose up to fill the room.

Even though she's been a Vu Trin apprentice for only half a month's time, Tierney has already heard countless stories about the last Black Witch's reign of fire, everyone in the Noi lands having lost family members in the Realm War.

During Carnissa Gardner's push East.

Everyone is clear on what the last Black Witch would have done to the Eastern Realm if the blessed Keltish Icaral hadn't cut her down.

Now the Prophecy that's being sounded by every seer in the Eastern Realm is coming to pass.

A new Black Witch looms on the horizon.

Even more powerful than Carnissa Gardner.

*And it's Elloren.*

Tierney clutches at the terrace's slick stone banister as rain streams down her slender form, thunder crashing overhead.

*How did Elloren gain control of her power? And how did the Vu Trin find out about it?*

*How did* Elloren *find out about it?*

*Why was Elloren in the line of fire during a strike on the Mage Council?*

*And why were the Vu Trin attacking the Mage Council to begin with?*

Tierney's knife-sharp intellect works to assemble the pieces.

So many questions unanswered, but there's one question Tierney already knows the answer to, her internal water magic upsurging around this intuitive certainty.

Elloren Gardner is alive.

And both the Gardnerians and the Vu Trin know what she is.

*Oh, Elloren,* Tierney grimly marvels, *you've triggered a war, haven't you? A war that was coming regardless, but a war sparked now because of you.*

But if Vogel doesn't have Elloren and there's serious conjecture that Elloren might come to the Eastern Realm...

That means that she's on the run.

And likely not just from Vogel.

A tremor shivers through Tierney as she pictures her close friend's face on all those postings and everything snaps into lethal clarity.

This isn't a search for Elloren's protection. This is a manhunt. Tierney is bone-deep certain of it.

If the Vu Trin find Elloren, they'll kill her.

Subversive resolve coalesces inside Tierney as she comes to terms with what she must do. She holds her palms out toward the Vo and sounds a beckoning call to summon her kelpies.

*You fear for her.*

Alarm spears through Tierney in response to the preternaturally deep voice sounding inside her mind. She lowers her palms to the terrace railing, teeth gritted, as her heart pounds against her chest and she keeps her eyes focused on the storming Vo.

Lightning flashes.

"Get out of my mind, Viger," she snarls, struggling to hide her desperation to force him out of her thoughts.

Because what she's going to do could get her thrown into military prison. And if Viger senses it...

"Why do you fear for the granddaughter of the Black Witch?" Viger presses in that insidious tone of his.

In a flash of anger, Tierney rounds on the dark-eyed young Fae, the sheeting rain around him turned to a shroud of mist that's halted by the dark aura swirling around him. His gaze is a compelling pool, and Tierney is immediately caught up in the sensation of falling toward him.

The whites of Viger's eyes ink to black as Tierney's fear swirls around her, like a pond stirred by a stick.

"Keep your thrall off me, Viger," Tierney snaps. "I'm warning you. You're not the only one with power."

Viger's form instantly morphs to dark mist then disappears as Tierney internally curses him, curses the entire situation, her fists tightly balled.

"Why do you fear for her?"

Her ire spikes as Tierney whips around to find Viger's tall form now calmly reclining against the terrace rail, uncharacteristically devoid of his usual covering of snakes, his horns absent, the whites of his eyes back, his claws retracted.

"If I talk to you," Tierney says sharply, "will you stay put and spare me your Death Fae theatrics? It's impressive and spooky, but I'm in no mood for it."

Viger goes silent as only a Death Fae can. It's not a normal silence. It's a stillness that seems to reverberate through the air on some low, bone-deep frequency that feels like being buried in the very center of Erthia.

In this moment, Tierney finds him oddly comforting—his strange thrall, his pale, morbid appearance. His complete outcast status.

Tierney considers how the Death Fae are famous for their

nonalignment with any group. How they stand apart from any mob.

Which seems like a very large mark in Viger's favor at this moment, frightening as he can be.

"You've become a friend to Elloren Gardner's brother," Tierney notes with a trace of challenge. Wanting to assess where he really stands.

"He's not what they think," Viger states as the rain picks up, casting his form in mist. All except those hypnotic, dark eyes of his, their focus intensifying. "You're summoning the Deathkin water horses to find the Black Witch," Viger reads with unflinching accuracy.

Tierney's magic seizes as she struggles to find a plausible lie to refute this. But she's devastatingly clear on one of the main reasons the Death Fae are mistrusted and often flat-out reviled here.

It's impossible to lie to them.

Tierney holds Viger's unsettling stare and decides to go for broke and let him in. It's the only chance she has to make him *see*. He has to understand her completely, otherwise he'll likely turn her in for treason.

Tierney pulls in a long, wavering breath and internally lets go, opening up all her fears to him.

Viger's eyes widen a fraction then narrow in tight.

Tierney gasps as everything darkens and she's cast into the sense of hurtling down from a great height, her breath shuddering as Viger's thrall takes rigid hold, a deeper darkness enfolding them both as everything cuts out—the rain, the wind, the riot of sapphire rune light tossed about by the waves, all vanished.

All except for Viger and his all-encompassing *stare*.

"Elloren Gardner is not what they think," Tierney says

against his darkness, the two of them now encased in it, Viger's form dimly lined in silver.

A raven blinks into view, perched on his shoulder.

"She is the Black Witch," he states with chilling certainty. "The forest echoes this. My ravens echo this." His voice deepens to the point that Tierney can feel it low in her center. "Their *fear* echoes this."

Rebellion rises in Tierney. "She may well be, Viger. But... don't you believe that things can run deeper than everyone thinks?"

"Like you?" Viger says, silky smooth. The words send a warm disturbance through Tierney's magic, and she struggles to ignore how enticing it feels. Tierney knows it's odd that she's both intrigued by Viger as well as terrified and repulsed by aspects of him. These Death Fae are all like mythical figures hovering around the edges of this place, unsettling the comforting sense of order.

Throwing Death into the mix.

*I will not reveal you*, Viger sounds in her mind.

Tierney's apprehension whirls around the thought.

Is he saying he won't turn her in?

"If you could be a tad less cryptic, Viger," she snaps, "it would be helpful."

*They're coming*, Viger responds, a slight smile lifting his mouth as he draws back his thrall. The wind, the rain, the flash of lightning all rush back in and around them both, soaking his coal-dark uniform, his spiky hair, his pale face and pointed ears.

A huge wave crests and crashes over the banister as kelpies form and leap onto the huge platform.

Tierney turns to face them, their hooves splashing as they take solid, rippling form, limned by the terrace's sapphire rune light.

Es'tryl'lyan comes forward, and Tierney moves to meet with him, thrown by the strange terror in his eyes. The kelpie lowers his powerful head, and Tierney raises her arm to hold his flowing, watery form, her kelpie smooth and solid but covered in rushing water that flows over Tierney's hand.

And that's when she feels it—the intense rush of alarm flowing from the army of kelpies.

*Warning. Warning. Warning.*

She's accosted by a sudden vision, thrust into her from the kelpies' minds.

Tierney closes her own eyes as she reads their collective thoughts, reads what they've found in the Vo forest.

Viger's darkness is suddenly whipping around the edges of her mind along with the kelpies' images.

*What are you reading in them, Tierney Calix?* His words seem to come from everywhere at once.

"Something unnatural," Tierney says, her throat cinching tight. "Animals that should not be here. Some of them filled with an unbalancing power. Something...unnatural in it that could shred the matrix of nature."

*What have they found?* Viger thinks again, his presence in her mind sending the hairs on the back of Tierney's neck prickling, his dark thrall intensifying.

"They're creatures I've seen only in books. Creatures of the desert. Insects. Like something from a nightmare." Tierney turns away from Es'tryl'lyan's dark, feral stare and meets Viger's. "Scorpios," she tells him breathlessly, her heartbeat picking up speed. "They found a swarm of desert scorpios, here in the forests of the Eastern Realm."

# PART SIX

# CHAPTER ONE

# WRAITH BATS
## ELLOREN GREY

*Sixth Month*
*Northwestern Agolith Desert*

Lukas, Valasca, and Chi Nam begin my intensive runic training that first full day in Chi Nam's desert Vonor, a sense of urgency in the air.

Valasca opens a thick Noi runic text on the low circular table before me. We're all seated around the onyx table in Chi Nam's cavernous front room. Several more runic texts as well as a number of rune blades, including the Ash'rion, are spread out before us.

I take in the long columns of complicated runic shapes as Valasca brings her index finger to a line of angular Noi script.

"These all draw on fire elementals," Valasca says. "We'll start there."

"How quickly can you memorize?" Chi Nam asks me.

"Pretty fast," I say as I study the shapes, comfortingly aware of Lukas's arm sliding around my waist. "I had to memorize hundreds of apothecary formulas at university."

I visually match three of the runes on the page with runes marked on the Ash'rion blade's hilt. "Did you fashion the runes on some of these blades?" I ask Valasca and Chi Nam.

"A few of them," Valasca says, her finger flicking toward three of the smaller blades. "And I charged them too."

"Sage must be able to charge runes on weapons as well, correct?" I ask.

All three of them nod.

"Sagellyn Gaffney can charge runes because she is a Light Mage," Chi Nam explains. "Only runic sorcerers or Light Mages can charge runes."

I look to Lukas, trying to work it all out. "But you can use a rune blade without being either of those things."

"I can," Lukas concurs. "Because the runes have been pre-charged with power by a rune sorcerer, and I know the runic spells that can unlock some of them. I don't possess the ability to charge runes since I'm not a Light Mage."

"He can amplify the charged magic with his affinity power, though," Chi Nam adds as she and Lukas exchange a conspiratorial look. She turns to me. "And so can you."

"Only exponentially stronger," Lukas says, flashing me a sly grin as his finger traces a provocative circle against my waist, trailing heat.

"All right, then," I say, gesturing toward the text as my resolve to learn how to fight strengthens. "Let's begin."

Chi Nam spends the rest of the day setting up complicated rune-amplification sorcery around our charging portal, while Lukas, Valasca, and I pore over the rune texts for countless hours until I'm bleary-eyed from sustained focus on the intricate shapes.

Evening arrives without my noticing, time seeming suspended within the walls of Chi Nam's windowless, cavernous Vonor. We've somehow slipped into speaking Noi exclusively as Lukas and Valasca drill me relentlessly, first on individual runes, and then on increasingly complex runic combinations and their corresponding spells.

"Feh, Ur, Tey, Oth..." Valasca calls out the names of Noi fire-and earth-based runes in varying sequences to prompt me to find the runes on the Ash'rion blade's hilt.

I slide my fingers along the hilt's smooth surface, locating the rune combinations faster and faster, my violin training proving to be invaluable for speed in this.

One combination to throw out an explosion of fire along with the weapon.

Another to pull lightning into the blade.

Another to hurl stones alongside the weapon.

Another to open up a chasm below the target upon contact.

"Good," Valasca finally says as the Vonor's sapphire runic light flickers over her angular face, enhancing her vivid sky blue hue. She smiles at Lukas. "We'll take her out tomorrow and see how much havoc she's capable of wreaking."

That evening, I take a walk outside the Vonor's shielded ledge, needing to stretch my legs and clear my head. My mind is swimming with runic shapes and combinations, the Ash'rion sheathed at my side along with my Wand.

The crimson moon is high in the sky, ruby stars strewn all over the heavens. The stormwall that limns the horizon flashes with puffs of muted white light, its thunder a soft, disjointed rhythm.

For a moment, I'm filled with the melancholy desire to have my violin with me. To sound out a melody over this vast, otherworldly landscape.

I walk along the flat, curving ledge that seems to encircle the Vonor's rocky mountain. The night air is cool against my skin as I take in the translucent dome-shield that Chi Nam has cast over her Vonor's entire mountain exterior, including this ledge. Faint blue runes rotate slowly against the shield's entire surface, the motion soothing.

Feeling momentarily safe here, I continue walking, curious about this strange, new place I've landed in. The world darkens as I move away from both the Vonor's lantern-lit entrance and the adjacent portal's bright blue glow.

I pause as I round a sharp curve.

Ruby moonlight spills over the scene before me, glinting purple off the edges of the Vonor's shield runes. Countless gigantic rock formations arc over the desert, as if some god has drawn the cascading curves with an enormous brush, the sweeps of crimson paint turned to stone.

The horizon's stormwall has begun flashing a gauzy amber light, and in the closer distance, a moonlit herd of some type of huge, lumbering beast is lazily moving away across the desert's ruddy sands.

I crane my neck toward the gem-like splash of garnet stars, a feeling of unreality washing over me, and not just from being in the middle of this dreamlike desert landscape, clear out of the Western Realm.

A small cinder of possibility has lit inside me.

I have power. True power that I can access. Because I can amplify elemental runes with the aura of my affinity magic, even though the trees have bound my lines.

My gaze falls to the dark silhouettes of the treetops that rise past my elevated ledge.

*Agolith Mesquite trees.*

The grove's branches writhe upward toward the starry sky, and I've an intrinsic sense of how the taproots of all these desert trees burrow down deep for water, tangle, then extend outward for leagues and leagues, bringing them into communion with the distant forests of all the lands.

An amorphous sense of unease begins to prick at my skin.

They're watching me.

Closely.

*Black Witch.*

The whisper brushes me on the slight breeze coming from the desert, and it sends a chill down my spine. I can feel the trees' sharpened focus hovering in the air.

Tension burrows under my skin.

It's like they're waiting for something.

Something that's coming for me.

I take a reflexive step back as I peer into the trees' dark hollows and my eyes catch on a hulking black shape hidden there.

My heart flies into my throat, terror piercing me as I take another reflexive step away.

Perched on a branch and camouflaged by the dark of night is a horrific bat-like beast. Big as a panther, hunched and muscular and black as the darkest mahogany wood, its gleaming dark eyes slitted like a lizard's. Leathery wings, no neck. Just huge jaws, silently grinding its teeth.

And there isn't just one.

There's a whole flock of them just past the shield, hidden inside the tree canopy.

All of their focus set on me.

I move to flee and back into a warm, hard person whose hands reach up to take hold of my arms. I whip my head around, my heartbeat slamming against my chest.

"Lukas…" I can barely get the words out as I point toward the canopy. "In the trees."

"I know," he says, lethally calm, as he takes in the night-camouflaged beasts.

I glance back at the bat things, desperately grateful for the shield. "Are they wraith bats?"

"They are," he states, loosening his hold on me a bit.

"I think they're *hunting* me."

Lukas studies them. "They're drawn to prey that cowers easily. And they can sense fear and amplify it."

The creatures bare their daggerlike teeth, and gooseflesh breaks out along my neck as Lukas's hands slide away from my arms. I turn to face him. "So they *are* hunting me."

Lukas's voice is unsympathetic when it comes. "Because you cower when faced with a physical threat."

Ire rises, cutting through the edge of my terror. "Fear is a reasonable response to them, Lukas."

"No, it isn't," he counters. "Not with your aim. And you're armed with one of the most powerful rune blades in existence. You're thinking with your fear. Not your common sense."

"So, if there was no shield, you wouldn't be the least bit afraid of them?" I hate that I can't keep a tremor out of my voice.

"I don't fear them in the slightest." Lukas eyes them coldly. "I see them like I see most enemies. As a puzzle to pick apart. To find the best way to dominate."

He sets his relentless gaze back on me, and I hold his formidable stare. It's brutal, the way he looks at things. But I realize, in one all-encompassing swoop, that I need to learn to think like a warrior.

"How do you manage to be so fearless?" I ask him, frustrated tears glazing my eyes as I wrestle with my terrified awareness of the bat things.

"Control," Lukas says. "And skill. You have vast power, Elloren. The reasons you cower are your lack of control and skills, and your lack of belief in yourself. You need to strike away this weakness, or your enemies will take advantage of it." He glances pointedly at the lurking bat monsters, and my fear spikes anew at the sight of their dark forms. A heightened tension shivers through my body as their thrall worms its way into me, seeking to break down every last shred of my resolve.

To immobilize me.

My airway constricts.

"Lukas..." I force out through the rise of a swamping terror.

Lukas flashes me an intense look, then walks past me toward the edge of the ledge. Without breaking his stride, he throws his palm out toward the shield, blue rays of light flashing from the contact, and then he moves straight through the translucent dome wall.

My fear explodes as he walks over the remaining ledge and stops at its cliff–edge, right in front of the wraith bat–infested treetops.

Breaking through my terror, I rush toward the shield as another wave of horror explodes through my knotted lines, constricting my lungs anew and halting my steps.

I struggle to pull in air, paralyzed to the spot, as I shiver with terror for Lukas.

The wraith bats grow agitated as they watch him, rustling in the trees and snapping their jaws threateningly. Getting no reaction from him, they begin to sniff at the air with their flat, slender nostrils, making wet, snuffling sounds.

They draw back, as if fearful of Lukas's scent. Four of them flap their powerful wings and fly away.

Lukas draws two rune blades and hurls them forward with sudden, violent force.

I flinch as both knives impale the trees' trunks with whip-like *cracks*, thin white lightning exploding from the blades sideways in a burst of light that startles the remaining creatures.

Disoriented and enraged, the beasts let out low, snarling growls as they struggle to keep their balance on the jostled branches and Lukas holds out his rune-marked palms, his blades flying back into his hands.

Snarling and snapping teeth, the bats launch themselves from the branches and fly away.

Lukas resheaths his blades, turns, and holds up his palm toward the shield, then strides back inside it in a flash of blue light.

He stops before me, a challenging look in his eyes.

I gape at him in amazement as the bats' psychic effect on my fear dissipates like a vise slowly releasing, but my own underlying fear remains, its daunting echo racing through me.

Lukas flicks his finger against the hilt of the Ash'rion blade sheathed at my side. "You could have taken those creatures down or driven them off solely with what we taught you today. You don't need to cower before them." His brow tenses. "That's why, starting tomorrow, we're going to be hard on you. Because a lot of what you need to learn has nothing to do with magic. You need to build up your confidence."

Sobered by what he's telling me, I look past him and watch the silhouette of the deadly flock as it flies away over the moonlit sands.

The fear they've amplified in me slides down into a sullen sense of foreboding.

We're both quiet for a moment, the air cool and still as I move toward the shield. I can feel Lukas's gaze on me.

I take a long, shuddering breath as I stare at the barrier of storms in the distance, lightning forking all over the stormwall. We're hidden for the moment, in the middle of nowhere, but eventually, Vogel will find me.

"I want to learn how to be truly brave," I say, my voice low and firm. "Like you."

A ripple of Lukas's fire rushes through me, and after a moment his arms slide around my waist as he folds himself against my back. A tide of emotion rushes through me, like a storm breaking open.

"I'm going to learn how to face down those bats without a shred of fear," I say in a harsh whisper as I watch the flash of lightning in the stormwall. "And I'm going to fight Marcus Vogel. Without backing down."

"You will," Lukas agrees as our fires feed into each other, pulsing heat. "We'll help you learn to harness your power." He leans down to softly nuzzle my neck, his voice pitched lower when it comes. "You could start by learning how to dominate me." I feel his mouth tilt into a slight smile against my neck.

He sends out more fire, and his heat tingles straight down my spine, catching on my affinity lines and sparking a hard flash of desire that has me flushing.

I give him a wry look over my shoulder, increasingly flustered by his power as I slide my hands along his muscular arms. "I have a feeling you're a lot harder to dominate than the wraith bats."

Lukas gives a low laugh. "I am. Which is why learning to dominate me would be well worth your effort." He leans in closer, his lips brushing my ear, suddenly serious. "Come back with me, Elloren."

It's clear what he's offering. To bed me, yes, but more than that. I can feel the longing in his fire, how everything in him is oriented toward me. And suddenly... I want him. And not just physically. I want to merge with what he is and claim it for my own. Because he's everything, in this moment, that I desperately want and need to be.

I turn around, take his hand...and bring him back inside with me.

We pass by Chi Nam and Valasca exiting as we enter the Vonor's cavernous front room en route to Chi Nam's meditation chamber. Lukas grabs our bedding and the Sanjire root, then leads me through a long and winding passage that eventually comes to what appears to be a small map room inside one of the Vonor's many caverns, rolls of maps lining shelves hewn into the stone and affixed to the walls, a black carpet marked with an ivory dragon image under our feet. The walls are a gleaming onyx stone that glitters sapphire from the runic light that emanates from a single lantern set on a small shelf.

I close the doorway's rune-marked curtain with a decided yank that I feel straight down my spine, because this feels like something new. Like my heart is opening up to him more than it ever has before.

Lukas lays the bedrolls side by side, pulls the Sanjire root bottle from his tunic's pocket, and sets it on a small alcove in the cavern wall, eyeing me poignantly as he does so.

We remove our tunics and weapons, Lukas's eyes flicking up to meet mine every so often, his muscles flexing as he moves. I let my gaze roam freely over the hard planes of his rune-marked chest and his muscular arms as he pulls off his boots and the blades he has strapped just under his pants, fire rising in me and simmering through my lines in a slow burn.

Lukas straightens, unfastens his wand sheath, the wand still inside, and sets it aside as I pull off the black Noi pants I'm wearing, now dressed only in a black linen Noi camisole and pantalets.

His gaze fixes on my body and travels over my thin, sparse garments.

We both still as our eyes meet and Lukas's fire flashes out to ripple through my lines.

An invitation.

My breath stutters as I take him in. The familiar lines of his face. His deep-green eyes. His hard body and the way his skin glimmers green. The fastlines on his hands.

The Sealinglines on his wrists.

Heat blooms on my face, my chest, as I remember the wild thrill of our joinings. And the feel of his unrestrained *power*.

He's all mine. I know it to be true. He's given himself to me fully over and over again.

I walk to where the Sanjire root bottle rests on stone, pick it up, and clumsily unstopper it, feeling breathless and giddy with nerves. As if this is our first time again.

I look down into the bottle and realize there's only one tendril of the root left.

"This is the last one," I tell him.

Lukas's expression tenses.

It doesn't need to be said. We both know that any one of these moments could be our last time together.

"Well, then," he says, his fire pulsing, "we'll just have to make it count."

I pull the root from the bottle and place it in my mouth, feeling Lukas's attention tight on me as I set the bottle back on the ledge. The glass scrapes against the stone with a *clink* that sounds loud in the silent room, a combustive tension charging the air between us.

I turn to find Lukas's eyes trained on me, his fire ratcheting up to a blaze and shuddering through me, and I'm lit up and intimidated and excited by the wild desire that's riding with it.

I walk over and pause before him.

"So," I say with a nervous half smile, suddenly wanting him with everything in me. "You think I'm good with my hands."

Lukas doesn't hesitate. He slides his arms around me and pulls me close, his lips coming to my temple as he kisses me there fervently and his fire breaks loose, intense emotion in the way he's holding me now, in the way his fire is covetously encircling my lines.

Suddenly, it all washes over me. How I've held myself back

from him. Not able to move past my grief over someone lost to me forever. While Lukas has risked his life for me again and again and thrown his lot in with me completely. And that look on his face last night...

*I want you more than I've ever wanted anything in my entire life.*

Casting off the last of my heart's hesitation, I release my fire to him in a shuddering rush, and Lukas inhales sharply, his gaze growing even more impassioned.

"I'm sorry," I tell him ardently, my voice breaking even as a tighter desire for him takes hold. "I'm sorry it's taken me so long to care for you like you care for—"

"Shh," he says with real tenderness as his fingers thread through my hair.

And then he pulls me closer, his fire blazing through me as our lips meet and he kisses me, long and deep.

"Give me your fire, Elloren," Lukas whispers as my power streams into his. "Give me all of it."

Flames rearing, I press him against the wall and kiss him passionately, my soft curves fitting against the hard lines of his body as Lukas embraces me, our lines fuse, and we give each other everything.

# SHADOW FIRE

## ELLOREN GREY

*Sixth Month*
*Northwestern Agolith Desert*

I wake to a shock of painful, wet cold.

My panicked heart races as I spring up to a sitting position, my gaze darting wildly around as I shake my wet head. The fog of sleep rapidly clears as I struggle to adjust to what's before me.

I blink up at Valasca, my whole body shivering. She's dressed in Vu Trin fighting gear, her expression blade-hard, a wooden bucket in her hands that I realize she's just used to douse me with water. I clasp my wet blanket around my gray naked self as embarrassment and blistering outrage surge through me.

Lukas stands just behind Valasca, dressed in a dark Noi tunic and pants as well, weapons strapped all over his body. His gaze on me is devoid of any of the affection and passion from last night, his fire held completely back.

"What are you doing?" I cry at them, stunned.

"Get up," Valasca orders.

"What? N-n-no!" My teeth chatter as I protest. "I—I'm un-c-clothed!"

"Learn not to care," Valasca says, her voice hard.

"Well, I do care!"

Valasca darts toward me and roughly grabs my arm, wrenching me up as I futilely hold the blanket to myself. Valasca tears the blanket away as I pointlessly try to cover my chest with my arm.

"What are you *doing*?" I cry at her.

Valasca leans in, her mouth a snarl. "Your training starts now, as we agreed."

"Not this way!"

"*Yes*, this way!" Valasca vehemently snarls back. "Completely our way, Elloren! This is *exactly* how it works in Amazakaraan."

I want to scream at her. I want to lash out at them both. I glare at Lukas, stunned by his change in demeanor from last night, but he simply looks back at me with an expression of immovable resolve.

"Fine!" I cry, furious and humiliated as Valasca tugs me along beside her, Lukas following, as I shiver and hurl epithets at them in my mind.

Valasca yanks me down a tunneling passage that descends into the Vonor mountain's base. Sparsely placed lanterns emit faint blue light to cut through the darkness, the rhythmic *plink* of water on stone becoming audible as the narrow passage eventually opens to reveal a vaulted cavern. A dark river of water courses through it, the space lit by several huge Noi runes marked on the deep-gray rocky walls.

Water-drawing runes.

I fleetingly wonder if Chi Nam built this entire river.

Either Valasca or Lukas—or both—has already been here

this morning, I can tell. There are a variety of weapons lined up on the surface of a huge, broad stone, and Vu Trin clothing and gear, including a folded towel, is neatly set out on another rocky table near the stream's edge.

"Get in," Valasca orders as we halt just before the streaming water.

Shivering, I dip my toe in the water and find it painfully cold. I whip my head around toward her. "It's too cold…"

"Learn not to care," Valasca says as she shoves me forward.

I fall face-first into the icy water and gasp, a blast of frigid pain knifing through me as I fall under its rune-lit surface, lines of black and blue rippling before my eyes, the stream deep with no solid purchase. My arms and legs flail against the freezing current as I fight back to the surface, coughing and sputtering as I break through and grab hold of some slick, irregular rock along the stone bank, my skin almost burning from the cold.

My feet make contact with a rocky shelf, and I scramble to find some purchase to lift myself out of the stream, almost slipping back in.

I finally manage to hoist myself onto the stone ledge, scraping my knee in the process. Trembling violently from the cold, I grab the towel to dry myself and glare hatefully at Valasca and Lukas, cursing under my breath.

Lukas is leaning against the cave's wall, arms crossed, watching me unsympathetically with none of his usual heat.

"Are you done?" I cry at them both. "What is this accomplishing?"

Valasca shoves a clean undergarment at me. Noi garb. Loose black linen pantalets embroidered with a small white dragon.

"Just the dhunya for now," Valasca orders, and I throw the undergarment on, cinching the drawstring tight, the embarrassment from being so undressed rapidly overtaken by angry resentment.

Valasca pulls out her rune stylus, all business as she surveys my form and I stand there shivering.

I look to Lukas, searching for something of who he was last night. The man I completely gave myself to and took as mine in return. But he's all hard edges and closed off. Almost confrontational. On some level I understand his sudden harshness, even though it stings. This shift had to happen. My encounter with the wraith bats made it clear that I'm too emotional. Too quick to panic.

Too quick to cave in.

I pull in a wavering breath and rein in my anger.

They're trying to help me.

Valasca surveys the tattoo-like rune chains that are draped all over my chest, as if checking on the source of my glamour. Then she touches her rune stylus to my abdomen.

Sage's Smaragdalfar demon-sensing rune lights up a glowing emerald through my gray Elfhollen glamour.

"Amazing," Valasca mutters with a pointed glance toward Lukas. "The potency of a Light Mage's markings." She shakes her head, as if in awe of Sage's artistry, then lowers herself onto one knee beside me and begins drawing glowing blue Noi runes down the side of my leg, a harder, fleeting sting following her marks than when Sage drew her emerald runes.

"What are you marking on me?" I begrudgingly ask, my mortification over standing here topless rapidly dissipating.

"A series of runes that will draw on your affinity auras," Valasca replies as she concentrates on forming the runes. "They'll amplify the elemental power in all the Noi and Amaz weapon runes that resonate with your affinities."

"Where's Chi Nam?" I ask as Valasca painstakingly draws, wondering if Chi Nam knows about these harsh Amaz ways.

"Strengthening the shield around the Vonor," Lukas replies.

A tense silence falls as Valasca draws lines of glowing sapphire runes down the sides of both my thighs and arms, her brow knotted in concentration, and I suppress a shiver from the cave's cool air on my exposed and increasingly lit-up skin.

Seeming finished with the runes on my limbs, Valasca studies them appraisingly, then moves in front of me to draw a series of blue Noi runes all around Sage's green demon-sensing rune. She then slips behind me to draw another row of runes straight down my spine.

My tangled firelines prickle to life, firing gold, my invisible earth power branching toward her stylus as Valasca continues to draw. My weaker water-and windlines stir under her sorcery, and surprisingly, I've the faintest awareness, for the first time ever, of a thread-slim line of light magic tangled with the rest of my lines.

A barely perceptible glowing green line.

Valasca strides back around to my front. "Splay your hands out," she orders.

I comply, and Valasca proceeds to draw a luminous Noi rune in the center of my palms, just like the ones she and Chi Nam have on theirs.

"Are those weapon-retrieval runes?" I ask.

Valasca nods. "They are. Press their center after deploying your weapon, and the weapon will fly right back into your hand."

I glance at Lukas, who opens his own palms to display identical glowing blue runes on his hands, his expression still dauntingly severe.

Finally done marking me, Valasca murmurs a runic spell and taps her stylus on the center of my chest.

All the runes pull in under the glamour, no longer visible under my false gray hue.

Valasca hands me the Vu Trin uniform, and I throw on the black fireproof battle tunic and pants. Then I sit down on a rocky outcropping and jerk on socks and my boots and weapons belt, taking out all my residual ire over Valasca's roughness and Lukas's emotional distance on my boots as I cinch the laces tight.

Valasca pulls out my newly green Wand from a long sack propped by the cave's wall and I'm filled with an inexplicable relief as I take it in hand and slide it into the belt sheath, knowing they made a point of bringing it here for me.

Lukas strides forward and begins fastening runic weapons to me along with Valasca, who throws a series of silver Vu Trin star weapons diagonally over my chest while Lukas attaches the sheathed Ash'rion blade to my upper arm. Valasca then secures a cunning sheath around my shoulder that holds three additional blades as Lukas comes down on one knee before me, yanks up my pant leg's hem, and straps another sheathed knife around my lower leg. Valasca expeditiously does the same on my other side.

I swallow as Lukas checks the fit of the sheath with a look of grim concentration, his hands on me sparking a remembrance of his hands caressing me last night. His sinuous touch down my legs, along my thighs. How he murmured my name over and over. There's no trace of this ardent affection now, and I feel his emotional withdrawal acutely, even as I struggle to see past my own reflexive emotions and understand.

The knives fastened, they let the hems of my pant legs drop to cover them. Then the two of them rise to their feet, step back, and survey my form.

"I think we're ready to take her out," Valasca says to Lukas as if I'm not even there, my wet hair in limp tangles against my face.

Lukas scrutinizes me once more, like I'm a thing. A sword. A weapon to be wielded. He nods and meets Valasca's gaze. "Let's see what she can do."

For the next few weeks, as the portal knits together and charges, Valasca and Lukas work me hard.

Chi Nam is a constant presence in the background, calmly splitting her time between strengthening the Vonor's shield, charging the portal, and silently overseeing my weapons training. I can sense her guiding hand at work in everything, both Lukas and Valasca often exchanging wordless looks with her that are met with Chi Nam's quick, almost imperceptible nod.

Each morning, Valasca wakes me with a dousing of icy water, which I now know is a trial that all Amaz soldier apprentices endure to learn to control their response to discomfort. I learned this the second time she threw me in the painfully chilly water, after I cursed her up and down and she snarled out the motives for her actions.

Defiantly rising to her challenge, I soon learn to wake and get myself to the freezing pool just before she and Lukas arrive, confrontationally stripping off my clothes while they stand there, arms crossed. Then I grit my teeth and jump into the freezing cold water before Valasca can push me in.

And every day, before dawn, Valasca enhances the charge in the runes on my body, and I'm outfitted by the two of them with weapons then brought to a makeshift practice area they've assembled at the far end of the broad curving ledge outside the Vonor. Lukas and Valasca have thrown up a series of wooden targets marked with concentric circles and shapes of various sizes. Some of the targets are hung from ropes strung on the mesquite tree limbs just past the ledge, these targets teaching me to deal with a moving target.

They instruct me in how to throw stars and blades and spears and how to wield a runic crossbow, zeroing in on blades when it becomes apparent I'm the most comfortable with the weight and feel of these weapons.

They drive me relentlessly, push me to do exercises to strengthen my arms and shoulders and chest, and teach me martial arts sequences to improve my control over my body and my balance. Every muscle in my body aches and burns, but they drive me until pain is cramping through me and I can barely manage another throw, my shoulders screaming with discomfort.

They have me practice in extreme heat. In the dead of the frigid night. And through it all, they purposefully keep me sleep-deprived by waking me with water or harsh taunts or simply grabbing hold of my arms and forcing me to my feet.

When I'm not training with them, I'm with Chi Nam as she drills me in the runic systems, my proficiency in the violin giving me a blessed edge in learning to rapidly slide my fingers over a rune-blade hilt to find the proper runic combinations faster and faster and faster.

I'm so exhausted at night that I fall asleep in Chi Nam's meditation room the moment my head hits my bedroll, all alone in the space since Lukas now sleeps in another cavern far removed from me.

All this time, Lukas remains aloof and closed off, and my emotions become increasingly tumultuous in response to the jarring withdrawal of his ardent attentions and bolstering fire, even though I understand with my rational mind why he's doing it.

Both he and Valasca have tersely laid out that I have to adjust to forcing my emotions aside. To stand firm in the face of loneliness and isolation and exhaustion and even terror. But it's becoming near impossible. I'm like a frayed rope, dangerously close to snapping, and my pained resentment builds and builds in me until I want to hurl every weapon I'm wielding straight at Lukas to assuage the hurt that's rising.

On our twentieth night here, Valasca goes out to hunt and scout the periphery of our location, and I'm alone with Lukas for the first time since we were last intimate.

A late-night chill has fallen over the stone ledge outside the Vonor, a sliver of the crimson-hued moon rising above the mesquite treetops.

My exhaustion is so acute that I can barely function.

They woke me hours before dawn, and every part of me hurts. I might be growing stronger and more adept at using rune weaponry, but Lukas and Valasca add drill after drill, never letting up.

I throw the last blade, the wooden target before me riddled with knives and stars, all perfectly lined up from the perfect aim the Wand has conferred to me, my speed and agility vastly improving. My anger over their relentless, overly harsh training mounts with each blade I throw, pain knifing up and down my arm. I throw the last star and turn to Lukas, my eyes blazing with refusal to do more.

He looks at me coldly. "Again," he says.

Anger ignites.

I hold out my palms and use the retrieval runes to draw star after star out of the target hung from the tree before me, the weapons flying through the air and hitting my rune-marked palms with painful force, one after another, as I grasp hold of them each in turn and fasten them to the diagonal sheath across my chest. Then I draw two of the knives back into my palms, angry tears welling. Suddenly, my anger and hurt and exhaustion are like a vicious tide that I can't beat down. I throw the knives to the ground with a growl and yank the star sheath off and hurl that to the ground as well, then round on Lukas and throw as much angry affinity fire toward him as I can. As my invisible fire power batters into him, he stands firm and glares at me, unmoved by my magical protest.

"Where are you, Lukas?" I cry, feeling like a shattered fragment of myself. "I *gave* myself to you the last time we were together. And now…it's like I'm *nothing* to you. You say it's to train me, but it's like I'm a weapon now and that's *it*." Pain strafes through me as my fire chaotically knifes out at him then falls apart into a frenzy of unfocused heat, my voice cracking. "I need you, Lukas. And I want to be more than just a weapon to you!" And suddenly, I'm on the brink of emotional and physical collapse, tears stinging at my eyes as it all rushes over me. What we're up against. How he's broken our connection just when I need him the most.

For a moment, we're locked in a silent battle, Lukas's gaze on me so severe that it's almost violent in its intensity.

And then he strides toward me, his expression fierce as he comes at me at the same time as his fire roars into me. His lips come down on mine as his body makes contact, pressing me against the stone wall behind me as he grasps hold of me and drives all of his fire and all of his earth affinity branches straight into me in an overpowering rush.

Lit up by the force of his magic, my desperate want for him breaks free and I throw my own fire, my own branches into him, our magery grasping for each other and taking fierce hold as I kiss him back just as intensely, his tongue in my mouth, my tongue around his as our power merges and builds into a fiery cyclone.

Lukas draws back, both of us breathing heavily as he holds tight to me, his eyes wild.

"I *love* you, Elloren. Is that what you want to hear?"

Stunned, I can't speak.

"Is that it?" he demands, his voice rough. "Is that what you want?"

"Yes," I rasp as his hands hold tight to my arms, ferocity in his fire. I swallow, overcome.

"I *love* you," he says again, lashing the words out with a vehemence that takes my breath away. "But you're the *Black Witch*. And if you're going to survive Vogel, we *cannot* coddle you. And I want you to survive him! But it's going to be nearly *impossible* to survive him! Do you understand?"

I swallow again and nod stiffly, barely able to take a breath. So shocked by his fierce declaration.

Lukas steps back and pulls in his fire, but I can still feel it, whipping out at the edges.

He collects himself, hands on his hips, his breathing forced into a more even cadence. When he looks back at me, his face is once again remote, his fire held back. He glances at the weapons I threw down.

"Again, Elloren," he demands.

Twelve nights later, I'm sitting around the ledge fire with Lukas, Valasca, and Chi Nam, every muscle hurting, but I'm getting used to the constant ache as they all push me harder and harder. Every day and night.

I'm changing. I can feel it. The weapons strapped all over my body are starting to feel like an extension of myself. Like extra limbs. And I'm starting to intimately know every inch of these weapons, every rune on their hilts and what they can do, the finger arrangements of their combinations beginning to feel as natural as the finger positions on the frets of a violin.

Lukas and Valasca have sparred with me in the middle of the night, dragging me, disoriented, out of sleep more than once as they yelled and shoved me and tried to intimidate me and throw me off balance before pulling me into mock battles in which I've been mock slain every single time.

But I'm feeling leaner. More honed. And I've begun going off on my own in the few spare moments they allow me to experiment with some of my throws and runic combinations. I'm starting to effectively wield more than one weapon at a time, following the Wand's gift of guidance, to level them at my targets, even when driven to complete mental and physical and emotional exhaustion.

I may not be a warrior yet, but I feel like a true soldier apprentice. I've also settled more fully into my Elfhollen glamour, getting used to the gray as I fall into my new, manufactured identity.

No longer Elloren Gardner but Ny'laea Shizoryn.

I'm drilled in this new identity until I'm fluent in my fictional history and answer to the name Ny'laea, speaking almost exclusively now in the Elfhollen language and outfitted in gray Elfhollen garb that's internally warded with Noi military runes.

Ever since Lukas's blazing declaration of love, I feel different around all of them, their aloof severity no longer a source of chafing pain, no matter how hard they drive me. Lukas has remained closed off to me, but I fully understand, both rationally and emotionally, why he's being harsh, and I accept it.

But every now and then, I catch him giving me a stray ardent look and sense the heated arc of his power reaching toward me before he carefully reins it all back in.

On my thirty-sixth day here, the sun blazes fiercely down on the world, pouring heat into the motionless desert air. The shade cast over me offers only a slim respite from the unforgiving heat.

I tighten my grip on the rune blades in my hands, the charged runes prickling under my fingers as they draw on my affinity auras.

Rivulets of sweat drip down my scorching neck as I face off with both Lukas and Valasca on the crimson sands of the desert plain, the air like a kiln, my gray Elfhollen garb oppressively hot. Chi Nam calmly watches from the sidelines as she leans into her rune staff. A great arc of red stone rises behind her and swoops over Lukas, Valasca, and me before descending to the sands.

Lukas and Valasca attack from opposite sides.

They draw their weapons in a blur, and I sense, immediately, the affinities they're powering up—

Lukas is drawing fire into his blade. I can both see it and sense it if I look at his weapon, my fire affinity lines tightening as the image of flickering heat flashes inside the blade's hilt. Valasca is pulling on runic power to weave complicated earth sorcery into a swarm of metallic darts, their translucent auras emanating from the runes on her weapon to hover around her form.

By pure muscle memory, my fingers slide into the corresponding defensive runic combination as they hurl their weapons at me in unison.

Lukas's fire bursts to searing life around his incoming weapon, and hundreds of spearing darts blink into existence around Valasca's as their weapons and magic barrel toward me.

I splay my arms out and flip my blades' gleaming sides toward Lukas's and Valasca's incoming power.

Their magic is the first thing that slams into my blades, Lukas's fire immediately snuffed out in a dramatic puff of steam by my blast of wintry water from one blade, and Valasca's darts singed to a bright red spray of molten ash by my blaze of concentrated fire from my other weapon, both of their blades hurled off through the sky in opposite directions from the sheer force of my magic.

They both whip out new blades, but before they can charge the weapons, I draw my blades back into my palms and amplify the knives' sorcery with rapid fingerwork. Then I hurl both blades at Lukas and Valasca, following the Wand's guiding green lines.

The blades slam into them and ricochet to the side as Lukas and Valasca promptly explode into balls of churning golden flame.

I gape at their twin conflagrations in complete open-mouthed astonishment as the fire quickly dissipates against the translucent shields both Lukas and Valasca have thrown up over themselves.

They exchange smiles full of blazing satisfaction before looking to me with obvious pride.

I turn toward Chi Nam, stunned beyond belief. "I did it, didn't I?" I marvel. "I finally did it. I killed them."

Chi Nam grins. "You did, Ny'laea. They are both most thoroughly and unequivocally dead."

A few nights later, Lukas and I stand just inside Chi Nam's shield on the cave's outside ledge and study the six wraith bats that lurk in the trees, silently watching us through merciless eyes.

I managed to suppress my fear and use runic sorcery to startle the beasts into leaving last night, but Lukas feels it's time to face them without the protection of Vonor's dome-shield. Exposed.

To practice holding my fear at bay while we have the

chance, since tomorrow we'll be stepping through the portal and leaving the desert and its wraith creatures behind.

I swallow as Lukas's hand comes to my arm, his gaze steady on the camouflaged beasts. The desert's night air is a cool, still embrace around us.

"I'm going to drop part of the shield in a moment," he says. "So, prepare yourself."

I pull in a deep breath and force fire into my lines as I clench and unclench my fist around my rune blade and picture the burning away of all emotion. I know that even the smallest rise in fear will be amplified by the monstrous bats and they'll try to immobilize me with it. But still, a spark of trepidation manages to weave through, and I struggle to tamp it down.

"There're so many of them," I say warily. And they're fast, I've found. Unexpectedly fast for their size.

I can sense their aura gathering around my mind, like a poison mist, seeking to stir my emotions into a panic.

I grip the Ash'rion blade tighter and stare them down in turn, battling back the encroaching fear with a steady stream of my invisible fire power as I prepare to startle them into fleeing with lightning.

"You can handle them," Lukas prods. "You've bested both Val and myself."

His tone is so unexpectedly warm, a rush of affection washes over me. I glance appreciatively at him, drawn to the sight of his lean, rune-marked chest in the garnet moonlight, the red glinting off his skin's deep-green glimmer. A slim, silvery scar from the scorpio attack transverses his chest and shoulder.

He threw off his tunic during this night's vigorous sparring, much of it a demonstration in how to deflect a physical attack that required quite a few close holds.

Heat simmers along my lines, hot as a brazier, as I take in his handsome form and consider how our nearness affected the two of us as we grappled with each other. Lukas's fire escaped his tight hold a number of times this evening, his lines heated to a scald by the time we were done.

Feeling brazen, I resheathe my blade and pivot to face him fully, then send out a hot, looping tendril of flame to tease his lines and draw his attention away from the bats.

Lukas's fire gives a hard flare as his eyes flick toward me, a question in them.

My fierce affinity draw to him rears hotter, overtaking all caution. Because I miss him. Desperately, in this moment. Touching him, being close to him—it's the only place my power feels free, loosened from the bonds of the trees. And I miss the way he sends fire through his kiss. Through his touch...

My fire pulses toward Lukas, unrestrained, as I reach up and trace a finger down his chest. Across the scar he got protecting me. Then I slide my hand up and over the hard musculature of his taut shoulder, quickly growing dazed with both heat and want.

I meet his eyes and a current of his power ripples through me.

Lukas's green gaze has gone dark as midnight, feral desire now in it.

Emboldened, I slide my hand up his neck and thread my fingers through his thick black hair. Then I bunch it in my fist.

I want him. Beyond all reason or caution. I want him.

Reckless desire sweeps through me as I pull Lukas toward me and into a deep kiss.

I can feel the curve of his mouth, his lips briefly tightening with amusement that's soon whisked away by the force of my invisible fire as I blast it into him in a rush, wave after wave of fire, and I don't stop. I keep filling him with a blazing stream of it, wanting to consume us both as his own fire mounts, his powerful flames spiraling around my sudden inferno.

And then Lukas's hands are around my wrists, pushing me firmly away as his fire whips toward me with searing force and my own fire surges relentlessly toward him.

"Stop," he says, all command as he breathes hard, his eyes glazed with passion. "We've no Sanjire root."

My power rushes harder toward him, feeding the flames and whipping them into a frenzy. "I wish we had Sanjire root," I say, frustrated hunger in the words. I want him so badly that I'm almost ready to be completely reckless.

"If we had Sanjire root," Lukas says, his eyes burning with desire, "I'd take you right here. Against that wall."

I smirk at this. "Maybe I'd take you first."

Lukas's feral look takes a turn for the darkly amused. He reaches up and brushes a finger along the side of my breast, trailing invisible flame. "Once you gain control over your lines," he says, his voice deep and velvet smooth, "I'll be completely at your mercy."

My smile inches higher. "That's how I'll begin my Black Witch reign over both Realms, then. By having you do my bidding."

Lukas's answering look of humor drops away as if he's been suddenly overwhelmed by emotion, his fire raging fitfully now. "We can't do this," he says, his tone flinty. "I need to be hard on you and training you like a soldier, not flirting with you." The harsh edge of his tone softens slightly. "I need to keep some semblance of distance from you."

I scowl in frustration, all of my fire straining toward him, desperate for release. "Am I truly in the military now?"

The edge of his mouth twitches up. "You've been drafted."

"Really? Into what army?"

Lukas's even stare doesn't waver. *"Mine."*

I step back slightly from him and take a deep, ragged breath, eyeing him and his handsome form with open want. "What happens when we get to Noi lands, Lukas?" I ask, frustration making my tone harsh. I motion between us. "What happens with us?"

Lukas's smile is subtle as his eyes flick over me. "We'll obtain a large supply of Sanjire root."

"You're assuming the Noi don't kill you as soon as you step foot over their border."

Lukas gives a short laugh. "They won't kill me. I have information about the Gardnerian military that they sorely need. And I'm powerful. The Vu Trin aren't fools. They'll want to make good use of my power. *You*, on the other hand, they'll want to kill. You'll need to remain glamoured for a bit."

"So, we won't be living together, I take it."

Lukas smiles. "Do you want to live with me, Elloren?"

*Yes, I want to live with you*, I think. *And share your bed.*

But it's more than that, I realize. It runs so much deeper than that.

I hold Lukas's searching gaze. "I do," I tell him. "I want to make my life with you." Even as I say it, I'm hit by a pang of sorrow.

*Yvan.*

*He's gone*, I harshly remind myself, pushing away the grief that rises at unexpected moments. *You're fasted. And sealed. To someone you've grown to care deeply for. You need to let Yvan go.*

"We won't be able to live together initially," Lukas says, growing thoughtful. "It would draw the Vu Trin straight to you." He moves closer and enfolds me in his arms, his lips brushing against my hair. I can feel his sultry smile in his tone. "We'll have to meet in back alleys and sordid taverns."

I pull back a fraction, serious. "I want to stay together. No matter what comes."

Lukas's gaze turns as serious as mine, strong emotion flashing in it as something new takes root between us. "I want that," he says. "I want to be with you. Always. No matter what."

Tears fill my eyes as affection wells inside me with unexpected force.

And love.

Love for Lukas Grey.

"Elloren," Lukas says, his voice thick with passion as he pulls me in for a heated kiss.

Our affinity branches twine as tightly as our embrace as we give in to our craving for each other.

And our love for each other.

Overcome, I start to close my eyes as I let myself fall even more deeply into both Lukas's kiss and his ardent affection, just as movement in a nearby tree catches my gaze.

A glint of predatory eyes.

Many eyes.

Many eyes on the same strangely elongated bat, Shadow tendriling up from its leathery wings as the rune on my abdomen starts to sting.

Fear strikes through me like a hammer to an anvil.

I push away from Lukas and grab tight hold of his arm, my lungs constricting as confusion ignites in his eyes and his fire.

Lukas whips his head around to follow my line of sight just as Chi Nam's military-grade runic dome barrier around the Vonor blinks out of sight, like a candle effortlessly snuffed out.

"Lukas," I rasp out as the wraith bat and several others extend their wings and begin to lift off from the tree as one, the many-eyed bat trailing smoke. My wand hand reflexively reaches for the Ash'rion blade as I notice the deflection rune marked on the many-eyed creature's chest. "Don't use magic!" I cry.

Lukas's expression turns savage as he pulls me back, lifts

his wand, and throws out a slashing line of fire to whip out across the unmarked bats as they launch themselves into the air.

Every bat save the many-eyed, elongated one bursts into flames and hurtles to the ground with an earsplitting shriek.

Lukas yanks me roughly behind him as the elongated, rune-marked bat lands before us with a hard thud and darts at Lukas with cobra-fast speed.

Lukas ducks to the side and the incoming beast crashes against the Vonor's stone wall, quickly righting itself as Lukas pulls his sword, lunges at the bat, and slashes the beast in two.

One wing and half its lower body severed, the elongated bat sets every eye on me and throws down its remaining wing. It thrusts its taloned tip down into the stone like a dagger as it lets out a rasping shriek, snaps its teeth, and pulls its mutilated body toward me, trailing dark blood as I ready my blade.

Enraged, Lukas lunges forward, lifts his sword, and brings it down, slicing the beast's head off, its eyes remaining open and pinned on me.

Dragon shrieks split the sky, and our heads whip up as several dragons soar in. The image of a dark tree made of Shadow shudders through my mind as the dragons begin to circle the Vonor in a wide arc and alarm spasms inside me.

Lukas's gaze meets mine with horrified urgency as he grabs hold of me once more and pulls me into a sprint toward the entrance to the Vonor.

Valasca and Chi Nam are already there, Valasca strapping on runic weapons and Chi Nam repetitively tapping runic codes with a rune stone into the portal's frame, the portal's center a stubbornly uncharged silver.

Valasca spits out a curse as her eyes meet Lukas's. "Vogel's forces can shut down advanced runic systems. We're in trouble."

"Vogel's here," I say, taking in Lukas's momentarily dire look.

But then a steely expression descends on Lukas's face. He looks to Chi Nam. "How long until the portal's ready?"

"Soon," she says as she holds a rune stone against the portal's frame, the central silver brightening in a sweeping ripple. She gives him a level look. "But for only one passage. Maybe two, but the second might fly off course."

"Can you speed it up?" he presses.

"I'm trying."

Lukas turns to me, looking fiercely decided. He grips my arms, his voice rough. "Elloren. When you get to Noi lands, find your brothers. And then, if she's still there, find Kam Vin. Warn them. Warn the Wyvernguard about what's coming."

Terror spikes. "No! I'm not going without all of you!"

"Be quiet!" Lukas snarls. "Listen to me! Tell them Vogel can shut down advanced military runes. Tell Kam Vin. She'll believe you. She understands what's happening in the Western Realm."

What he's saying smashes through me in a terrible wave. I attempt to twist out of his grip, shaking my head vehemently, panic building. "*No.* I won't go without you!"

"Elloren." Lukas's voice is hard, his grasp on my arms relentless as Valasca begins attaching additional blades to me. "You *will*."

Valasca stuffs a money purse into my tunic's pocket, then straightens and grabs hold of my arm as well, her expression both desperate and ironhard. "Find Ni," she says with great urgency, a beseeching edge to her tone. "Promise me you'll find Ni and tell her what Vogel can do. Warn her. And…" Her expression momentarily shatters, her voice breaking. "Tell her I love her. Promise me, Elloren. Promise me you'll tell her."

They're sacrificing their lives for me.

Tears blur my vision as I shake my head, desperation overtaking me. "No. Please. *No.*"

The dragons stop circling and fly in to land on the flat expanse of desert in front of the Vonor mountain.

Lukas's tone gains an impassioned edge. "Elloren, you are *not* weak. You're a *warrior*. I have *always* known that you're powerful. But now, *you* have to believe it. You need to survive. You need to fight Vogel. And you need to *win*."

Tears sheen my eyes as I glance toward the dragons, their seven riders now striding toward us, dark and small from this distance.

I look back at Lukas, both terrified and devastated. "I love you," I tell him.

Lukas's expression tightens, almost a flinch followed by a look of excruciating pain. We can't lie to each other, so he knows that what I've just said is true. I loved Yvan. That will never change. But I've grown to love Lukas too.

My fastmate. My lover. My friend.

When it comes, Lukas's voice is thick with emotion, his voice on the edge of breaking. "There are no words for what I feel for you. There never have been." He glances toward the incoming Mages, releases my arms, then turns and draws his wand, his demeanor turning deadly.

I can feel his magic consolidating into a honed, lethal spear.

He steps away from me and follows Chi Nam as she moves toward the end of the stony ledge and slams her staff down onto stone. Another runic shield flies up and over us that pulses with blue light and a denser constellation of runes.

Lukas positions himself just behind her, wand readied. Valasca moves to his side with two blades clenched in her fists.

Heart pounding, I ready my own blades as Vogel comes into sharper view as he strides toward us, the white bird emblazoned on his priestly tunic, his Shadow Wand in hand.

Four Level Five Mage soldiers flank him along with his two envoys, but the envoys are terrifyingly altered. Shadow horns have begun a slow curl up from their heads, their eyes simmering red as coals, the rune on my abdomen heating up to a scald.

*They're demons*, I realize, terror spiking.

Without warning, Vogel's dark tree blasts into me like an affinity fist, my hands and wrists shot through with pain as if stabbed with countless needles. Both his power and the pain drive me back a step, cinching the air from my lungs as Vogel's Shadow branches lash themselves around my lines, bearing down, rooting me to the spot, and tying me there as I struggle against his invisible bindings, a vengeful cry of protest rising in my throat.

I wrestle against Vogel's power, tensing my lines in an effort to throw off his thrall, but his hold is too strong.

Multiple many-eyed wraith bats alight in the nearby trees and on the arcing stone formations all around us, and my desperation spikes as my green Wand begins to hum with frantic energy against my side.

I want to lash out and fight Vogel but I can't move. He's taken complete hold of my knotted lines.

I've a sudden, internal sense of shimmering green branches curling up from my Wand around the dark tree in my mind.

The Shadow around my lines rears back in an explosion of what feels like furious surprise. Hissing from the contact, it surges in to take an even more vicious hold of my lines.

I rage against Vogel's hold on me, but it's no use. My bound-up magic and my Wand and all of my allies are no match for Vogel and his Shadow Wand—it's too strong.

Vogel is too strong.

Vogel and his Mages stride right up to Chi Nam's shield and come to a stop before it.

He smiles at Chi Nam, slow and merciless. "You have something that belongs to me, Chilon. Give me my Black Witch."

Chi Nam raises her chin as she stares Vogel down. "You can't have her, you fiend." She slams her staff down onto stone once more, blue light raying out from both her staff and the shield around us.

Vogel scrutinizes Chi Nam without a trace of emotion, as if she's a particularly diverting insect, as blue rune light flickers over the elegant planes of his face.

All of a sudden, everything is washed in an eruption of golden light that's burst to life behind me.

Valasca's head whips back, her eyes widening as she peers just past me. "It's charged for one," she rasps out, a new defiance lighting her eyes as her gaze flicks to mine.

It all happens in a split second.

Vogel's whole demeanor turns vicious as the wraith bats launch themselves from the trees with a collective shriek and all Vogel's Shadow Mages lift their wands in unison.

Shadow fire bursts from their wands.

Lukas turns and hurls himself toward me just as the Shadow Mages' wall of flame blazes into Chi Nam's shield, exploding it in a flash of blue as it ignites Chi Nam's form and races toward us.

Lukas picks me up and throws me, and then Valasca, into the portal, Valasca rapidly whisked off to the side as I'm pulled straight backward into the portal's shimmering golden depths.

Lukas's eyes meet mine as the black fire hits his back, his mouth forming one word that's snuffed out by the roar of the fire.

*Elloren.*

A wave of shimmering gold cuts him from sight and swallows the sound as I scream his name.

# CONFLAGRATION

## ELLOREN GREY

*Seventh Month*
*Dyoi Forest, Eastern Realm*

I fall through the portal's glimmering gold center headfirst and hit the ground hard as I'm thrust into a dense purple forest under stormy daylit skies.

Wildly disoriented, I push myself up, palms to the mossy ground, and whip my head around.

Behind me, the portal stands suspended in the air. Its golden haze is fog-like and insubstantial, the runes of the portal's frame dissipating to transparency and wavering like water.

My heart slams against my chest, panic cresting as I lurch toward the portal even as it fades to a vaporous echo.

*"Lukas!"* I cry into the rapidly erasing portal. *"Chi Nam! Valasca!"*

Shaking, I thrust my arm toward it, but my arm passes straight through. *"Lukas!"* I scream, desperate for sound to carry to them all.

*Ancient One, no. No. He gave his life for me. And Chi Nam…*

The image of powerful Chi Nam being instantly consumed by Vogel's Shadow fire, of the fire hitting Lukas's back just before I was whisked away from them over an impossible distance, is like a knife straight through my heart.

*"Lukas!"* I cry out at the portal. *"Chi! Valasca!"* Where is Valasca? Did she get whisked leagues away from me? Or could she be somewhere in this forest?

Devastated, I look up and all around me through tear-streaked eyes and take in the shocking sight of the largest trees I've ever seen, rising to mammoth proportions all around me.

All of them purple.

The massive trunks are a blackened nightshade hue, their teardrop leaves a vivid violet. The forest floor is covered with curling ferns colored a muted amethyst. A small lizard with an intricate purple geometric pattern on its back scurries up the broad trunk beside me.

A silent vein of bright white lightning forks through the sky. The sudden, hard *crack* of thunder makes me flinch as if struck, my heart wrenching anew.

I frantically look toward the portal, its internal golden fog now gone, the surrounding arc a faint, ghostly echo of blue rune light.

"Lukas!" I cry again, choking on tears. Unfamiliar birdsong sounds out, low and whooping, as a silver crane with a curling tail soars through the canopy.

*I'm in Noi lands*, I realize. In the Dyoi Forest. Leagues and leagues and leagues away from them.

Leagues away from Lukas.

"Valasca!" I cry into the forest, distraught. I scan the trees for some sight of her, calling out her name again and again with desperate force in every direction.

No answer.

Just the chirring of insects and unfamiliar birdsong and the rustling of violet leaves.

The image of Lukas being hit by Vogel's black fire plays again in my mind, along with the heart-shattering realization.

*He's dead.*

And if, by some miracle, the fire didn't kill him, Vogel and his soldiers have surely murdered him by now.

My head falls into my hands as a rush of fresh tears glaze my eyes and I struggle to breathe.

I replay it again and again in my mind. My last glimpse of Lukas. That blazing look in his eyes. How he called out my name just before I was whisked away from him.

*He saved me. He saved my life. They all did.*

I glance up to find the last of the portal vanishing from sight.

"Lukas!" I sob into the empty air. "Valasca. Chi..." My voice trails into nothing, choked off by grief, a nauseated heartbreak taking hold.

Another bolt of lightning scythes through the sky with an earsplitting crack, my face twisting with misery as a palpable ripple of awareness comes to life in the snaking root beneath my palm. It's quickly followed by a wave of amorphous hostility rushing in from the forest all around me, along with a sharp tug on my tangled affinity lines, pulling them in every direction.

Tethering them anew.

*They know.*

Even here in the Eastern Realm, the trees know what I am.

I imagine their leagues-long network of roots, leading from the Western Realm's forests and over the desert's expanse to the East, sending their message from root to root.

*Black Witch.*

Outrage kindles deep in my core with surprising force. I draw my palm away from the root and push myself to my feet.

"So, you know," I quietly seethe at the forest, my lips turning down into a trembling grimace as I face down the trees. "You all know what I am."

A wave of panic suddenly overtakes my outrage.

*I'm alone. In a hostile forest. In a land where the military wants to kill me. And I have no idea how to get out of here.*

*And Vogel is going to come for both me and this entire Realm.*

The ground seems to shift beneath my feet, and I lean down and brace my hands on my thighs as I force even breaths and battle back the fear.

Lukas's words come to me, filling my mind.

*You're a warrior. I have always known that you're powerful. But now, you* have *to believe it.*

Fresh tears sting my eyes at the remembrance of Lukas's deep, bolstering voice. And Lukas's, Valasca's, and Chi Nam's unwavering conviction that I could be strong.

*They all believed you could be a warrior,* I rage as the anguished grief sweeps through me. *And they gave up everything to help you escape.*

*You have to be strong.*

I glance down at the crushed ferns where I was crumpled up a moment ago, my rune blades lying on the ground, as an even starker realization grips hold.

*Vogel can destroy the Noi military's runes. He can march up to the most powerful sorceress in Noilaan and effortlessly cut her down. Which means he's going to be able to march right into the Eastern Realm and destroy everything and everyone in it.*

Determination bolts through me.

*You have to get to the Wyvernguard and warn the Vu Trin.*

I press the runes on my palms, my rune blades flying up from the forest floor and into my hands.

Then I close my fists around their hilts.

*No more falling apart,* I order myself, grasping the blades tight. *You're on your own now.*

Grief burning in my chest, I sheathe my blades, wipe away my tears, and feel for my other weapons, the knives strapped to my arms and just under my pant legs' hems, the Wand sheathed at my side.

All there.

Lightning flashes, the air charged with the incoming storm's energy as urgency rises, sparking an answering flush of energy through my tangled lines. I need to get to the Noi city of Voloi, home of the Wyvernguard. And I need to get there fast.

Because Vogel is coming for the Eastern Realm.

The Shadow Wand is rising.

I tense my brow at the purple forest surrounding me, picturing Chi Nam's map of the East. If this is truly the Dyoi Forest, then I need to travel east and get past both the Zonor River and the Vo Mountain Range. And beyond that, over the Vo River to reach Voloi.

But I've no compass...

A child's scream splits the air, the sound piercing my thoughts as my whole body tenses.

Another scream in the same direction. And then an insectile screech that ends on a chittering note.

I pale as I remember that sound.

*Scorpios.*

Terror blasts through me, momentarily rooting me to the spot.

And then another heart-wrenching scream sounds out. A woman crying out in distress in Uriskal.

Their cries break through my fear like a hammer shattering glass. I pull my rune blades from their sheaths and set out at a run toward the sounds, dodging trees, leaping over thick roots, crushing ferns beneath my boots.

The trees thin ahead, the dense forest giving way to a shallow, bowl-shaped valley, pale lilac grass swaying in the prestorm wind, lightning flashing from the angry clouds massing overhead.

I pause as I take in the nightmare scene before me in one sweeping glance.

A purple-hued Urisk woman and little girl are huddled against a large boulder at the edge of the field, backed against it and cowering. A skinny, fierce-looking Gardnerian girl who looks to be about thirteen stands before them, a knife raised in her trembling hand as she faces off against the three huge scorpios that are closing in on them all. One of the scorpios is taller than the others and chillingly elongated in shape, Shadow runes marked on its chitinous thorax and back, including a deflection rune.

For a moment, I remain frozen as the young child screams and the horrible things repeatedly make a play for the older girl with the knife, clicking and screeching, rearing up to make threatening jabs toward her with lethal forelimbs and poison-tipped tails.

Rage rises, freeing me as my military training takes hold. I grip my rune blades tighter and carefully move forward.

My foot skids on a loose root, my heel thumping down onto the forest floor.

The scorpios' heads twitch toward me in one unified motion.

Alarm leaps in my chest as a sting ripples through the demon-detecting rune on my abdomen. Two of the scorpios are looking at me with depthless insect eyes. But the third, the elongated one, is not only looking at me with its bulging insect eyes, but the countless eyes scattered around these eyes. And in the center of the swarm is an eye that's not insectile at all. It's a pale green knowing eye.

A Vogel eye.

All hesitation breaks apart like a storm coming untethered. Rampant fury washes over me in a blinding flash as white-hot Magefire rushes through my lines.

Lukas. Chi Nam. The Lupines. Yvan. Everyone Vogel's killed. It all strikes through me as my fire blasts into a violent conflagration.

A snarl erupts from deep inside me, quickly building to a roar. "Get away from them, you *bastard*!"

I charge into the valley, my training overtaking me as my fingers slide over the runes on the hilts of both blades and I power up the fire runes.

The smaller scorpios fall back into a protective crouch as the green Wand buzzes against my side and I raise the blades, shimmering green lines forming in my vision and tracking straight to the beasts as I slide my fingers over the runes and sound the Noi spells.

With a guttural cry I hurl both blades forward, aiming for the scorpios' necks.

The knives find their marks, and both creatures' heads explode into churning golden fire, the bodies flailing and gurgling as they fall to the ground twitching and the larger scorpio starts for me on huge, scuttling legs.

Fury snapping through my blood, I press the runes on my palms, and the knives fly back across the field and into my hands with hard thwacks.

"You see me?" I growl out at the Shadow-marked scorpio, fisting the blades as I stalk toward it. "*Good!* Go ahead, Vogel! Come at me, you bastard!"

The thing makes a sudden leap for me, flying high into the air, verdant lines forming in my vision as I throw both blades straight at the thing's vulnerable neck.

The scorpio screeches as my blades sink right into its throat and I hurl myself to the side just as it crashes down, the taloned edge of its massive forearm barely missing my shoulder.

Black ichor explodes from its neck as it thrashes, and I roll away as its forearm crashes down toward me again and again and again. I keep rolling and rolling through the grass as the little girl screams. Then I scramble upright as the thing bucks and writhes.

Fury still ripping through me, I unsheathe another blade and approach the vile thing to find its one pale green Vogel eye open and alert as the creature gobbles and chitters, then grows completely still.

Nothing can slake my thirst for vengeance in that moment as a berserker rage overtakes me.

I stride right up to the monster and look straight into its pale green eye.

"I'm going to come for you," I seethe at Vogel, scoured out by my fury, nothing but rage inside me now, "and I'm going to be your worst nightmare."

There's no way for the thing to have an expression, but I can feel the cold, vicious spite that flickers in that one eye.

*"Go straight to hell, Vogel,"* I hiss, then bring my blade down to impale his eye.

I dig into the creature, gouging out the Vogel eye and all the other eyes. Driving my knife into its head again and again and again. Then I straighten and pull in a quavering breath, blood-lust still strafing through my lines as I blink at what's before me, reality warping as I survey the wreckage I've wrought.

The two smaller scorpios are splayed out, their charred heads still smoking and bent back at odd angles where my blades impaled their necks, black ichor staining the surrounding lavender grass. The Vogel scorpio's head is a mound of gore.

Magefire whips through my tangled lines, hot and furious. But there's something more. Another line of fire, golden-hot and mounting in strength. A spike of grief hits me as I realize it's an echo of Yvan's Wyvernfire.

In a disbelieving daze, I lean to wipe the black mucous coating my blade on the pale lilac grass, then rise and resheathe my weapon as my Wyvernfire ripples through my lines.

I hold up my hands and press the retrieval runes on my palms with my thumbs.

The two other blades embedded in the Vogel scorpio's neck fly toward me with such force that they almost sever the beast's head, their hilts slapping into my palms.

I wipe them on the grass as well, straighten, and calmly resheathe them both.

The woman, the teenage girl, and the child are all clinging to each other and eyeing me with looks of pure shock. They're sick, the woman and the young child, I swiftly realize. Quite sick. With bloodshot eyes and red sores thick around their mouths. There's a feverish, strung-out look about them, and they're skeletally thin.

The Red Grippe.

The final stages of it, from the looks of them both.

The Gardnerian girl sets herself staunchly before them, her green-eyed glare fixed on me, her blade still in hand. Her whole self seems tightly strung, like a violin string wound to the near breaking point. I notice that they all have similar heart-shaped faces.

I look closer.

My eyes linger on the ears that are poking through the Gardnerian girl's long, unwashed black hair. Her ears are jagged—scarred—and I realize, in a horrified flash, that they've been cropped. Like Olilly's were, that horrible night when Gardnerian mobs attacked Urisk all over Verpacia.

Which means they were once pointed.

I set my eyes on the little Urisk girl and note the emerald flecks in her amethyst eyes, the strands of Gardnerian black mingled in with her violet hair.

In a burst of comprehension, I realize that both of these children are part Gardnerian and part Urisk and would not be looked at kindly in the Western Realm by practically anyone.

It all comes together in my mind—the myriad reasons these three are likely fleeing East.

Concerned, I lift a hand toward them, palm out. "Don't be alarmed," I say, not sure if I'm talking to them or myself, astonished by what I've just done. I turn and blink at the decimated scorpio carcasses, the image surreal.

*I took down three scorpios.*

*Three.*

Tears blur my vision as Lukas's and Chi Nam's and Valasca's unwavering belief in me fills my mind.

*You were right*, I tell them, my heart aching. *I can fight back. I can be a warrior.*

"Who...who are you?" the Urisk woman asks me waveringly in the Common Tongue, her heavily accented voice stitched tight.

I turn toward her and take in the stark fear in her reddened amethyst eyes.

*The Black Witch*, I almost say.

"I'm..." I begin then pause, struggling to quickly assemble my thoughts, remembering the false Elfhollen name I'm supposed to use in the Eastern Realm, the Elfhollen identity that Valasca and Lukas and Chi Nam drilled into me.

"My name is Ny'laea Shizoryn," I tell them as my voice breaks around another painful wave of grief.

Their wide-eyed stares remain fixed on me.

I step toward them but stop when they collectively flinch, the little girl whimpering and coughing up thick phlegm as she clings to who I assume is her mother. The young child's green-flecked eyes are wide and haunted, as if she's replaying the scorpio attack over and over in her mind. She's so thin. Much too thin. Like her mother...

Dread gathers in me like a deep, welling pool as my apothecary mind savagely ticks off the cold facts about their illness.

They'll be dead in a matter of days if they don't get hold of Norfure tincture. The immediacy of their situation momentarily sweeps away my own pain.

"Where are we?" I ask them as another flash of golden warmth shimmers through my lines.

The teenage girl looks to the woman questioningly, her expression growing conflicted when the woman remains cautiously silent. But then the girl straightens with an air of defiance, as if fighting against her own intimidation, as she sets her piercing forest green eyes on me.

"We're in the Dyoi Forest," she says, clutching her blade.

It strikes me anew, the sheer impossibility of it.

I'm here, in the Eastern Realm, along with my brothers and so many loved ones. Trystan and Rafe. Diana and Jarod and Andras. Tierney and Naga and Sage, and other allies and friends. All of them probably here, somewhere.

"Do you have a compass?" I ask the girl as lightning forks through the sky above, sending out a resounding crack.

She nods, her brow furrowed tight as she pulls a golden compass from her pocket, seeming braced like a soldier and ready to press through hell itself to get the woman and child to safety.

"I need your help," I level with the girl. "I don't know which way to go."

She considers this, her mouth thinning, the force of her gaze a formidable thing.

"I'll help you," she finally blurts out. There's a rushed, reckless quality to the words, like she's made the sudden decision to jump off a cliff.

I nod at this, both heartened and overcome with emotion over her obvious bravery in the face of such great difficulty. "And I'll protect you," I promise her.

The air seems to flicker and warp, translucent white birds

flashing into view and settling on the shoulders of the girl, the child, and the woman as the Wand pulses against my side.

My heart twists as I remember all the other times the ethereal Watchers have shown themselves.

To prompt compassion for heroic Ariel.

To lead me to Marina.

I've seen the Watchers on the shoulders of Smaragdalfar refugee children. And Watchers in terrible mourning when the Lupines were murdered.

Watchers led me to the Wand sheathed at my side.

And now, they're here, with this girl and her sick family.

It's a heartening thought, that there could be a larger force at play in the world. A force for good that cares about the oppressed.

Even though its power pales in comparison to the power of the Shadow Wand.

I remember talking to Sage about the Wand of Myth, the Wand we've both been the Bearers of.

*The force of good seems very, very weak*, I rued to her.

*Then we strengthen it*, Sage answered me with unflinching resolve. *I think it needs us in that way.*

I look at the people before me as the Watchers blink out of view and the Wand goes silent once more.

*Perhaps this is how it starts*, I consider as tears glaze my eyes. *By helping each other.*

Another fiercer shot of warmth suddenly jets through my lines, fiery gold and blisteringly powerful.

My eyes widen.

Shocked, I glance around, the power of the trees palpably retreating from the sudden rush of heat.

"What's the matter?" the girl worriedly asks me.

The golden fire roars through me again, and before I can answer her, the flames intensify. Not Mage heat, I realize. No.

I recognize the unique, golden-blaze quality of this heat. The signature sting of it.

There's nothing vague or amorphous about this heat. It's directional. Blasting toward me from the northeast and as familiar to me as my own heart, my own lines. Heat I've felt intimately in more than one kiss. Heat that's been sent through me at close range.

A light-headed swoop flashes through me as I'm seized by the realization.

*Yvan. This is Yvan's heat.*

I'm sure of it. As sure as I am of my own existence.

*Sweet Ancient One.*

My breath catches in my throat as the Wyvernfire whips through my lines and circles around me with overwhelming force, fierce recognition and yearning in it.

*Is Yvan alive?*

Tears slide down my eyes and I send out my own fire toward the blaze that's rushing through me. Twining the flames tightly together as the golden fire fills every part of me and I can see it burning in the back of my mind, suffused with the echo of one word. One word, sent out over Ancient One knows how many leagues of Eastern land. A word with so much passion invested in it, it releases a cyclone of longing and want and fierce grief inside me.

*Elloren.*

★ ★ ★ ★ ★

*The enthralling saga continues in*
The Demon Tide,
*book four of The Black Witch Chronicles!*

# ACKNOWLEDGMENTS

First of all, thank you to my husband, Walter, for his unflinching and enthusiastic support. I love you.

To my epic daughters—Alex, Willow, Taylor, and Schuyler—thank you for supporting me in this author thing and being so all-around great. I love you.

Love going out to my late mother, Mary Jane Sexton, and to my late close friend, Diane Dexter. In the moments that seemed most daunting, I remembered how much you both believed in me and this series. Your feisty legacy continues to inspire me.

A special thank-you to author Ileana for helping me through the most difficult part of this book's edit—your encouragement and insights were everything—thank you for sharing your friendship and immense talent.

Thank you to my mother-in-law, Gail Kamaras, and my sister-in-law, Jessica Bowers, for all your support. I love you guys. A shout-out to my brilliant author brother, Mr. Beanbag, for always being awesome and always being supportive of me.

To authors Cam M. Sato and K., my international writing group cohorts—thank you for sharing your incredible talent and friendship with me week after week. I feel privileged to be on this writing journey with you both.

Thank you to author/editor Dian Parker for sharing your incredible talent with me, and to author Eva Gumprecht for being an inspiration. Thank you to Liz Zundel for sharing your writing talent and for your friendship, especially during this challenging edit. Love you, Liz. And thank you, Betty—much love going out to you. Thank you, Suzanne. Your support this past year has been everything.

A million thanks to my fellow authors at Inkyard Press. I'm not only starstruck by all of you and your talent, I'm also so grateful for your support and friendship. To the authors of Utah and the librarians of Texas—I am so happy to know all of you. Thank you for all the support. To YALSA and all the librarians who have supported me and my series—you are the definition of awesome. Thank you to Jessie.

And thank you to authors Cerece, Nan, Kelly, Abigail, Laura, A., Shaila, Jennifer, Summer, Ira, Erin, Stephanie, Keira, G., Abby, McCall, Liz, Lia, P., Joel, Laura, R., C., Meg, Sierra, Jon, J., and V., and thank you to all the other authors who have supported me throughout the past year (a special thank-you to that private author Facebook community—so lucky to have all of you). Thanks going out to Lorraine for so much positive support. Love you, college roomie :) Thank you to the Burlington Writers' Workshop for sharing your talent and insight with me. Thank you, Mike Marcotte, for all the tech support with my website. Thank you to all the Vermont authors (you are legion) who are so supportive of my series. I'm so grateful to you all. Also, thank you to the Vermont College of Fine Arts for all the support throughout the year. You are a magical place of inspiration. Thank you to the League of Vermont Writers for being awesome. Thank you to Dan and Bronwyn (I love you guys), and thank you, John G., for your support and friendship. To all the librarians at the Kellogg Hubbard Library for being so enthusiastic and supportive of my series—a giant thank-you. Thank you to all the bookstores that have been so enthusiastic about this series, including Phoenix Books in Burlington, Vermont; Bear Pond Books in Montpelier, Vermont; and Next Chapter Bookstore in Barre, Vermont. Also, thank you to the booksellers working in the YA section at the Burlington, Vermont, Barnes & Noble, for your boundless enthusiasm.

To all the bloggers and readers from all over the world who have been so supportive of me online—you are all so fun and great. I'm enjoying being on this series journey with you all. Thank you for all the notes and letters and great ideas! To my sensitivity readers: thank you for making this book so much better with your insightful suggestions and inclusive vision. Any flaws that remain are completely my own.

Thank you to two of my favorite authors, Tamora Pierce and Robin Hobb, for your support and praise. I'll never be able to thank you enough.

Thank you to my phenomenally talented audio readers for the series—Julia Whelan, Jesse Vilinsky, and Amy McFadden.

And a huge thank-you to everyone at Inkyard Press and HarperCollins who have supported both me and this series. I can't believe I get to work with people of your caliber. Thank you to Natashya Wilson, executive editor at Inkyard Press and my wonderful editor, and Connolly Bottum, assistant editor, for everything. Tashya, I'm so grateful to be working with you on the rest of these series. And thank you to editor Lauren Smulski, for making every one of the books we worked on together miles better. Thank you to Reka Rubin and Christine Tsai on the Harlequin subrights team, for being such huge fans of The Black Witch Chronicles, and for your efforts to bring my books to readers all over the world. Thank you to Shara Alexander, Laura Gianino, Linette Kim, Bess Braswell, Brittany Mitchell, and everyone else in marketing and publicity who helped to promote this series. To Kathleen Oudit and Mary Luna of Harlequin's talented art department—I can never thank you enough for my spectacular covers and maps. Many thanks to the sales team for their support—and especially Gillian Wise, for your boundless enthusiasm for The Black Witch Chronicles. A big thank-you to Inkyard Press's digital promoters/social media team: Eleanor Elliott, Larissa Walker, and Olivia Gissing, Marianna Ricciuto, Brendan Flattery, and the Digital Assets team. And thank you to Ingrid Dolan, head of copy editing, copy editor Gina Macedo for doing such a beautiful job (loved your notes!), and Tamara Shifman, head of proofreading.

And lastly, thank you to my wonderful agent, Carrie Hannigan, Ellen Goff, and everyone else at HG Literary, for all your support and for believing in The Black Witch Chronicles for so many years. Much love going out to all of you.